PHILO VANCE

FOUR COMPLETE NOVELS

By S. S. VAN DINE

ABOUT THE AUTHOR

S. S. VAN DINE was the pseudonym adopted by Willard Huntington Wright when he published his first detective novel, *The Benson Murder Case,* in 1926. A distinguished art and literary critic during the early part of his writing career, Wright began penning detective stories following a severe breakdown suffered in 1923 as a result of the heavy work load he endured as columnist, editor, and aspiring fiction writer. During the two years Wright remained bedridden, he read more than 2,000 detective stories. As his health improved, he turned to writing the Philo Vance detective stories, adopting the pseudonym to protect himself from possible ridicule from his literary peers.

Wright was born in Charlottesville, Virginia, in 1888. He was educated at St. Vincent and Pomona colleges in California and at Harvard University and studied art in Munich and Paris. He became a noted art critic, worked as editor of *The Smart Set* magazine, and collaborated with H. L. Mencken and George Jean Nathan on a series of sketches about European nightlife. His sole literary novel, *The Man of Promise,* was published in 1916.

The amateur detective Philo Vance appeared for the first time in *The Benson Murder Case* in 1926. Ten more Philo Vance novels followed before Wright's death in 1939, and a final work, *The Winter Murder Case,* appeared posthumously. The books became overwhelming successes, making Philo Vance the most popular literary detective in the world at that time.

PHILO VANCE

FOUR COMPLETE NOVELS

By S. S. VAN DINE

The Benson Murder Case

The "Canary" Murder Case

The Bishop Murder Case

The Scarab Murder Case

AVENEL BOOKS • NEW YORK

This omnibus edition contains the complete and unabridged texts of the original editions.
It has been completely reset for this volume.

This 1984 edition is published by Avenel Books,
distributed by Crown Publishers, Inc., by arrangement with
Charles Scribner's Sons.

Manufactured in the United States of America

Library of Congress Cataloging in Publication Data

Van Dine, S.S.
Philo Vance 4 complete S.S. Van Dine novels.
Originally published separately 1926-1930.
Contents: The scarab murder case—The Bishop murder case—The "Canary" murder case—[etc.]
1. Detective and mystery stories, American.
I. Title: Philo Vance four complete S.S. Van Dine novels. II. Title.
PS3545.R846A6   1984   813'.52   83-21346

ISBN: 0-517-432889

h g f e d c b a

CONTENTS

The Benson Murder Case

"Mr. Mason," he said, "I wish to thank you for my life."

"Sir," said Mason, "I had no interest in your life. The adjustment of your problem was the only thing of interest to me."

—Randolph Mason: Corrector of Destinies

INTRODUCTORY

IF YOU will refer to the municipal statistics of the City of New York, you will find that the number of unsolved major crimes during the four years that John F.-X. Markham was district attorney, was far smaller than under any of his predecessors' administrations. Markham projected the district attorney's office into all manner of criminal investigations; and, as a result, many abstruse crimes on which the police had hopelessly gone aground were eventually disposed of.

But although he was personally credited with the many important indictments and subsequent convictions that he secured, the truth is that he was only an instrument in many of his most famous cases. The man who actually solved them and supplied the evidence for their prosecution was in no way connected with the city's administration and never once came into the public eye.

At that time I happened to be both legal advisor and personal friend of this other man, and it was thus that the strange and amazing facts of the situation became known to me. But not until recently have I been at liberty to make them public. Even now I am not permitted to divulge the man's name, and for that reason I have chosen, arbitrarily, to refer to him throughout these *ex officio* reports as Philo Vance.

It is, of course, possible that some of his acquaintances may, through my revelations, be able to guess his identity; and if such should prove the case, I beg of them to guard that knowledge; for though he has now gone to Italy to live and has given me permission to record the exploits of which he was the unique central character, he has very emphatically imposed his anonymity upon me; and I should not like to feel that, through any lack of discretion or delicacy, I have been the cause of his secret becoming generally known.

The present chronicle has to do with Vance's solution of the notorious Benson murder which, due to the unexpectedness of the crime, the prominence of the persons involved, and the startling evidence adduced, was invested with an interest rarely surpassed in the annals of New York's criminal history.

This sensational case was the first of many in which Vance figured as a kind of *amicus curiæ* in Markham's investigations.

S. S. VAN DINE

New York

5

CHARACTERS OF THE BOOK

PHILO VANCE

JOHN F.-X. MARKHAM
District Attorney of New York County

ALVIN H. BENSON
Well-known Wall Street broker and man-about-town, who was mysteriously murdered in his home

MAJOR ANTHONY BENSON
Brother of the murdered man

MRS. ANNA PLATZ
Housekeeper for Alvin Benson

MURIEL ST. CLAIR
A young singer

CAPTAIN PHILIP LEACOCK
Miss St. Clair's fiancé

LEANDER PFYFE
Intimate friend of Alvin Benson's

MRS. PAULA BANNING
A friend of Leander Pfyfe's

ELSIE HOFFMAN
Secretary of the firm of Benson and Benson

COLONEL BIGSBY OSTRANDER
A retired army officer

WILLIAM H. MORIARTY
An alderman, Borough of the Bronx

JACK PRISCO
Elevator boy at the Chatham Arms

GEORGE G. STITT
Of the firm of Stitt and McCoy, Public Accountants

MAURICE DINWIDDIE
Assistant District Attorney

CHIEF INSPECTOR O'BRIEN
Of the Police Department of New York City

WILLIAM M. MORAN
Commanding Officer of the Detective Bureau

ERNEST HEATH
  Sergeant of the Homicide Bureau
BURKE
  Detective of the Homicide Bureau
SNITKIN
  Detective of the Homicide Bureau
EMERY
  Detective of the Homicide Bureau
BEN HANLON
  Commanding Officer of Detectives assigned to District Attorney's office
PHELPS
  Detective assigned to District Attorney's office
TRACY
  Detective assigned to District Attorney's office
SPRINGER
  Detective assigned to District Attorney's office
HIGGINBOTHAM
  Detective assigned to District Attorney's office
CAPTAIN CARL HAGEDORN
  Firearms expert
DR. DOREMUS
  Medical Examiner
FRANCIS SWACKER
  Secretary to the District Attorney
CURRIE
  Vance's valet

1

PHILO VANCE AT HOME

(*Friday, June 14; 8:30 A.M.*)

IT HAPPENED that, on the morning of the momentous June the fourteenth when the discovery of the murdered body of Alvin H. Benson created a sensation which, to this day, has not entirely died away, I had breakfasted with Philo Vance in his apartment. It was not unusual for me to share Vance's luncheons and dinners, but to have breakfast with him was something of an occasion. He was a late riser, and it was his habit to remain incommunicado until his midday meal.

The reason for this early meeting was a matter of business—or, rather, of aesthetics. On the afternoon of the previous day Vance had attended a preview of Vollard's collection of Cézanne watercolors at the Kessler Galleries and, having seen several pictures he particularly wanted, he had invited me to an early breakfast to give me instructions regarding their purchase.

A word concerning my relationship with Vance is necessary to clarify my role of narrator in this chronicle. The legal tradition is deeply imbedded in my family, and when my preparatory-school days were over, I was sent, almost as a matter of course, to Harvard to study law. It was there I met Vance, a reserved, cynical, and caustic freshman who was the bane of his professors and the fear of his fellow classmen. Why he should have chosen me, of all the students at the university, for his extrascholastic association, I have never been able to understand fully. My own liking for Vance was simply explained: he fascinated and interested me, and supplied me with a novel kind of intellectual diversion. In his liking for me, however, no such basis of appeal was present. I was (and am now) a commonplace fellow, possessed of a conservative and rather conventional mind. But, at least, my mentality was not rigid, and the ponderosity of the legal procedure did not impress me greatly—which is why, no doubt, I had little taste for my inherited profession—; and it is possible that these traits found certain affinities in Vance's unconscious mind. There is, to be sure, the less consoling explanation that I appealed to Vance as a kind of foil, or anchorage, and that he sensed in my nature a complementary antithesis to his own. But whatever the explanation, we were much together;

9

and, as the years went by, that association ripened into an inseparable friendship.

Upon graduation I entered my father's law firm—Van Dine and Davis—and after five years of dull apprenticeship I was taken into the firm as the junior partner. At present I am the second Van Dine of Van Dine, Davis, and Van Dine, with offices at 120 Broadway. At about the time my name first appeared on the letterheads of the firm, Vance returned from Europe, where he had been living during my legal novitiate, and, an aunt of his having died and made him her principal beneficiary, I was called upon to discharge the technical obligations involved in putting him in possession of his inherited property.

This work was the beginning of a new and somewhat unusual relationship between us. Vance had a strong distaste for any kind of business transaction, and in time I became the custodian of all his monetary interests and his agent at large. I found that his affairs were various enough to occupy as much of my time as I cared to give to legal matters, and as Vance was able to indulge the luxury of having a personal legal factotum, so to speak, I permanently closed my desk at the office and devoted myself exclusively to his needs and whims.

If, up to the time when Vance summoned me to discuss the purchase of the Cézannes, I had harbored any secret or repressed regrets for having deprived the firm of Van Dine, Davis, and Van Dine of my modest legal talents, they were permanently banished on that eventful morning; for, beginning with the notorious Benson murder, and extending over a period of nearly four years, it was my privilege to be a spectator of what I believe was the most amazing series of criminal cases that ever passed before the eyes of a young lawyer. Indeed, the grim dramas I witnessed during that period constitute one of the most astonishing secret documents in the police history of this country.

Of these dramas Vance was the central character. By an analytical and interpretative process which, as far as I know, has never before been applied to criminal activities, he succeeded in solving many of the important crimes on which both the police and the district attorney's office had hopelessly fallen down.

Due to my peculiar relations with Vance it happened that not only did I participate in all the cases with which he was connected but I was also present at most of the informal discussions concerning them which took place between him and the district attorney; and, being of methodical temperament, I kept a fairly complete record of them. In addition, I noted down (as accurately as memory permitted) Vance's unique psychological methods of determining guilt, as he explained them from time to time. It is fortunate that I performed this gratuitous labor of accumulation and transcription, for now that circumstances have unexpectedly rendered possible my making the cases public, I am able to present them in full detail and with all their various sidelights and succeeding steps—a task that would be impossible were it not for my numerous clippings and *adversaria*.

Fortunately, too, the first case to draw Vance into its ramifications was that of Alvin Benson's murder. Not only did it prove one of the most famous of New York's *causes célèbres,* but it gave Vance an excellent opportunity of displaying his rare talents of deductive reasoning, and, by its nature and magnitude, aroused his interest in a branch of activity which heretofore had been alien to his temperamental promptings and habitual predilections.

The case intruded upon Vance's life suddenly and unexpectedly, although he himself had, by a casual request made to the district attorney over a month before, been the involuntary agent of this destruction of his normal routine. The thing, in fact, burst upon us before we had quite finished our breakfast on that mid-June morning, and put an end temporarily to all business connected with the purchase of the Cézanne paintings. When, later in the day, I visited the Kessler Galleries, two of the watercolors that Vance had particularly desired had been sold; and I am convinced that, despite his success in the unraveling of the Benson murder mystery and his saving of at least one innocent person from arrest, he has never to this day felt entirely compensated for the loss of those two little sketches on which he had set his heart.

As I was ushered into the living room that morning by Currie, a rare old English servant who acted as Vance's butler, valet, majordomo and, on occasions, specialty cook, Vance was sitting in a large armchair, attired in a surah silk dressing gown and gray suede slippers, with Vollard's book on Cézanne open across his knees.

"Forgive my not rising, Van." He greeted me casually. "I have the whole weight of the modern evolution in art resting on my legs. Furthermore, this plebeian early rising fatigues me, y'know."

He riffled the pages of the volume, pausing here and there at a reproduction.

"This chap Vollard," he remarked at length, "has been rather liberal with our art-fearing country. He has sent a really goodish collection of his Cézannes here. I viewed 'em yesterday with the proper reverence and, I might add, unconcern, for Kessler was watching me; and I've marked the ones I want you to buy for me as soon as the gallery opens this morning."

He handed me a small catalog he had been using as a bookmark.

"A beastly assignment, I know," he added, with an indolent smile. "These delicate little smudges with all their blank paper will prob'ly be meaningless to your legal mind—they're so unlike a neatly typed brief, don't y' know. And you'll no doubt think some of 'em are hung upside-down—one of 'em is, in fact, and even Kessler doesn't know it. But don't fret, Van old dear. They're very beautiful and valuable little knickknacks, and rather inexpensive when one considers what they'll be bringing in a few years. Really an excellent investment for some money-loving soul, y' know—inf'nitely better than that Lawyer's Equity Stock over which you grew so eloquent at the time of my dear Aunt Agatha's death."*

Vance's one passion (if a purely intellectual enthusiasm may be called a passion) was art—not art in its narrow, personal aspects, but in its broader, more universal significance. And art was not only his dominating interest but his chief diversion. He was something of an authority on Japanese and Chinese prints; he knew tapestries and ceramics; and once I heard him give an impromptu *causerie* to a few guests on Tanagra figurines, which, had it been transcribed, would have made a most delightful and instructive monograph.

Vance had sufficient means to indulge his instinct for collecting, and pos-

* As a matter of fact, the same watercolors that Vance obtained for $250 and $300 were bringing three times as much four years later.

sessed a fine assortment of pictures and *objets d'art*. His collection was hetero-geneous only in its superficial characteristics: every piece he owned embodied some principle of form or line that related it to all the others. One who knew art could feel the unity and consistency in all the items with which he sur-rounded himself, however widely separated they were in point of time or *métier* or surface appeal. Vance, I have always felt, was one of those rare human beings, a collector with a definite philosophic point of view.

His apartment in East Thirty-eighth Street—actually the two top floors of an old mansion, beautifully remodeled and in part rebuilt to secure spacious rooms and lofty ceilings—was filled, but not crowded, with rare specimens of oriental and occidental, ancient and modern, art. His paintings ranged from the Italian primitives to Cézanne and Matisse; and among his collection of original drawings were works as widely separated as those of Michelangelo and Picasso. Vance's Chinese prints constituted one of the finest private col-lections in this country. They included beautiful examples of the work of Ririomin, Rianchu, Jinkomin, Kakei, and Mokkei.

"The Chinese," Vance once said to me, "are the truly great artists of the East. They were the men whose work expressed most intensely a broad philo-sophic spirit. By contrast the Japanese were superficial. It's a long step be-tween the little more than decorative *souci* of a Hokusai and the profoundly thoughtful and conscious artistry of a Ririomin. Even when Chinese art de-generated under the Manchus, we find in it a deep philosophic quality—a spiritual *sensibilité*, so to speak. And in the modern copies of copies—what is called the *bunjinga* style—we still have pictures of profound meaning."

Vance's catholicity of taste in art was remarkable. His collection was as var-ied as that of a museum. It embraced a black-figured amphora by Amasis, a proto-Corinthian vase in the Ægean style, Koubatcha and Rhodian plates, Athenian pottery, a sixteenth-century Italian holywater stoup of rock crystal, pewter of the Tudor period (several pieces bearing the double-rose hallmark), a bronze plaque by Cellini, a triptych of Limoges enamel, a Spanish retable of an altarpiece by Vallfogona, several Etruscan bronzes, an Indian Greco Bud-dhist, a statuette of the Goddess Kuan Yin from the Ming Dynasty, a number of very fine Renaissance woodcuts, and several specimens of Byzantine, Carolingian, and early French ivory carvings.

His Egyptian treasures included a gold jug from Zakazik, a statuette of the Lady Nai (as lovely as the one in the Louvre), two beautifully carved steles of the First Theban Age, various small sculptures comprising rare representa-tions of Hapi and Amset, and several Arrentine bowls carved with Kala-thiskos dancers. On top of one of his embayed Jacobean bookcases in the library, where most of his modern paintings and drawings were hung, was a fascinating group of African sculpture—ceremonial masks and statuette fe-tishes from French Guinea, the Sudan, Nigeria, the Ivory Coast, and the Congo.

A definite purpose has animated me in speaking at such length about Vance's art instinct, for, in order to understand fully the melodramatic adven-tures which began for him on that June morning, one must have a general idea of the man's penchants and inner promptings. His interest in art was an im-portant—one might almost say the dominant—factor in his personality. I have never met a man quite like him—a man so apparently diversified and yet so fundamentally consistent.

Vance was what many would call a dilettante. But the designation does him injustice. He was a man of unusual culture and brilliance. An aristocrat by birth and instinct, he held himself severely aloof from the common world of men. In his manner there was an indefinable contempt for inferiority of all kinds. The great majority of those with whom he came in contact regarded him as a snob. Yet there was in his condescension and disdain no trace of spuriousness. His snobbishness was intellectual as well as social. He detested stupidity even more, I believe, than he did vulgarity or bad taste. I have heard him on several occasions quote Fouché's famous line: *C'est plus qu'un crime; c'est une faute.* And he meant it literally.

Vance was frankly a cynic, but he was rarely bitter; his was a flippant, Juvenalian cynicism. Perhaps he may best be described as a bored and supercilious, but highly conscious and penetrating, spectator of life. He was keenly interested in all human reactions; but it was the interest of the scientist, not the humanitarian. Withal he was a man of rare personal charm. Even people who found it difficult to admire him found it equally difficult not to like him. His somewhat quixotic mannerisms and his slightly English accent and inflection—a heritage of his postgraduate days at Oxford—impressed those who did not know him well as affectations. But the truth is, there was very little of the *poseur* about him.

He was unusually good-looking, although his mouth was ascetic and cruel, like the mouths on some of the Medici portraits*; moreover, there was a slightly derisive hauteur in the lift of his eyebrows. Despite the aquiline severity of his lineaments, his face was highly sensitive. His forehead was full and sloping—it was the artist's, rather than the scholar's, brow. His cold gray eyes were widely spaced. His nose was straight and slender, and his chin narrow but prominent, with an unusually deep cleft. When I saw John Barrymore recently in *Hamlet,* I was somehow reminded of Vance; and once before, in a scene of *Caesar and Cleopatra* played by Forbes-Robertson, I received a similar impression.†

Vance was slightly under six feet, graceful, and giving the impression of sinewy strength and nervous endurance. He was an expert fencer and had been the captain of the university's fencing team. He was mildly fond of outdoor sports and had a knack of doing things well without any extensive practice. His golf handicap was only three; and one season he had played on our championship polo team against England. Nevertheless, he had a positive antipathy to walking and would not go a hundred yards on foot if there was any possible means of riding.

In his dress he was always fashionable—scrupulously correct to the smallest detail—yet unobtrusive. He spent considerable time at his clubs; his favorite

* I am thinking particularly of Bronzino's portraits of Pietro de' Medici and Cosimo de' Medici, in the National Gallery, and of Vasari's medallion portrait of Lorenzo de' Medici in the Vecchio Palazzo, Florence.

† Once when Vance was suffering from sinusitis, he had an X-ray photograph of his head made; and the accompanying chart described him as a "marked dolichocephalic" and a "disharmonious Nordic." It also contained the following data:—cephalic index 75; nose, leptorhine, with an index of 48; facial angle, 85°; vertical index, 72; upper facial index, 54; interpupilary width, 67; chin, masognathous, with an index of 103; sella turcica, abnormally large.

was the Stuyvesant, because, as he explained to me, its membership was drawn largely from the political and commercial ranks, and he was never drawn into a discussion which required any mental effort. He went occasionally to the more modern operas and was a regular subscriber to the symphony concerts and chamber music recitals.

Incidentally, he was one of the most unerring poker players I have ever seen. I mention this fact not merely because it was unusual and significant that a man of Vance's type should have preferred so democratic a game to bridge or chess, for instance, but because his knowledge of the science of human psychology involved in poker had an intimate bearing on the chronicles I am about to set down.

Vance's knowledge of psychology was indeed uncanny. He was gifted with an instinctively accurate judgment of people, and his study and reading had coordinated and rationalized this gift to an amazing extent. He was well grounded in the academic principles of psychology, and all his courses at college had either centered about this subject or been subordinated to it. While I was confining myself to a restricted area of torts and contracts, constitutional and common law, equity, evidence, and pleading, Vance was reconnoitering the whole field of cultural endeavor. He had courses in the history of religions, the Greek classics, biology, civics, and political economy, philosophy, anthropology, literature, theoretical and experimental psychology, and ancient and modern languages.* But it was, I think, his courses under Münsterberg and William James that interested him the most.

Vance's mind was basically philosophical—that is, philosophical in the more general sense. Being singularly free from the conventional sentimentalities and current superstitions, he could look beneath the surface of human acts into actuating impulses and motives. Moreover, he was resolute both in his avoidance of any attitude that savored of credulousness and in his adherence to cold, logical exactness in his mental processes.

"Until we can approach all human problems," he once remarked, "with the clinical aloofness and cynical contempt of a doctor examining a guinea pig strapped to a board, we have little chance of getting at the truth."

Vance led an active, but by no means animated, social life—a concession to various family ties. But he was not a social animal—I cannot remember ever having met a man with so undeveloped a gregarious instinct—and when he went forth into the social world, it was generally under compulsion. In fact, one of his "duty" affairs had occupied him on the night before that memorable June breakfast; otherwise, we would have consulted about the Cézannes the evening before; and Vance groused a good deal about it while Currie was serving our strawberries and eggs *Bénédictine*. Later on I was to give profound

---

* "Culture," Vance said to me shortly after I had met him, "is polyglot; and the knowledge of many tongues is essential to an understanding of the world's intellectual and æsthetic achievements. Especially are the Greek and Latin classics vitiated by translation." I quote the remark here because his omnivorous reading in languages other than English, coupled with his amazingly retentive memory, had a tendency to affect his own speech. And while it may appear to some that his speech was at times pedantic, I have tried, throughout these chronicles to quote him literally, in the hope of presenting a portrait of the man as he was.

thanks to the God of Coincidence that the blocks had been arranged in just that pattern; for had Vance been slumbering peacefully at nine o'clock when the district attorney called, I would probably have missed four of the most interesting and exciting years of my life; and many of New York's shrewdest and most desperate criminals might still be at large.

Vance and I had just settled back in our chairs for our second cup of coffee and a cigarette when Currie, answering an impetuous ringing of the front door bell, ushered the district attorney into the living room.

"By all that's holy!" he exclaimed, raising his hands in mock astonishment. "New York's leading *flâneur* and art connoisseur is up and about!"

"And I am suffused with blushes at the disgrace of it," Vance replied.

It was evident, however, that the district attorney was not in a jovial mood. His face suddenly sobered. "Vance, a serious thing has brought me here. I'm in a great hurry and merely dropped by to keep my promise. . . . The fact is, Alvin Benson has been murdered."

Vance lifted his eyebrows languidly. "Really, now," he drawled. "How messy! But he no doubt deserved it. In any event, that's no reason why you should repine. Take a chair and have a cup of Currie's incomp'rable coffee." And before the other could protest, he rose and pushed a bell-button.

Markham hesitated a second or two.

"Oh, well. A couple of minutes won't make any difference. But only a gulp." And he sank into a chair facing us.

2

AT THE SCENE OF THE CRIME

(*Friday, June 14; 9 A.M.*)

JOHN F.-X. Markham, as you remember, had been elected district attorney of New York County on the Independent Reform Ticket during one of the city's periodical reactions against Tammany Hall. He served his four years and would probably have been elected to a second term had not the ticket been hopelessly split by the political juggling of his opponents. He was an indefatigable worker and projected the district attorney's office into all manner of criminal and civil investigations. Being utterly incorruptible, he not only aroused the fervid admiration of his constituents but produced an almost unprecedented sense of security in those who had opposed him on partisan lines.

He had been in office only a few months when one of the newspapers referred to him as the Watch Dog; and the sobriquet clung to him until the end of his administration. Indeed, his record as a successful prosecutor during the four years of his incumbency was such a remarkable one that even today it is not infrequently referred to in legal and political discussions.

Markham was a tall, strongly built man in the middle forties, with a clean-shaven, somewhat youthful face which belied his uniformly gray hair. He was not handsome according to conventional standards, but he had an unmistakable air of distinction, and was possessed of an amount of social culture rarely found in our latter-day political officeholders. Withal he was a man of brusque and vindictive temperament; but his brusqueness was an incrustation on a solid foundation of good breeding, not—as is usually the case—the roughness of substructure showing through an inadequately superimposed crust of gentility.

When his nature was relieved of the stress of duty and care, he was the most gracious of men. But early in my acquaintance with him I had seen his attitude of cordiality suddenly displaced by one of grim authority. It was as if a new personality—hard, indomitable, symbolic of eternal justice—had in that moment been born in Markham's body. I was to witness this transformation many times before our association ended. In fact, this very morning, as he sat opposite to me in Vance's living room, there was more than a hint of it in the aggressive sternness of his expression; and I knew that he was deeply troubled over Alvin Benson's murder.

He swallowed his coffee rapidly and was setting down the cup, when Vance, who had been watching him with quizzical amusement, remarked, "I say, why this sad preoccupation over the passing of one Benson? You weren't, by any chance, the murderer, what?"

Markham ignored Vance's levity. "I'm on my way to Benson's. Do you care to come along? You asked for the experience, and I dropped in to keep my promise."

I then recalled that several weeks before at the Stuyvesant Club, when the subject of the prevalent homicides in New York was being discussed, Vance had expressed a desire to accompany the district attorney on one of his investigations, and that Markham had promised to take him on his next important case. Vance's interest in the psychology of human behavior had prompted the desire, and his friendship with Markham, which had been of long standing, had made the request possible.

"You remember everything, don't you?" Vance replied lazily. "An admirable gift, even if an uncomfortable one." He glanced at the clock on the mantel, it lacked a few minutes of nine. "But what an indecent hour! Suppose someone should see me."

Markham moved forward impatiently in his chair. "Well, if you think the gratification of your curiosity would compensate you for the disgrace of being seen in public at nine o'clock in the morning, you'll have to hurry. I certainly won't take you in dressing gown and bedroom slippers. And I most certainly won't wait over five minutes for you to get dressed."

"Why the haste, old dear?" Vance asked, yawning. "The chap's dead, don't y' know; he can't possibly run away."

"Come, get a move on, you orchid," the other urged. "This affair is no joke. It's damned serious, and from the looks of it, it's going to cause an ungodly scandal. What are you going to do?"

"Do? I shall humbly follow the great avenger of the common people," returned Vance, rising and making an obsequious bow.

He rang for Currie and ordered his clothes brought to him.

"I'm attending a levee which Mr. Markham is holding over a corpse and I want something rather spiffy. Is it warm enough for a silk suit? . . . And a lavender tie, by all means."

"I trust you won't also wear your green carnation," grumbled Markham.

"Tut! Tut!" Vance chided him. "You've been reading Mr. Hitchens. Such heresy in a district attorney! Anyway, you know full well I never wear boutonnieres. The decoration has fallen into disrepute. The only remaining devotees of the practice are roués and saxophone players. . . . But tell me about the departed Benson."

Vance was now dressing, with Currie's assistance, at a rate of speed I had rarely seen him display in such matters. Beneath his bantering pose I recognized the true eagerness of the man for a new experience and one that promised such dramatic possibilities for his alert and observing mind.

"You knew Alvin Benson casually, I believe," the district attorney said. "Well, early this morning his housekeeper phoned the local precinct station that she had found him shot through the head, fully dressed and sitting in his favorite chair in his living room. The message, of course, was put through at once to the telegraph bureau at headquarters, and my assistant on duty notified me immediately. I was tempted to let the case follow the regular police routine. But half an hour later Major Benson, Alvin's brother, phoned me and asked me, as a special favor, to take charge. I've known the major for twenty years and I couldn't very well refuse. So I took a hurried breakfast and started for Benson's house. He lived in West Forty-eighth Street; and as I passed your corner I remembered your request and dropped by to see if you cared to go along."

"Most consid'rate," murmured Vance, adjusting his four-in-hand before a small polychrome mirror by the door. Then he turned to me. "Come, Van. We'll all gaze upon the defunct Benson. I'm sure some of Markham's sleuths will unearth the fact that I detested the bounder and accuse me of the crime; and I'll feel safer, don't y' know, with legal talent at hand. . . . No objections—eh, what, Markham?"

"Certainly not," the other agreed readily, although I felt that he would rather not have had me along. But I was too deeply interested in the affair to offer any ceremonious objections and I followed Vance and Markham downstairs.

As we settled back in the waiting taxicab and started up Madison Avenue, I marveled a little, as I had often done before, at the strange friendship of these two dissimilar men beside me—Markham forthright, conventional, a trifle austere, and overserious in his dealings with life; and Vance casual, mercurial, debonair, and whimsically cynical in the face of the grimmest realities. And yet this temperamental diversity seemed, in some wise, the very cornerstone of their friendship; it was as if each saw in the other some unattainable field of experience and sensation that had been denied himself. Markham represented to Vance the solid and immutable realism of life, whereas Vance symbolized for Markham the carefree, exotic, gypsy spirit of intellectual adventure. Their intimacy, in fact, was even greater than showed on the surface; and despite Markham's exaggerated deprecations of the other's attitudes and opinions, I believe he respected Vance's intelligence more profoundly than that of any other man he knew.

As we rode uptown that morning Markham appeared preoccupied and gloomy. No word had been spoken since we left the apartment; but as we turned west into Forty-eighth Street Vance asked; "What is the social etiquette of these early-morning murder functions, aside from removing one's hat in the presence of the body?"

"You keep your hat on," growled Markham.

"My word! Like a synagogue, what? Most int'restin'! Perhaps one takes off one's shoes so as not to confuse the footprints."

"No," Markham told him. "The guests remain fully clothed—in which the function differs from the ordinary evening affairs of your smart set."

"My *dear* Markham!"—Vance's tone was one of melancholy reproof—"The horrified moralist in your nature is at work again. That remark of yours was pos'tively Epworth Leaguish."

Markham was too abstracted to follow up Vance's badinage. "There are one or two things," he said soberly, "that I think I'd better warn you about. From the looks of it, this case is going to cause considerable noise, and there'll be a lot of jealousy and battling for honors. I won't be fallen upon and caressed affectionately by the police for coming in at this stage of the game; so be careful not to rub their bristles the wrong way. My assistant, who's there now, tells me he thinks the inspector has put Heath in charge. Heath's a sergeant in the homicide bureau and is undoubtedly convinced at the present moment that I'm taking hold in order to get the publicity."

"Aren't you his technical superior?" asked Vance.

"Of course; and that makes the situation just so much more delicate. . . . I wish to God the major hadn't called me up."

"*Eheu!*" sighed Vance. "The world is full of Heaths. Beastly nuisances."

"Don't misunderstand me," Markham hastened to assure him. "Heath is a good man—in fact, as good a man as we've got. The mere fact that he was assigned to the case shows how seriously the affair is regarded at headquarters. There'll be no unpleasantness about my taking charge, you understand; but I want the atmosphere to be as halcyon as possible. Heath'll resent my bringing along you two chaps as spectators, anyway; so I beg of you, Vance, emulate the modest violet."

"I prefer the blushing rose, if you don't mind," Vance protested. "However, I'll instantly give the hypersensitive Heath one of my choicest Régie cigarettes with the rose-petal tips."

"If you do," smiled Markham, "he'll probably arrest you as a suspicious character."

We had drawn up abruptly in front of an old brownstone residence on the upper side of Forty-eighth Street, near Sixth Avenue. It was a house of the better class, built on a twenty-five foot lot in a day when permanency and beauty were still matters of consideration among the city's architects. The design was conventional, to accord with the other houses in the block, but a touch of luxury and individuality was to be seen in its decorative copings and in the stone carvings about the entrance and above the windows.

There was a shallow paved areaway between the street line and the front elevation of the house; but this was enclosed in a high iron railing, and the only entrance was by way of the front door, which was about six feet above the street level at the top of a flight of ten broad stone stairs. Between the entrance and the right-hand wall were two spacious windows covered with heavy iron grilles.

A considerable crowd of morbid onlookers had gathered in front of the house; and on the steps lounged several alert-looking young men whom I took to be newspaper reporters. The door of our taxicab was opened by a uniformed patrolman who saluted Markham with exaggerated respect and ostentatiously cleared a passage for us through the gaping throng of idlers. Another uniformed patrolman stood in the little vestibule and, on recognizing Markham, held the outer door open for us and saluted with great dignity.

"*Ave, Cæsar, te salutamus,*" whispered Vance, grinning.

"Be quiet," Markham grumbled. "I've got troubles enough without your garbled questions."

As we passed through the massive carved-oak front door into the main hallway we were met by Assistant District Attorney Dinwiddie, a serious, swarthy young man with a prematurely lined face, whose appearance gave one the impression that most of the woes of humanity were resting upon his shoulders.

"Good morning, Chief," he greeted Markham, with eager relief. "I'm damned glad you've got here. This case'll rip things wide open. Cut-and-dried murder, and not a lead."

Markham nodded gloomily and looked past him into the living room. "Who's here?" he asked.

"The whole works, from the chief inspector down," Dinwiddie told him, with a hopeless shrug, as if the fact boded ill for all concerned.

At that moment a tall, massive, middle-aged man with a pink complexion and a closely cropped white moustache, appeared in the doorway of the living room. On seeing Markham he came forward stiffly with outstretched hand. I recognized him at once as Chief Inspector O'Brien, who was in command of the entire police department. Dignified greetings were exchanged between him and Markham, and then Vance and I were introduced to him. Inspector O'Brien gave us each a curt, silent nod and turned back to the living room, with Markham, Dinwiddie, Vance, and myself following.

The room, which was entered by a wide double door about ten feet down the hall, was a spacious one, almost square, and with high ceilings. Two windows gave on the street; and on the extreme right of the north wall, opposite to the front of the house, was another window opening on a paved court. To the left of this window were the sliding doors leading into the dining room at the rear.

The room presented an appearance of garish opulence. About the walls hung several elaborately framed paintings of race horses and a number of mounted hunting trophies. A highly colored oriental rug covered nearly the entire floor. In the middle of the east wall, facing the door, was an ornate fireplace and carved marble mantel. Placed diagonally in the corner on the right stood a walnut upright piano with copper trimmings. Then there was a mahogany bookcase with glass doors and figured curtains, a sprawling tapestried davenport, a squat Venetian tabouret with inlaid mother-of-pearl, a teakwood stand containing a large brass samovar, and a buhl-topped center table nearly six feet long. At the side of the table nearest the hallway, with its back to the front windows, stood a large wicker lounge chair with a high, fan-shaped back.

In this chair reposed the body of Alvin Benson.

Though I had served two years at the front in the World War and had seen

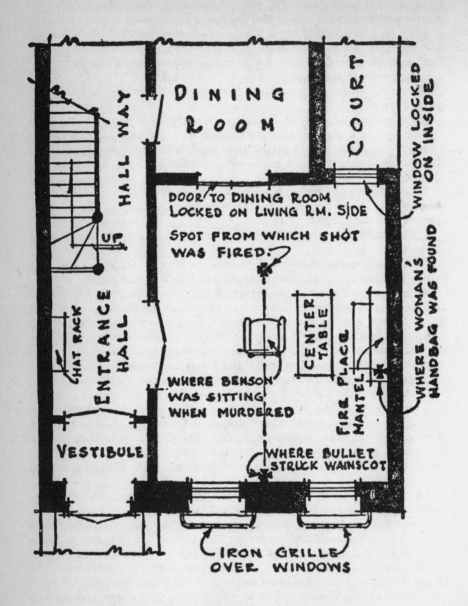

DINING ROOM

COURT

WINDOW LOCKED ON INSIDE

HALL WAY

UP

DOOR TO DINING ROOM LOCKED ON LIVING RM. S|DE

SPOT FROM WHICH SHOT WAS FIRED.

CENTER TABLE

WHERE WOMAN'S HANDBAG WAS FOUND

HAT RACK

ENTRANCE HALL

WHERE BENSON WAS SITTING WHEN MURDERED

FIRE PLACE MANTEL

VESTIBULE

WHERE BULLET STRUCK WAINSCOT

IRON GRILLE OVER WINDOWS

WEST 48TH. STREET

death in many terrible guises, I could not repress a strong sense of revulsion at the sight of this murdered man. In France death had seemed an inevitable part of my daily routine, but here all the organisms of environment were opposed to the idea of fatal violence. The bright June sunshine was pouring into the room, and through the open windows came the continuous din of the city's noises, which, for all their cacophony, are associated with peace and security and the orderly social processes of life.

Benson's body was reclining in the chair in an attitude so natural that one almost expected him to turn to us and ask why we were intruding upon his privacy. His head was resting against the chair's back. His right leg was crossed over his left in a position of comfortable relaxation. His right arm was resting easily on the center table, and his left arm lay along the chair's arm. But that which most strikingly gave his attitude its appearance of naturalness was a small book which he held in his right hand with his thumb still marking the place where he had evidently been reading.*

He had been shot through the forehead from in front; and the small circular bullet mark was now almost black as a result of the coagulation of the blood. A large dark spot on the rug at the rear of the chair indicated the extent of the hemorrhage caused by the grinding passage of the bullet through his brain. Had it not been for these grisly indications, one might have thought that he had merely paused momentarily in his reading to lean back and rest.

He was attired in an old smoking jacket and red felt bedroom slippers but still wore his dress trousers and evening shirt, though he was collarless, and the neckband of the shirt had been unbuttoned as if for comfort. He was not an attractive man physically, being almost completely bald and more than a little stout. His face was flabby, and the puffiness of his neck was doubly conspicuous without its confining collar. With a slight shudder of distaste I ended my brief contemplation of him and turned to the other occupants of the room.

Two burly fellows with large hands and feet, their black felt hats pushed far back on their heads, were minutely inspecting the iron grillwork over the front windows. They seemed to be giving particular attention to the points where the bars were cemented into the masonry; and one of them had just taken hold of a grille with both hands and was shaking it, simian-wise, as if to test its strength. Another man, of medium height and dapper appearance, with a small blond moustache, was bending over in front of the grate looking intently, so it seemed, at the dusty gas logs. On the far side of the table a thickset man in blue serge and a derby hat, stood with arms akimbo scrutinizing the silent figure in the chair. His eyes, hard and pale blue, were narrowed, and his square prognathous jaw was rigidly set. He was gazing with rapt intensity at Benson's body, as though he hoped, by the sheer power of concentration, to probe the secret of the murder.

Another man, of unusual mien, was standing before the rear window, with a jeweler's magnifying glass in his eye, inspecting a small object held in the palm of his hand. From pictures I had seen of him I knew he was Captain Carl Hagedorn, the most famous firearms expert in America. He was a large, cumbersome, broad-shouldered man of about fifty; and his black, shiny clothes

---

* The book was O. Henry's *Strictly Business*, and the place at which it was being held open was, curiously enough, the story entitled "A Municipal Report."

were several sizes too large for him. His coat hitched up behind, and in front hung halfway down to his knees; and his trousers were baggy and lay over his ankles in grotesquely comic folds. His head was round and abnormally large, and his ears seemed sunken into his skull. His mouth was entirely hidden by a scraggly, gray-shot moustache, all the hairs of which grew downward, forming a kind of lambrequin to his lips. Captain Hagedorn had been connected with the New York Police Department for thirty years, and though his appearance and manner were ridiculed at headquarters, he was profoundly respected. His word on any point pertaining to firearms and gunshot wounds was accepted as final by headquarters men.

In the rear of the room, near the dining room door, stood two other men talking earnestly together. One was Inspector William M. Moran, commanding officer of the detective bureau; the other, Sergeant Ernest Heath of the homicide bureau, of whom Markham had already spoken to us.

As we entered the room in the wake of Chief Inspector O'Brien everyone ceased his occupation for a moment and looked at the district attorney in a spirit of uneasy, but respectful, recognition. Only Captain Hagedorn, after a cursory squint at Markham, returned to the inspection of the tiny object in his hand, with an abstracted unconcern which brought a faint smile to Vance's lips.

Inspector Moran and Sergeant Heath came forward with stolid dignity; and after the ceremony of handshaking (which I later observed to be a kind of religious rite among the police and the members of the district attorney's staff), Markham introduced Vance and me and briefly explained our presence. The inspector bowed pleasantly to indicate his acceptance of the intrusion, but I noticed that Heath ignored Markham's explanation and proceeded to treat us as if we were nonexistent.

Inspector Moran was a man of different quality from the others in the room. He was about sixty, with white hair and a brown moustache, and was immaculately dressed. He looked more like a successful Wall Street broker of the better class than a police official.*

"I've assigned Sergeant Heath to the case, Mr. Markham," he explained in a low, well-modulated voice. "It looks as though we are in for a bit of trouble before it's finished. Even the chief inspector thought it warranted his lending the moral support of his presence to the preliminary rounds. He has been here since eight o'clock."

Inspector O'Brien had left us immediately upon entering the room and now stood between the front windows, watching the proceedings with a grave, indecipherable face.

"Well, I think I'll be going," Moran added. "They had me out of bed at seven thirty, and I haven't had any breakfast yet. I won't be needed anyway now that you're here. . . . Good morning." And again he shook hands.

When he had gone, Markham turned to the assistant district attorney.

"Look after these two gentlemen, will you, Dinwiddie? They're babes in the wood and want to see how these affairs work. Explain things to them while I have a little confab with Sergeant Heath."

---

* Inspector Moran (as I learned later) had once been the president of a large upstate bank that had failed during the panic of 1907, and during the Gaynor Administration had been seriously considered for the post of Police Commissioner.

Dinwiddie accepted the assignment eagerly. I think he was glad of the opportunity to have someone to talk to by way of venting his pent-up excitement.

As the three of us turned rather instinctively toward the body of the murdered man—he was, after all, the hub of this tragic drama—I heard Heath say in a sullen voice:

"I suppose you'll take charge now, Mr. Markham."

Dinwiddie and Vance were talking together, and I watched Markham with interest after what he had told us of the rivalry between the police department and the district attorney's office.

Markham looked at Heath with a slow, gracious smile and shook his head. "No, Sergeant," he replied. "I'm here to work with you, and I want that relationship understood from the outset. In fact, I wouldn't be here now if Major Benson hadn't phoned me and asked me to lend a hand. And I particularly want my name kept out of it. It's pretty generally known—and if it isn't, it will be—that the major is an old friend of mine; so, it will be better all round if my connection with the case is kept quiet."

Heath murmured something I did not catch, but I could see that he had, in large measure, been placated. He, in common with all other men who were acquainted with Markham, knew his word was good; and he personally liked the district attorney.

"If there's any credit coming from this affair," Markham went on, "the police department is to get it; therefore I think it best for you to see the reporters.... And, by the way," he added good-naturedly, "if there's any blame coming, you fellows will have to bear that, too."

"Fair enough," assented Heath.

"And now, Sergeant, let's get to work," said Markham.

3

A LADY'S HANDBAG

(Friday, June 14; 9:30 A.M.)

THE DISTRICT attorney and Heath walked up to the body and stood regarding it.

"You see," Heath explained; "he was shot directly from the front. A pretty powerful shot, too, for the bullet passed through the head and struck the woodwork over there by the window." He pointed to a place on the wainscot a short distance from the floor near the drapery of the window nearest the hallway. "We found the expelled shell, and Captain Hagedorn's got the bullet."

He turned to the firearms expert. "How about it, Captain? Anything special?"

Hagedorn raised his head slowly and gave Heath a myopic frown. Then, after a few awkward movements, he answered with unhurried precision. "A forty-five army bullet—Colt automatic."

"Any idea how close to Benson the gun was held?" asked Markham.

"Yes, sir, I have," Hagedorn replied, in his ponderous monotone. "Between five and six feet—probably."

Heath snorted. " 'Probably,' " he repeated to Markham with good-natured contempt. "You can bank on it if the captain says so. . . . You see, sir, nothing smaller than a forty-four or forty-five will stop a man, and these steel-capped army bullets go through a human skull like it was cheese. But in order to carry straight to the woodwork the gun had to be held pretty close; and, as there aren't any powder marks on the face, it's a safe bet to take the captain's figures as to distance."

At this point we heard the front door open and close, and Dr. Doremus, the chief medical examiner, accompanied by his assistant, bustled in. He shook hands with Markham and Inspector O'Brien, and gave Heath a friendly salutation.

"Sorry I couldn't get here sooner," he apologized.

He was a nervous man with a heavily seamed face and the manner of a real estate salesman.

"What have we got here?" he asked, in the same breath, making a wry face at the body in the chair.

"You tell us, Doc," retorted Heath.

Dr. Doremus approached the murdered man with a callous indifference indicative of a long process of hardening. He first inspected the face closely. He was, I imagine, looking for powder marks. Then he glanced at the bullet hole in the forehead and at the ragged wound in the back of the head. Next he moved the dead man's arm, bent the fingers, and pushed the head a little to the side. Having satisfied himself as to the state of *rigor mortis,* he turned to Heath.

"Can we get him on the settee there?"

Heath looked at Markham inquiringly. "All through, sir?"

Markham nodded, and Heath beckoned to the two men at the front windows and ordered the body placed on the davenport. It retained its sitting posture, due to the hardening of the muscles after death, until the doctor and his assistant straightened out the limbs. The body was then undressed, and Dr. Doremus examined it carefully for other wounds. He paid particular attention to the arms; and he opened both hands wide and scrutinized the palms. At length he straightened up and wiped his hands on a large colored silk handkerchief.

"Shot through the left frontal," he announced. "Direct angle of fire. Bullet passed completely through the skull. Exit wound in the left occipital region— base of skull. You found the bullet, didn't you? He was awake when shot, and death was immediate—probably never knew what hit him. . . . He's been dead about—well, I should judge, eight hours, maybe longer."

"How about twelve thirty for the exact time?" asked Heath.

The doctor looked at his watch.

"Fits O.K. . . . Anything else?"

No one answered, and after a slight pause the chief inspector spoke. "We'd like a postmortem report today, Doctor."

"That'll be all right," Dr. Doremus answered, snapping shut his medical case and handing it to his assistant. "But get the body to the mortuary as soon as you can."

After a brief handshaking ceremony, he went out hurriedly.

Heath turned to the detective who had been standing by the table when we entered. "Burke, you phone headquarters to call for the body, and tell 'em to get a move on. Then go back to the office and wait for me."

Burke saluted and disappeared.

Heath then addressed one of the two men who had been inspecting the grilles of the front windows. "How about that ironwork, Snitkin?"

"No chance, Sergeant," was the answer. "Strong as a jail—both of 'em. Nobody never got in through those windows."

"Very good," Heath told him. "Now you two fellows chase along with Burke."

When they had gone, the dapper man in the blue serge suit and derby, whose sphere of activity had seemed to be the fireplace, laid two cigarette butts on the table.

"I found these under the gas logs, Sergeant," he explained unenthusiastically. "Not much, but there's nothing else laying around."

"All right, Emery." Heath gave the butts a disgruntled look. "You needn't wait, either. I'll see you at the office later."

Hagedorn came ponderously forward. "I guess I'll be getting along, too," he rumbled. "But I'm going to keep this bullet awhile. It's got some peculiar rifling marks on it. You don't want it specially, do you, Sergeant?"

Heath smiled tolerantly. "What'll I do with it, Captain? You keep it. But don't you dare lose it."

"I won't lose it," Hagedorn assured him, with stodgy seriousness; and, without so much as a glance at either the district attorney or the chief inspector, he waddled from the room with a slightly rolling movement which suggested that of some huge amphibious mammal.

Vance, who was standing beside me near the door, turned and followed Hagedorn into the hall. The two stood talking in low tones for several minutes. Vance appeared to be asking questions, and although I was not close enough to hear their conversation, I caught several words and phrases—"trajectory," "muzzle velocity," "angle of fire," "impetus," "impact," "deflection," and the like—and wondered what on earth had prompted this strange interrogation.

As Vance was thanking Hagedorn for his information Inspector O'Brien entered the hall. "Learning fast?" he asked, smiling patronizingly at Vance. Then, without waiting for a reply: "Come along, Captain; I'll drive you downtown."

Markham heard him. "Have you got room for Dinwiddie, too, Inspector?"

"Plenty, Mr. Markham."

The three of them went out.

Vance and I were now left alone in the room with Heath and the district attorney, and, as if by common impulse, we all settled ourselves in chairs, Vance taking one near the dining room door directly facing the chair in which Benson had been murdered.

I had been keenly interested in Vance's manner and actions from the moment of his arrival at the house. When he had first entered the room he had adjusted his monocle carefully—an act which, despite his air of passivity, I recognized as an indication of interest. When his mind was alert and he wished to take on external impressions quickly, he invariably brought out his monocle. He could see adequately enough without it, and his use of it, I had observed, was largely the result of an intellectual dictate. The added clarity of vision it gave him seemed subtly to affect his clarity of mind.*

At first he had looked over the room incuriously and watched the proceedings with bored apathy; but during Heath's brief questioning of his subordinates, an expression of cynical amusement had appeared on his face. Following a few general queries to Assistant District Attorney Dinwiddie, he had sauntered, with apparent aimlessness, about the room, looking at the various articles and occasionally shifting his gaze back and forth between different pieces of furniture. At length he had stooped down and inspected the mark made by the bullet on the wainscot; and once he had gone to the door and looked up and down the hall.

The only thing that had seemed to hold his attention to any extent was the body itself. He had stood before it for several minutes, studying its position, and had even bent over the outstretched arm on the table as if to see just how the dead man's hand was holding the book. The crossed position of the legs, however, had attracted him most, and he had stood studying them for a considerable time. Finally, he had returned his monocle to his waistcoat pocket and joined Dinwiddie and me near the door, where he had stood, watching Heath and the other detectives with lazy indifference, until the departure of Captain Hagedorn.

The four of us had no more than taken seats when the patrolman stationed in the vestibule appeared at the door. "There's a man from the local precinct station here, sir," he announced, "who wants to see the officer in charge. Shall I send him in?"

Heath nodded curtly, and a moment later a large red-faced Irishman, in civilian clothes, stood before us. He saluted Heath, but on recognizing the district attorney, made Markham the recipient of his report.

"I'm Officer McLaughlin, sir—West Forty-seventh Street station," he informed us; "and I was on duty on this beat last night. Around midnight, I guess it was, there was a big gray Cadillac standing in front of this house—I noticed it particular, because it had a lot of fishing tackle sticking out the back, and all of its lights were on. When I heard of the crime this morning, I reported the car to the station sergeant, and he sent me around to tell you about it."

"Excellent," Markham commented; and then, with a nod, referred the matter to Heath.

"May be something in it," the latter admitted dubiously. "How long would you say the car was here, Officer?"

"A good half hour anyway. It was here before twelve, and when I come back at twelve thirty or thereabouts, it was still here. But the next time I come by, it was gone."

"You saw nothing else? Nobody in the car, or anyone hanging around who might have been the owner?"

---

* Vance's eyes were slightly bifocal. His right eye was 1.2 astigmatic, whereas his left eye was practically normal.

"No, sir, I did not."

Several other questions of a similar nature were asked him; but nothing more could be learned, and he was dismissed.

"Anyway," remarked Heath, "the car story will be good stuff to hand the reporters."

Vance had sat through the questioning of McLaughlin with drowsy inattention—I doubt if he even heard more than the first few words of the officer's report—and now, with a stifled yawn, he rose and, sauntering to the center table, picked up one of the cigarette butts that had been found in the fireplace. After rolling it between his thumb and forefinger and scrutinizing the tip, he ripped the paper open with his thumbnail and held the exposed tobacco to his nose.

Heath, who had been watching him gloweringly, leaned suddenly forward in his chair.

"What are you doing there?" he demanded, in a tone of surly truculence.

Vance lifted his eyes in decorous astonishment.

"Merely smelling of the tobacco," he replied, with condescending unconcern. "It's rather mild, y' know, but delicately blended."

The muscles in Heath's cheeks worked angrily. "Well, you'd better put it down, sir," he advised. Then he looked Vance up and down. "Tobacco expert?" he asked, with ill-disguised sarcasm.

"Oh, dear no." Vance's voice was dulcet. "My specialty is scarab-cartouches of the Ptolemaic dynasties."

Markham interposed diplomatically. "You really shouldn't touch anything around here, Vance, at this stage of the game. You never know what'll turn out to be important. Those cigarette stubs may quite possibly be significant evidence."

"Evidence?" repeated Vance sweetly. "My word! You don't say, really! Most amusin'!"

Markham was plainly annoyed; and Heath was boiling inwardly but made no further comment; he even forced a mirthless smile. He evidently felt that he had been a little too abrupt with this friend of the district attorney's, however much the friend might have deserved being reprimanded.

Heath, however, was no sycophant in the presence of his superiors. He knew his worth and lived up to it with his whole energy, discharging the tasks to which he was assigned with a dogged indifference to his own political well-being. This stubbornness of spirit, and the solidity of character it implied, were respected and valued by the men over him.

He was a large, powerful man but agile and graceful in his movements, like a highly trained boxer. He had hard blue eyes, remarkably bright and penetrating, a small nose, a broad, oval chin, and a stern, straight mouth with lips that appeared always compressed. His hair, which, though he was well along in his forties, was without a trace of grayness, was cropped about the edges and stood upright in a short bristly pompadour. His voice had an aggressive resonance, but he rarely blustered. In many ways he accorded with the conventional notion of what a detective is like. But there was something more to the man's personality, an added capability and strength, as it were; and as I sat watching him that morning I felt myself unconsciously admiring him, despite his very obvious limitations.

"What's the exact situation, Sergeant?" Markham asked. "Dinwiddie gave me only the barest facts."

Heath cleared his throat. "We got the word a little before seven. Benson's housekeeper, a Mrs. Platz, called up the local station and reported that she'd found him dead, and asked that somebody be sent over at once. The message, of course, was relayed to headquarters. I wasn't there at the time, but Burke and Emery were on duty, and after notifying Inspector Moran, they came on up here. Several of the men from the local station were already on the job doing the usual nosing about. When the inspector had got here and looked the situation over, he telephoned me to hurry along. When I arrived, the local men had gone, and three more men from the homicide bureau had joined Burke and Emery. The inspector also phoned Captain Hagedorn—he thought the case big enough to call him in on it at once—and the captain had just got here when you arrived. Mr. Dinwiddie had come in right after the inspector and phoned you at once. Chief Inspector O'Brien came along a little ahead of me. I questioned the Platz woman right off; and my men were looking the place over when you showed up."

"Where's this Mrs. Platz now?" asked Markham.

"Upstairs being watched by one of the local men. She lives in the house."

"Why did you mention the specific hour of twelve thirty to the doctor?"

"Platz told me she heard a report at that time, which I thought might have been the shot. I guess now it *was* the shot—it checks up with a number of things."

"I think we'd better have another talk with Mrs. Platz," Markham suggested. "But first: did you find anything suggestive in the room here—anything to go on?"

Heath hesitated almost imperceptibly; then he drew from his coat pocket a woman's handbag and a pair of long white kid gloves, and tossed them on the table in front of the district attorney.

"Only these," he said. "One of the local men found them on the end of the mantel over there."

After a casual inspection of the gloves Markham opened the handbag and turned its contents out onto the table. I came forward and looked on, but Vance remained in his chair, placidly smoking a cigarette.

The handbag was of fine gold mesh with a catch set with small sapphires. It was unusually small and obviously designed only for evening wear. The objects which it had held, and which Markham was now inspecting, consisted of a flat watered-silk cigarette case, a small gold phial of Roger and Gallet's Fleurs d'Amour perfume, a *cloisonné* vanity compact, a short delicate cigarette holder of inlaid amber, a gold-cased lipstick, a small embroidered French-linen handkerchief with "M. St.C." monogrammed in the corner, and a Yale latchkey.

"This ought to give us a good lead," said Markham, indicating the handkerchief. "I suppose you went over the articles carefully, Sergeant."

Heath nodded. "Yes, and I imagine the bag belongs to the woman Benson was out with last night. The housekeeper told me he had an appointment and went out to dinner in his dress clothes. She didn't hear Benson when he came back, though. Anyway, we ought to be able to run down 'M. St.C.' without much trouble.

Markham had taken up the cigarette case again, and as he held it upside down a little shower of loose dried tobacco fell onto the table.

Heath stood up suddenly. "Maybe those cigarettes came out of that case," he suggested. He picked up the intact butt and looked at it. "It's a lady's cigarette, all right. It looks as though it might have been smoked in a holder, too."

"I beg to differ with you, Sergeant," drawled Vance. "You'll forgive me, I'm sure. But there's a bit of lip rouge on the end of the cigarette. It's hard to see, on account of the gold tip."

Heath looked at Vance sharply; he was too much surprised to be resentful. After a closer inspection of the cigarette, he turned again to Vance.

"Perhaps you could also tell us from these tobacco grains, if the cigarettes came from this case," he suggested, with gruff irony.

"One never knows, does one?" Vance replied, indolently rising.

Picking up the case, he pressed it wide open and tapped it on the table. Then he looked into it closely, and a humorous smile twitched the corners of his mouth. Putting his forefinger deep into the case, he drew out a small cigarette which had evidently been wedged flat along the bottom of the pocket.

"My olfact'ry gifts won't be necess'ry now," he said. "It is apparent even to the naked eye that the cigarettes are, to speak loosely, identical—eh what, Sergeant?"

Heath grinned good-naturedly. "That's one on us, Mr. Markham." And he carefully put the cigarette and the stub in an envelope, which he marked and pocketed.

"You now see, Vance," observed Markham, "the importance of those cigarette butts."

"Can't say that I do," responded the other. "Of what possible value is a cigarette butt? You can't smoke it, y' know."

"It's evidence, my dear fellow," explained Markham patiently. "One knows that the owner of this bag returned with Benson last night and remained long enough to smoke two cigarettes."

Vance lifted his eyebrows in mock amazement. "One does, does one? Fancy that, now."

"It only remains to locate her," interjected Heath.

"She's a rather decided brunette, at any rate—if that fact will facilitate your quest any," said Vance easily; "though why you should desire to annoy the lady, I can't for the life of me imagine—really I can't, don't y' know."

"Why do you say she's a brunette?" asked Markham.

"Well, if she isn't," Vance told him, sinking listlessly back in his chair, "then she should consult a cosmetician as to the proper way to make up. I see she uses 'Rachel' powder and Guerlain's dark lipstick. And it simply isn't done among blondes, old dear."

"I defer, of course, to your expert opinion," smiled Markham. Then, to Heath: "I guess we'll have to look for a brunette, Sergeant."

"It's all right with me," agreed Heath jocularly. By this time, I think, he had entirely forgiven Vance for destroying the cigarette butt.

4

THE HOUSEKEEPER'S STORY

(*Friday, June 14; 11 A.M.*)

"Now," SUGGESTED Markham, "suppose we take a look over the house. I imagine you've done that pretty thoroughly already, Sergeant, but I'd like to see the layout. Anyway, I don't want to question the housekeeper until the body has been removed."

Heath rose. "Very good, sir. I'd like another look myself."

The four of us went into the hall and walked down the passageway to the rear of the house. At the extreme end, on the left, was a door leading downstairs to the basement; but it was locked and bolted.

"The basement is only used for storage now," Heath explained; "and the door which opens from it into the street areaway is boarded up. The Platz woman sleeps upstairs—Benson lived here alone, and there's plenty of spare room in the house—and the kitchen is on this floor."

He opened a door on the opposite side of the passageway, and we stepped into a small, modern kitchen. Its two high windows, which gave into the paved rear yard at a height of about eight feet from the ground, were securely guarded with iron bars, and, in addition, the sashes were closed and locked. Passing through a swinging door, we entered the dining room, which was directly behind the living room. The two windows here looked upon a small stone court, really no more than a deep airwell between Benson's house and the adjoining one; and these also were iron-barred and locked.

We now reentered the hallway and stood for a moment at the foot of the stairs leading above.

"You can see, Mr. Markham," Heath pointed out, "that whoever shot Benson must have gotten in by the front door. There's no other way he could have entered. Living alone, I guess Benson was a little touchy on the subject of burglars. The only window that wasn't barred was the rear one in the living room; and that was shut and locked. Anyway, it only leads into the inside court. The front windows of the living room have that ironwork over them; so they couldn't have been used even to shoot through, for Benson was shot from the opposite direction.... It's pretty clear the gunman got in the front door."

"Looks that way," said Markham.

"And pardon me for saying so," remarked Vance, "but Benson let him in."

"Yes?" retorted Heath unenthusiastically. "Well, we'll find all that out later, I hope."

"Oh, doubtless," Vance drily agreed.

We ascended the stairs and entered Benson's bedroom, which was directly over the living room. It was severely but well furnished and in excellent order. The bed was made, showing it had not been slept in that night; and the window shades were drawn. Benson's dinner jacket and white piqué waistcoat were hanging over a chair. A winged collar and a black bowtie were on the bed, where they had evidently been thrown when Benson had taken them off on returning home. A pair of low evening shoes were standing by the bench at the foot of the bed. In a glass of water on the night table was a platinum plate of four false teeth; and a toupee of beautiful workmanship was lying on the chiffonier.

This last item aroused Vance's special interest. He walked up to it and regarded it closely.

"Most int'restin'," he commented. "Our departed friend seems to have worn false hair; did you know that, Markham?"

"I always suspected it," was the indifferent answer.

Heath, who had remained standing on the threshold, seemed a little impatient.

"There's only one other room on this floor," he said, leading the way down the hall. "It's also a bedroom—for guests, so the housekeeper explained."

Markham and I looked in through the door, but Vance remained lounging against the balustrade at the head of the stairs. He was manifestly uninterested in Alvin Benson's domestic arrangements; and when Markham and Heath and I went up to the third floor, he sauntered down into the main hallway. When at length we descended from our tour of inspection he was casually looking over the titles in Benson's bookcase.

We had just reached the foot of the stairs when the front door opened and two men with a stretcher entered. The ambulance from the Department of Welfare had arrived to take the corpse to the Morgue; and the brutal, businesslike way in which Benson's body was covered up, lifted onto the stretcher, carried out and shoved into the wagon, made me shudder. Vance, on the other hand, after the merest fleeting glance at the two men, paid no attention to them. He had found a volume with a beautiful Humphrey-Milford binding, and was absorbed in its Roger Payne tooling and powdering.

"I think an interview with Mrs. Platz is indicated now," said Markham; and Heath went to the foot of the stairs and gave a loud, brisk order.

Presently a gray-haired, middle-aged woman entered the living room accompanied by a plainclothesman smoking a large cigar. Mrs. Platz was of the simple, old-fashioned, motherly type, with a calm, benevolent countenance. She impressed me as highly capable, and as a woman given little to hysteria—an impression strengthened by her attitude of passive resignation. She seemed, however, to possess that taciturn shrewdness that is so often found among the ignorant.

"Sit down, Mrs. Platz." Markham greeted her kindly. "I'm the district attorney, and there are some questions I want to ask you."

She took a straight chair by the door and waited, gazing nervously from one to the other of us. Markham's gentle, persuasive voice, though, appeared to encourage her; and her answers became more and more fluent.

The main facts that transpired from a quarter-of-an-hour's examination may be summed up as follows:

Mrs. Platz had been Benson's housekeeper for four years and was the only servant employed. She lived in the house, and her room was on the third, or top, floor in the rear.

On the afternoon of the preceding day Benson had returned from his office at an unusually early hour—around four o'clock—announcing to Mrs. Platz that he would not be home for dinner that evening. He had remained in the living room, with the hall door closed, until half past six and had then gone upstairs to dress.

He had left the house about seven o'clock but had not said where he was going. He had remarked casually that he would return in fairly good season but had told Mrs. Platz she need not wait up for him—which was her custom whenever he intended bringing guests home. This was the last she had seen him alive. She had not heard him when he returned that night.

She had retired about half past ten and, because of the heat, had left the door ajar. She had been awakened some time later by a loud detonation. It had startled her, and she had turned on the light by her bed, noting that it was just half past twelve by the small alarm clock she used for rising. It was, in fact, the early hour which had reassured her. Benson, whenever he went out for the evening, rarely returned home before two; and this fact, coupled with the stillness of the house, had made her conclude that the noise which had aroused her had been merely the backfiring of an automobile in Forty-ninth Street. Consequently, she had dismissed the matter from her mind, and gone back to sleep.

At seven o'clock the next morning she came downstairs as usual to begin her day's duties and, on her way to the front door to bring in the milk and cream, had discovered Benson's body. All the shades in the living room were down.

At first she thought Benson had fallen asleep in his chair, but when she saw the bullet hole and noticed that the electric lights had been switched off, she knew he was dead. She had gone at once to the telephone in the hall and, asking the operator for the police station, had reported the murder. She had then remembered Benson's brother, Major Anthony Benson, and had telephoned him also. He had arrived at the house almost simultaneously with the detectives from the West Forty-seventh Street station. He had questioned her a little, talked with the plainclothesmen, and gone away before the men from headquarters arrived.

"And now, Mrs. Platz," said Markham, glancing at the notes he had been making, "one or two more questions, and we won't trouble you further. . . . Have you noticed anything in Mr. Benson's actions lately that might lead you to suspect that he was worried—or, let us say, in fear of anything happening to him?"

"No sir," the woman answered readily. "It looked like he was in special good humor for the last week or so."

"I notice that most of the windows on this floor are barred. Was he particularly afraid of burglars, or of people breaking in?"

"Well—not exactly," was the hesitant reply. "But he did use to say as how the police were no good—begging your pardon, sir—and how a man in this city had to look out for himself if he didn't want to get held up."

Markham turned to Heath with a chuckle. "You might make a special note of that for your files, Sergeant." Then to Mrs. Platz: "Do you know of anyone who had a grudge against Mr. Benson?"

"Not a soul, sir," the housekeeper answered emphatically. "He was a queer man in many ways, but everybody seemed to like him. He was all the time going to parties or giving parties. I just can't see why anybody'd want to kill him."

Markham looked over his notes again. "I don't think there's anything else for the present. . . . How about it, Sergeant? Anything further you want to ask?"

Heath pondered a moment. "No, I can't think of anything more just now. . . . But you, Mrs. Platz," he added, turning a cold glance on the woman, "will stay here in this house till you're given permission to leave. We'll want to question you later. But you're not to talk to anyone else—understand? Two of my men will be here for a while yet."

Vance, during the interview, had been jotting down something on the fly-leaf of a small pocket address book and as Heath was speaking he tore out the page and handed it to Markham. Markham glanced at it frowningly and pursed his lips. Then after a few moments' hesitation, he addressed himself again to the housekeeper.

"You mentioned, Mrs. Platz, that Mr. Benson was liked by everyone. Did you yourself like him?"

The woman shifted her eyes to her lap. "Well, sir," she replied reluctantly, "I was only working for him and I haven't got any complaint about the way he treated me."

Despite her words, she gave the impression that she either disliked Benson extremely or greatly disapproved of him. Markham, however, did not push the point.

"And, by the way, Mrs. Platz," he said next, "did Mr. Benson keep any fire-arms about the house? For instance, do you know if he owned a revolver?"

For the first time during the interview, the woman appeared agitated, even frightened.

"Yes, sir, I—think he did," she admitted, in an unsteady voice.

"Where did he keep it?"

The woman glanced up apprehensively and rolled her eyes slightly as if weighing the advisability of speaking frankly. Then she replied in a low voice, "In that hidden drawer there in the center table. You—you use that little brass button to open it with."

Heath jumped up, and pressed the button she had indicated. A tiny, shallow drawer shot out; and in it lay a Smith and Wesson thirty-eight revolver with an inlaid pearl handle. He picked it up, broke the carriage, and looked at the head of the cylinder.

"Full," he announced laconically.

An expression of tremendous relief spread over the woman's features, and she sighed audibly.

Markham had risen and was looking at the revolver over Heath's shoulder.

"You'd better take charge of it, Sergeant," he said; "though I don't see ex-actly how it fits in with the case."

He resumed his seat and, glacing at the notation Vance had given him, turned again to the housekeeper.

"One more question, Mrs. Platz. You said Mr. Benson came home early and spent his time before dinner in this room. Did he have any callers during that time?"

I was watching the woman closely, and it seemed to me that she quickly compressed her lips. At any rate, she sat up a little straighter in her chair be-fore answering.

"There wasn't no one, as far as I know."

"But surely you would have known if the bell rang," insisted Markham. "You would have answered the door, wouldn't you?"

"There wasn't no one," she repeated, with a trace of sullenness.

"And last night—did the doorbell ring at all after you had retired?"

"No, sir."

"You would have heard it, even if you'd been asleep?"

"Yes, sir. There's a bell just outside my door, the same as in the kitchen. It rings in both places. Mr. Benson had it fixed that way."

Markham thanked her and dismissed her. When she had gone, he looked at Vance questioningly. "What idea did you have in your mind when you handed me those questions?"

"I might have been a bit presumptuous, y' know," said Vance; "but when the lady was extolling the deceased's popularity, I rather felt she was overdoing it a bit. There was an unconscious implication of antithesis in her eulogy, which suggested to me that she herself was not ardently enamored of the gentleman."

"And what put the notion of firearms into your mind?"

"That query," explained Vance, "was a corollary of your own questions about barred windows and Benson's fear of burglars. If he was in a funk about housebreakers or enemies, he'd be likely to have weapons at hand—eh, what?"

"Well, anyway, Mr. Vance," put in Heath, "your curiosity unearthed a nice little revolver that's probably never been used."

"By the bye, Sergeant," returned Vance, ignoring the other's good-humored sarcasm, "just what do you make of that nice little revolver?"

"Well, now," Heath replied, with ponderous facetiousness, "I deduct that Mr. Benson kept a pearl-handled Smith and Wesson in a secret drawer of his center table."

"You don't say—really!" exclaimed Vance in mock admiration. "Pos'tively illuminatin'!"

Markham broke up this raillery. "Why did you want to know about visitors, Vance? There obviously hadn't been anyone here."

"Oh, just a whim of mine. I was assailed by an impulsive yearning to hear what La Platz would say."

Heath was studying Vance curiously. His first impressions of the man were being dispelled, and he had begun to suspect that beneath the other's casual and debonair exterior there was something of a more solid nature than he had at first imagined. He was not altogether satisfied with Vance's explanations to Markham and seemed to be endeavoring to penetrate to his real reasons for supplementing the district attorney's interrogation of the housekeeper. Heath was astute, and he had the worldly man's ability to read people; but Vance, being different from the men with whom he usually came in contact, was an enigma to him.

At length he relinquished his scrutiny and drew up his chair to the table with a spirited air.

"And now, Mr. Markham," he said crisply, "we'd better outline our activities so as not to duplicate our efforts. The sooner I get my men started, the better."

Markham assented readily. "The investigation is entirely up to you, Sergeant. I'm here to help wherever I'm needed."

"That's very kind of you, sir," Heath returned. "But it looks to me as though there'd be enough work for all parties. . . . Suppose I get to work on running down the owner of the handbag, and send some men out scouting among Benson's night-life cronies—I can pick up some names from the housekeeper, and they'll be a good starting point. And I'll get after that Cadillac, too. . . . Then we ought to look into his lady friends—I guess he had enough of 'em."

"I may get something out of the major along that line," supplied Markham. "He'll tell me anything I want to know. And I can also look into Benson's business associates through the same channel."

"I was going to suggest that you could do that better than I could," Heath rejoined. "We ought to run into something pretty quick that'll give us a line to go on. And I've got an idea that when we locate the lady he took to dinner last night and brought back here, we'll know a lot more than we do now."

"Or a lot less," murmured Vance.

Heath looked up quickly and grunted with an air of massive petulance.

"Let me tell you something, Mr. Vance," he said, "since I understand you want to learn something about these affairs: when anything goes seriously wrong in this world, it's pretty safe to look for a woman in the case."

"Ah, yes," smiled Vance. "*Cherchez la femme*—an aged notion. Even the Romans labored under the superstition. They expressed it with *Dux femina facti.*"

"However they expressed it," retorted Heath, "they had the right idea. And don't let 'em tell you different."

Again Markham diplomatically intervened.

"That point will be settled very soon, I hope. . . . And now, Sergeant, if you've nothing else to suggest, I'll be getting along. I told Major Benson I'd see him at lunchtime; and I may have some news for you by tonight."

"Right," assented Heath. "I'm going to stick around here awhile and see if there's anything I overlooked. I'll arrange for a guard outside and also for a man inside to keep an eye on the Platz woman. Then I'll see the reporters and let them in on the disappearing Cadillac and Mr. Vance's mysterious revolver in the secret drawer. I guess that ought to hold 'em. If I find out anything, I'll phone you."

When he had shaken hands with the district attorney, he turned to Vance. "Good-bye, sir," he said pleasantly, much to my surprise, and to Markham's, too, I imagine. "I hope you learned something this morning."

"You'd be pos'tively dumfounded, Sergeant, at all I did learn," Vance answered carelessly.

Again I noted the look of shrewd scrutiny in Heath's eyes; but in a second it was gone. "Well, I'm glad of that," was his perfunctory reply.

Markham, Vance, and I went out, and the patrolman on duty hailed a taxicab for us.

"So that's the way our lofty *gendarmerie* approaches the mysterious wherefores of criminal enterprise—eh?" mused Vance, as we started on our way across town. "Markham, old dear, how do those robust lads ever succeed in running down a culprit?"

"You have witnessed only the barest preliminaries," Markham explained. "There are certain things that must be done as a matter of routine—*ex abundantia cautelæ,* as we lawyers say."

"But, my word!—such technique!" sighed Vance. "Ah, well, *quantum est in rubus inane!* as we laymen say."

"You don't think much of Heath's capacity, I know"—Markham's voice was patient—"but he's a clever man and one that it's very easy to underestimate."

"I daresay," murmured Vance. "Anyway, I'm deuced grateful to you, and all that, for letting me behold the solemn proceedings. I've been vastly amused, even if not uplifted. Your official Æsculapius rather appealed to me, y' know—such a brisk, unemotional chap, and utterly unimpressed with the corpse. He really should have taken up crime in a serious way, instead of studying medicine."

Markham lapsed into gloomy silence and sat looking out of the window in troubled meditation until we reached Vance's house.

"I don't like the looks of things," he remarked, as we drew up to the curb. "I have a curious feeling about this case."

Vance regarded him a moment from the corner of his eye. "See here, Markham," he said with unwonted seriousness; "haven't you any idea who shot Benson?"

Markham forced a faint smile, "I wish I had. Crimes of willful murder are not so easily solved. And this case strikes me as a particularly complex one."

"Fancy, now!" said Vance, as he stepped out of the machine. "And I thought it extr'ordin'rily simple."

5

GATHERING INFORMATION

(Saturday, June 15; forenoon.)

YOU WILL remember the sensation caused by Alvin Benson's murder. It was one of those crimes that appeal irresistibly to the popular imagination. Mystery is the basis of all romance, and about the Benson case there hung an impenetrable aura of mystery. It was many days before any definite light was shed on the circumstances surrounding the shooting; but numerous *ignes fatui* arose to beguile the public's imagination, and wild speculations were heard on all sides.

Alvin Benson, while not a romantic figure in any respect, had been well known; and his personality had been a colorful and spectacular one. He had been a member of New York's wealthy bohemian social set—an avid sportsman, a rash gambler, and professional man-about-town; and his life, led on the borderland of the demimonde, had contained many highlights. His exploits in the nightclubs and cabarets had long supplied the subject matter for exaggerated stories and comments in the various local papers and magazines which batten on Broadway's scandalmongers.

Benson and his brother, Anthony, had, at the time of the former's sudden death, been running a brokerage office at 21 Wall Street, under the name of

Benson and Benson. Both were regarded by the other brokers of the Street as shrewd businessmen, though perhaps a shade unethical when gauged by the constitution and bylaws of the New York Stock Exchange. They were markedly contrasted as to temperament and taste and saw little of each other outside the office. Alvin Benson devoted his entire leisure to pleasure-seeking and was a regular patron of the city's leading cafes; whereas Anthony Benson, who was the older and had served as a major in the late war, followed a sedate and conventional existence, spending most of his evenings quietly at his clubs. Both, however, were popular in their respective circles, and between them they had built up a large clientele.

The glamour of the financial district had much to do with the manner in which the crime was handled by the newspapers. Moreover, the murder had been committed at a time when the metropolitan press was experiencing a temporary lull in sensationalism; and the story was spread over the front pages of the papers with a prodigality rarely encountered in such cases.* Eminent detectives throughout the country were interviewed by enterprising reporters. Histories of famous unsolved murder cases were revived; and clairvoyants and astrologers were engaged by the Sunday editors to solve the mystery by various metaphysical devices. Photographs and detailed diagrams were the daily accompaniments of these journalistic outpourings.

In all the news stories the gray Cadillac and the pearl-handled Smith and Wesson were featured. There were pictures of Cadillac cars, "touched up" and reconstructed to accord with Patrolman McLaughlin's description, some of them even showing the fishing tackle protruding from the tonneau. A photograph of Benson's center table had been taken, with the secret drawer enlarged and reproduced in an "inset." One Sunday magazine went so far as to hire an expert cabinetmaker to write a dissertation on secret compartments in furniture.

The Benson case from the outset had proved a trying and difficult one from the police standpoint. Within an hour of the time that Vance and I had left the scene of the crime a systematic investigation had been launched by the men of the homicide bureau in charge of Sergeant Heath. Benson's house was again gone over thoroughly, and all his private correspondence read; but nothing was brought forth that could throw any light on the tragedy. No weapon was found aside from Benson's own Smith and Wesson; and though all the window grilles were again inspected, they were found to be secure, indicating that the murderer had either let himself in with a key or else been admitted by Benson. Heath, by the way, was unwilling to admit this latter possibility despite Mrs. Platz's positive assertion that no other person besides herself and Benson had a key.

Because of the absence of any definite clue, other than the handbag and the gloves, the only proceeding possible was the interrogating of Benson's friends and associates in the hope of uncovering some fact which would furnish a

---

* Even the famous Elwell case, which came several years later and bore certain points of similarity to the Benson case, created no greater sensation, despite the fact that Elwell was more widely known than Benson, and the persons involved were more prominent socially. Indeed, the Benson case was referred to several times in descriptions of the Elwell case; and one antiadministration paper regretted editorially that John F.-X. Markham was no longer district attorney of New York.

trail. It was by this process also that Heath hoped to establish the identity of the owner of the handbag. A special effort was therefore made to ascertain where Benson had spent the evening; but though many of his acquaintances were questioned, and the cafes where he habitually dined were visited, no one could at once be found who had seen him that night; nor, as far as it was possible to learn, had he mentioned to anyone his plans for the evening. Furthermore, no general information of a helpful nature came to light immediately, although the police pushed their inquiry with the utmost thoroughness. Benson apparently had no enemies; he had not quarreled seriously with anyone; and his affairs were reported in their usual orderly shape.

Major Anthony Benson was naturally the principal person looked to for information, because of his intimate knowledge of his brother's affairs; and it was in this connection that the district attorney's office did its chief functioning at the beginning of the case. Markham had lunched with Major Benson the day the crime was discovered, and though the latter had shown a willingness to cooperate—even to the detriment of his brother's character—his suggestions were of little value. He explained to Markham that, though he knew most of his brother's associates, he could not name anyone who would have any reason for committing such a crime or anyone who, in his opinion, would be able to help in leading the police to the guilty person. He admitted frankly, however, that there was a side to his brother's life with which he was unacquainted and regretted that he was unable to suggest any specific way of ascertaining the hidden facts. But he intimated that his brother's relations with women were of a somewhat unconventional nature; and he ventured the opinion that there was a bare possibility of a motive being found in that direction.

Pursuant of the few indefinite and unsatisfactory suggestions of Major Benson, Markham had immediately put to work two good men from the detective division assigned to the district attorney's office, with instructions to confine their investigations to Benson's women acquaintances so as not to appear in any way to be encroaching upon the activities of the central office men. Also, as a result of Vance's apparent interest in the housekeeper at the time of the interrogation, he had sent a man to look into the woman's antecedents and relationships.

Mrs. Platz, it was learned, had been born in a small Pennsylvania town, of German parents both of whom were dead; and had been a widow for over sixteen years. Before coming to Benson, she had been with one family for twelve years and had left the position only because her mistress had given up housekeeping and moved into a hotel. Her former employer, when questioned, said she thought there had been a daughter but had never seen the child and knew nothing of it. In these facts there was nothing to take hold of, and Markham had merely filed the report as a matter of form.

Heath had instigated a citywide search for the gray Cadillac, although he had little faith in its direct connection with the crime; and in this the newspapers helped considerably by the extensive advertising given the car. One curious fact developed that fired the police with the hope that the Cadillac might indeed hold some clue to the mystery. A street cleaner, having read or heard about the fishing tackle in the machine, reported the finding of two jointed fishing rods, in good condition, at the side of one of the drives in Central Park near Columbus Circle. The question was: were these rods part of the equipment Patrolman McLaughlin had seen in the Cadillac? The owner of the car might conceivably have thrown them away in his flight; but, on the other hand, they might have been lost by someone else while driving through the park. No further information was forthcoming, and on the morning of the day following the discovery of the crime the case, so far as any definite progress toward a solution was concerned, had taken no perceptible forward step.

That morning Vance had sent Currie out to buy him every available newspaper; and he had spent over an hour perusing the various accounts of the crime. It was unusual for him to glance at a newspaper, even casually, and I could not refrain from expressing my amazement at his sudden interest in a subject so entirely outside his normal routine.

"No, Van old dear," he explained languidly, "I am not becoming sentimental or even human, as that word is erroneously used today. I can not say with Terence, 'Homo sum, humani nihil a me alienum puto,' because I regard most things that are called human as decidedly alien to myself. But, y' know, this little flurry in crime has proved rather int'restin', or, as the magazine writers say, intriguing—beastly word! . . . Van, you really should read this precious interview with Sergeant Heath. He takes an entire column to say, 'I know nothing.' A priceless lad! I'm becoming pos'tively fond of him."

"It may be," I suggested, "that Heath is keeping his true knowledge from the papers as a bit of tactical diplomacy."

"No," Vance returned, with a sad wag of the head, "no man has so little vanity that he would delib'rately reveal himself to the world as a creature with no perceptible powers of human reasoning—as he does in all these morning journals—for the mere sake of bringing one murderer to justice. That would be martyrdom gone mad."

"Markham, at any rate, may know or suspect something that hasn't been revealed," I said.

Vance pondered a moment. "That's not impossible," he admitted. "He has kept himself modestly in the background in all this journalistic palaver. Suppose we look into the matter more thoroughly—eh, what?"

Going to the telephone, he called the district attorney's office, and I heard him make an appointment with Markham for lunch at the Stuyvesant Club.

"What about that Nadelmann statuette at Stieglitz's," I asked, remembering the reason for my presence at Vance's that morning.

"I ain't* in the mood for Greek simplifications today," he answered, turning again to his newspapers.

To say that I was surprised at his attitude is to express it mildly. In all my association with him I had never known him to forgo his enthusiasm for art in favor of any other divertisement; and heretofore anything pertaining to the law and its operations had failed to interest him. I realized, therefore that something of an unusual nature was at work in his brain and I refrained from further comment.

---

* Vance, who had lived many years in England, frequently said "ain't"—a contraction which is regarded there more leniently than in this country. He also pronounced *ate* as if it were spelled *et;* and I can not remember his ever using the word "stomach" or "bug," both of which are under the social ban in England.

Markham was a little late for the appointment at the club, and Vance and I were already at our favorite corner table when he arrived.

"Well, my good Lycurgus," Vance greeted him, "aside from the fact that several new and significant clues have been unearthed and that the public may expect important developments in the very near future, and all that sort of tosh, how are things really going?"

Markham smiled. "I see you have been reading the newspapers. What do you think of the accounts?"

"Typical, no doubt," replied Vance. "They carefully and painstakingly omit nothing but the essentials."

"Indeed?" Markham's tone was jocular. "And what, may I ask, do you regard as the essentials of the case?"

"In my foolish amateur way," said Vance, "I looked upon dear Alvin's toupee as a rather conspicuous essential, don't y' know."

"Benson, at any rate, regarded it in that light, I imagine. . . . Anything else?"

"Well, there was the collar and the tie on the chiffonier."

"And," added Markham chaffingly, "don't overlook the false teeth in the tumbler."

"You're pos'tively coruscatin'!" Vance exclaimed. "Yes, they, too, were an essential of the situation. And I'll warrant the incomp'rable Heath didn't even notice them. But the other Aristotles present were equally sketchy in their observations."

"You weren't particularly impressed by the investigation yesterday, I take it," said Markham.

"On the contrary," Vance assured him, "I was impressed to the point of stupefaction. The whole proceedings constituted a masterpiece of absurdity. Everything relevant was sublimely ignored. There were at least a dozen *points de départ*, all leading in the same direction, but not one of them apparently was even noticed by any of the officiating *pourparleurs*. Everybody was too busy at such silly occupations as looking for cigarette ends and inspecting the ironwork at the windows. Those grilles, by the way, were rather attractive— Florentine design."

Markham was both amused and ruffled.

"One's pretty safe with the police, Vance," he said. "They get there eventually."

"I simply adore your trusting nature," murmured Vance. "But confide in me: what do you know regarding Benson's murderer?"

Markham hesitated. "This is, of course, in confidence," he said at length; "but this morning, right after you phoned, one of the men I had put to work on the amatory end of Benson's life reported that he had found the woman who left her handbag and gloves at the house that night—the initials on the handkerchief gave him the clue. And he dug up some interesting facts about her. As I suspected, she was Benson's dinner companion that evening. She's an actress—musical comedy, I believe. Muriel St. Clair by name."

"Most unfortunate," breathed Vance. "I was hoping, y' know, your myrmidons wouldn't discover the lady. I haven't the pleasure of her acquaintance or I'd send her a note of commiseration. . . . Now, I presume, you'll play the *juge d'instruction* and chivvy her most horribly, what?"

"I shall certainly question her, if that's what you mean."

Markham's manner was preoccupied, and during the rest of the lunch we spoke but little.

As we sat in the club's lounge room later having our smoke, Major Benson, who had been standing dejectedly at a window close by, caught sight of Markham and came over to us. He was a full-faced man of about fifty, with grave, kindly features and a sturdy, erect body.

He greeted Vance and me with a casual bow and turned at once to the district attorney. "Markham, I've been thinking things over constantly since our lunch yesterday," he said, "and there's one other suggestion I think I might make. There's a man named Leander Pfyfe who was very close to Alvin; and it's possible he could give you some helpful information. His name didn't occur to me yesterday, for he doesn't live in the city; he's on Long Island somewhere—Port Washington, I think. It's just an idea. The truth is, I can't seem to figure out anything that makes sense in this terrible affair."

He drew a quick, resolute breath, as if to check some involuntary sign of emotion. It was evident that the man, for all his habitual passivity of nature, was deeply moved.

"That's a good suggestion, Major," Markham said, making a notation on the back of a letter. "I'll get after it immediately."

Vance, who, during this brief interchange, had been gazing unconcernedly out of the window, turned and addressed himself to the major. "How about Colonel Ostrander? I've seen him several times in the company of your brother."

Major Benson made a slight gesture of depreciation.

"Only an acquaintance. He'd be of no value." Then he turned to Markham. "I don't imagine it's time even to hope that you've run across anything."

Markham took his cigar from his mouth and turning it about in his fingers, contemplated it thoughtfully.

"I wouldn't say that," he remarked, after a moment. "I've managed to find out whom your brother dined with Thursday night; and I know that this person returned home with him shortly after midnight." He paused as if deliberating the wisdom of saying more. Then: "The fact is, I don't need a great deal more evidence than I've got already to go before the grand jury and ask for an indictment."

A look of surprised admiration flashed in the major's sombre face.

"Thank God for that, Markham!" he said. Then, setting his heavy jaw, he placed his hand on the district attorney's shoulder. "Go the limit—for my sake!" he urged. "If you want me for anything, I'll be here at the club till late."

With this he turned and walked from the room.

"It seems a bit cold-blooded to bother the major with questions so soon after his brother's death," commented Markham. "Still, the world has got to go on."

Vance stifled a yawn. "Why—in Heaven's name?" he murmured listlessly.

6

VANCE OFFERS AN OPINION

(*Saturday, June 15; 2 P.M.*)

WE SAT for a while smoking in silence, Vance gazing lazily out into Madison Square, Markham frowning deeply at the faded oil portrait of old Peter Stuyvesant that hung over the fireplace.

Presently Vance turned and contemplated the district attorney with a faintly sardonic smile.

"I say, Markham," he drawled; "it has always been a source of amazement to me how easily you investigators of crime are misled by what you call clues. You find a footprint, or a parked automobile, or a monogrammed handkerchief, and then dash off on a wild chase with your eternal *Ecce signum!* 'Pon my word, it's as if you chaps were all under the spell of shillin' shockers. Won't you ever learn that crimes can't be solved by deductions based merely on material clues and circumst'ntial evidence?"

I think Markham was as much surprised as I at this sudden criticism; yet we both knew Vance well enough to realize that, despite his placid and almost flippant tone, there was a serious purpose behind his words.

"Would you advocate ignoring all the tangible evidence of a crime?" asked Markham, a bit patronizingly.

"Most emphatically," Vance declared calmly. "It's not only worthless but dangerous. . . . The great trouble with you chaps, d' ye see, is that you approach every crime with a fixed and unshakable assumption that the criminal is either half-witted or a colossal bungler. I say, has it never by any chance occurred to you that if a detective could see a clue, the criminal would also have seen it and would either have concealed it or disguised it, if he had not wanted it found? And have you never paused to consider that anyone clever enough to plan and execute a successful crime these days is, *ipso facto*, clever enough to manufacture whatever clues suit his purpose? Your detective seems wholly unwilling to admit that the surface appearance of a crime may be delib'rately deceptive or that the clues may have been planted for the def'nite purpose of misleading him."

"I'm afraid," Markham pointed out, with an air of indulgent irony, "that we'd convict very few criminals if we were to ignore all indicatory evidence, cogent circumstances, and irresistible inferences. . . . As a rule, you know, crimes are not witnessed by outsiders."

"That's your fundamental error, don't y' know," Vance observed impassively. "Every crime is witnessed by outsiders, just as is every work of art. The fact that no one sees the criminal, or the artist, actu'lly at work, is wholly incons'quential. The modern investigator of crime would doubtless refuse to believe that Rubens painted the *Descent from the Cross* in the Cathedral at Antwerp if there was sufficient circumst'ntial evidence to indicate that he had been away on diplomatic business, for instance, at the time it was painted. And yet, my dear fellow, such a conclusion would be prepost'rous. Even if the inf'rences to the contr'ry were so irresistible as to be legally overpowering,

42

the picture itself would prove conclusively that Rubens did paint it. Why? For the simple reason, d' ye see, that no one but Rubens could have painted it. It bears the indelible imprint of his personality and genius—and his alone."

"I'm not an æsthetician," Markham reminded him, a trifle testily. "I'm merely a practical lawyer and when it comes to determining the authorship of a crime, I prefer tangible evidence to metaphysical hypotheses."

"Your pref'rence, my dear fellow," Vance returned blandly, "will inev'tably involve you in all manner of embarrassing errors."

He slowly lit another cigarette and blew a wreath of smoke toward the ceiling. "Consider, for example, your conclusions in the present murder case," he went on, in his emotionless drawl. "You are laboring under the grave misconception that you know the person who prob'bly killed the unspeakable Benson. You admitted as much to the major; and you told him you had nearly enough evidence to ask for an indictment. No doubt, you do possess a number of what the learned Solons of today regard as convincing clues. But the truth is, don't y' know, you haven't your eye on the guilty person at all. You're about to bedevil some poor girl who had nothing whatever to do with the crime."

Markham swung about sharply.

"So!" he retorted. "I'm about to bedevil an innocent person, eh? Since my assistants and I are the only ones who happen to know what evidence we hold against her, perhaps you will explain by what occult process you acquired your knowledge of this person's innocence."

"It's quite simple, y' know," Vance replied, with a quizzical twitch of the lips. "You haven't your eye on the murderer for the reason that the person who committed this particular crime was sufficiently shrewd and perspicacious to see to it that no evidence which you or the police were likely to find would even remotely indicate his guilt."

He had spoken with the easy assurance of one who enunciates an obvious fact—a fact which permits of no argument.

Markham gave a disdainful laugh. "No lawbreaker," he asserted oracularly, "is shrewd enough to see all contingencies. Even the most trivial event has so many intimately related and serrated points of contact with other events which precede and follow, that it is a known fact that every criminal—however long and carefully he may plan—leaves some loose end to his preparations, which in the end betrays him."

"A known fact?" Vance repeated. "No, my dear fellow—merely a conventional superstition, based on the childish idea of an implacable, avenging Nemesis. I can see how this esoteric notion of the inev'tability of divine punishment would appeal to the popular imagination, like fortune-telling and Ouija boards, don't y' know; but—my word!—it desolates me to think that you, old chap, would give credence to such mystical moonshine."

"Don't let it spoil your entire day," said Markham acridly.

"Regard the unsolved, or successful, crimes that are taking place every day," Vance continued, disregarding the other's irony, "—crimes which completely baffle the best detectives in the business, what? The fact is, the only crimes that are ever solved are those planned by stupid people. That's why, whenever a man of even mod'rate sagacity decides to commit a crime, he accomplishes it with but little diff'culty and fortified with the pos'tive assurance of his immunity to discovery."

"Undetected crimes," scornfully submitted Markham, "result, in the main, from official bad luck, not from superior criminal cleverness."

"Bad luck"—Vance's voice was almost dulcet—"is merely a defensive and self-consoling synonym for inefficiency. A man with ingenuity and brains is not harassed by bad luck. . . . No, Markham old dear; unsolved crimes are simply crimes which have been intelligently planned and executed. And, d' ye see, it happens that the Benson murder falls into that categ'ry. Therefore, when, after a few hours' investigation, you say you're pretty sure who committed it, you must pardon me if I take issue with you."

He paused and took a few meditative puffs on his cigarette. "The factitious and casuistic methods of deduction you chaps pursue are apt to lead almost anywhere. In proof of which assertion I point triumphantly to the unfortunate young lady whose liberty you are now plotting to take away."

Markham. who had been hiding his resentment behind a smile of tolerant contempt, now turned on Vance and fairly glowered.

"It so happens—and I'm speaking *ex cathedra,*" he proclaimed defiantly, "that I come pretty near having the goods on your 'unfortunate young lady.'"

Vance was unmoved. "And yet, y' know," he observed drily, "no woman could possibly have done it."

I could see that Markham was furious. When he spoke he almost spluttered.

"A woman couldn't have done it, eh—no matter what the evidence?"

"Quite so," Vance rejoined placidly; "not if she herself swore to it and produced a tome of what you scions of the law term, rather pompously, incontrovertible evidence."

"Ah!" There was no mistaking the sarcasm of Markham's tone. "I am to understand, then, that you even regard confessions as valueless?"

"Yes, my dear Justinian," the other reponded, with an air of complacency; "I would have you understand precisely that. Indeed, they are worse than valueless—they're downright misleading. The fact that occasionally they may prove to be correct—like woman's prepost'rously overrated intuition—renders them just so much more unreliable."

Markham grunted disdainfully.

"Why should any person confess something to his detriment unless he felt that the truth had been found out or was likely to be found out?"

" 'Pon my word, Markham, you astound me! Permit me to murmur, *privatissime et gratis,* into your innocent ear that there are many other presumable motives for confessing. A confession may be the result of fear, or duress, or expediency, or mother-love, or chivalry, or what the psychoanalysts call the inferiority complex, or delusions, or a mistaken sense of duty, or a perverted egotism, or sheer vanity, or any other of a hundred causes. Confessions are the most treach'rous and unreliable of all forms of evidence; and even the silly and unscientific law repudiates them in murder cases unless substantiated by other evidence."

"You are eloquent; you wring me," said Markham. "But if the law threw out all confessions and ignored all material clues, as you appear to advise, then society might as well close down all its courts and scrap all its jails."

"A typical *non sequitur* of legal logic," Vance replied.

"But how would you convict the guilty, may I ask?"

"There is one infallible method of determining human guilt and responsibility," Vance explained; "but as yet the police are as blissfully unaware of its possibilities as they are ignorant of its operations. The truth can be learned only by an analysis of the psychological factors of a crime and an application of them to the individual. The only real clues are psychological—not material. Your truly profound art expert, for instance, does not judge and authenticate pictures by an inspection of the underpainting and a chemical analysis of the pigments, but by studying the creative personality revealed in the picture's conception and execution. He asks himself: Does this work of art embody the qualities of form and technique and mental attitude that made up the genius—namely, the personality—of Rubens, or Michelangelo, or Veronese, or Titian, or Tintoretto, or whoever may be the artist to whom the work has been tentatively credited."

"My mind is, I fear," Markham confessed, "still sufficiently primitive to be impressed by vulgar facts; and in the present instance—unfortunately for your most original and artistic analogy—I possess quite an array of such facts, all of which indicate that a certain young woman is the—shall we say?—creator of the criminal opus entitled *The Murder of Alvin Benson.*"

Vance shrugged his shoulders almost imperceptibly.

"Would you mind telling me—in confidence, of course—what these facts are?"

"Certainly not," Markham acceded. *"Imprimis:* the lady was in the house at the time the shot was fired."

Vance affected incredibility. "Eh—my word! She was actu'lly there? Most extr'ordin'ry!"

"The evidence of her presence is unassailable," pursued Markham. "As you know, the gloves she wore at dinner and the handbag she carried with her were both found on the mantel in Benson's living room."

"Oh!" murmured Vance, with a faintly deprecating smile. "It was not the lady, then, but her gloves and bag which were present—a minute and unimportant distinction, no doubt, from the legal point of view.... Still," he added, "I deplore the inability of my layman's untutored mind to accept the two conditions as identical. My trousers are at the dry cleaners; therefore, I am at the dry cleaners, what?"

Markham turned on him with considerable warmth.

"Does it mean nothing in the way of evidence, even to your layman's mind, that a woman's intimate and necessary articles, which she has carried throughout the evening, are found in her escort's quarters the following morning?"

"In admitting that it does not," Vance acknowledged quietly, "I no doubt expose a legal perception lamentably inefficient."

"But since the lady certainly wouldn't have carried these particular objects during the afternoon, and since she couldn't have called at the house that evening during Benson's absence without the housekeeper knowing it, how, may one ask, did these articles happen to be there the next morning if she herself did not take them there late that night?"

" 'Pon my word, I haven't the slightest notion," Vance rejoined. "The lady, herself could doubtless appease your curiosity. But there are any number of possible explanations, y' know. Our departed Chesterfield might have brought them home in his coat pocket—women are eternally handing men all manner of gewgaws and bundles to carry for 'em, with the cooing request: 'Can you put this in your pocket for me?' . . . Then again, there is the possibility that the real murderer secured them in some way and placed them on the mantel delib'rately to mislead the *Polizei*. Women, don't y' know, never put their belongings in such neat, out-of-the-way places as mantels and hatracks. They invariably throw them down on your fav'rite chair or your center table."

"And, I suppose," Markham interjected, "Benson also brought the lady's cigarette butts home in his pocket?"

"Stranger things have happened," returned Vance equably; "though I sha'n't accuse him of it in this instance. . . . The cigarette butts may, y' know, be evidence of a previous *conversazione.*"

"Even your despised Heath," Markham informed him, "had sufficient intelligence to ascertain from the housekeeper that she sweeps out the grate every morning."

Vance sighed admiringly. "You're *so* thorough, aren't you? . . . But, I say, that can't be, by any chance, your only evidence against the lady?"

"By no means," Markham assured him. "But, despite your superior distrust, it's good corroboratory evidence nevertheless."

"I daresay," Vance agreed, "seeing with what frequency innocent persons are condemned in our courts. . . . But tell me more."

Markham proceeded with an air of quiet self-assurance. "My man learned, first, that Benson dined alone with this woman at the Marseilles, a little bohemian restaurant in West Fortieth Street; secondly, that they quarreled; and thirdly, that they departed at midnight, entering a taxicab together. . . . Now, the murder was committed at twelve-thirty; but since the lady lives on Riverside Drive, in the Eighties, Benson couldn't possibly have accompanied her home—which obviously he would have done had he not taken her to his own house—and returned by the time the shot was fired. But we have further proof pointing to her being at Benson's. My man learned, at the woman's apartment house, that actually she did not get home until shortly after one. Moreover, she was without gloves and handbag and had to be let in to her rooms with a passkey, because, as she explained, she had lost hers. As you remember, we found the key in her bag. And—to clinch the whole matter—the smoked cigarettes in the grate corresponded to the one you found in her case."

Markham paused to relight his cigar.

"So much for that particular evening," he resumed. "As soon as I learned the woman's identity this morning, I put two more men to work on her private life. Just as I was leaving the office this noon the men phoned in their reports. They had learned that the woman has a fiancé, a chap named Leacock, who was a captain in the army, and who would be likely to own just such a gun as Benson was killed with. Furthermore, this Captain Leacock lunched with the woman the day of the murder and also called on her at her apartment the morning after."

Markham leaned slightly forward, and his next words were emphasized by the tapping of his fingers on the arm of the chair.

"As you see, we have the motive, the opportunity, and the means. . . .

Perhaps you will tell me now that I possess no incriminating evidence."

"My dear Markham," Vance affirmed calmly, "you haven't brought out a single point which could not easily be explained away by any bright school-boy." He shook his head lugubriously. "And on such evidence people are deprived of their life and liberty! 'Pon my word, you alarm me. I tremble for my personal safety."

Markham was nettled.

"Would you be so good as to point out, from your dizzy pinnacle of sapi-ence, the errors in my reasoning?"

"As far as I can see," returned Vance evenly, "your particularization concerning the lady is innocent of reasoning. You've simply taken several unaf-fined facts and jumped to a false conclusion. I happen to know the conclusion is false because all the psychological indications of the crime contradict it—that is to say, the only real evidence in the case points unmistakably in another direction."

He made a gesture of emphasis, and his tone assumed an unwonted gravity.

"And if you arrest any woman for killing Alvin Benson, you will simply be adding another crime—a crime of delib'rate and unpardonable stupidity—to the one already committed. And between shooting a bounder like Benson and ruining an innocent woman's reputation, I'm inclined to regard the latter as the more reprehensible."

I could see a flash of resentment leap into Markham's eyes; but he did not take offense. Remember: these two men were close friends; and, for all their divergency of nature, they understood and respected each other. Their frank-ness—severe and even mordant at times—was, indeed, a result of that respect.

There was a moment's silence; then Markham forced a smile. "You fill me with misgivings," he averred mockingly; but, despite the lightness of his tone, I felt that he was half in earnest. "However, I hadn't exactly planned to arrest the lady just yet."

"You reveal commendable restraint," Vance complimented him. "But I'm sure you've already arranged to ballyrag the lady and perhaps trick her into one or two of those contradictions so dear to every lawyer's heart—just as if any nervous or high-strung person could help indulging in apparent contra-dictions while being cross-questioned as a suspect in a crime they had nothing to do with. . . . To 'put 'em on the grill'—a most accurate designation. So remi-niscent of burning people at the stake, what?"

"Well, I'm most certainly going to question her," replied Markham firmly, glancing at his watch. "And one of my men is escorting her to the office in half an hour; so I must break up this most delightful and edifying chat."

"You really expect to learn something incriminating by interrogating her?" asked Vance. "Y' know, I'd jolly well like to witness your humiliation. But I presume your heckling of suspects is a part of the legal arcana."

Markham had risen and turned toward the door, but at Vance's words he paused and appeared to deliberate. "I can't see any particular objection to your being present," he said, "if you really care to come."

I think he had an idea that the humiliation of which the other had spoken would prove to be Vance's own; and soon we were in a taxicab headed for the Criminal Courts Building.

REPORTS AND AN INTERVIEW

(*Saturday, June 15; 3 P.M.*)

WE ENTERED the ancient building, with its discolored marble pillars and balustrades and its old-fashioned iron scrollwork, by the Franklin Street door and went directly to the district attorney's office on the fourth floor. The office, like the building, breathed an air of former days. Its high ceilings, its massive golden-oak woodwork, its elaborate low-hung chandelier of bronze and china, its dingy bay walls of painted plaster, and its four high narrow windows to the south—all bespoke a departed era in architecture and decoration.

On the floor was a large velvet carpet-rug of dingy brown; and the windows were hung with velour draperies of the same color. Several large, comfortable chairs stood about the walls and before the long oak table in front of the district attorney's desk. This desk, directly under the windows and facing the room, was broad and flat, with carved uprights and two rows of drawers extending to the floor. To the right of the high-backed swivel desk-chair, was another table of carved oak. There were also several filing cabinets in the room and a large safe. In the center of the east wall a leather-covered door, decorated with large brass nailheads, led into a long narrow room, between the office and the waiting room, where the district attorney's secretary and several clerks had their desks. Opposite to this door was another one opening into the district attorney's inner sanctum; and still another door, facing the windows, gave on the main corridor.

Vance glanced over the room casually.

"So this is the matrix of municipal justice—eh, what?" He walked to one of the windows and looked out upon the gray circular tower of the Tombs opposite. "And there, I take it, are the oubliettes where the victims of our law are incarc'rated so as to reduce the competition of criminal activity among the remaining citizenry. A most distressin' sight, Markham."

The district attorney had sat down at his desk and was glancing at several notations on his blotter.

"There are a couple of my men waiting to see me," he remarked, without looking up; "so, if you'll be good enough to take a chair over here, I'll proceed with my humble efforts to undermine society still further."

He pressed a button under the edge of his desk, and an alert young man with thick-lensed glasses appeared at the door.

"Swacker, tell Phelps to come in," Markham ordered. "And also tell Springer, if he's back from lunch, that I want to see him in a few minutes."

The secretary disappeared, and a moment later a tall, hawk-faced man, with stoop shoulders and an awkward, angular gait, entered.

"What news?" asked Markham.

"Well, Chief," the detective replied in a low, grating voice, "I just found out something I thought you could use right away. After I reported this noon, I ambled around to this Captain Leacock's house, thinking I might learn something from the houseboys, and ran into the captain coming out. I tailed along;

and he went straight up to the lady's house on the Drive and stayed there over an hour. Then he went back home, looking worried."

Markham considered a moment.

"It may mean nothing at all, but I'm glad to know it anyway. St. Clair'll be here in a few minutes, and I'll find out what she has to say. There's nothing else for today. . . . Tell Swacker to send Tracy in."

Tracy was the antithesis of Phelps. He was short, a trifle stout, and exuded an atmosphere of studied suavity. His face was rotund and genial; he wore a pince nez; and his clothes were modish and fitted him well.

"Good-morning, Chief." He greeted Markham in a quiet, ingratiating tone. "I understand the St. Clair woman is to call here this afternoon, and there are a few things I've found out that may assist in your questioning."

He opened a small notebook and adjusted his pince nez.

"I thought I might learn something from her singing teacher, an Italian formerly connected with the Metropolitan but now running a sort of choral society of his own. He trains aspiring prima donnas in their roles with a chorus and settings, and Miss St. Clair is one of his pet students. He talked to me without any trouble; and it seems he knew Benson well. Benson attended several of St. Clair's rehearsals and sometimes called for her in a taxicab. Rinaldo—that's the man's name—thinks he had a bad crush on the girl. Last winter when she sang at the Criterion in a small part, Rinaldo was back stage coaching, and Benson sent her enough hothouse flowers to fill the star's dressing room and have some left over. I tried to find out if Benson was playing 'angel' for her, but Rinaldo either didn't know or pretended he didn't." Tracy closed his notebook and looked up. "That any good to you Chief?"

"First-rate," Markham told him. "Keep at work along that line and let me hear from you again about this time Monday."

Tracy bowed, and as he went out the secretary again appeared at the door. "Springer's here now, sir," he said. "Shall I send him in?"

Springer proved to be a type of detective quite different from either Phelps or Tracy. He was older, and had the gloomy capable air of a hardworking bookkeeper in a bank. There was no initiative in his bearing, but one felt that he could discharge a delicate task with extreme competency.

Markham took from his pocket the envelope on which he had noted the name given him by Major Benson.

"Springer, there's a man down on Long Island that I want to interview as soon as possible. It's in connection with the Benson case, and I wish you'd locate him and get him up here as soon as possible. If you can find him in the telephone book, you needn't go down personally. His name is Leander Pfyfe, and he lives, I think, at Port Washington."

Markham jotted down the name on a card and handed it to the detective.

"This is Saturday, so if he comes to town tomorrow, have him ask for me at the Stuyvesant Club. I'll be there in the afternoon."

When Springer had gone, Markham again rang for his secretary and gave instructions that the moment Miss St. Clair arrived she was to be shown in.

"Sergeant Heath is here," Swacker informed him, "and wants to see you if you're not too busy."

Markham glanced at the clock over the door. "I guess I'll have time. Send him in."

Heath was surprised to see Vance and me in the district attorney's office, but after greeting Markham with the customary handshake, he turned to Vance with a good-natured smile.

"Still acquiring knowledge, Mr. Vance?"

"Can't say that I am, Sergeant," returned Vance lightly. "But I'm learning a number of most int'restin' errors. . . . How goes the sleuthin'?"

Heath's face became suddenly serious.

"That's what I'm here to tell the chief about." He addressed himself to Markham. "This case is a jawbreaker, sir. My men and myself have talked to a dozen of Benson's cronies, and we can't worm a single fact of any value out of 'em. They either don't know anything or they're giving a swell imitation of a lot of clams. They all appear to be greatly shocked—bowled over, floored, flabbergasted—by the news of the shooting. And have they got any idea as to why or how it happened? They'll tell the world they haven't. You know the line of talk: Who'd want to shoot good old Al? Nobody could've done it but a burglar who didn't know good old Al. If he'd known good old Al, even the burglar wouldn't have done it. . . . 🔲 I felt like killing off a few of those birds myself so they could go and join their good old Al."

"Any news of the car?" asked Markham.

Heath grunted his disgust. "Not a word. And that's funny, too, seeing all the advertising it got. Those fishing rods are the only thing we've got. . . . The inspector, by the way, sent me the postmortem report this morning; but it didn't tell us anything we didn't know. Translated into human language, it said Benson died from a shot in the head, with all his organs sound. It's a wonder, though, they didn't discover that he'd been poisoned with a Mexican bean or bit by an African snake, or something, so's to make the case a little more intrikkit than it already is."

"Cheer up, Sergeant," Markham exhorted him. "I've had a little better luck. Tracy ran down the owner of the handbag and found out she'd been to dinner with Benson that night. He and Phelps also learned a few other supplementary facts that fit in well; and I'm expecting the lady here at any minute. I'm going to find out what she has to say for herself."

An expression of resentment came into Heath's eyes as the district attorney was speaking, but he erased it at once and began asking questions. Markham gave him every detail and also informed him of Leander Pfyfe.

"I'll let you know immediately how the interview comes out," he concluded.

As the door closed on Heath, Vance looked up at Markham with a sly smile.

"Not exactly one of Nietzsche's *Übermenschen*—eh, what? I fear the subtleties of this complex world bemuse him a bit, y' know. . . . And he's so disappointin'. I felt pos'tively elated when the bustling lad with the thick glasses announced his presence. I thought surely he wanted to tell you he had jailed at least six of Benson's murderers."

"Your hopes run too high, I fear," commented Markham.

"And yet, that's the usual procedure—if the headlines in our great moral dailies are to be credited. I always thought that the moment a crime was committed the police began arresting people promiscuously—to maintain the excitement, don't y' know. Another illusion gone! . . . Sad, sad," he murmured. "I sha'n't forgive our Heath; he has betrayed my faith in him."

At this point Markham's secretary came to the door and announced the arrival of Miss St. Clair.

I think we were all taken a little aback at the spectacle presented by this young woman as she came slowly into the room with a firm graceful step, and with her head held slightly to one side in an attitude of supercilious inquiry. She was small and strikingly pretty, although "pretty" is not exactly the word with which to describe her. She possessed that faintly exotic beauty that we find in the portraits of the Carracci, who sweetened the severity of Leonardo and made it at once intimate and decadent. Her eyes were dark and widely spaced; her nose was delicate and straight, and her forehead broad. Her full sensuous lips were almost sculpturesque in their linear precision, and her mouth wore an enigmatic smile, or hint of a smile. Her rounded, firm chin was a bit heavy when examined apart from the other features, but not in the ensemble. There was poise and a certain strength of character in her bearing; but one sensed the potentialities of powerful emotions beneath her exterior calm. Her clothes harmonized with her personality; they were quiet and apparently in the conventional style, but a touch of color and originality here and there conferred on them a fascinating distinction.

Markham rose and bowing, with formal courtesy, indicated a comfortable upholstered chair directly in front of his desk. With a barely perceptible nod, she glanced at the chair and then seated herself in a straight armless chair standing next to it.

"You won't mind, I'm sure," she said, "if I choose my own chair for the inquisition."

Her voice was low and resonant—the speaking voice of the highly trained singer. She smiled as she spoke, but it was not a cordial smile; it was cold and distant, yet somehow indicative of levity.

"Miss St. Clair," began Markham, in a tone of polite severity, "the murder of Mr. Alvin Benson has intimately involved yourself. Before taking any definite steps, I have invited you here to ask you a few questions. I can, therefore, advise you quite honestly that frankness will best serve your interests."

He paused, and the woman looked at him with an ironically questioning gaze. "Am I supposed to thank you for your generous advice?"

Markham's scowl deepened as he glanced down at a typewritten page on his desk.

"You are probably aware that your gloves and handbag were found in Mr. Benson's house the morning after he was shot."

"I can understand how you might have traced the handbag to me," she said; "but how did you arrive at the conclusion that the gloves were mine?"

Markham looked up sharply. "Do you mean to say the gloves are not yours?"

"Oh, no." She gave him another wintry smile. "I merely wondered how you knew they belonged to me, since you couldn't have known either my taste in gloves or the size I wore."

"They're your gloves, then?"

"If they are Tréfousse, size five-and-three-quarters, of white kid and elbow length, they are certainly mine. And I'd so like to have them back, if you don't mind."

"I'm sorry," said Markham, "but it is necessary that I keep them for the present."

She dismissed the matter with a slight shrug of the shoulders. "Do you mind if I smoke?" she asked.

Markham instantly opened a drawer of his desk and took out a box of Benson and Hedges cigarettes.

"I have my own, thank you," she informed him. "But I would so appreciate my holder. I've missed it horribly."

Markham hesitated. He was manifestly annoyed by the woman's attitude. "I'll be glad to lend it to you," he compromised; and reaching into another drawer of his desk, he laid the holder on the table before her.

"Now, Miss St. Clair," he said, resuming his gravity of manner, "will you tell me how these personal articles of yours happened to be in Mr. Benson's living room?"

"No, Mr. Markham, I will not," she answered.

"Do you realize the serious construction your refusal places upon the circumstances?"

"I really hadn't given it much thought." Her tone was indifferent.

"It would be well if you did," Markham advised her. "Your position is not an enviable one; and the presence of your belongings in Mr. Benson's room is, by no means, the only thing that connects you directly with the crime."

The woman raised her eyes inquiringly, and again the enigmatic smile appeared at the corners of her mouth. "Perhaps you have sufficient evidence to accuse me of the murder?"

Markham ignored this question. "You were well acquainted with Mr. Benson, I believe?"

"The finding of my handbag and gloves in his apartment might lead one to assume as much, mightn't it?" she parried.

"He was, in fact, much interested in you?" persisted Markham.

She made a *moue* and sighed. "Alas, yes! Too much for my peace of mind. . . . Have I been brought here to discuss the attentions this gentleman paid me?"

Again Markham ignored her query. "Where were you, Miss St. Clair, between the time you left the Marseilles at midnight and the time you arrived home—which, I understand, was after one o'clock?"

"You are simply wonderful!" she exclaimed. "You seem to know everything. . . . Well, I can only say that during that time I was on my way home."

"Did it take you an hour to go from Fortieth Street to Eighty-first and Riverside Drive?"

"Just about, I should say—a few minutes more or less, perhaps."

"How do you account for that?" Markham was becoming impatient.

"I can't account for it," she said, "except by the passage of time. Time does fly, doesn't it, Mr. Markham?"

"By your attitude you are only working detriment to yourself," Markham warned her, with a show of irritation. "Can you not see the seriousness of your position? You are known to have dined with Mr. Benson, to have left the restaurant at midnight, and to have arrived at your own apartment after one o'clock. At twelve-thirty, Mr. Benson was shot; and your personal articles were found in the same room the morning after."

"It looks terribly suspicious, I know," she admitted, with whimsical seriousness. "And I'll tell you this, Mr. Markham: if my thoughts could have killed

Mr. Benson, he would have died long ago. I know I shouldn't speak ill of the dead—there's a saying about it beginning *'de mortuis,'* isn't there?—but the truth is, I had reason to dislike Mr. Benson exceedingly."

"Then, why did you go to dinner with him?"

"I've asked myself the same question a dozen times since," she confessed dolefully. "We women are such impulsive creatures—always doing things we shouldn't. . . . But I know what you're thinking: if I had intended to shoot him, that would have been a natural preliminary. Isn't that what's in your mind? I suppose all murderesses do go to dinner with their victims first."

While she spoke she opened her vanity case and looked at her reflection in its mirror. She daintily adjusted several imaginary stray ends of her abundant dark brown hair, and touched her arched eyebrows gently with her little finger as if to rectify some infinitesimal disturbance in their penciled contour. Then she tilted her head, regarded herself appraisingly, and returned her gaze to the district attorney only as she came to the end of her speech. Her actions had perfectly conveyed to her listeners the impression that the subject of the conversation was, in her scheme of things, of secondary importance to her personal appearance. No words could have expressed her indifference so convincingly as had her little pantomime.

Markham was becoming exasperated. A different type of district attorney would no doubt have attempted to use the pressure of his office to force her into a more amenable frame of mind. But Markham shrank instinctively from the bludgeoning, threatening methods of the ordinary public prosecutor, especially in his dealings with women. In the present case, however, had it not been for Vance's strictures at the club, he would no doubt have taken a more aggressive stand. But it was evident he was laboring under a burden of uncertainty superinduced by Vance's words and augmented by the evasive deportment of the woman herself.

After a moment's silence he asked grimly, "You did considerable speculating through the firm of Benson and Benson, did you not?"

A faint ring of musical laughter greeted this question. "I see that the dear major has been telling tales. . . . Yes, I've been gambling most extravagantly. And I had no business to do it. I'm afraid I'm avaricious."

"And is it not true that you've lost heavily of late—that, in fact, Mr. Alvin Benson called upon you for additional margin and finally sold out your securities?"

"I wish to Heaven it were not true," she lamented, with a look of simulated tragedy. Then: "Am I supposed to have done away with Mr. Benson out of sordid revenge or as an act of just retribution?" She smiled archly and waited expectantly, as if her question had been part of a guessing game.

Markham's eyes hardened as he coldly enunciated his next words.

"Is it not a fact that Captain Philip Leacock owned just such a pistol as Mr. Benson was killed with—a forty-five army Colt automatic?"

At the mention of her fiancé's name she stiffened perceptibly and caught her breath. The part she had been playing fell from her, and a faint flush suffused her cheeks and extended to her forehead. But almost immediately she had reassumed her role of playful indifference.

"I never inquired into the make or caliber of Captain Leacock's firearms," she returned carelessly.

"And is it not a fact," pursued Markham's imperturbable voice, "that Captain Leacock lent you his pistol when he called at your apartment on the morning before the murder?"

"It's most ungallant of you, Mr. Markham," she reprimanded him coyly, "to inquire into the personal relations of an engaged couple; for I am betrothed to Captain Leacock—though you probably know it already."

Markham stood up, controlling himself with effort.

"Am I to understand that you refuse to answer any of my questions, or to endeavor to extricate yourself from the very serious position you are in?"

She appeared to consider. "Yes," she said slowly, "I haven't anything I care especially to say just now."

Markham leaned over and rested both hands on the desk. "Do you realize the possible consequences of your attitude?" he asked ominously. "The facts I know regarding your connection with the case, coupled with your refusal to offer a single extenuating explanation, give me more grounds than I actually need to order your being held."

I was watching her closely as he spoke, and it seemed to me that her eyelids drooped involuntarily the merest fraction of an inch. But she gave no other indication of being affected by the pronouncement, and merely looked at the district attorney with an air of defiant amusement.

Markham, with a sudden contraction of the jaw, turned and reached toward a bell button beneath the edge of his desk. But, in doing so, his glance fell upon Vance; and he paused indecisively. The look he had encountered on the other's face was one of reproachful amazement; not only did it express complete surprise at his apparent decision but it stated, more eloquently than words could have done, that he was about to commit an act of irreparable folly.

There were several moments of tense silence in the room. Then calmly and unhurriedly Miss St. Clair opened her vanity case and powdered her nose. When she had finished, she turned a serene gaze upon the district attorney.

"Well, do you want to arrest me now?" she asked.

Markham regarded her for a moment, deliberating. Instead of answering at once, he went to the window and stood for a full minute looking down upon the Bridge of Sighs which connects the Criminal Courts Building with the Tombs.

"No, I think not today," he said slowly.

He stood awhile longer in absorbed contemplation; then, as if shaking off his mood of irresolution, he swung about and confronted the woman.

"I'm not going to arrest you—yet," he reiterated, a bit harshly. "But I'm going to order you to remain in New York for the present. And if you attempt to leave, you *will* be arrested. I hope that is clear."

He pressed a button, and his secretary entered.

"Swacker, please escort Miss St. Clair downstairs, and call a taxicab for her. . . . Then you can go home yourself."

She rose and gave Markham a little nod.

"You were very kind to lend me my cigarette holder," she said pleasantly, laying it on his desk.

Without another word, she walked calmly from the room.

The door had no more than closed behind her when Markham pressed another button. In a few moments the door leading into the outer corridor opened, and a white-haired, middle-aged man appeared.

"Ben," ordered Markham hurriedly, "have that woman that Swacker's taking downstairs followed. Keep her under surveillance and don't let her get lost. She's not to leave the city—understand? It's the St. Clair woman Tracy dug up."

When the man had gone, Markham turned and stood glowering at Vance.

"What do you think of your innocent young lady now?" he asked, with an air of belligerent triumph.

"Nice gel—eh, what?" replied Vance blandly. "Extr'ordin'ry control. And she's about to marry a professional milit'ry man! Ah, well. *De gustibus*. . . . Y' know, I was afraid for a moment you were actu'lly going to send for the manacles. And if you had, Markham old dear, you'd have regretted it to your dying day."

Markham studied him for a few seconds. He knew there was something more than a mere whim beneath Vance's certitude of manner; and it was this knowledge that had stayed his hand when he was about to have the woman placed in custody.

"Her attitude was certainly not conducive to one's belief in her innocence," Markham objected. "She played her part damned cleverly, though. But it was just the part a shrewd woman, knowing herself guilty, would have played."

"I say, didn't it occur to you," asked Vance, "that perhaps she didn't care a farthing whether you thought her guilty or not?—that, in fact, she was a bit disappointed when you let her go?"

"That's hardly the way I read the situation," returned Markham. "Whether guilty or innocent, a person doesn't ordinarily invite arrest."

"By the bye," asked Vance, "where was the fortunate swain during the hour of Alvin's passing?"

"Do you think we didn't check up on that point?" Markham spoke with disdain. "Captain Leacock was at his own apartment that night from eight o'clock on."

"Was he, really?" airily retorted Vance. "A most model young fella!"

Again Markham looked at him sharply. "I'd like to know what weird theory has been struggling in your brain today," he mused. "Now that I've let the lady go temporarily—which is what you obviously wanted me to do—and have stultified my own better judgment in so doing, why not tell me frankly what you've got up your sleeve?"

" 'Up my sleeve?' Such an inelegant metaphor! One would think I was a prestidig'tator, what?"

Whenever Vance answered in this fashion, it was a sign that he wished to avoid making a direct reply; and Markham dropped the matter.

"Anyway," he submitted, "you didn't have the pleasure of witnessing my humiliation, as you prophesied."

Vance looked up in simulated surprise. "Didn't I, now?" Then he added sorrowfully, "Life is so full of disappointments, y' know."

8

VANCE ACCEPTS A CHALLENGE

(*Saturday, June 15; 4 P.M.*)

AFTER MARKHAM had telephoned Heath the details of the interview, we returned to the Stuyvesant Club. Ordinarily the district attorney's office shuts down at one o'clock on Saturdays; but today the hour had been extended because of the importance attaching to Miss St. Clair's visit. Markham had lapsed into an introspective silence which lasted until we were again seated in the alcove of the club's lounge-room. Then he spoke irritably.

"Dammit! I shouldn't have let her go. . . . I still have a feeling she's guilty."

Vance assumed an air of gushing credulousness.

"Oh, really? I daresay you're *so* psychic. Been that way all your life, no doubt. And haven't you had lots and lots of dreams that came true? I'm sure you've often had a phone call from someone you were thinking about at the moment. A delectable gift. Do you read palms, also? . . . Why not have the lady's horoscope cast?"

"I have no evidence as yet," Markham retorted, "that your belief in her innocence is founded on anything more substantial than your impressions."

"Ah, but it is," averred Vance. "I *know* she's innocent. Furthermore, I know that no woman could possibly have fired the shot."

"Don't get the erroneous idea in your head that a woman couldn't have manipulated a forty-five army Colt."

"Oh, that?" Vance dismissed the notion with a shrug. "The material indications of the crime don't enter into my calculations, y' know—I leave 'em entirely to you lawyers and the lads with the bulging deltoids. I have other, and surer, ways of reaching conclusions. That's why I told you that if you arrested any woman for shooting Benson, you'd be blundering most shamefully."

Markham grunted indignantly. "And yet you seem to have repudiated all processes of deduction whereby the truth may be arrived at. Have you, by any chance, entirely renounced your faith in the operations of the human mind?"

"Ah, there speaks the voice of God's great common people!" exclaimed Vance. "Your mind is so typical, Markham. It works on the principle that what you don't know isn't knowledge, and that, since you don't understand a thing there is no explanation. A comfortable point of view. It relieves one from all care and uncertainty. Don't you find the world a very sweet and wonderful place?"

Markham adopted an attitude of affable forbearance. "You spoke at lunch-time, I believe, of one infallible method of detecting crime. Would you care to divulge this profound and priceless secret to a mere district attorney?"

Vance bowed with exaggerated courtesy.*

---

* The following conversation in which Vance explains his psychological methods of criminal analysis, is, of course, set down from memory. However, a proof of this passage was sent to him with a request that he revise and alter it in whatever manner he chose; so that, as it now stands, it describes Vance's theory in practically his own words.

"Delighted, I'm sure," he returned. "I referred to the science of individual character and the psychology of human nature. We all do things, d' ye see, in a certain individual way, according to our temp'raments. Every human act, no matter how large or how small, is a direct expression of a man's personality and bears the inev'table impress of his nature. Thus, a musician, by looking at a sheet of music, is able to tell at once whether it was composed, for example, by Beethoven, or Schubert, or Debussy, or Chopin. And an artist, by looking at a canvas, knows immediately whether it is a Corot, a Harpignies, a Rembrandt, or a Franz Hals. And just as no two faces are exactly alike, so no two natures are exactly alike; the combination of ingredients which go to make up our personalities, varies in each individual. That is why, when twenty artists, let us say, sit down to paint the same subject, each one conceives and executes it in a different manner. The result in each case is a distinct and unmistakable expression of the personality of the painter who did it. . . . It's really rather simple, don't y' know."

"Your theory, doubtless, would be comprehensible to an artist," said Markham, in a tone of indulgent irony. "But its metaphysical refinements are, I admit, considerably beyond the grasp of a vulgar worldling like myself."

" 'The mind inclined to what is false rejects the nobler course,' " murmured Vance, with a sigh.

"There is," argued Markham, "a slight difference between art and crime."

"Psychologically, old chap, there's none," Vance amended evenly. "Crimes possess all the basic factors of a work of art—approach, conception, technique, imagination, attack, method, and organization. Moreover, crimes vary fully as much in their manner, their aspects, and their general nature, as do works of art. Indeed, a carefully planned crime is just as direct an expression of the individual as is a painting, for instance. And therein lies the one great possibility of detection. Just as an expert æsthetician can analyze a picture and tell you who painted it, or the personality and temp'rament of the person who painted it, so can the expert psychologist analyze a crime and tell you who committed it—that is, if he happens to be acquainted with the person—or else can describe to you, with almost mathematical surety, the criminal's nature and character. . . . And that, my dear Markham, is the only sure and inev'table means of determining human guilt. All others are mere guesswork, unscientific, uncertain, and—perilous."

Throughout this explanation Vance's manner had been almost casual; yet the very serenity and assurance of his attitude conferred upon his words a curious sense of authority. Markham had listened with interest, though it could be seen that he did not regard Vance's theorizing seriously.

"Your system ignores motive altogether," he objected.

"Naturally," Vance replied, "since it's an irrelevant factor in most crimes. Every one of us, my dear chap, has just as good a motive for killing at least a score of men as the motives which actuate ninety-nine crimes out of a hundred. And, when anyone is murdered, there are dozens of innocent people who had just as strong a motive for doing it as had the actual murderer. Really, y' know, the fact that a man has a motive is no evidence whatever that he's guilty—such motives are too universal a possession of the human race. Suspecting a man of murder because he has a motive is like suspecting a man of running away with another man's wife because he has two legs. The reason that some people kill and others don't, is a matter of temp'rament—of individual psychology. It all comes back to that. . . . And another thing: when a person does possess a real motive—something tremendous and overpowering—he's pretty apt to keep it to himself, to hide it and guard it carefully—eh, what? He may even have disguised the motive through years of preparation; or the motive may have been born within five minutes of the crime through the unexpected discovery of facts a decade old. . . . So, d' ye see, the absence of any apparent motive in a crime might be regarded as more incriminating than the presence of one."

"You are going to have some difficulty in eliminating the idea of *cui bono* from the consideration of crime."

"I daresay," agreed Vance. "The idea of *cui bono* is just silly enough to be impregnable. And yet, many persons would be benefited by almost anyone's death. Kill Sumner, and, on that theory, you could arrest the entire membership of the Authors' League."

"Opportunity, at any rate," persisted Markham, "is an insuperable factor in crime—and by opportunity, I mean that affinity of circumstances and conditions which make a particular crime possible, feasible, and convenient for a particular person."

"Another irrelevant factor," asserted Vance. "Think of the opportunities we have every day to murder people we dislike! Only the other night I had ten insuff'rable bores to dinner in my apartment—a social devoir. But I refrained—with consid'rable effort, I admit—from putting arsenic in the Pontet Canet. The Borgias and I, y' see, merely belong in different psychological categ'ries. On the other hand, had I been resolved to do murder, I would—like those resourceful *cinquecenio* patricians—have created my own opportunity. . . . And there's the rub:—one can either make an opportunity or disguise the fact that he had it, with false alibis and various other tricks. You remember the case of the murderer who called the police to break into his victim's house before the latter had been killed, saying he suspected foul play, and who then preceded the policemen indoors and stabbed the man as they were trailing up the stairs."*

"Well, what of actual proximity, or presence—the proof of a person being on the scene of the crime at the time it was committed?"

"Again misleading," Vance declared. "An innocent person's presence is too often used as a shield by the real murderer, who is actu'lly absent. A clever criminal can commit a crime from a distance through an agency that is present. Also, a clever criminal can arrange an alibi and then go to the scene of the crime disguised and unrecognized. There are far too many convincing ways of being present when one is believed to be absent—and vice versa. . . . But we can never part from our individualities and our natures. And that is why all crime inev'tably comes back to human psychology—the one fixed, undisguisable basis of deduction."

"It's a wonder to me," said Markham, "in view of your theories, that you don't advocate dismissing nine-tenths of the police force and installing a gross

---

* I don't know what case Vance was referring to; but there are several instances of this device on record, and writers of detective fiction have often used it. The latest instance is to be found in G. K. Chesterton's *The Innocence of Father Brown*, in the story entitled "The Wrong Shape."

or two of those psychological machines so popular with the Sunday Supplement editor."

Vance smoked a minute meditatively.

"I've read about 'em. Int'restin' toys. They can no doubt indicate a certain augmented emotional stress when the patient transfers his attention from the pious platitudes of Dr. Frank Crane to a problem in spherical trigonometry. But if an innocent person were harnessed up to the various tubes, galvanometers, electromagnets, glass plates, and brass knobs of one of these apparatuses, and then quizzed about some recent crime, your indicat'ry needle would cavort about like a Russian dancer as a result of sheer nervous panic on the patient's part."

Markham smiled patronizingly.

"And I suppose the needle would remain static with a guilty person in contact?"

"Oh, on the contr'ry," Vance's tone was unruffled. "The needle would bob up and down just the same—but not *because* he was guilty. If he was stupid, for instance, the needle would jump as a result of his resentment at a seemingly newfangled third-degree torture. And if he was intelligent, the needle would jump because of his suppressed mirth at the puerility of the legal mind for indulging in such nonsense."

"You move me deeply," said Markham. "My head is spinning like a turbine. But there are those of us poor worldlings who believe that criminality is a defect of the brain."

"So it is," Vance readily agreed. "But unfortunately the entire human race possesses the defect. The virtuous ones haven't, so to speak, the courage of their defects. . . . However, if you were referring to a criminal type, then, alas! we must part company. It was Lombrosco, that darling of the yellow journals, who invented the idea of the congenital criminal. Real scientists like DuBois, Karl Pearson, and Goring have shot his idiotic theories full of holes."*

"I am floored by your erudition," declared Markham, as he signaled to a passing attendant and ordered another cigar. "I console myself, however, with the fact that, as a rule, murder will leak out."

Vance smoked his cigarette in silence, looking thoughtfully out through the window up at the hazy June sky.

"Markham," he said at length, "the number of fantastic ideas extant about criminals is pos'tively amazing. How a sane person can subscribe to that ancient hallucination that 'murder will out' is beyond me. It rarely 'outs,' old dear. And, if it did 'out,' why a homicide bureau? Why all this whirlin'-dervish activity by the police whenever a body is found? . . . The poets are to blame for this bit of lunacy. Chaucer probably started it with his 'Mordre wol out,' and Shakespeare helped it along by attributing to murder a miraculous organ that speaks in lieu of a tongue. It was some poet, too, no doubt, who conceived the fancy that carcasses bleed at the sight of the murderer. . . . Would you, as the

* It was Pearson and Goring who, about twenty years ago, made an extensive investigation and tabulation of professional criminals in England, the results of which showed (1) that criminal careers began mostly between the ages of 16 and 21; (2) that over ninety percent of criminals were mentally normal; and (3) that more criminals had criminal older brothers than criminal fathers.

great Protector of the Faithful, dare tell the police to wait calmly in their offices, or clubs, or favorite beauty parlors—or wherever policemen do their waiting—until a murder 'outs'? Poor dear!—if you did, they'd ask the governor for your detention as *particeps criminis,* or apply for a *de lunatico inquirendo.*"*

Markham grunted good-naturedly. He was busy cutting and lighting his cigar.

"I believe you chaps have another hallucination about crime," continued Vance, "namely, that the criminal always returns to the scene of the crime. This weird notion is even explained on some recondite and misty psychological ground. But, I assure you, psychology teaches no such prepost'rous doctrine. If ever a murderer returned to the body of his victim for any reason other than to rectify some blunder he had made, then he is a subject for Broadmoor—or Bloomingdale. . . . How easy it would be for the police if this fanciful notion were true! They'd merely have to sit down at the scene of the crime, play bezique or Mah Jongg until the murderer returned, and then escort him to the bastille, what? The true psychological instinct in anyone having committed a punishable act is to get as far away from the scene of it as the limits of this world will permit."†

"In the present case, at any rate," Markham reminded him, "we are neither waiting inactively for the murder to out, nor sitting in Benson's living room trusting to the voluntary return of the criminal."

"Either course would achieve success as quickly as the one you are now pursuing," Vance said.

"Not being gifted with your singular insight," retorted Markham, "I can only follow the inadequate processes of human reasoning."

"No doubt," Vance agreed commiseratingly. "And the results of your activities thus far force me to the conclusion that a man with a handful of legalistic logic can successfully withstand the most obst'nate and heroic assaults of ordin'ry common sense."

Markham was piqued. "Still harping on the St. Clair woman's innocence, eh? However, in view of the complete absence of any tangible evidence pointing elsewhere, you must admit I have no choice of courses."

"I admit nothing of the kind," Vance told him, "for, I assure you, there is an abundance of evidence pointing elsewhere. You simply failed to see it."

"You think so!" Vance's nonchalant cocksureness had at last overthrown Markham's equanimity. "Very well, old man; I hereby enter an emphatic denial to all your fine theories; and I challenge you to produce a single piece of this evidence which you say exists."

* Sir Basil Thomson, K.C.B., former Assistant Commissioner of Metropolitan Police, London, writing in the *Saturday Evening Post* several years after this conversation, said: "Take, for example, the proverb that murder will out, which is employed whenever one out of many thousands of undiscovered murderers is caught through a chance coincidence that captures the popular imagination. It is because murder will not out that the pleasant shock of surprise when it does out calls for a proverb to enshrine the phenomenon. The poisoner who is brought to justice has almost invariably proved to have killed other victims without exciting suspicion until he has grown careless."

† In "Popular Fallacies About Crime" (*Saturday Evening Post*; April 21, 1923, p. 8) Sir Basil Thomson also upheld this point of view.

He threw his words out with asperity, and gave a curt, aggressive gesture with his extended fingers, to indicate that, as far as he was concerned, the subject was closed.

Vance, too, I think, was pricked a little.

"Y'know, Markham old dear, I'm no avenger of blood or vindicator of the honor of society. The role would bore me."

Markham smiled loftily but made no reply.

Vance smoked meditatively for a while. Then, to my amazement, he turned calmly and deliberately to Markham, and said in a quiet, matter-of-fact voice, "I'm going to accept your challenge. It's a bit alien to my tastes; but the problem, y' know, rather appeals to me; it presents the same diff'culties as the *Concert Champêtre* affair—a question of disputed authorship, as it were."*

Markham abruptly suspended the motion of lifting his cigar to his lips. He had scarcely intended his challenge literally; it had been uttered more in the nature of a verbal defiance; and he scrutinized Vance a bit uncertainly. Little did he realize that the other's casual acceptance of his unthinking and but half-serious challenge was to alter the entire criminal history of New York.

"Just how do you intend to proceed?" he asked.

Vance waved his hand carelessly. "Like Napoleon, *je m'en gage, et puis je vois*. However, I must have your word that you'll give me every possible assistance and will refrain from all profound legal objections."

Markham pursed his lips. He was frankly perplexed by the unexpected manner in which Vance had met his defiance. But immediately he gave a good-natured laugh, as if, after all, the matter was of no serious consequence.

"Very well," he assented. "You have my word. . . . And now what?"

After a moment Vance lit a fresh cigarette and rose languidly. "First," he announced, "I shall determine the exact height of the guilty person. Such a fact will, no doubt, come under the head of indicat'ry evidence—eh, what?"

Markham stared at him incredulously.

"How, in Heaven's name, are you going to do that?"

"By those primitive deductive methods to which you so touchingly pin your faith," he answered easily. "But come; let us repair to the scene of the crime."

He moved toward the door, Markham reluctantly following in a state of perplexed irritation. "But you know the body was removed," the latter protested; "and the place by now has no doubt been straightened up."

"Thank Heaven for that!" murmured Vance. "I'm not particularly fond of corpses; and untidiness, y' know, annoys me frightfully."

As we emerged into Madison Avenue, he signaled to the *commissionnaire* for a taxicab, and without a word, urged us into it.

"This is all nonsense," Markham declared ill-naturedly, as we started on our journey uptown. "How do you expect to find any clues now? By this time everything has been obliterated."

"Alas, my dear Markham," lamented Vance, in a tone of mock solicitude, "how woefully deficient you are in philosophic theory! If anything, no matter how inf'nitesimal, could really be obliterated, the universe, y' know, would

---

* For years the famous *Concert Champêtre* in the Louvre was officially attributed to Titian. Vance, however, took it upon himself to convince the Curator, M. Lepelletier, that it was a Giorgione, with the result that the painting is now credited to that artist.

cease to exist—the cosmic problem would be solved, and the Creator would write Q.E.D. across an empty firmament. Our only chance of going on with this illusion we call Life, d' ye see, lies in the fact that consciousness is like an inf'nite decimal point. Did you, as a child, ever try to complete the decimal one-third by filling a whole sheet of paper with the numeral three? You always had the fraction one-third left, don't y' know. If you could have eliminated the smallest one-third, after having set down ten thousand threes, the problem would have ended. So with life, my dear fellow. It's only because we can't erase or obliterate anything that we go on existing."

He made a movement with his fingers, putting a sort of tangible period to his remarks, and looked dreamily out of the window up at the fiery film of sky.

Markham had settled back into his corner and was chewing morosely at his cigar. I could see he was fairly simmering with impotent anger at having let himself be goaded into issuing his challenge. But there was no retreating now. As he told me afterward, he was fully convinced he had been dragged forth out of a comfortable chair on a patent and ridiculous fool's errand.

9

THE HEIGHT OF THE MURDERER

(*Saturday, June 15; 5 P.M.*)

WHEN WE arrived at Benson's house, a patrolman leaning somnolently against the iron paling of the areaway came suddenly to attention and saluted. He eyed Vance and me hopefully, regarding us no doubt as suspects being taken to the scene of the crime for questioning by the district attorney. We were admitted by one of the men from the homicide bureau who had been in the house on the morning of the investigation.

Markham greeted him with a nod.

"Everything going all right?"

"Sure," the man replied good-naturedly. "The old lady's as meek as a cat—and a swell cook."

"We want to be alone for a while, Sniffin," said Markham, as we passed into the living room.

"The gastronome's name is Snitkin, not Sniffin," Vance corrected him, when the door had closed on us.

"Wonderful memory," muttered Markham churlishly.

"A failing of mine," said Vance. "I suppose you are one of those rare persons who never forget a face but just can't recall names, what?"

But Markham was in no mood to be twitted. "Now that you've dragged me here, what are you going to do?" He waved his hand depreciatingly and sank into a chair with an air of contemptuous abdication.

The living room looked much the same as when we saw it last, except that it had been put neatly in order. The shades were up, and the late afternoon light was flooding in profusely. The ornateness of the room's furnishings seemed intensified by the glare.

Vance glanced about him and gave a shudder. "I'm half inclined to turn back," he drawled. "It's a clear case of justifiable homicide by an outraged interior decorator."

"My dear æsthete," Markham urged impatiently, "be good enough to bury your artistic prejudices and to proceed with your problem. . . . Of course," he added, with a malicious smile, "if you fear the result, you may still withdraw and thereby preserve your charming theories in their present virgin state."

"And permit you to send an innocent maiden to the chair!" exclaimed Vance, in mock indignation. "Fie, fie! *La politesse* alone forbids my withdrawal. May I never have to lament, with Prince Henry, that 'to my shame I have a truant been to chivalry.' "

Markham set his jaw and gave Vance a ferocious look. "I'm beginning to think that, after all, there is something in your theory that every man has some motive for murdering another."

"Well," replied Vance cheerfully, "now that you have begun to come round to my way of thinking, do you mind if I send Mr. Snitkin on an errand?"

Markham sighed audibly and shrugged his shoulders. "I'll smoke during the *opéra bouffe,* if it won't interfere with your performance."

Vance went to the door and called Snitkin.

"I say, would you mind going to Mrs. Platz and borrowing a long tape measure and a ball of string. . . . The district attorney wants them," he added, giving Markham a sycophantic bow.

"I can't hope that you're going to hang yourself, can I?" asked Markham.

Vance gazed at him reprovingly. "Permit me," he said sweetly, "to command *Othello* to your attention:

> 'How poor are they that have not patience!
> What wound did ever heal but by degrees?'

Or—to descend from a poet to a platitudinarian—let me present for your consid'ration a pentameter from Longfellow: 'All things come round to him who will but wait.' Untrue, of course, but consolin'. Milton said it much better in his 'They also serve—.' But Cervantes said it best: 'Patience and shuffle the cards.' Sound advice, Markham—and advice expressed rakishly, as all good advice should be. . . . To be sure, patience is a sort of last resort—a practice to adopt when there's nothing else to do. Still, like virtue, it occasionally rewards the practitioner; although I'll admit that, as a rule, it is—again like virtue—bootless. That is to say, it is its own reward. It has, however, been swathed in many verbal robes. It is 'sorrows's slave,' and the 'sov'reign o'er transmuted ills,' as well as 'all the passion of great hearts.' Rousseau wrote, *La patience est amère mais son fruit est doux.* But perhaps your legal taste runs to Latin. *Superanda omnis fortuna ferendo est,* quoth Vergil. And Horace also spoke on the subject. *Durum!* said he, *sed levius fit patientia——*"

"Why ⬛⬛⬛⬛ doesn't Snitkin come?" growled Markham.

Almost as he spoke the door opened, and the detective handed Vance the tape measure and string.

"And now, Markham, for your reward!"

Bending over the rug Vance moved the large wicker chair into the exact position it had occupied when Benson had been shot. The position was easily determined, for the impressions of the chair's castors on the deep nap of the rug were plainly visible. He then ran the string through the bullet hole in the back of the chair and directed me to hold one end of it against the place where the bullet had struck the wainscot. Next he took up the tape measure and, extending the string through the hole, measured a distance of five feet and six inches along it, starting at the point which corresponded to the location of Benson's forehead as he sat in the chair. Tying a knot in the string to indicate the measurement, he drew the string taut, so that it extended in a straight line from the mark on the wainscot, through the hole in the back of the chair, to a point five feet and six inches in front of where Benson's head had rested.

"This knot in the string," he explained, "now represents the exact location of the muzzle of the gun that ended Benson's career. You see the reasoning— eh, what? Having two points in the bullet's course—namely, the hole in the chair and the mark on the wainscot—and also knowing the approximate vertical line of explosion, which was between five and six feet from the gentleman's skull, it was merely necess'ry to extend the straight line of the bullet's course to the vertical line of explosion in order to ascertain the exact point at which the shot was fired."

"Theoretically very pretty," commented Markham; "though why you should go to so much trouble to ascertain this point in space I can't imagine. . . . Not that it matters, for you have overlooked the possibility of the bullet's deflection."

"Forgive me for contradicting you,"—Vance smiled—"but yesterday morning I questioned Captain Hagedorn at some length and learned that there had been no deflection of the bullet. Hagedorn had inspected the wound before we arrived; and he was really pos'tive on that point. In the first place, the bullet struck the frontal bone at such an angle as to make deflection practically impossible even had the pistol been of smaller caliber. And in the second place, the pistol with which Benson was shot was of so large a bore—a point-forty-five—and the muzzle velocity was so great, that the bullet would have taken a straight course even had it been held at a greater distance from the gentleman's brow."

"And how," asked Markham, "did Hagedorn know what the muzzle velocity was?"

"I was inquis'tive on that point myself," answered Vance; "and he explained that the size and character of the bullet and the expelled shell told him the whole tale. That's how he knew the gun was an army Colt automatic—I believe he called it a U.S. Government Colt—and not the ordinary Colt automatic. The weight of the bullets of these two pistols is slightly different: the ordinary Colt bullet weighs 200 grains, whereas the army Colt bullet weighs 230 grains. Hagedorn, having a hypersensitive tactile sense, was able, I presume, to distinguish the diff'rence at once, though I didn't go into his physiological gifts with him—my reticent nature, you understand. . . . However, he could tell it was a forty-five army Colt automatic bullet; and knowing this, he knew that the muzzle velocity was 809 feet, and that the striking energy was 329— which gives a six-inch penetration in white pine at a distance of twenty-five yards. . . . An amazin' creature, this Hagedorn. Imagine having one's head full of such entrancing information! The old mysteries of why a man should take up the bass fiddle as a life work and where all the pins go are babes' conundrums compared with the one of why a human being should devote his years to the idiosyncrasies of bullets."

"The subject is not exactly an enthralling one," said Markham wearily; "so, for the sake of argument, let us admit that you have now found the precise point of the gun's explosion. Where do we go from there?"

"While I hold the string on a straight line," directed Vance, "be good enough to measure the exact distance from the floor to the knot. Then my secret will be known."

"This game doesn't enthrall me, either," Markham protested. "I'd much prefer 'London Bridge.' "

Nevertheless he made the measurement.

"Four feet, eight and a half inches," he announced indifferently.

Vance laid a cigarette on the rug at a point directly beneath the knot.

"We now know the exact height at which the pistol was held when it was fired.... You grasp the process by which this conclusion was reached, I'm sure."

"It seems rather obvious," answered Markham.

Vance again went to the door and called Snitkin.

"The district attorney desires the loan of your gun for a moment," he said. "He wishes to make a test."

Snitkin stepped up to Markham and held out his pistol wonderingly.

"The safety's on, sir. Shall I shift it?"

Markham was about to refuse the weapon when Vance interposed.

"That's quite all right. Mr. Markham doesn't intend to fire it—I hope."

When the man had gone, Vance seated himself in the wicker chair and placed his head in juxaposition with the bullet hole.

"Now, Markham," he requested, "will you please stand on the spot where the murderer stood, holding the gun directly above that cigarette on the floor, and aim delib'rately at my left temple.... Take care," he cautioned, with an engaging smile, "not to pull the trigger, or you will never learn who killed Benson."

Reluctantly Markham complied. As he stood taking aim Vance asked me to measure the height of the gun muzzle from the floor.

The distance was four feet and nine inches.

"Quite so," he said, rising. "Y' see, Markham, you are five feet, eleven inches tall; therefore the person who shot Benson was very nearly your own height—certainly not under five feet, ten.... That, too, is rather obvious, what?"

His demonstration had been simple and clear. Markham was frankly impressed; his manner had become serious. He regarded Vance for a moment with a meditative frown; then he said, "That's all very well; but the person who fired the shot might have held the pistol relatively higher than I did."

"Not tenable," returned Vance. "I've done too much shooting myself not to know that when an expert takes delib'rate aim with a pistol at a small target, he does it with a stiff arm and with a slightly raised shoulder, so as to bring the sight on a straight line between his eye and the object at which he aims. The height at which one holds a revolver, under such conditions, pretty accurately determines his own height."

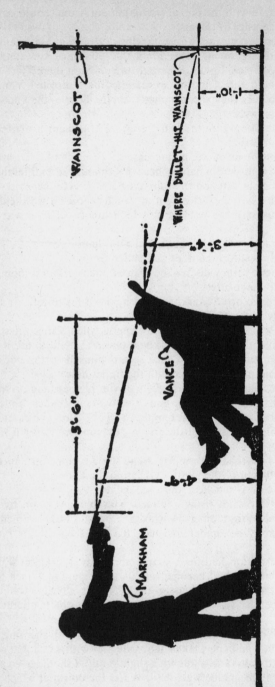

Diagram of shooting.

"Your argument is based on the assumption that the person who killed Benson was an expert taking deliberate aim at a small target?"

"Not an assumption, but a fact," declared Vance. "Consider: had the person not been an expert shot, he would not—at a distance of five or six feet—have selected the forehead but a larger target—namely, the breast. And having selected the forehead, he most certainly took delib'rate aim, what? Furthermore, had he not been an expert shot, and had he pointed the gun at the breast without taking delib'rate aim, he would, in all prob'bility, have fired more than one shot."

Markham pondered. "I'll grant that, on the face of it, your theory sounds plausible," he conceded at length. "On the other hand, the guilty man could have been almost any height over five feet, ten; for certainly a man may crouch as much as he likes and still take deliberate aim."

"True," agreed Vance. "But don't overlook the fact that the murderer's position, in this instance, was a perfectly natural one. Otherwise, Benson's attention would have been attracted, and he would not have been taken unawares. That he was shot unawares was indicated by his attitude. Of course, the assassin might have stooped a little without causing Benson to look up. . . . Let us say, therefore, that the guilty person's height is somewhere between five feet, ten, and six feet, two. Does that appeal to you?"

Markham was silent.

"The delightful Miss St. Clair, y' know," remarked Vance, with a japish smile, "can't possibly be over five feet, five or six."

Markham grunted and continued to smoke abstractedly.

"This Captain Leacock, I take it," said Vance, "is over six feet—eh, what?"

Markham's eyes narrowed. "What makes you think so?"

"You just told me, don't y' know."

"I told you!"

"Not in so many words," Vance pointed out. "But after I had shown you the approximate height of the murderer, and it didn't correspond at all to that of the young lady you suspected, I knew your active mind was busy looking around for another possibility. And, as the lady's *inamorato* was the only other possibility on your horizon, I concluded that you were permitting your thoughts to play about the captain. Had he, therefore, been the stipulated height, you would have said nothing; but when you argued that the murderer might have stooped to fire the shot, I decided that the captain was inord'nately tall. . . . Thus, in the pregnant silence that emanated from you, old dear, your spirit held sweet communion with mine and told me that the gentleman was a six-footer no less."

"I see that you include mind reading among your gifts," said Markham. "I now await an exhibition of slate writing."

His tone was irritable, but his irritation was that of a man reluctant to admit the alteration of his beliefs. He felt himself yielding to Vance's guiding rein, but he still held stubbornly to the course of his own previous convictions.

"Surely you don't question my demonstration of the guilty person's height?" asked Vance mellifluously.

"Not altogether," Markham replied. "It seems colorable enough. . . . But why, I wonder, didn't Hagedorn work the thing out, if it was so simple?"

"Anaxagoras said that those who have occasion for a lamp supply it with oil. A profound remark, Markham—one of those seemingly simple quips that contain a great truth. A lamp without oil, y' know, is useless. The police always have plenty of lamps—every variety, in fact—but no oil, as it were. That's why they never find anyone unless it's broad daylight."

Markham's mind was now busy in another direction, and he rose and began to pace the floor. "Until now I hadn't thought of Captain Leacock as the actual agent of the crime."

"Why hadn't you thought of him? Was it because one of your sleuths told you he was at home like a good boy that night?"

"I suppose so." Markham continued pacing thoughtfully. Then suddenly he swung about. "That wasn't it, either. It was the amount of damning circumstantial evidence against the St. Clair woman. . . . And, Vance, despite your demonstration here today, you haven't explained away any of the evidence against her. Where was she between twelve and one? Why did she go with Benson to dinner? How did her handbag get here? And what about those burned cigarettes of hers in the grate?—they're the obstacle, those cigarette butts; and I can't admit that your demonstration wholly convinces me—despite the fact that it *is* convincing—as long as I've got the evidence of those cigarettes to contend with, for that evidence is also convincing."

"My word!" sighed Vance. "You're in a pos'tively ghastly predic'ment. However, maybe I can cast illumination on those disquietin' cigarette butts."

Once more he went to the door and, summoning Snitkin, returned the pistol.

"The district attorney thanks you," he said. "And will you be good enough to fetch Mrs. Platz. We wish to chat with her."

Turning back to the room, he smiled amiably at Markham. "I desire to do all the conversing with the lady this time, if you don't mind. There are potentialities in Mrs. Platz which you entirely overlooked when you questioned her yesterday."

Markham was interested, though sceptical. "You have the floor," he said.

10

ELIMINATING A SUSPECT

(Saturday, June 15; 5:30 P.M.)

WHEN THE housekeeper entered, she appeared even more composed than when Markham had first questioned her. There was something at once sullen and indomitable in her manner, and she looked at me with a slightly challenging expression. Markham merely nodded to her, but Vance stood up and indicated a low tufted Morris chair near the fireplace, facing the front windows. She sat down on the edge of it, resting her elbows on its broad arms.

"I have some questions to ask you, Mrs. Platz," Vance began, fixing her sharply with his gaze; "and it will be best for everyone if you tell the whole truth. You understand me—eh, what?"

The easygoing, half-whimsical manner he had taken with Markham had disappeared. He stood before the woman, stern and implacable.

At his words she lifted her head. Her face was blank, but her mouth was set stubbornly, and a smouldering look in her eyes told of a suppressed anxiety.

Vance waited a moment and then went on, enunciating each word with distinctness.

"At what time, on the day Mr. Benson was killed, did the lady call here?"

The woman's gaze did not falter, but the pupils of her eyes dilated. "There was nobody here."

"Oh, yes, there was, Mrs. Platz." Vance's tone was assured. "What time did she call?"

"Nobody was here, I tell you," she persisted.

Vance lit a cigarette with interminable deliberation, his eyes resting steadily on hers. He smoked placidly until her gaze dropped. Then he stepped nearer to her, and said firmly, "If you tell the truth, no harm will come to you. But if you refuse any information you will find yourself in trouble. The withholding of evidence is a crime, y' know, and the law will show you no mercy."

He made a sly grimace at Markham, who was watching the proceedings with interest.

The woman now began to show signs of agitation. She drew in her elbows, and her breathing quickened. "In God's name, I swear it!—there wasn't anybody here." A slight hoarseness gave evidence of her emotion.

"Let us not invoke the Deity," suggested Vance carelessly. "What time was the lady here?"

She set her lips stubbornly, and for a whole minute there was silence in the room. Vance smoked quietly, but Markham held his cigar motionless between his thumb and forefinger in an attitude of expectancy.

Again Vance's impassive voice demanded: "What time was she here?"

The woman clinched her hands with a spasmodic gesture, and thrust her head forward.

"I tell you—I swear it——"

Vance made a peremptory movement of his hand and smiled coldly. "It's no go," he told her. "You're acting stupidly. We're here to get the truth—and you're going to tell us."

"I've told you the truth."

"Is it going to be necess'ry for the district attorney here to order you placed in custody?"

"I've told you the truth," she repeated.

Vance crushed out his cigarette decisively in an ash receiver on the table.

"Right-o, Mrs. Platz. Since you refuse to tell me about the young woman who was here that afternoon, I'm going to tell you about her."

His manner was easy and cynical, and the woman watched him suspiciously.

"Late in the afternoon of the day your employer was shot the doorbell rang. Perhaps you had been informed by Mr. Benson that he was expecting a caller, what? Anyhow, you answered the door and admitted a charming young lady. You showed her into this room . . . and—what do you think, my dear Madam!—she took that very chair on which you are resting so uncomfortably."

He paused and smiled tantalizingly.

"Then," he continued, "you served tea to the young lady and Mr. Benson. After a bit she departed, and Mr. Benson went upstairs to dress for dinner. . . . Y' see, Mrs. Platz, I happen to know."

He lit another cigarette.

"Did you notice the young lady particularly? If not, I'll describe her to you. She was rather short—*petite* is the word. She had dark hair and dark eyes and she was dressed quietly."

A change had come over the woman. Her eyes stared; her cheeks were now gray; and her breathing had become audible.

"Now, Mrs. Platz," demanded Vance sharply, "what have you to say?"

She drew a deep breath. "There wasn't anybody here," she said doggedly. There was something almost admirable in her obstinacy.

Vance considered a moment. Markham was about to speak but evidently thought better of it and sat watching the woman fixedly.

"Your attitude is understandable," Vance observed finally. "The young lady, of course, was well known to you, and you had a personal reason for not wanting it known she was here."

At these words she sat up straight, a look of terror in her face. "I never saw her before!" she cried, then stopped abruptly.

"Ah!" Vance gave her an amused leer. "You had never seen the young lady before—eh, what? . . . That's quite possible. But it's immaterial. She's a nice girl, though, I'm sure—even if she did have a dish of tea with your employer alone in his home."

"Did she tell you she was here?" The woman's voice was listless. The reaction to her tense obduracy had left her apathetic.

"Not exactly," Vance replied. "But it wasn't necess'ry. I knew without her informing me. . . . Just when did she arrive, Mrs. Platz?"

"About a half hour after Mr. Benson got here from the office." She had at last given over all denials and evasions. "But he didn't expect her—that is, he didn't say anything to me about her coming; and he didn't order tea until after she came."

Markham thrust himself forward. "Why didn't you tell me she'd been here when I asked you yesterday morning?"

The woman cast an uneasy glance about the room.

"I rather fancy," Vance intervened pleasantly, "that Mrs. Platz was afraid you might unjustly suspect the young lady."

She grasped eagerly at his words. "Yes sir—that was all. I was afraid you might think she—did it. And she was such a quiet, sweet-looking girl. . . . That was the only reason, sir."

"Quite so," agreed Vance consolingly. "But tell me: did it not shock you to see such a quiet, sweet-looking young lady smoking cigarettes?"

Her apprehension gave way to astonishment. "Why—yes, sir, it did. . . . But she wasn't a bad girl—I could tell that. And most girls smoke nowadays. They don't think anything of it, like they used to."

"You're quite right," Vance assured her. "Still young ladies really shouldn't throw their cigarettes in tiled, gas-log fireplaces, should they, now?"

The woman regarded him uncertainly; she suspected him of jesting. "Did she do that?" She leaned over and looked into the fireplace. "I didn't see any cigarettes there this morning."

"No, you wouldn't have," Vance informed her. "One of the district attorney's sleuths, d' ye see, cleaned it all up nicely for you yesterday."

She shot Markham a questioning glance. She was not sure whether Vance's remark was to be taken seriously; but his casualness of manner and pleasantness of voice tended to put her at ease.

"Now that we understand each other, Mrs. Platz," he was saying, "was there anything else you particularly noticed when the young lady was here? You will be doing her a good service by telling us, because both the district attorney and I happen to know she is innocent."

She gave Vance a long, shrewd look, as if appraising his sincerity. Evidently the results of her scrutiny were favorable, for her answer left no doubt as to her complete frankness.

"I don't know if it'll help, but when I came in with the toast, Mr. Benson looked like he was arguing with her. She seemed worried about something that was going to happen and asked him not to hold her to some promise she'd made. I was only in the room a minute and I didn't hear much. But just as I was going out he laughed and said it was only a bluff and that nothing was going to happen."

She stopped and waited anxiously. She seemed to fear that her revelation might, after all, prove injurious rather than helpful to the girl.

"Was that all?" Vance's tone indicated that the matter was of no consequence.

The woman demurred.

"That was all I heard; but . . . there was a small blue box of jewelry sitting on the table."

"My word!—a box of jewelry! Do you know whose it was?"

"No, sir, I don't. The lady hadn't brought it, and I never saw it in the house before."

"How did you know it was jewelry?"

"When Mr. Benson went upstairs to dress, I came in to clear the tea things away, and it was still sitting on the table."

Vance smiled. "And you played Pandora and took a peep—eh, what? Most natural—I'd have done it myself."

He stepped back and bowed politely.

"That will be all, Mrs. Platz. . . . And you needn't worry about the young lady. Nothing is going to happen to her."

When she had left us, Markham leaned forward and shook his cigar at Vance. "Why didn't you tell me you had information about the case unknown to me?"

"My dear chap!" Vance lifted his eyebrows in protestation. "To what do you refer specifically?"

"How did you know this St. Clair woman had been here in the afternoon?"

"I didn't; but I surmised it. There were cigarette butts of hers in the grate; and, as I knew she hadn't been here on the night Benson was shot, I thought it rather likely she had been here earlier in the day. And since Benson didn't arrive from his office until four, I whispered into my ear that she had called sometime between four and the hour of his departure for dinner. . . . An element'ry syllogism, what?"

"How did you know she wasn't here that night?"

"The psychological aspects of the crime left me in no doubt. As I told you, no woman commited it—my metaphysical hypotheses again; but never mind. . . . Furthermore, yesterday morning I stood on the spot where the murderer stood and sighted with my eye along the line of fire, using Benson's head and the mark on the wainscot as my points of coinc'dence. It was evident to me then, even without measurements, that the guilty person was rather tall."

"Very well. . . . But how did you know she left here that afternoon before Benson did?" persisted Markham.

"How else could she have changed into an evening gown? Really, y' know, ladies don't go about *décolletées* in the afternoon."

"You assume, then, that Benson himself brought her gloves and handbag back here that night?"

"Someone did—and it certainly wasn't Miss St. Clair."

"All right," conceded Markham. "And what about this Morris chair?—how did you know she sat in it?"

"What other chair could she have sat in and still thrown her cigarettes into the fireplace? Women are notoriously poor shots, even if they were given to hurling their cigarette stubs across the room."

"That deduction is simple enough," admitted Markham. "But suppose you tell me how you know she had tea here unless you were privy to some information on the point?"

"It pos'tively shames me to explain it. But the humiliating truth is that I inferred the fact from the condition of yon samovar. I noted yesterday that it had been used and had not been emptied or wiped off."

Markham nodded with contemptuous elation.

"You seem to have sunk to the despised legal level of material clues."

"That's why I'm blushing so furiously. . . . However, psychological deductions alone do not determine facts *in esse,* but only *in posse.* Other conditions must, of course, be considered. In the present instance the indications of the samovar served merely as the basis for an assumption, or guess, with which to draw out the housekeeper."

"Well, I won't deny that you succeeded," said Markham. "I'd like to know, though, what you had in mind when you accused the woman of a personal interest in the girl. That remark certainly indicated some preknowledge of the situation."

Vance's face became serious.

"Markham, I give you my word," he said earnestly, "I had nothing in mind. I made the accusation, thinking it was false, merely to trap her into a denial. And she fell into the trap. But—deuce take it!—I seemed to hit some nail squarely on the head, what? I can't for the life of me imagine why she was frightened. But it really doesn't matter."

"Perhaps not," agreed Markham, but his tone was dubious. "What do you make of the box of jewelry and the disagreement between Benson and the girl?"

"Nothing yet. They don't fit in, do they?"

He was silent a moment. Then he spoke with unusual seriousness. "Markham, take my advice and don't bother with these side issues. I'm telling you the girl had no part in the murder. Let her alone—you'll be happier in your old age if you do."

Markham sat scowling, his eyes in space. "I'm convinced that you *think* you know something."

"*Cogito, ergo sum,*" murmured Vance. "Y' know, the naturalistic philosophy of Descartes has always rather appealed to me. It was a departure from universal doubt and a seeking for positive knowledge in self-consciousness. Spinoza in his pantheism, and Berkeley in his idealism, quite misunderstood the significance of their precursor's favorite enthymeme. Even Descartes' errors were brilliant. His method of reasoning, for all its scientific inaccuracies, gave new signif'cation to the symbols of the analyst. The mind, after all, if it is to function effectively, must combine the mathematical precision of a natural science with such pure speculations as astronomy. For instance, Descartes' doctrine of Vortices——"

"Oh, be quiet," growled Markham. "I'm not insisting that you reveal your precious information. So why burden me with a dissertation on seventeenth-century philosophy?"

"Anyhow, you'll admit, won't you," asked Vance lightly, "that, in elim'nating those disturbing cigarette butts, so to speak, I've elim'nated Miss St. Clair as a suspect?"

Markham did not answer at once. There was no doubt that the developments of the past hour had made a decided impression upon him. He did not underestimate Vance, despite his persistent opposition; and he knew that, for all his flippancy, Vance was fundamentally serious. Furthermore, Markham had a finely developed sense of justice. He was not narrow, even though obstinate at times; and I have never known him to close his mind to the possibilities of truth, however opposed to his own interests. It did not, therefore, surprise me in the least when, at last, he looked up with a gracious smile of surrender.

"You've made your point," he said; "and I accept it with proper humility. I'm most grateful to you."

Vance walked indifferently to the window and looked out. "I am happy to learn that you are capable of accepting such evidence as the human mind could not possibly deny."

I had always noticed, in the relationship of these two men, that whenever either made a remark that bordered on generosity, the other answered in a manner which ended all outward show of sentiment. It was as if they wished to keep this more intimate side of their mutual regard hidden from the world.

Markham therefore ignored Vance's thrust. "Have you perhaps any enlightening suggestions, other than negative ones, to offer as to Benson's murderer?" he asked.

"Rather!" said Vance. "No end of suggestions."

"Could you spare me a good one?" Markham imitated the other's playful tone.

Vance appeared to reflect. "Well, I should advise that, as a beginning, you look for a rather tall man, cool-headed, familiar with firearms, a good shot, and fairly well known to the deceased—a man who was aware that Benson was going to dinner with Miss St. Clair, or who had reason to suspect the fact."

Markham looked narrowly at Vance for several moments.

"I think I understand. . . . Not a bad theory, either. You know, I'm going to suggest immediately to Heath that he investigate more thoroughly Captain Leacock's activities on the night of the murder."

"Oh, by all means," said Vance carelessly, going to the piano.

Markham watched him with an expression of puzzled interrogation. He was about to speak when Vance began playing a rollicking French cafe song which opens, I believe, with *"Ils sont dans les vignes les moineaux."*

11

A MOTIVE AND A THREAT

(*Sunday, June 16; afternoon.*)

THE FOLLOWING day, which was Sunday, we lunched with Markham at the Stuyvesant Club. Vance had suggested the appointment the evening before; for, as he explained to me, he wished to be present in case Leander Pfyfe should arrive from Long Island.

"It amuses me tremendously," he had said, "the way human beings delib'rately complicate the most ordin'ry issues. They have a downright horror of anything simple and direct. The whole modern commercial system is nothing but a colossal mechanism for doing things in the most involved and roundabout way. If one makes a ten-cent purchase at a department store nowadays, a complete history of the transaction is written out in triplicate, checked by a dozen floorwalkers and clerks, signed and countersigned, entered into innum'rable ledgers with various colored inks, and then elab'rately secreted in steel filing cabinets. And not content with all this superfluous *chinoiserie,* our businessmen have created a large and expensive army of efficiency experts whose sole duty it is to complicate and befuddle this system still further. . . . It's the same with everything else in modern life. Regard that insup'rable mania called golf. It consists merely of knocking a ball into a hole with a stick. But the devotees of this pastime have developed a unique and distinctive livery in which to play it. They concentrate for twenty years on the correct angulation of their feet and the proper method of entwining their fingers about the stick. Moreover, in order to discuss the pseudointr'cacies of this idiotic sport, they've invented an outlandish vocabulary which is unintelligible even to an English scholar."

He pointed disgustedly at a pile of Sunday newspapers.

"Then here's this Benson murder—a simple and incons'quential affair. Yet the entire machinery of the law is going at high pressure and blowing off jets of steam all over the community, when the matter could be settled quietly in five minutes with a bit of intelligent thinking."

At lunch, however, he did not refer to the crime; and, as if by tacit agreement, the subject was avoided. Markham had merely mentioned casually to us as we went into the dining room that he was expecting Heath a little later.

The sergeant was waiting for us when we retired to the lounge room for our smoke, and by his expression it was evident he was not pleased with the way things were going.

"I told you, Mr. Markham," he said, when he had drawn up our chairs, "that this case was going to be a tough one. . . . Could you get any kind of a lead from the St. Clair woman?"

Markham shook his head.

"She's out of it." And he recounted briefly the happenings at Benson's house the preceding afternoon.

"Well, if you're satisfied," was Heath's somewhat dubious comment, "that's good enough for me. But what about this Captain Leacock?"

"That's what I asked you here to talk about," Markham told him. "There's no direct evidence against him, but there are several suspicious circumstances that tend to connect him with the murder. He seems to meet the specifications as to height; and we mustn't overlook the fact that Benson was shot with just such a gun as Leacock would be likely to possess. He was engaged to the girl, and a motive might be found in Benson's attentions to her."

"And ever since the big scrap," supplemented Heath, "these Army boys don't think anything of shooting people. They got used to blood on the other side."

"The only hitch," resumed Markham, "is that Phelps, who had the job of checking up on the captain, reported to me that he was home that night from eight o'clock on. Of course, there may be a loophole somewhere, and I was going to suggest that you have one of your men go into the matter thoroughly and see just what the situation is. Phelps got his information from one of the hallboys; and I think it might be well to get hold of the boy again and apply a little pressure. If it was found that Leacock was not at home at twelve-thirty that night, we might have the lead you've been looking for."

"I'll attend to it myself," said Heath. "I'll go round there tonight, and if this boy knows anything, he'll spill it before I'm through with him."

We had talked but a few minutes longer when a uniformed attendant bowed deferentially at the district attorney's elbow and announced that Mr. Pfyfe was calling.

Markham requested that his visitor be shown into the lounge room, and then added to Heath, "You'd better remain, and hear what he has to say."

Leander Pfyfe was an immaculate and exquisite personage. He approached us with a mincing gate of self-approbation. His legs, which were very long and thin, with knees that seemed to bend slightly inward, supported a short bulging torso; and his chest curved outward in a generous arc, like that of a pouter pigeon. His face was rotund, and his jowls hung in two loops over a collar too tight for comfort. His blond sparse hair was brushed back sleekly; and the ends of his narrow, silken moustache were waxed into needlepoints. He was dressed in light gray summer flannels and wore a pale turquoise-green silk shirt, a vivid foulard tie, and gray suede Oxfords. A strong odor of oriental perfume was given off by the carefully arranged batiste handkerchief in his breast pocket.

He greeted Markham with viscid urbanity and acknowledged his introduction to us with a patronizing bow. After posing himself in a chair the attendant placed for him, he began polishing a gold-rimmed eyeglass which he wore on a ribbon, and fixed Markham with a melancholy gaze.

"A very sad occasion, this," he sighed.

"Realizing your friendship for Mr. Benson," said Markham, "I deplore the necessity of appealing to you at this time. It was very good of you, by the way, to come to the city today."

Pfyfe made a mildly deprecating movement with his carefully manicured fingers. He was, he explained with an air of ineffable self-complacency, only too glad to discommode himself to give aid to servants of the public. A distressing necessity, to be sure; but his manner conveyed unmistakably that he knew and recognized the obligations attaching to the dictum of *noblesse oblige* and was prepared to meet them.

He looked at Markham with a self-congratulatory air, and his eyebrows queried: "What can I do for you?" though his lips did not move.

"I understand from Major Anthony Benson," Markham said, "that you were very close to his brother and therefore might be able to tell us something of his personal affairs, or private social relationships, that would indicate a line of investigation."

Pfyfe gazed sadly at the floor. "Ah, yes. Alvin and I were very close—we were, in fact, the most intimate of friends. You can not imagine how broken up I was at hearing of the dear fellow's tragic end." He gave the impression that here was a modern instance of Æneas and Achates. "And I was deeply grieved at not being able to come at once to New York to put myself at the service of those that needed me."

"I'm sure it would have been a comfort to his other friends," remarked Vance, with cool politeness. "But in the circumst'nces you will be forgiven."

Pfyfe blinked regretfully. "Ah, but I shall never forgive myself—though I cannot hold myself altogether blameworthy. Only the day before the tragedy I had started on a trip to the Catskills. I had even asked dear Alvin to go along; but he was too busy." Pfyfe shook his head as if lamenting the incomprehensible irony of life. "How much better—ah, how infinitely much better—if only——"

"You were gone a very short time," commented Markham, interrupting what promised to be a homily on perverse providence.

"True," Pfyfe indulgently admitted. "But I met with a most unfortunate accident." He polished his eyeglass a moment. "My car broke down, and I was necessitated to return."

"What road did you take?" asked Heath.

Pfyfe delicately adjusted his eyeglass and regarded the sergeant with an intimation of boredom.

"My advice, Mr.—ah—Sneed——"

"Heath," the other corrected him surlily.

"Ah, yes—Heath. . . . My advice, Mr. Heath, is that if you are contemplating a motor trip to the Catskills, you apply to the Automobile Club of America for a roadmap. My choice of itinerary might very possibly not suit you."

He turned back to the district attorney with an air that implied he preferred talking to an equal.

"Tell me, Mr. Pfyfe," Markham asked; "did Mr. Benson have any enemies?"

The other appeared to think the matter over. "No-o. Not one, I should say, who would actually have killed him as a result of animosity."

"You imply nevertheless that he had enemies. Could you not tell us a little more?"

Pfyfe passed his hand gracefully over the tips of his golden moustache and then permitted his index-finger to linger on his cheek in an attitude of meditative indecision.

"Your request, Mr. Markham,"—he spoke with pained reluctance—"brings up a matter which I hesitate to discuss. But perhaps it is best that I confide in you—as one gentleman to another. Alvin, in common with many other admirable fellows, had a—what shall I say?—a weakness let me put it that way—for the fair sex."

He looked at Markham, seeking approbation for his extreme tact in stating an indelicate truth.

"You undersand," he continued, in answer to the other's sympathetic nod, "Alvin was not a man who possessed the personal characteristics that women hold attractive. (I somehow got the impression that Pfyfe considered himself as differing radically from Benson in this respect.) Alvin was aware of his physical deficiency, and the result was—I trust you will understand my hesitancy in mentioning this distressing fact—but the result was that Alvin used certain—ah—methods in his dealings with women, which you and I could never bring ourselves to adopt. Indeed—though it pains me to say it—he often took unfair advantage of women. He used underhand methods, as it were."

He paused, apparently shocked by this heinous imperfection of his friend and by the necessity of his own seemingly disloyal revelation.

"Was it one of these women whom Benson had dealt with unfairly that you had in mind?" asked Markham.

"No—not the woman herself," Pfyfe replied; "but a man who was interested in her. In fact, this man threatened Alvin's life. You will appreciate my reluctance in telling you this; but my excuse is that the threat was made quite openly. There were several others besides myself who heard it."

"That, of course, relieves you from any technical breach of confidence," Markham observed.

Pfyfe acknowledged the other's understanding with a slight bow.

"It happened at a little party of which I was the unfortunate host," he confessed modestly.

"Who was the man?" Markham's tone was polite but firm.

"You will comprehend my reticence. . . ." Pfyfe began. Then, with an air of righteous frankness, he leaned forward. "It might prove unfair to Alvin to withhold the gentleman's name. . . . He was Captain Philip Leacock."

He allowed himself the emotional outlet of a sigh.

"I trust you won't ask me for the lady's name."

"It won't be necessary," Markham assured him. "But I'd appreciate your telling us a little more of the episode."

Pfyfe complied with an expression of patient resignation.

"Alvin was considerably taken with the lady in question and showed her many attentions which were, I am forced to admit, unwelcome. Captain Leacock resented these attentions; and at the little affair to which I had invited him and Alvin some unpleasant and, I must say, unrefined words passed between them. I fear the wine had been flowing too freely, for Alvin was always punctilious—he was a man, indeed, skilled in the niceties of social intercourse; and the captain, in an outburst of temper, told Alvin that, unless he left the lady strictly alone in the future, he would pay with his life. The captain even went so far as to draw a revolver halfway out of his pocket."

"Was it a revolver or an automatic pistol?" asked Heath.

Pfyfe gave the district attorney a faint smile of annoyance, without deigning even to glance at the sergeant.

"I misspoke myself; forgive me. It was not a revolver. It was, I believe, an automatic army pistol—though, you understand, I didn't see it in its entirety."

"You say there were others who witnessed the altercation?"

"Several of my guests were standing about," Pfyfe explained; "but, on my word, I couldn't name them. The fact is, I attached little importance to the threat—indeed, it had entirely slipped my memory until I read the account of poor Alvin's death. Then I thought at once of the unfortunate incident and said to myself: Why not tell the district attorney. . . ?"

"Thoughts that breathe and words that burn," murmured Vance, who had been sitting through the interview in oppressive boredom.

Pfyfe once more adjusted his eyeglass and gave Vance a withering look.

"I beg your pardon, sir?"

Vance smiled disarmingly. "Merely a quotation from Gray. Poetry appeals to me in certain moods, don't y' know. . . . Do you, by any chance, know Colonel Ostrander?"

Pfyfe looked at him coldly, but only a vacuous countenance met his gaze. "I am acquainted with the gentleman," he replied haughtily.

"Was Colonel Ostrander present at this delightful little social affair of yours?" Vance's tone was artlessly innocent.

"Now that you mention it, I believe he was," admitted Pfyfe, and lifted his eyebrows inquisitively.

But Vance was again staring disinterestedly out of the window.

Markham, annoyed at the interruption, attempted to reestablish the conversation on a more amiable and practical basis. But Pfyfe, though loquacious, had little more information to give. He insisted constantly on bringing the talk back to Captain Leacock, and, despite his eloquent protestations, it was obvious he attached more importance to the threat than he chose to admit. Markham questioned him for fully an hour but could learn nothing else of a suggestive nature.

When Pfyfe rose to go, Vance turned from his contemplation of the outside world and, bowing affably, let his eyes rest on the other with ingenuous good nature.

"Now that you are in New York, Mr. Pfyfe, and were so unfortunate as to be unable to arrive earlier, I assume that you will remain until after the investigation."

Pfyfe's studied and habitual calm gave way to a look of oily astonishment. "I hadn't contemplated doing so."

"It would be most desirable if you could arrange it," urged Markham; though I am sure he had no intention of making the request until Vance suggested it.

Pfyfe hesitated and then made an elegant gesture of resignation. "Certainly I shall remain. When you have further need of my services, you will find me at the Ansonia."

He spoke with exalted condescension and magnanimously conferred upon

Markham a parting smile. But the smile did not spring from within. It appeared to have been adjusted upon his features by the unseen hands of a sculptor; and it affected only the muscles about his mouth.

When he had gone, Vance gave Markham a look of suppressed mirth.

" 'Elegancy, facility, and golden cadence.' . . . But put not your faith in poesy, old dear. Our Ciceronian friend is an unmitigated fashioner of deceptions."

"If you're trying to say that he's a smooth liar," remarked Heath, "I don't agree with you. I think that story about the captain's threat is straight goods."

"Oh, that! Of course, it's true. . . . And, y' know, Markham, the knightly Mr. Pfyfe was frightfully disappointed when you didn't insist on his revealing Miss St. Clair's name. This Leander, I fear, would never have swum the Hellespont for a lady's sake."

"Whether he's a swimmer or not," said Heath impatiently, "he's given us something to go on."

Markham agreed that Pfyfe's recital had added materially to the case against Leacock.

"I think I'll have the captain down to my office tomorrow, and question him," he said.

A moment later Major Benson entered the room, and Markham invited him to join us.

"I just saw Pfyfe get into a taxi," he said, when he had sat down. "I suppose you've been asking him about Alvin's affairs. . . . Did he help you any?"

"I hope so, for all our sakes," returned Markham kindly. "By the way, Major, what do you know about a Captain Philip Leacock?"

Major Benson lifted his eyes to Markham's in surprise.

"Didn't you know? Leacock was one of the captains in my regiment—a first-rate man. He knew Alvin pretty well, I think; but my impression is they didn't hit it off very chummily. . . . Surely you don't connect him with this affair?"

Markham ignored the question. "Did you happen to attend a party of Pfyfe's the night the captain threatened your brother?"

"I went, I remember, to one or two of Pfyfe's parties," said the major. "I don't, as a rule, care for such gatherings, but Alvin convinced me it was a good business policy."

He lifted his head and frowned fixedly into space, like one searching for an elusive memory.

"However, I don't recall—By George! Yes, I believe I do. . . . But if the instance I am thinking of is what you have in mind, you can dismiss it. We were all a little moist that night."

"Did you see the gun?" pursued Heath.

The major pursed his lips. "Now that you mention it, I think he did make some motion of the kind."

"Did you see the gun?" pursued Heath.

"No, I can't say that I did."

Markham put the next question. "Do you think Captain Leacock capable of the act of murder?"

"Hardly," Major Benson answered with emphasis. "Leacock isn't cold-blooded. The woman over whom the tiff occurred is more capable of such an act than he is."

A short silence followed, broken by Vance.

"What do you know, Major, about this glass of fashion and mold of form, Pfyfe? He appears a rare bird. Has he a history, or is his presence his life's document?"

"Leander Pfyfe," said the major, "is a typical specimen of the modern young do-nothing—I say young, though I imagine he's around forty. He was pampered in his upbringing—had everything he wanted, I believe; but he became restless and followed several different fads till he tired of them. He was two years in South Africa hunting big game and, I think, wrote a book recounting his adventures. Since then he has done nothing that I know of. He married a wealthy shrew some years ago—for her money, I imagine. But the woman's father controls the purse strings and holds him down to a rigid allowance. . . . Pfyfe's a waster and an idler, but Alvin seemed to find some attraction in the man."

The major's words had been careless in inflection and undeliberated, like those of a man discussing a neutral matter; but all of us, I think, received the impression that he had a strong personal dislike for Pfyfe.

"Not a ravishing personality, what?" remarked Vance. "And he uses far too much *Jicky.*"

"Still," supplied Heath, with a puzzled frown, "a fellow's got to have a lot of nerve to shoot big game. . . . And, speaking of nerve, I've been thinking that the guy who shot your brother, Major, was a mighty cool-headed proposition. He did it from the front when his man was wide awake and with a servant upstairs. That takes nerve."

"Sergeant, you're pos'tively brilliant!" exclaimed Vance.

12

THE OWNER OF A COLT .45

(*Monday, June 17; forenoon.*)

THOUGH VANCE and I arrived at the district attorney's office the following morning a little after nine, the captain had been waiting twenty minutes; and Markham directed Swacker to send him in at once.

Captain Philip Leacock was a typical army officer, very tall—fully six feet, two inches—clean-shaven, straight, and slender. His face was grave and immobile; and he stood before the district attorney in the erect, earnest attitude of a soldier awaiting orders from his superior officer.

"Take a seat, Captain," said Markham, with a formal bow. "I have asked you here, as you probably know, to put a few questions to you concerning Mr. Alvin Benson. There are several points regarding your relationship with him which I want you to explain."

"Am I suspected of complicity in the crime?" Leacock spoke with a slight southern accent.

"That remains to be seen," Markham told him coldly. "It is to determine that point that I wish to question you."

The other sat rigidly in his chair and waited.

Markham fixed him with a direct gaze.

"You recently made a threat on Mr. Alvin Benson's life, I believe."

Leacock started, and his fingers tightened over his knees. But before he could answer, Markham continued: "I can tell you the occasion on which the threat was made—it was at a party given by Mr. Leander Pfyfe."

Leacock hesitated, then thrust forward his jaw. "Very well, sir; I admit I made the threat. Benson was a cad—he deserved shooting. . . . That night he had become more obnoxious than usual. He'd been drinking too much—and so had I, I reckon."

He gave a twisted smile and looked nervously past the district attorney out of the window.

"But I didn't shoot him, sir. I didn't even know he'd been shot until I read the paper next day."

"He was shot with an army Colt, the kind you fellows carried in the war," said Markham, keeping his eyes on the man.

"I know," Leacock replied. "The papers said so."

"You have such a gun, haven't you, Captain?"

Again the other hesitated. "No, sir." His voice was barely audible.

"What became of it?"

The man glanced at Markham and then quickly shifted his eyes. "I—I lost it . . . in France."

Markham smiled faintly.

"Then how do you account for the fact that Mr. Pfyfe saw the gun the night you made the threat?"

"Saw the gun?" He looked blankly at the district attorney.

"Yes, saw it and recognized it as an army gun," persisted Markham, in a level voice. "Also, Major Benson saw you make a motion as if to draw a gun."

Leacock drew a deep breath, and set his mouth doggedly.

"I tell you sir, I haven't a gun. . . . I lost it in France."

"Perhaps you didn't lose it, Captain. Perhaps you lent it to someone."

"I didn't sir!" the words burst from his lips.

"Think a minute, Captain. . . . Didn't you lend it to someone?"

"No—I did not!"

"You paid a visit—yesterday—to Riverside Drive. . . . Perhaps you took it there with you."

Vance had been listening closely. "Oh, deuced clever!" he now murmured in my ear.

Captain Leacock moved uneasily. His face, even with its deep coat of tan, seemed to pale, and he sought to avoid the implacable gaze of his questioner by concentrating his attention upon some object on the table. When he spoke, his voice, heretofore truculent, was colored by anxiety.

"I didn't have it with me. . . . And I didn't lend it to anyone."

Markham sat leaning forward over the desk, his chin on his hand, like a minatory graven image. "It may be you lent it to someone prior to that morning."

"Prior to . . . ?" Leacock looked up quickly and paused, as if analyzing the other's remark.

Markham took advantage of his perplexity.

"Have you lent your gun to anyone since you returned from France?"

"No, I've never lent it——" he began, but suddenly halted and flushed. Then he added hastily, "How could I lend it? I just told you, sir——"

"Never mind that!" Markham cut in. 'So you had a gun, did you, Captain? . . . Have you still got it?"

Leacock opened his lips to speak but closed them again tightly.

Markham relaxed and leaned back in his chair.

"You were aware, of course, that Benson had been annoying Miss St. Clair with his attentions?"

At the mention of the girl's name the captain's body became rigid; his face turned a dull red, and he glared menacingly at the district attorney. At the end of a slow, deep inhalation he spoke through clenched teeth.

"Suppose we leave Miss St. Clair out of this." He looked as though he might spring at Markham.

"Unfortunately, we can't." Markham's words were sympathetic but firm. "Too many facts connect her with the case. Her handbag, for instance, was found in Benson's living room the morning after the murder."

"That's a lie, sir!"

Markham ignored the insult.

"Miss St. Clair herself admits the circumstance." He held up his hand, as the other was about to answer. "Don't misinterpret my mentioning the fact. I am not accusing Miss St. Clair of having anything to do with the affair. I'm merely endeavoring to get some light on your own connection with it."

The captain studied Markham with an expression that clearly indicated he doubted these assurances. Finally he set his mouth and announced with determination:

"I haven't anything more to say on the subject, sir."

"You knew, didn't you," continued Markham, "that Miss St. Clair dined with Benson at the Marseilles on the night he was shot?"

"What of it?" retorted Leacock sullenly.

"And you knew, didn't you, that they left the restaurant at midnight, and that Miss St. Clair did not reach home until after one?"

A strange look came into the man's eyes. The ligaments of his neck tightened, and he took a deep, resolute breath. But he neither glanced at the district attorney nor spoke.

"You know, of course," pursued Markham's monotonous voice, "that Benson was shot at half past twelve?" He waited, and for a whole minute there was silence in the room.

"You have nothing more to say, Captain?" he asked at length; "no further explanations to give me?"

Leacock did not answer. He sat gazing imperturbably ahead of him; and it was evident he had sealed his lips for the time being.

Markham rose.

"In that case, let us consider the interview at an end."

The moment Captain Leacock had gone, Markham rang for one of his clerks.

"Tell Ben to have that man followed. Find out where he goes and what he does. I want a report at the Stuyvesant Club tonight."

When we were alone, Vance gave Markham a look of half-bantering admiration.

"Ingenious, not to say artful.... But, y' know, your questions about the lady were shocking bad form."

"No doubt," Markham agreed. "But it looks now as if we were on the right track. Leacock didn't create an impression of unassailable innocence."

"Didn't he?" asked Vance. "Just what were the signs of his assailable guilt?"

"You saw him turn white when I questioned him about the weapon. His nerves were on edge—he was genuinely frightened."

Vance sighed. "What a perfect ready-made set of notions you have, Markham! Don't you know that an innocent man, when he comes under suspicion, is apt to be more nervous than a guilty one, who, to begin with, had enough nerve to commit the crime and, secondly, realizes that any show of nervousness is regarded as guilt by you lawyer chaps? 'My strength is as the strength of ten because my heart is pure' is a mere Sunday school pleasantry. Touch almost any innocent man on the shoulder and say 'You're arrested,' and his pupils will dilate, he'll break out in a cold sweat, the blood will rush from his face, and he'll have tremors and dyspnea. If he's a *hystérique,* or a cardiac neurotic, he'll probably collapse completely. It's the guilty person who, when thus accosted, lifts his eyebrows in bored surprise and says, 'You don't mean it, really—here have a cigar.' "

"The hardened criminal may act as you say," Markham conceded; "but an honest man who's innocent doesn't go to pieces, even when accused."

Vance shook his head hopelessly. "My dear fellow, Crile and Voronoff might have lived in vain for all of you. Manifestations of fear are the result of glandular secretions—nothing more. All they prove is that the person's thyroid is undeveloped or that his adrenals are subnormal. A man accused of a crime, or shown the bloody weapon with which it was committed, will either smile serenely, or scream, or have hysterics, or faint, or appear disint'rested according to his hormones and irrespective of his guilt. Your theory, d' ye see, would be quite all right if everyone had the same amount of the various internal secretions. But they haven't.... Really, y' know, you shouldn't send a man to the electric chair simply because he's deficient in endocrines. It isn't cricket."

Before Markham could reply, Swacker appeared at the door and said Heath had arrived.

The sergeant, beaming with satisfaction, fairly burst into the room. For once he forgot to shake hands. "Well, it looks like we've got hold of something workable. I went to this Captain Leacock's apartment house last night, and here's the straight of it:—Leacock was at home the night of the thirteenth all right; but shortly after midnight he went out, headed west—get that!—and he didn't return till about quarter of one!"

"What about the hallboy's original story?" asked Markham.

"That's the best part of it. Leacock had the boy fixed. Gave him money to swear he hadn't left the house that night. What do you think of that, Mr. Markham? Pretty crude—huh? . . . The kid loosened up when I told him I was thinking of sending him up the river for doing the job himself." Heath laughed unpleasantly. "And he won't spill anything to Leacock, either."

Markham nodded his head slowly.

"What you tell me, Sergeant, bears out certain conclusions I arrived at when I talked to Captain Leacock this morning. Ben put a man on him when he left here, and I'm to get a report tonight. Tomorrow may see this thing through. I'll get in touch with you in the morning, and if anything's to be done, you understand, you'll have the handling of it."

When Heath had left us, Markham folded his hands behind his head and leaned back contentedly.

"I think I've got the answer," he said. "The girl dined with Benson and returned to his house afterward. The captain, suspecting the fact, went out, found her there, and shot Benson. That would account not only for her gloves and handbag but for the hour it took her to go from the Marseilles to her home. It would also account for her attitude here Saturday and for the captain's lying about the gun. . . . There. I believe, I have my case. The smashing of the captain's alibi about clinches it."

"Oh, quite," said Vance airily. " 'Hope springs exulting on triumphant wing.' "

Markham regarded him a moment. "Have you entirely forsworn human reason as a means of reaching a decision? Here we have an admitted threat, a motive, the time, the place, the opportunity, the conduct, and the criminal agent."

"Those words sound strangely familiar," Vance smiled. "Didn't most of 'em fit the young lady also? . . . And you really haven't got the criminal agent, y' know. But it's no doubt floating about the city somewhere. A mere detail, however."

"I may not have it in my hand," Markham countered. "But with a good man on watch every minute, Leacock won't find much opportunity of disposing of the weapon."

Vance shrugged indifferently.

"In any event, go easy," he admonished. "My humble opinion is that you've merely unearthed a conspiracy."

"Conspiracy? . . . Good Lord! What kind?"

"A conspiracy of circumst'nces, don't y' know."

"I'm glad, at any rate, it hasn't to do with international politics," returned Markham good-naturedly.

He glanced at the clock. "You won't mind if I get to work? I've a dozen things to attend to and a couple of committees to see. . . . Why don't you go across the hall and have a talk with Ben Hanlon and then come back at twelve thirty? We'll have lunch together at the Bankers' Club. Ben's our greatest expert on foreign extradition and has spent most of his life chasing about the world after fugitives from justice. He'll spin you some good yarns."

"How perfectly fascinatin'!" exclaimed Vance, with a yawn. But instead of taking the suggestion, he walked to the window and lit a cigarette. He stood for a while puffing at it, rolling it between his fingers, and inspecting it critically.

"Y'know, Markham," he observed, "everything's going to pot these days. It's this silly democracy. Even the nobility is degen'rating. These Régie cigarettes, now; they've fallen off frightfully. There was a time when no self-respecting potentate would have smoked such inferior tobacco."

Markham smiled. "What's the favor you want to ask?"

"Favor? What has that to do with the decay of Europe's aristocracy?"

"I've noticed that whenever you want to ask a favor which you consider questionable etiquette, you begin with a denunciation of royalty."

"Observin' fella," commented Vance dryly. Then he, too, smiled. "Do you mind if I invite Colonel Ostrander along to lunch?"

Markham gave him a sharp look. "Bigsby Ostrander, you mean? . . . Is he the mysterious colonel you've been asking people about for the past two days?"

"That's the lad. Pompous ass and that sort of thing. Might prove a bit edi-fyin', though. He's the papa of Benson's crowd, so to speak; knows all parties. Regular old scandalmonger."

"Have him along, by all means," agreed Markham. Then he picked up the telephone. "Now I'm going to tell Ben you're coming over for an hour or so."

13

THE GRAY CADILLAC

(*Monday, June 17; 12:30 P.M.*)

WHEN, AT half past twelve, Markham, Vance, and I entered the Grill of the Bankers' Club in the Equitable Building, Colonel Ostrander was already at the bar engaged with one of Charlie's prohibition clam-broth-and-Worcester-shire-sauce cocktails. Vance had telephoned him immediately upon our leaving the district attorney's office, requesting him to meet us at the club; and the colonel had seemed eager to comply.

"Here is New York's gayest dog," said Vance, introducing him to Markham (I had met him before); "a sybarite and a hedonist. He sleeps till noon, and makes no appointments before tiffin-time. I had to knock him up and threaten him with your official ire to get him downtown at this early hour."

"Only too pleased to be of any service," the colonel assured Markham grandiloquently. "Shocking affair! Gad! I couldn't credit it when I read it in the papers. Fact is, though—I don't mind sayin' it—I've one or two ideas on the subject. Came very near calling you up myself, sir."

When we had taken our seats at the table, Vance began interrogating him without preliminaries.

"You know all the people in Benson's set, Colonel. Tell us something about Captain Leacock. What sort of chap is he?"

"Ha! So you have your eye on the gallant captain?"

Colonel Ostrander pulled importantly at his white moustache. He was a large pink-faced man with bushy eyelashes and small blue eyes; and his manner and bearing were those of a pompous light-opera general.

"Not a bad idea. Might possibly have done it. Hotheaded fellow. He's badly smitten with a Miss St. Clair—fine girl, Muriel. And Benson was smitten, too. If I'd been twenty years younger myself——"

"You're too fascinatin' to the ladies, as it is, Colonel," interrupted Vance. "But tell us about the captain."

"Ah, yes—the captain. Comes from Georgia originally. Served in the war—some kind of decoration. He didn't care for Benson—disliked him, in fact. Quick-tempered, single-track-minded sort of person. Jealous, too. You know the type—a product of that tribal etiquette below the Mason and Dixon line. Puts women on a pedestal—not that they shouldn't be put there, God bless 'em! But he'd go to jail for a lady's honor. A shielder of womanhood. Sentimental cuss, full of chivalry; just the kind to blow out a rival's brains:— no questions asked—*pop*—and it's all over. Dangerous chap to monkey with. Benson was a confounded idiot to bother with the girl when he knew she was engaged to Leacock. Playin' with fire. I don't mind sayin' I was tempted to warn him. But it was none of my affair—I had no business interferin'. Bad taste."

"Just how well did Captain Leacock know Benson?" asked Vance. "By that I mean, how intimate were they?"

"Not intimate at all," the colonel replied.

He made a ponderous gesture of negation, and added, "I should say not! Formal, in fact. They met each other here and there a good deal, though. Knowing 'em both pretty well, I've often had 'em to little affairs at my humble diggin's."

"You wouldn't say Captain Leacock was a good gambler—levelheaded and all that?"

"Gambler—huh!" The colonel's manner was heavily contemptuous. "Poorest I ever saw. Played poker worse than a woman. Too excitable— couldn't keep his feelin's to himself. Altogether too rash."

Then, after a momentary pause: "By George! I see what you're aimin' at. . . . And you're dead right. It's rash young puppies just like him that go about shootin' people they don't like."

"The captain, I take it, is quite different in that regard from your friend, Leander Pfyfe," remarked Vance.

The colonel appeared to consider. "Yes and no," he decided. "Pfyfe's a cool gambler—that I'll grant you. He once ran a private gambling place of his own down on Long Island—roulette, monte, baccarat, that sort of thing. And he popped tigers and wild boars in Africa for a while. But Pfyfe's got his senti- mental side, and he'd plunge on a pair of deuces with all the betting odds against him. Not a good scientific gambler. Flighty in his impulses, if you un- derstand me. I don't mind admittin', though, that he could shoot a man and forget all about it in five minutes. But he'd need a lot of provocation. . . . He may have had it—you can't tell."

"Pfyfe and Benson were rather intimate, weren't they?"

"Very—very. Always saw 'em together when Pfyfe was in New York. Known each other years. Boon companions, as they called 'em in the old days. Actually lived together before Pfyfe got married. An exacting woman, Pfyfe's wife; makes him toe the mark. But loads of money."

"Speaking of the ladies," said Vance, "what was the situation between Ben- son and Miss St. Clair?"

"Who can tell?" asked the colonel sententiously. "Muriel didn't cotton to Benson—that's sure. And yet . . . women are strange creatures——"

"Oh, no end strange," agreed Vance, a trifle wearily. "But really, y' know, I wasn't prying into the lady's personal relations with Benson. I thought you might know her mental attitude concerning him."

"Ah—I see. Would she, in short, have been likely to take desperate measures against him? . . . Egad! That's an idea!"

The colonel pondered the point.

"Muriel, now, is a girl of strong character. Works hard at her art. She's a singer and, I don't mind tellin' you, a mighty fine one. She's deep, too—deuced deep. And capable. Not afraid of taking a chance. Independent. I myself wouldn't want to be in her path if she had it in for me. Might stick at nothing."

He nodded his head sagely.

"Women are funny that way. Always surprisin' you. No sense of values. The most peaceful of 'em will shoot a man in cold blood without warnin'——"

He suddenly sat up, and his little blue eyes glistened like china. "By gad!" He fairly blurted the ejaculation. "Muriel had dinner alone with Benson the night he was shot—the very night. Saw 'em together myself at the Marseilles."

"You don't say, really!" muttered Vance incuriously. "But I suppose we all must eat. . . . By the bye, how well did you yourself know Benson?"

The colonel looked startled, but Vance's innocuous expression seemed to reassure him.

"I? My dear fellow! I've known Alvin Benson fifteen years. At least fifteen—maybe longer. Showed him the sights in this old town before the lid was put on. A live town it was then. Wide open. Anything you wanted. Gad—what times we had! Those were the days of the old Haymarket. Never thought of toddlin' home till breakfast——"

Vance again interrupted his irrelevancies.

"How intimate are your relations with Major Benson?"

"The major? . . . That's another matter. He and I belong to different schools. Dissimilar tastes. We never hit it off. Rarely see each other."

He seemed to think that some explanation was necessary, for before Vance could speak again, he nodded, "The major, you know, was never one of the boys, as we say. Disapproved of gaiety. Didn't mix with our little set. Considered me and Alvin too frivolous. Serious-minded chap."

Vance ate in silence for a while, then asked in an offhand way, "Did you do much speculating through Benson and Benson?"

For the first time the colonel appeared hesitant about answering. He ostentatiously wiped his mouth with his napkin.

"Oh—dabbled a bit," he at length admitted airily. "Not very lucky, though. . . . We all flirted now and then with the Goddess of Chance in Benson's office."

Throughout the lunch Vance kept plying him with questions along these lines; but at the end of an hour he seemed to be no nearer anything definite than when he began. Colonel Ostrander was voluble, but his fluency was vague and disorganized. He talked mainly in parentheses and insisted on elaborating his answers with rambling opinions, until it was almost impossible to extract what little information his words contained.

Vance, however, did not appear discouraged. He dwelt on Captain Leacock's character and seemed particularly interested in his personal relationship with Benson. Pfyfe's gambling proclivities also occupied his attention, and he let the colonel ramble on tiresomely about the man's gambling house on Long Island and his hunting experiences in South Africa. He asked numerous questions about Benson's other friends but paid scant attention to the answers.

The whole interview impressed me as pointless, and I could not help wondering what Vance hoped to learn. Markham, I was convinced, was equally at sea. He pretended polite interest and nodded appreciatively during the colonel's incredibly drawn-out periods; but his eyes wandered occasionally, and several times I saw him give Vance a look of reproachful inquiry. There was no doubt, however, that Colonel Ostrander knew his people.

When we were back in the district attorney's office, having taken leave of our garrulous guest at the subway entrance, Vance threw himself into one of the easy chairs with an air of satisfaction.

"Most entertainin', what? As an elim'nator of suspects the colonel has his good points."

"Eliminator!" retorted Markham. "It's a good thing he's not connected with the police; he'd have half the community jailed for shooting Benson."

"He *is* a bit bloodthirsty," Vance admitted. "He's determined to get somebody jailed for the crime."

"According to that old warrior, Benson's coterie was a camorra of gunmen—not forgetting the women. I couldn't help getting the impression, as he talked, that Benson was miraculously lucky not to have been riddled with bullets long ago."

"It's obvious," commented Vance, "that you overlooked the illuminatin' flashes in the colonel's thunder."

"Were there any?" Markham asked. "At any rate, I can't say that they exactly blinded me by their brilliance."

"And you received no solace from his words?"

"Only those in which he bade me a fond farewell. The parting didn't exactly break my heart. . . . What the old boy said about Leacock, however, might be called a confirmatory opinion. It verified—if verification had been necessary—the case against the captain."

Vance smiled cynically. "Oh, to be sure. And what he said about Miss St. Clair would have verified the case against her, too—last Saturday. Also, what he said about Pfyfe would have verified the case against that Beau Sabreur, if you had happened to suspect him—eh, what?"

Vance had scarcely finished speaking when Swacker came in to say that Emery from the homicide bureau had been sent over by Heath and wished, if possible, to see the district attorney.

When the man entered, I recognized him at once as the detective who had found the cigarette butts in Benson's grate.

With a quick glance at Vance and me, he went directly to Markham. "We've found the gray Cadillac, sir; and Sergeant Heath thought you might want to know about it right away. It's in a small, one-man garage on Seventy-fourth Street near Amsterdam Avenue, and has been there three days. One of the men from the Sixty-eighth Street station located it and phoned in to headquarters; and I hopped uptown at once. It's the right car—fishing tackle and all, except for the rods; so I guess the ones found in Central Park belonged to the car after all; fell out probably. . . . It seems a fellow drove the car into the garage about noon last Friday, and gave the garage-man twenty dollars to keep his mouth shut. The man's a wop and says he don't read the papers. Anyway, he came across pronto when I put the screws on."

The detective drew out a small notebook.

"I looked up the car's number. . . . It's listed in the name of Leander Pfyfe, 24 Elm Boulevard, Port Washington, Long Island."

Markham received this piece of unexpected information with a perplexed frown. He dismissed Emery almost curtly and sat tapping thoughtfully on his desk.

Vance watched him with an amused smile.

"It's really not a madhouse, y' know," he observed comfortingly. "I say, don't the colonel's words bring you any cheer, now that you know Leander was hovering about the neighborhood at the time Benson was translated into the Beyond?"

"Damn your old colonel!" snapped Markham. "What interests me at present is fitting this new development into the situation."

"It fits beautifully," Vance told him. "It rounds out the mosaic, so to speak. . . . Are you actu'lly disconcerted by learning that Pfyfe was the owner of the mysterious car?"

"Not having your gift of clairvoyance, I am, I confess, disturbed by the fact."

Markham lit a cigar—an indication of worry. "You, of course," he added, with sarcasm, "knew before Emery came here that it was Pfyfe's car."

"I didn't know," Vance corrected him; "but I had a strong suspicion. Pfyfe overdid his distress when he told us of his breakdown in the Catskills. And Heath's question about his itiner'ry annoyed him frightfully. His hauteur was too melodramatic."

"Your *ex post facto* wisdom is most useful!"

Markham smoked awhile in silence.

"I think I'll find out about this matter."

He rang for Swacker. "Call up the Ansonia," he ordered angrily; "locate Leander Pfyfe, and say I want to see him at the Stuyvesant Club at six o'clock. And tell him he's to be there."

"It occurs to me," said Markham, when Swacker had gone, "that this car episode may prove helpful, after all. Pfyfe was evidently in New York that night, and for some reason he didn't want it known. Why, I wonder? He tipped us off about Leacock's threat against Benson and hinted strongly that we'd better get on the fellow's track. Of course, he may have been sore at Leacock for winning Miss St. Clair away from his friend, and taken this means of wreaking a little revenge on him. On the other hand, if Pfyfe was at Benson's house the night of the murder, he may have some real information. And now that we've found out about the car, I think he'll tell us what he knows."

"He'll tell you something anyway," said Vance. "He's the type of congenital liar that'll tell anybody anything as long as it doesn't involve himself unpleasantly."

"You and the Cumean Sibyl, I presume, could inform me in advance what he's going to tell me."

"I couldn't say as to the Cumean Sibyl, don't y' know," Vance returned lightly; "but speaking for myself, I rather fancy he'll tell you that he saw the impetuous captain at Benson's house that night."

Markham laughed. "I hope he does. You'll want to be on hand to hear him, I suppose."

"I couldn't bear to miss it."

Vance was already at the door, preparatory to going, when he turned again to Markham. "I've another slight favor to ask. Get a dossier on Pfyfe—there's a good fellow. Send one of your innumerable Dogberrys to Port Washington and have the gentleman's conduct and social habits looked into. Tell your emiss'ry to concentrate on the woman question. . . . I promise you, you sha'n't regret it."

Markham, I could see, was decidedly puzzled by this request and half inclined to refuse it. But after deliberating a few moments, he smiled and pressed a button on his desk.

"Anything to humor you," he said. "I'll send a man down at once."

14

LINKS IN THE CHAIN

(*Monday, June 17; 6 P.M.*)

VANCE AND I spent an hour or so that afternoon at the Anderson Galleries looking at some tapestries which were to be auctioned the next day, and afterward had tea at Sherry's. We were at the Stuyvesant Club a little before six. A few minutes later Markham and Pfyfe arrived; and we went at once into one of the conference rooms.

Pfyfe was as elegant and superior as at the first interview. He wore a ratcatcher suit and Newmarket gaiters of unbleached linen, and was redolent of perfume.

"An unexpected pleasure to see you gentlemen again so soon," he greeted us, like one conferring a blessing.

Markham was far from amiable, and gave him an almost brusque salutation. Vance had merely nodded, and now sat regarding Pfyfe drearily as if seeking to find some excuse for his existence but utterly unable to do so.

Markham went directly to the point. "I've found out, Mr. Pfyfe, that you placed your machine in a garage at noon on Friday and gave the man twenty dollars to say nothing about it."

Pfyfe looked up with a hurt look. "I've been deeply wronged," he complained sadly. "I gave the man fifty dollars."

"I am glad you admit the fact so readily," returned Markham. "You knew, by the newspapers, of course, that your machine was seen outside Benson's house the night he was shot."

"Why else should I have paid so liberally to have its presence in New York kept secret?" His tone indicated that he was pained at the other's obtuseness.

"In that case, why did you keep it in the city at all?" asked Markham. "You could have driven it back to Long Island."

Pfyfe shook his head sorrowfully, a look of commiseration in his eyes. Then he leaned forward with an air of benign patience:—he would be gentle with this dull-witted district attorney, like a fond teacher with a backward child, and would strive to lead him out of the tangle of his uncertainties.

"I am a married man, Mr. Markham." He pronounced the fact as if some special virtue attached to it. "I started on my trip for the Catskills Thursday after dinner, intending to stop a day in New York to make my adieus to some-one residing here. I arrived quite late—after midnight—and decided to call on Alvin. But when I drove up, the house was dark. So, without even ringing the bell, I walked to Pietro's in Forty-third Street to get a nightcap,—I keep a bit of my own pinch-bottle Haig and Haig there—but, alas! the place was closed, and I strolled back to my car. . . . To think that while I was away poor Alvin was shot!"

He stopped and polished his eyeglass.

"The irony of it! . . . I didn't even guess that anything had happened to the dear fellow—how could I? I drove, all unsuspecting of the tragedy, to a Turk-ish bath and remained there the night. The next morning I read of the murder; and in the later editions I saw the mention of my car. It was then I became— shall I say worried? But no. *Worried* is a misleading word. Let me say, rather, that I became aware of the false position I might be placed in if the car were traced to me. So I drove it to the garage and paid the man to say nothing of its whereabouts, lest its discovery confuse the issue of Alvin's death."

One might have thought, from his tone and the self-righteous way he looked at Markham, that he had bribed the garageman wholly out of consid-eration for the district attorney and the police.

"Why didn't you continue on your trip?" asked Markham. "That would have made the discovery of the car even less likely."

Pfyfe adopted an air of compassionate surprise.

"With my dearest friend foully murdered? How could one have the heart to seek diversion at such a sad moment? . . . I returned home and informed Mrs. Pfyfe that my car had broken down."

"You might have driven home in your car, it seems to me," observed Markham.

Pfyfe offered a look of infinite forbearance for the other's inspection and took a deep sigh, which conveyed the impression that, though he could not sharpen the world's perceptions, he at least could mourn for its deplorable lack of understanding.

"If I had been in the Catskills away from any source of information, where Mrs. Pfyfe believed me to be, how would I have heard of Alvin's death until, perhaps, days afterward? You see, unfortunately I had not mentioned to Mrs. Pfyfe that I was stopping over in New York. The truth is, Mr. Markham, I had reason for not wishing my wife to know I was in the city. Consequently, if I had driven back at once, she would, I regret to say, have suspected me of breaking my journey. I therefore pursued the course which seemed simplest."

Markham was becoming annoyed at the man's fluent hypocrisy. After a brief silence he asked abruptly, "Did the presence of your car at Benson's house that night have anything to do with your apparent desire to implicate Captain Leacock in the affair?"

Pfyfe lifted his eyebrows in pained astonishment and made a gesture of polite protestation.

"My dear sir!" His voice betokened profound resentment of the other's unjust imputation. "If yesterday you detected in my words an undercurrent of suspicion against Captain Leacock, I can account for it only by the fact that I actually saw the captain in front of Alvin's house when I drove up that night."

Markham shot a curious look at Vance, then said to Pfyfe, "You are sure you saw Leacock?"

"I saw him quite distinctly. And I would have mentioned the fact yesterday had it not involved the tacit confession of my own presence there."

"What if it had?" demanded Markham. "It was vital information, and I could have used it this morning. You were placing your comfort ahead of the legal demands of justice; and your attitude puts a very questionable aspect on your own alleged conduct that night."

"You are pleased to be severe, sir," said Pfyfe with self-pity. "But having placed myself in a false position, I must accept your criticism."

"Do you realize," Markham went on, "that many a district attorney, if he knew what I know about your movements and had been treated the way you've treated me, would arrest you on suspicion?"

"Then I can only say," was the suave response, "that I am most fortunate in my inquisitor."

Markham rose.

"That will be all for today, Mr. Pfyfe. But you are to remain in New York until I give you permission to return home. Otherwise, I will have you held as a material witness."

Pfyfe made a shocked gesture in deprecation of such acerbities and bade us a ceremonious good-afternoon.

When we were alone, Markham looked seriously at Vance. "Your prophecy was fulfilled, though I didn't dare hope for such luck. Pfyfe's evidence puts the final link in the chain against the captain."

Vance smoked languidly.

"I'll admit your theory of the crime is most satisfyin'. But alas! the psychological objection remains. Everything fits, with the one exception of the captain; and he doesn't fit at all. . . . Silly idea, I know. But he has no more business being cast as the murderer of Benson than the bisonic Tetrazzini had being cast as the phthisical Mimi."*

"In any other circumstances," Markham answered, "I might defer reverently to your charming theories. But with all the circumstantial and presumptive evidence I have against Leacock, it strikes my inferior legal mind as sheer nonsense to say, 'He just couldn't be guilty because his hair is parted in the middle and he tucks his napkin in his collar.' There's too much logic against it."

"I'll grant your logic is irrefutable—as all logic is, no doubt. You've prob'bly convinced many innocent persons by sheer reasoning that they were guilty."

Vance stretched himself wearily.

* Obviously a reference to Tetrazzini's performance in *La Bohème* at the Manhattan Opera House in 1908.

"What do you say to a light repast on the roof? The unutt'rable Pfyfe has tired me."

In the summer dining room on the roof of the Stuyvesant Club we found Major Benson sitting alone, and Markham asked him to join us.

"I have good news for you, Major," he said, when we had given our order. "I feel confident I have my man; everything points to him. Tomorrow will see the end, I hope."

The major gave Markham a questioning frown.

"I don't understand exactly. From what you told me the other day, I got the impression there was a woman involved."

Markham smiled awkwardly and avoided Vance's eyes. "A lot of water has run under the bridge since then," he said. "The woman I had in mind was eliminated as soon as we began to check up on her. But in the process I was led to the man. There's little doubt of his guilt. I felt pretty sure about it this morning, and just now I learned that he was seen by a credible witness in front of your brother's house within a few minutes of the time the shot was fired."

"Is there any objection to your telling me who it was?" The major was still frowning.

"None whatsoever. The whole city will probably know it tomorrow. . . . It was Captain Leacock."

Major Benson stared at him in unbelief. "Impossible! I simply can't credit it. That boy was with me three years on the other side, and I got to know him pretty well. I can't help feeling there's a mistake somewhere. . . . The police," he added quickly, "have got on the wrong track."

"It's not the police," Markham informed him. "It was my own investigations that turned up the captain."

The major did not answer, but his silence bespoke his doubt.

"Y' know," put in Vance, "I feel the same way about the captain that you do, Major. It rather pleases me to have my impressions verified by one who has known him so long."

"What, then, was Leacock doing in front of the house that night?" urged Markham acidulously.

"He might have been singing carols beneath Benson's window," suggested Vance.

Before Markham could reply, he was handed a card by the headwaiter. When he glanced at it, he gave a grunt of satisfaction and directed that the caller be sent up immediately. Then, turning back to us, he said, "We may learn something more now. I've been expecting this man Higginbotham. He's the detective that followed Leacock from my office this morning."

Higginbotham was a wiry, pale-faced youth with fishy eyes and a shifty manner. He slouched up to the table and stood hesitantly before the district attorney.

"Sit down and report, Higginbotham," Markham ordered. "These gentlemen are working with me on the case."

"I picked up the bird while he was waiting for the elevator," the man began, eyeing Markham craftily. "He went to the subway and rode uptown to Seventy-ninth and Broadway. He walked through Eightieth to Riverside Drive and went in the apartment-house at No. 94. Didn't give his name to the boy—got right in the elevator. He stayed upstairs a coupla hours, come down at one twenty, and hopped a taxi. I picked up another one and followed him. He went down the Drive to Seventy-second, through Central Park, and east on Fifty-ninth. Got out at Avenue A, and walked out on the Queensborough Bridge. About halfway to Blackwell's Island he stood leaning over the rail for five or six minutes. Then he took a small package out of his pocket and dropped it in the river."

"What size was the package?" There was repressed eagerness in Markham's question.

Higginbotham indicated the measurements with his hands.

"How thick was it?"

"Inch or so, maybe."

Markham leaned forward.

"Could it have been a gun—a Colt automatic?"

"Sure, it could. Just about the right size. And it was heavy, too—I could tell by the way he handled it, and the way it hit the water."

"All right." Markham was pleased. "Anything else?"

"No, sir. After he'd ditched the gun, he went home and stayed. I left him there."

When Higginbotham had gone, Markham nodded at Vance with melancholy elation.

"There's your criminal agent. . . . What more would you like?"

"Oh, lots," drawled Vance.

Major Benson looked up, perplexed.

"I don't quite grasp the situation. Why did Leacock have to go to Riverside Drive for his gun?"

"I have reason to think," said Markham, "that he took it to Miss St. Clair the day after the shooting—for safekeeping probably. He wouldn't have wanted it found in his place."

"Might he not have taken it to Miss St. Clair's before the shooting?"

"I know what you mean," Markham answered. (I, too, recalled the major's assertion the day before that Miss St. Clair was more capable of shooting his brother than was the captain.) "I had the same idea myself. But certain evidential facts have eliminated her as a suspect."

"You've undoubtedly satisfied yourself on the point," returned the major; but his tone was dubious. "However, I can't see Leacock as Alvin's murderer."

He paused and laid a hand on the district attorney's arm. "I don't want to appear presumptuous, or unappreciative of all you've done; but I really wish you'd wait a bit before clapping that boy into prison. The most careful and conscientious of us are liable to error: Even facts sometimes lie damnably; and I can't help believing that the facts in this instance have deceived you."

It was plain that Markham was touched by this request of his old friend; but his instinctive fidelity to duty helped him to resist the other's appeal.

"I must act according to my convictions, Major," he said firmly, but with a great kindness.

15

"PFYFE—PERSONAL"

(*Tuesday, June 18; 9 A.M.*)

THE NEXT day—the fourth of the investigation—was an important and, in some ways, a momentous one in the solution of the problem posed by Alvin Benson's murder. Nothing of a definite nature came to light, but a new element was injected into the case; and this new element eventually led to the guilty person.

Before we parted from Markham after our dinner with Major Benson, Vance had made the request that he be permitted to call at the district attorney's office the next morning. Markham, both disconcerted and impressed by his unwonted earnestness, had complied; although, I think, he would rather have made his arrangements for Captain Leacock's arrest without the disturbing influence of the other's protesting presence. It was evident that, after Higginbotham's report, Markham had decided to place the captain in custody and to proceed with his preparation of data for the grand jury.

Although Vance and I arrived at the office at nine o'clock, Markham was already there. As we entered the room, he picked up the telephone receiver and asked to be put through to Sergeant Heath.

At that moment Vance did an amazing thing. He walked swiftly to the district attorney's desk and, snatching the receiver out of Markham's hand, clamped it down on the hook. Then he placed the telephone to one side and laid both hands on the other's shoulders.

Markham was too astonished and bewildered to protest; and before he could recover himself, Vance said in a low, firm voice, which was all the more impelling because of its softness, "I'm not going to let you jail Leacock—that's what I came here for this morning. You're not going to order his arrest as long as I'm in this office and can prevent it by any means whatever. There's only one way you can accomplish this act of unmitigated folly, and that's by summoning your policemen and having me forcibly ejected. And I advise you to call a goodly number of 'em, because I'll give 'em the battle of their bellicose lives!"

The incredible part of this threat was that Vance meant it literally. And Markham knew he meant it.

"If you do call your henchmen," he went on, "you'll be the laughing stock of the city inside of a week; for, by that time, it'll be known who really did shoot Benson. And I'll be a popular hero and a martyr—God save the mark!—for defying the district attorney and offering up my sweet freedom on the altar of truth and justice and that sort of thing. . . ."

The telephone rang, and Vance answered it.

"Not wanted," he said, closing off immediately. Then he stepped back and folded his arms.

At the end of the brief silence Markham spoke, his voice quavering with rage. "If you don't go at once, Vance, and let me run this office myself, I'll have no choice but to call in those policemen."

Vance smiled. He knew Markham would take no such extreme measures. After all, the issue between these two friends was an intellectual one; and though Vance's actions had placed it for a moment on a physical basis, there was no danger of its so continuing.

Markham's belligerent gaze slowly turned to one of profound perplexity. "Why are you so damned interested in Leacock?" he asked gruffly. "Why this irrational insistence that he remain at large?"

"You priceless, inexpressible ass!" Vance strove to keep all hint of affection out of his voice. "Do you think I care particularly what happens to a southern army captain? There are hundreds of Leacocks, all alike—with their square shoulders and square chins, and their knobby clothes, and their totemistic codes of barbaric chivalry. Only a mother could tell 'em apart. . . . I'm int'rested in *you,* old chap. I don't want to see you make a mistake that's going to injure you more than it will Leacock."

Markham's eyes lost their hardness; he understood Vance's motive and forgave him. But he was still firm in his belief of the captain's guilt. He remained thoughtful for some time. Then, having apparently arrived at a decision, he rang for Swacker and asked that Phelps be sent for.

"I've a plan that may nail this affair down tight," he said. "And it'll be evidence that not even you, Vance, can gainsay."

Phelps came in, and Markham gave him instructions.

"Go and see Miss St. Clair at once. Get to her some way, and ask her what was in the package Captain Leacock took away from her apartment yesterday and threw in the East River." He briefly summarized Higginbotham's report of the night before. "Demand that she tell you and intimate that you know it was the gun with which Benson was shot. She'll probably refuse to answer and will tell you to get out. Then go downstairs and wait developments. If she phones, listen in at the switchboard. If she happens to send a note to anyone, intercept it. And if she goes out—which I hardly think likely—follow her and learn what you can. Let me hear from you the minute you get hold of anything."

"I get you, Chief." Phelps seemed pleased with the assignment, and departed with alacrity.

"Are such burglarious and eavesdropping methods considered ethical by your learned profession?" asked Vance. "I can't harmonize such conduct with your other qualities, y' know."

Markham leaned back and gazed up at the chandelier. "Personal ethics don't enter into it. Or, if they do, they are crowded out by greater and graver considerations—by the higher demands of justice. Society must be protected; and the citizens of this county look to me for their security against the encroachments of criminals and evildoers. Sometimes, in the pursuance of my duty, it is necessary to adopt courses of conduct that conflict with my personal instincts. I have no right to jeopardize the whole of society because of an assumed ethical obligation to an individual. . . . You understand, of course, that I would not use any information obtained by these unethical methods, unless it pointed to criminal activities on the part of that individual. And in such a case, I would have every right to use it, for the good of the community."

"I daresay you're right," yawned Vance. "But society doesn't int'rest me particularly. And I inf'nitely prefer good manners to righteousness."

As he finished speaking Swacker announced Major Benson, who wanted to see Markham at once.

The major was accompanied by a pretty young woman of about twenty-two with yellow bobbed hair, dressed daintily and simply in light blue *crêpe de Chine*. But for all her youthful and somewhat frivolous appearance, she possessed a reserve and competency of manner that immediately evoked one's confidence.

Major Benson introduced her as his secretary, and Markham placed a chair for her facing his desk.

"Miss Hoffman has just told me something that I think is vital for you to know," said the major; "and I brought her directly to you."

He seemed unusually serious, and his eyes held a look of expectancy colored with doubt.

"Tell Mr. Markham exactly what you told me, Miss Hoffman."

The girl raised her head prettily and related her story in a capable, well-modulated voice.

"About a week ago—I think it was Wednesday—Mr. Pfyfe called on Mr. Alvin Benson in his private office. I was in the next room, where my typewriter is located. There's only a glass partition between the two rooms, and when anyone talks loudly in Mr. Benson's office, I can hear them. In about five minutes, Mr. Pfyfe and Mr. Benson began to quarrel. I thought it was funny, for they were such good friends; but I didn't pay much attention to it and went on with my typing. Their voices got very loud, though, and I caught several words. Major Benson asked me this morning what the words were; so I suppose you want to know, too. Well, they kept referring to a note; and once or twice a check was mentioned. Several times I caught the word *father-in-law,* and once Mr. Benson said 'nothing doing.' . . . Then Mr. Benson called me in and told me to get him an envelope marked 'Pfyfe-Personal' out of his private drawer in the safe. I got it for him, but right after that our bookkeeper wanted me for something, so I didn't hear any more. About fifteen minutes later, when Mr. Pfyfe had gone, Mr. Benson called me to put the envelope back. And he told me that if Mr. Pfyfe ever called again, I wasn't, under any circumstances, to let him into the private office unless he himself was there. He also told me that I wasn't to give the envelope to anybody—not even on a written order. . . . And that is all, Mr. Markham."

During her recital I had been as much interested in Vance's actions as in what she had been saying. When first she had entered the room, his casual glance had quickly changed to one of attentive animation, and he had studied her closely. When Markham had placed the chair for her, he had risen and reached for a book lying on the table near her; and, in doing so, he had leaned unnecessarily close to her in order to inspect—or so it appeared to me—the side of her head. And during her story he had continued his observation, at times bending slightly to the right or left to better his view of her. Unaccountable as his actions had seemed, I knew that some serious consideration had prompted the scrutiny.

When she finished speaking, Major Benson reached in his pocket, and tossed a long manila envelope on the desk before Markham.

"Here it is," he said. "I got Miss Hoffman to bring it to me the moment she told me her story."

Markham picked it up hesitantly, as if doubtful of his right to inspect its contents.

"You'd better look at it," the major advised. "That envelope may very possibly have an important bearing on the case."

Markham removed the elastic band and spread the contents of the envelope before him. They consisted of three items—a canceled check for $10,000 made out to Leander Pfyfe and signed by Alvin Benson; a note for $10,000 to Alvin Benson signed by Pfyfe, and a brief confession, also signed by Pfyfe, saying the check was a forgery. The check was dated March 20th of the current year. The confession and the note were dated two days later. The note—which was for ninety days—fell due on Friday, June 21st, only three days off.

For fully five minutes Markham studied these documents in silence. Their sudden introduction into the case seemed to mystify him. Nor had any of the perplexity left his face when he finally put them back in the envelope.

He questioned the girl carefully and had her repeat certain parts of her story. But nothing more could be learned from her; and at length he turned to the major.

"I'll keep this envelope awhile, if you'll let me. I don't see its significance at present, but I'd like to think it over."

When Major Benson and his secretary had gone, Vance rose and extended his legs.

"*À la fin!*" he murmured. " 'All things journey: sun and moon, morning, noon, and afternoon, night and all her stars.' *Videlicet:* we begin to make progress."

"What the devil are you driving at?" The new complication of Pfyfe's peccadilloes had left Markham irritable.

"Int'restin' young woman, this Miss Hoffman—eh, what?" Vance rejoined irrelevantly. "Didn't care especially for the deceased Benson. And she fairly detests the aromatic Leander. He has prob'bly told her he was misunderstood by Mrs. Pfyfe and invited her to dinner."

"Well, she's pretty enough," commented Markham indifferently. "Benson, too, may have made advances—which is why she disliked him."

"Oh, absolutely." Vance mused a moment. "Pretty—yes; but misleadin'. She's an ambitious gel and capable, too—knows her business. She's no ball of fluff. She has a solid, honest streak in her—a bit of Teutonic blood, I'd say." He paused meditatively. "Y' know, Markham, I have a suspicion you'll hear from little Miss Katinka again."

"Crystal-gazing, eh?" mumbled Markham.

"Oh, dear no!" Vance was looking lazily out of the window. "But I did enter the silence, so to speak, and indulged in a bit of craniological contemplation."

"I thought I noticed you ogling the girl," said Markham. "But since her hair was bobbed and she had her hat on, how could you analyze the bumps?—if that's the phrase you phrenologists use."

"Forget not Goldsmith's preacher," Vance admonished. "Truth from his lips prevailed, and those who came to scoff remained et cetera. . . . To begin with, I'm no phrenologist. But I believe in epochal, racial, and heredit'ry variations in skulls. In that respect I'm merely an old-fashioned Darwinian. Every child knows that the skull of the Piltdown man differs from that of the Cromagnard; and even a lawyer could distinguish an Aryan head from a

Ural-Altaic head, or a Maylaic from a Negrillo. And, if one is versed at all in the Mendelian theory, heredit'ry cranial similarities can be detected. . . . But all this erudition is beyond you, I fear. Suffice it to say that, despite the young woman's hat and hair, I could see the contour of her head and the bone structure in her face; and I even caught a glimpse of her ear."

"And thereby deduced that we'd hear from her again," added Markham scornfully.

"Indirectly—yes," admitted Vance. Then, after a pause: "I say, in view of Miss Hoffman's revelation, do not Colonel Ostrander's comments of yesterday begin to take on a phosph'rescent aspect?"

"Look here!" said Markham impatiently. "Cut out these circumlocutions and get to the point."

Vance turned slowly from the window and regarded him pensively. "Markham—I put the question academically—doesn't Pfyfe's forged check, with its accompanying confession and its shortly due note, constitute a rather strong motive for doing away with Benson?"

Markham sat up suddenly. "You think Pfyfe guilty—is that it?"

"Well, here's the touchin' situation: Pfyfe obviously signed Benson's name to a check, told him about it, and got the surprise of his life when his dear old pal asked him for a ninety-day note to cover the amount and also for a written confession to hold over him to insure payment. . . . Now consider the subs'quent facts:—First, Pfyfe called on Benson a week ago and had a quarrel in which the check was mentioned—Damon was prob'bly pleading with Pythias to extend the note and was vulgarly informed that there was 'nothing doing.' Secondly, Benson was shot two days later, less than a week before the note fell due. Thirdly, Pfyfe was at Benson's house the hour of the shooting, and not only lied to you about his whereabouts but bribed a garage owner to keep silent about his car. Fourthly, his explanation, when caught, of his unrewarded search for Haig and Haig was, to say the least, a bit thick. And don't forget that the original tale of his lonely quest for nature's solitudes in the Catskills—with his mysterious stopover in New York to confer a farewell benediction upon some anonymous person—was not all that one could have hoped for in the line of plausibility. Fifthly, he is an impulsive gambler, given to taking chances; and his experiences in South Africa would certainly have familiarized him with firearms. Sixthly, he was rather eager to involve Leacock and did a bit of caddish talebearing to that end, even informing you that he saw the captain on the spot at the fatal moment. Seventhly—but why bore you? Have I not supplied you with all the factors you hold so dear—what are they now?—motive, time, place, opportunity, conduct? All that's wanting is the criminal agent. But then, the captain's gun is at the bottom of the East River; so you're not very much better off in his case, what?"

Markham had listened attentively to Vance's summary. He now sat in rapt silence gazing down at the desk.

"How about a little chat with Pfyfe before you make any final move against the captain?" suggested Vance.

"I think I'll take your advice," answered Markham slowly, after several minutes' reflection. Then he picked up the telephone. "I wonder if he's at his hotel now."

"Oh, he's there," said Vance. "Watchful waitin' and all that."

Pfyfe was in; and Markham requested him to come at once to the office.

"There's another thing I wish you'd do for me," said Vance, when the other had finished telephoning. "The fact is, I'm longing to know what everyone was doing during the hour of Benson's dissolution—that is, between midnight and one A.M. on the night of the thirteenth, or to speak pedantically, the morning of the fourteenth."

Markham looked at him in amazement.

"Seems silly, doesn't it?" Vance went on blithely. "But you put such faith in alibis—though they do prove disappointin' at times, what? There's Leacock, for instance. If that hallboy had told Heath to toddle along and sell his violets, you couldn't do a blessed thing to the captain. Which shows, d' ye see, that you're too trustin'. . . . Why not find out where everyone was? Pfyfe and the captain were at Benson's; and they're about the only ones whose whereabouts you've looked into. Maybe there were others hovering around Alvin that night. There may have been a crush of friends and acquaintances on hand—a regular soiree, y' know. . . . Then again, checking up on all these people will supply the desolate sergeant with something to take his mind off his sorrows."

Markham knew, as well as I, that Vance would not have made a suggestion of this kind unless actuated by some serious motive; and for several moments he studied the other's face intently, as if trying to read his reason for this unexpected request.

"Who, specifically," he asked, "is included in your 'everyone'?" He took up his pencil and held it poised above a sheet of paper.

"No one is to be left out," replied Vance. "Put down Miss St. Clair—Captain Leacock—the Major—Pfyfe—Miss Hoffman——"

"Miss Hoffman!"

"Everyone! . . . Have you Miss Hoffman? Now jot down Colonel Ostrander——"

"Look here!" cut in Markham.

"——and I may have one or two others for you later. But that will do nicely for a beginning."

Before Markham could protest further, Swacker came in to say that Heath was waiting outside.

"What about our friend Leacock, sir?" was the sergeant's first question.

"I'm holding that up for a day or so," explained Markham. "I want to have another talk with Pfyfe before I do anything definite." And he told Heath about the visit of Major Benson and Miss Hoffman.

Heath inspected the envelope and its enclosures and then handed them back.

"I don't see anything in that," he said. "It looks to me like a private deal between Benson and this fellow Pfyfe. Leacock's our man; and the sooner I get him locked up, the better I'll feel."

"That may be tomorrow," Markham encouraged him. "So don't feel downcast over this little delay. . . . You're keeping the captain under surveillance, aren't you?"

"I'll say so," grinned Heath.

Vance turned to Markham. "What about that list of names you made out for the sergeant?" he asked ingenuously. "I understood you to say something about alibis."

Markham hesitated, frowning. Then he handed Heath the paper containing the names Vance had called off to him. "As a matter of caution, Sergeant," he said morosely, "I wish you'd get me the alibis of all these people on the night of the murder. It may bring something contributory to light. Verify those you already know, such as Pfyfe's; and let me have the reports as soon as you can."

When Heath had gone, Markham turned a look of angry exasperation upon Vance.

"Of all the confounded troublemakers——" he began.

But Vance interrupted him blandly.

"Such ingratitude! If only you knew it, Markham, I'm your tutelary genius, your *deus ex machina,* your fairy godmother."

16

ADMISSIONS AND SUPPRESSIONS

(*Tuesday, June 18; afternoon.*)

AN HOUR later Phelps, the operative Markham had sent to 94 Riverside Drive, came in radiating satisfaction.

"I think I've got what you want, Chief." His raucous voice was covertly triumphant. "I went up to the St. Clair woman's apartment and rang the bell. She came to the door herself, and I stepped into the hall and put my questions to her. She sure refused to answer. When I let on I knew the package contained the gun Benson was shot with, she just laughed and jerked the door open. 'Leave this apartment, you vile creature,' she says to me."

He grinned.

"I hurried downstairs, and I hadn't any more than got to the switchboard when her signal flashed. I let the boy get the number and then I stood him to one side and listened in. . . . She was talking to Leacock, and her first words were: 'They know you took the pistol from here yesterday and threw it in the river.' That must've knocked him out, for he didn't say anything for a long time. Then he answered, perfectly calm and kinda sweet: 'Don't worry, Muriel; and don't say a word to anybody for the rest of the day. I'll fix everything in the morning.' He made her promise to keep quiet until tomorrow, and then he said good-bye."

Markham sat awhile digesting the story.

"What impression did you get from the conversation?"

"If you ask me, Chief," said the detective, "I'd lay ten to one that Leacock's guilty and the girl knows it."

Markham thanked him and let him go.

"This sub-Potomac chivalry," commented Vance, "is a frightful nuisance. . . . But aren't we about due to hold polite converse with the genteel Leander?"

Almost as he spoke the man was announced. He entered the room with his habitual urbanity of manner, but for all his suavity, he could not wholly disguise his uneasiness of mind.

"Sit down, Mr. Pfyfe," directed Markham brusquely. "It seems you have a little more explaining to do."

Taking out the manilla envelope, he laid its contents on the desk where the other could see them.

"Will you be so good as to tell me about these?"

"With the greatest pleasure," said Pfyfe; but his voice had lost its assurance. Some of his poise, too, had deserted him, and as he paused to light a cigarette I detected a slight nervousness in the way he manipulated his gold match safe.

"I really should have mentioned these before," he confessed, indicating the papers with a delicately inconsequential wave of the hand.

He leaned forward on one elbow, taking a confidential attitude, and as he talked, the cigarette bobbed up and down between his lips.

"It pains me deeply to go into this matter," he began; "but since it is in the interests of truth, I shall not complain. . . . My—ah—domestic arrangements are not all that one could desire. My wife's father has, curiously enough, taken a most unreasonable dislike to me; and it pleases him to deprive me of all but the meagerest financial assistance, although it is really my wife's money that he refuses to give me. A few months ago I made use of certain funds—ten thousand dollars, to be exact—which, I learned later, had not been intended for me. When my father-in-law discovered my error, it was necessary for me to return the full amount to avoid a misunderstanding between Mrs. Pfyfe and myself—a misunderstanding which might have caused my wife great unhappiness. I regret to say, I used Alvin's name on a check. But I explained it to him at once, you understand, offering him the note and this little confession as evidence of my good faith. . . . And that is all, Mr. Markham."

"Was that what your quarrel with him last week was about?"

Pfyfe gave him a look of querulous surprise. "Ah, you heard of our little contretemps? . . . Yes—we had a slight disagreement as to the—shall I say terms of the transaction?"

"Did Benson insist that the note be paid when due?"

"No—not exactly." Pfyfe's manner became unctuous. "I beg of you, sir, not to press me as to my little chat with Alvin. It was, I assure you, quite irrelevant to the present situation. Indeed, it was of a most personal and private nature." He smiled confidingly. "I will admit, however, that I went to Alvin's house the night he was shot, intending to speak to him about the check; but, as you already know, I found the house dark and spent the night in a Turkish bath."

"Parden me, Mr. Pfyfe"—it was Vance who spoke—"but did Mr. Benson take your note without security?"

"Of course!" Pfyfe's tone was a rebuke. "Alvin and I, as I have explained, were the closest friends."

"But even a friend, don't y' know," Vance submitted, "might ask for security on such a large amount. How did Benson know that you'd be able to repay him?"

"I can only say that he did know," the other answered, with an air of patient deliberation.

Vance continued to be doubtful. "Perhaps it was because of the confession you had given him."

Pfyfe rewarded him with a look of beaming approval. "You grasp the situation perfectly," he said.

Vance withdrew from the conversation, and though Markham questioned Pfyfe for nearly half an hour, nothing further transpired. Pfyfe clung to his story in every detail and politely refused to go deeper into his quarrel with Benson, insisting that it had no bearing on the case. At last he was permitted to go.

"Not very helpful," Markham observed. "I'm beginning to agree with Heath that we've turned up a mare's nest in Pfyfe's frenzied financial deal."

"You'll never be anything but your own sweet trusting self, will you?" lamented Vance sadly. "Pfyfe has just given you your first intelligent line of investigation, and you say he's not helpful! ... Listen to me and *nota bene.* Pfyfe's story about the ten thousand dollars is undoubtedly true; he appropriated the money and forged Benson's name to a check with which to replace it. But I don't for a second believe there was no security in addition to the confession. Benson wasn't the type of man—friend or no friend—who'd hand over that amount without security. He wanted his money back, not somebody in jail. That's why I put my oar in and asked about the security. Pfyfe, of course, denied it; but when pressed as to how Benson knew he'd pay the note, he retired into a cloud. I had to suggest the confession as the possible explanation; which showed that something else was in his mind—something he didn't care to mention. And the way he jumped at my suggestion bears out my theory."

"Well, what of it?" Markham asked impatiently.

"Oh, for the gift of tears!" moaned Vance. "Don't you see that there's someone in the background—someone connected with the security? It must be so, y' know; otherwise Pfyfe would have told you the entire tale of the quarrel, if only to clear himself from suspicion. Yet, knowing that his position is an awkward one, he refused to divulge what passed between him and Benson in the office that day. ... Pfyfe is shielding someone—and he is not the soul of chivalry, y' know. Therefore, I ask: Why?"

He leaned back and gazed at the ceiling.

"I have an idea, amounting to a cerebral cyclone," he added, "that when we put our hands on that security, we'll also put our hands on the murderer."

At this moment the telephone rang, and when Markham answered it, a look of startled amusement came into his eyes. He made an appointment with the speaker for half past five that afternoon. Then, hanging up the receiver, he laughed outright at Vance.

"Your auricular researches have been confirmed," he said. "Miss Hoffman just called me confidentially on an outside phone to say she has something to add to her story. She's coming here at five thirty."

Vance was unimpressed by the announcement. "I rather imagined she'd telephone during her lunch hour."

Again Markham gave him one of his searching scrutinies. "There's something damned queer going on around here," he observed.

"Oh, quite," returned Vance carelessly. "Queerer than you could possibly imagine."

For fifteen or twenty minutes Markham endeavored to draw him out; but Vance seemed suddenly possessed of an ability to say nothing with the blandest fluency. Markham finally became exasperated.

"I'm rapidly coming to the conclusion," he said, "that either you had a hand in Benson's murder or you're a phenomenally good guesser."

"There is, y' know, an alternative," rejoined Vance. "It might be that my æsthetic hypotheses and metaphysical deductions, as you call 'em, are working out—eh, what?"

A few minutes before we went to lunch, Swacker announced that Tracy had just returned from Long Island with his report.

"Is he the lad you sent to look into Pfyfe's *affaires du cover?*" Vance asked Markham. "For, if he is, I am all a-flutter."

"He's the man. . . . Send him in, Swacker."

Tracy entered smiling silkily, his black notebook in one hand, his pince nez in the other.

"I had no trouble learning about Pfyfe," he said. "He's well known in Port Washington—quite a character, in fact—and it was easy to pick up gossip about him."

He adjusted his glasses carefully and referred to his notebook. "He married a Miss Hawthorn in nineteen ten. She's wealthy, but Pfyfe doesn't benefit much by it, because her father sits on the moneybags——"

"Mr. Tracy, I say," interrupted Vance; "never mind the *née*-Hawthorn and her doting papa—Mr. Pfyfe himself has confided in us about his sad marriage. Tell us, if you can, about Mr. Pfyfe's extranuptial affairs. Are there any other ladies?"

Tracy looked inquiringly at the district attorney; he was uncertain as to Vance's *locus standi.* Receiving a nod from Markham, he turned a page in his notebook and proceeded.

"I found one other woman in the case. She lives in New York and often telephones to a drugstore near Pfyfe's house and leaves messages for him. He uses the same phone to call her by. He had made some deal with the proprietor, of course; but I was able to obtain her phone number. As soon as I came back to the city, I got her name and address from Information and made a few inquiries. . . . She's a Mrs. Paula Banning, a widow, and a little fast, I should say; and she lives in an apartment at 268 West Seventy-fifth Street."

This exhausted Tracy's information; and when he went out, Markham smiled broadly at Vance.

"He didn't supply you with very much fuel."

"My word! I think he did unbelievably well," said Vance. "He unearthed the very information we wanted."

"*We* wanted?" echoed Markham. "I have more important things to think about than Pfyfe's amours."

"And yet, y' know, this particular amour of Pfyfe's is going to solve the problem of Benson's murder," replied Vance; and would say no more.

Markham, who had an accumulation of other work awaiting him and numerous appointments for the afternoon, decided to have his lunch served in the office; so Vance and I took leave of him.

We lunched at the Élysée, dropped in at Knoedler's to see an exhibition of French Pointillism, and then went to Aeolian Hall, where a string quartet from San Francisco was giving a program of Mozart. A little before half past five we were again at the district attorney's office, which at that hour was deserted except for Markham.

Shortly after our arrival Miss Hoffman came in and told the rest of her story in direct, businesslike fashion.

"I didn't give you all the particulars this morning," she said; "and I wouldn't care to do so now unless you are willing to regard them as confidential, for my telling you might cost me my position."

"I promise you," Markham assured her, "that I will entirely respect your confidence."

She hesitated a moment and then continued. "When I told Major Benson this morning about Mr. Pfyfe and his brother, he said at once that I should come with him to your office and tell you also. But on the way over, he suggested that I might omit a part of the story. He didn't exactly tell me not to mention it; but he explained that it had nothing to do with the case and might only confuse you. I followed his suggestion; but after I got back to the office, I began thinking it over, and knowing how serious a matter Mr. Benson's death was, I decided to tell you anyway. In case it did have some bearing on the situation, I didn't want to be in the position of having withheld anything from you."

She seemed a little uncertain as to the wisdom of her decision.

"I do hope I haven't been foolish. But the truth is, there was something else besides that envelope which Mr. Benson asked me to bring him from the safe the day he and Mr. Pfyfe had their quarrel. It was a square, heavy package, and, like the envelope, was marked 'Pfyfe-Personal.' And it was over this package that Mr. Benson and Mr. Pfyfe seemed to be quarreling."

"Was it in the safe this morning when you went to get the envelope for the major?" asked Vance.

"Oh, no. After Mr. Pfyfe left last week, I put the package back in the safe along with the envelope. But Mr. Benson took it home with him last Thursday—the day he was killed."

Markham was but mildly interested in the recital and was about to bring the interview to a close when Vance spoke up.

"It was very good of you, Miss Hoffman, to take this trouble to tell us about the package; and now that you are here, there are one or two questions I'd like to ask. . . . How did Mr. Alvin Benson and the major get along together?"

She looked at Vance with a curious little smile.

"They didn't get along very well," she said. "They were so different. Mr. Alvin Benson was not a very pleasant person, and not very honorable, I'm afraid. You'd never have thought they were brothers. They were constantly disputing about the business; and they were terribly suspicious of each other."

"That's not unnatural," commented Vance, "seeing how incompatible their temp'raments were. . . . By the bye, how did this suspicion show itself?"

"Well, for one thing, they sometimes spied on each other. You see, their offices were adjoining, and they would listen to each other through the door. I did the secretarial work for both of them, and I often saw them listening. Several times they tried to find out things from me about each other."

Vance smiled at her appreciatively.

"Not a pleasant position for you."

"Oh, I didn't mind it." She smiled back. "It amused me."

"When was the last time you caught either one of them listening?" he asked.

The girl quickly became serious. "The very last day Mr. Alvin Benson was alive, I saw the major standing by the door. Mr. Benson had a caller—a lady—and the major seemed very much interested. It was in the afternoon. Mr. Benson went home early that day—only about half an hour after the lady had gone. She called at the office again later, but he wasn't there, of course, and I told her he had already gone home."

"Do you know who the lady was?" Vance asked her.

"No, I don't," she said. "She didn't give her name."

Vance asked a few other questions, after which we rode uptown in the subway with Miss Hoffman, taking leave of her at Twenty-third Street.

Markham was silent and preoccupied during the trip. Nor did Vance make any comment until we were comfortably relaxed in the easy chairs of the Stuyvesant Club's lounge room. Then, lighting a cigarette lazily, he said, "You grasp the subtle mental processes leading up to my prophecy about Miss Hoffman's second coming—eh, what, Markham? Y'see, I knew friend Alvin had not paid that forged check without security, and I also knew that the tiff must have been about the security, for Pfyfe was not really worrying about being jailed by his alter ego. I rather suspect Pfyfe was trying to get the security back before paying off the note and was told there was 'nothing doing.' . . . Moreover, Little Goldilocks may be a nice girl and all that; but it isn't in the feminine temp'rament to sit next door to an altercation beween two such rakes and not listen attentively. I shouldn't care, y' know, to have to decipher the typing she said she did during the episode. I was quite sure she heard more than she told; and I asked myself: Why this curtailment? The only logical answer was: Because the major had suggested it. And since the *gnädiges Fräulein* was a forthright Germanic soul, with an inbred streak of selfish and cautious honesty, I ventured the prognostication that as soon as she was out from under the benev'lent jurisdiction of her tutor, she would tell us the rest in order to save her own skin if the matter should come up later. . . . Not so cryptic when explained, what?"

"That's all very well," conceded Markham petulantly. "But where does it get us?"

"I shouldn't say that the forward movement was entirely imperceptible."

Vance smoked awhile impassively. "You realize, I trust," he said, "that the mysterious package contained the security."

"One might form such a conclusion," agreed Markham. "But the fact doesn't dumbfound me—if that's what you're hoping for."

"And, of course," pursued Vance easily, "your legal mind, trained in the technique of ratiocination, has already identified it as the box of jewels that Mrs. Platz espied on Benson's table that fatal afternoon."

Markham sat up suddenly, then sank back with a shrug.

"Even if it was," he said, "I don't see how that helps us. Unless the major knew the package had nothing to do with the case, he would not have suggested to his secretary that she omit telling us about it."

"Ah! But if the major knew that the package was an irrelevant item in the case, then he must also know something about the case—eh, what? Otherwise, he couldn't determine what was, and what was not, irrelevant. . . . I have felt all along that he knew more than he admitted. Don't forget that he put us on the track of Pfyfe, and also that he was quite pos'tive Captain Leacock was innocent."

Markham thought for several minutes.

"I'm beginning to see what you're driving at," he remarked slowly. "Those jewels, after all, may have an important bearing on the case. . . . I think I'll have a chat with the major about things."

Shortly after dinner at the club that night Major Benson came into the lounge room where we had retired for our smoke; and Markham accosted him at once.

"Major, aren't you willing to help me a little more in getting at the truth about your brother's death?" he asked.

The other gazed at him searchingly; the inflection of Markham's voice belied the apparent casualness of the question.

"God knows it's not my wish to put obstacles in your way," he said, carefully weighing each word. "I'd gladly give you any help I could. But there are one or two things I cannot tell you at this time. . . . If there was only myself to be considered," he added, "it would be different."

"But you do suspect someone?" Vance put the question.

"In a way—yes. I overheard a conversation in Alvin's office one day that took on added significance after his death."

"You shouldn't let chivalry stand in the way," urged Markham. "If your suspicion is unfounded, the truth will surely come out."

"But when I don't *know,* I certainly ought not to hazard a guess," affirmed the major. "I think it best that you solve this problem without me."

Despite Markham's importunities, he would say no more; and shortly afterward he excused himself and went out.

Markham, now profoundly worried, sat smoking restlessly, tapping the arm of his chair with his fingers.

"Well, old bean, a bit involved, what?" commented Vance.

"It's not so damned funny," Markham grumbled. "Everyone seems to know more about the case than the police or the district attorney's office."

"Which wouldn't be so disconcertin' if they all weren't so deuced reticent," supplemented Vance cheerfully. "And the touchin' part of it is that each of 'em appears to be keeping still in order to shield someone else. Mrs. Platz began it; she lied about Benson's having any callers that afternoon because she didn't want to involve his tea companion. Miss St. Clair declined point-blank to tell you anything because she obviously didn't desire to cast suspicion on another. The captain became voiceless the moment you suggested his affianced bride was entangled. Even Leander refused to extricate himself from a delicate situation lest he implicate another. And now the major! . . . Most annoyin'. On the other hand, don't y' know, it's comfortin'—not to say upliftin'—to be dealing exclusively with such noble, self-sacrificin' souls."

"Hell!" Markham put down his cigar and rose. "The case is getting on my nerves. I'm going to sleep on it and tackle it in the morning."

"That ancient idea of sleeping on a problem is a fallacy," said Vance, as we walked out into Madison Avenue, "—an apologia, as it were, for one's not being able to think clearly. Poetic idea, y' know. All poets believe in it—nature's soft nurse, the balm of woe, childhood's mandragora, tired nature's sweet restorer, and that sort of thing. Silly notion. When the brain is keyed up and alive, it works far better than when apathetic from the torpor of sleep. Slumber is an anodyne—not a stimulus."

"Well, you sit up and think," was Markham's surly advice.

"That's what I'm going to do," blithely returned Vance; "but not about the Benson case. I did all the thinking I'm going to do along that line four days ago."

17

THE FORGED CHECK

(*Wednesday, June 19; forenoon.*)

WE RODE downtown with Markham the next morning, and though we arrived at his office before nine o'clock, Heath was already there waiting. He appeared worried, and when he spoke, his voice held an ill-disguised reproof for the district attorney.

"What about this Leacock, Mr. Markham?" he asked. "It looks to me like we'd better grab him quick. We've been tailing him right along; and there's something funny going on. Yesterday morning he went to his bank and spent half an hour in the chief cashier's office. After that he visited his lawyer's and was there over an hour. Then he went back to the bank for another half hour. He dropped in to the Astor Grill for lunch but didn't eat anything—sat staring at the table. About two o'clock he called on the realty agents who have the handling of the building he lives in; and after he'd left, we found out he'd offered his apartment for sublease beginning tomorrow. Then he paid six calls on friends of his and went home. After dinner my man rang his apartment bell and asked for Mr. Hoozitz;—Leacock was packing up! . . . It looks to me like a getaway."

Markham frowned. Heath's report clearly troubled him; but before he could answer, Vance spoke. "Why this perturbation, Sergeant? You're watching the captain. I'm sure he can't slip from your vigilant clutches."

Markham looked at Vance a moment, then turned to Heath. "Let it go at that. But if Leacock attempts to leave the city, nab him."

Heath went out sullenly.

"By the bye, Markham," said Vance; "don't make an appointment for half past twelve today. You already have one, don't y' know. And with a lady."

Markham put down his pen and stared. "What new damned nonsense is this?"

"I made an engagement for you. Called the lady by phone this morning. I'm sure I woke the dear up."

Markham spluttered, striving to articulate his angry protest.

Vance held up his hand soothingly.

"And you simply must keep the engagement. Y' see, I told her it was you speaking; and it would be shocking taste not to appear. . . . I promise, you won't regret meeting her," he added. "Things looked so sadly befuddled last night—I couldn't bear to see you suffering so. Cons'quently, I arranged for you to see Mrs. Paula Banning, Pfyfe's Éloïse, y' know. I'm pos'tive she'll be able to dispel some of this inspissated gloom that's enveloping you."

"See here, Vance!" Markham growled. "I happen to be running this office——" He stopped abruptly, realizing the hopelessness of making headway against the other's blandness. Moreover, I think, the prospect of interviewing Mrs. Paula Banning was not wholly alien to his inclinations. His resentment slowly ebbed, and when he again spoke, his voice was almost matter-of-fact.

"Since you've committed me, I'll see her. But I'd rather Pfyfe wasn't in such close communication with her. He's apt to drop in—with preconcerted unexpectedness."

"Funny," murmured Vance. "I thought of that myself.... That's why I phoned him last night that he could return to Long Island."

"You phoned him——!"

"Awf'lly sorry and all that," Vance apologized. "But you'd gone to bed. Sleep was knitting up your raveled sleave of care; and I couldn't bring myself to disturb you.... Pfyfe was so grateful, too. Most touchin'. Said his wife also would be grateful. He was pathetically consid'rate about Mrs. Pfyfe. But I fear he'll need all his velvety forensic powers to explain his absence."

"In what other quarters have you involved me during my absence?" asked Markham acrimoniously.

"That's all," replied Vance, rising and strolling to the window.

He stood looking out, smoking thoughtfully. When he turned back to the room, his bantering air had gone. He sat down facing Markham.

"The major has practically admitted to us," he said, "that he knows more about this affair than he has told. You naturally can't push the point, in view of his hon'rable attitude in the matter. And yet, he's willing for you to find out what he knows, as long as he doesn't tell you himself—that was unquestionably the stand he took last night. Now, I believe there's a way you can find out without calling upon him to go against his principles.... You recall Miss Hoffman's story of the eavesdropping; and you also recall that he told you he heard a conversation which, in the light of Benson's murder, became significant. It's quite prob'ble, therefore, that the major's knowledge has to do with something connected with the business of the firm, or at least with one of the firm's clients."

Vance slowly lit another cigarette.

"My suggestion is this: Call up the major and ask permission to send a man to take a peep at his ledger accounts and his purchase and sales books. Tell him you want to find out about the transactions of one of his clients. Intimate that it's Miss St. Clair—or Pfyfe, if you like. I have a strange mediumistic feeling that, in this way, you'll get on the track of the person he's shielding. And I'm also assailed by the premonition that he'll welcome your interest in his ledger."

The plan did not appeal to Markham as feasible or fraught with possibilities; and it was evident he disliked making such a request of Major Benson. But so determined was Vance, so earnestly did he argue his point, that in the end Markham acquiesced.

"He was quite willing to let me send a man," said Markham, hanging up the receiver. "In fact, he seemed eager to give me every assistance."

"I thought he'd take kindly to the suggestion," said Vance. "Y' see, if you discover for yourself whom he suspects, it relieves him of the onus of having tattled."

Markham rang for Swacker. "Call up Stitt and tell him I want to see him here before noon—that I have an immediate job for him."

"Stitt," Markham explained to Vance, "is the head of a firm of public accountants over in the New York Life Building. I use him a good deal on work like this."

Shortly before noon Stitt came. He was a prematurely old young man, with a sharp, shrewd face and a perpetual frown. The prospect of working for the district attorney pleased him.

Markham explained briefly what was wanted, and revealed enough of the case to guide him in his task. The man grasped the situation immediately and made one or two notes on the back of a dilapidated envelope.

Vance also, during the instructions, had jotted down some notations on a piece of paper.

Markham stood up and took his hat.

"Now, I suppose, I must keep the appointment you made for me," he complained to Vance. Then: "Come, Stitt, I'll take you down with us in the judges' private elevator."

"If you don't mind," interposed Vance, "Mr. Stitt and I will forgo the honor and mingle with the commoners in the public lift. We'll meet you downstairs."

Taking the accountant by the arm, he led him out through the main waiting room. It was ten minutes, however, before he joined us.

We took the subway to Seventy-second Street and walked up West End Avenue to Mrs. Paula Banning's address. She lived in a small apartment house just around the corner in Seventy-fifth Street. As we stood before her door, waiting for an answer to our ring, a strong odor of Chinese incense drifted out to us.

"Ah! That facilitates matters," said Vance, sniffing. "Ladies who burn joss sticks are invariably sentimental."

Mrs. Banning was a tall, slightly adipose woman of indeterminate age, with straw-colored hair and a pink-and-white complexion. Her face in repose possessed a youthful and vacuous innocence; but the expression was only superficial. Her eyes, a very light blue, were hard; and a slight puffiness about her cheekbones and beneath her chin attested to years of idle and indulgent living. She was not unattractive, however, in a vivid, flamboyant way; and her manner, when she ushered us into her overfurnished and rococo living room, was one of easygoing good-fellowship.

When we were seated and Markham had apologized for our intrusion, Vance at once assumed the role of interviewer. During his opening explanatory remarks he appraised the woman carefully, as if seeking to determine the best means of approaching her for the information he wanted.

After a few minutes of verbal reconnoitering, he asked permission to smoke and offered Mrs. Banning one of his cigarettes, which she accepted. Then he smiled at her in a spirit of appreciative geniality and relaxed comfortably in his chair. He conveyed the impression that he was fully prepared to sympathize with anything she might tell him.

"Mr. Pfyfe strove very hard to keep you entirely out of this affair," said Vance; "and we fully appreciate his delicacy in so doing. But certain circumst'nces connected with Mr. Benson's death have inadvertently involved you in the case; and you can best help us and yourself—and particularly Mr.

Pfyfe—by telling us what we want to know and trusting to our discretion and understanding."

He had emphasized Pfyfe's name, giving it a significant intonation; and the woman had glanced down uneasily. Her apprehension was apparent, and when she looked up into Vance's eyes, she was asking herself: How much does he know? as plainly as if she had spoken the words audibly.

"I can't imagine what you want me to tell you," she said, with an effort at astonishment. "You know that Andy was not in New York that night." (Her designating of the elegant and superior Pfyfe as "Andy" sounded almost like *lèse-majesté*.) "He didn't arrive in the city until nearly nine the next morning."

"Didn't you read in the newspapers about the gray Cadillac that was parked in front of Benson's house?" Vance, in putting the question, imitated her own astonishment.

She smiled confidently. "That wasn't Andy's car. He took the eight o'clock train to New York the next morning. He said it was lucky that he did, seeing that a machine just like his had been at Mr. Benson's the night before."

She had spoken with the sincerity of complete assurance. It was evident that Pfyfe had lied to her on this point.

Vance did not disabuse her; in fact, he gave her to understand that he accepted her explanation and consequently dismissed the idea of Pfyfe's presence in New York on the night of the murder.

"I had in mind a connection of a somewhat diff'rent nature when I mentioned you and Mr. Pfyfe as having been drawn into the case. I referred to a personal relationship between you and Mr. Benson."

She assumed an attitude of smiling indifference.

"I'm afraid you've made another mistake." She spoke lightly. "Mr. Benson and I were not even friends. Indeed, I scarcely knew him."

There was an overtone of emphasis in her denial—a slight eagerness which, in indicating a conscious desire to be believed, robbed her remark of the complete casualness she had intended.

"Even a business relationship may have its personal side," Vance reminded her; "especially when the intermediary is an intimate friend of both parties to the transaction."

She looked at him quickly, then turned her eyes away. "I really don't know what you're talking about," she affirmed; and her face for a moment lost its contours of innocence and became calculating. "You're surely not implying that I had any business dealings with Mr. Benson?"

"Not directly," replied Vance. "But certainly Mr. Pfyfe had business dealings with him; and one of them, I rather imagined, involved you consid'rably."

"Involved me?" She laughed scornfully, but it was a strained laugh.

"It was a somewhat unfortunate transaction, I fear," Vance went on, "—unfortunate in that Mr. Pfyfe was necessitated to deal with Mr. Benson; and doubly unfortunate, y' know, in that he should have had to drag you into it."

His manner was easy and assured, and the woman sensed that no display of scorn or contempt, however well simulated, would make an impression upon him. Therefore, she adopted an attitude of tolerantly incredulous amusement.

"And where did you learn about all this?" she asked playfully.

"Alas! I didn't learn about it," answered Vance, falling in with her manner. "That's the reason, d' ye see, that I indulged in this charming little visit. I was foolish enough to hope that you'd take pity on my ignorance and tell me all about it."

"But I wouldn't think of doing such a thing," she said, "even if this mysterious transaction had really taken place."

"My word!" sighed Vance. "That *is* disappointin'. . . . Ah, well. I see that I must tell you what little I know about it and trust to your sympathy to enlighten me further."

Despite the ominous undercurrent of his words, his levity acted like a sedative to her anxiety. She felt that he was friendly, however much he might know about her.

"Am I bringing you news when I tell you that Mr. Pfyfe forged Mr. Benson's name to a check for ten thousand dollars?" he asked.

She hesitated, gauging the possible consequences of her answer. "No, that isn't news. Andy tells me everything."

"And did you also know that Mr. Benson, when informed of it, was rather put out?—that, in fact, he demanded a note and a signed confession before he would pay the check?"

The woman's eyes flashed angrily.

"Yes, I knew that too. And after all Andy had done for him! If ever a man deserved shooting, it was Alvin Benson. He was a dog. And he pretended to be Andy's best friend. Just think of it—refusing to lend Andy the money without a confession! . . . You'd hardly call that a business deal, would you? I'd call it a dirty, contemptible, underhand trick."

She was enraged. Her mask of breeding and good-fellowship had fallen from her; and she poured out vituperation on Benson with no thought of the words she was using. Her speech was devoid of all the ordinary reticencies of intercourse between strangers.

Vance nodded consolingly during her tirade.

"Y' know, I sympathize fully with you." The tone in which he made the remark seemed to establish a closer rapprochement.

After a moment he gave her a friendly smile. "But, after all, one could almost forgive Benson for holding the confession, if he hadn't also demanded security."

"What security?"

Vance was quick to sense the change in her tone. Taking advantage of her rage, he had mentioned the security while the barriers of her pose were down. Her frightened, almost involuntary query told him that the right moment had arrived. Before she could gain her equilibrium or dispel the momentary fear which had assailed her, he said, with suave deliberation:

"The day Mr. Benson was shot, he took home with him from the office a small blue box of jewels."

She caught her breath but otherwise gave no outward sign of emotion. "Do you think he had stolen them?"

The moment she had uttered the question, she realized that it was a mistake in technique. An ordinary man might have been momentarily diverted from the truth by it. But by Vance's smile she recognized that he had accepted it as an admission.

"It was rather fine of you, y' know, to lend Mr. Pfyfe your jewels to cover the note with."

At this she threw her head up. The blood had left her face, and the rouge on her cheeks took on a mottled and unnatural hue.

"You say I lent my jewels to Andy! I swear to you——"

Vance halted her denial with a slight movement of the hand and a *coup d'œil*. She saw that his intention was to save her from the humiliation she might feel later at having made too emphatic and unqualified a statement; and the graciousness of his action, although he was an antagonist, gave her more confidence in him.

She sank back into her chair, and her hands relaxed.

"What makes you think I lent Andy my jewels?"

Her voice was colorless, but Vance understood the quesion. It was the end of her deceptions. The pause which followed was an amnesty—recognized as such by both. The next spoken words would be the truth.

"Andy had to have them," she said, "or Benson would have put him in jail." One read in her words a strange, self-sacrificing affection for the worthless Pfyfe. "And if Benson hadn't done it, and had merely refused to honor the check, his father-in-law would have done it. . . . Andy is so careless, so unthinking. He does things without weighing the consequences. I am all the time having to hold him down. . . . But this thing has taught him a lesson—I'm sure of it."

I felt that if anything in the world could teach Pfyfe a lesson, it was the blind loyalty of this woman.

"Do you know what he quarreled about with Mr. Benson in his office last Wednesday?" asked Vance.

"That was all my fault," she explained, with a sigh. "It was getting very near to the time when the note was due, and I knew Andy didn't have all the money. So I asked him to go to Benson and offer him what he had, and see if he couldn't get my jewels back. . . . But he was refused—I thought he would be."

Vance looked at her for a while sympathetically.

"I don't want to worry you any more than I can help," he said; "but won't you tell me the real cause of your anger against Benson a moment ago?"

She gave him an admiring nod. "You're right—I had good reason to hate him." Her eyes narrowed unpleasantly. "The day after he had refused to give Andy the jewels, he called me up—it was in the afternoon—and asked me to have breakfast with him at his house the next morning. He said he was home and had the jewels with him; and he told me—hinted, you understand—that maybe—*maybe* I could have them. That's the kind of beast he was! . . . I telephoned to Port Washington to Andy and told him about it, and he said he'd be in New York the next morning. He got here about nine o'clock, and we read in the paper that Benson had been shot that night."

Vance was silent for a long time. Then he stood up and thanked her.

"You have helped us a great deal. Mr. Markham is a friend of Major Benson's, and, since we have the check and the confession in our possession, I shall ask him to use his influence with the major to permit us to destroy them—very soon."

18

A CONFESSION

(*Wednesday, June 19; 1 P.M.*)

WHEN WE were again outside Markham asked, "How in Heaven's name did you know she had put up her jewels to help Pfyfe?"

"My charmin' metaphysical deductions, don't y' know," answered Vance. "As I told you, Benson was not the openhanded, bighearted altruist who would have lent money without security; and certainly the impecunious Pfyfe had no collateral worth ten thousand dollars or he wouldn't have forged the check. *Ergo:* someone lent him the security. Now, who would be so trustin' as to lend Pfyfe that amount of security except a sentimental woman who was blind to his amazin' defects? Y'know, I was just evil-minded enough to suspect there was a Calypso in the life of this Ulysses when he told us of stopping over in New York to murmur *au revoir* to someone. When a man like Pfyfe fails to specify the sex of a person, it is safe to assume the feminine gender. So I suggested that you send a Paul Pry to Port Washington to peer into his transmatrimonial activities; I felt certain a *bonne amie* would be found. Then, when the mysterious package, which obviously was the security, seemed to identify itself as the box of jewels seen by the inquisitive housekeeper, I said to myself: 'Ah! Leander's misguided Dulcinea has lent him her gewgaws to save him from the yawning dungeon.' Nor did I overlook the fact that he had been shielding someone in his explanation about the check. Therefore, as soon as the lady's name and address were learned by Tracy, I made the appointment for you. . . ."

We were passing the Gothic-Renaissance Schwab residence which extends from West End Avenue to Riverside Drive at Seventy-third Street; and Vance stopped for a moment to contemplate it.

Markham waited patiently. At length Vance walked on.

". . . Y' know, the moment I saw Mrs. Banning, I knew my conclusions were correct. She was a sentimental soul and just the sort of professional good sport who would have handed over her jewels to her *amoroso*. Also, she was bereft of gems when we called—and a woman of her stamp always wears her jewels when she desires to make an impression on strangers. Moreover, she's the kind that would have jewelry even if the larder was empty. It was therefore merely a question of getting her to talk."

"On the whole, you did very well," observed Markham.

Vance gave him a condescending bow. "Sir Hubert is too generous. But tell me, didn't my little chat with the lady cast a gleam into your darkened mind?"

"Naturally," said Markham. "I'm not utterly obtuse. She played unconsciously into our hands. She believed Pfyfe did not arrive in New York until the morning after the murder, and therefore told us quite frankly that she had phoned him that Benson had the jewels at home. The situation now is: Pfyfe knew they were in Benson's house and was there himself at about the time the shot was fired. Furthermore, the jewels are gone; and Pfyfe tried to cover up his tracks that night."

Vance sighed hopelessly. "Markham, there are altogether too many trees for you in this case. You simply can't see the forest, y' know, because of 'em."

"There is the remote possibility that you are so busily engaged in looking at one particular tree that you are unaware of the others."

A shadow passed over Vance's face. "I wish you were right," he said.

It was nearly half past one, and we dropped into the Fountain Room of the Ansonia Hotel for lunch. Markham was preoccupied throughout the meal, and when we entered the subway later, he looked uneasily at his watch.

"I think I'll go on down to Wall Street and call on the major a moment before returning to the office. I can't understand his asking Miss Hoffman not to mention the package to me. . . . It might not have contained the jewels, after all."

"Do you imagine for one moment," rejoined Vance, "that Alvin told the major the truth about the package? It was not a very cred'table transaction, y' know; and the major most likely would have given him what-for."

Major Benson's explanation bore out Vance's surmise. Markham, in telling him of the interview with Paula Banning, emphasized the jewel episode in the hope that the major would voluntarily mention the package; for his promise to Miss Hoffman prevented him from admitting that he was aware of the other's knowledge concerning it.

The major listened with considerable astonishment, his eyes gradually growing angry. "I'm afraid Alvin deceived me," he said. He looked straight ahead for a moment, his face softening. "And I don't like to think it, now that he's gone. But the truth is, when Miss Hoffman told me this morning about the envelope, she also mentioned a small parcel that had been in Alvin's private safe-drawer; and I asked her to omit any reference to it from her story to you. I knew the parcel contained Mrs. Banning's jewels, but I thought the fact would only confuse matters if brought to your attention. You see, Alvin told me that a judgment had been taken against Mrs. Banning, and that, just before the Supplementary Proceedings, Pfyfe had brought her jewels here and asked him to sequester them temporarily in his safe."

On our way back to the Criminal Courts Building, Markham took Vance's arm and smiled. "Your guessing luck is holding out, I see."

"Rather!" agreed Vance. "It would appear that the late Alvin, like Warren Hastings, resolved to die in the last dyke of prevarication. . . . *Splendide mendax,* what?"

"In any event," replied Markham, "the major has unconsciously added another link in the chain against Pfyfe."

"You seem to be making a collection of chains," commented Vance drily. "What have you done with the ones you forged about Miss St. Clair and Leacock?"

"I haven't entirely discarded them—if that's what you think," asserted Markham gravely.

When we reached the office, Sergeant Heath was awaiting us with a beatific grin.

"It's all over, Mr. Markham," he announced. "This noon, after you'd gone, Leacock came here looking for you. When he found you were out, he phoned headquarters, and they connected him with me. He wanted to see me—very important, he said; so I hurried over. He was sitting in the waiting room when

I came in and he called me over and said: 'I came to give myself up. I killed Benson.' I got him to dictate a confession to Swacker, and then he sighed it. . . . Here it is." He handed Markham a typewritten sheet of paper.

Markham sank wearily into a chair. The strain of the past few days had begun to tell on him. He signed heavily. "Thank God! Now our troubles are ended."

Vance looked at him lugubriously and shook his head.

"I rather fancy, y' know, that your troubles are only beginning," he drawled.

When Markham had glanced through the confession, he handed it to Vance, who read it carefully with an expression of growing amusement.

"Y' know," he said, "this document isn't at all legal. Any judge worthy the name would throw it precip'tately out of court. It's far too simple and precise. It doesn't begin with 'greetings'; it doesn't contain a single 'wherefore-be-it' or 'be-it-known' or 'do-hereby'; it says nothing about 'free will' or 'sound mind' or 'disposin' mem'ry'; and the captain doesn't once refer to himself as 'the party of the first part'. . . . Utterly worthless, Sergeant. If I were you, I'd chuck it."

Heath was feeling too complacently triumphant to be annoyed. He smiled with magnanimous tolerance.

"It strikes you as funny, doesn't it, Mr. Vance?"

"Sergeant, if you knew how inord'nately funny this confession is, you'd pos'tively have hysterics."

Vance then turned to Markham. "Really, y' know, I shouldn't put too much stock in this. It may, however, prove a valuable lever with which to prise open the truth. In fact, I'm jolly glad the captain has gone in for imag'native lit'rature. With this entrancin' fable in our possession, I think we can overcome the major's scruples and get him to tell us what he knows. Maybe I'm wrong, but it's worth trying."

He stepped to the district attorney's desk and leaned over it cajolingly.

"I haven't led you astray yet, old dear; and I'm going to make another suggestion. Call up the major and ask him to come here at once. Tell him you've secured a confession—but don't you dare say whose. Imply it's Miss St. Clair's, or Pfyfe's—or Pontius Pilate's. But urge his immediate presence. Tell him you want to discuss it with him before proceeding with the indictment."

"I can't see the necessity of doing that," objected Markham. "I'm pretty sure to see him at the club tonight and I can tell him then."

"That wouldn't do at all," insisted Vance. "If the major can enlighten us on any point, I think Sergeant Heath should be present to hear him."

"I don't need any enlightenment," cut in Heath.

Vance regarded him with admiring surprise.

"What a wonderful man! Even Goethe cried for *mehr Licht;* and here are you in a state of luminous saturation! . . . Astonishin'!"

"See here, Vance," said Markham: "why try to complicate the matter? It strikes me as a waste of time, besides being an imposition, to ask the major here to discuss Leacock's confession. We don't need his evidence now, anyway."

Despite his gruffness there was a hint of reconsideration in his voice; for though his instinct had been to dismiss the request out of hand, the experiences of the past few days had taught him that Vance's suggestions were not made without an object.

Vance, sensing the other's hesitancy, said, "My request is based on something more than an idle desire to gaze upon the major's rubicund features at this moment. I'm telling you, with all the meager earnestness I possess, that his presence here now would be most helpful."

Markham deliberated and argued the point at some length. But Vance was so persistent that in the end he was convinced of the advisability of complying.

Heath was patently disgusted, but he sat down quietly and sought solace in a cigar.

Major Benson arrived with astonishing promptness, and when Markham handed him the confession, he made little attempt to conceal his eagerness. But as he read it his face clouded, and a look of puzzlement came into his eyes.

At length he looked up, frowning.

"I don't quite understand this; and I'll admit I'm greatly surprised. It doesn't seem credible that Leacock shot Alvin. . . . And yet, I may be mistaken, of course."

He laid the confession on Markham's desk with an air of disappointment, and sank into a chair.

"Do *you* feel satisfied?" he asked.

"I don't see any way around it," said Markham. "If he isn't guilty, why should he come forward and confess? God knows, there's plenty of evidence against him. I was ready to arrest him two days ago."

"He's guilty all right," put in Heath. "I've had my eye on him from the first."

Major Benson did not reply at once; he seemed to be framing his next words.

"It might be—that is, there's the bare possibility—that Leacock had an ulterior motive in confessing."

We all, I think, recognized the thought which his words strove to conceal.

"I'll admit," acceded Markham, "that at first I believed Miss St. Clair guilty, and I intimated as much to Leacock. But later I was persuaded that she was not directly involved."

"Does Leacock know this?" the major asked quickly.

Markham thought a moment. "No, I can't say that he does. In fact, it's more than likely he still thinks I suspect her."

"Ah!" The major's exclamation was almost involuntary.

"But what's that got to do with it?" asked Heath irritably. "Do you think he's going to the chair to save her reputation?—Bunk! That sort of thing's all right in the movies, but no man's that crazy in real life."

"I'm not so sure, Sergeant," ventured Vance lazily. "Women are too sane and practical to make such foolish gestures; but men, y' know, have an illim'table capacity for idiocy."

He turned an inquiring gaze on Major Benson.

"Won't you tell us why you think Leacock is playing Sir Galahad?"

But the major took refuge in generalities, and was disinclined even to follow up his original intimation as to the cause of the captain's action. Vance questioned him for some time but was unable to penetrate his reticence.

Heath, becoming restless, finally spoke up.

"You can't argue Leacock's guilt away, Mr. Vance. Look at the facts. He threatened Benson that he'd kill him if he caught him with the girl again. The next time Benson goes out with her, he's found shot. Then Leacock hides his gun at her house, and when things begin to get hot, he takes it away and ditches it in the river. He bribes the hallboy to alibi him; and he's seen at Benson's house at twelve thirty that night. When he's questioned, he can't explain anything.... If that ain't an open-and-shut case, I'm a mock-turtle."

"The circumstances are convincing," admitted Major Benson. "But couldn't they be accounted for on other grounds?"

Heath did not deign to answer the question.

"The way I see it," he continued, "is like this: Leacock gets suspicious along about midnight, takes his gun and goes out. He catches Benson with the girl, goes in, and shoots him like he threatened. They're both mixed up in it, if you ask me; but Leacock did the shooting. And now we got his confession.... There isn't a jury in the country that wouldn't convict him."

"*Probi et legales homines*—oh, quite!" murmured Vance.

Swacker appeared at the door. "The reporters are clamoring for attention," he announced with a wry face.

"Do they know about the confession?" Markham asked Heath.

"Not yet. I haven't told 'em anything so far—that's why they're clamoring, I guess. But I'll give 'em an earful now, if you say the word."

Markham nodded, and Heath started for the door. But Vance quickly planted himself in the way.

"Could you keep this thing quiet till tomorrow, Markham?" he asked.

Markham was annoyed. "I could if I wanted to—yes. But why should I?"

"For your own sake, if for no other reason. You've got your prize safely locked up. Control your vanity for twenty-four hours. The major and I both know that Leacock's innocent, and by this time tomorrow the whole country'll know it."

Again an argument ensued; but the outcome, like that of the former argument, was a foregone conclusion. Markham had realized for some time that Vance had reason to be convinced of something which as yet he was unwilling to divulge. His opposition to Vance's requests were, I had suspected, largely the result of an effort to ascertain this information; and I was positive of it now as he leaned forward and gravely debated the advisability of making public the captain's confession.

Vance, as heretofore, was careful to reveal nothing; but in the end his sheer determination carried his point; and Markham requested Heath to keep his own council until the next day. The major, by a slight nod, indicated his approbation of the decision.

"You might tell the newspaper lads, though," suggested Vance, "that you'll have a rippin' sensation for 'em tomorrow."

Heath went out, crestfallen and glowering.

"A rash fella, the sergeant—so impetuous!"

Vance again picked up the confession and perused it.

"Now, Markham, I want you to bring your prisoner forth—habeas corpus and that sort of thing. Put him in that chair facing the window, give him one of the good cigars you keep for influential politicians, and then listen attentively while I politely chat with him. . . . The major, I trust, will remain for the interlocut'ry proceedings."

"That request, at least, I'll grant without objections," smiled Markham. "I had already decided to have a talk with Leacock."

He pressed a buzzer, and a brisk, ruddy-faced clerk entered.

"A requisition for Captain Philip Leacock," he ordered.

When it was brought to him, he initialed it. "Take it to Ben, and tell him to hurry."

The clerk disappeared through the door leading to the outer corridor. Ten minutes later a deputy sheriff from the Tombs entered with the prisoner.

19

VANCE CROSS-EXAMINES

(*Wednesday, June 19; 3:30 P.M.*)

CAPTAIN LEACOCK walked into the room with a hopeless indifference of bearing. His shoulders drooped; his arms hung listlessly. His eyes were haggard like those of a man who had not slept for days. On seeing Major Benson, he straightened a little and, stepping toward him, extended his hand. It was plain that, however much he may have disliked Alvin Benson, he regarded the major as a friend. But suddenly, realizing the situation, he turned away, embarrassed.

The major went quickly to him and touched him on the arm. "It's all right, Leacock," he said softly. "I can't think that you really shot Alvin."

The captain turned apprehensive eyes upon him. "Of course, I shot him." His voice was flat. "I told him I was going to."

Vance came forward and indicated a chair.

"Sit down, Captain. The district attorney wants to hear your story of the shooting. The law, you understand, does not accept murder confessions without corroborat'ry evidence. And since, in the present case, there are suspicions against others than yourself, we want you to answer some questions in order to substantiate your guilt. Otherwise, it will be necess'ry for us to follow up our suspicions."

Taking a seat facing Leacock, he picked up the confession.

"You say here you were satisfied that Mr. Benson had wronged you, and you went to his house at about half past twelve on the night of the thirteenth. . . . When you speak of his wronging you, do you refer to his attentions to Miss St. Clair?"

Leacock's face betrayed a sulky belligerence.

"It doesn't matter why I shot him. Can't you leave Miss St. Clair out of it?"

"Certainly," agreed Vance. "I promise you she shall not be brought into it. But we must understand your motive thoroughly."

After a brief silence Leacock said, "Very well, then. That was what I referred to."

"How did you know Miss St. Clair went to dinner with Mr. Benson that night?"

"I followed them to the Marseilles."

"And then you went home?"

"Yes."

"What made you go to Mr. Benson's house later?"

"I got to thinking about it more and more, until I couldn't stand it any longer. I began to see red, and at last I took my Colt and went out, determined to kill him."

A note of passion had crept into his voice. It seemed unbelievable that he could be lying.

Vance again referred to the confession.

"You dictated: 'I went to 87 West Forty-eighth Street and entered the house by the front door.' ... Did you ring the bell? Or was the front door unlatched?"

Leacock was about to answer but hesitated. Evidently he recalled the newspaper accounts of the housekeeper's testimony in which she asserted positively that the bell had not rung that night.

"What difference does it make?" He was sparring for time.

"We'd like to know—that's all," Vance told him. "But no hurry."

"Well, if it's so important to you: I didn't ring the bell; and the door was unlocked." His hesitancy was gone. "Just as I reached the house, Benson drove up in a taxicab——"

"Just a moment. Did you happen to notice another car standing in front of the house? A gray Cadillac?"

"Why—yes."

"Did you recognize its occupant?"

There was another short silence.

"I'm not sure. I think it was a man named Pfyfe."

"He and Mr. Benson were outside at the same time, then?"

Leacock frowned. "No—not at the same time. There was nobody there when I arrived. ... I didn't see Pfyfe until I came out a few minutes later."

"He arrived in his car when you were inside—is that it?"

"He must have."

"I see. ... And now to go back a little: Benson drove up in a taxicab. Then what?"

"I went up to him and said I wanted to speak to him. He told me to come inside, and we went in together. He used his latchkey."

"And now, Captain, tell us just what happened after you and Mr. Benson entered the house."

"He laid his hat and stick on the hatrack, and we walked into the living room. He sat down by the table, and I stood up and said—what I had to say. Then I drew my gun and shot him."

Vance was closely watching the man, and Markham was leaning forward tensely.

"How did it happen that he was reading at the time?"

"I believe he did pick up a book while I was talking. ... Trying to appear indifferent, I reckon."

"Think now: you and Mr. Benson went into the living room directly from the hall, as soon as you entered the house?"

"Yes."

"Then how do you account for the fact, Captain, that when Mr. Benson was shot, he had on his smoking jacket and slippers?"

Leacock glanced nervously about the room. Before he answered, he wet his lips with his tongue.

"Now that I think of it, Benson did go upstairs for a few minutes first. . . . I guess I was too excited," he added desperately, "to recollect everything."

"That's natural," Vance said sympathetically. "But when he came downstairs, did you happen to notice anything peculiar about his hair?"

Leacock looked up vaguely. "His hair? I—don't understand."

"The color of it, I mean. When Mr. Benson sat before you under the table lamp, didn't you remark some—difference, let us say—in the way his hair looked?"

The man closed his eyes, as if striving to visualize the scene. "No—I don't remember."

"A minor point," said Vance indifferently. "Did Benson's speech strike you as peculiar when he came downstairs—that is, was there a thickness, or slight impediment of any kind, in his voice?"

Leacock was manifestly puzzled.

"I don't know what you mean," he said. "He seemed to talk the way he always talked."

"And did you happen to see a blue jewel case on the table?"

"I didn't notice."

Vance smoked a moment thoughtfully.

"When you left the room after shooting Mr. Benson, you turned out the lights, of course?"

When no immediate answer came, Vance volunteered the suggestion: "You must have done so, for Mr. Pfyfe says the house was dark when he drove up."

Leacock then nodded an affirmative. "That's right. I couldn't recollect for the moment."

"Now that you remember the fact, just how did you turn them off?"

"I——" he began, and stopped. Then, finally: "At the switch."

"And where is that switch located, Captain?"

"I can't just recall."

"Think a moment. Surely you can remember."

"By the door leading into the hall, I think."

"Which side of the door?"

"How can I tell?" the man asked piteously. "I was too—nervous. . . . But I think it was on the right-hand side of the door."

"The right-hand side when entering or leaving the room?"

"As you go out."

"That would be where the bookcase stands?"

"Yes."

Vance appeared satisfied.

"Now, there's the question of the gun," he said. "Why did you take it to Miss St. Clair?"

"I was a coward," the man replied. "I was afraid they might find it at my apartment. And I never imagined she would be suspected."

"And when she was suspected, you at once took the gun away and threw it into the East River?"

"Yes."

"I suppose there was one cartridge missing from the magazine, too—which in itself would have been a suspicious circumstance."

"I thought of that. That's why I threw the gun away."

Vance frowned. "That's strange. There must have been two guns. We dredged the river, y' know, and found a Colt automatic, but the magazine was full. . . . Are you sure, Captain, that it was *your* gun you took from Miss St. Clair's and threw over the bridge?"

I knew no gun had been retrieved from the river and I wondered what he was driving at. Was he, after all, trying to involve the girl? Markham, too, I could see, was in doubt.

Leacock made no answer for several moments. When he spoke, it was with dogged sullenness.

"There weren't two guns. The one you found was mine. . . . I refilled the magazine myself."

"Ah, that accounts for it." Vance's tone was pleasant and reassuring. "Just one more question, Captain. Why did you come here today and confess?"

Leacock thrust his chin out, and for the first time during the cross-examination his eyes became animated. "Why? It was the only honorable thing to do. You have unjustly suspected an innocent person; and I didn't want anyone else to suffer."

This ended the interview. Markham had no questions to ask; and the deputy sheriff led the captain out.

When the door had closed on him, a curious silence fell over the room. Markham sat smoking furiously, his hands folded behind his head, his eyes fixed on the ceiling. The major had settled back in his chair, and was gazing at Vance with admiring satisfaction. Vance was watching Markham out of the corner of his eye, a drowsy smile on his lips. The expressions and attitudes of the three men conveyed perfectly their varying individual reactions to the interview—Markham troubled, the major pleased, Vance cynical.

It was Vance who broke the silence. He spoke easily, almost lazily. "You see how silly the confession is, what? Our pure and lofty captain is an incredibly poor Munchausen. No one could lie as badly as he did who hadn't been born into the world that way. It's simply impossible to imitate such stupidity. And he did so want us to think him guilty. Very affectin'. He prob'bly imagined you'd merely stick the confession in his shirtfront and send him to the hangman. You noticed, he hadn't even decided how he got into Benson's house that night. Pfyfe's admitted presence outside almost spoiled his impromptu explanation of having entered *bras dessus bras dessous* with his intended victim. And he didn't recall Benson's semi-négligé attire. When I reminded him of it, he had to contradict himself and send Benson trotting upstairs to make a rapid change. Luckily, the toupee wasn't mentioned by the newspapers. The captain couldn't imagine what I meant when I intimated that Benson had dyed his hair when changing his coat and shoes. . . . By the bye, Major, did your brother speak thickly when his false teeth were out?"

"Noticeably so," answered the major. "If Alvin's plate had been removed that night—as I gathered it had been from your question—Leacock would surely have noticed it."

"There were other things he didn't notice," said Vance: "the jewel case, for instance, and the location of the electric light switch."

"He went badly astray on that point," added the major. "Alvin's house is old-fashioned, and the only switch in the room is a pendant one attached to the chandelier."

"Exactly," said Vance. "However, his worst break was in connection with the gun. He gave his hand away completely there. He said he threw the pistol into the river largely because of the missing cartridge, and when I told him the magazine was full, he explained that he had refilled it, so I wouldn't think it was anyone else's gun that was found. . . . It's plain to see what's the matter. He thinks Miss St. Clair is guilty, and is determined to take the blame."

"That's my impression," said Major Benson.

"And yet," mused Vance, "the captain's attitude bothers me a little. There's no doubt he had something to do with the crime, else why should he have concealed his pistol the next day in Miss St. Clair's apartment? He's just the kind of silly beggar, d' ye see, who would threaten any man he thought had designs on his fiancée and then carry out the threat if anything happened. And he has a guilty conscience—that's obvious. But for what? Certainly not the shooting. The crime was planned; and the captain never plans. He's the kind that gets an *idée fixe,* girds up his loins, and does the deed in knightly fashion, prepared to take the cons'quences. That sort of chivalry, y' know, is sheer *beau geste:* its acolytes want everyone to know of their valor. And when they go forth to rid the world of a Don Juan, they're always clear-minded. The captain, for instance, wouldn't have overlooked his Lady Fair's gloves and handbag, he would have taken 'em away. In fact, it's just as certain he would have shot Benson as it is he didn't shoot him. That's the beetle in the amber. It's psychologically possible he would have done it, and psychologically impossible he would have done it the way it was done."

He lit a cigarette and watched the drifting spirals of smoke.

"If it wasn't so fantastic, I'd say he started out to do it and found it already done. And yet, that's about the size of it. It would account for Pfyfe's seeing him there, and for his secreting the gun at Miss St. Clair's the next day."

The telephone rang: Colonel Ostrander wanted to speak to the district attorney. Markham, after a short conversation, turned a disgruntled look upon Vance.

"Your bloodthirsty friend wanted to know if I'd arrested anyone yet. He offered to confer more of his invaluable suggestions upon me in case I was still undecided as to who was guilty."

"I heard you thanking him fulsomely for something or other. . . . What did you give him to understand about your mental state?"

"That I was still in the dark."

Markham's answer was accompanied by a somber, tired smile. It was his way of telling Vance that he had entirely rejected the idea of Captain Leacock's guilt.

The major went to him and held out his hand.

"I know how you feel," he said. "This sort of thing is discouraging; but it's better that the guilty person should escape altogether than that an innocent man should be made to suffer. . . . Don't work too hard, and don't let these disappointments get to you. You'll soon hit on the right solution, and when you do"—his jaw snapped shut, and he uttered the rest of the sentence between clenched teeth—"you'll meet with no opposition from me. I'll help you put the thing over."

He gave Markham a grim smile and took up his hat.

"I'm going back to the office now. If you want me at any time, let me know. I may be able to help you—later on."

With a friendly, appreciative bow to Vance, he went out.

Markham sat in silence for several minutes.

"Damn it, Vance!" he said irritably. "This case gets more difficult by the hour. I feel worn out."

"You really shouldn't take it so seriously, old dear," Vance advised lightly. "It doesn't pay, y' know, to worry over the trivia of existence.

> 'Nothing's new,
> And nothing's true,
> And nothing really matters.'

Several million johnnies were killed in the war, and you don't let the fact bedevil your phagocytes or inflame your brain cells. But when one rotter is mercifully shot in your district, you lie awake nights perspiring over it, what? My word! You're deucedly inconsistent."

"Consistency——" began Markham; but Vance interrupted him.

"Now don't quote Emerson. I inf'nitely prefer Erasmus. Y' know, you ought to read his *Praise of Folly;* it would cheer you no end. That goaty old Dutch professor would never have grieved inconsolably over the destruction of Alvin *Le Chauve.*"

"I'm not a *fruges consumere natus* like you," snapped Markham. "I was elected to this office——"

"Oh, quite—'loved I not honor more' and all that," Vance chimed in. "But don't be so sens'tive. Even if the captain has succeeded in bungling his way out of jail, you have at least five possibilities left. There's Mrs. Platz . . . and Pfyfe . . . and Colonel Ostrander . . . and Miss Hoffman . . . and Mrs. Banning.—I say! Why don't you arrest 'em all, one at a time, and get 'em to confess? Heath would go crazy with joy."

Markham was in too crestfallen a mood to resent this chaffing. Indeed, Vance's lightheartedness seemed to buoy him up.

"If you want the truth," he said; "that's exactly what I feel like doing. I am restrained merely by my indecision as to which one to arrest first."

"Stout fella!" Then Vance asked: "What are you going to do with the captain now? It'll break his heart if you release him."

"His heart'll have to break, I'm afraid." Markham reached for the telephone. "I'd better see to the formalities now."

"Just a moment!" Vance put forth a restraining hand. "Don't end his rapturous martyrdom just yet. Let him be happy for another day at least. I've a notion he may be most useful to us, pining away in his lonely cell like the prisoner of Chillon."

Markham put down the telephone without a word. More and more, I had noticed, he was becoming inclined to accept Vance's leadership. This attitude was not merely the result of the hopeless confusion in his mind, though his uncertainty probably influenced him to some extent; but it was due in large measure to the impression Vance had given him of knowing more than he cared to reveal.

"Have you tried to figure out just how Pfyfe and his Turtledove fit into the case?" Vance asked.

"Along with a few thousand other enigmas—yes," was the petulant reply. "But the more I try to reason it out, the more of a mystery the whole thing becomes."

"Loosely put, my dear Markham," criticized Vance. "There are no mysteries originating in human beings, y' know; there are only problems. And any problem originating in one human being can be solved by another human being. It merely requires a knowledge of the human mind, and the application of that knowledge to human acts. Simple, what?"

He glanced at the clock.

"I wonder how your Mr. Stitt is getting along with the Benson and Benson books. I await his report with anticipat'ry excitement."

This was too much for Markham. The wearing-down process of Vance's intimations and veiled innuendoes had at last dissipated his self-control. He bent forward and struck the desk angrily with his hand.

"I'm damned tired of this superior attitude of yours," he complained hotly. "Either you know something or you don't. If you don't know anything, do me the favor of dropping these insinuations of knowledge. If you do know anything, it's up to you to tell me. You've been hinting around in one way or another ever since Benson was shot. If you've got any idea who killed him, I want to know it."

He leaned back and took out a cigar. Not once did he look up as he carefully clipped the end and lit it. I think he was a little ashamed at having given way to his anger.

Vance had sat apparently unconcerned during the outburst. At length he stretched his legs and gave Markham a long contemplative look.

"Y' know, Markham old bean, I don't blame you a bit for your unseemly ebullition. The situation has been most provokin'. But now, I fancy, the time has come to put an end to the comedietta. I really haven't been spoofing, y' know. The fact is, I've some most int'restin' ideas on the subject."

He stood up and yawned.

"It's a beastly hot day, but it must be done—eh, what?

> 'So nigh is grandeur to our dust,
>   So near is God to man.
> When duty whispers low, *Thou must,*
>   The youth replies, *I can.*'

I'm the noble youth, don't y' know. And you're the voice of duty—though you didn't exactly whisper, did you? . . . *Was aber ist deine Pflicht?* And Goethe answered: *Die Forderung des Tages.* But—deuce take it!—I wish the demand had come on a cooler day."

He handed Markham his hat.

"Come, *Postume.* To everything there is a season, and a time to every purpose under the heaven.* You are through with the office for today. Inform Swacker of the fact, will you?—there's a dear! We attend upon a lady—Miss St. Clair, no less."

Markham realized that Vance's jesting manner was only the masquerade of a very serious purpose. Also, he knew that Vance would tell him what he knew or suspected only in his own way, and that, no matter how circuitous and unreasonable that way might appear, Vance had excellent reasons for following it. Furthermore, since the unmasking of Captain Leacock's purely fictitious confession, he was in a state of mind to follow any suggestion that held the faintest hope of getting at the truth. He therefore rang at once for Swacker and informed him he was quitting the office for the day.

In ten minutes we were in the subway on our way to 94 Riverside Drive.

20

A LADY EXPLAINS

(*Wednesday, June 19; 4:30 P.M.*)

"THE QUEST for enlightenment upon which we are now embarked," said Vance, as we rode uptown, "may prove a bit tedious. But you must exert your willpower and bear with me. You can't imagine what a ticklish task I have on my hands. And it's not a pleasant one either. I'm a bit too young to be sentimental and yet, d' ye know, I'm half inclined to let your culprit go."

"Would you mind telling me why we are calling on Miss. St. Clair?" asked Markham resignedly.

Vance amiably complied. "Not at all. Indeed, I deem it best for you to know. There are several points connected with the lady that need eluc'dation. First, there are the gloves and the handbag. Nor poppy nor mandragora shall ever medicine thee to that sweet sleep which thou ow'dst yesterday until you have learned about those articles—eh, what? Then, you recall, Miss Hoffman told us that the major was lending an ear when a certain lady called upon Benson the day he was shot. I suspect that the visitor was Miss St. Clair; and I am rather curious to know what took place in the office that day and why she came back later. Also, why did she go to Benson's for tea that afternoon? And what part did the jewels play in the chit-chat? But there are other items. For example: Why did the captain take his gun to her? What makes him think she shot Benson?—he really believes it, y' know. And why did she think that he was guilty from the first?"

Markham looked skeptical.

"You expect her to tell us all this?"

"My hopes run high," returned Vance. "With her verray parfit gentil knight

---

* This quotation from Ecclesiastes reminds me that Vance regularly read the Old Testament. "When I weary of the professional liter'ry man," he once said, "I find stimulation in the majestic prose of the Bible. If the moderns feel that they simply must write, they should be made to spend at least two hours a day with the Biblical historians."

jailed as a self-confessed murderer, she will have nothing to lose by unburdening her soul. . . . But we must have no blustering. Your police brand of aggressive cross-examination will, I assure you, have no effect upon the lady."

"Just how do you propose to elicit your information?"

"With *morbidezza,* as the painters say. Much more refined and gentlemanly, y' know."

Markham considered a moment. "I think I'll keep out of it, and leave the Socratic elenctus entirely to you."

"An extr'ordin'rily brilliant suggestion," said Vance.

When we arrived Markham announced over the house telephone that he had come on a vitally important mission; and we were received by Miss St. Clair without a moment's delay. She was apprehensive, I imagine, concerning the whereabouts of Captain Leacock.

As she sat before us in her little drawing room overlooking the Hudson, her face was quite pale, and her hands, though tightly clasped, trembled a little. She had lost much of her cold reserve, and there were unmistakable signs of sleepless worry about her eyes.

Vance went directly to the point. His tone was almost flippant in its lightness: it at once relieved the tension of the atmosphere, and gave an air bordering on inconsequentiality to our visit.

"Captain Leacock has, I regret to inform you, very foolishly confessed to the murder of Mr. Benson. But we are not entirely satisfied with his *bona fides.* We are, alas! awash between Scylla and Charybdis. We can not decide whether the captain is a deep-dyed villain or a *chevalier sans peur et sans reproche.* His story of how he accomplished the dark deed is a bit sketchy; he is vague on certain essential details; and—what's most confusin'—he turned the lights off in Benson's hideous living room by a switch which pos'tively doesn't exist. Cons'quently, the suspicion has crept into my mind that he has concocted this tale of derring-do in order to shield someone whom he really believes guilty."

He indicated Markham with a slight movement of the head.

"The district attorney here does not wholly agree with me. But then, d' ye see, the legal mind is incredibly rigid and unreceptive once it has been invaded by a notion. You will remember that, because you were with Mr. Alvin Benson on his last evening on earth, and for other reasons equally irrelevant and trivial, Mr. Markham actu'lly concluded that you had had something to do with the gentleman's death."

He gave Markham a smile of waggish reproach, and went on: "Since you, Miss St. Clair, are the only person whom Captain Leacock would shield so heroically, and since I, at least, am convinced of your own innocence, will you not clear up for us a few of those points where your orbit crossed that of Mr. Benson? . . . Such information cannot do the captain or yourself any harm, and it very possibly will help to banish from Mr. Markham's mind his lingering doubts as to the captain's innocence."

Vance's manner had an assuaging effect upon the woman; but I could see that Markham was boiling inwardly at Vance's animadversions on him, though he refrained from any interruption.

Miss St. Clair stared steadily at Vance for several minutes.

"I don't know why I should trust you, or even believe you," she said evenly;

"but now that Captain Leacock has confessed—I was afraid he was going to, when he last spoke to me—I see no reason why I should not answer your questions. . . . Do you truly think he is innocent?"

The question was like an involuntary cry; her pent-up emotion had broken through her carapace of calm.

"I truly do," Vance avowed soberly. "Mr. Markham will tell you that before we left his office, I pleaded with him to release Captain Leacock. It was with the hope that your explanations would convince him of the wisdom of such a course that I urged him to come here."

Something in his tone and manner seemed to inspire her confidence.

"What do you wish to ask me?" she asked.

Vance cast another reproachful glance at Markham, who was restraining his outraged feelings only with difficulty; and then turned back to the woman.

"First of all, will you explain how your gloves and handbag found their way into Mr. Benson's house? Their presence there has been preying most distressin'ly on the district attorney's mind."

She turned a direct, frank gaze upon Markham.

"I dined with Mr. Benson at his invitation. Things between us were not pleasant, and when we started for home, my resentment of his attitude increased. At Times Square I ordered the chauffeur to stop—I preferred returning home alone. In my anger and my haste to get away, I must have dropped my gloves and bag. It was not until Mr. Benson had driven off that I realized my loss, and having no money, I walked home. Since my things were found in Mr. Benson's house, he must have taken them there himself."

"Such was my own belief," said Vance. "And—my word!—it's a deucedly long walk out here, what?"

He turned to Markham with a tantalizing smile.

"Really, y' know, Miss St. Clair couldn't have been expected to reach here before one."

Markham, grim and resolute, made no reply.

"And now," pursued Vance, "I should love to know under what circumst'nces the invitation to dinner was extended."

A shadow darkened her face, but her voice remained even.

"I had been losing a lot of money through Mr. Benson's firm, and suddenly my intuition told me that he was purposely seeing to it that I did lose, and that he could, if he desired, help me to recoup." She dropped her eyes. "He had been annoying me with his attentions for some time; and I didn't put any despicable scheme past him. I went to his office and told him quite plainly what I suspected. He replied that if I'd dine with him that night, we could talk it over. I knew what his object was, but I was so desperate I decided to go anyway, hoping I might plead with him."

"And how did you happen to mention to Mr. Benson the exact time your little dinner party would terminate?"

She looked at Vance in astonishment but answered unhesitatingly.

"He said something about making a gay night of it; and then I told him—very emphatically—that if I went, I would leave him sharply at midnight, as was my invariable rule on all parties. . . . You see," she added, "I study very hard at my singing, and going home at midnight, no matter what the occasion, is one of the sacrifices—or rather, restrictions—I impose on myself."

"Most commendable and most wise!" commented Vance. "Was this fact generally known among your acquaintances?"

"Oh, yes. It even resulted in my being nicknamed Cinderella."

"Specifically, did Colonel Ostrander and Mr. Pfyfe know it?"

"Yes."

Vance thought a moment.

"How did you happen to go to tea at Mr. Benson's home the day of the murder, if you were to dine with him that night?"

A flush stained her cheeks. "There was nothing wrong in that," she declared. "Somehow, after I had left Mr. Benson's office, I revolted against my decision to dine with him, and I went to his house—I had gone back to the office first, but he had left—to make a final appeal and to beg him to release me from my promise. But he laughed the matter off and, after insisting that I have tea, sent me home in a taxicab to dress for dinner. He called for me about half past seven."

"And when you pleaded with him to release you from your promise, you sought to frighten him by recalling Captain Leacock's threat; and he said it was only a bluff."

Again the woman's astonishment was manifest. "Yes," she murmured.

Vance gave her a soothing smile.

"Colonel Ostrander told me he saw you and Mr. Benson at the Marseilles."

"Yes, and I was terribly ashamed. He knew what Mr. Benson was and had warned me against him only a few days before."

"I was under the impression the colonel and Mr. Benson were good friends."

"They were—up to a week ago. But the colonel lost more money than I did in a stock pool which Mr. Benson engineered recently, and he intimated to me very strongly that Mr. Benson had deliberately misadvised us to his own benefit. He didn't even speak to Mr. Benson that night at the Marseilles."

"What about these rich and precious stones that accompanied your tea with Mr. Benson?"

"Bribes," she answered; and her contemptuous smile was a more eloquent condemnation of Benson than if she had resorted to the bitterest castigation. "The gentleman sought to turn my head with them. I was offered a string of pearls to wear to dinner, but I declined them. And I was told that if I saw things in the right light—or some such charming phrase—I could have jewels just like them for my very, very own—perhaps even those identical ones, on the twenty-first."

"Of course—the twenty-first." Vance grinned. "Markham, are you listening? On the twenty-first Leander's note falls due, and if it's not paid, the jewels are forfeited."

He addressed himself again to Miss St. Clair.

"Did Mr. Benson have the jewels with him at dinner?"

"Oh, no! I think my refusal of the pearls rather discouraged him."

Vance paused, looking at her with ingratiating cordiality.

"Tell us now, please, of the gun episode—in your own words, as the lawyers say, hoping to entangle you later."

But she evidently feared no entanglement.

"The morning after the murder Captain Leacock came here and said he had

gone to Mr. Benson's house about half past twelve with the intention of
shooting him. But he had seen Mr. Pfyfe outside and, assuming he was calling,
had given up the idea and gone home. I feared that Mr. Pfyfe had seen him,
and I told him it would be safer to bring his pistol to me and to say, if questioned, that he'd lost it in France. . . . You see, I really thought he had shot Mr.
Benson and was—well, lying like a gentleman, to spare my feelings. Then,
when he took the pistol from me with the purpose of throwing it away altogether, I was even more certain of it."

She smiled faintly at Markham.

"That was why I refused to answer your questions. I wanted you to think
that maybe I had done it, so you'd not suspect Captain Leacock."

"But he wasn't lying at all," said Vance.

"I know now that he wasn't. And I should have known it before. He'd never
have brought the pistol to me if he'd been guilty."

A film came over her eyes.

"And—poor boy!—he confessed because he thought that I was guilty."

"That's precisely the harrowin' situation," nodded Vance. "But where did
he think you had obtained a weapon?"

"I know many army men, friends of his and of Major Benson's. And last
summer at the mountains I did considerable pistol practice for the fun of it.
Oh, the idea was reasonable enough."

Vance rose and made a courtly bow.

"You've been most gracious—and most helpful," he said. "Y' see, Mr.
Markham had various theories about the murder. The first, I believe, was that
you alone were the Madam Borgia. The second was that you and the captain
did the deed together—*à quatre mains,* as it were. The third was that the captain pulled the trigger *a cappella.* And the legal mind is so exquisitely developed that it can believe in several conflicting theories at the same time. The
sad thing about the present case is that Mr. Markham still leans toward the
belief that both of you are guilty, individually and collectively. I tried to reason with him before coming here; but I failed. Therefore, I insisted upon his
hearing from your own charming lips your story of the affair."

He went up to Markham, who sat glaring at him with lips compressed.

"Well, old chap," he remarked pleasantly, "surely you are not going to per-
sist in your obsession that either Miss St. Clair or Captain Leacock is guilty,
what? . . . And won't you relent and unshackle the captain as I begged you
to?"

He extended his arms in a theatrical gesture of supplication.

Markham's wrath was at the breaking point, but he got up deliberately and,
going to the woman, held out his hand. "Miss St. Clair," he said kindly—and
again I was impressed by the bigness of the man—, "I wish to assure you that I
have dismissed the idea of your guilt, and also Captain Leacock's, from what
Mr. Vance terms my incredibly rigid and unreceptive mind. . . . I forgive him,
however, because he has saved me from doing you a very grave injustice. And
I will see that you have your captain back as soon as the papers can be signed
for his release."

As we walked out onto Riverside Drive, Markham turned savagely on
Vance.

"So! *I* was keeping her precious captain locked up, and *you* were pleading with me to let him go! You know damned well I didn't think either one of them was guilty—you—you lounge lizard!"

Vance sighed. "Dear me! Don't you want to be of any help at all in this case?" he asked sadly.

"What good did it do you to make an ass of me in front of that woman?" spluttered Markham. "I can't see that you got anywhere, with all your tom-foolery."

"What!" Vance registered utter amazement. "The testimony you've heard today is going to help immeasurably in convicting the culprit. Furthermore, we now know about the gloves and handbag, and who the lady was that called at Benson's office, and what Miss St. Clair did between twelve and one, and why she dined alone with Alvin, and why she first had tea with him, and how the jewels came to be there, and why the captain took her his gun and then threw it away, and why he confessed. . . . My word! Doesn't all this knowledge soothe you? It rids the situation of so much debris."

He stopped and lit a cigarette.

"The really important thing the lady told us was that her friends knew she invariably departed at midnight when she went out of an evening. Don't overlook or belittle that point, old dear; it's most pert'nent. I told you long ago that the person who shot Benson knew she was dining with him that night."

"You'll be telling me next you know who killed him," Markham scoffed.

Vance sent a ring of smoke circling upward.

"I've known all along who shot the blighter."

Markham snorted derisively.

"Indeed! And when did this revelation burst upon you?"

"Oh, not more than five minutes after I entered Benson's house that first morning," replied Vance.

"Well, well! Why didn't you confide in me and avoid all these trying activities?"

"Quite impossible," Vance explained jocularly. "You were not ready to receive my apocryphal knowledge. It was first necess'ry to lead you patiently by the hand out of the various dark forests and morasses into which you insisted upon straying. You're so dev'lishly unimag'native, don't y' know."

A taxicab was passing and he hailed it.

"Eighty-seven West Forty-eighth Street," he directed.

Then he took Markham's arm confidingly. "Now for a brief chat with Mrs. Platz. And then—then I shall pour into your ear all my maidenly secrets."

21

SARTORIAL REVELATIONS

(*Wednesday, June 19; 5:30 P.M.*)

THE HOUSEKEEPER regarded our visit that afternoon with marked uneasiness.
Though she was a large, powerful woman, her body seemed to have lost some
of its strength, and her face showed signs of prolonged anxiety. Snitkin informed us, when we entered, that she had carefully read every newspaper account of the progress of the case and had questioned him interminably on the
subject.

She entered the living room with scarcely an acknowledgment of our presence and took the chair Vance placed for her like a woman resigning herself to
a dreaded but inevitable ordeal. When Vance looked at her keenly, she gave
him a frightened glance and turned her face away, as if, in the second their
eyes met, she had read his knowledge of some secret she had been jealously
guarding.

Vance began his questioning without prelude or protasis.

"Mrs. Platz, was Mr. Benson very particular about his toupee—that is, did
he often receive his friends without having it on?"

The woman appeared relieved. "Oh, no, sir—never."

"Think back, Mrs. Platz. Has Mr. Benson never, to your knowledge, been in
anyone's company without his toupee?"

She was silent for some time, her brows contracted.

"Once I saw him take off his wig and show it to Colonel Ostrander, an el-
derly gentleman who used to call here very often. But Colonel Ostrander was
an old friend of his. He told me they lived together once."

"No one else?"

Again she frowned thoughtfully. "No," she said, after several minutes.

"What about the tradespeople?"

"He was very particular about them. . . . And strangers, too," she added.
"When he used to sit in here in hot weather without his wig, he always pulled
the shade on that window." She pointed to the one nearest the hallway. "You
can look in it from the steps."

"I'm glad you brought up that point," said Vance. "And anyone standing
on the steps could tap on the window or the iron bars, and attract the attention
of anyone in this room?"

"Oh, yes, sir—easily. I did it myself once, when I went on an errand and
forgot my key."

"It's quite likely, don't you think, that the person who shot Mr. Benson obtained admittance that way?"

"Yes, sir." She grasped eagerly at the suggestion.

"The person would have had to know Mr. Benson pretty well to tap on the
window instead of ringing the bell. Don't you agree with me, Mrs. Platz?"

"Yes, sir." Her tone was doubtful; evidently the point was a little beyond
her.

"If a stranger had tapped on the window, would Mr. Benson have admitted
him without his toupee?"

"Oh, no—he wouldn't have let a stranger in."

"You are sure the bell didn't ring that night?"

"Positive, sir." The answer was very emphatic.

"Is there a light on the front steps?"

"No, sir."

"If Mr. Benson had looked out of the window to see who was tapping, could he have recognized the person at night?"

The woman hesitated. "I don't know—I don't think so."

"Is there any way you can see through the front door who is outside without opening it?"

"No, sir. Sometimes I wished there was."

"Then, if the person knocked on the window, Mr. Benson must have recognized the voice?"

"It looks that way, sir."

"And you're certain no one could have got in without a key?"

"How could they? The door locks by itself."

"It's the regulation spring lock, isn't it?"

"Yes, sir."

"Then it must have a catch you can turn off so that the door will open from either side even though it's latched."

"It did have a catch like that," she explained, "but Mr. Benson had it fixed so's it wouldn't work. He said it was too dangerous—I might go out and leave the house unlocked."

Vance stepped into the hallway, and I heard him opening and shutting the front door.

"You're right, Mrs. Platz," he observed, when he came back. "Now tell me: are you quite sure no one had a key?"

"Yes, sir. No one but me and Mr. Benson had a key."

Vance nodded his acceptance of her statement.

"You said you left your bedroom door open on the night Mr. Benson was shot. . . . Do you generally leave it open?"

"No, I 'most always shut it. But it was terrible close that night."

"Then it was merely an accident you left it open?"

"As you might say."

"If your door had been closed as usual, could you have heard the shot, do you think?"

"If I'd been awake, maybe. Not if I was sleeping, though. They got heavy doors in these old houses, sir."

"And they're beautiful, too," commented Vance.

He looked admiringly at the massive mahogany double door that opened into the hall.

"Y' know, Markham, our so-called civ'lization is nothing more than the persistent destruction of everything that's beautiful and enduring, and the designing of cheap makeshifts. You should read Oswald Spengler's *Untergang des Abendlands*—a most penetratin' document. I wonder some enterprisin' publisher hasn't embalmed it in our native argot.* The whole history of this degen'rate era we call modern civ'lization can be seen in our woodwork. Look

* The book—or a part of it—has, I believe, been recently translated into English.

at that fine old door, for instance, with its beveled panels and ornamented bo-lection, and its Ionic pilasters and carved lintel. And then compare it with the flat, flimsy, machine-made, shellacked boards which are turned out by the thousand today. *Sic transit. . . .*"

He studied the door for some time; then turned abruptly back to Mrs. Platz, who was eyeing him curiously and with mounting apprehension.

"What did Mr. Benson do with the box of jewels when he went out to din-ner?" he asked.

"Nothing, sir," she answered nervously. "He left them on the table there."

"Did you see them after he had gone?"

"Yes; and I was going to put them away. But I decided I'd better not touch them."

"And nobody came to the door, or entered the house, after Mr. Benson left?"

"No, sir."

"You're quite sure?"

"I'm positive, sir."

Vance rose, and began to pace the floor. Suddenly, just as he was passing the woman, he stopped and faced her.

"Was your maiden name Hoffman, Mrs. Platz?"

The thing she had been dreading had come. Her face paled, her eyes opened wide, and her lower lip drooped a little.

Vance stood looking at her, not unkindly. Before she could regain control of herself, he said, "I had the pleasure of meeting your charmin' daughter re-cently."

"My daughter. . . ?" the woman managed to stammer.

"Miss Hoffman, y' know—the attractive young lady with the blond hair. Mr. Benson's secret'ry."

The woman sat erect and spoke through clamped teeth. "She's not my daughter."

"Now, now, Mrs. Platz!" Vance chided her, as if speaking to a child. "Why this foolish attempt at deception? You remember how worried you were when I accused you of having a personal interest in the lady who was here to tea with Mr. Benson? You were afraid I thought it was Miss Hoffman. . . . But why should you be anxious about her, Mrs. Platz? I'm sure she's a very nice girl. And you really can't blame her for preferring the name of Hoffman to that of Platz. *Platz* means generally a place, though it also means a crash or an explosion; and sometimes a *Platz* is a bun or a yeast cake. But a *Hoffman* is a courtier—much nicer than being a yeast cake, what?"

He smiled engagingly, and his manner had a quieting effect upon her.

"It isn't that, sir," she said, looking at him appealingly. "I made her take the name. In this country any girl who's smart can get to be a lady if she's given a chance. And——"

"I understand perfectly," Vance interposed pleasantly. "Miss Hoffman is clever, and you feared that the fact of your being a housekeeper, if it became known, would stand in the way of her success. So you elim'nated yourself, as it were, for her welfare. I think it was very generous of you. . . . Your daughter lives alone?"

"Yes, sir—in Morningside Heights. But I see her every week." Her voice was barely audible.

"Of course—as often as you can, I'm sure. . . . Did you take the position as Mr. Benson's housekeeper because she was his secret'ry?"

She looked up, a bitter expression in her eyes. "Yes, sir—I did. She told me the kind of man he was; and he often made her come to the house here in the evenings to do extra work."

"And you wanted to be here to protect her?"

"Yes, sir—that was it."

"Why were you so worried the morning after the murder, when Mr. Markham here asked you if Mr. Benson kept any firearms around the house?"

The woman shifted her gaze. "I—wasn't worried."

"Yes, you were, Mrs. Platz. And I'll tell you why. You were afraid we might think Miss Hoffman shot him."

"Oh, no, sir, I wasn't!" she cried. "My girl wasn't even here that night—I swear it!—she wasn't here. . . ."

She was badly shaken; the nervous tension of a week had snapped, and she looked helplessly about her.

"Come, come, Mrs. Platz," pleaded Vance consolingly. "No one believes for a moment that Miss Hoffman had a hand in Mr. Benson's death."

The woman peered searchingly into his face. At first she was loath to believe him—it was evident that fear had long been preying on her mind—and it took him fully a quarter of an hour to convince her that what he had said was true. When, finally, we left the house, she was in a comparatively peaceful state of mind.

On our way to the Stuyvesant Club Markham was silent, completely engrossed with his thoughts. It was evident that the new facts educed by the interview with Mrs. Platz troubled him considerably.

Vance sat smoking dreamily, turning his head now and then to inspect the buildings we passed. We drove east through Forty-eighth Street, and when we came abreast of the New York Bible Society House, he ordered the chauffeur to stop and insisted that we admire it.

"Christianity," he remarked, "has almost vindicated itself by its architecture alone. With few exceptions, the only buildings in this city that are not eyesores are the churches and their allied structures. The American æsthetic credo is: Whatever's big is beautiful. These depressin' gargantuan boxes with rectangular holes in 'em, which are called skyscrapers, are worshiped by Americans simply because they're huge. A box with forty rows of holes is twice as beautiful as a box with twenty rows. Simple formula, what? . . . Look at this little five-story affair across the street. It's inf'nitely lovelier—and more impressive, too—than any skyscraper in the city. . . ."

Vance referred but once to the crime during our ride to the club and then only indirectly.

"Kind hearts, y' know, Markham, are more than coronets. I've done a good deed today and I feel pos'tively virtuous. Frau Platz will *schlafen* much better tonight. She has been frightfully upset about little Gretchen. She's a doughty old soul; motherly and all that. And she couldn't bear to think of the future Lady Vere de Vere being suspected. . . . Wonder why she worried so?" And he gave Markham a sly look.

Nothing further was said until after dinner, which we ate in the Roof Garden. We had pushed back our chairs, and sat looking out over the treetops of Madison Square.

"Now, Markham," said Vance, "give over all prejudices, and consider the situation judiciously—as you lawyers euphemistically put it. . . . To begin with, we now know why Mrs. Platz was so worried at your question regarding firearms and why she was upset by my ref'rence to her personal int'rest in Benson's tea companion. So, those two mysteries are elim'nated. . . ."

"How did you find out about her relation to the girl?" interjected Markham.

" 'Twas my ogling did it." Vance gave him a reproving look. "You recall that I 'ogled' the young lady at our first meeting—but I forgive you. . . . And you remember our little discussion about cranial idiosyncrasies? Miss Hoffman, I noticed at once, possessed all the physical formations of Benson's housekeeper. She was brachycephalic; she had overarticulated cheekbones, an orthognathous jaw, a low, flat parietal structure, and a mesorrhinian nose. . . . Then I looked for her ear, for I had noted that Mrs. Platz had the pointed, lobeless, 'satyr' ear—sometimes called the Darwin ear. These ears run in families; and when I saw that Miss Hoffman's were of the same type, even though modified, I was fairly certain of the relationship. But there were other similarities—in pigment, for instance, and in height—both are tall, y' know. And the central masses of each were very large in comparison with the peripheral masses; the shoulders were narrow and the wrists and ankles small, while the hips were bulky. . . . That Hoffman was Platz's maiden name was only a guess. But it didn't matter."

Vance adjusted himself more comfortably in his chair.

"Now for your judicial considerations. . . . First, let us assume that at a little before half past twelve on the night of the thirteenth the villain came to Benson's house, saw the light in the living room, tapped on the window, and was instantly admitted. . . . What, would you say, do these assumptions indicate regarding the visitor?"

"Merely that Benson was acquainted with him," returned Markham. "But that doesn't help us any. We can't extend the *sus. per coll.* to everybody the man knew."

"The indications go much further than that, old chap," Vance retorted. "They show unmistakably that Benson's murderer was a most intimate crony, or, at least, a person before whom he didn't care how he looked. The absence of the toupee, as I once suggested to you, was a prime essential of the situation. A toupee, don't y' know, is the sartorial *sine qua non* of every middle-aged Beau Brummel afflicted with baldness. You heard Mrs. Platz on the subject. Do you think for a second that Benson, who hid his hirsute deficiency even from the grocer's boy, would visit with a mere acquaintance thus bereft of his crowning glory? And besides being thus denuded, he was without his full complement of teeth. Moreover, he was without collar or tie, and attired in an old smoking jacket and bedroom slippers! Picture the spectacle, my dear fellow. . . . A man does not look fascinatin' without his collar and with his shirtband and gold stud exposed. Thus attired, he is the equiv'lent of a lady in curl papers. . . . How many men do you think Benson knew with whom he would have sat down to a tête-à-tête in this undress condition?"

"Three or four, perhaps," answered Markham. "But I can't arrest them all."

"I'm sure you would if you could. But it won't be necess'ry."

Vance selected another cigarette from his case and went on. "There are other helpful indications, y' know. For instance, the murderer was fairly well acquainted with Benson's domestic arrangements. He must have known that the housekeeper slept a good distance from the living room and would not be startled by the shot if her door was closed as usual. Also, he must have known there was no one else in the house at that hour. And another thing: don't forget that his voice was perfectly familiar to Benson. If there had been the slightest doubt about it, Benson would not have let him in, in view of his natural fear of housebreakers and with the captain's threat hanging over him."

"That's a tenable hypothesis. . . . What else?"

"The jewels, Markham—those orators of love. Have you thought of them? They were on the center table when Benson came home that night; and they were gone in the morning. Wherefore, it seems inev'table that the murderer took 'em—eh, what? . . . And may they not have been one reason for the murderer's coming there that night? If so, who of Benson's most intimate *personae gratae* knew of their presence in the house? And who wanted 'em particularly?"

"Exactly, Vance." Markham nodded his head slowly. "You've hit it. I've had an uneasy feeling about Pfyfe right along. I was on the point of ordering his arrest today when Heath brought word of Leacock's confession; and then, when that blew up, my suspicions reverted to him. I said nothing this afternoon because I wanted to see where your ideas had led you. What you've been saying checks up perfectly with my own notions. Pfyfe's our man——"

He brought the front legs of his chair down suddenly.

"And now, damn it, you've let him get away from us!"

"Don't fret, old dear," said Vance. "He's safe with Mrs. Pfyfe, I fancy. And anyhow, your friend, Mr. Ben Hanlon, is well versed in retrieving fugitives. . . . Let the harassed Leander alone for the moment. You don't need him tonight—and tomorrow you won't want him."

Markham wheeled about.

"What's that! I won't want him? . . . And why, pray?"

"Well," Vance explained indolently, "he hasn't a congenial and lovable nature, has he? And he's not exactly an object of blindin' beauty. I shouldn't want him around me more than was necess'ry, don't y' know. . . . Incidentally, he's not guilty."

Markham was too nonplussed to be exasperated. He regarded Vance searchingly for a full minute.

"I don't follow you," he said. "If you think Pfyfe's innocent, who, in God's name, do you think is guilty?"

Vance glanced at his watch.

"Come to my house tomorrow for breakfast and bring those alibis you asked Heath for; and I'll tell you who shot Benson."

Something in his tone impressed Markham. He realized that Vance would not have made so specific a promise unless he was confident of his ability to keep it. He knew Vance too well to ignore, or even minimize, his statement.

"Why not tell me now?" he asked.

"Awf'lly sorry, y' know," apologized Vance; "but I'm going to the Philharmonic's 'special' tonight. They're playing César Franck's D-Minor, and Stransky's temp'rament is em'nently suited to its diatonic sentimentalities. . . . You'd better come along, old man. Soothin' to the nerves and all that."

"Not me!" grumbled Markham. "What I need is a brandy-and-soda."

He walked down with us to the taxicab.

"Come at nine tomorrow," said Vance, as we took our seats. "Let the office wait a bit. And don't forget to phone Heath for those alibis."

Then, just as we started off, he leaned out of the car. "And I say, Markham: how tall would you say Mrs. Platz is?"

22

VANCE OUTLINES A THEORY

(*Thursday, June 20; 9 A.M.*)

MARKHAM CAME to Vance's apartment at promptly nine o'clock the next morning. He was in a bad humor.

"Now, see here, Vance," he said, as soon as he was seated at the table, "I want to know what was the meaning of your parting words last night."

"Eat your melon, old dear," said Vance. "It comes from northern Brazil and is very delicious. But don't devitalize its flavor with pepper or salt. An amazin' practice, that, though not as amazin' as stuffing a melon with ice cream. The American does the most dumbfoundin' things with ice cream. He puts it on pie; he puts it in soda water; he encases it in hard chocolate like a bonbon; he puts it between sweet biscuits and calls the result an ice cream sandwich; he even uses it instead of whipped cream in a Charlotte Russe. . . ."

"What I want to know——" began Markham; but Vance did not permit him to finish.

"It's surprisin', y' know, the erroneous ideas people have about melons. There are only two species, the muskmelon and the watermelon. All breakfast melons—like cantaloupes, citrons, nutmegs, Cassabas, and honeydews—are varieties of the muskmelon. But people have the notion, d' ye see, that cantaloupe is a generic term. Philadelphians call all melons cantaloupes; whereas this type of muskmelon was first cultivated in Cantalupo, Italy. . . ."

"Very interesting," said Markham, with only partly disguised impatience. "Did you intend by your remark last night——"

"And after the melon, Currie has prepared a special dish for you. It's my own gustat'ry *chef-d'œuvre*—with Currie's collaboration, of course. I've spent months on its conception—composing and organizing it, so to speak. I haven't named it yet; perhaps you can suggest a fitting appellation. . . . To achieve this dish, one first chops up a hard-boiled egg and mixes it with grated *Port du Salut* cheese, adding a soupçon of tarragon. This paste is then enclosed in a filet of white perch, like a French pancake. It is tied with silk, rolled in a specially prepared almond batter, and cooked in sweet butter. That, of course, is the barest outline of its manufacture, with all the truly exquisite details omitted."

"It sounds appetizing." Markham's tone was devoid of enthusiasm. "But I didn't come here for a cooking lesson."

"Y' know, you underestimate the importance of your ventral pleasures," pursued Vance. "Eating is the one infallible guide to a people's intellectual advancement, as well as the inev'table gauge of the individual's temp'rament. The savage cooked and ate like a savage. In the early days of the human race mankind was cursed with one vast epidemic of indigestion. There's where his devils and demons and ideas of hell came from: they were the nightmares of his dyspepsia. Then, as man began to master the technique of cooking, he became civilized; and when he achieved the highest pinnacles of the culin'ry art, he also achieved the highest pinnacles of cultural and intellectual glory. When the art of the gourmet retrogressed, so did man. The tasteless, standardized cookery of America is typical of our decadence. A perfectly blended soup, Markham, is more ennoblin' than Beethoven's C-Minor Symphony. . . ."

Markham listened stolidly to Vance's chatter during breakfast. He made several attempts to bring up the subject of the crime, but Vance glibly ignored each essay. It was not until Currie had cleared away the dishes that he referred to the object of Markham's visit.

"Did you bring the alibi reports?" was his first question.

Markham nodded. "And it took me two hours to find Heath after you'd gone last night."

"Sad," breathed Vance.

He went to the desk and took a closely written double sheet of foolscap from one of the compartments.

"I wish you'd glance this over and give me your learned opinion," he said, handing the paper to Markham. "I prepared it last night after the concert."

I later took possession of the document and filed it with my other notes and papers pertaining to the Benson case. The following is a verbatim copy:

HYPOTHESIS

Mrs. Anna Platz shot and killed Alvin Benson on the night of June 13th.

PLACE

She lived in the house and admitted being there at the time the shot was fired.

OPPORTUNITY

She was alone in the house with Benson.

All the windows were either barred or locked on the inside. The front door was locked. There was no other means of ingress.

Her presence in the living room was natural; she might have entered ostensibly to ask Benson a domestic question.

Her standing directly in front of him would not necessarily have caused him to look up. Hence, his reading attitude.

Who else could have come so close to him for the purpose of shooting him without attracting his attention?

He would not have cared how he appeared before his housekeeper. He had become accustomed to being seen by her without his teeth and toupee and in négligé condition.

Living in the house, she was able to choose a propitious moment for the crime.

TIME

She waited up for him. Despite her denial, he might have told her when he would return.

When he came in alone and changed to his smoking jacket, she knew he was not expecting any late visitors.

She chose a time shortly after his return because it would appear that he had brought someone home with him, and that this other person had killed him.

MEANS

She used Benson's own gun. Benson undoubtedly had more than one; for he would have been more likely to keep a gun in his bedroom than in his living room; and since a Smith and Wesson was found in the living room, there probably was another in the bedroom.

Being his housekeeper, she knew of the gun upstairs. After he had gone down to the living room to read, she secured it and took it with her, concealed under her apron.

She threw the gun away or hid it after the shooting. She had all night in which to dispose of it.

She was frightened when asked what firearms Benson kept about the house, for she was not sure whether or not we knew of the gun in the bedroom.

MOTIVE

She took the position of housekeeper because she feared Benson's conduct toward her daughter. She always listened when her daughter came to his house at night to work.

Recently she discovered that Benson had dishonorable intentions and believed her daughter to be in imminent danger.

A mother who would sacrifice herself for her daughter's future, as she has done, would not hesitate at killing to save her.

And there are the jewels. She has them hidden and is keeping them for her daughter. Would Benson have gone out and left them on the table? And if he had put them away, who but she, familiar with the house and having plenty of time, could have found them?

CONDUCT

She lied about St. Clair's coming to tea, explaining later that she knew St. Clair could not have had anything to do with the crime. Was this feminine intuition? No. She could know St. Clair was innocent only because she herself was guilty. She was too motherly to want an innocent person suspected.

She was markedly frightened yesterday when her daughter's name was mentioned, because she feared the discovery of the relationship might reveal her motive for shooting Benson.

She admitted hearing the shot, because, if she had denied it, a test might have proved that a shot in the living room would have sounded loudly in her room; and this would have aroused suspicion against her. Does a person, when awakened, turn on the lights and determine the exact hour? And if she had heard a report which sounded like a shot being fired in the house, would she not have investigated or given an alarm?

When first interviewed, she showed plainly she disliked Benson.

Her apprehension has been pronounced each time she has been questioned.

She is the hardheaded, shrewd, determined German type, who could both plan and perform such a crime.

HEIGHT

She is about five feet, ten inches tall—the demonstrated height of the murderer.

Markham read this précis through several times—he was fully fifteen minutes at the task—and when he had finished, he sat silent for ten minutes more. Then he rose and walked up and down the room.

"Not a fancy legal document, that," remarked Vance. "But I think even a grand juror could understand it. You, of course, can rearrange and elab'rate it, and bedeck it with innum'rable meaningless phrases and recondite legal idioms."

Markham did not answer at once. He paused by the French windows and looked down into the street. Then he said, "Yes, I think you've made out a case. . . . Extraordinary! I've wondered from the first what you were getting at; and your questioning of Platz yesterday impressed me as pointless. I'll admit it never occurred to me to suspect her. Benson must have given her good cause."

He turned and came slowly toward us, his head down, his hands behind him.

"I don't like the idea of arresting her. . . . Funny I never thought of her in connection with it."

He stopped in front of Vance.

"And you yourself didn't think of her at first, despite your boast that you knew who did it after you'd been in Benson's house five minutes."

Vance smiled mirthfully and sprawled in his chair.

Markham became indignant. "Damn it! You told me the next day that no woman could have done it, no matter what evidence was adduced, and harangued me about art and psychology and God knows what."

"Quite right," murmured Vance, still smiling. "No woman did it."

"No woman did it!" Markham's gorge was rising rapidly.

"Oh, dear no!"

He pointed to the sheet of paper in Markham's hand.

"That's just a bit of spoofing, don't y' know. . . . Poor old Mrs. Platz!—she's as innocent as a lamb."

Markham threw the paper on the table and sat down. I had never seen him so furious; but he controlled himself admirably.

"Y' see, my dear old bean," explained Vance, in his unemotional drawl, "I had an irresistible longing to demonstrate to you how utterly silly your circumst'ntial and material evidence is. I'm rather proud, y' know, of my case against Mrs. Platz. I'm sure you could convict her on the strength of it. But, like the whole theory of your exalted law, it's wholly specious and erroneous. . . . Circumst'ntial evidence, Markham, is the utt'rest tommyrot imag'nable. Its theory is not unlike that of our present-day democracy. The democratic theory is that if you accumulate enough ignorance at the polls, you produce intelligence; and the theory of circumst'ntial evidence is that if you accumulate a sufficient number of weak links, you produce a strong chain."

"Did you get me here this morning," demanded Markham coldly, "to give me a dissertation on legal theory?"

"Oh, no," Vance blithely assured him. "But I simply must prepare you for the acceptance of my revelation; for I haven't a scrap of material or circumst'ntial evidence against the guilty man. And yet, Markham, I know he's guilty as well as I know you're sitting in that chair planning how you can torture and kill me without being punished."

"If you have no evidence, how did you arrive at your conclusion?" Markham's tone was vindictive.

"Solely by psychological analysis—by what might be called the science of personal possibilities. A man's psychological nature is as clear a brand to one who can read it as was Hester Prynne's scarlet letter. . . . I never read Hawthorne, by the bye. I can't abide the New England temp'rament."

Markham set his jaw, and gave Vance a look of arctic ferocity.

"You expect me to go into court, I suppose, leading your victim by the arm, and say to the judge, 'Here's the man that shot Alvin Benson. I have no evidence against him, but I want you to sentence him to death because my brilliant and sagacious friend, Mr. Philo Vance, the inventor of stuffed perch, says this man has a wicked nature.' "

Vance gave an almost imperceptible shrug.

"I sha'n't wither away with grief if you don't even arrest the guilty man. But I thought it no more than humane to tell you who he was, if only to stop you from chivvying all these innocent people."

"All right—tell me, and let me get on about my business."

I don't believe there was any longer a question in Markham's mind that Vance actually knew who had killed Benson. But it was not until considerably later in the morning that he fully understood why Vance had kept him for days upon tenterhooks. When at last he did understand it, he forgave Vance; but at the moment he was angered to the limit of his control.

"There are one or two things that must be done before I can reveal the gentleman's name," Vance told him. "First, let me have a peep at those alibis."

Markham took from his pocket a sheaf of typewritten pages and passed them over.

Vance adjusted his monocle and read through them carefully. Then he stepped out of the room; and I heard him telephoning. When he returned, he reread the reports. One in particular he lingered over, as if weighing its possibilities.

"There's a chance, y' know," he murmured at length, gazing indecisively into the fireplace.

He glanced at the report again.

"I see here," he said, "that Colonel Ostrander, accompanied by a Bronx alderman named Moriarty, attended the Midnight Follies at the Piccadilly Theatre in Forty-seventh Street on the night of the thirteenth, arriving there a little before twelve and remaining through the performance, which was over about half past two A.M. . . . Are you acquainted with this particular alderman?"

Markham's eyes lifted sharply to the other's face. "I've met Mr. Moriarty. What about him?" I thought I detected a note of suppressed excitement in his voice.

"Where do Bronx aldermen loll about in the forenoons?" asked Vance.

"At home, I should say. Or possibly at the Samoset Club.... Sometimes they have business at City Hall."

"My word!—such unseemly activity for a politician!... Would you mind ascertaining if Mr. Moriarty is at home or at his club. If it's not too much bother, I'd like to have a brief word with him."

Markham gave Vance a penetrating gaze. Then, without a word, he went to the telephone in the den.

"Mr. Moriarty was at home, about to leave for City Hall," he announced on returning. "I asked him to drop by here on his way downtown."

"I do hope he doesn't disappoint us," sighed Vance. "But it's worth trying."

"Are you composing a charade?" asked Markham; but there was neither humor nor good nature in the question.

" 'Pon my word, old man, I'm not trying to confuse the main issue," said Vance. "Exert a little of that simple faith with which you are so gen'rously supplied—it's more desirable than Norman blood, y' know. I'll give you the guilty man before the morning's over. But, d' ye see, I must make sure that you'll accept him. These alibis are, I trust, going to prove most prof'table in paving the way for my *coup de boutoir*.... An alibi, as I recently confided to you, is a tricky and dang'rous thing, and open to grave suspicion. And the absence of an alibi means nothing at all. For instance, I see by these reports that Miss Hoffman has no alibi for the night of the thirteenth. She says she went to a motion picture theater and then home. But no one saw her at any time. She was prob'bly at Benson's visiting mama until late. Looks suspicious—eh, what? And yet, even if she was there, her only crime that night was filial affection.... On the other hand, there are several alibis here which are, as one says, cast iron—silly metaphor: cast iron's easily broken—and I happen to know one of 'em is spurious. So be a good fellow and have patience; for it's most necess'ry that these alibis be minutely inspected."

Fifteen minutes later Mr. Moriarty arrived. He was a serious, good-looking, well-dressed youth in his late twenties—not at all my idea of an alderman— and he spoke clear and precise English with almost no trace of the Bronx accent.

Markham introduced him and briefly explained why he had been requested to call.

"One of the men from the homicide bureau," answered Moriarty, "was asking me about the matter only yesterday."

"We have the report," said Vance, "but it's a bit too general. Will you tell us exactly what you did that night after you met Colonel Ostrander?"

"The colonel had invited me to dinner and the Follies. I met him at the Marseilles at ten. We had dinner there and went to the Picadilly a little before twelve, where we remained until about two thirty. I walked to the colonel's apartment with him, had a drink and a chat, and then took the subway home about three thirty."

"You told the detective yesterday you sat in a box at the theater."

"That's correct."

"Did you and the colonel remain in the box throughout the performance?"

"No. After the first act a friend of mine came to the box, and the colonel excused himself and went to the washroom. After the second act the colonel and I stepped outside into the alleyway and had a smoke."

"What time, would you say, was the first act over?"

"Twelve thirty or thereabouts."

"And where is this alleyway situated?" asked Vance. "As I recall, it runs along the side of the theater to the street."

"You're right."

"And isn't there an exit door very near the boxes, which leads into the alleyway?"

"There is. We used it that night."

"How long was the colonel gone after the first act?"

"A few minutes—I couldn't say exactly."

"Had he returned when the curtain went up on the second act?"

Moriarty reflected. "I don't believe he had. I think he came back a few minutes after the act began."

"Ten minutes?"

"I couldn't say. Certainly no more."

"Then, allowing for a ten-minute intermission, the colonel might have been away twenty minutes?"

"Yes—it's possible."

This ended the interview; and when Moriarty had gone, Vance lay back in his chair and smoked thoughtfully.

"Surprisin' luck!" he commented. "The Piccadilly Theatre, y' know, is practically round the corner from Benson's house. You grasp the possibilities of the situation, what? . . . The colonel invites an alderman to the Midnight Follies and gets box seats near an exit giving on an alley. At a little before half past twelve he leaves the box, sneaks out via the alley, goes to Benson's, taps and is admitted, shoots his man, and hurries back to the theater. Twenty minutes would have been ample."

Markham straightened up but made no comment.

"And now," continued Vance, "let's look at the indicat'ry circumst'nces and the confirmat'ry facts. . . . Miss St. Clair told us the colonel had lost heavily in a pool of Benson's manipulation and had accused him of crookedness. He hadn't spoken to Benson for a week; so it's plain there was bad blood between 'em. He saw Miss St. Clair at the Marseilles with Benson; and, knowing she always went home at midnight, he chose half past twenve as a propitious hour; although originally he may have intended to wait until much later, say, one thirty or two, before sneaking out of the theater. Being an army officer, he would have had a Colt forty-five, and he was probably a good shot. He was most anxious to have you arrest someone—he didn't seem to care who; and he even phoned you to inquire about it. He was one of the very few persons in the world whom Benson would have admitted, attired as he was. He'd known Benson int'mately for fifteen years, and Mrs. Platz once saw Benson take off his toupee and show it to him. Moreover, he would have known all about the domestic arrangements of the house; he no doubt had slept there many a time when showing his old pal the wonders of New York's night life. . . . How does all that appeal to you?"

Markham had risen and was pacing the floor, his eyes almost closed.

"So that was why you were so interested in the colonel—asking people if they knew him and inviting him to lunch? . . . What gave you the idea, in the first place, that he was guilty?"

"Guilty!" exclaimed Vance. "That priceless old dunderhead guilty! Really, Markham, the notion's prepost'rous. I'm sure he went to the washroom that night to comb his eyebrows and arrange his tie. Sitting, as he was, in a box, the gels on the stage could see him, y' know."

Markham halted abruptly. An ugly color crept into his cheeks, and his eyes blazed. But before he could speak, Vance went on, with serene indifference to his anger.

"And I played in the most astonishin' luck. Still, he's just the kind of ancient popinjay who'd go to the washroom and dandify himself—I rather counted on that, don't y' know. . . . My word! We've made amazin' progress this morning, despite your injured feelings. You now have five different people, any one of whom you can, with a little legal ingenuity, convict of the crime—in any event, you can get indictments against 'em."

He leaned his head back meditatively.

"First, there's Miss St. Clair. You were quite pos'tive she did the deed, and you told the major you were all ready to arrest her. My demonstration of the murderer's height could be thrown out on the grounds that it was intelligent and conclusive and therefore had no place in a court of law. I'm sure the judge would concur. Secondly, I give you Captain Leacock. I actu'lly had to use physical force to keep you from jailing the chap. You had a beautiful case against him—to say nothing of his delightful confession. And if you met with any diff'culties, he'd help you out; he'd adore having you convict him. Thirdly, I submit Leander the Lovely. You had a better case against him than against almost any one of the others—a perfect wealth of circumst'ntial evidence—an *embarras de richesse,* in fact. And any jury would delight in convicting him. I would, myself, if only for the way he dresses. Fourthly, I point with pride to Mrs. Platz. Another perfect circumst'ntial case, fairly bulging with clues and inf'rences and legal whatnots. Fifthly, I present the colonel. I have just rehearsed your case against him; and I could elab'rate it touchin'ly, given a little more time."

He paused and gave Markham a smile of cynical affability.

"Observe, please, that each member of this quintet meets all the demands of presumptive guilt: each one fulfills the legal requirements as to time, place, opportunity, means, motive, and conduct. The only drawback, d' ye see, is that all five are quite innocent. A most discomposin' fact, but there you are. . . . Now, if all the people against whom there's the slightest suspicion are innocent, what's to be done? . . . Annoyin', ain't it?"

He picked up the alibi reports.

"There's pos'tively nothing to be done but to go on checking up these alibis."

I could not imagine what goal he was trying to reach by these apparently irrelevant digressions; and Markham, too, was mystified. But neither of us doubted for a moment that there was method in his madness.

"Let's see," he mused. "The major's is the next in order. What do you say to tackling it? It shouldn't take long—he lives near here; and the entire alibi hinges on the evidence of the nightboy at his apartment house. Come!" He got up.

"How do you know the boy is there now?" objected Markham.

"I phoned a while ago and found out."

"But this is damned nonsense!"

Vance now had Markham by the arm, playfully urging him toward the door. "Oh, undoubtedly," he agreed. "But I've often told you, old dear, you take life much too seriously."

Markham, protesting vigorously, held back and endeavored to disengage his arm from the other's grip. But Vance was determined; and after a somewhat heated dispute, Markham gave in.

"I'm about through with this hocus-pocus," he growled, as we got into a taxicab.

"I'm through already," said Vance.

23

CHECKING AN ALIBI

(*Thursday, June 20; 10:30 A.M.*)

THE CHATHAM ARMS, where Major Benson lived, was a small exclusive bachelor apartment house in Forty-sixth Street, midway between Fifth and Sixth Avenues. The entrance, set in a simple and dignified façade, was flush with the street and only two steps above the pavement. The front door opened into a narrow hallway with a small reception room, like a cul-de-sac, on the left. At the rear could be seen the elevator; and beside it, tucked under a narrow flight of iron stairs which led round the elevator shaft, was a telephone switchboard.

When we arrived, two youths in uniform were on duty, one lounging in the door of the elevator, the other seated at the switchboard.

Vance halted Markham near the entrance.

"One of these boys, I was informed over the telephone, was on duty the night of the thirteenth. Find out which one it was and scare him into submission by your exalted title of District Attorney. Then turn him over to me."

Reluctantly Markham walked down the hallway. After a brief interrogation of the boys he led one of them into the reception room, and peremptorily explained what he wanted.*

Vance began his questioning with the confident air of one who has no doubt whatever as to another's exact knowledge.

"What time did Major Benson get home the night his brother was shot?"

The boy's eyes opened wide. "He came in about 'leven—right after show time," he answered, with only a momentary hesitation.

(I have set down the rest of the questions and answers in dramatic-dialogue form, for purposes of space economy.)

VANCE: He spoke to you, I suppose?

BOY: Yes, sir. He told me he'd been to the theater, and said what a rotten show it was—and that he had an awful headache.

---

* The boy was Jack Prisco, of 621 Kelly Street.

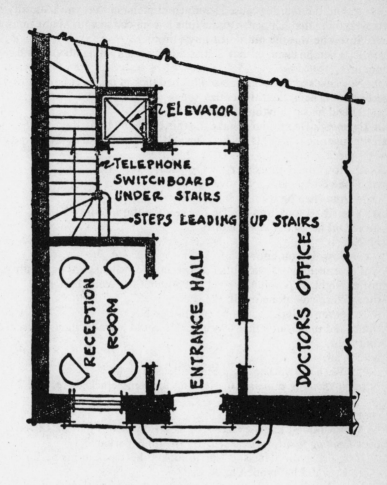

WEST 46TH. STREET

FIRST FLOOR OF CHATHAM ARMS APARTMENT IN
WEST FORTY-SIXTH STREET

VANCE: How do you happen to remember so well what he said a week ago?

BOY: Why, his brother was murdered that night!

VANCE: And the murder caused so much excitement that you naturally re-called everything that happened at the time in connection with Major Benson?

BOY: Sure—he was the murdered guy's brother.

VANCE: When he came in that night, did he say anything about the day of the month?

BOY: Nothin' except that he guessed his bad luck in pickin' a bum show was on account of it bein' the thirteenth.

VANCE: Did he say anything else?

BOY (grinning): He said he'd make the thirteenth my lucky day, and he gave me all the silver he had in his pocket—nickels and dimes and quarters and one fifty-cent piece.

VANCE: How much altogether?

BOY: Three dollars and forty-five cents.

VANCE: And then he went to his room?

BOY: Yes, sir—I took him up. He lives on the third floor.

VANCE: Did he go out again later?

BOY: No, sir.

VANCE: How do you know?

BOY: I'd've seen him. I was either answerin' the switchboard or runnin' the elevator all night. He couldn't've got out without my seein' him.

VANCE: Were you alone on duty?

BOY: After ten o'clock there's never but one boy on.

VANCE: And there's no other way a person could leave the house except by the front door?

BOY: No, sir.

VANCE: When did you next see Major Benson?

BOY (after thinking a moment): He rang for some cracked ice, and I took it up.

VANCE: What time?

BOY: Why—I don't know exactly. . . . Yes, I do! It was half past twelve.

VANCE (smiling faintly): He asked you the time, perhaps?

BOY: Yes, sir, he did. He asked me to look at his clock in his parlor.

VANCE: How did he happen to do that?

BOY: Well, I took up the ice, and he was in bed; and he asked me to put it in his pitcher in the parlor. When I was doin' it, he called me to look at the clock on the mantel and tell him what time it was. He said his watch had stopped and he wanted to set it.

VANCE: What did he say then?

BOY: Nothin' much. He told me not to ring his bell, no matter who called up. He said he wanted to sleep, and didn't want to be woke up.

VANCE: Was he emphatic about it?

BOY: Well—he meant it, all right.

VANCE: Did he say anything else?

BOY: No. He just said good night and turned out the light, and I came on downstairs.

VANCE: What light did he turn out?

BOY: The one in his bedroom.

VANCE: Could you see into his bedroom from the parlor?

BOY: No. The bedroom's off the hall.

VANCE: How could you tell the light was turned off then?

BOY: The bedroom door was open, and the light was shinin' into the hall.

VANCE: Did you pass the bedroom door when you went out?

BOY: Sure—you have to.

VANCE: And was the door still open?

BOY: Yes.

VANCE: Is that the only door to the bedroom?

BOY: Yes.

VANCE: Where was Major Benson when you entered the apartment?

BOY: In bed.

VANCE: How do you know?

BOY (*mildly indignant*): I saw him.

VANCE (*after a pause*): You're quite sure he didn't come downstairs again?

BOY: I told you I'd've seen him if he had.

VANCE: Couldn't he have walked down at some time when you had the elevator upstairs, without your seeing him?

BOY: Sure, he could. But I didn't take the elevator up after I'd took the major his cracked ice until around two thirty, when Mr. Montagu came in.

VANCE: You took no one up in the elevator, then, between the time you brought Major Benson the ice and when Mr. Montagu came in at two thirty?

BOY: Nobody.

VANCE: And you didn't leave the hall here between those hours?

BOY: No. I was sittin' here all the time.

VANCE: Then the last time you saw him was in bed at twelve thirty?

BOY: Yes—until early in the morning when some dame* phoned him and said his brother had been murdered. He came down and went out about ten minutes after.

VANCE (*giving the boy a dollar*): That's all. But don't you open your mouth to anyone about our being here, or you may find yourself in the lockup—understand? . . . Now, get back to your job.

When the boy had left us, Vance turned a pleading gaze upon Markham.

"Now, old man, for the protection of society, and the higher demands of justice, and the greatest good for the greatest number, and *pro bono publico,* and that sort of thing, you must once more adopt a course of conduct contr'ry to your innate promptings—or whatever the phrase you used. Vulgarly put, I want to snoop through the major's apartment at once."

"What for?" Markham's tone was one of exclamatory protest. "Have you completely lost your senses? There's no getting round the boy's testimony. I may be weakminded, but I know when a witness like that is telling the truth."

"Certainly, he's telling the truth," agreed Vance serenely. "That's just why I want to go up. Come, my Markham. There's no danger of the major returning *en surprise* at this hour. . . . And"—he smiled cajolingly—"you promised me every assistance, don't y' know."

Markham was vehement in his remonstrances, but Vance was equally ve-

---

* Obviously Mrs. Platz.

hement in his insistence; and a few minutes later we were trespassing, by means of a passkey, in Major Benson's apartment.

The only entrance was a door leading from the public hall into a narrow passageway which extended straight ahead into the living room at the rear. On the right of this passageway, near the entrance, was a door opening into the bedroom.

Vance walked directly back into the living room. On the right-hand wall was a fireplace and a mantel on which sat an old-fashioned mahogany clock. Near the mantel, in the far corner, stood a small table containing a silver ice-water service consisting of a pitcher and six goblets.

"There is our very convenient clock," said Vance. "And there is the pitcher in which the boy put the ice—imitation Sheffield plate."

Going to the window, he glanced down into the paved rear court twenty-five or thirty feet below.

"The major certainly couldn't have escaped through the window," he remarked.

He turned and stood a moment looking into the passageway.

"The boy could easily have seen the light go out in the bedroom, if the door was open. The reflection on the glazed white wall of the passage would have been quite brilliant."

Then, retracing his steps, he entered the bedroom. It contained a small canopied bed facing the door, and beside it stood a night table on which was an electric lamp. Sitting down on the edge of the bed, he looked about him and turned the lamp on and off by the socket chain. Presently he fixed his eyes on Markham.

"You see how the major got out without the boy's knowing it—eh, what?"

"By levitation, I suppose," submitted Markham.

"It amounted to that, at any rate," replied Vance. "Deuced ingenious, too. . . . Listen, Markham:—At half past twelve the major rang for cracked ice. The boy brought it, and when he entered, he looked in through the door, which was open, and saw the major in bed. The major told him to put the ice in the pitcher in the living room. The boy walked on down the passage and across the living room to the table in the corner. The major then called to him to learn the time by the clock on the mantel. The boy looked: it was half past twelve. The major replied that he was not to be disturbed again, said good night, turned off this light on this night table, jumped out of bed—he was dressed, of course—and stepped quickly out into the public hall before the boy had time to empty the ice and return to the passage. The major ran down the stairs and was in the street before the elevator descended. The boy, when he passed the bedroom door on his way out, could not have seen whether the major was still in bed or not, even if he had looked in, for the room was then in darkness.—Clever, what?"

"The thing would have been possible, of course," conceded Markham. "But your specious imaginings fail to account for his return."

"That was the simplest part of the scheme. He prob'bly waited in a doorway across the street for some other tenant to go in. The boy said a Mr. Montagu returned about two thirty. Then the major slipped in when he knew the elevator had ascended, and walked up the stairs."

Markham, smiling patiently, said nothing.

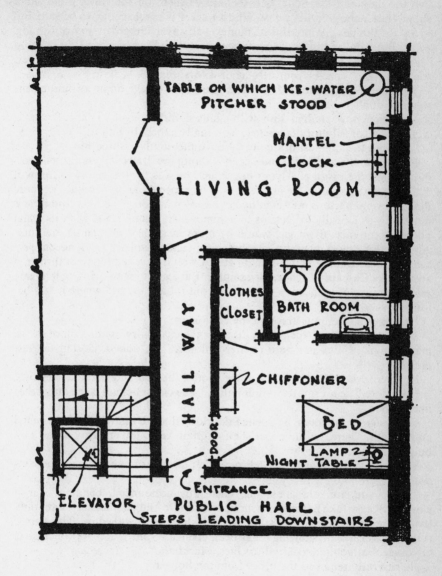

THIRD FLOOR OF CHATHAM ARMS APARTMENT IN
WEST FORTY-SIXTH STREET

"You perceived," continued Vance, "the pains taken by the major to establish the date and the hour, and to impress them on the boy's mind. Poor show—headache—unlucky day. Why unlucky? The thirteenth, to be sure. But lucky for the boy. A handful of money—all silver. Singular way of tipping, what? But a dollar bill might have been forgotten."

A shadow clouded Markham's face, but his voice was as indulgently impersonal as ever. "I prefer your case against Mrs. Platz."

"Ah, but I've not finished." Vance stood up. "I have hopes of finding the weapon, don't y' know."

Markham now studied him with amused incredulity. "That, of course, would be a contributory factor. . . . You really expect to find it?"

"Without the slightest diff'culty," Vance pleasantly assured him.

He went to the chiffonier and began opening the drawers. "Our absent host didn't leave the pistol at Alvin's house; and he was far too canny to throw it away. Being a major in the late war, he'd be expected to have such a weapon: in fact, several persons may actu'lly have known he possessed one. And if he is innocent—as he fully expects us to assume—why shouldn't it be in its usual place? Its absence, d' ye see, would be more incriminatin' than its presence. Also, there's a most int'restin' psychological factor involved. An innocent person who was afraid of being thought guilty, would have hidden it, or thrown it away—like Captain Leacock, for example. But a guilty man, wishing to create an appearance of innocence, would have put it back exactly where it was before the shooting."

He was still searching through the chiffonier.

"Our only problem, then, is to discover the custom'ry abiding place of the major's gun. . . . It's not here in the chiffonier," he added, closing the last drawer.

He opened a kit bag standing at the foot of the bed and rifled its contents.

"Nor here," he murmured indifferently. "The clothes closet is the only other likely place."

Going across the room, he opened the closet door. Unhurriedly he switched on the light. There, on the upper shelf, in plain view, lay an army belt with a bulging holster.

Vance lifted it with extreme delicacy and placed it on the bed near the window.

"There you are, old chap," he cheerfully announced, bending over it closely. "Please take particular note that the entire belt and holster—with only the exception of the holster's flap—is thickly coated with dust. The flap is comparatively clean, showing it has been opened recently. . . . Not conclusive, of course; but you're so partial to clues, Markham."

He carefully removed the pistol from the holster.

"Note, also, that the gun itself is innocent of dust. It has been recently cleaned, I surmise."

His next act was to insert a corner of his handkerchief into the barrel. Then, withdrawing it, he held it up.

"You see—eh, what? Even the inside of the barrel is immaculate. . . . And I'll wager all my Cézannes against an LL.B. degree that there isn't a cartridge missing."

He extracted the magazine and poured the cartridges onto the night table, where they lay in a neat row before us. There were seven—the full number for that style of gun.

"Again, Markham, I present you with one of your revered clues. Cartridges that remain in a magazine for a long time become slightly tarnished, for the catch plate is not airtight. But a fresh box of cartridges is well sealed, and its contents retain their luster much longer."

He pointed to the first cartridge that had rolled out of the magazine.

"Observe that this one cartridge—the last to be inserted into the magazine—is a bit brighter than its fellows. The inf'rence is—you're an adept at inf'rences, y' know—that it is a newer cartridge and was placed in the magazine rather recently."

He looked straight into Markham's eyes. "It was placed there to take the place of the one which Captain Hagedorn is keeping."

Markham lifted his head jerkily, as if shaking himself out of an encroaching spell of hypnosis. He smiled but with an effort.

"I still think your case against Mrs. Platz is your masterpiece."

"My picture of the major is merely blocked in," answered Vance. "The revealin' touches are to come. But first, a brief catechism:—How did the major know that brother Alvin would be home at twelve thirty on the night of the thirteenth?—He heard Alvin invite Miss St. Clair to dinner—remember Miss Hoffman's story of his eavesdropping?—and he also heard her say she'd unfailingly leave at midnight. When I said yesterday, after we had left Miss St. Clair, that something she told us would help convict the guilty person, I referred to her statement that midnight was her invariable hour of departure. The major therefore knew Alvin would be home about half past twelve, and he was pretty sure that no one else would be there. In any event, he could have waited for him, what? . . . Could he have secured an immediate audience with his brother *en déshabillé?*—Yes. He tapped on the window; his voice was recognized beyond any shadow of doubt; and he was admitted instanter. Alvin had no sartorial modesties in front of his brother and would have thought nothing of receiving him without his teeth and toupee. . . . Is the major the right height?—He is. I purposely stood beside him in your office the other day; and he is almost exactly five feet, ten and a half."

Markham sat staring silently at the disemboweled pistol. Vance had been speaking in a voice quite different from that he had used when constructing his hypothetical cases against the others; and Markham had sensed the change.

"We now come to the jewels," Vance was saying. "I once expressed the belief, you remember, that when we found the security for Pfyfe's note, we would put our hands on the murderer. I thought then the major had the jewels; and after Miss Hoffman told us of his requesting her not to mention the package, I was sure of it. Alvin took them home on the afternoon of the thirteenth, and the major undoubtedly knew it. This fact, I imagine, influenced his decision to end Alvin's life that night. He wanted those baubles, Markham."

He rose jauntily and stepped to the door.

"And now it remains only to find 'em. . . . The murderer took 'em away with him; they couldn't have left the house any other way. Therefore, they're in this apartment. If the major had taken them to the office, someone might have seen them; and if he had placed them in a safe deposit box, the clerk at the bank might have remembered the episode. Moreover, the same psychology that applied to the gun applies to the jewels. The major has acted throughout on the assumption of his innocence; and, as a matter of fact, the trinkets were safer here than elsewhere. There'd be time enough to dispose of them when the affair blew over.... Come with me a moment, Markham. It's painful, I know; and your heart's too weak for an anæsthetic."

Markham followed him down the passageway in a kind of daze. I felt a great sympathy for the man, for now there was no question that he knew Vance was serious in his demonstration of the major's guilt. Indeed, I have always felt that Markham suspected the true purpose of Vance's request to investigate the major's alibi, and that his opposition was due as much to his fear of the results as to his impatience with the other's irritating methods. Not that he would have balked ultimately at the truth, despite his long friendship for Major Benson; but he was struggling—as I see it now—with the inevitability of circumstances, hoping against hope that he had read Vance incorrectly and that, by vigorously contesting each step of the way, he might alter the very shape of destiny itself.

Vance led the way to the living room and stood for five minutes inspecting the various pieces of furniture, while Markham remained in the doorway watching him through narrowed lids, his hands crowded deep into his pockets.

"We could, of course, have an expert searcher rake the apartment over inch by inch," observed Vance. "But I don't think it necess'ry. The major's a bold, cunning soul. Witness his wide square forehead, the dominating stare of his globular eyes, the perpendicular spine, and the indrawn abdomen. He's forthright in all his mental operations. Like Poe's Minister D——, he would recognize the futility of painstakingly secreting the jewels in some obscure corner. And anyhow, he had no object in secreting them. He merely wished to hide 'em where there'd be no chance of their being seen. This naturally suggests a lock and key, what? There was no such cache in the bedroom—which is why I came here."

He walked to a squat rosewood desk in the corner, and tried all its drawers; but they were unlocked. He next tested the table drawer; but that, too, was unlocked. A small Spanish cabinet by the window proved equally disappointing.

"Markham, I simply must find a locked drawer," he said.

He inspected the room again and was about to return to the bedroom when his eye fell on a Circassian-walnut humidor half hidden by a pile of magazines on the undershelf of the center table. He stopped abruptly and, going quickly to the box, endeavored to lift the top. It was locked.

"Let's see," he mused: "what does the major smoke? Romeo y Julieta Perfeccionados, I believe—but they're not sufficiently valuable to keep under lock and key."

He picked up a strong bronze paper knife lying on the table and forced its point into the crevice of the humidor just above the lock.

"You can't do that!" cried Markham; and there was as much pain as reprimand in his voice.

Before he could reach Vance, however, there was a sharp click, and the lid flew open. Inside was a blue velvet jewel case.

"Ah! 'Dumb jewels more quick than words,' " said Vance, stepping back.

Markham stood staring into the humidor with an expression of tragic distress. Then slowly he turned and sank heavily into a chair.

"Good God!" he murmured. "I don't know what to believe."

"In that respect," returned Vance, "you're in the same disheartenin' predic'ment as all the philosophers. But you were ready enough, don't y' know, to believe in the guilt of half a dozen innocent people. Why should you gag at the major, who actu'lly is guilty?"

His tone was contemptuous, but a curious, inscrutable look in his eyes belied his voice; and I remembered that, although these two men were welded in an indissoluble friendship, I had never heard a word of sentiment, or even sympathy, pass between them.

Markham had leaned forward in an attitude of hopelessness, elbows on knees, his head in his hands.

"But the motive!" he urged. "A man doesn't shoot his brother for a handful of jewels."

"Certainly not," agreed Vance. "The jewels were a mere addendum. There was a vital motive—rest assured. And, I fancy, when you get your report from the expert accountant, all—or at least a goodly part—will be revealed."

"So that was why you wanted his books examined?"

Markham stood up resolutely. "Come. I'm going to see this thing through."

Vance did not move at once. He was intently studying a small antique candlestick of oriental design on the mantel.

"I say!" he muttered. "That's a dev'lish fine copy!"

24

THE ARREST

(Thursday, June 20; noon.)

ON LEAVING the apartment, Markham took with him the pistol and the case of jewels. In the drug store at the corner of Sixth Avenue he telephoned Heath to meet him immediately at the office and to bring Captain Hagedorn. He also telephoned Stitt, the public accountant, to report as soon as possible.

"You observe, I trust," said Vance, when we were in the taxicab headed for the Criminal Courts Building, "the great advantage of my methods over yours. When one knows at the outset who committed a crime, one isn't misled by appearances. Without that foreknowledge, one is apt to be deceived by a clever alibi, for example. . . . I asked you to secure the alibis because, knowing the major was guilty, I thought he'd have prepared a good one."

"But why ask for all of them? And why waste time trying to disprove Colonel Ostrander's?"

"What chance would I have had of securing the major's alibi if I had not injected his name surreptitiously, as it were, into a list of other names? . . . And had I asked you to check the major's alibi first, you'd have refused. I chose the colonel's alibi to start with because it seemed to offer a loophole—and I was lucky in the choice. I knew that if I could puncture one of the other alibis, you would be more inclined to help me test the major's."

"But if, as you say, you knew from the first that the major was guilty, why, in God's name, didn't you tell me, and save me this week of anxiety?"

"Don't be ingenuous, old man," returned Vance. "If I had accused the major at the beginning, you'd have had me arrested for *scandalum magnatum* and criminal libel. It was only by deceivin' you every minute about the major's guilt, and drawing a whole school of red herrings across the trail, that I was able to get you to accept the fact even today. And yet, not once did I actu'lly lie to you. I was constantly throwing out suggestions, and pointing to significant facts, in the hope that you'd see the light for yourself; but you ignored all my intimations, or else misinterpreted them, with the most irritatin' perversity."

Markham was silent a moment. "I see what you mean. But why did you keep setting up these straw men and then knocking them over?"

"You were bound, body and soul, to circumst'ntial evidence," Vance pointed out. "It was only by letting you see that it led you nowhere that I was able to foist the major on you. There was no evidence against him—he naturally saw to that. No one even regarded him as a possibility: fratricide has been held as inconceivable—a *lusus naturae*—since the days of Cain. Even with all my finessing you fought every inch of the way, objectin' to this and that, and doing everything imag'nable to thwart my humble efforts . . . Admit, like a good fellow, that, had it not been for my assiduousness, the major would never have been suspected."

Markham nodded slowly.

"And yet, there are some things I don't understand even now. Why, for instance, should he have objected so strenuously to my arresting the captain?"

Vance wagged his head.

"How deuced obvious you are! Never attempt a crime, my Markham, you'd be instantly apprehended. I say, can't you see how much more impregnable the major's position would be if he showed no int'rest in your arrests—if, indeed, he appeared actu'lly to protest against your incarc'ration of a victim. Could he, by any other means, have elim'nated so completely all possible suspicion against himself? Moreover, he knew very well that nothing he could say would swerve you from your course. You're so noble, don't y' know."

"But he did give me the impression once or twice that he thought Miss St. Clair was guilty."

"Ah! There you have a shrewd intelligence taking advantage of an opportunity. The major unquestionably planned the crime so as to cast suspicion on the captain. Leacock had publicly threatened his brother in connection with Miss St. Clair; and the lady was about to dine alone with Alvin. When, in the morning, Alvin was found shot with an army Colt, who but the captain would be suspected? The major knew the captain lived alone, and that he would have diff'culty in establishing an alibi. Do you now see how cunning he was in recommending Pfyfe as a source of information? He knew that if you interviewed Pfyfe, you'd hear of the threat. And don't ignore the fact that his suggestion of Pfyfe was an apparent afterthought; he wanted to make it appear casual, don't y' know.—Astute devil, what?"

Markham, sunk in gloom, was listening closely.

"Now for the opportunity of which he took advantage," continued Vance. "When you upset his calculations by telling him you knew whom Alvin dined with, and that you had almost enough evidence to ask for an indictment, the idea appealed to him. He knew no charmin' lady could ever be convicted of murder in this most chivalrous city, no matter what the evidence; and he had enough of the sporting instinct in him to prefer that no one should actu'lly be punished for the crime. Cons'quently, he was willing to switch you back to the lady. And he played his hand cleverly, making it appear that he was most reluctant to involve her."

"Was that why, when you wanted me to examine his books and to ask him to the office to discuss the confession, you told me to intimate that I had Miss St. Clair in mind?"

"Exactly!"

"And the person the major was shielding——"

"Was himself. But he wanted you to think it was Miss St. Clair."

"If you were certain he was guilty, why did you bring Colonel Ostrander into the case?"

"In the hope that he could supply us with faggots for the major's funeral pyre. I knew he was acquainted intimately with Alvin Benson and his entire camarilla; and I knew, too, that he was an egregious quidnunc who might have got wind of some enmity between the Benson boys and have suspected the truth. And I also wanted to get a line on Pfyfe, by way of elim'nating every remote counterpossibility."

"But we already had a line on Pfyfe."

"Oh, I don't mean material clues. I wanted to learn about Pfyfe's nature—his psychology, y' know—particularly his personality as a gambler. Y' see, it was the crime of a calculating, cold-blooded gambler; and no one but a man of that particular type could possibly have committed it."

Markham apparently was not interested just now in Vance's theories.

"Did you believe the major," he asked, "when he said his brother had lied to him about the presence of the jewels in the safe?"

"The wily Alvin prob'bly never mentioned 'em to Anthony," rejoined Vance. "An ear at the door during one of Pfyfe's visits was, I fancy, his source of information. . . . And speaking of the major's eavesdropping, it was that which suggested to me a possible motive for the crime. Your man Stitt, I hope, will clarify that point."

"According to your theory, the crime was rather hastily conceived." Markham's statement was in reality a question.

"The details of its execution were hastily conceived," corrected Vance. "The major undoubtedly had been contemplating for some time elim'nating his brother. Just how or when he was to do it he hadn't decided. He may have thought out and rejected a dozen plans. Then, on the thirteenth, came the opportunity: all the conditions adjusted themselves to his purpose. He heard Miss St. Clair's promise to go to dinner; and he therefore knew that Alvin would prob'bly be home alone at twelve thirty, and that, if he were done away with at that hour, suspicion would fall on Captain Leacock. He saw Alvin take home the jewels—another prov'dential circumst'nce. The propitious moment for which he had been waiting, d' ye see, was at hand. All that remained was to establish an alibi and work out a *modus operandi*. How he did this, I've already eluc'dated."

Markham sat thinking for several minutes. At last he lifted his head.

"You've about convinced me of his guilt," he admitted. "But damn it, man! I've got to prove it; and there's not much actual legal evidence."

Vance gave a slight shrug.

"I'm not int'rested in your stupid courts and your silly rules of evidence. But, since I've convinced you, you can't charge me with not having met your challenge, don't y' know."

"I suppose not," Markham assented gloomily.

Slowly the muscles about his mouth tightened.

"You've done your share, Vance, I'll carry on."

Heath and Captain Hagedorn were waiting when we arrived at the office, and Markham greeted them in his customary reserved, matter-of-fact way. By now he had himself well in hand and he went about the task before him with the somber forcefulness that characterized him in the discharge of all his duties.

"I think we at last have the right man, Sergeant," he said. "Sit down, and I'll go over the matter with you in a moment. There are one or two things I want to attend to first."

He handed Major Benson's pistol to the firearms expert.

"Look that gun over, Captain, and tell me if there's any way of identifying it as the weapon that killed Benson."

Hagedorn moved ponderously to the window. Laying the pistol on the sill, he took several tools from the pockets of his voluminous coat and placed them beside the weapon. Then, adjusting a jeweler's magnifying glass to his eye, he began what seemed an interminable series of tinkerings. He opened the plates of the stock and, drawing back the sear, took out the firing pin. He removed the slide, unscrewed the link, and extracted the recoil spring. I thought he was going to take the weapon entirely apart, but apparently he merely wanted to let light into the barrel; for presently he held the gun to the window and placed his eye at the muzzle. He peered into the barrel for nearly five minutes, moving it slightly back and forth to catch the reflection of the sun on different points of the interior.

At last, without a word, he slowly and painstakingly went through the operation of redintegrating the weapon. Then he lumbered back to his chair and sat blinking heavily for several moments.

"I'll tell you," he said, thrusting his head forward and gazing at Markham over the tops of his steel-rimmed spectacles. "This, now, may be the right gun. I wouldn't say for sure. But when I saw the bullet the other morning, I noticed some peculiar rifling marks on it; and the rifling in this gun here looks to me as though it would match up with the marks on the bullet. I'm not certain. I'd like to look at this barrel through my helixometer.*"

"But you believe it's the gun?" insisted Markham.

"I couldn't say, but I think so. I might be wrong."

"Very good, Captain. Take it along and call me the minute you've inspected it thoroughly."

"It's the gun, all right," asserted Heath, when Hagedorn had gone. "I know

---

* A helixometer, I learned later, is an instrument that makes it possible to examine every portion of the inside of a gun's barrel through a microscope.

that bird. He wouldn't've said as much as he did if he hadn't been sure. . . .
Whose gun is it, sir?"

"I'll answer you presently." Markham was still battling against the truth—
withholding, even from himself, his pronouncement of the major's guilt until
every loophole of doubt should be closed. "I want to hear from Stitt before I
say anything. I sent him to look over Benson and Benson's books. He'll be
here any moment."

After a wait of a quarter of an hour, during which time Markham attempted
to busy himself with other matters, Stitt came in. He said a somber good-
morning to the district attorney and Heath; then, catching sight of Vance,
smiled appreciatively.

"That was a good tip you gave me. You had the dope. If you'd kept Major
Benson away longer, I could have done more. While he was there he was
watching me every minute."

"I did the best I could," sighed Vance. He turned to Markham. "Y' know, I
was wondering all through lunch yesterday how I could remove the major
from his office during Mr. Stitt's investigation; and when we learned of Leacock's confession, it gave me just the excuse I needed. I really didn't want the
major here—I simply wished to give Mr. Stitt a free hand."

"What did you find out?" Markham asked the accountant.

"Plenty!" was the laconic reply.

He took a sheet of paper from his pocket and placed it on the desk.

"There's a brief report. . . . I followed Mr. Vance's suggestion and took a
look at the stock record and the cashier's collateral blotter, and traced the
transfer receipts. I ignored the journal entries against the ledger, and concentrated on the activities of the firm heads. Major Benson, I found, has been
consistently hypothecating securities transferred to him as collateral for marginal trading, and has been speculating steadily in mercantile curb stocks. He
has lost heavily—how much, I can't say."

"And Alvin Benson?" asked Vance.

"He was up to the same tricks. But he played in luck. He made a wad on a
Columbus Motors pool a few weeks back; and he has been salting the money
away in his safe—or, at least, that's what the secretary told me."

"And if Major Benson has possession of the key to that safe," suggested
Vance, "then it's lucky for him his brother was shot."

"Lucky?" retorted Stitt. "It'll save him from state prison."

When the accountant had gone, Markham sat like a man of stone, his eyes
fixed on the wall opposite. Another straw at which he had grasped in his instinctive denial of the major's guilt had been snatched from him.

The telephone rang. Slowly he took up the receiver, and as he listened I saw
a look of complete resignation come into his eyes. He leaned back in his chair,
like a man exhausted.

"It was Hagedorn," he said. "That was the right gun."

Then he drew himself up and turned to Heath. "The owner of that gun,
Sergeant, was Major Benson."

The detective whistled softly and his eyes opened slightly with astonishment. But gradually his face assumed its habitual stolidity of expression.
"Well, it don't surprise me any," he said.

Markham rang for Swacker.

"Get Major Benson on the wire and tell him—tell him I'm about to make an arrest and would appreciate his coming here immediately." His deputizing of the telephone call to Swacker was understood by all of us, I think.

Markham then summarized, for Heath's benefit, the case against the major. When he had finished, he rose and rearranged the chairs at the table in front of his desk.

"When Major Benson comes, Sergeant," he said, "I am going to seat him here." He indicated a chair directly facing his own. "I want you to sit at his right; and you'd better get Phelps—or one of the other men, if he isn't in—to sit at his left. But you're not to make any move until I give the signal. Then you can arrest him."

When Heath had returned with Phelps and they had taken their seats at the table, Vance said, "I'd advise you, Sergeant, to be on your guard. The minute the major knows he's in for it, he'll go bald-headed for you."

Heath smiled with heavy contempt.

"This isn't the first man I've arrested, Mr. Vance—with many thanks for your advice. And what's more, the major isn't that kind; he's too nervy."

"Have it your own way," replied Vance indifferently. "But I've warned you. The major is cool-headed; he'd take big chances and he could lose his last dollar without turning a hair. But when he is finally cornered and sees ultimate defeat, all his repressions of a lifetime, having had no safety valve, will explode physically. When a man lives without passions or emotions or enthusiasms, there's bound to be an outlet sometime. Some men explode and some commit suicide—the principle is the same: it's a matter of psychological reaction. The major isn't the self-destructive type—that's why I say he'll blow up."

Heath snorted. "We may be short on psychology down here," he rejoined, "but we know human nature pretty well."

Vance stifled a yawn and carelessly lit a cigarette. I noticed, however, that he pushed his chair back a little from the end of the table where he and I were sitting.

"Well, Chief," rasped Phelps, "I guess your troubles are about over—though I sure did think that fellow Leacock was your man. . . . Who got the dope on this Major Benson?"

"Sergeant Heath and the homicide bureau will receive entire credit for the work," said Markham; and added, "I'm sorry, Phelps, but the district attorney's office, and everyone connected with it, will be kept out of it altogether."

"Oh, well, it's all in a lifetime," observed Phelps philosophically.

We sat in strained silence until the major arrived. Markham smoked abstractedly. He glanced several times over the sheet of notations left by Stitt and once he went to the water cooler for a drink. Vance opened at random a law book before him and perused with an amused smile a bribery case decision by a Western judge. Heath and Phelps, habituated to waiting, scarcely moved.

When Major Benson entered Markham greeted him with exaggerated casualness and busied himself with some papers in a drawer to avoid shaking hands. Heath, however, was almost jovial. He drew out the major's chair for him and uttered a ponderous banality about the weather. Vance closed the law book and sat erect with his feet drawn back.

Major Benson was cordially dignified. He gave Markham a swift glance; but if he suspected anything, he showed no outward sign of it.

"Major, I want you to answer a few questions—if you care to." Markham's voice, though low, had in it a resonant quality.

"Anything at all," returned the other easily.

"You own an army pistol, do you not?"

"Yes—a Colt automatic," he replied, with a questioning lift of the eyebrows.

"When did you last clean and refill it?"

Not a muscle of the major's face moved. "I don't exactly remember," he said. "I've cleaned it several times. But it hasn't been refilled since I returned from overseas."

"Have you lent it to anyone recently?"

"Not that I recall."

Markham took up Stitt's report and looked at it a moment. "How did you hope to satisfy your clients if suddenly called upon for their marginal securities?"

The major's upper lip lifted contemptuously, exposing his teeth.

"So! That was why, under the guise of friendship, you sent a man to look over my books!" I saw a red blotch of color appear on the back of his neck and swell upward to his ears.

"It happens that I didn't send him there for that purpose." The accusation had cut Markham. "But I did enter your apartment this morning."

"You're a housebreaker, too, are you?" The man's face was now crimson; the veins stood out on his forehead.

"And I found Mrs. Banning's jewels. . . . How did they get there, Major?"

"It's none of your damned business how they got there," he said, his voice as cold and even as ever.

"Why did you tell Miss Hoffman not to mention them to me?"

"That's none of your damned business either."

"Is it any of my business," asked Markham quietly, "that the bullet which killed your brother was fired from your gun?"

The major looked at him steadily, his mouth a sneer.

"That's the kind of double-crossing you do!—invite me here to arrest me and then ask me questions to incriminate myself when I'm unaware of your suspicions. A fine dirty sport *you* are!"

Vance leaned forward. "You fool!" His voice was very low, but it cut like a whip. "Can't you see he's your friend and is asking you these questions in a last desp'rate hope that you're not guilty?"

The major swung round on him hotly. "Keep out of this—you damned sissy!"

"Oh, quite," murmured Vance.

"And as for *you*"—he pointed a quivering finger at Markham—"I'll make you sweat for this! . . ."

Vituperation and profanity poured from the man. His nostrils were expanded, his eyes blazing. His wrath seemed to surpass all human bounds; he was like a person in an apoplectic fit—contorted, repulsive, insensate.

Markham sat through it patiently, his head resting on his hands, his eyes closed. When, at length, the major's rage became inarticulate, he looked up and nodded to Heath. It was the signal the detective had been watching for.

But before Heath could make a move, the major sprang to his feet. With the motion of rising he swung his body swiftly about and brought his fist against

Heath's face with terrific impact. The sergeant went backward in his chair and lay on the floor dazed. Phelps leaped forward, crouching; but the major's knee shot upward and caught him in the lower abdomen. He sank to the floor, where he rolled back and forth groaning.

The major then turned on Markham. His eyes were glaring like a maniac's, and his lips were drawn back. His nostrils dilated with each stertorous breath. His shoulders were hunched, and his arms hung away from his body, his fingers rigidly flexed. His attitude was the embodiment of a terrific, uncontrolled malignity.

"You're next!" The words, guttural and venomous, were like a snarl.

As he spoke he sprang forward.

Vance, who had sat quietly during the melee, looking on with half-closed eyes and smoking indolently, now stepped sharply round the end of the table. His arms shot forward. With one hand he caught the major's right wrist; with the other he grasped the elbow. Then he seemed to fall back with a swift pivotal motion. The major's pinioned arm was twisted upward behind his shoulder blades. There was a cry of pain, and the man suddenly relaxed in Vance's grip.

By this time Heath had recovered. He scrambled quickly to his feet and stepped up. There was the click of handcuffs, and the major dropped heavily into a chair, where he sat moving his shoulder back and forth painfully.

"It's nothing serious," Vance told him. "The capsular ligament is torn a little. It'll be all right in a few days."

Heath came forward and, without a word, held out his hand to Vance. The action was at once an apology and a tribute. I liked Heath for it.

When he and his prisoner had gone, and Phelps had been assisted into an easy chair, Markham put his hand on Vance's arm.

"Let's get away," he said. "I'm done up."

25

VANCE EXPLAINS HIS METHODS

(*Thursday, June 20; 9 P.M.*)

THAT SAME evening, after a Turkish bath and dinner, Markham, grim and weary, and Vance, bland and debonair, and myself were sitting together in the alcove of the Stuyvesant Club's lounge room.

We had smoked in silence for half an hour or more, when Vance, as if giving articulation to his thoughts, remarked, "And it's stubborn, unimag'native chaps like Heath who constitute the human barrage between the criminal and society! . . . Sad, sad."

"We have no Napoleons today," Markham observed. "And if we had, they'd probably not be detectives."

"But even should they have yearnings toward that profession," said Vance, "they would be rejected on their physical measurements. As I understand it, your policemen are chosen by their height and weight; they must meet certain requirements as to heft—as though the only crimes they had to cope with were riots and gang feuds. Bulk—the great American ideal, whether in art, architecture, table d'hôte meals, or detectives. An entrancin' notion."

"At any rate, Heath has a generous nature," said Markham palliatingly. "He has completely forgiven you for everything."

Vance smiled. "The amount of credit and emulsification he received in the afternoon papers would have mellowed anyone. He should even forgive the major for hitting him. A clever blow, that, based on rotary leverage. Heath's constitution must be tough, or he wouldn't have recovered so quickly. . . . And poor Phelps! He'll have a horror of knees the rest of his life."

"You certainly guessed the major's reaction," said Markham. "I'm almost ready to grant there's something in your psychological flummery, after all. Your æsthetic deductions seemed to put you on the right track."

After a pause he turned and looked inquisitively at Vance. "Tell me exactly why, at the outset, you were convinced of the major's guilt?"

Vance settled back in his chair.

"Consider, for a moment, the characteristics—the outstanding features—of the crime. Just before the shot was fired, Benson and the murderer undoubtedly had been talking or arguing, the one seated, the other standing. Then Benson had pretended to read, he had said all he had to say. His reading was his gesture of finality; for one doesn't read when conversing with another unless for a purpose. The murderer, seeing the hopelessness of the situation and having come prepared to meet it heroically, took out a gun, aimed it at Benson's temple, and pulled the trigger. After that, he turned out the lights and went away. . . . Such are the facts indicated and actual."

He took several puffs on his cigarette.

"Now, let's analyze 'em. . . . As I pointed out to you, the murderer didn't fire at the body, where, though the chances of hitting would have been much greater, the chances of death would have been less. He chose the more diff'cult and hazardous—and, at the same time, the more certain and efficient—course. His technique, so to speak, was bold, direct, and fearless. Only a man with iron nerves and a highly developed gambler's instinct would have done it in just this forthright and audacious fashion. Therefore, all nervous, hotheaded, impulsive, or timid persons were automatically elim'nated as suspects. The neat, businesslike aspect of the crime, together with the absence of any material clues that could possibly have imcrim'nated the culprit, indicated unmistakably that it had been premeditated and planned with coolness and precision, by a person of tremendous self-assurance, and one used to taking risks. There was nothing subtle or in the least imag'native about the crime. Every feature of it pointed to an aggressive, blunt mind—a mind at once static, determined, and intrepid, and accustomed to dealing with facts and situations in a direct, concrete, and unequivocal manner. . . . I say, Markham, surely you're a good enough judge of human nature to read the indications, what?"

"I think I get the drift of your reasoning," the other admitted a little doubtfully.

"Very well, then," Vance continued. "Having determined the exact psychological nature of the deed, it only remained to find some int'rested person whose mind and temp'rament were such that if he undertook a task of this kind in the given circumst'nces, he would inev'tably do it in precisely the manner in which it was done. As it happened, I had known the major for a long time; and so it was obvious to me, the moment I had looked over the situation that first morning, that he had done it. The crime, in every respect and feature, was a perfect psychological expression of his character and mentality. But even had I not known him personally, I would have been able—since I possessed so clear and accurate a knowledge of the murderer's personality—to pick him out from any number of suspects."

"But suppose another person of the major's type had done it?" asked Markham.

"We all differ in our natures, however similar two persons may appear at times," Vance explained. "And while, in the present case, it is barely conceivable that another man of the major's type and temp'rament might have done it, the law of probability must be taken into account. Even supposing there were two men almost identical in personality and instincts in New York, what would be the chance of their both having had a reason to kill Benson? However, despite the remoteness of the possibility, when Pfyfe came into the case and I learned he was a gambler and a hunter, I took occasion to look into his qualifications. Not knowing him personally, I appealed to Colonel Ostrander for my information; and what he told me put Pfyfe at once *hors de propos.*"

"But he had nerve. He was a rash plunger; and he certainly had enough at stake," objected Markham.

"Ah! But between a rash plunger and a bold, levelheaded gambler like the major there is a great difference—a psychological abyss. In fact, their animating impulses are opposites. The plunger is actuated by fear and hope and desire; the cool-headed gambler is actuated by expediency and belief and judgment. The one is emotional, the other mental. The major, unlike Pfyfe, is a born gambler and inf'nitely self-confident. This kind of self-confidence, however, is not the same as recklessness, though superficially the two bear a close resemblance. It is based on an instinctive belief in one's own infallibility and safety. It's the reverse of what the Freudians call the inferiority complex—a form of egomania, a variety of *folie de grandeur.* The major possessed it, but it was absent from Pfyfe's composition; and as the crime indicated its possession by the perpetrator, I knew Pfyfe was innocent."

"I begin to grasp the thing in a nebulous sort of way," said Markham after a pause.

"But there were other indications, psychological and otherwise," Vance went on "—the undress attire of the body, the toupee and teeth upstairs, the inferred familiarity of the murderer with the domestic arrangements, the fact that he had been admitted by Benson himself, and his knowledge that Benson would be at home alone at that time—all pointing to the major as the guilty person. Another thing—the height of the murderer corresponded to the major's height. This indication, though, was of minor importance; for had my measurements not tallied with the major, I would have known that the bullet had been deflected, despite the opinions of all the Captain Hagedorns in the universe."

"Why were you so positive a woman couldn't have done it?"

"To begin with, it wasn't a woman's crime—that is, no woman would have done it in the way it was done. The most mentalized women are emotional when it comes to a fundamental issue like taking a life. That a woman could have coldly planned such a murder and then executed it with such business-like efficiency—aiming a single shot at her victim's temple at a distance of five or six feet—would be contr'ry, d' ye see, to everything we know of human nature. Again, women don't stand up to argue a point before a seated antagonist. Somehow they seem to feel more secure sitting down. They talk better sitting; whereas men talk better standing. And even had a woman stood before Benson, she could not have taken out a gun and aimed it without his looking up. A man's reaching in his pocket is a natural action; but a woman has no pockets and no place to hide a gun except her handbag. And a man is always on guard when an angry woman opens a handbag in front of him—the very uncertainty of women's natures has made men suspicious of their actions when aroused. . . . But—above all—it was Benson's bald pate and bedroom slippers that made the woman hypothesis untenable."

"You remarked a moment ago," said Markham, "that the murderer went there that night prepared to take heroic measures if necessary. And yet you say he planned the murder."

"True. The two statements don't conflict, y' know. The murder was planned—without doubt. But the major was willing to give his victim a last chance to save his life. My theory is this: The major, being in a tight financial hole with state prison looming before him, and knowing that his brother had sufficient funds in the safe to save him, plotted the crime and went to the house that night prepared to commit it. First, however, he told his brother of his predic'ment and asked for the money; and Alvin prob'bly told him to go to the devil. The major may even have pleaded a bit in order to avoid killing him; but when the liter'ry Alvin turned to reading, he saw the futility of appealing further, and proceeded with the dire business."

Markham smoked awhile.

"Granting all you've said," he remarked at length, "I still don't see how you could know, as you asserted this morning, that the major had planned the murder so as to throw suspicion deliberately on Captain Leacock."

"Just as a sculptor, who thoroughly understands the principles of form and composition, can accurately supply any missing integral part of a statue," Vance explained, "so can the psychologist who understands the human mind supply any missing factor in a given human action. I might add, parenthetically, that all this blather about the missing arms of the Aphrodite of Melos—the Milo Venus, y' know—is the utt'rest fiddle-faddle. Any competent artist who knew the laws of æsthetic organization could restore the arms exactly as they were originally. Such restorations are merely a matter of context—the missing factor, d' ye see, simply has to conform and harmonize with what is already known."

He made one of his rare gestures of delicate emphasis.

"Now, the problem of circumventing suspicion is an important detail in every deliberated crime. And since the general conception of this particular crime was pos'tive, conclusive, and concrete, it followed that each one of its component parts would be pos'tive, conclusive, and concrete. Therefore, for the major merely to have arranged things so that he himself should *not* be suspected would have been too negative a conception to fit consistently with the

other psychological aspects of the deed. It would have been too vague, too indirect, too indef'nite. The type of literal mind which conceived this crime
would logically have provided a specific and tangible object of suspicion.
Cons'quently, when the material evidence began to pile up against the captain, and the major waxed vehement in defending him, I knew he had been
chosen as the dupe. At first, I admit, I suspected the major of having selected
Miss St. Clair as the victim; but when I learned that the presence of her gloves
and handbag at Benson's was only an accident, and remembered that the
major had given us Pfyfe as a source of information about the captain's threat,
I realized that her projection into the role of murderer was unpremeditated."

A little later Markham rose and stretched himself.

"Well, Vance," he said, "your task is finished. Mine has just begun. And I
need sleep."

Before a week had passed, Major Anthony Benson was indicted for the
murder of his brother. His trial before Judge Rudolph Hansacker, as you remember, created a nationwide sensation. The Associated Press sent columns
daily to its members; and for weeks the front pages of the country's newspapers were emblazoned with spectacular reports of the proceedings. How the
district attorney's office won the case after a bitter struggle; how, because of
the indirect character of the evidence, the verdict was for murder in the second
degree; and how, after a retrial in the court of appeals, Anthony Benson finally received a sentence of from twenty years to life—all these facts are a
matter of official and public record.

Markham personally did not appear as public prosecutor. Having been a
lifelong friend of the defendant's, his position was an unenviable and difficult
one, and no word of criticism was directed against his assignment of the case
to Chief Assistant District Attorney Sullivan. Major Benson surrounded himself with an array of counsel such as is rarely seen in our criminal courts. Both
Blashfield and Bauer were among the attorneys for the defense—Blashfield
fulfilling the duties of the English solicitor, and Bauer acting as advocate.
They fought with every legal device at their disposal, but the accumulation of
evidence against their client overwhelmed them.

After Markham had been convinced of the major's guilt, he had made a
thorough examination of the business affairs of the two brothers and found
the situation even worse than had been indicated by Stitt's first report. The
firm's securities had been systematically appropriated for private speculations;
but whereas Alvin Benson had succeeded in covering himself and making a
large profit, the major had been almost completely wiped out by his invest-
ments. Markham was able to show that the major's only hope of replacing the
diverted securities and saving himself from criminal prosecution lay in Alvin
Benson's immediate death. It was also brought out at the trial that the major,
on the very day of the murder, had made emphatic promises which could have
been kept only in the event of his gaining access to his brother's safe. Furthermore, these promises had involved specific amounts in the other's possession;
and, in one instance, he had put up, on a forty-eight-hour note, a security already pledged—a fact which, in itself would have exposed his hand had his
brother lived.

Miss Hoffman was a helpful and intelligent witness for the prosecution. Her
knowledge of conditions at the Benson and Benson offices went far toward
strengthening the case against the major.

Mrs. Platz also testified to overhearing acrimonious arguments between the brothers. She stated that less than a fortnight before the murder the major, after an unsuccessful attempt to borrow $50,000 from Alvin, had threatened him, saying, "If I ever have to choose between your skin and mine, it won't be mine that'll suffer."

Theodore Montagu, the man who, according to the story of the elevator boy at the Chatham Arms, had returned at half past two on the night of the murder, testified that as his taxicab turned in front of the apartment house the headlights flashed on a man standing in a tradesmen's entrance across the street, and that the man looked like Major Benson. This evidence would have had little effect had not Pfyfe come forward after the arrest and admitted seeing the major crossing Sixth Avenue at Forty-sixth Street when he had walked to Pietro's for his drink of Haig and Haig. He explained that he had attached no importance to it at the time, thinking the major was merely returning home from some Broadway restaurant. He himself had not been seen by the major.

This testimony, in connection with Mr. Montagu's, annihilated the major's carefully planned alibi; and though the defense contended stubbornly that both witnesses had been mistaken in their identification, the jury was deeply impressed by the evidence, especially when Assistant District Attorney Sullivan, under Vance's tutoring, painstakingly explained, with diagrams, how the major could have gone out and returned that night without being seen by the boy.

It was also shown that the jewels could not have been taken from the scene of the crime except by the murderer; and Vance and I were called as witnesses to the finding of them in the major's apartment. Vance's demonstration of the height of the murderer was shown in court, but, curiously, it carried little weight, as the issue was confused by a mass of elaborate scientific objections. Captain Hagedorn's identification of the pistol was the most difficult obstacle with which the defense had to contend.

The trial lasted three weeks, and much evidence of a scandalous nature was taken, although, at Markham's suggestion, Sullivan did his best to minimize the private affairs of those innocent persons whose lives unfortunately touched upon the episode. Colonel Ostrander, however, has never forgiven Markham for not having had him called as a witness.

During the last week of the trial Miss Muriel St. Clair appeared as prima donna in a large Broadway light opera production which ran successfully for nearly two years. She has since married her chivalrous Captain Leacock, and they appear perfectly happy.

Pfyfe is still married and as elegant as ever. He visits New York regularly, despite the absence of his "dear old Alvin"; and I have occasionally seen him and Mrs. Banning together. Somehow, I shall always like that woman. Pfyfe raised the $10,000—how, I have no idea—and reclaimed her jewels. Their ownership, by the way, was not divulged at the trial, for which I was very glad.

On the evening of the day the verdict was brought in against the major, Vance and Markham and I were sitting in the Stuyvesant Club. We had dined together, but no word of the events of the past few weeks had passed between us. Presently, however, I saw an ironic smile creep slowly to Vance's lips.

"I say, Markham," he drawled, "what a grotesque spectacle the trial was! The real evidence, y' know, wasn't even introduced. Benson was convicted entirely on suppositions, presumptions, implications and inf'rences. . . . God help the innocent Daniel who inadvertently falls into a den of legal lions!"

Markham, to my surprise, nodded gravely.

"Yes," he concurred; "but if Sullivan had tried to get a conviction on your so-called psychological theories, he'd have been adjudged insane."

"Doubtless," sighed Vance. "You illuminati of the law would have little to do if you went about your business intelligently."

"Theoretically," replied Markham at length, "your theories are clear enough; but I'm afraid I've dealt too long with material facts to forsake them for psychology and art. . . . However," he added lightly, "if my legal evidence should fail me in the future, may I call on you for assistance?"

"I'm always at your service, old chap, don't y' know," Vance rejoined. "I rather fancy, though, that it's when your legal evidence is leading you irresistibly to your victim that you'll need me most, what?"

And the remark, though intended merely as a good-natured sally, proved strangely prophetic.

The "Canary" Murder Case

CHARACTERS OF THE BOOK

PHILO VANCE

JOHN F.-X. MARKHAM
    District Attorney of New York County

MARGARET ODELL (THE "CANARY")
    Famous Broadway beauty and ex-Follies girl, who was mysteriously murdered in her apartment

AMY GIBSON
    Margaret Odell's maid

CHARLES CLEAVER
    A man-about-town

KENNETH SPOTSWOODE
    A manufacturer

LOUIS MANNIX
    An importer

DR. AMBROISE LINDQUIST
    A fashionable neurologist

TONY SKEEL
    A professional burglar

WILLIAM ELMER JESSUP
    Telephone operator

HARRY SPIVELY
    Telephone operator

ALYS LA FOSSE
    A musical-comedy actress

WILEY ALLEN
    A gambler

POTTS
    A street cleaner

AMOS FEATHERGILL
    Assistant District Attorney

WILLIAM M. MORAN
    Commanding Officer of the Detective Bureau

ERNEST HEATH
    Sergeant of the Homicide Bureau

SNITKIN
: *Detective of the Homicide Bureau*

GUILFOYLE
: *Detective of the Homicide Bureau*

BURKE
: *Detective of the Homicide Bureau*

TRACY
: *Detective assigned to District Attorney's office*

DEPUTY INSPECTOR CONRAD BRENNER
: *Burglar-tools expert*

CAPTAIN DUBOIS
: *Fingerprint expert*

DETECTIVE BELLAMY
: *Fingerprint expert*

PETER QUACKENBUSH
: *Official photographer*

DR. DOREMUS
: *Medical examiner*

SWACKER
: *Secretary to the district attorney*

CURRIE
: *Vance's valet*

1

THE "CANARY"

IN THE offices of the Homicide Bureau of the Detective Division of the New York Police Department, on the third floor of the police headquarters building in Centre Street, there is a large steel filing cabinet; and within it, among thousands of others of its kind, there reposes a small green index card on which is typed: "ODELL, MARGARET. 184 West 71st Street. Sept. 10. Murder: Strangled about 11 P.M. Apartment ransacked. Jewelry stolen. Body found by Amy Gibson, maid."

Here, in a few commonplace words, is the bleak, unadorned statement of one of the most astonishing crimes in the police annals of this country—a crime so contradictory, so baffling, so ingenious, so unique, that for many days the best minds of the police department and the district attorney's office were completely at a loss as to even a method of approach. Each line of investigation only tended to prove that Margaret Odell could not possibly have been murdered. And yet, huddled on the great silken davenport in her living room lay the girl's strangled body, giving the lie to so grotesque a conclusion.

The true story of this crime, as it eventually came to light after a disheartening period of utter darkness and confusion, revealed many strange and bizarre ramifications, many dark recesses of man's unexplored nature, and the uncanny subtlety of a human mind sharpened by desperate and tragic despair. And it also revealed a hidden page of passional melodrama which, in its essence and organisms, was no less romantic and fascinating than that vivid, theatrical section of the *Comédie Humaine* which deals with the fabulous love of Baron Nucingen for Esther van Gobseck, and with the unhappy Torpille's tragic death.

Margaret Odell was a product of the bohemian demimonde of Broadway—a scintillant figure who seemed somehow to typify the gaudy and spurious romance of transient gaiety. For nearly two years before her death she had been the most conspicuous and, in a sense, popular figure of the city's night life. In our grandparents' day she might have had conferred upon her that somewhat questionable designation "the toast of the town"; but today there are too many

173

aspirants for this classification, too many cliques and violent schisms in the Lepidoptera of our cafe life, to permit of any one competitor being thus singled out. But, for all the darlings of both professional and lay press agents, Margaret Odell was a character of unquestioned fame in her little world.

Her notoriety was due in part to certain legendary tales of her affairs with one or two obscure potentates in the backwashes of Europe. She had spent two years abroad after her first success in *The Bretonne Maid*—a popular musical comedy in which she had been mysteriously raised from obscurity to the rank of "star"—and, one may cynically imagine, her press agent took full advantage of her absence to circulate vermilion tales of her conquests.

Her appearances went far toward sustaining her somewhat equivocal fame. There was no question that she was beautiful in a hard, slightly flamboyant way. I remember seeing her dancing one night at the Antlers Club—a famous rendezvous for postmidnight pleasure-seekers, run by the notorious Red Raegan.* She impressed me then as a girl of uncommon loveliness, despite the calculating, predatory cast of her features. She was of medium height, slender, graceful in a leonine way, and, I thought, a trifle aloof and even haughty in manner—a result, perhaps, of her reputed association with European royalty. She had the traditional courtesan's full, red lips, and the wide, mongoose eyes of Rossetti's "Blessed Damozel." There was in her face that strange combination of sensual promise and spiritual renunciation with which the painters of all ages have sought to endow their conceptions of the Eternal Magdalene. Hers was the type of face, voluptuous and with a hint of mystery, which rules man's emotions and, by subjugating his mind, drives him to desperate deeds.

Margaret Odell had received the sobriquet of Canary as a result of a part she had played in an elaborate ornithological ballet of the *Follies*, in which each girl had been gowned to represent a variety of bird. To her had fallen the role of canary; and her costume of white and yellow satin, together with her mass of shining golden hair and pink and white complexion, had distinguished her in the eyes of the spectators as a creature of outstanding charm. Before a fortnight had passed—so eulogistic were her press notices, and so unerringly did the audience single her out for applause—the "Bird Ballet" was changed to the "Canary Ballet," and Miss Odell was promoted to the rank of what might charitably be called *première danseuse,* at the same time having a solo waltz and a song† interpolated for the special display of her charms and talents.

She had quitted the *Follies* at the close of the season, and during her subsequent spectacular career in the haunts of Broadway's night life she had been popularly and familiarly called the Canary. Thus it happened that when her dead body was found, brutally strangled, in her apartment, the crime immediately became known, and was always thereafter referred to, as the Canary murder.

My own participation in the investigation of the Canary murder case—or rather my role of Boswellian spectator—constituted one of the most memorable experiences of my life. At the time of Margaret Odell's murder John F.-X. Markham was district attorney of New York, having taken office the preced-

* The Antlers Club has since been closed by the police; and Red Raegan is now serving a long term in Sing Sing for grand larceny.

† Written especially for her by B. G. De Sylva.

ing January. I need hardly remind you that during the four years of his incumbency he distinguished himself by his almost uncanny success as a criminal investigator. The praise which was constantly accorded him, however, was highly distasteful to him; for, being a man with a keen sense of honor, he instinctively shrank from accepting credit for achievements not wholly his own. The truth is that Markham played only a subsidiary part in the majority of his most famous criminal cases. The credit for their actual solution belonged to one of Markham's very close friends, who refused, at the time, to permit the facts to be made public.

This man was a young social aristocrat, whom, for purposes of anonymity, I have chosen to call Philo Vance.

Vance had many amazing gifts and capabilities. He was an art collector in a small way, a fine amateur pianist, and a profound student of æsthetics and psychology. Although an American, he had largely been educated in Europe, and still retained a slight English accent and intonation. He had a liberal independent income, and spent considerable time fulfilling the social obligations which devolved on him as a result of family connections; but he was neither an idler nor a dilettante. His manner was cynical and aloof; and those who met him only casually set him down as a snob. But knowing Vance, as I did, intimately, I was able to glimpse the real man beneath the surface indications; and I knew that his cynicism and aloofness, far from being a pose, sprang instinctively from a nature which was at once sensitive and solitary.

Vance was not yet thirty-five, and, in a cold, sculptural fashion, was impressively good-looking. His face was slender and mobile; but there was a stern, sardonic expression to his features, which acted as a barrier between him and his fellows. He was not emotionless, but his emotions were, in the main, intellectual. He was often criticized for his asceticism, yet I have seen him exhibit rare bursts of enthusiasm over an æsthetic or psychological problem. However, he gave the impression of remaining remote from all mundane matters; and, in truth, he looked upon life like a dispassionate and impersonal spectator at a play, secretly amused and debonairly cynical at the meaningless futility of it all. Withal, he had a mind avid for knowledge, and few details of the human comedy that came within his sphere of vision escaped him.

It was as a direct result of this intellectual inquisitiveness that he became actively, though unofficially, interested in Markham's criminal investigations.

I kept a fairly complete record of the cases in which Vance participated as a kind of *amicus curiae,* little thinking that I would ever be privileged to make them public; but Markham, after being defeated, as you remember, on a hopelessly split ticket at the next election, withdrew from politics; and last year Vance went abroad to live, declaring he would never return to America. As a result, I obtained permission from both of them to publish my notes in full. Vance stipulated only that I should not reveal his name; but otherwise no restrictions were placed upon me.

I have related elsewhere* the peculiar circumstances which led to Vance's participation in criminal research, and how, in the face of almost insuperable contradictory evidence, he solved the mysterious shooting of Alvin Benson. The present chronical deals with his solution of Margaret Odell's murder, which took place in the early fall of the same year, and which, you

* "The Benson Murder Case"

will recall, created an even greater sensation than its predecessor.*

A curious set of circumstances was accountable for the way in which Vance was shouldered with this new investigation. Markham for weeks had been badgered by the antiadministration newspapers for the signal failures of his office in obtaining convictions against certain underworld offenders whom the police had turned over to him for prosecution. As a result of prohibition a new and dangerous, and wholly undesirable, kind of night life had sprung up in New York. A large number of well-financed cabarets, calling themselves nightclubs, had made their appearance along Broadway and in its side streets; and already there had been an appalling number of serious crimes, both passional and monetary, which, it was said, had had their inception in these unsavory resorts.

At last, when a case of murder accompanying a holdup and jewel robbery in one of the family hotels uptown was traced directly to plans and preparations made in one of the nightclubs, and when two detectives of the Homicide Bureau investigating the case were found dead one morning in the neighborhood of the club, with bullet wounds in their backs, Markham decided to pigeonhole the other affairs of his office and take a hand personally in the intolerable criminal conditions that had arisen.†

2

FOOTPRINTS IN THE SNOW

(Sunday, September 9)

ON THE day following his decision, Markham and Vance and I were sitting in a secluded corner of the lounge room of the Stuyvesant Club. We often came together there, for we were all members of the club, and Markham frequently used it as a kind of unofficial uptown headquarters.‡

---

* The Loeb-Leopold crime, the Dorothy King case, and the Hall-Mills murder came later; but the Canary murder proved fully as conspicuous a case as the Nan Patterson-"Cæsar" Young affair, Durant's murder of Blanche Lamont and Minnie Williams in San Francisco, the Molineux arsenic-poisoning case, and the Carlyle Harris morphine murder. To find a parallel in point of public interest one must recall the Borden double-murder in Fall River, the Thaw case, the shooting of Elwell, and the Rosenthal murder.

† The case referred to here was that of Mrs. Elinor Quiggly, a wealthy widow living at the Adlon Hotel in West 96th Street. She was found on the morning of September 5 suffocated by a gag which had been placed on her by robbers who had evidently followed her home from the Club Turque—a small but luxurious all-night cafe at 89 West 48th Street. The killing of the two detectives, McQuade and Cannison, was, the police believe, due to the fact that they were in possession of incriminating evidence against the perpetrators of the crime. Jewelry amounting to over $50,000 was stolen from the Quiggly apartment.

‡ The Stuyvesant was a large club, somewhat in the nature of a glorified hotel; and its extensive membership was drawn largely from the political, legal, and financial ranks.

"It's bad enough to have half the people in this city under the impression that the district attorney's office is a kind of high-class collection agency," he remarked that night, "without being necessitated to turn detective because I'm not given sufficient evidence, or the right kind of evidence, with which to secure convictions."

Vance looked up with a slow smile and regarded him quizzically.

"The difficulty would seem to be," he returned, with an indolent drawl, "that the police, being unversed in the exquisite abracadabra of legal procedure, labor under the notion that evidence which would convince a man of ordin'ry intelligence, would also convince a court of law. A silly notion, don't y' know. Lawyers don't really want evidence; they want erudite technicalities. And the average policeman's brain is too forthright to cope with the pedantic demands of jurisprudence."

"It's not as bad as that," Markham retorted, with an attempt at good nature, although the strain of the past few weeks had tended to upset his habitual equanimity. "If there weren't rules of evidence, grave injustice would too often be done innocent persons. And even a criminal is entitled to protection in our courts."

Vance yawned mildly.

"Markham, you should have been a pedagogue. It's positively amazin' how you've mastered all the standard oratorical replies to criticism. And yet, I'm unconvinced. You remember the Wisconsin case of the kidnapped man whom the courts declared presumably dead. Even when he reappeared, hale and hearty, among his former neighbors, his status of being presumably dead was not legally altered. The visible and demonstrable fact that he was actually alive was regarded by the court as an immaterial and impertinent side issue.* . . . Then there's the touchin' situation—so prevalent in this fair country—of a man being insane in one state and sane in another. . . . Really, y' know, you can't expect a mere lay intelligence, unskilled in the benign processes of legal logic, to perceive such subtle nuances. Your layman, swaddled in the darkness of ordin'ry common sense, would say that a person who is a lunatic on one bank of a river would still be a lunatic if he was on the opposite bank. And he'd also hold—erroneously, no doubt—that if a man was living, he would presumably be alive."

"Why this academic dissertation?" asked Markham, this time a bit irritably.

"It seems to touch rather vitally on the source of your present predicament," Vance explained equably. "The police, not being lawyers, have apparently got you into hot water, what? . . . Why not start an agitation to send all detectives to law school?"

"You're a great help," retorted Markham.

Vance raised his eyebrows slightly.

"Why disparage my suggestion? Surely you must perceive that it has merit. A man without legal training, when he knows a thing to be true, ignores all incompetent testimony to the contr'ry, and clings to the facts. A court of law listens solemnly to a mass of worthless testimony, and renders a decision not on the facts but according to a complicated set of rules. The result, d' ye see, is that a court often acquits a prisoner, realizing full well that he is guilty. Many

* The case to which Vance referred, I ascertained later, was Shatterham v. Shatterham, 417 Mich., 79—a testamentary case.

a judge has said, in effect, to a culprit, 'I know, and the jury knows, that you committed the crime, but in view of the legally admissible evidence, I declare you innocent. Go and sin again.' "

Markham grunted. "I'd hardly endear myself to the people of this country if I answered the current strictures against me by recommending law courses for the police department."

"Permit me, then, to suggest the alternative of Shakespeare's butcher: 'Let's kill all the lawyers.' "

"Unfortunately, it's a situation, not a utopian theory, that has to be met."

"And just how," asked Vance lazily, "do you propose to reconcile the sensible conclusions of the police with what you touchingly call correctness of legal procedure?"

"To begin with," Markham informed him, "I've decided henceforth to do my own investigating of all important nightclub criminal cases. I called a conference of the heads of my departments yesterday, and from now on there's going to be some real activity radiating direct from my office. I intend to produce the kind of evidence I need for convictions."

Vance slowly took a cigarette from his case and tapped it on the arm of his chair. "Ah! So you are going to substitute the conviction of the innocent for the acquittal of the guilty?"

Markham was nettled; turning in his chair, he frowned at Vance. "I won't pretend not to understand your remark," he said acidulously. "You're back again on your favorite theme of the inadequacy of circumstantial evidence as compared with your psychological theories and æsthetic hypotheses."

"Quite so," agreed Vance carelessly. "Y' know, Markham, your sweet and charmin' faith in circumstantial evidence is positively disarming. Before it, the ordin'ry powers of ratiocination are benumbed. I tremble for the innocent victims you are about to gather into your legal net. You'll eventually make the mere attendance at any cabaret a frightful hazard."

Markham smoked awhile in silence. Despite the seeming bitterness at times in the discussions of these two men, there was at bottom no animosity in their attitude toward each other. Their friendship was of long standing, and, despite the dissimilarity of their temperaments and the marked difference in their points of view, a profound mutual respect formed the basis of their intimate relationship.

At length Markham spoke. "Why this sweeping deprecation of circumstantial evidence? I admit that at times it may be misleading; but it often forms powerful presumptive proof of guilt. Indeed, Vance, one of our greatest legal authorities has demonstrated that it is the most powerful actual evidence in existence. Direct evidence, in the very nature of crime, is almost always unavailable. If the courts had to depend on it, the great majority of criminals would still be at large."

"I was under the impression that this precious majority had always enjoyed its untrammeled freedom."

Markham ignored the interruption. "Take this example: A dozen adults see an animal running across the snow, and testify that it was a chicken; whereas a child sees the same animal, and declares it was a duck. They thereupon examine the animal's footprints and find them to be the webfooted tracks made by a duck. Is it not conclusive, then, that the animal was a duck and not a chicken, despite the preponderance of direct evidence?"

"I'll grant you your duck," acceded Vance indifferently.

"And having gratefully accepted the gift," pursued Markham, "I propound a corollary: A dozen adults see a human figure crossing the snow, and take oath it was a woman; whereas a child asserts that the figure was a man. Now, will you not also grant that the circumstantial evidence of a man's footprints in the snow would supply incontrovertible proof that it was, in fact, a man, and not a woman?"

"Not at all, my dear Justinian," replied Vance, stretching his legs languidly in front of him; "unless, of course, you could show that a human being possesses no higher order of brain than a duck."

"What have brains to do with it?" Markham asked impatiently. "Brains don't affect one's footprints."

"Not those of a duck, certainly. But brains might very well—and, no doubt, often do—affect the footprints of a human being."

"Am I having a lesson in anthropology, Darwinian adaptability, or merely metaphysical speculation?"

"In none of those abstruse subjects," Vance assured him. "I'm merely stating a simple fact culled from observation."

"Well, according to your highly and peculiarly developed processes of reasoning, would the circumstantial evidence of those masculine footprints indicate a man or a woman?"

"Not necessarily either," Vance answered, "or, rather, a possibility of each. Such evidence, when applied to a human being—to a creature, that is, with a reasoning mind—would merely mean to me that the figure crossing the snow was either a man in his own shoes or a woman in man's shoes; or perhaps, even, a long-legged child. In short, it would convey to my purely unlegal intelligence only that the tracks were made by some descendant of the *Pithecanthropus erectus* wearing men's shoes on his nether limbs—sex and age unknown. A duck's spoors, on the other hand, I might be tempted to take at their face value."

"I'm delighted to observe," said Markham, "that at least you repudiate the possibility of a duck dressing itself up in the gardener's boots."

Vance was silent for a moment; then he said, "The trouble with you modern Solons, d' ye see, is that you attempt to reduce human nature to a formula; whereas the truth is that man, like life, is infinitely complex. He's shrewd and tricky—skilled for centuries in all the most diabolical chicaneries. He is a creature of low cunning, who, even in the normal course of his vain and idiotic struggle for existence, instinctively and deliberately tells ninety-nine lies to one truth. A duck, not having had the heaven-kissing advantages of human civilization, is a straightforward and eminently honest bird."

"How," asked Markham, "since you jettison all the ordinary means of arriving at a conclusion, would you decide the sex or species of this person who left the masculine footprints in the snow?"

Vance blew a spiral of smoke toward the ceiling.

"First, I'd repudiate all the evidence of the twelve astigmatic adults and the one bright-eyed child. Next, I'd ignore the footprints in the snow. Then, with a mind unprejudiced by dubious testimony and uncluttered with material clues,

I'd determine the exact nature of the crime which this fleeing person had committed. After having analyzed its various factors, I could infallibly tell you not only whether the culprit was a man or a woman, but I could describe his habits, character, and personality. And I could do all this whether the fleeing figure left male or female or kangaroo tracks, or used stilts, or rode off on a velocipede, or levitated without leaving tracks at all."

Markham smiled broadly. "You'd be worse than the police in the matter of supplying me legal evidence, I fear."

"I, at least, wouldn't procure evidence against some unsuspecting person whose boots had been appropriated by the real culprit," retorted Vance. "And, y' know, Markham, as long as you pin your faith to footprints, you'll inevitably arrest just those persons whom the actual criminals want you to— namely, persons who have had nothing to do with the criminal conditions you're about to investigate."

He became suddenly serious.

"See here, old man; there are some shrewd intelligences at present allied with what the theologians call the powers of darkness. The surface appearances of many of these crimes that are worrying you are palpably deceptive. Personally, I don't put much stock in the theory that a malevolent gang of cutthroats have organized an American camorra and made the silly nightclubs their headquarters. The idea is too melodramatic. It smacks too much of the gaudy journalistic imagination; it's too Eugène Sue-ish. Crime isn't a mass instinct except during wartime, and then it's merely an obscene sport. Crime, d' ye see, is a personal and individual business. One doesn't make up a *partie carée* for a murder as one does for a bridge game. . . . Markham, old dear, don't let this romantic criminological idea lead you astray. And don't scrutinize the figurative footprints in the snow too closely. They'll confuse you most horribly—you're far too trustin' and literal for this wicked world. I warn you that no clever criminal is going to leave his own footprints for your tape measure and calipers."

He sighed deeply and gave Markham a look of bantering commiseration.

"And have you paused to consider that your first case may even be devoid of footprints? . . . Alas! What, then, will you do?"

"I could overcome that difficulty by taking you along with me," suggested Markham, with a touch of irony. "How would you like to accompany me on the next important case that breaks?"

"I am ravished by the idea," said Vance.

Two days later the front pages of our metropolitan press carried glaring headlines telling of the murder of Margaret Odell.

3

THE MURDER

(Tuesday, September 11; 8:30 A.M.)

It was barely half past eight on that momentous morning of September the 11th when Markham brought word to us of the event.

I was living temporarily with Vance at his home in East 38th Street—a large remodeled apartment occupying the two top floors of a beautiful mansion. For several years I had been Vance's personal legal representative and adviser, having resigned from my father's law firm of Van Dine, Davis, and Van Dine to devote myself to his needs and interests. His affairs were by no means voluminous, but his personal finances, together with his numerous purchases of paintings and *objets d'art,* occupied my full time without burdening me. This monetary and legal stewardship was eminently congenial to my tastes; and my friendship with Vance, which had dated from our undergraduate days at Harvard, supplied the social and human element in an arrangement which otherwise might easily have degenerated into one of mere drab routine.

On this particular morning I had risen early and was working in the library when Currie, Vance's valet and majordomo, announced Markham's presence in the living room. I was considerably astonished at this early morning visit, for Markham well knew that Vance, who rarely rose before noon, resented any intrusion upon his matutinal slumbers. And in that moment I received the curious impression that something unusual and portentous was toward.

I found Markham pacing restlessly up and down, his hat and gloves thrown carelessly on the center table. As I entered he halted and looked at me with harassed eyes. He was a moderately tall man, clean-shaven, gray-haired, and firmly set up. His appearance was distinguished, and his manner courteous and kindly. But beneath his gracious exterior there was an aggressive sternness, an indomitable, grim strength, that gave one the sense of dogged efficiency and untiring capability.

"Good morning, Van," he greeted me, with impatient perfunctoriness. "There's been another half-world murder—the worst and ugliest thus far. . . ." He hesitated and regarded me searchingly. "You recall my chat with Vance at the club the other night? There was something damned prophetic in his remarks. And you remember I half promised to take him along on the next important case. Well, the case has broken—with a vengeance. Margaret Odell, whom they called the Canary, has been strangled in her apartment; and from what I just got over the phone, it looks like another nightclub affair. I'm headed for the Odell apartment now. . . . What about rousing out the sybarite?"

"By all means," I agreed, with an alacrity which, I fear, was in large measure prompted by purely selfish motives. The Canary! If one had sought the city over for a victim whose murder would stir up excitement, there could have been but few selections better calculated to produce this result.

Hastening to the door, I summoned Currie and told him to call Vance at once.

181

"I'm afraid, sir——" began Currie, politely hesitant.

"Calm your fears," cut in Markham. "I'll take all responsibility for waking him at this indecent hour."

Currie sensed an emergency and departed.

A minute or two later Vance, in an elaborately embroidered silk kimono and sandals, appeared at the living room door.

"My word!" he greeted us, in mild astonishment, glancing at the clock. "Haven't you chaps gone to bed yet?"

He strolled to the mantel and selected a gold-tipped Régie cigarette from a small Florentine humidor.

Markham's eyes narrowed; he was in no mood for levity.

"The Canary has been murdered," I blurted out.

Vance held his wax vesta poised and gave me a look of indolent inquisitiveness. "Whose canary?"

"Margaret Odell was found strangled this morning," amended Markham brusquely. "Even *you,* wrapped in your scented cotton-wool, have heard of her. And you can realize the significance of the crime. I'm personally going to look for those footprints in the snow; and if you want to come along, as you intimated the other night, you'll have to get a move on."

Vance crushed out his cigarette.

"Margaret Odell, eh?—Broadway's blond Aspasia—or was it Phryne who had the *coiffure d'or?* . . . Most distressin'!" Despite his offhand manner, I could see he was deeply interested. "The base enemies of law and order are determined to chivvy you most horribly, aren't they, old dear? Deuced inconsiderate of 'em! . . . Excuse me while I seek habiliments suitable to the occasion."

He disappeared into his bedroom, while Markham took out a large cigar and resolutely prepared it for smoking, and I returned to the library to put away the papers on which I had been working.

In less than ten minutes Vance reappeared, dressed for the street.

"Bien, mon vieux," he announced gaily, as Currie handed him his hat and gloves and a malacca cane. *"Allons-y!"*

We rode uptown along Madison Avenue, turned into Central Park, and came out by the West 72d Street entrance. Margaret Odell's apartment was at 184 West 71st Street, near Broadway; and as we drew up to the curb, it was necessary for the patrolman on duty to make a passage for us through the crowd that had already gathered as a result of the arrival of the police.

Feathergill, an assistant district attorney, was waiting in the main hall for his chief's arrival.

"It's too bad, sir," he lamented. "A rotten show all round. And just at this time! . . ." He shrugged his shoulders discouragingly.

"It may collapse quickly," said Markham, shaking the other's hand. "How are things going? Sergeant Heath phoned me right after you called, and said that, at first glance, the case looked a bit stubborn."

"Stubborn?" repeated Feathergill lugubriously. "It's downright impervious. Heath is spinning round like a turbine. He was called off the Boyle case, by the way, to devote his talents to this new shocker. Inspector Moran arrived ten minutes ago and gave him the official imprimatur."

"Well, Heath's a good man," declared Markham. "We'll work it out. . . . Which is the apartment?"

Feathergill led the way to a door at the rear of the main hall. "Here you are, sir," he announced. "I'll be running along now. I need sleep. Good luck!" And he was gone.

It will be necessary to give a brief description of the house and its interior arrangement, for the somewhat peculiar structure of the building played a vital part in the seemingly insoluble problem posed by the murder.

The house, which was a four-story stone structure originally built as a residence, had been remodeled, both inside and outside, to meet the requirements of an exclusive individual apartment dwelling. There were, I believe, three or four separate suites on each floor; but the quarters upstairs need not concern us. The main floor was the scene of the crime, and here there were three apartments and a dentist's office.

The main entrance to the building was directly on the street, and extending straight back from the front door was a wide hallway. Directly at the rear of this hallway, and facing the entrance, was the door to the Odell apartment, which bore the numeral "3." About halfway down the front hall, on the right-hand side, was the stairway leading to the floors above; and directly beyond the stairway, also on the right, was a small reception room with a wide archway instead of a door. Directly opposite to the stairway, in a small recess, stood the telephone switchboard. There was no elevator in the house.

Another important feature of this ground-floor plan was a small passageway at the rear of the main hall and at right angles to it, which led past the front walls of the Odell apartment to a door opening on a court at the west side of the building. This court was connected with the street by an alley four feet wide.

In the accompanying diagram this arrangement of the ground floor can be easily visualized, and I suggest that the reader fix it in his mind; for I doubt if ever before so simple and obvious an architectural design played such an important part in a criminal mystery. By its very simplicity and almost conventional familiarity—indeed, by its total lack of any puzzling complications—it proved so baffling to the investigators that the case threatened, for many days, to remain forever insoluble.

As Markham entered the Odell apartment that morning Sergeant Ernest Heath came forward at once and extended his hand. A look of relief passed over his broad, pugnacious features and it was obvious that the animosity and rivalry which always exist between the detective division and the district attorney's office during the investigation of any criminal case had no place in his attitude on this occasion.

"I'm glad you've come, sir," he said, and meant it.

He then turned to Vance with a cordial smile, and held out his hand.*

"So the amachoor sleuth is with us again!" His tone held a friendly banter.

"Oh, quite," murmured Vance. "How's your induction coil working this beautiful September morning, Sergeant?"

"I'd hate to tell you!" Then Heath's face grew suddenly grave, and he turned to Markham. "It's a raw deal, sir. Why in hell couldn't they have picked someone besides the Canary for their dirty work? There's plenty of

---

* Heath had become acquainted with Vance during the investigation of the Benson murder case two months previously.

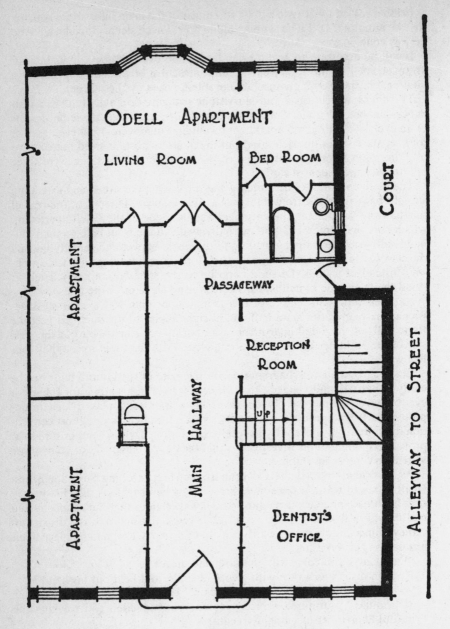

ODELL APARTMENT

LIVING ROOM

BED ROOM

COURT

APARTMENT

PASSAGEWAY

RECEPTION
ROOM

MAIN HALLWAY

ALLEYWAY TO STREET

UP

APARTMENT

DENTIST'S
OFFICE

WEST SEVENTY-FIRST STREET

Janes on Broadway who coulda faded from the picture without causing a second alarm; but they gotta go and bump off the Queen of Sheba!"

As he spoke, William M. Moran, the commanding officer of the detective bureau, came into the little foyer and performed the usual handshaking ceremony. Though he had met Vance and me but once before, and then casually, he remembered us both and addressed us courteously by name.

"Your arrival," he said to Markham, in a well-bred, modulated voice, "is very welcome. Sergeant Heath will give you what preliminary information you want. I'm still pretty much in the dark myself—only just arrived."

"A lot of information *I've* got to give," grumbled Heath, as he led the way into the living room.

Margaret Odell's apartment was a suite of two fairly large rooms connected by a wide archway draped with heavy damask portieres. The entrance door from the main hall of the building led into a small rectangular foyer about eight feet long and four feet deep, with double Venetian-glass doors opening into the main room beyond. There was no other entrance to the apartment, and the bedroom could be reached only through the archway from the living room.

There was a large davenport, covered with brocaded silk, in front of the fireplace in the left-hand wall of the living room, with a long narrow library table of inlaid rosewood extending along its back. On the opposite wall, between the foyer and the archway into the bedroom, hung a triplicate Marie Antoinette mirror, beneath which stood a mahogany gate-legged table. On the far side of the archway, near the large oriel window, was a baby grand Steinway piano with a beautifully designed and decorated case of Louis-Seize ornamentation. In the corner to the right of the fireplace was a spindle-legged escritoire and a square hand-painted wastepaper basket of vellum. To the left of the fireplace stood one of the loveliest Boule cabinets I have ever seen. Several excellent reproductions of Boucher, Fragonard, and Watteau hung about the walls. The bedroom contained a chest of drawers, a dressing table, and several gold-leaf chairs. The whole apartment seemed eminently in keeping with the Canary's fragile and evanescent personality.

As we stepped from the little foyer into the living room and stood for a moment looking about, a scene bordering on wreckage met our eyes. The rooms had apparently been ransacked by someone in a frenzy of haste, and the disorder of the place was appalling.

"They didn't exactly do the job in dainty fashion," remarked Inspector Moran.

"I suppose we oughta be grateful they didn't blow the joint up with dynamite," returned Heath acridly.

But it was not the general disorder that most attracted us. Our gaze was almost immediately drawn and held by the body of the dead girl, which rested in an unnatural, semirecumbent attitude in the corner of the davenport nearest to where we stood. Her head was turned backward, as if by force, over the silken tufted upholstery; and her hair had come unfastened and lay beneath her head and over her bare shoulder like a frozen cataract of liquid gold. Her face, in violent death, was distorted and unlovely. Her skin was discolored; her eyes were staring; her mouth was open, and her lips were drawn back. Her neck, on either side of the thyroid cartilage, showed ugly dark

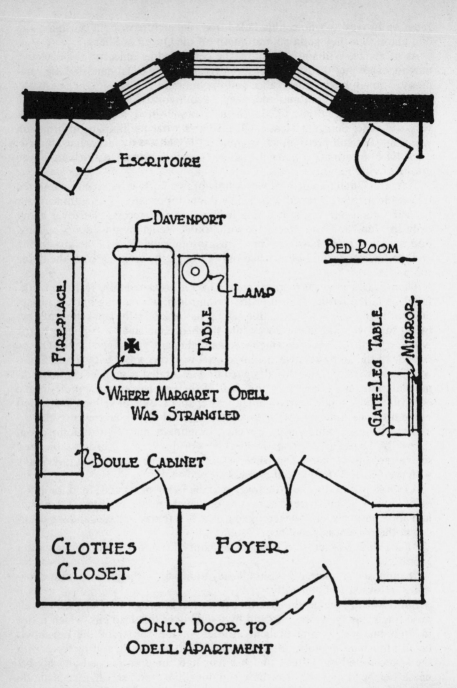

ESCRITOIRE

DAVENPORT

BED ROOM

FIREPLACE

LAMP

TABLE

GATE-LEG TABLE

MIRROR

WHERE MARGARET ODELL
WAS STRANGLED

BOULE CABINET

CLOTHES
CLOSET

FOYER

ONLY DOOR TO
ODELL APARTMENT

bruises. She was dressed in a flimsy evening gown of black Chantilly lace over cream-colored chiffon, and across the arm of the davenport had been thrown an evening cape of cloth-of-gold trimmed with ermine.

There were evidences of her ineffectual struggle with the person who had strangled her. Besides the disheveled condition of her hair, one of the shoulder straps of her gown had been severed, and there was a long rent in the fine lace across her breast. A small corsage of artificial orchids had been torn from her bodice, and lay crumpled in her lap. One satin slipper had fallen off, and her right knee was twisted inward on the seat of the davenport, as if she had sought to lift herself out of the suffocating clutches of her antagonist. Her fingers were still flexed, no doubt as they had been at the moment of her capitulation to death, when she had relinquished her grip upon the murderer's wrists.

The spell of horror cast over us by the sight of the tortured body was broken by the matter-of-fact tones of Heath.

"You see, Mr. Markham, she was evidently sitting in the corner of this settee when she was grabbed suddenly from behind."

Markham nodded. "It must have taken a pretty strong man to strangle her so easily."

"I'll say!" agreed Heath. He bent over and pointed to the girl's fingers, on which showed several abrasions. "They stripped her rings off, too; and they didn't go about it gentle, either." Then he indicated a segment of fine platinum chain, set with tiny pearls, which hung over one of her shoulders. "And they grabbed whatever it was hanging around her neck, and broke the chain doing it. They weren't overlooking anything, or losing any time. . . . A swell, gentlemanly job. Nice and refined."

"Where's the medical examiner?" asked Markham.

"He's coming," Heath told him. "You can't get Doc Doremus to go anywheres without his breakfast."

"He may find something else—something that doesn't show."

"There's plenty showing for me," declared Heath. "Look at this apartment. It wouldn't be much worse if a Kansas cyclone had struck it."

We turned from the depressing spectacle of the dead girl and moved toward the center of the room.

"Be careful not to touch anything, Mr. Markham," warned Heath. "I've sent for the fingerprint experts—they'll be here any minute now."

Vance looked up in mock astonishment.

"Fingerprints? You don't say—really! How delightful!—Imagine a johnnie in this enlightened day leaving his fingerprints for you to find."

"All crooks aren't clever, Mr. Vance," declared Heath combatively.

"Oh, dear, no! They'd never be apprehended if they were. But, after all, Sergeant, even an authentic fingerprint merely means that the person who made it was dallying around at some time or other. It doesn't indicate guilt."

"Maybe so," conceded Heath doggedly. "But I'm here to tell you that if I get any good honest-to-God fingerprints outa this devastated area, it's not going so easy with the bird that made 'em."

Vance appeared to be shocked. "You positively terrify me, Sergeant. Henceforth I shall adopt mittens as a permanent addition to my attire. I'm always handling the furniture and the teacups and the various knickknacks in the houses where I call, don't y' know."

Markham interposed himself at this point and suggested they make a tour of inspection while waiting for the medical examiner.

"They didn't add anything much to the usual methods," Heath pointed out. "Killed the girl, and then ripped things wide open."

The two rooms had apparently been thoroughly ransacked. Clothes and various articles were strewn about the floor. The doors of both clothes closets (there was one in each room) were open, and to judge from the chaos in the bedroom closet, it had been hurriedly searched; although the closet off the living room, which was given over to the storage of infrequently used items, appeared to have been ignored. The drawers of the dressing table and chest had been partly emptied on to the floor, and the bedclothes had been snatched away and the mattress turned back. Two chairs and a small occasional table were upset; several vases were broken, as if they had been searched and then thrown down in the wrath of disappointment; and the Marie Antoinette mirror had been broken. The escritoire was open, and its pigeonholes had been emptied in a jumbled pile upon the blotter. The doors of the Boule cabinet swung wide, and inside there was the same confusion of contents that marked the interior of the escritoire. The bronze-and-porcelain lamp on the end of the library table was lying on its side, its satin shade torn where it had struck the sharp corner of a silver bonbonnière.

Two objects in the general disarray particularly attracted my attention—a black metal document box of the kind purchasable at any stationery store, and a large jewel case of sheet steel with a circular inset lock. The latter of these objects was destined to play a curious and sinister part in the investigation to follow.

The document box, which was now empty, had been placed on the library table, next to the overturned lamp. Its lid was thrown back, and the key was still in the lock. In all the litter and disorganization of the room, this box seemed to be the one outstanding indication of calm and orderly activity on the part of the wrecker.

The jewel case, on the other hand, had been violently wrenched open. It sat on the dressing table in the bedroom, dented and twisted out of shape by the terrific leverage that had been necessary to force it, and beside it lay a brass-handled, cast iron poker which had evidently been brought from the living room and used as a makeshift chisel with which to prize open the lock.

Vance had glanced but casually at the different objects in the rooms as we made our rounds, but when he came to the dressing table, he paused abruptly. Taking out his monocle, he adjusted it carefully, and leaned over the broken jewel case.

"Most extr'ordin'ry!" he murmured, tapping the edge of the lid with his gold pencil. "What do you make of that, Sergeant?"

Heath had been eyeing Vance with narrowed lids as the latter bent over the dressing table.

"What's in your mind, Mr. Vance?" he, in turn, asked.

"Oh, more than you could ever guess," Vance answered lightly. "But just at the moment I was toying with the idea that this steel case was never torn open by that wholly inadequate iron poker, what?"

Heath nodded his head approvingly. "So you, too, noticed that, did you? . . . And you're dead right. That poker might've twisted the box a little, but it never snapped that lock."

He turned to Inspector Moran.

"That's the puzzler I've sent for 'Prof' Brenner to clean up—*if* he can. The jimmying of that jewel case looks to me like a high-class professional job. No Sunday school superintendent did it."

Vance continued for a while to study the box, but at length he turned away with a perplexed frown.

"I say!" he commented. "Something devilish queer took place here last night."

"Oh, not so queer," Heath amended. "It was a thorough job, all right, but there's nothing mysterious about it."

Vance polished his monocle and put it away.

"If you go to work on that basis, Sergeant," he returned carelessly, "I greatly fear you'll run aground on a reef. And may kind Heaven bring you safe to shore!"

4

THE PRINT OF A HAND

(*Tuesday, September 11; 9:30 A.M.*)

A FEW minutes after we had returned to the living room Doctor Doremus, the chief medical examiner, arrived, jaunty and energetic. Immediately in his train came three other men, one of whom carried a bulky camera and a folded tripod. These were Captain Dubois and Detective Bellamy, fingerprint experts, and Peter Quackenbush, the official photographer.

"Well, well, well!" exclaimed Doctor Doremus. "Quite a gathering of the clans. More trouble, eh? . . . I wish your friends, Inspector, would choose a more respectable hour for their little differences. This early rising upsets my liver."

He shook hands with everybody in a brisk, businesslike manner.

"Where's the body?" he demanded breezily, looking about the room. He caught sight of the girl on the davenport. "Ah! A lady."

Stepping quickly forward, he made a rapid examination of the dead girl, scrutinizing her neck and fingers, moving her arms and head to determine the condition of *rigor mortis,* and finally unflexing her stiffened limbs and laying her out straight on the long cushions, preparatory to a more detailed necropsy.

The rest of us moved toward the bedroom, and Heath motioned to the fingerprint men to follow.

"Go over everything," he told them. "But take a special look at this jewel case and the handle of this poker, and give that document box in the other room a close up-and-down."

"Right," assented Captain Dubois. "We'll begin in here while the doc's busy in the other room." And he and Bellamy set to work.

Our interest naturally centered on the captain's labors. For fully five minutes we watched him inspecting the twisted steel sides of the jewel case and the smooth, polished handle of the poker. He held the objects gingerly by their edges, and, placing a jeweler's glass in his eye, flashed his pocket light on every square inch of them. At length he put them down, scowling.

"No fingerprints here," he announced. "Wiped clean."

"I mighta known it," grumbled Heath. "It was a professional job, all right." He turned to the other expert. "Found anything, Bellamy?"

"Nothing to help," was the grumpy reply. "A few old smears with dust over 'em."

"Looks like a washout," Heath commented irritably; "though I'm hoping for something in the other room."

At this moment Doctor Doremus came into the bedroom and, taking a sheet from the bed, returned to the davenport and covered the body of the murdered girl. Then he snapped shut his case and, putting on his hat at a rakish angle, stepped forward with the air of a man in great haste to be on his way.

"Simple case of strangulation from behind," he said, his words running together. "Digital bruises about the front of the throat; thumb bruises in the suboccipital region. Attack must have been unexpected. A quick, competent job though deceased evidently battled a little."

"How do you suppose her dress became torn, Doctor?" asked Vance.

"Oh, that? Can't tell. She may have done it herself—instinctive motions of clutching for air."

"Not likely though, what?"

"Why not? The dress was torn and the bouquet was ripped off, and the fellow who was choking her had both hands on her throat. Who else could've done it?"

Vance shrugged his shoulders and began lighting a cigarette.

Heath, annoyed by his apparently inconsequential interruption, put the next question.

"Don't those marks on the fingers mean that her rings were stripped off?"

"Possibly. They're fresh abrasions. Also, there's a couple of lacerations on the left wrist and slight contusions on the thenar eminence, indicating that a bracelet may have been forcibly pulled over her hand."

"That fits O.K.," pronounced Heath, with satisfaction. "And it looks like they snatched a pendant of some kind off her neck."

"Probably," indifferently agreed Doctor Doremus. "The piece of chain had cut into her flesh a little behind the right shoulder."

"And the time?"

"Nine or ten hours ago. Say, about eleven thirty—maybe a little before. Not after midnight, anyway." He had been teetering restlessly on his toes. "Anything else?"

Heath pondered.

"I guess that's all, doc," he decided. "I'll get the body to the mortuary right away. Let's have the postmortem as soon as you can."

"You'll get a report in the morning." And despite his apparent eagerness to be off, Doctor Doremus stepped into the bedroom and shook hands with Heath and Markham and Inspector Moran before he hurried out.

Heath followed him to the door, and I heard him direct the officer outside to telephone the Department of Public Welfare to send an ambulence at once for the girl's body.

"I positively adore that official archiater of yours," Vance said to Markham. "Such detachment! Here are you stewing most distressingly over the passing of one damsel fair and frail, and that blithe *medicus* is worrying only over a sluggish liver brought on by early rising."

"What has he to be upset over?" complained Markham. "The newspapers are not riding him with spurs. . . . And by the way, what was the point of your questions about the torn dress?"

Vance lazily inspected the tip of his cigarette. "Consider," he said. "The lady was evidently taken by surprise; for, had there been a struggle beforehand, she would not have been strangled from behind while sitting down. Therefore, her gown and corsage were undoubtedly intact at the time she was seized. But, despite the conclusion of your dashing Paracelsus, the damage to her toilet was not of a nature that could have been self-inflicted in her struggle for air. If she had felt the constriction of the gown across her breast, she would have snatched the bodice itself by putting her fingers inside the band. But, if you noticed, her bodice was intact; the only thing that had been torn was the deep lace flounce on the outside; and it had been torn, or rather ripped, by a strong lateral pull; whereas, in the circumstances, any wrench on her part would have been downward or outward."

Inspector Moran was listening intently, but Heath seemed restless and impatient; apparently he regarded the torn gown as irrelevant to the simple main issue.

"Moreover," Vance went on, "there is the corsage. If she herself had torn it off while being strangled, it would doubtless have fallen to the floor; for, remember, she offered considerable resistance. Her body was twisted sidewise; her knee was drawn up, and one slipper had been kicked off. Now, no bunch of silken posies is going to remain in a lady's lap during such a commotion. Even when ladies sit still, their gloves and handbags and handkerchiefs and programs and serviettes are forever sliding off of their laps onto the floor, don't y' know."

"But if your argument's correct," protested Markham, "then, the tearing of the lace and the snatching off of the corsage could have been done only after she was dead. And I can't see any object in such senseless vandalism."

"Neither can I," sighed Vance. "It's all devilish queer."

Heath looked up at him sharply. "That's the second time you've said that. But there's nothing what you'd call queer about this mess. It is a straightaway case." He spoke with an overtone of insistence, like a man arguing against his own insecurity of opinion. "The dress might've been torn almost anytime," he went on stubbornly. "And the flower might've got caught in the lace of her skirt so it couldn't roll off."

"And how would you explain the jewel case, Sergeant?" asked Vance.

"Well, the fellow might've tried the poker and then, finding it wouldn't work, used his jimmy."

"If he had the efficient jimmy," countered Vance, "why did he go to the trouble of bringing the silly poker from the living room?"

The sergeant shook his head perplexedly.

"You never can tell why some of these crooks act the way they do."

"Tut, tut!" Vance chided him. "There should be no such word as *never* in the bright lexicon of detecting."

Heath regarded him sharply. "Was there anything else that struck you as queer?" His subtle doubts were welling up again.

"Well, there's the lamp on the table in the other room."

We were standing near the archway between the two rooms, and Heath turned quickly and looked blankly at the fallen lamp.

"I don't see anything queer about that."

"It has been upset—eh, what?" suggested Vance.

"What if it has?" Health was frankly puzzled. "Damn near everything in this apartment has been knocked crooked."

"Ah! But there's a reason for most of the other things having been disturbed—like the drawers and pigeonholes and closets and vases. They all indicate a search; they're consistent with a raid for loot. But that lamp, now, d' ye see, doesn't fit into the picture. It's a false note. It was standing on the opposite end of the table to where the murder was committed, at least five feet away; and it couldn't possibly have been knocked over in the struggle. . . . No, it won't do. It's got no business being upset, any more than that pretty mirror over the gate-legged table has any business being broken. That's why it's queer."

"What about those chairs and the little table?" asked Heath, pointing to two small gilded chairs which had been overturned, and a fragile tip-table that lay on its side near the piano.

"Oh, they fit into the ensemble," returned Vance. "They're all light pieces of furniture which could easily have been knocked over, or thrown aside, by the hasty gentleman who rifled these rooms."

"The lamp might've been knocked over in the same way," argued Heath.

Vance shook his head. "Not tenable, Sergeant. It has a solid bronze base and isn't at all top-heavy; and, being set well back on the table, it wasn't in anyone's way. . . . That lamp was upset deliberately."

The sergeant was silent for a while. Experience had taught him not to underestimate Vance's observations; and, I must confess, as I looked at the lamp lying on its side on the end of the library table, well removed from any of the other disordered objects in the room, Vance's argument seemed to possess considerable force. I tried hard to fit it into a hasty reconstruction of the crime but was utterly unable to do so.

"Anything else that don't seem to fit into the picture?" Heath at length asked.

Vance pointed with his cigarette toward the clothes closet in the living room. This closet was alongside of the foyer, in the corner near the Boule cabinet, directly opposite to the end of the davenport.

"You might let your mind dally a moment with the condition of that clothes press," suggested Vance carelessly. "You will note that, though the door's ajar, the contents have not been touched. And it's about the only area in the apartment that hasn't been disturbed."

Heath walked over and looked into the closet.

"Well, anyway, I'll admit that's queer," he finally conceded.

Vance had followed him indolently and stood gazing over his shoulder.

"And my word!" he exclaimed suddenly. "The key's on the inside of the lock. Fancy that, now! One can't lock a closet door with the key on the inside—can one, Sergeant?"

"The key may not mean anything," Heath observed hopefully. "Maybe the door was never locked. Anyhow, we'll find out about that pretty soon. I'm holding the maid outside, and I'm going to have her on the carpet as soon as the captain finishes his job here."

He turned to Dubois, who, having completed his search for fingerprints in the bedroom, was now inspecting the piano.

"Any luck yet?"

The captain shook his head.

"Gloves," he answered succinctly.

"Same here," supplemented Bellamy gruffly, on his knees before the escritoire.

Vance, with a sardonic smile, turned and walked to the window, where he stood looking out and smoking placidly, as if his entire interest in the case had evaporated.

At this moment the door from the main hall opened, and a short, thin little man, with gray hair and a scraggly gray beard, stepped inside and stood blinking against the vivid sunlight.

"Good morning, Professor," Heath greeted the newcomer. "Glad to see you. I've got something nifty, right in your line."

Deputy Inspector Conrad Brenner was one of that small army of obscure, but highly capable, experts who are connected with the New York Police Department, and who are constantly being consulted on abstruse technical problems, but whose names and achievements rarely get into the public prints. His specialty was locks and burglars' tools; and I doubt if, even among those exhaustively painstaking criminologists of the University of Lausanne, there was a more accurate reader of the evidential signs left by the implements of housebreakers. In appearance and bearing he was like a withered little college professor.* His black, unpressed suit was old-fashioned in cut; and he wore a very high stiff collar, like a *fin-de-siècle* clergyman, with a narrow black string tie. His gold-rimmed spectacles were so thick-lensed that the pupils of his eyes gave the impression of acute belladonna poisoning.

When Heath had spoken to him, he merely stood staring with a sort of detached expectancy; he seemed utterly unaware that there was anyone else in the room. The sergeant, evidently familiar with the little man's idiosyncrasies of manner, did not wait for a response, but started at once for the bedroom.

"This way, please, Professor," he directed cajolingly, going to the dressing table and picking up the jewel case. "Take a squint at this and tell me what you see."

Inspector Brenner followed Heath, without looking to right or left, and, taking the jewel case, went silently to the window and began to examine it. Vance, whose interest seemed suddenly to be reawakened, came forward and stood watching him.

For fully five minutes the little expert inspected the case, holding it within a few inches of his myopic eyes. Then he lifted his glance to Heath and winked several times rapidly.

---

* It is an interesting fact that for the nineteen years he had been connected with the New York Police Department, he had been referred to, by his superiors and subordinates alike, as "the Professor."

"Two instruments were used in opening this case." His voice was small and high-pitched, but there was in it an undeniable quality of authority. "One bent the lid and made several fractures on the baked enamel. The other was, I should say, a steel chisel of some kind, and was used to break the lock. The first instrument, which was blunt, was employed amateurishly, at the wrong angle of leverage; and the effort resulted only in twisting the overhang of the lid. But the steel chisel was inserted with a knowledge of the correct point of oscillation, where a minimum of leverage would produce the counteracting stress necessary to displace the lockbolts."

"A professional job?" suggested Heath.

"Highly so," answered the inspector, again blinking. "That is to say, the forcing of the lock was professional. And I would even go so far as to advance the opinion that the instrument used was one especially constructed for such illegal purposes."

"Could this have done the job?" Heath held out the poker.

The other looked at it closely and turned it over several times. "It might have been the instrument that bent the cover, but it was not the one used for prying open the lock. This poker is cast iron and would have snapped under any great pressure; whereas this box is of cold rolled eighteen-gauge steel plate, with an inset cylinder pin-tumbler lock taking a paracentric key. The leverage force necessary to distort the flange sufficiently to lift the lid could have been made only by a steel chisel."

"Well, that's that." Heath seemed well satisfied with Inspector Brenner's conclusion. "I'll send the box down to you, Professor, and you can let me know what else you find out."

"I'll take it along, if you have no objection." And the little man tucked it under his arm and shuffled out without another word.

Heath grinned at Markham. "Queer bird. He ain't happy unless he's measuring jimmy marks on doors and windows and things. He couldn't wait till I sent him the box. He'll hold it lovingly on his lap all the way down in the subway, like a mother with a baby."

Vance was still standing near the dressing table, gazing perplexedly into space. "Markham," he said, "the condition of that jewel case is positively astounding. It's unreasonable, illogical—insane. It complicates the situation most damnably. That steel box simply couldn't have been chiseled open by a professional burglar . . . and yet, don't y' know, it actually was."

Before Markham could reply, a satisfied grunt from Captain Dubois attracted our attention. "I've got something for you, Sergeant," he announced.

We moved expectantly into the living room. Dubois was bending over the end of the library table almost directly behind the place where Margaret Odell's body had been found. He took out an insufflator, which was like a very small hand bellows, and blew a fine light-yellow powder evenly over about a square foot of the polished rosewood surface of the table top. Then he gently blew away the surplus powder, and there appeared the impression of a human hand distinctly registered in saffron. The bulb of the thumb and each fleshy hummock between the joints of the fingers and around the palm stood out like tiny circular islands. All the papillary ridges were clearly discernible. The photographer then hooked his camera to a peculiar adjustable tripod and, carefully focusing his lens, took two flashlight pictures of the hand mark.

"This ought to do." Dubois was pleased with his find. "It's the right hand—a clear print—and the guy who made it was standing right behind the dame.... And it's the newest print in the place."

"What about this box?" Heath pointed to the black document box on the table near the overturned lamp.

"Not a mark—wiped clean."

Dubois began putting away his paraphernalia.

"I say, Captain Dubois," interposed Vance, "did you take a good look at the inside doorknob of that clothes press?"

The man swung about abruptly and gave Vance a glowering look. "People ain't in the habit of handling the inside knobs of closet doors. They open and shut closets from the outside."

Vance raised his eyebrows in simulated astonishment.

"Do they, now, really?—Fancy that! ... Still, don't y' know, if one were inside the closet, one couldn't reach the outside knob."

"The people *I* know don't shut themselves in clothes closets." Dubois' tone was ponderously sarcastic.

"You positively amaze me!" declared Vance. "All the people I know are addicted to the habit—a sort of daily pastime, don't y' know."

Markham, always diplomatic, intervened. "What idea have you about that closet, Vance?"

"Alas! I wish I had one," was the dolorous answer. "It's because I can't, for the life of me, make sense of its neat and orderly appearance that I'm so interested in it. Really, y' know, it should have been artistically looted."

Heath was not entirely free from the same vague misgivings that were disturbing Vance, for he turned to Dubois and said, "You might go over the knob, Captain. As this gentleman says, there's something funny about the condition of that closet."

Dubois, silent and surly, went to the closet door and sprayed his yellow powder over the inside knob. When he had blown the loose particles away, he bent over it with his magnifying glass. At length he straightened up and gave Vance a look of ill-natured appraisal.

"There's fresh prints on it, all right," he grudgingly admitted; "and, unless I'm mistaken, they were made by the same hand as those on the table. Both thumb marks are ulnar loops, and the index fingers are both whorl patterns. ... Here, Pete," he ordered the photographer, "make some shots of that knob."

When this had been done, Dubois, Bellamy, and the photographer left us.

A few minutes later, after an interchange of pleasantries, Inspector Moran also departed. At the door he passed two men in the white uniforms of interns, who had come to take away the girl's body.

5

THE BOLTED DOOR

(Tuesday, September 11; 10:30 A.M.)

MARKHAM AND Heath and Vance and I were now alone in the apartment. Dark, low-hanging clouds had drifted across the sun, and the gray spectral light intensified the tragic atmosphere of the rooms. Markham had lighted a cigar, and stood leaning against the piano, looking about him with a disconsolate but determined air. Vance had moved over to one of the pictures on the side wall of the living room—Boucher's "La Bergère Endormie" I think it was—and stood looking at it with cynical contempt.

"Dimpled nudities, gamboling Cupids and woolly clouds for royal cocottes," he commented. His distaste for all the painting of the French decadence under Louis XV was profound. "One wonders what pictures courtesans hung in their boudoirs before the invention of these amorous eclogues, with their blue verdure and beribboned sheep."

"I'm more interested at present in what took place in this particular boudoir last night," retorted Markham impatiently.

"There's not much doubt about that, sir," said Heath encouragingly. "And I've an idea that when Dubois checks up those fingerprints with our files, we'll about know who did it."

Vance turned toward him with a rueful smile. "You're so trusting, Sergeant. I, in turn, have an idea that, long before this touchin' case is clarified, you'll wish the irascible captain with the insect powder had never found those fingerprints." He made a playful gesture of emphasis. "Permit me to whisper into your ear that the person who left his sign manuals on yonder rosewood table and cutglass doorknob had nothing whatever to do with the precipitate demise of the fair Mademoiselle Odell."

"What is it you suspect?" demanded Markham sharply.

"Not a thing, old dear," blandly declared Vance. "I'm wandering about in a mental murk as empty of signposts as interplanetary space. The jaws of darkness do devour me up; I'm in the dead vast and middle of the night. My mental darkness is Egyptian, Stygian, Cimmerian—I'm in a perfect Erebus of tenebrosity."

Markham's jaw tightened in exasperation; he was familiar with this evasive loquacity of Vance's. Dismissing the subject, he addressed himself to Heath.

"Have you done any questioning of the people in the house here?"

"I talked to Odell's maid and to the janitor and the switchboard operators, but I didn't go much into details—I was waiting for you. I'll say this, though: what they did tell me made my head swim. If they don't back down on some of their statements, we're up against it."

"Let's have them in now, then," suggested Markham; "the maid first." He sat down on the piano bench with his back to the keyboard.

Heath rose but, instead of going to the door, walked to the oriel window.

"There's one thing I want to call your attention to, sir, before you interview these people, and that's the matter of entrances and exits in this apartment."

196

He drew aside the gold-gauze curtain. "Look at that iron grating. All the windows in this place, including the ones in the bathroom, are equipped with iron bars just like these. It's only eight or ten feet to the ground here, and whoever built this house wasn't taking any chances of burglars getting in through the windows."

He released the curtain and strode into the foyer. "Now, there's only one entrance to this apartment, and that's this door here opening off the main hall. There isn't a transom or an airshaft or a dumbwaiter in the place, and that means that the only way—*the only way*—that anybody can get in or out of this apartment is through this door. Just keep that fact in your mind, sir, while you're listening to the stories of these people. . . . Now, I'll have the maid brought in."

In response to Heath's order a detective led in a mulatto woman about thirty years old. She was neatly dressed and gave one the impression of capability. When she spoke, it was with a quiet, clear enunciation which attested to a greater degree of education than is ordinarily found in members of her class.

Her name, we learned, was Amy Gibson; and the information elicited by Markham's preliminary questioning consisted of the following facts:

She had arrived at the apartment that morning a few minutes after seven, and, as was her custom, had let herself in with her own key, as her mistress generally slept till late.

Once or twice a week she came early to do sewing and mending for Miss Odell before the latter arose. On this particular morning she had come early to make an alteration in a gown.

As soon as she had opened the door, she had been confronted by the disorder of the apartment, for the Venetian-glass doors of the foyer were wide open; and almost simultaneously she had noticed the body of her mistress on the davenport.

She had called at once to Jessup, the night telephone operator then on duty, who, after one glance into the living room, had notified the police. She had then sat down in the public reception room and waited for the arrival of the officers.

Her testimony had been simple and direct and intelligently stated. If she was nervous or excited, she managed to keep her feelings well under control.

"Now," continued Markham, after a short pause, "let us go back to last night. At what time did you leave Miss Odell?"

"A few minutes before seven, sir," the woman answered, in a colorless, even tone which seemed to be characteristic of her speech.

"Is that your usual hour for leaving?"

"No; I generally go about six. But last night Miss Odell wanted me to help her dress for dinner."

"Don't you always help her dress for dinner?"

"No, sir. But last night she was going with some gentleman to dinner and the theater, and wanted to look specially nice."

"Ah!" Markham leaned forward. "And who was this gentleman?"

"I don't know, sir—Miss Odell didn't say."

"And you couldn't suggest who it might have been?"

"I couldn't say, sir."

"And when did Miss Odell tell you that she wanted you to come early this morning?"

"When I was leaving last night."

"So she evidently didn't anticipate any danger, or have any fear of her companion."

"It doesn't look that way." The woman paused, as if considering. "No, I know she didn't. She was in good spirits."

Markham turned to Heath.

"Any other questions you want to ask, Sergeant?"

Heath removed an unlighted cigar from his mouth, and bent forward, resting his hands on his knees.

"What jewelry did this Odell woman have on last night?" he demanded gruffly.

The maid's manner became cool and a bit haughty.

"Miss Odell"—she emphasized the "Miss," by way of reproaching him for the disrespect implied in his omission—"wore all her rings, five or six of them, and three bracelets—one of square diamonds, one of rubies, and one of diamonds and emeralds. She also had on a sunburst of pear-shaped diamonds on a chain round her neck, and she carried a platinum lorgnette set with diamonds and pearls."

"Did she own any other jewelry?"

"A few small pieces, maybe, but I'm not sure."

"And did she keep 'em in the steel jewel case in the room?"

"Yes—when she wasn't wearing them." There was more than a suggestion of sarcasm in the reply.

"Oh, I thought maybe she kept 'em locked up when she had 'em on." Heath's antagonism had been aroused by the maid's attitude; he could not have failed to note that she had consistently omitted the punctilious "sir" when answering him. He now stood up and pointed loweringly to the black document box on the rosewood table.

"Ever see that before?"

The woman nodded indifferently. "Many times."

"Where was it generally kept?"

"In that thing." She indicated the Boule cabinet with a motion of the head.

"What was in the box?"

"How should I know?"

"You don't know—huh?" Heath thrust out his jaw, but his bullying attitude had no effect upon the impassive maid.

"I've got no idea," she replied calmly. "It was always kept locked, and I never saw Miss Odell open it."

The sergeant walked over to the door of the living room closet.

"See that key?" he asked angrily.

Again the woman nodded; but this time I detected a look of mild astonishment in her eyes.

"Was that key always kept on the inside of the door?"

"No, it was always on the outside."

Heath shot Vance a curious look. Then, after a moment's frowning contemplation of the knob, he waved his hand to the detective who had brought the maid in.

"Take her back to the reception room, Snitkin, and get a detailed description from her of all the Odell jewelry. . . . And keep her outside; I'll want her again."

When Snitkin and the maid had gone out, Vance lay back lazily on the davenport, where he had sat during the interview, and sent a spiral of cigarette smoke toward the ceiling.

"Rather illuminatin', what?" he remarked. "The dusky demoiselle got us considerably forrader. Now we know that the closet key is on the wrong side of the door, and that our *fille de joie* went to the theater with one of her favorite *inamorati,* who presumably brought her home shortly before she took her departure from this wicked world."

"You think that's helpful, do you?" Heath's tone was contemptuously triumphant. "Wait till you hear the crazy story the telephone operator's got to tell."

"All right, Sergeant," put in Markham impatiently. "Suppose we get on with the ordeal."

"I'm going to suggest, Mr. Markham, that we question the janitor first. And I'll show you why." Heath went to the entrance door of the apartment, and opened it. "Look here for just a minute, sir."

He stepped out into the main hall and pointed down the little passageway on the left. It was about ten feet in length and ran between the Odell apartment and the blank rear wall of the reception room. At the end of it was a solid oak door which gave on the court at the side of the house.

"That door," explained Heath, "is the only side or rear entrance to this building; and when that door is bolted, nobody can get into the house except by the front entrance. You can't even get into the building through the other apartments, for every window on this floor is barred. I checked up on that point as soon as I got here."

He led the way back into the living room.

"Now, after I'd looked over the situation this morning," he went on, "I figured that our man had entered through that side door at the end of the passageway, and had slipped into this apartment without the night operator seeing him. So I tried the side door to see if it was open. But it was bolted on the inside—not locked, mind you, but bolted. And it wasn't a slip bolt, either, that could have been jimmied or worked open from the outside, but a tough old-fashioned turn bolt of solid brass. . . . And now I want you to hear what the janitor's got to say about it."

Markham nodded acquiescence, and Heath called an order to one of the officers in the hall. A moment later a stolid, middle-aged German, with sullen features and high cheekbones, stood before us. His jaw was clamped tight, and he shifted his eyes from one to the other of us suspiciously.

Heath straightway assumed the role of inquisitor. "What time do you leave here at night?" He had, for some reason, assumed a belligerent manner.

"Six o'clock—sometimes earlier, sometimes later." The man spoke in a surly monotone. He was obviously resentful at this unexpected intrusion upon his orderly routine.

"And what time do you get here in the morning?"

"Eight o'clock, regular."

"What time did you go home last night?"

"About six—maybe quarter past."

Heath paused and finally lighted the cigar on which he had been chewing at intervals during the past hour.

"Now, tell me about that side door," he went on, with undiminished aggressiveness. "You told me you lock it every night before you leave—is that right?"

"*Ja*—that's right." The man nodded his head affirmatively several times. "Only I don't lock it—I bolt it."

"All right, you bolt it, then." As Heath talked his cigar bobbed up and down between his lips; smoke and words came simultaneously from his mouth. "And last night you bolted it as usual about six o'clock?"

"Maybe a quarter past," the janitor amended, with Germanic precision.

"You're sure you bolted it last night?" The question was almost ferocious.

"*Ja, ja.* Sure, I am. I do it every night. I never miss."

The man's earnestness left no doubt that the door in question had indeed been bolted on the inside at about six o'clock of the previous evening. Heath, however, belabored the point for several minutes, only to be reassured doggedly that the door had been bolted. At last the janitor was dismissed.

"Really, y' know, Sergeant," remarked Vance with an amused smile, "that honest Rheinlander bolted the door."

"Sure, he did," spluttered Heath, "and I found it still bolted this morning at quarter of eight. That's just what messes things up so nice and pretty. If that door was bolted from six o'clock last evening until eight o'clock this morning, I'd appreciate having someone drive up in a hearse and tell me how the Canary's little playmate got in here last night. And I'd also like to know how he got out."

"Why not through the main entrance?" asked Markham. "It seems the only logical way left, according to your own findings."

"That's how I had it figured out, sir," returned Heath. "But wait till you hear what the phone operator has to say."

"And the phone operator's post," mused Vance, "'is in the main hall halfway between the front door and this apartment. Therefore, the gentleman who caused all the disturbance hereabouts last night would have had to pass within a few feet of the operator both on arriving and departing—eh, what?"

"That's it!" snapped Heath. "And, according to the operator, no such person came or went."

Markham seemed to have absorbed some of Heath's irritability. "Get the fellow in here, and let me question him," he ordered.

Heath obeyed with a kind of malicious alacrity.

6

A CALL FOR HELP

JESSUP MADE a good impression from the moment he entered the room. He was a serious, determined-looking man in his early thirties, rugged and well built; and there was a squareness to his shoulders that carried a suggestion of military training. He walked with a decided limp—his right foot dragged perceptibly—and I noted that his left arm had been stiffened into a permanent arc, as if by an unreduced fracture of the elbow. He was quiet and reserved, and his eyes were steady and intelligent. Markham at once motioned him to a wicker chair beside the closet door, but he declined it, and stood before the district attorney in a soldierly attitude of respectful attention. Markham opened the interrogation with several personal questions. It transpired that Jessup had been a sergeant in the World War,* had twice been seriously wounded, and had been invalided home shortly before the armistice. He had held his present post of telephone operator for over a year.

"Now, Jessup," continued Markham, "there are things connected with last night's tragedy that you can tell us."

"Yes, sir." There was no doubt that this ex-soldier would tell us accurately anything he knew, and also that, if he had any doubt as to the correctness of his information, he would frankly say so. He possessed all the qualities of a careful and well-trained witness.

"First of all, what time did you come on duty last night?"

"At ten o'clock, sir." There was no qualification to this blunt statement; one felt that Jessup would arrive punctually at whatever hour he was due. "It was my short shift. The day man and myself alternate in long and short shifts."

"And did you see Miss Odell come in last night after the theater?"

"Yes, sir. Everyone who comes in has to pass the switchboard."

"What time did she arrive?"

"It couldn't have been more than a few minutes after eleven."

"Was she alone?"

"No, sir. There was a gentleman with her."

"Do you know who he was?"

"I don't know his name, sir. But I have seen him several times before when he has called on Miss Odell."

"You could describe him, I suppose."

"Yes, sir. He's tall and clean-shaven except for a very short gray moustache, and is about forty-five, I should say. He looks—if you understand me, sir— like a man of wealth and position."

Markham nodded. "And now, tell me: did he accompany Miss Odell into her apartment or did he go immediately away?"

---

* His full name was William Elmer Jessup, and he had been attached to the 308th Infantry of the 77th Division of the Overseas Forces.

201

"He went in with Miss Odell and stayed about half an hour."

Markham's eyes brightened, and there was a suppressed eagerness in his next words. "Then he arrived about eleven, and was alone with Miss Odell in her apartment until about half past eleven. You're sure of these facts?"

"Yes, sir, that's correct," the man affirmed.

Markham paused and leaned forward.

"Now, Jessup, think carefully before answering: did any one else call on Miss Odell at any time last night?"

"No one, sir," was the unhesitating reply.

"How can you be so sure?"

"I would have seen them, sir. They would have had to pass the switchboard in order to reach this apartment."

"And don't you ever leave the switchboard?" asked Markham.

"No, sir," the man assured him vigorously, as if protesting against the implication that he would desert a post of duty. "When I want a drink of water, or go to the toilet, I use the little lavatory in the reception room; but I always hold the door open and keep my eye on the switchboard in case the pilot light should show up for a telephone call. Nobody could walk down the hall, even if I was in the lavatory, without my seeing them."

One could well believe that the conscientious Jessup kept his eye at all times on the switchboard lest a call should flash and go unanswered. The man's earnestness and reliability were obvious; and there was no doubt in any of our minds, I think, that if Miss Odell had had another visitor that night, Jessup would have known of it.

But Heath, with the thoroughness of his nature, rose quickly and stepped out into the main hall. In a moment he returned, looking troubled but satisfied.

"Right!" He nodded to Markham. "The lavatory door's on a direct unobstructed line with the switchboard."

Jessup took no notice of this verification of his statement, and stood, his eyes attentively on the district attorney, awaiting any further questions that might be asked him. There was something both admirable and confidence-inspiring in his unruffled demeanor.

"What about last night?" resumed Markham. "Did you leave the switchboard often, or for long?"

"Just once, sir; and then only to go to the lavatory for a minute or two. But I watched the board the whole time."

"And you'd be willing to state on oath that no one else called on Miss Odell from ten o'clock on, and that no one, except her escort, left her apartment after that hour?"

"Yes, sir, I would."

He was plainly telling the truth, and Markham pondered several moments before proceeding.

"What about the side door?"

"That's kept locked all night, sir. The janitor bolts it when he leaves and unbolts it in the morning. I never touch it."

Markham leaned back and turned to Heath.

"The testimony of the janitor and Jessup here," he said, "seems to limit the situation pretty narrowly to Miss Odell's escort. If, as seems reasonable to assume, the side door was bolted all night, and if no other caller came or went through the front door, it looks as if the man we wanted to find was the one who brought her home."

Heath gave a short, mirthless laugh. "That would be fine, sir, if something else hadn't happened around here last night." Then to Jessup: "Tell the district attorney the rest of the story about this man."

Markham looked toward the operator with expectant interest; and Vance, lifting himself on one elbow, listened attentively.

Jessup spoke in a level voice, with the alert and careful manner of a soldier reporting to his superior officer.

"It was just this, sir. When the gentleman came out of Miss Odell's apartment at about half past eleven, he stopped at the switchboard and asked me to get him a Yellow Taxicab. I put the call through, and while he was waiting for the car, Miss Odell screamed and called for help. The gentleman turned and rushed to the apartment door, and I followed quickly behind him. He knocked; but at first there was no answer. Then he knocked again, and at the same time called out to Miss Odell and asked her what was the matter. This time she answered. She said everything was all right, and told him to go home and not to worry. Then he walked back with me to the switchboard, remarking that he guessed Miss Odell must have fallen asleep and had a nightmare. We talked for a few minutes about the war, and then the taxicab came. He said good night and went out, and I heard the car drive away."

It was plain to see that this epilogue of the departure of Miss Odell's anonymous escort completely upset Markham's theory of the case. He looked down at the floor with a baffled expression and smoked vigorously for several moments. At last he said:

"How long was it after this man came out of the apartment that you heard Miss Odell scream?"

"About five minutes. I had put my connection through to the taxicab company, and it was a minute or so later that she screamed."

"Was the man near the switchboard?"

"Yes, sir. In fact, he had one arm resting on it."

"How many times did Miss Odell scream? And just what did she say when she called for help?"

"She screamed twice and then cried, 'Help! Help!' "

"And when the man knocked on the door the second time, what did he say?"

"As near as I can recollect, sir, he said, 'Open the door, Margaret! What's the trouble?' "

"And can you remember her exact words when she answered him?"

Jessup hesitated and frowned reflectively. "As I recall, she said, 'There's nothing the matter. I'm sorry I screamed. Everything's all right, so please go home, and don't worry.' . . . Of course, that may not be exactly what she said, but it was something very close to it."

"You could hear her plainly through the door, then?"

"Oh, yes. These doors are not very thick."

Markham rose and began pacing meditatively. At length, halting in front of the operator, he asked another question:

"Did you hear any other suspicious sounds in this apartment after the man left?"

"Not a sound of any kind, sir," Jessup declared. "Someone from outside the building, however, telephoned Miss Odell about ten minutes later, and a man's voice answered from her apartment."

"What's this!" Markham spun round, and Heath sat up at attention, his eyes wide. "Tell me every detail of that call."

Jessup complied unemotionally.

"About twenty minutes to twelve a trunk light flashed on the board, and when I answered it, a man asked for Miss Odell. I plugged the connection through, and after a short wait the receiver was lifted from her phone—you can tell when a receiver's taken off the hook, because the guide light on the board goes out—and a man's voice answered 'Hello.' I pulled the listening-in key over, and, of course, didn't hear any more."

There was silence in the apartment for several minutes. Then Vance, who had been watching Jessup closely during the interview, spoke.

"By the bye, Mr. Jessup," he asked carelessly, "were you yourself, by any chance, a bit fascinated—let us say—by the charming Miss Odell?"

For the first time since entering the room the man appeared ill at ease. A dull flush overspread his cheeks. "I thought she was a very beautiful lady," he answered resolutely.

Markham gave Vance a look of disapproval, and then addressed himself abruptly to the operator. "That will be all for the moment, Jessup."

The man bowed stiffly and limped out.

"This case is becoming positively fascinatin'," murmured Vance, relaxing once more upon the davenport.

"It's comforting to know that someone's enjoying it." Markham's tone was irritable. "And what, may I ask, was the object of your question concerning Jessup's sentiments toward the dead woman?"

"Oh, just a vagrant notion struggling in my brain," returned Vance. "And then, y' know, a bit of *boudoir racontage* always enlivens a situation, what?"

Heath, rousing himself from gloomy abstraction, spoke up.

"We've still got the fingerprints, Mr. Markham. And I'm thinking that they're going to locate our man for us."

"But even if Dubois does identify those prints," said Markham, "we'll have to show how the owner of them got into this place last night. He'll claim, of course, they were made prior to the crime."

"Well, it's a sure thing," declared Heath stubbornly, "that there was some man in here last night when Odell got back from the theater, and that he was still here until after the other man left at half past eleven. The woman's screams and the answering of that phone call at twenty minutes to twelve prove it. And since Doc Doremus said that the murder took place before midnight, there's no getting away from the fact that the guy who was hiding in here did the job."

"That appears incontrovertible," agreed Markham. "And I'm inclined to think it was someone she knew. She probably screamed when he first revealed himself, and then, recognizing him, calmed down and told the other man out in the hall that nothing was the matter. . . . Later on he strangled her."

"And, I might suggest," added Vance, "that his place of hiding was that clothes press."

"Sure," the sergeant concurred. "But what's bothering me is how he got in here. The day operator who was at the switchboard until ten last night told me that the man who called and took Odell out to dinner was the only visitor she had."

Markham gave a grunt of exasperation.

"Bring the day man in here," he ordered. "We've got to straighten this thing out. *Somebody* got in here last night, and before I leave, I'm going to find out how it was done."

Vance gave him a look of patronizing amusement.

"Y' know, Markham," he said, "I'm not blessed with the gift of psychic inspiration, but I have one of those strange, indescribable feelings, as the minor poets say, that if you really contemplate remaining in this bestrewn boudoir till you've discovered how the mysterious visitor gained admittance here last night, you'd do jolly well to send for your toilet access'ries and several changes of fresh linen—not to mention your pyjamas. The chap who engineered this little soiree planned his entrance and exit most carefully and perspicaciously."

Markham regarded Vance dubiously but made no reply.

6

A NAMELESS VISITOR

(*Tuesday, September 11; 11:15 A.M.*)

HEATH HAD stepped out into the hall, and now returned with the day telephone operator, a sallow, thin young man who, we learned, was named Spively. His almost black hair, which accentuated the pallor of his face, was sleeked back from his forehead with pomade; and he wore a very shallow moustache which barely extended beyond the alæ of his nostrils. He was dressed in an exaggeratedly dapper fashion, in a dazzling chocolate-colored suit cut very close to his figure, a pair of cloth-topped buttoned shoes, and a pink shirt with a stiff turn-over collar to match. He appeared nervous, and immediately sat down in the wicker chair by the door, fingering the sharp creases of his trousers, and running the tip of his tongue over his lips.

Markham went straight to the point.

"I understand you were at the switchboard yesterday afternoon and last night until ten o'clock. Is that correct?"

Spively swallowed hard and nodded his head. "Yes, sir."

"What time did Miss Odell go out to dinner?"

"About seven o'clock. I'd just sent to the restaurant next door for some sandwiches——"

"Did she go alone?" Markham interrupted his explanation.

"No. A fella called for her."

"Did you know this 'fella'?"

"I'd seen him a couple of times calling on Miss Odell, but I didn't know who he was."

"What did he look like?" Markham's question was uttered with hurried impatience.

Spively's description of the girl's escort tallied with Jessup's description of the man who had accompanied her home, though Spively was more voluble and less precise than Jessup had been. Patently, Miss Odell had gone out at seven and returned at eleven with the same man.

"Now," resumed Markham, putting an added stress on his words, "I want to know who else called on Miss Odell between the time she went out to dinner and ten o'clock when you left the switchboard."

Spively was puzzled by the question, and his thin arched eyebrows lifted and contracted. "I—don't understand," he stammered. "How could any one call on Miss Odell when she was out?"

"Someone evidently did," said Markham. "And he got into her apartment and was there when she returned at eleven."

The youth's eyes opened wide, and his lips fell apart. "My God, sir!" he exclaimed. "So that's how they murdered her!—laid in wait for her!..." He stopped abruptly, suddenly realizing his own proximity to the mysterious chain of events that had led up to the crime. "But nobody got into her apartment while I was on duty," he blurted, with frightened emphasis. "Nobody! I never left the board from the time she went out until quitting time."

"Couldn't anyone have come in the side door?"

"What! Was it unlocked?" Spively's tone was startled. "It never is unlocked at night. The janitor bolts it when he leaves at six."

"And you didn't unbolt it last night for any purpose? Think!"

"No, sir, I didn't!" He shook his head earnestly.

"And you are positive that no one got into the apartment through the front door after Miss Odell left?"

"Positive! I tell you I didn't leave the board the whole time, and nobody could've got by me without my knowing it. There was only one person that called and asked for her—"

"Oh! So someone did call!" snapped Markham. "When was it? And what happened?—Jog your memory before you answer."

"It wasn't anything important," the youth assured him, genuinely frightened. "Just a fella who came in and rang her bell and went right out again."

"Never mind whether it was important or not." Markham's tone was cold and peremptory. "What time did he call?"

"About half past nine."

"And who was he?"

"A young fella I've seen come here several times to see Miss Odell. I don't know his name."

"Tell me exactly what took place," pursued Markham.

Again Spively swallowed hard and wetted his lips.

"It was like this," he began, with effort. "The fella came in and started walking down the hall and I said to him, 'Miss Odell isn't in.' But he kept on going and said, 'Oh, well, I'll ring the bell anyway to make sure.' A telephone call came through just then, and I let him go on. He rang the bell and knocked on the door, but of course there wasn't any answer; and pretty soon he came on back and said, 'I guess you were right.' Then he tossed me half a dollar and went out."

"You actually saw him go out?" There was a note of disappointment in Markham's voice.

"Sure, I saw him go out. He stopped just inside the front door and lit a cigarette. Then he opened the door and turned toward Broadway."

" 'One by one the rosy petals fall,' " came Vance's indolent voice. "A most amusin' situation!"

Markham was loath to relinquish his hope in the criminal possibilities of this one caller who had come and gone at half past nine.

"What was this man like?" he asked. "Can you describe him?"

Spively sat up straight, and when he answered, it was with an enthusiasm that showed he had taken special note of the visitor.

"He was good-looking, not so old—maybe thirty. And he had on a full-dress suit and patent-leather pumps, and a pleated silk shirt——"

"What, what?" demanded Vance, in simulated unbelief, leaning over the back of the davenport. "A silk shirt with evening dress! Most extr'ordin'ry!"

"Oh, a lot of the best dressers are wearing them," Spively explained, with condescending pride. "It's all the fashion for dancing."

"You don't say—really!" Vance appeared dumbfounded. "I must look into this. . . . And, by the bye, when this Beau Brummel of the silk shirt paused by the front door, did he take his cigarette from a long flat silver case carried in his lower waistcoat pocket?"

The youth looked at Vance in admiring astonishment.

"How did you know?" he exclaimed.

"Simple deduction," Vance explained, resuming his recumbent posture. "Large metal cigarette cases carried in the waistcoat pocket somehow go with silk shirts for evening wear."

Markham, clearly annoyed at the interruption, cut in sharply with a demand for the operator to proceed with his description.

"He wore his hair smoothed down," Spively continued, "and you could see it was kind of long; but it was cut in the latest style. And he had a small waxed moustache; and there was a big carnation in the lapel of his coat, and he had on chamois gloves. . . ."

"My word!" murmured Vance. "A gigolo!"

Markham, with the incubus of the nightclubs riding him heavily, frowned and took a deep breath. Vance's observation evidently had launched him on an unpleasant train of thought.

"Was this man short or tall?" he asked next.

"He wasn't so tall—about my height," Spively explained. "And he was sort of thin."

There was an easily recognizable undercurrent of admiration in his tone, and I felt that this youthful telephone operator had seen in Miss Odell's caller a certain physical and sartorial ideal. This palpable admiration, coupled with the somewhat *outré* clothes affected by the youth, permitted us to read between the lines of his remarks a fairly accurate description of the man who had unsuccessfully rung the dead girl's bell at half past nine the night before.

When Spively had been dismissed, Markham rose and strode about the room, his head enveloped in a cloud of cigar smoke, while Heath sat stolidly watching him, his brows knit.

Vance stood up and stretched himself.

"The absorbin' problem, it would seem, remains *in statu quo*," he remarked airily. "How, oh, how, did the fair Margaret's executioner get in?"

"You know, Mr. Markham," rumbled Heath sententiously, "I've been thinking that the fellow may have come here earlier in the afternoon—say, before that side door was locked. Odell herself may have let him in and hidden him when the other man came to take her to dinner."

"It looks that way," Markham admitted. "Bring the maid in here again, and we'll see what we can find out."

When the woman had been brought in, Markham questioned her as to her actions during the afternoon, and learned that she had gone out at about four to do some shopping and had returned about half past five.

"Did Miss Odell have any visitor with her when you got back?"

"No, sir," was the prompt answer. "She was alone."

"Did she mention that anyone had called?"

"No, sir."

"Now," continued Markham, "could anyone have been hidden in this apartment when you went home at seven?"

The maid was frankly astonished and even a little horrified. "Where could anyone hide?" she asked, looking round the apartment.

"There are several possible places," Markham suggested: "in the bathroom, in one of the clothes closets, under the bed, behind the window draperies. . . ."

The woman shook her head decisively. "No one could have been hidden," she declared. "I was in the bathroom half a dozen times, and I got Miss Odell's gown out of the clothes closet in the bedroom. As soon as it began to get dark, I drew all the window shades myself. And as for the bed, it's built almost down to the floor; no one could squeeze under it." (I glanced closely at the bed and realized that this statement was quite true.)

"What about the clothes closet in this room?" Markham put the question hopefully, but again the maid shook her head.

"Nobody was in there. That's where I keep my own hat and coat, and I took them out myself when I was getting ready to go. I even put away one of Miss Odell's old dresses in that closet before I left."

"And you are absolutely certain," reiterated Markham, "that no one could have been hidden anywhere in these rooms at the time you went home?"

"Absolutely, sir."

"Do you happen to remember if the key of this clothes closet was on the inside or the outside of the lock when you opened the door to get your hat?"

The woman paused and looked thoughtfully at the closet door. "It was on the outside, where it always was," she announced, after several moments' reflection. "I remember because it caught in the chiffon of the old dress I put away."

Markham frowned and then resumed his questioning. "You say you don't know the name of Miss Odell's dinner companion last night. Can you tell us the names of any men she was in the habit of going out with?"

"Miss Odell never mentioned any names to me," the woman said. "She was very careful about it, too—secretive, you might say. You see, I'm only here in the daytime, and the gentlemen she knew generally came in the evening."

"And you never heard her speak of anyone of whom she was frightened—anyone she had reason to fear?"

"No, sir—although there was one man she was trying to get rid of. He was a bad character—I wouldn't have trusted him anywhere—and I told Miss Odell she'd better look out for him. But she'd known him a long time, I guess, and had been pretty soft on him once."

"How do you happen to know this?"

"One day, about a week ago," the maid explained, "I came in after lunch, and he was with her in the other room. They didn't hear me, because the portieres were drawn. He was demanding money, and when she tried to put him off, he began threatening her. And she said something that showed she'd given him money before. I made a noise, and then they stopped arguing; and pretty soon he went out."

"What did this man look like?" Markham's interest was reviving.

"He was kind of thin—not very tall—and I'd say he was around thirty. He had a hard face—good-looking, some would say—and pale blue eyes that gave you the shivers. He always wore his hair greased back, and he had a little yellow moustache pointed at the ends."

"Ah!" said Vance. "Our gigolo!"

"Has this man been here since?" asked Markham.

"I don't know, sir—not when I was here."

"That will be all," said Markham; and the woman went out.

"She didn't help us much," complained Heath.

"What!" exclaimed Vance. "I think she did remarkably well. She cleared up several moot points."

"And just what portions of her information do you consider particularly illuminating?" asked Markham, with ill-concealed annoyance.

"We now know, do we not," rejoined Vance serenely, "that no one was lying *perdu* in here when the *bonne* departed yesterevening."

"Instead of that fact being helpful," retorted Markham, "I'd say it added materially to the complications of the situation."

"It would appear that way, wouldn't it, now? But, then—who knows?—it may prove to be your brightest and most comfortin' clue. . . . Furthermore, we learned that someone evidently locked himself in that clothes press, as witness the shifting of the key, and that, moreover, this occulation did not occur until the abigail had gone, or, let us say, after seven o'clock."

"Sure," said Heath with sour facetiousness; "when the side door was bolted and an operator was sitting in the front hall, who swears nobody came in that way."

"It is a bit mystifyin'," Vance conceded sadly.

"Mystifying? It's impossible!" grumbled Markham.

Heath, who was now staring with meditative pugnacity into the closet, shook his head helplessly.

"What I don't understand," he ruminated, "is why, if the fellow was hiding in the closet, he didn't ransack it when he came out, like he did all the rest of the apartment."

"Sergeant," said Vance, "you've put your finger on the crux of the matter. . . . Y' know, the neat, undisturbed aspect of that closet rather suggests that the crude person who rifled these charming rooms omitted to give it his attention because it was locked on the inside and he couldn't open it."

"Come, come!" protested Markham. "That theory implies that there were two unknown persons in here last night."

Vance sighed. "Harrow and alas! I know it. And we can't introduce even one into this apartment logically. . . . Distressin', ain't it?"

Heath sought consolation in a new line of thought.

"Anyway," he submitted, "we know that the fancy fellow with the patent-leather pumps who called here last night at half past nine was probably Odell's lover, and was grafting on her."

"And in just what recondite way does that obvious fact help to roll the clouds away?" asked Vance. "Nearly every modern Delilah has an avaricious *amoroso*. It would be rather singular if there wasn't such a chap in the offing, what?"

"That's all right, too," returned Heath. "But I'll tell you something, Mr. Vance, that maybe you don't know. The men that these girls lose their heads over are generally crooks of some kind—professional criminals, you understand. That's why, knowing that this job was the work of a professional, it don't leave me cold, as you might say, to learn that this fellow who was threatening Odell and grafting on her was the same one who was prowling round· here last night. . . . And I'll say this, too: the description of him sounds a whole lot like the kind of high-class burglars that hang out at these swell all-night cafes."

"You're convinced, then," asked Vance mildly, "that this job, as you call it, was done by a professional criminal?"

Heath was almost contemptuous in his reply. "Didn't the guy wear gloves and use a jimmy? It was a yeggman's job, all right."

7

THE INVISIBLE MURDERER

(Tuesday, September 11; 11:45 A.M.)

MARKHAM WENT to the window and stood, his hands behind him, looking down into the little paved rear yard. After several minutes he turned slowly.

"The situation, as I see it," he said, "boils down to this:—The Odell girl has an engagement for dinner and the theater with a man of some distinction. He calls for her a little after seven, and they go out together. At eleven o'clock they return. He goes with her into her apartment and remains half an hour. He leaves at half past eleven and asks the phone operator to call him a taxi. While he is waiting the girl screams and calls for help, and, in response to his inquiries, she tells him nothing is wrong and bids him go away. The taxi arrives, and he departs in it. Ten minutes later someone telephones her, and a man answers from her apartment. This morning she is found murdered, and the apartment ransacked."

He took a long draw on his cigar.

"Now, it is obvious that when she and her escort returned last night, there was another man in this place somewhere; and it is also obvious that the girl was alive after her escort had departed. Therefore, we must conclude that the man who was already in the apartment was the person who murdered her. This conclusion is further corroborated by Doctor Doremus's report that the crime occurred between eleven and twelve. But since her escort did not leave till half past eleven, and spoke with her after that time, we can put the actual hour of the murder as between half past eleven and midnight. . . . These are the inferable facts from the evidence thus far adduced."

"There's not much getting away from 'em," agreed Heath.

"At any rate, they're interestin'," murmured Vance.

Markham, walking up and down earnestly, continued: "The features of the situation revolving round these inferable facts are as follows:—There was no one hiding in the apartment at seven o'clock—the hour the maid went home. Therefore, the murderer entered the apartment later. First, then, let us consider the side door. At six o'clock, an hour before the maid's departure, the janitor bolted it on the inside, and both operators disavow emphatically that they went near it. Moreover, you, Sergeant, found it bolted this morning. Hence, we may assume that the door was bolted on the inside all night, and that nobody could have entered that way. Consequently, we are driven to the inevitable alternative that the murderer entered by the front door. Now, let us consider this other means of entry. The phone operator who was on duty until ten o'clock last night asserts positively that the only person who entered the front door and passed down the main hall to this apartment was a man who rang the bell and, getting no answer, immediately walked out again. The other operator, who was on duty from ten o'clock until this morning, asserts with equal positiveness that no one entered the front door and passed the switchboard coming to this apartment. Add to all this the fact that every window on this floor is barred, and that no one from upstairs can descend into the main hall without coming face to face with the operator, and we are, for the moment, confronted with an impasse."

Heath scratched his head and laughed mirthlessly. "It don't make sense, does it, sir?"

"What about the next apartment?" asked Vance, "the one with the door facing the rear passageway—No. 2, I think?"

Heath turned to him patronizingly. "I looked into that the first thing this morning. Apartment No. 2 is occupied by a single woman; and I woke her up at eight o'clock and searched the place. Nothing there. Anyway, you have to walk past the switchboard to reach her apartment the same as you do to reach this one; and nobody called on her or left her apartment last night. What's more, Jessup, who's a shrewd sound lad, told me this woman is a quiet, ladylike sort, and that she and Odell didn't even know each other."

"You're so thorough, Sergeant!" murmured Vance.

"Of course," put in Markham, "it would have been possible for someone from the other apartment to have slipped in here behind the operator's back between seven and eleven, and then to have slipped back after the murder. But as Sergeant Heath's search this morning failed to uncover anyone, we can eliminate the possibility of our man having operated from that quarter."

"I dare say you're right," Vance indifferently admitted. "But it strikes me, Markham old dear, that your own affectin' recapitulation of the situation jolly well eliminates the possibility of your man's having operated from any quarter. . . . And yet he came in, garroted the unfortunate damsel, and departed—

eh, what? . . . It's a charmin' little problem. I wouldn't have missed it for worlds."

"It's uncanny," pronounced Markham gloomily.

"It's positively spiritualistic," amended Vance. "It has the caressin' odor of a séance. Really, y' know, I'm beginning to suspect that some medium was hovering in the vicinage last night doing some rather tip-top materializations. . . . I say, Markham, could you get an indictment against an ectoplasmic emanation?"

"It wasn't no spook that made those fingerprints," growled Heath, with surly truculence.

Markham halted his nervous pacing and regarded Vance irritably. "Damn it! This is rank nonsense. The man got in some way, and he got out, too. There's something wrong somewhere. Either the maid is mistaken about someone being here when she left, or else one of those phone operators went to sleep and won't admit it."

"Or else one of 'em's lying," supplemented Heath.

Vance shook his head. "The dusky *fille de chambre,* I'd say, is eminently trustworthy. And if there was any doubt about anyone's having come in the front door unnoticed, the lads on the switchboard would, in the present circumstances, be only too eager to admit it. . . . No, Markham, you'll simply have to approach this affair from the astral plane, so to speak."

Markham grunted his distaste of Vance's jocularity. "That line of investigation I leave to you with your metaphysical theories and esoteric hypotheses."

"But, consider," protested Vance banteringly. "You've proved conclusively—or, rather, you've demonstrated legally—that no one could have entered or departed from this apartment last night; and, as you've often told me, a court of law must decide all matters, not in accord with the known or suspected facts, but according to the evidence; and the evidence in this case would prove a sound alibi for every corporeal being extant. And yet, it's not exactly tenable, d' ye see, that the lady strangled herself. If only it had been poison, what an exquisite and satisfyin' suicide case you'd have! . . . Most inconsiderate of her homicidal visitor not to have used arsenic instead of his hands!"

"Well, he strangled her," pronounced Heath. "Furthermore, I'll lay my money on the fellow who called here last night at half past nine and couldn't get in. He's the bird I want to talk to."

"Indeed?" Vance produced another cigarette. "I shouldn't say, to judge from our description of him, that his conversation would prove particularly fascinatin'."

An ugly light came into Heath's eyes. "We've got ways," he said through his teeth, "of getting damn interesting conversation outta people who haven't no great reputation for repartee."

Vance sighed. "How the Four Hundred needs you, my Sergeant!"

Markham looked at his watch.

"I've got pressing work at the office," he said, "and all this talk isn't getting us anywhere." He put his hand on Heath's shoulder. "I leave you to go ahead. This afternoon I'll have these people brought down to my office for another questioning—maybe I can jog their memories a bit. . . . You've got some line of investigation planned?"

"The usual routine," replied Heath drearily. "I'll go through Odell's papers, and I'll have three or four of my men check up on her."

"You'd better get after the Yellow Taxicab Company right away," Markham suggested. "Find out, if you can, who the man was who left here at half past eleven last night, and where he went."

"Do you imagine for one moment," asked Vance, "that if this man knew anything about the murder, he would have stopped in the hall and asked the operator to call a taxi for him?"

"Oh, I don't look for much in that direction." Markham's tone was almost listless. "But the girl may have said something to him that'll give us a lead."

Vance shook his head facetiously. "O welcome pure-ey'd Faith, white-handed Hope, thou hovering angel, girt with golden wings!"

Markham was in no mood for chaffing. He turned to Heath, and spoke with forced cheeriness. "Call me up later this afternoon. I may get some new evidence out of the outfit we've just interviewed. . . . And," he added, "be sure to put a man on guard here. I want this apartment kept just as it is until we see a little more light."

"I'll attend to that," Heath assured him.

Markham and Vance and I went out and entered the car. A few minutes later we were winding rapidly across town through Central Park.

"Recall our recent *conversazione* about footprints in the snow?" asked Vance, as we emerged into Fifth Avenue and headed south.

Markham nodded abstractedly.

"As I remember," mused Vance, "in the hypothetical case you presented there were not only footprints but a dozen or more witnesses—including a youthful prodigy—who saw a figure of some kind cross the hibernal landscape. . . . *Grau, teurer Freund, ist alle Theorie!* Here you are in a most beastly pother because of the disheartenin' fact that there are neither footprints in the snow nor witnesses who saw a fleeing figure. In short, you are bereft of both direct and circumstantial evidence. . . . Sad, sad."

He wagged his head dolefully.

"Y' know, Markham, it appears to me that the testimony in this case constitutes conclusive legal proof that no one could have been with the deceased at the hour of her passing, and that, *ergo,* she is presumably alive. The strangled body of the lady is, I take it, simply an irrelevant circumstance from the standpoint of legal procedure. I know that you learned lawyers won't admit a murder without a body; but how, in sweet Heaven's name, do you get around a *corpus delicti* without a murder?"

"You're talking nonsense," Markham rebuked him, with a show of anger.

"Oh, quite," agreed Vance. "And yet, it's a distressin' thing for a lawyer not to have footprints of some kind, isn't it, old dear? It leaves one so up in the air."

Suddenly Markham swung round. "*You,* of course, don't need footprints, or any other kind of material clues," he flung at Vance tauntingly. "*You* have powers of divination such as are denied ordinary mortals. If I remember correctly, you informed me, somewhat grandiloquently, that, knowing the nature and conditions of a crime, you could lead me infallibly to the culprit, whether he left footprints or not. You recall that boast? . . . Well, here's a crime, and the perpetrator left no footprints coming or going. Be so kind as to end my suspense by confiding in me who killed the Odell girl."

Vance's serenity was not ruffled by Markham's ill-humored challenge. He sat smoking lazily for several minutes; then he leaned over and flicked his cigarette ash out of the window.

" 'Pon my word, Markham," he rejoined evenly, "I'm half inclined to look into this silly murder. I think I'll wait, though, and see whom the nonplussed Heath turns up with his inquiries."

Markham grunted scoffingly and sank back on the cushions. "Your generosity wrings me," he said.

9

THE PACK IN FULL CRY

(*Tuesday, September 11; afternoon*)

ON OUR WAY downtown that morning we were delayed for a considerable time in the traffic congestion just north of Madison Square, and Markham anxiously looked at his watch.

"It's past noon," he said. "I think I'll stop at the club and have a bite of lunch. . . . I presume that eating at this early hour would be too plebeian for so exquisite a hothouse flower as you."

Vance considered the invitation.

"Since you deprived me of my breakfast," he decided, "I'll permit you to buy me some eggs *Bénédictine.*"

A few minutes later we entered the almost empty grill of the Stuyvesant Club and took a table near one of the windows looking southward over the treetops of Madison Square.

Shortly after we had given our order a uniformed attendant entered and, bowing deferentially at the district attorney's elbow, held out an unaddressed communication sealed in one of the club's envelopes. Markham read it with an expression of growing curiosity, and as he studied the signature a look of mild surprise came into his eyes. At length he looked up and nodded to the waiting attendant. Then, excusing himself, he left us abruptly. It was fully twenty minutes before he returned.

"Funny thing," he said. "That note was from the man who took the Odell woman to dinner and the theater last night. . . . A small world," he mused. "He's staying here at the club—he's a nonresident member and makes it his headquarters when he's in town."

"You know him?" Vance put the question disinterestedly.

"I've met him several times—chap named Spotswoode." Markham seemed perplexed. "He's a man of family, lives in a country house on Long Island, and is regarded generally as a highly respectable member of society—one of the last persons I'd suspect of being mixed up with the Odell girl. But, according to his own confession, he played around a good deal with her during his visits to New York—'sowing a few belated wild oats,' as he expressed it—and last night took her to Francelle's for dinner and to the Winter Garden afterwards."

"Not my idea of an intellectual, or even edifyin', evening," commented Vance. "And he selected a deuced unlucky day for it. . . . I say, imagine opening the morning paper and learning that your *petite dame* of the preceding evening had been strangled! Disconcertin', what?"

"He's certainly disconcerted," said Markham. "The early afternoon papers were out about an hour ago, and he'd been phoning my office every ten minutes, when I suddenly walked in here. He's afraid his connection with the girl will leak out and disgrace him."

"And won't it?"

"I hardly see the necessity. No one knows who her escort was last evening; and since he obviously had nothing to do with the crime, what's to be gained by dragging him into it? He told me the whole story, and offered to stay in the city as long as I wanted him to."

"I infer, from the cloud of disappointment that enveloped you when you returned just now, that his story held nothing hopeful for you in the way of clues."

"No," Markham admitted. "The girl apparently never spoke to him of her intimate affairs; and he couldn't give me a single helpful suggestion. His account of what happened last night agreed perfectly with Jessup's. He called for the girl at seven, brought her home at about eleven, stayed with her half an hour or so, and then left her. When he heard her call for help, he was frightened, but on being assured by her there was nothing wrong, he concluded she had dozed off into a nightmare, and thought no more of it. He drove direct to the club here, arriving about ten minutes to twelve. Judge Redfern, who saw him descend from the taxi, insisted on his coming upstairs and playing poker with some men who were waiting in the judge's rooms for him. They played until three o'clock this morning."

"Your Long Island Don Juan has certainly not supplied you with any footprints in the snow."

"Anyway, his coming forward at this time closes one line of inquiry over which we might have wasted considerable time."

"If many more lines of inquiry are closed," remarked Vance dryly, "you'll be in a distressin' dilemma, don't y' know."

"There are enough still open to keep me busy," said Markham, pushing back his plate and calling for the check. He rose; then pausing, regarded Vance meditatingly. "Are you sufficiently interested to want to come along?"

"Eh, what? My word! . . . Charmed, I'm sure. But, I say, sit down just a moment—there's a good fellow!—till I finish my coffee."

I was considerably astonished at Vance's ready acceptance, careless and bantering though it was, for there was an exhibition of old Chinese prints at the Montross Galleries that afternoon, which he had planned to attend. A Riokai and a Moyeki, said to be very fine examples of Sung painting, were to be shown; and Vance was particularly eager to acquire them for his collection.

We rode with Markham to the Criminal Courts building and, entering by the Franklin Street door, took the private elevator to the district attorney's spacious but dingy private office, which overlooked the gray-stone ramparts of the Tombs. Vance seated himself in one of the heavy leather-upholstered chairs near the carved oak table on the right of the desk and lighted a cigarette with an air of cynical amusement.

"I await with anticipat'ry delight the grinding of the wheels of justice," he confided, leaning back lazily.

"You are doomed not to hear the first turn of those wheels," retorted Markham. "The initial revolution will take place outside of this office." And he disappeared through a swinging door which led to the judge's chambers.

Five minutes later he returned and sat down in the high-backed swivel chair at his desk, with his back to the four tall narrow windows in the south wall of the office.

"I just saw Judge Redfern," he explained—"it happened to be the midday recess—and he verified Spotswoode's statement in regard to the poker game. The judge met him outside of the club at ten minutes before midnight, and was with him until three in the morning. He noted the time because he had promised his guests to be back at half past eleven and was twenty minutes late."

"Why all this substantiation of an obviously unimportant fact?" asked Vance.

"A matter of routine," Markham told him, slightly impatient. "In a case of this kind every factor, however seemingly remote to the main issue, must be checked."

"Really, y' know, Markham"—Vance laid his head back on the chair and gazed dreamily at the ceiling—"one would think that this eternal routine, which you lawyer chaps worship so devoutly, actually got one somewhere occasionally; whereas it never gets one anywhere. Remember the Red Queen in 'Through the Looking-Glass——' "

"I'm too busy at present to debate the question of routine *versus* inspiration," Markham answered brusquely, pressing a button beneath the edge of his desk.

Swacker, his youthful and energetic secretary, appeared at the door which communicated with a narrow inner chamber between the district attorney's office and the main waiting room.

"Yes, Chief?" The secretary's eyes gleamed expectantly behind his enormous horn-rimmed glasses.

"Tell Ben to send me in a man at once."*

Swacker went out through the corridor door, and a minute or two later a suave, rotund man, dressed immaculately and wearing a pince-nez, entered, and stood before Markham with an ingratiating smile.

"Morning, Tracy." Markham's tone was pleasant but curt. "Here's a list of four witnesses in connection with the Odell case that I want brought down here at once—the two phone operators, the maid, and the janitor. You'll find them at 184 West 71st Street. Sergeant Heath is holding them there."

"Right, sir." Tracy took the memorandum, and with a priggish, but by no means inelegant, bow went out.

During the next hour Markham plunged into the general work that had accumulated during the forenoon, and I was amazed at the man's tremendous vitality and efficiency. He disposed of as many important matters as would

* "Ben" was Colonel Benjamin Hanlon, the commanding officer of the Detective Division attached to the district attorney's office.

have occupied the ordinary businessman for an entire day. Swacker bobbed in and out with electric energy, and various clerks appeared at the touch of a buzzer, took their orders, and were gone with breathless rapidity. Vance, who had sought diversion in a tome of famous arson trials, looked up admiringly from time to time and shook his head in mild reproach at such spirited activity.

It was just half past two when Swacker announced the return of Tracy with the four witnesses; and for two hours Markham questioned and cross-questioned them with a thoroughness and an insight that even I, as a lawyer, had rarely seen equaled. His interrogation of the two phone operators was quite different from his casual questioning of them earlier in the day; and if there had been a single relevant omission in their former testimony, it would certainly have been caught now by Markham's grueling catechism. But when, at last, they were told they could go, no new information had been brought to light. Their stories now stood firmly grounded: no one—with the exception of the girl herself and her escort, and the disappointed visitor at half past nine—had entered the front door and passed down the hall to the Odell apartment from seven o'clock on; and no one had passed out that way. The janitor reiterated stubbornly that he had bolted the side door a little after six, and no amount of wheedling or aggression could shake his dogged certainty on that point. Amy Gibson, the maid, could add nothing to her former testimony. Markham's intensive examination of her produced only repetitions of what she had already told him.

Not one new possibility—not one new suggestion—was brought out. In fact, the two hours' interlocutory proceedings resulted only in closing up every loophole in a seemingly incredible situation. When, at half past four, Markham sat back in his chair with a weary sigh, the chance of unearthing a promising means of approach to the astonishing problem seemed more remote than ever.

Vance closed his treatise on arson and threw away his cigarette.

"I tell you, Markham old chap"—he grinned—"this case requires umbilical contemplation, not routine. Why not call in an Egyptian seeress with a *flair* for crystal-gazing?"

"If this sort of thing goes on much longer," returned Markham dispiritedly, "I'll be tempted to take your advice."

Just then Swacker looked in through the door to say that Inspector Brenner was on the wire. Markham picked up the telephone receiver, and as he listened he jotted down some notes on a pad. When the call had ended, he turned to Vance.

"You seemed disturbed over the condition of the steel jewel case we found in the bedroom. Well, the expert on burglar tools just called up; and he verifies his opinion of this morning. The case was pried open with a specially-made cold chisel such as only a professional burglar would carry or would know how to use. It had an inch-and-three-eighths beveled bit and a one-inch flat handle. It was an old instrument—there was a peculiar nick in the blade—and is the same one that was used in a successful housebreak on upper Park Avenue early last summer.... Does that highly exciting information ameliorate your anxiety?"

"Can't say that it does." Vance had again become serious and perplexed.

"In fact, it makes the situation still more fantastic. . . . I could see a glimmer of light—eerie and unearthly, perhaps, but still a perceptible illumination—in all this murkiness if it wasn't for that jewel case and the steel chisel."

Markham was about to answer when Swacker again looked in and informed him that Sergeant Heath had arrived and wanted to see him.

Heath's manner was far less depressed than when we had taken leave of him that morning. He accepted the cigar Markham offered him, and seating himself at the conference table in front of the district attorney's desk, drew out a battered notebook.

"We've had a little good luck," he began. "Burke and Emery—two of the men I put on the case—got a line on Odell at the first place they made inquiries. From what they learned, she didn't run around with many men—limited herself to a few live wires, and played the game with what you'd call *finesse*. . . . The principal one—the man who's been seen most with her—is Charles Cleaver."

Markham sat up. "I know Cleaver—if it's the same one."

"It's him, all right," declared Heath. "Former Brooklyn Tax Commissioner; been interested in a poolroom for pony-betting over in Jersey City ever since. Hangs out at the Stuyvesant Club, where he can hobnob with his old Tammany Hall cronies."

"That's the one," nodded Markham. "He's a kind of professional gay dog—known as Pop, I believe."

Vance gazed into space.

"Well, well," he murmured. "So old Pop Cleaver was also entangled with our subtle and sanguine Dolores. She certainly couldn't have loved him for his *beaux yeux*."

"I thought, sir," went on Heath, "that, seeing as how Cleaver is always in and out of the Stuyvesant Club, you might ask him some questions about Odell. He ought to know something."

"Glad to, Sergeant." Markham made a note on his pad. "I'll try to get in touch with him tonight. . . . Anyone else on your list?"

"There's a fellow named Mannix—Louis Mannix—who met Odell when she was in the 'Follies'; but she chucked him over a year ago, and they haven't been seen together since. He's got another girl now. He's the head of the firm of Mannix and Levine, fur importers, and is one of your nightclub rounders—a heavy spender. But I don't see much use of barking up that tree—his affair with Odell went cold too long ago."

"Yes," agreed Markham; "I think we can eliminate him."

"I say, if you keep up this elimination much longer," observed Vance, "you won't have anything left but the lady's corpse."

"And then, there's the man who took her out last night," pursued Heath. "Nobody seems to know his name—he must've been one of those discreet, careful old boys. I thought at first he might have been Cleaver, but the descriptions don't tally. . . . And by the way, sir, here's a funny thing: when he left Odell last night he took the taxi down to the Stuyvesant Club and got out there."

Markham nodded. "I know all about that, Sergeant. And I know who the man was; and it wasn't Cleaver."

Vance was chuckling. "The Stuyvesant Club seems to be well in the forefront of this case," he said. "I do hope it doesn't suffer the sad fate of the Knickerbocker Athletic."*

Heath was intent on the main issue.

"Who was the man, Mr. Markham?"

Markham hesitated, as if pondering the advisability of taking the other into his confidence. Then he said: "I'll tell you his name, but in strict confidence. The man was Kenneth Spotswoode."

He then recounted the story of his being called away from lunch, and of his failure to elicit any helpful suggestions from Spotswoode. He also informed Heath of his verification of the man's statements regarding his movements after meeting Judge Redfern at the club.

"And," added Markham, "since he obviously left the girl before she was murdered, there's no necessity to bother him. In fact, I gave him my word I'd keep him out of it for his family's sake."

"If you're satisfied, sir, I am." Heath closed his notebook and put it away. "There's just one other little thing. Odell used to live on 110th Street, and Emery dug up her former landlady and learned that this fancy guy the maid told us about used to call on her regularly."

"That reminds me, Sergeant." Markham picked up the memorandum he had made during Inspector Brenner's phone call. "Here's some data the Professor gave me about the forcing of the jewel case."

Heath studied the paper with considerable eagerness. "Just as I thought!" He nodded his head with satisfaction. "Clear-cut professional job, by somebody who's been in the line of work before."

Vance roused himself. "Still, if such is the case," he said, "why did this experienced burglar first use the insufficient poker? And why did he overlook the living room clothes press?"

"I'll find all that out, Mr. Vance, when I get my hands on him," asserted Heath, with a hard look in his eyes. "And the guy I want to have a nice quiet little chat with is the one with the pleated silk shirt and the chamois gloves."

"*Chacun à son goût*," sighed Vance. "For myself, I have no yearning whatever to hold converse with him. Somehow, I can't just picture a professional looter trying to rend a steel box with a cast iron poker."

"Forget the poker," Heath advised gruffly. "He jimmied the box with a steel chisel; and that same chisel was used last summer in another burglary on Park Avenue. What about *that?*"

"Ah! That's what torments me, Sergeant. If it wasn't for that disturbin' fact, d' ye see, I'd be lightsome and *sans souci* this afternoon, inviting my soul over a dish of tea at Claremont."

Detective Bellamy was announced, and Heath sprang to his feet. "That'll mean news about those fingerprints," he prophesied hopefully.

Bellamy entered unemotionally and walked up to the district attorney's desk.

---

* Vance was here referring to the famous Molineux case, which, in 1898, sounded the death knell of the old Knickerbocker Athletic Club at Madison Avenue and 45th Street. But it was commercialism that ended the Stuyvesant's career. This club, which stood on the north side of Madison Square, was razed a few years later to make room for a skyscraper.

"Cap'n Dubois sent me over," he said. "He thought you'd want the report on those Odell prints." He reached into his pocket and drew out a small flat folder which, at a sign from Markham, he handed to Heath. "We identified 'em. Both made by the same hand, like Cap'n Dubois said: and that hand belonged to Tony Skeel."

" 'Dude' Skeel, eh?" The sergeant's tone was vibrant with suppressed excitement. "Say, Mr. Markham, that gets us somewhere. Skeel's an ex-convict and an artist in his line."

He opened the folder and took out an oblong card and a sheet of blue paper containing eight or ten lines of typewriting. He studied the card, gave a satisfied grunt, and handed it to Markham. Vance and I stepped up and looked at it. At the top was the familiar rogues' gallery photograph showing the full face and profile of a regular-featured youth with thick hair and a square chin. His eyes were wide-set and pale, and he wore a small, evenly trimmed moustache with waxed, needlepoint ends. Below the double photograph was a brief tabulated description of its sitter, giving his name, aliases, residence, and Bertillon measurements, and designating the character of his illegal profession. Underneath were ten little squares arranged in two rows, each containing a fingerprint impress made in black ink—the upper row being the impressions of the right hand, the lower row those of the left.

"So that's the *arbiter elegantiarum* who introduced the silk shirt for full-dress wear! My word!" Vance regarded the identification card satirically. "I wish he'd start a craze for gaiters with dinner jackets—these New York theaters are frightfully drafty in winter."

Heath put the card back in the folder and glanced over the typewritten paper that had accompanied it.

"He's our man, and no mistake, Mr. Markham. Listen to this: 'Tony (Dude) Skeel. Two years Elmira Reformatory, 1902 to 1904. One year in the Baltimore County jail for petit larceny, 1906. Three years in San Quentin for assault and robbery, 1908 to 1911. Arrested Chicago for housebreaking, 1912; case dismissed. Arrested and tried for burglary in Albany, 1913; no conviction. Served two years and eight months in Sing-Sing for housebreaking and burglary, 1914 to 1916.' " He folded the paper and put it, with the card, into his breast pocket. "Sweet little record."

"That dope what you wanted?" asked the imperturbable Bellamy.

"I'll say!" Heath was almost jovial.

Bellamy lingered expectantly with one eye on the district attorney; and Markham, as if suddenly remembering something, took out a box of cigars and held it out.

"Much obliged, sir," said Bellamy, helping himself to two Mi Favoritas; and putting them into his waistcoat pocket with great care, he went out.

"I'll use your phone now, if you don't mind, Mr. Markham," said Heath. He called the Homicide Bureau.

"Look up Tony Skeel—Dude Skeel—pronto, and bring him in as soon as you find him," were his orders to Snitkin. "Get his address from the files and take Burke and Emery with you. If he's hopped it, send out a general alarm and have him picked up—some of the boys'll have a line on him. Lock him up without booking him, see? . . . And, listen. Search his room for burglar tools: he probably won't have any laying around, but I specially want a one-and-three-eighths-inch chisel with a nick in the blade. . . . I'll be at headquarters in half an hour."

He hung up the receiver and rubbed his hands together.

"Now we're sailing," he rejoiced.

Vance had gone to the window and stood staring down on the "Bridge of Sighs," his hands thrust deep into his pockets. Slowly he turned, and fixed Heath with a contemplative eye.

"It simply won't do, don't y' know," he asserted. "Your friend, the Dude, may have ripped open that bally box, but his head isn't the right shape for the rest of last evening's performance."

Heath was contemptuous. "Not being a phrenologist, I'm going by the shape of his fingerprints."

"A woeful error in the technic of criminal approach, *sergente mio,*" replied Vance dulcetly. "The question of culpability in this case isn't so simple as you imagine. It's deuced complicated. And this glass of fashion and mold of form whose portrait you're carryin' next to your heart has merely added to its intricacy."

10

A FORCED INTERVIEW

(*Tuesday, September 11; 8 P.M.*)

MARKHAM DINED at the Stuyvesant Club, as was his custom, and at his invitation Vance and I remained with him. He no doubt figured that our presence at the dinner table would act as a bulwark against the intrusion of casual acquaintances; for he was in no mood for the pleasantries of the curious. Rain had begun to fall late in the afternoon, and when dinner was over, it had turned into a steady downpour which threatened to last well into the night. Dinner over, the three of us sought a secluded corner of the lounge room, and settled ourselves for a protracted smoke.

We had been there less than a quarter of an hour when a slightly rotund man, with a heavy, florid face and thin gray hair, strolled up to us with a stealthy, self-assured gait, and wished Markham a jovial good evening. Though I had not met the newcomer I knew him to be Charles Cleaver.

"Got your note at the desk saying you wanted to see me." He spoke with a voice curiously gentle for a man of his size; but, for all its gentleness, there was in it a timbre of calculation and coldness.

Markham rose and, after shaking hands, introduced him to Vance and me—though, it seemed, Vance had known him slightly for some time. He took the chair Markham indicated, and, producing a Corona Corona, he carefully cut the end with a gold clipper attached to his heavy watch chain, rolled the cigar between his lips to dampen it and lighted it in closely cupped hands.

"I'm sorry to trouble you, Mr. Cleaver," began Markham, "but, as you probably have read, a young woman by the name of Margaret Odell was murdered last night in her apartment in 71st Street. . . ."

He paused. He seemed to be considering just how he could best broach a subject so obviously delicate; and perhaps he hoped that Cleaver would volunteer the fact of his acquaintance with the girl. But not a muscle of the man's face moved; and, after a moment, Markham continued.

"In making inquiries into the young woman's life I learned that you, among others, were fairly well acquainted with her."

Again he paused. Cleaver lifted his eyebrows almost imperceptibly but said nothing.

"The fact is," went on Markham, a trifle annoyed by the other's deliberately circumspect attitude, "my report states that you were seen with her on many occasions during a period of nearly two years. Indeed, the only inference to be drawn from what I've learned is that you were more than casually interested in Miss Odell."

"Yes?" The query was as noncommital as it was gentle.

"Yes," repeated Markham. "And I may add, Mr. Cleaver, that this is not the time for pretenses or suppressions. I am talking to you tonight, in large measure *ex officio,* because it occurred to me that you could give me some assistance in clearing the matter up. I think it only fair to say that a certain man is now under grave suspicion, and we hope to arrest him very soon. But, in any event, we will need help, and that is why I requested this little chat with you at the club."

"And how can I assist you?" Cleaver's face remained blank; only his lips moved as he put the question.

"Knowing this young woman as well as you did," explained Markham patiently, "you are no doubt in possession of some information—certain facts or confidences, let us say—which would throw light on her brutal, and apparently unexpected, murder."

Cleaver was silent for some time. His eyes had shifted to the wall before him, but otherwise his features remained set.

"I'm afraid I can't accommodate you," he said at length.

"Your attitude is not quite what might be expected in one whose conscience is entirely clear," returned Markham, with a show of resentment.

The man turned a mildly inquisitive gaze upon the district attorney.

"What has my knowing the girl to do with her being murdered? She didn't confide in me who her murderer was to be. She didn't even tell me that she knew anyone who intended to strangle her. If she'd known, she most likely could have avoided being murdered."

Vance was sitting close to me, a little removed from the others, and, leaning over, murmured in my ear *sotto voce:* "Markham's up against another lawyer—poor dear! . . . A crumplin' situation."

But however inauspiciously this interlocutory skirmish may have begun, it soon developed into a grim combat which ended in Cleaver's complete surrender. Markham, despite his suavity and graciousness, was an unrelenting and resourceful antagonist; and it was not long before he had forced from Cleaver some highly significant information.

In response to the man's ironically evasive rejoinder, he turned quickly and leaned forward.

"You're not on the witness stand in your own defense, Mr. Cleaver," he said sharply, "however much you appear to regard yourself as eligible for that position."

Cleaver glared back fixedly without replying; and Markham, his eyelids level, studied the man opposite, determined to decipher all he could from the other's phlegmatic countenance. But Cleaver was apparently just as determined that his *vis-à-vis* should decipher absolutely nothing; and the features that met Markham's scrutiny were as arid as a desert. At length Markham sank back in his chair.

"It doesn't matter particularly," he remarked indifferently, "whether you discuss the matter or not here in the club tonight. If you prefer to be brought to my office in the morning by a sheriff with a subpœna, I'll be only too glad to accommodate you."

"That's up to you," Cleaver told him hostilely.

"And what's printed in the newspapers about it will be up to the reporters," rejoined Markham. "I'll explain the situation to them and give them a verbatim report of the interview."

"But I've nothing to tell you." The other's tone was suddenly conciliatory; the idea of publicity was evidently highly distasteful to him.

"So you informed me before," said Markham coldly. "Therefore I wish you good evening."

He turned to Vance and me with the air of a man who had terminated an unpleasant episode.

Cleaver, however, made no move to go. He smoked thoughtfully for a minute or two; then he gave a short, hard laugh which did not even disturb the contours of his face.

"Oh, hell!" he grumbled, with forced good nature. "As you said, I'm not on the witness stand. . . . What do you want to know?"

"I've told you the situation." Markham's voice betrayed a curious irritation. "You know the sort of thing I want. How did this Odell girl live? Who were her intimates? Who would have been likely to want her out of the way? What enemies had she?—Anything that might lead us to an explanation of her death. . . . And incidentally," he added with tartness, "anything that'll eliminate yourself from any suspected participation, direct or indirect, in the affair."

Cleaver stiffened at these last words and started to protest indignantly. But immediately he changed his tactics. Smiling contemptuously, he took out a leather pocket case and, extracting a small folded paper, handed it to Markham.

"I can eliminate myself easily enough," he proclaimed, with easy confidence. "There's a speeding summons from Boonton, New Jersey. Note the date and the time: September the tenth—last night—at half past eleven. Was driving down to Hopatcong, and was ticketed by a motorcycle cop just as I had passed Boonton and was heading for Mountain Lakes. Got to appear in court there tomorrow morning. Damn nuisance, these country constables." He gave Markham a long, calculating look. "You couldn't square it for me, could you? It's a rotten ride to Jersey, and I've got a lot to do tomorrow."

Markham, who had inspected the summons casually, put it in his pocket.

"I'll attend to it for you," he promised, smiling amiably. "Now tell me what you know."

Cleaver puffed meditatively on his cigar. Then, leaning back and crossing his knees, he spoke with apparent candor.

"I doubt if I know much that'll help you. . . . I liked the Canary, as she was called—in fact, was pretty much attached to her at one time. Did a number of foolish things; wrote her a lot of damn-fool letters when I went to Cuba last year. Even had my picture taken with her down at Atlantic City." He made a self-condemnatory grimace. "Then she began to get cool and distant; broke several appointments with me. I raised the devil with her, but the only answer I got was a demand for money. . . ."

He stopped and looked down at his cigar ash. A venomous hatred gleamed from his narrowed eyes, and the muscles of his jowls hardened.

"No use lying about it. She had those letters and things, and she touched me for a neat little sum before I got 'em back. . . ."

"When was this?"

There was a momentary hesitation. "Last June," Cleaver replied. Then he hurried on: "Mr. Markham"—his voice was bitter—"I don't want to throw mud on a dead person; but that woman was the shrewdest, coldest-blooded blackmailer it's ever been my misfortune to meet. And I'll say this, too: I wasn't the only easy mark she squeezed. She had others on her string. . . . I happen to know she once dug into old Louey Mannix for a plenty—he told me about it."

"Could you give me the names of any of these other men?" asked Markham, attempting to dissemble his eagerness. "I've already heard of the Mannix episode."

"No, I couldn't." Cleaver spoke regretfully. "I've seen the Canary here and there with different men; and there's one in particular I've noticed lately. But they were all strangers to me."

"I suppose the Mannix affair is dead and buried by this time?"

"Yes—ancient history. You won't get any line on the situation from that angle. But there are others—more recent than Mannix—who might bear looking into, if you could find them. I'm easygoing myself; take things as they come. But there's a lot of men who'd go red-headed if she did the things to them that she did to me."

Cleaver, despite his confession, did not strike me as easygoing, but rather as a cold, self-contained, nerveless person whose immobility was at all times dictated by policy and expediency.

Markham studied him closely.

"You think, then, her death may have been due to vengeance on the part of some disillusioned admirer?"

Cleaver carefully considered his answer. "Seems reasonable," he said finally. "She was riding for a fall."

There was a short silence; then Markham asked: "Do you happen to know of a young man she was interested in—good-looking, small, blond moustache, light blue eyes—named Skeel?"

Cleaver snorted derisively. "That wasn't the Canary's specialty—she let the young ones alone, as far as I know."

At this moment a pageboy approached Cleaver and bowed. "Sorry to disturb you, sir, but there's a phone call for your brother. Party said it was important and, as your brother isn't in the club now, the operator thought you might know where he'd gone."

"How would I know?" fumed Cleaver. "Don't ever bother me with his calls."

"Your brother in the city?" asked Markham casually. "I met him years ago. He's a San Franciscan, isn't he?"

"Yes—rabid Californian. He's visiting New York for a couple of weeks so he'll appreciate Frisco more when he gets back."

It seemed to me that this information was given reluctantly; and I got the impression that Cleaver, for some reason, was annoyed. But Markham, apparently, was too absorbed in the problem before him to take notice of the other's disgruntled air, for he reverted at once to the subject of the murder.

"I happen to know one man who has been interested in the Odell woman recently; he may be the same one you've seen her with—tall, about forty-five, and wears a gray, closed-cropped moustache." (He was, I knew, describing Spotswoode.)

"That's the man," averred Cleaver. "Saw them together only last week at Mouquin's."

Markham was disappointed. "Unfortunately, he's checked off the list. . . . But there must be somebody who was in the girl's confidence. You're sure you couldn't cudgel your brains to my advantage?"

Cleaver appeared to think.

"If it's merely a question of someone who had her confidence," he said, "I might suggest Doctor Lindquist—first name's Ambroise, I think; and he lives somewhere in the Forties near Lexington Avenue. But I don't know that he'd be of any value to you. Still, he was pretty close to her at one time."

"You mean that this Doctor Lindquist might have been interested in her otherwise than professionally?"

"I wouldn't like to say." Cleaver smoked for a while as if inwardly debating the situation. "Anyway, here are the facts: Lindquist is one of these exclusive society specialists—a neurologist he calls himself—and I believe he's the head of a private sanitarium of some kind for nervous women. He must have money, and, of course, his social standing is a vital asset to him—just the sort of man the Canary might have selected as a source of income. And I know this: he came to see her a good deal oftener than a doctor of his type would be apt to. I ran into him one night at her apartment, and when she introduced us, he wasn't even civil."

"It will at least bear looking into," replied Markham unenthusiastically. "You've no one else in mind who might know something helpful?"

Cleaver shook his head.

"No—no one."

"And she never mentioned anything to you that indicated she was in fear of anyone, or anticipated trouble?"

"Not a word. Fact is, I was bowled over by the news. I never read any paper but the morning *Herald*—except, of course, *The Daily Racing Form* at night. And as there was no account of the murder in this morning's paper, I didn't hear about it until just before dinner. The boys in the billiard room were talking about it, and I went out and looked at an afternoon paper. If it hadn't been for that, I might not have known of it till tomorrow morning."

Markham discussed the case with him until half past eight but could elicit no further suggestions. Finally Cleaver rose to go.

"Sorry I couldn't give you more help," he said. His rubicund face was beaming now, and he shook hands with Markham in the friendliest fashion.

"You wangled that viscid old sport rather cleverly, don't y' know," remarked Vance, when Cleaver had gone. "But there's something deuced queer about him. The transition from his gambler's glassy stare to his garrulous confidences was too sudden—suspiciously sudden, in fact. I may be evil-minded, but he didn't impress me as a luminous pillar of truth. Maybe it's because I don't like those cold, boiled eyes of his—somehow they didn't harmonize with his gushing imitation of openhearted frankness."

"We can allow him something for his embarrassing position," suggested Markham charitably. "It isn't exactly pleasant to admit having been taken in and blackmailed by a charmer."

"Still, if he got his letters back in June, why did he continue paying court to the lady? Heath reported he was active in that sector right up to the end."

"He may be the complete amorist," smiled Markham.

"Some like Abra, what?——

> 'Abra was ready ere I call'd her name;
> And, though I call'd another, Abra came.'

Maybe—yes. He might qualify as a modern Cayley Drummle."

"At any rate, he gave us, in Doctor Lindquist, a possible source of information."

"Quite so," agreed Vance. "And that's about the only point of his whole passionate unfoldment that I particularly put any stock in, because it was the only point he indicated with any decent reticence. . . . My advice is that you interview this Æsculapius of the fair sex without further delay."

"I'm dog-tired," objected Markham. "Let it wait till tomorrow."

Vance glanced at the great clock over the stone mantel.

"It's latish, I'll admit, but why not, as Pittacus advised, seize time by the forelock?

> 'Who lets slip fortune, her shall never find:
> Occasion once past by, is a bald behind.'

But the elder Cato anticipated Cowley. In his 'Disticha de Moribus' he wrote: *Fronte capillata*——"

"Come!" pleaded Markham, rising. "Anything to dam this flow of erudition."

11

SEEKING INFORMATION

(Tuesday September 11; 9 P.M.)

TEN MINUTES later we were ringing the bell of a stately old brownstone house in East 44th Street.

A resplendently caparisoned butler opened the door, and Markham presented his card.

"Take this to the doctor at once and say that it's urgent."

"The doctor is just finishing dinner," the stately seneschal informed him, and conducted us into a richly furnished reception room, with deep, comfortable chairs, silken draperies, and subdued lights.

"A typical gynecologist's seraglio," observed Vance, looking around. "I'm sure the pasha himself is a majestic and elegant personage."

The prediction proved true. Doctor Lindquist entered the room a moment later inspecting the district attorney's card as if it had been a cuneiform inscription whose import he could not quite decipher. He was a tall man in his late forties, with bushy hair and eyebrows, and a complexion abnormally pale. His face was long, and, despite the asymmetry of his features, he might easily have been called handsome. He was in dinner clothes, and he carried himself with the self-conscious precision of a man unduly impressed with his own importance. He seated himself at a kidney-shaped desk of carved mahogany and lifted his eyes with polite inquiry to Markham.

"To what am I indebted for the honor of this call?" he asked in a studiously melodious voice, lingering over each word caressingly. "You are most fortunate to have found me in," he added, before Markham could speak. "I confer with patients only by appointment." One felt that he experienced a certain humiliation at having received us without elaborate ceremonial preliminaries.

Markham, whose nature was opposed to all circumlocution and pretense, came direct to the point.

"This isn't a professional consultation, Doctor; but it happens that I want to speak to you about one of your former patients—a Miss Margaret Odell."

Doctor Lindquist regarded the gold paperweight before him with vacantly reminiscent eyes.

"Ah, yes. Miss Odell. I was just reading of her violent end. A most unfortunate and tragic affair. . . . In just what way can I be of service to you?—You understand, of course, that the relationship between a physician and his patient is one of sacred confidence——"

"I understand that thoroughly," Markham assured him abruptly. "On the other hand, it is the sacred duty of every citizen to assist the authorities in bringing a murderer to justice. And if there is anything you can tell me which will help toward that end, I shall certainly expect you to tell me."

The doctor raised his hand slightly in polite protestation. "I shall, of course, do all I can to assist you, if you will but indicate your desires."

"There's no need to beat about the bush, Doctor," said Markham. "I know that Miss Odell was a patient of yours for a long time; and I realize that it is highly possible, not to say probable, that she told you certain personal things which may have direct bearing on her death."

"But, my dear Mr.——," Doctor Lindquist glanced ostentatiously at the card, "ah—Markham, my relations with Miss Odell were of a purely professional character."

"I had understood, however," ventured Markham, "that, while what you say may be technically true, nevertheless there was an informality, let me say, in that relationship. Perhaps I may state it better by saying that your professional attitude transcended a merely scientific interest in her case."

I heard Vance chuckle softly; and I myself could hardly suppress a smile at Markham's verbose and orbicular accusation. But Doctor Lindquist, it seemed, was in no wise disconcerted. Assuming an air of beguiling pensiveness, he said: "I will confess, in the interests of strict accuracy, that during my somewhat protracted treatment of her case, I came to regard the young woman with a certain—shall I say, fatherly liking? But I doubt if she was even aware of this mild sentiment on my part."

The corners of Vance's mouth twitched slightly. He was sitting with drowsy eyes, watching the doctor with a look of studious amusement.

"And she never at any time told you of any private or personal affairs that were causing her anxiety?" persisted Markham.

Doctor Lindquist pyramided his fingers, and appeared to give the question his undivided thought.

"No, I can't recall a single statement of that nature." His words were measured and urbane. "I know, naturally, in a general way, her manner of living; but the details, you will readily perceive, were wholly outside my province as a medical consultant. The disorganization of her nerves was due—so my diagnosis led me to conclude—to late hours, excitement, irregular and rich eating—what, I believe, is referred to vulgarly as going the pace. The modern woman, in this febrile age, sir——"

"When did you see her last, may I ask?" Markham interrupted impatiently.

The doctor made a pantomime of eloquent surprise.

"When did I see her last? . . . Let me see." He could, apparently, recall the occasion only with considerable difficulty. "A fortnight ago, perhaps—though it may have been longer. I really can't recall. . . . Shall I refer to my files?"

"That won't be necessary," said Markham. He paused and regarded the doctor with a look of disarming affability. "And was this last visit a paternal or merely a professional one?"

"Professional, of course." Doctor Lindquist's eyes were impassive and only mildly interested; but his face, I felt, was by no means the unedited reflection of his thoughts.

"Did the meeting take place here or at her apartment?"

"I believe I called on her at her home."

"You called on her a great deal, Doctor—so I am informed—and at rather unconventional hours. . . . Is this entirely in accord with your practice of seeing patients only by appointment?"

Markham's tone was pleasant, but from the nature of his question I knew that he was decidedly irritated by the man's bland hypocrisy, and felt that he was deliberately withholding relevant information.

Before Doctor Lindquist could reply, however, the butler appeared at the door and silently indicated an extension telephone on a taboret beside the desk. With an unctuously murmured apology, the doctor turned and lifted the receiver.

Vance took advantage of this opportunity to scribble something on a piece of paper and pass it surreptitiously to Markham.

His call completed, Doctor Lindquist drew himself up haughtily and faced Markham with chilling scorn.

"Is it the function of the district attorney," he asked distantly, "to harrass respectable physicians with insulting questions? I did not know that it was illegal—or even original, for that matter—for a doctor to visit his patients."

"I am not discussing *now*"—Markham emphasized the adverb—"your infractions of the law; but since you suggest a possibility which, I assure you, was not in my mind, would you be good enough to tell me—merely as a matter of form—where you were last night between eleven and twelve?"

The question produced a startling effect. Doctor Lindquist became suddenly like a tautly drawn rope, and rising slowly and stiffly, he glared, with cold intense venom, at the district attorney. His velvety mask had fallen off; and I detected another emotion beneath his repressed anger: his expression cloaked a fear, and his wrath but partly veiled a passionate uncertainty.

"My whereabouts last night is no concern of yours." He spoke with great effort, his breath coming and going noisily.

Markham waited, apparently unmoved, his eyes riveted on the trembling man before him. This calm scrutiny completely broke down the other's self-control.

"What do you mean by forcing yourself in here with your contemptible insinuations?" he shouted. His face, now livid and mottled, was hideously contorted; his hands made spasmodic movements; and his whole body shook as with a tremor. "Get out of here—you and your two myrmidons! Get out, before I have you thrown out!"

Markham, himself enraged now, was about to reply, when Vance took him by the arm.

"The doctor is gently hinting that we go," he said. And with amazing swiftness he spun Markham round and led him firmly out of the room.

When we were again in the taxicab on our way back to the club, Vance sniggered gaily. "A sweet specimen, that! Paranoia. Or, more likely, manic-depressive insanity—the *folie circulaire* type: recurring periods of maniacal excitement alternating with periods of the clearest sanity, don't y' know. Anyway, the doctor's disorder belongs in the category of psychoses—associated with the maturation or waning of the sexual instinct. He's just the right age, too. Neurotic degenerate—that's what this oily Hippocrates is. In another minute he would have attacked you. . . . My word! It's a good thing I came to the rescue. Such chaps are about as safe as rattlesnakes."

He shook his head in a mock discouragement.

"Really, y' know, Markham, old thing," he added, "you should study the cranial indications of your fellow man more carefully—*vultus est index animi*. Did you, by any chance, note the gentleman's wide rectangular forehead, his irregular eyebrows, and pale luminous eyes, and his outstanding ears with their thin upper rims, their pointed tragi and split lobes? . . . A clever devil, this Ambroise—but a moral imbecile. Beware of those pseudopyriform faces, Markham; leave their Apollonian Greek suggestiveness to misunderstood women."

"I wonder what he really knows?" grumbled Markham irritably.

"Oh, he knows something—rest assured of that! And if only we knew it, too, we'd be considerably further along in the investigation. Furthermore, the information he is hiding is somewhat unpleasantly connected with himself. His euphoria is a bit shaken. He frightfully overdid the grand manner; his valedict'ry fulmination was the true expression of his feeling toward us."

"Yes," agreed Markham. "That question about last night acted like a petard. What prompted you to suggest my asking it?"

"A number of things—his gratuitous and obviously mendacious statement that he had just read of the murder; his wholly insincere homily on the sacredness of professional confidences; the cautious and Pecksniffian confession of his fatherly regard for the girl; his elaborate struggle to remember when he had last seen her—this particularly, I think, made me suspicious; and then, the psychopathic indicants of his physiognomy."

"Well," admitted Markham, "the question had its effect. . . . I feel that I shall see this fashionable M.D. again."

"You will," iterated Vance. "We took him unawares. But when he has had time to ponder the matter and concoct an appealin' tale, he'll become downright garrulous. . . . Anyhow, the evening is over, and you can meditate on buttercups till the morrow."

But the evening was not quite over as far as the Odell case was concerned. We had been back in the lounge room of the club but a short time when a man walked by the corner in which we sat, and bowed with formal courtesy to Markham. Markham, to my surprise, rose and greeted him, at the same time indicating a chair.

"There's something further I wanted to ask you, Mr. Spotswoode," he said, "if you can spare a moment."

At the mention of the name I regarded the man closely, for, I confess, I was not a little curious about the anonymous escort who had taken the girl to dinner and the theater the night before. Spotswoode was a typical New England aristocrat, inflexible, slow in his movements, reserved, and quietly but modishly dressed. His hair and moustache were slightly gray—which, no doubt, enhanced the pinkness of his complexion. He was just under six feet tall and well proportioned, but a trifle angular.

Markham introduced him to Vance and me, and briefly explained that we were working with him on the case and that he had thought it best to take us fully into his confidence.

Spotswoode gave him a dubious look but immediately bowed his acceptance of the decision.

"I'm in your hands, Mr. Markham," he replied, in a well-bred but somewhat high-pitched voice, "and I concur, of course, with whatever you think advisable." He turned to Vance with an apologetic smile. "I'm in a rather unpleasant position and naturally feel a little sensitive about it."

"I'm something of an antinomian," Vance pleasantly informed him. "At any rate, I'm not a moralist; so my attitude in the matter is quite academic."

Spotswoode laughed softly. "I wish my family held a similar point of view; but I'm afraid they would not be so tolerant of my foibles."

"It's only fair to tell you, Mr. Spotswoode," interposed Markham, "that there is a bare possibility I may have to call you as a witness."

The man looked up quickly, his face clouding over, but he made no comment.

"The fact is," continued Markham, "we are about to make an arrest, and your testimony may be needed to establish the time of Miss Odell's return to her apartment, and also to substantiate the fact that there was presumably someone in her room after you had left. Her screams and calls for help, which you heard, may prove vital evidence in obtaining a conviction."

Spotswoode seemed rather appalled at the thought of his relations with the girl becoming public, and for several minutes he sat with averted eyes.

"I see your point," he acknowledged at length. "But it would be a terrible thing for me if the fact of my delinquencies became known."

"That contingency may be entirely avoided," Markham encouraged him. "I promise you that you will not be called upon unless it is absolutely necessary. . . . And now, what I especially wanted to ask you is this: do you happen to know a Doctor Lindquist, who, I understand, was Miss Odell's personal physician?"

Spotswoode was frankly puzzled. "I never heard the name," he answered. "In fact, Miss Odell never mentioned any doctor to me."

"And did you ever hear her mention the name of Skeel . . . or refer to any one as Tony?"

"Never." His answer was emphatic.

Markham lapsed into a disappointed silence. Spotswoode, too, was silent; he sat as if in a revery.

"You know, Mr. Markham," he said, after several minutes, "I ought to be ashamed to admit it, but the truth is I cared a good deal for the girl. I suppose you've kept her apartment intact. . . ." He hesitated, and a look almost of appeal came into his eyes. "I'd like to see it again if I could."

Markham regarded him sympathetically but finally shook his head.

"It wouldn't do. You'd be sure to be recognized by the operator—or there might be a reporter about—and then I'd be unable to keep you out of the case."

The man appeared disappointed but did not protest; and for several minutes no one spoke. Then Vance raised himself slightly in his chair.

"I say, Mr. Spotswoode, do you happen to remember anything unusual occurring last night during the half hour you remained with Miss Odell after the theater?"

"Unusual?" the man's manner was eloquent of his astonishment. "To the contrary. We chatted awhile, and then, as she seemed tired, I said good night and came away, making a luncheon appointment with her for today."

"And yet, it now seems fairly certain that some other man was hiding in the apartment when you were there."

"There's little doubt on that point," agreed Spotswoode, with the suggestion of a shudder. "And her screams would seem to indicate that he came forth from hiding a few minutes after I went."

"And you had no suspicion of the fact when you heard her call for help?"

"I did at first—naturally. But when she assured me that nothing was the matter, and told me to go home, I attributed her screams to a nightmare. I knew she had been tired, and I had left her in the wicker chair near the door, from where her screams seemed to come; so I naturally concluded she had dozed off and called out in her sleep. . . . If only I hadn't taken so much for granted!"

"It's a harrowin' situation." Vance was silent for a while; then he asked: "Did you, by any chance, notice the door of the living room closet? Was it open or closed?"

Spotswoode frowned, as if attempting to visualize the picture; but the result was a failure.

"I suppose it was closed. I probably would have noticed it if it had been open."

"Then, you couldn't say if the key was in the lock or not?"

"Good Lord, no! I don't even know if it ever had a key."

The case was discussed for another half hour; then Spotswoode excused himself and left us.

"Funny thing," ruminated Markham, "how a man of his upbringing could be so attracted by the empty-headed, butterfly type."

"I'd say it was quite natural," returned Vance. . . . "You're such an incorrigible moralist, Markham."

12

CIRCUMSTANTIAL EVIDENCE

(*Wednesday, September 12; 9 A.M.*)

THE FOLLOWING day, which was Wednesday, not only brought forth an important and, as it appeared, conclusive development in the Odell case but marked the beginning of Vance's active cooperation in the proceedings. The psychological elements in the case had appealed to him irresistibly, and he felt, even at this stage of the investigation, that a final answer could never be obtained along the usual police lines. At his request Markham had called for him at a little before nine o'clock, and we had driven direct to the district attorney's office.

Heath was waiting impatiently when we arrived. His eager and covertly triumphant expression plainly indicated good news.

"Things are breaking fine and dandy," he announced, when we had sat down. He himself was too elated to relax, and stood between Markham's desk rolling a large black cigar between his fingers. "We got the Dude—six o'clock yesterday evening—and we got him right. One of the C. O. boys, named Riley, who was patroling Sixth Avenue in the Thirties, saw him swing off a surface car and head for McAnerny's Pawn Shop. Right away Riley wigwags the traffic officer on the corner and follows the Dude into McAnerny's. Pretty soon the traffic officer comes in with a patrolman, who he's picked up; and the three of 'em nab our stylish friend in the act of pawning this ring."

He tossed a square solitaire diamond in a filigreed platinum setting on the district attorney's desk.

"I was at the office when they brought him in, and I sent Snitkin with the ring up to Harlem to see what the maid had to say about it, and she identified it as belonging to Odell."

"But, I say, it wasn't a part of the *bijouterie* the lady was wearing that night, was it, Sergeant?" Vance put the question casually.

Heath jerked about and eyed him with sullen calculation.

"What if it wasn't? It came out of that jimmied jewel case—or I'm Ben Hur."

"Of course it did," murmured Vance, lapsing into lethargy.

"And that's where we're in luck," declared Heath, turning back to Markham. "It connects Skeel directly with the murder and the robbery."

"What has Skeel to say about it?" Markham was leaning forward intently. "I suppose you questioned him."

"I'll say we did," replied the sergeant; but his tone was troubled. "We had him up all night giving him the works. And the story he tells is this: he says the girl gave him the ring a week ago, and that he didn't see her again until the afternoon of the day before yesterday. He came to her apartment between four and five—you remember the maid said she was out then—and entered and left the house by the side door, which was unlocked at that time. He admits he called again at half past nine that night, but he says that when he found she was out, he went straight home and stayed there. His alibi is that he sat up with his landlady till after midnight playing Khun Khan and drinking beer. I hopped up to his place this morning, and the old girl verified it. But that don't mean anything. The house he lives in is a pretty tough hangout, and this landlady, besides being a heavy boozer, has been up the river a coupla times for shoplifting."

"What does Skeel say about the fingerprints?"

"He says, of course, he made 'em when he was there in the afternoon."

"And the one on the closet doorknob?"

Heath gave a derisive grunt.

"He's got an answer for that, too—says he thought he heard someone coming in, and locked himself in the clothes closet. Didn't want to be seen and spoil any game Odell mighta been playing."

"Most considerate of him to keep out of the way of the *belles poires*," drawled Vance. "Touchin' loyalty, what?"

"You don't believe the rat, do you, Mr. Vance?" asked Heath, with indignant surprise.

"Can't say that I do. But our Antonio at least spins a consistent yarn."

"Too damn consistent to suit me," growled the sergeant.

"That's all you could get out of him?" It was plain that Markham was not pleased with the results of Heath's third degree of Skeel.

"That's about all, sir. He stuck to his story like a leech."

"You found no chisel in his room?"

Heath admitted that he hadn't. "But you couldn't expect him to keep it around," he added.

Markham pondered the facts for several minutes. "I can't see that we've got a very good case, however much we may be convinced of Skeel's guilt. His alibi may be thin, but taken in connection with the phone operator's testimony, I'm inclined to think it would hold tight in court."

"What about the ring, sir?" Heath was desperately disappointed. "And what about his threats, and his fingerprints, and his record of similar burglaries?"

"Contributory factors only," Markham explained. "What we need for a murder is more than a *prima facie* case. A good criminal lawyer could have him discharged in twenty minutes, even if I could secure an indictment. It's not impossible, you know, that the woman gave him the ring a week ago—you recall that the maid said he was demanding money from her about that time. And there's nothing to show that the fingerprints were not actually made late Monday afternoon. Moreover, we can't connect him in any way with the chisel, for we don't know who did the Park Avenue job last summer. His whole story fits the facts perfectly; and we haven't anything contradictory to offer."

Heath shrugged helplessly; all the wind had been taken out of his sails.

"What do you want done with him?" he asked desolately.

Markham considered—he, too, was discomfited.

"Before I answer, I think I'll have a go at him myself."

He pressed a buzzer and ordered a clerk to fill out the necessary requisition. When it had been signed in duplicate, he sent Swacker with it to Ben Hanlon.

"Do ask him about those silk shirts," suggested Vance. "And find out, if you can, if he considers a white waistcoat *de rigueur* with a dinner jacket."

"This office isn't a male millinery shop," snapped Markham.

"But, Markham dear, you won't learn anything else from this Petronius."

Ten minutes later a deputy sheriff from the Tombs entered with his handcuffed prisoner.

Skeel's appearance that morning belied his sobriquet of "Dude." He was haggard and pale; his ordeal of the previous night had left its imprint upon him. He was unshaven; his hair was uncombed; the ends of his moustache drooped; and his cravat was awry. But despite his bedraggled condition, his manner was jaunty and contemptuous. He gave Heath a defiant leer and faced the district attorney with swaggering indifference.

To Markham's questions he doggedly repeated the same story he had told Heath. He clung tenaciously to every detail of it with the ready accuracy of a man who had painstakingly memorized a lesson and was thoroughly familiar with it. Markham coaxed, threatened, bullied. All hint of his usual affability was gone; he was like an inexorable dynamic machine. But Skeel, whose nerves seemed to be made of iron, withstood the vicious fire of his cross-questioning without wincing; and, I confess, his resistance somewhat aroused my admiration despite my revulsion toward him and all he stood for.

After half an hour Markham gave up, completely baffled in his efforts to elicit any damaging admissions from the man. He was about to dismiss him when Vance rose languidly and strolled to the district attorney's desk. Seating himself on the edge of it, he regarded Skeel with impersonal curiosity.

"So you're a devotee of Khun Khan, eh?" he remarked indifferently. "Silly game, what? More interestin' than Conquain or Rum, though. Used to be played in the London clubs. Of East Indian origin, I believe. . . . You still play it with two decks, I suppose, and permit round-the-corner mating?"

An involuntary frown gathered on Skeel's forehead. He was used to violent district attorneys and familiar with the bludgeoning methods of the police, but here was a type of inquisitor entirely new to him; and it was plain that he was both puzzled and apprehensive. He decided to meet this novel antagonist with a smirk of arrogant amusement.

"By the bye," continued Vance, with no change in tone, "can anyone hidden in the clothes press of the Odell living room see the davenport through the keyhole?"

Suddenly all trace of a smile was erased from the man's features.

"And I say," Vance hurried on, his eyes fixed steadily on the other, "why didn't you give the alarm?"

I was watching Skeel closely, and though his set expression did not alter, I saw the pupils of his eyes dilate. Markham, also, I think, noted this phenomenon.

"Don't bother to answer," pursued Vance, as the man opened his lips to speak. "But tell me: didn't the sight shake you up a bit?"

"I don't know what you're talking about," Skeel retorted with sullen impertinence. But, for all his sangfroid, one sensed an uneasiness in his manner. There was an overtone of effort in his desire to appear indifferent, which robbed his words of complete conviction.

"Not a pleasant situation, that." Vance ignored his retort. "How did you feel, crouching there in the dark, when the closet doorknob was turned and someone tried to get in?" His eyes were boring into the man, though his voice retained its casual intonation.

The muscles of Skeel's face tightened, but he did not speak.

"Lucky thing you took the precaution of locking yourself in—eh, what?" Vance went on. "Suppose he'd got the door open—my word! Then what? . . ."

He paused and smiled with a kind of silky sweetness which was more impressive than any glowering aggression.

"I say, did you have your steel chisel ready for him? Maybe he'd have been too quick and strong for you—maybe there would have been thumbs pressing against your larnyx, too, before you could have struck him—eh? . . . Did you think of that, there in the dark? . . . No, not precisely a pleasant situation. A bit gruesome, in fact."

"What are you raving about?" Skeel spat out insolently. "You're balmy." But his swagger had been forgotten, and a look akin to horror had passed across his face. This slackening of pose was momentary, however; almost at once his smirk returned, and his head swayed in contempt.

Vance sauntered back to his chair and stretched himself in it listlessly, as if all his interest in the case had again evaporated.

Markham had watched the little drama attentively, but Heath had sat smoking with ill-concealed annoyance. The silence that followed was broken by Skeel.

"Well, I suppose I'm to be railroaded. Got it all planned, have you? . . . Try and railroad me!" He laughed harshly. "My lawyer's Abe Rubin, and you might phone him that I'd like to see him."*

---

* Abe Rubin was at that time the most resourceful and unscrupulous criminal lawyer in New York. Since his disbarment two years ago, little has been heard from him.

Markham, with a gesture of annoyance, waved to the deputy sheriff to take Skeel back to the Tombs.

"What were you trying to get at?" he asked Vance when the man was gone.

"Just an elusive notion in the depths of my being struggling for the light." Vance smoked placidly a moment. "I thought Mr. Skeel might be persuaded to pour out his heart to us. So I wooed him with words."

"That's just bully," gibed Heath. "I was expecting you any minute to ask him if he played mumbly-peg or if his grandmother was a hootowl."

"Sergeant, dear Sergeant," pleaded Vance, "don't be unkind. I simply couldn't endure it. . . . And really, now, didn't my chat with Mr. Skeel suggest a possibility to you?"

"Sure," said Heath, "that he was hiding in the closet when Odell was killed. But where does that get us? It lets Skeel out, although the job was a professional one, and he was caught red-handed with some of the swag."

He turned disgustedly to the district attorney.

"And now what, sir?"

"I don't like the look of things," Markham complained. "If Skeel has Abe Rubin to defend him, we won't stand a chance with the case we've got. I feel convinced he was mixed up in it; but no judge will accept my personal feelings as evidence."

"We could turn the Dude loose and have him tailed," suggested Heath grudgingly. "We might catch him doing something that'll give the game away."

Markham considered.

"That might be a good plan," he acceded. "We'll certainly get no more evidence on him as long as he's locked up."

"It looks like our only chance, sir."

"Very well," agreed Markham. "Let him think we're through with him; he may get careless. I'll leave the whole thing to you, Sergeant. Keep a couple of good men on him day and night. Something may happen."

Heath rose, an unhappy man. "Right, sir. I'll attend to it."

"And I'd like to have more data on Charles Cleaver," added Markham. "Find out what you can of his relations with the Odell girl. Also, get me a line on Doctor Ambroise Lindquist. What's his history? What are his habits? You know the kind of thing. He treated the girl for some mysterious or imaginary ailment; and I think he has something up his sleeve. But don't go near him personally—yet."

Heath jotted the name down in his notebook, without enthusiasm.

"And before you set your stylish captive free," put in Vance, yawning, "you might, don't y' know, see if he carries a key that fits the Odell apartment."

Heath jerked up short and grinned. "Now, that idea's got some sense to it. . . . Funny I didn't think of it myself." And, shaking hands with all of us, he went out.

13

AN ERSTWHILE GALLANT

(Wednesday, September 12; 10:30 A.M.)

SWACKER WAS evidently waiting for an opportunity to interrupt, for, when Sergeant Heath had passed through the door, he at once stepped into the room.

"The reporters are here, sir," he announced, with a wry face. "You said you'd see them at ten thirty."

In response to a nod from his chief, he held open the door, and a dozen or more newspaper men came trooping in.

"No questions, please, this morning," Markham begged pleasantly. "It's too early in the game. But I'll tell you all I know. . . . I agree with Sergeant Heath that the Odell murder was the work of a professional criminal—the same who broke into Arnheim's house on Park Avenue last summer."

Briefly he told of Inspector Brenner's findings in connection with the chisel.

"We've made no arrest, but one may be expected in the very near future. In fact, the police have the case well in hand but are going carefully in order to avoid any chance of an acquittal. We've already recovered some of the missing jewelry. . . ."

He talked to the reporters for five minutes or so, but he made no mention of the testimony of the maid or the phone operators, and carefully avoided the mention of any names.

When we were again alone, Vance chuckled admiringly.

"A masterly evasion, my dear Markham! Legal training has its advantages—decidedly it has its advantages. . . . 'We've recovered some of the missing jewelry!' Sweet wingèd words! Not an untruth—oh, no!—but how deceivin'! Really, y' know, I must devote more time to the caressin' art of *suggestio falsi* and *suppressio veri.* You should be crowned with an anadem of myrtle."

"Leaving all that to one side," Markham rejoined impatiently, "suppose you tell me, now that Heath's gone, what was in your mind when you applied your verbal voodooism to Skeel. What was all the conjurer-talk about dark closets, and alarums, and pressing thumbs, and peering through keyholes?"

"Well, now, I didn't think my little chit-chat was so cryptic," answered Vance. "The *recherché* Tony was undoubtedly ambuscaded *à la sourdine* in the clothes press at some time during the fatal evening; and I was merely striving, in my amateurish way, to ascertain the exact hour of his concealment."

"And did you?"

"Not conclusively." Vance shook his head sadly. "Y' know, Markham, I'm the proud possessor of a theory—it's vague and obscure and unsubtantial; and it's downright unintelligible. And even if it were verified, I can't see how it would help us any, for it would leave the situation even more incomprehensible than it already is. . . . I almost wish I hadn't questioned Heath's Beau Nash. He upset my ideas frightfully."

"From what I could gather, you seem to think it possible that Skeel witnessed the murder. That couldn't, by any stretch of the imagination, be your precious theory?"

"That's part of it, anyway."

"My dear Vance, you do astonish me!" Markham laughed outright. "Skeel, then, according to you, is innocent; but he keeps his knowledge to himself, invents an alibi, and doesn't even tattle when he's arrested. . . . It won't hold water."

"I know," sighed Vance. "It's a veritable sieve. And yet, the notion haunts me—it rides me like a hag—it eats into my vitals."

"Do you realize that this mad theory of yours presupposes that, when Spotswoode and Miss Odell returned from the theater, there were *two* men hidden in the apartment—two men *unknown to each other*—namely Skeel and your hypothetical murderer?"

"Of couse I realize it; and the thought of it is breaking down my reason."

"Furthermore, they must have entered the apartment separately and hidden separately. . . . How, may I ask, did they get in? And how did they get out? And which one caused the girl to scream after Spotswoode had left? And what was the other one doing in the meantime? And if Skeel was a passive spectator, horrified and mute, how do you account for his breaking open the jewel case and securing the ring—?"

"Stop! Stop! Don't torture me so," Vance pleaded. "I know I'm insane. Been given to hallucinations since birth; but—Merciful Heaven!—I've never before had one as crazy as this."

"On that point at least, my dear Vance, we are in complete and harmonious agreement," smiled Markham.

Just then Swacker came in and handed Markham a letter.

"Brought by messenger, and marked 'immediate,' " he explained.

The letter, written on heavy engraved stationery, was from Doctor Lindquist, and explained that between the hours of 11 P.M. and 1 A.M. on Monday night he had been in attendance on a patient at his sanitarium. It also apologized for his actions when asked regarding his whereabouts, and offered a wordy, but not particularly convincing, explanation of his conduct. He had had an unusually trying day, it seemed—neurotic cases were trying, at best— and the suddenness of our visit, together with the apparently hostile nature of Markham's questions, had completely upset him. He was more than sorry for his outburst, he said, and stood ready to assist in any way he could. It was unfortunate for all concerned, he added, that he had lost his temper, for it would have been a simple matter for him to explain about Monday night.

"He has thought the situation over calmly," said Vance, "and hereby offers you a neat little alibi which, I think, you will have difficulty in shaking. . . . An artful beggar—like all these unbalanced pseudopsychiatrists. Observe: he was with a patient. To be sure! What patient? Why, one too ill to be questioned. . . . There you are. A cul-de-sac masquerading as an alibi. Not bad, what?"

"It doesn't interest me overmuch." Markham put the letter away. "That pompous professional ass could never have got into the Odell apartment without having been seen; and I can't picture him sneaking in by devious means." He reached for some papers. . . . "And now, if you don't object, I'll make an effort to earn my $15,000 salary."

But Vance, instead of making a move to go, sauntered to the table and opened a telephone directory.

"Permit me a suggestion, Markham," he said, after a moment's search. "Put off your daily grind for a bit, and let's hold polite converse with Mr. Louis Mannix. Y' know, he's the only presumptive swain of the inconstant Margaret, so far mentioned, who hasn't been given an audience. I hanker to gaze upon him and hearken to his rune. He'd make the family circle complete, so to speak. . . . He still holds forth in Maiden Lane, I see; and it wouldn't take long to fetch him here."

Markham had swung half round in his chair at the mention of Mannix's name. He started to protest, but he knew from experience that Vance's suggestions were not the results of idle whims; and he was silent for several moments weighing the matter. With practically every other avenue of inquiry closed for the moment, I think the idea of questioning Mannix rather appealed to him.

"All right," he consented, ringing for Swacker; "though I don't see how he can help. According to Heath, the Odell girl gave him his *congé* a year ago."

"He may still have hay on his horns, or, like Hotspur, be drunk with choler. You can't tell." Vance resumed his chair. "With such a name, he'd bear investigation *ipso facto.*"

Markham sent Swacker for Tracy; and when the latter arrived, suave and beaming, he was given instructions to take the district attorney's car and bring Mannix to the office.

"Get a subpœna," said Markham; "and use it if necessary."

Half an hour or so later Tracy returned.

"Mr. Mannix made no difficulty about coming," he reported. "Was quite agreeable, in fact. He's in the waiting room now."

Tracy was dismissed, and Mannix was ushered in.

He was a large man, and he walked with the forced elasticity of gait which epitomizes the silent struggle of incipiently corpulent middle age to deny the onrush of the years and cling to the semblance of youth. He carried a slender wanghee cane; and his checkered suit, brocaded waistcoat, pearl-gray gaiters, and gaily beribboned Homburg hat gave him an almost foppish appearance. But these various indications of sportiveness were at once forgotten when one inspected his features. His small eyes were bright and crafty; his nose was bibative, and appeared disproportionately small above his thick, sensual lips and prognathous jaw. There was an oiliness and shrewdness in the man's manner which were at once repulsive and arresting.

At a gesture from Markham he sat down on the edge of a chair, placing a podgy hand on each knee. His attitude was one of alert suspicion.

"Mr. Mannix," said Markham, an engaging note of apology in his voice, "I am sorry to have discommoded you; but the matter in hand is both serious and urgent. . . . A Miss Margaret Odell was murdered night before last, and in the course of inquiries we learned that you had at one time known her quite well. It occurred to me that you might be in possession of some facts about her that would assist us in our investigation."

A saponaceous smile, meant to be genial, parted the man's heavy lips.

"Sure, I knew the Canary—a long time ago, y' understand." He permitted himself a sigh. "A fine, high-class girl, if I do say so. A good looker and a good dresser. Too damn bad she didn't go on with the show business. But"—he made a repudiative motion with his hand—"I haven't seen the lady, y' understand, for over a year—not to speak to, if you know what I mean."

Mannix clearly was on his guard, and his beady little eyes did not once leave the district attorney's face.

"You had a quarrel with her perhaps?" Markham asked the question incuriously.

"Well, now, I wouldn't go so far as to say we quarreled. No." Mannix paused, seeking the correct word. "You might say we disagreed—got tired of the arrangement and decided to separate; kind of drifted apart. Last thing I told her was, if she ever needed a friend, she'd know where to find me."

"Very generous of you," murmured Markham. "And you never renewed your little affair?"

"Never—never. Don't remember ever speaking to her from that day to this."

"In view of certain things I've learned, Mr. Mannix"—Markham's tone was regretful—"I must ask you a somewhat personal question. Did she ever make an attempt to blackmail you?"

Mannix hesitated, and his eyes seemed to grow even smaller, like those of a man thinking rapidly.

"Certainly not!" he replied, with belated emphasis. "Not at all. Nothing of the kind." He raised both hands in protest against the thought. Then he asked furtively: "What gave you such an idea?"

"I have been told," explained Markham, "that she had extorted money from one or two of her admirers."

Mannix made a wholly unconvincing grimace of astonishment. "Well well! You don't tell me! Can it be possible?" He peered shrewdly at the district attorney. "Maybe it was Charlie Cleaver she blackmailed—yes?"

Markham picked him up quickly.

"Why do you say Cleaver?"

Again Mannix waved his thick hand, this time deprecatingly.

"No special reason, y' understand. Just thought it might be him. . . . No special reason."

"Did Cleaver ever tell you he'd been blackmailed?"

"Cleaver tell me? . . . Now, I ask you, Mr. Markham: why should Cleaver tell me such a story—why should he?"

"And you never told Cleaver that the Odell girl had blackmailed you?"

"Positively not!" Mannix gave a scornful laugh which was far too theatrical to have been genuine. "Me tell Cleaver I'd been blackmailed? Now, that's funny, that is."

"Then, why did you mention Cleaver a moment ago?"

"No reason at all—like I told you. . . . He knew the Canary; but that ain't no secret."

Markham dropped the subject. "What do you know about Miss Odell's relations with a Doctor Ambroise Lindquist?"

Mannix was now obviously perplexed. "Never heard of him—no, never. She didn't know him when I was taking her around."

"Whom else besides Cleaver did she know well?"

Mannix shook his head ponderously.

"Now, that I couldn't say—positively I couldn't say. Seen her with this man and that, same as everybody saw her; but who they were I don't know—absolutely."

"Ever hear of Tony Skeel?" Markham quickly leaned over and met the other's gaze inquiringly.

Once more Mannix hesitated, and his eyes glittered calculatingly. "Well, now that you ask me, I believe I did hear of the fellow. But I couldn't swear to it, y' understand. . . . What makes you think I heard of this Skeel fellow?"

Markham ignored the question.

"Can you think of no one who might have borne Miss Odell a grudge, or had cause to fear her?"

Mannix was volubly emphatic on the subject of his complete ignorance of any such person; and after a few more questions, which elicited only denials, Markham let him go.

"Not bad at all, Markham old thing—eh, what?" Vance seemed pleased with the conference. "Wonder why he's so coy? Not a nice person, this Mannix. And he's so fearful lest he be informative. Again, I wonder why. He was so careful—oh, so careful."

"He was sufficiently careful, at any rate, not to tell us anything," declared Markham gloomily.

"I shouldn't say that, don't y' know." Vance lay back and smoked placidly. "A ray of light filtered through here and there. Our fur-importing philogynist denied he'd been blackmailed—which was obviously untrue—and tried to make us believe that he and the lovely Margaret cooed like turtledoves at parting—Tosh! . . . And then, that mention of Cleaver. That wasn't spontaneous—dear me, no. Brother Mannix and spontaneity are as the poles apart. He had a reason for bringing Cleaver in; and I fancy that if you knew what that reason was, you'd feel like flinging roses riotously, and that sort of thing. Why Cleaver? That *secret-de-Polichinelle* explanation was a bit weak. The orbits of these two paramours cross somewhere. On that point, at least, Mannix inadvertently enlightened us. . . . Moreover, it's plain that he doesn't know our fashionable healer with the satyr ears. But, on the other hand, he's aware of the existence of Mr. Skeel, and would rather like to deny the acquaintance. . . . So—*voilà l'affaire*. Plenty of information; but—my word!—what to do with it?"

"I give it up," acknowledged Markham hopelessly.

"I know; it's a sad sad world," Vance commiserated him. "But you must face the olla podrida with a bright eye. It's time for lunch, and a fillet of sole *Marguéry* will cheer you no end."

Markham glanced at the clock and permitted himself to be led to the Lawyers Club.

14

VANCE OUTLINES A THEORY

(*Wednesday, September 12; evening*)

VANCE AND I did not return to the district attorney's office after lunch, for Markham had a busy afternoon before him, and nothing further was likely to transpire in connection with the Odell case until Sergeant Heath had completed his investigations of Cleaver and Doctor Lindquist. Vance had seats for Giordano's *Madame Sans-Gêne,* and two o'clock found us at the Metropolitan. Though the performance was excellent, Vance was too *distrait* to enjoy it; and it was significant that, after the opera, he directed the chauffeur to the Stuyvesant Club. I knew he had a tea appointment, and that he had planned to motor to Longue Vue for dinner; and the fact that he should have dismissed these social engagements from his mind in order to be with Markham showed how intensely the problem of the murder had absorbed his interest.

It was after six o'clock when Markham came in, looking harassed and tired. No mention of the case was made during dinner, with the exception of Markham's casual remark that Heath had turned in his reports on Cleaver and Doctor Lindquist and Mannix. (It seemed that, immediately after lunch, he had telephoned to the sergeant to add Mannix's name to the two others as a subject for inquiry.) It was not until we had retired to our favorite corner of the lounge room that the topic of the murder was brought up for discussion.

And that discussion, brief and one-sided, was the beginning of an entirely new line of investigation—a line which, in the end, led to the guilty person.

Markham sank wearily into his chair. He had begun to show the strain of the last two days of fruitless worry. His eyes were a trifle heavy, and there was a grim tenacity in the lines of his mouth. Slowly and deliberately he lighted a cigar, and took several deep inhalations.

"Damn the newspapers!" he grumbled. "Why can't they let the district attorney's office handle its business in its own way? . . . Have you seen the afternoon papers? They're all clamoring for the murderer. You'd think I had him up my sleeve."

"You forget, my dear chap," grinned Vance, "that we are living under the benign and upliftin' reign of Democritus, which confers upon every ignoramus the privilege of promiscuously criticising his betters."

Markham snorted. "I don't complain about criticism; it's the lurid imagination of these bright young reporters that galls me. They're trying to turn this sordid crime into a spectacular Borgia melodrama, with passion running rampant, and mysterious influences at work, and all the pomp and trappings of a medieval romance. . . . You'd think even a schoolboy could see that it was only an ordinary robbery and murder of the kind that's taking place regularly throughout the country."

Vance paused in the act of lighting a cigarette, and his eyebrows lifted. Turning, he regarded Markham with a look of mild incredulity. "I say! Do you really mean to tell me that your statement for the press was given out in good faith?"

Markham looked up in surprise. "Certainly it was. . . . What do you mean by 'good faith'?"

Vance smiled indolently. "I rather thought, don't y' know, that your oration to the reporters was a bit of strategy to lull the real culprit into a state of false security, and to give you a clear field for investigation."

Markham contemplated him a moment.

"See here, Vance," he demanded irritably, "what are you driving at?"

"Nothing at all—really, old fellow," the other assured him affably. "I knew that Heath was deadly sincere about his belief in Skeel's guilt, but it never occurred to me, d' ye see, that you yourself actually regarded the crime as one committed by a professional burglar. I foolishly thought that you let Skeel go this morning in the hope that he would lead you somehow to the guilty person. I rather imagined you were spoofing the trusting sergeant by pretending to fall in with his silly notion."

"Ah, I see! Still clinging to your weird theory that a brace of villains were present, hiding in separate clothes closets, or something of the kind." Markham made no attempt to temper his sarcasm. "A sapient idea—so much more intelligent that Heath's!"

"I know it's weird. But it happens not to be any weirder than your theory of a lone yeggman."

"And for what reason, pray," persisted Markham, with considerable warmth, "do you consider the yeggman theory weird?"

"For the simple reason that it was not the crime of a professional thief at all, but the willfully deceptive act of a particularly clever man who doubtless spent weeks in its preparation."

Markham sank back in his chair and laughed heartily. "Vance, you have contributed the one ray of sunshine to an otherwise gloomy and depressing case."

Vance bowed with mock humility.

"It gives me great pleasure," was his dulcet rejoinder, "to be able to bring even a wisp of light into so clouded a mental atmosphere."

A brief silence followed. Then Markham asked, "Is this fascinating and picturesque conclusion of yours regarding the highly intellectual character of the Odell woman's murderer based on your new and original psychological methods of deduction?" There was no mistaking the ridicule in his voice.

"I arrived at it," explained Vance sweetly, "by the same process of logic I used in determining the guilt of Alvin Benson's murderer."

Markham smiled. *Touché!* . . . Don't think I'm so ungrateful as to belittle the work you did in that case. But this time, I fear, you've permitted your theories to lead you hopelessly astray. The present case is what the police call an open-and-shut affair."

"Particularly shut," amended Vance dryly. "And both you and the police are in the distressin' situation of waiting inactively for your suspected victim to give the game away."

"I'll admit the situation is not all one could desire." Markham spoke morosely. "But even so, I can't see that there's any opportunity in this affair for your recondite psychological methods. The thing's too obvious—that's the trouble. What we need now is evidence, not theories. If it wasn't for the spacious and romantic imaginings of the newspaper men, public interest in the case would already have died out."

"Markham," said Vance quietly, but with unwonted seriousness, "if that's what you really believe, then you may as well drop the case now; for you're foredoomed to failure. You think it's an obvious crime. But let me tell you, it's a subtle crime, if ever there was one. And it's as clever as it is subtle. No common criminal committed it—believe me. It was done by a man of very superior intellect and astoundin' ingenuity."

Vance's assured, matter-of-fact tone had a curiously convincing quality; and Markham, restraining his impulse to scoff, assumed an air of indulgent irony.

"Tell me," he said, "by what cryptic mental process you arrived at so fantastic a conclusion."

"With pleasure." Vance took a few puffs on his cigarette and lazily watched the smoke curl upward.*

"Y' know, Markham," he began, in his emotionless drawl, "every genuine work of art has a quality which the critics call *élan*—namely, enthusiasm and spontaneity. A copy, or imitation, lacks that distinguishing characteristic; it's too perfect, too carefully done, too exact. Even enlightened scions of the law, I fancy, are aware that there is bad drawing in Botticelli and disproportions in Rubens, what? In an original, d' ye see, such flaws don't matter. But an imitator never puts 'em in: he doesn't dare—he's too intent on getting all the details correct. The imitator works with a self-consciousness and a meticulous care which the artist, in the throes of creative labor, never exhibits. And here's the point: there's no way of imitating that enthusiasm and spontaneity—that *élan*—which an original painting possesses. However closely a copy may resemble an original, there's a vast psychological difference between them. The copy breathes an air of insincerity, of ultra-perfection, of conscious effort. . . . You follow me, eh?"

"Most instructive, my dear Ruskin."

Vance meekly bowed his appreciation, and proceeded pleasantly. "Now, let us consider the Odell murder. You and Heath are agreed that it is a commonplace, brutal, sordid, unimaginative crime. But, unlike you two bloodhounds on the trail, I have ignored its mere appearances and have analyzed its various factors—I have looked at it psychologically, so to speak. And I have discovered that it is not a genuine and sincere crime—that is to say, an original—but only a sophisticated, self-conscious and clever imitation, done by a skilled copyist. I grant you it is correct and typical in every detail. But just there is where it fails, don't y' know. Its technic is too good, its craftsmanship too perfect. The ensemble, as it were, is not convincing—it lacks *élan*. Æsthetically speaking, it has all the earmarks of a *tour de force*. Vulgarly speaking, it's a fake." He paused and gave Markham an engaging smile. "I trust this somewhat oracular peroration has not bored you."

"Pray continue," urged Markham, with exaggerated politeness. His manner was jocular, but something in his tone led me to believe that he was seriously interested.

---

* I sent a proof of the following paragraphs to Vance, and he edited and corrected them; so that, as they now stand, they represent his theories in practically his own words.

"What is true of art is true of life," Vance resumed placidly. "Every human action, d' ye see, conveys unconsciously an impression either of genuineness or of spuriousness—of sincerity or calculation. For example, two men at table eat in a similar way, handle their knives and forks in the same fashion, and apparently do the identical things. Although the sensitive spectator cannot put his finger on the points of difference, he nonetheless senses at once which man's breeding is genuine and instinctive and which man's is imitative and self-conscious."

He blew a wreath of smoke toward the ceiling and settled more deeply into his chair.

"Now, Markham, just what are the universally recognized features of a sordid crime of robbery and murder? . . . Brutality, disorder, haste, ransacked drawers, cluttered desks, broken jewel cases, rings stripped from the victim's fingers, severed pendant chains, torn clothing, tipped-over chairs, upset lamps, broken vases, twisted draperies, strewn floors, and so forth. Such are the accepted immemorial indications—eh, what? But—consider a moment, old chap. Outside of fiction and the drama, in how many crimes do they *all* appear—all in perfect ordination, and without a single element to contradict the general effect? That is to say, how many actual crimes are technically perfect in their settings? . . . None! And why? Simply because nothing actual in this life—nothing that is spontaneous and genuine—runs to accepted form in every detail. The law of chance and fallibility invariably steps in."

He made a slight indicative gesture.

"But regard this particular crime: look at it closely. What do you find? You will perceive that its *mise en scène* has been staged, and its drama enacted, down to every minute detail—like a Zola novel. It is almost mathematically perfect. And therein, d' ye see, lies the irresistible inference of its having been carefully premeditated and planned. To use an art term, it is a tickled-up crime. Therefore, its conception was not spontaneous. . . . And yet, don't y' know, I can't point out any specific flaw; for its great flaw lies in its being flawless. And nothing flawless, my dear fellow, is natural or genuine."

Markham was silent for a while.

"You deny even the remote possibility of a common thief having murdered the girl?" he asked at length; and now there was no hint of sarcasm in his voice.

"If a common thief did it," contended Vance, "then there's no science of psychology, there are no philosophic truths, and there are no laws of art. If it was a genuine crime of robbery, then, by the same token, there is no difference whatever between an old master and a clever technician's copy."

"You'd entirely eliminate robbery as the motive, I take it."

"The robbery," Vance affirmed, "was only a manufactured detail. The fact that the crime was committed by a highly astute person indicates unquestionably that there was a far more potent motive behind it. Any man capable of so ingenious and clever a piece of deception is obviously a person of education and imagination; and he most certainly would not have run the stupendous risk of killing a woman unless he had feared some overwhelming disaster—unless, indeed, her continuing to live would have caused him greater mental anguish, and would have put him in greater jeopardy, even than the crime itself. Between two colossal dangers, he chose the murder as the lesser."

Markham did not speak at once; he seemed lost in reflection. But presently he turned and, fixing Vance with a dubious stare, said, "What about that chiselled jewel box? A professional burglar's jimmy wielded by an experienced hand doesn't fit into your æsthetic hypothesis—it is, in fact, diametrically opposed to such a theory."

"I know it only too well." Vance nodded slowly. "And I've been harried and hectored by that steel chisel ever since I beheld the evidence of its work that first morning. . . . Markham, that chisel is the one genuine note in an otherwise spurious performance. It's as if the real artist had come along at the moment the copyist had finished his faked picture, and painted in a single small object with the hand of a master."

"But doesn't that bring us back inevitably to Skeel?"

"Skeel—ah, yes. That's the explanation, no doubt; but not the way you conceive it. Skeel ripped the box open—I don't question that; but—deuce take it!—it's the only thing he did do; it's the only thing that was left for him to do. That's why he got only a ring which La Belle Marguerite was not wearing that night. All her other baubles—to wit, those that adorned her—had been stripped from her and were gone."

"Why are you so positive on this point?"

"The poker, man—the poker! . . . Don't you see? That amateurish assault upon the jewel case with a cast iron coal prodder couldn't have been made *after* the case had been prized open—it would have had to be made *before*. And that seemingly insane attempt to break steel with cast iron was part of the stage setting. The real culprit didn't care if he got the case open or not. He merely wanted it to look as if he had *tried* to get it open; so he used the poker and then left it lying beside the dented box."

"I see what you mean." This point, I think, impressed Markham more strongly than any other Vance had raised; for the presence of the poker on the dressing table had not been explained away either by Heath or Inspector Brenner. . . . "Is that the reason you questioned Skeel as if he might have been present when your other visitor was there?"

"Exactly. By the evidence of the jewel case I knew he either was in the apartment when the bogus crime of robbery was being staged, or else had come upon the scene when it was over and the stage director had cleared out. . . . From his reactions to my questions I rather fancy he was present."

"Hiding in the closet?"

"Yes. That would account for the closet not having been disturbed. As I see it, it wasn't ransacked, for the simple and rather grotesque reason that the elegant Skeel was locked within. How else could that one clothes press have escaped the rifling activities of the pseudoburglar? He wouldn't have omitted it deliberately, and he was far too thoroughgoing to have overlooked it accidentally. Then there are the fingerprints on the knob. . . ."

Vance lightly tapped on the arm of his chair.

"I tell you, Markham old dear, you simply must build your conception of the crime on this hypothesis and proceed accordingly. If you don't, each edifice you rear will come toppling about your ears."

15

FOUR POSSIBILITIES

(Wednesday, September 12; evening)

WHEN Vance finished speaking, there was a long silence. Markham, impressed by the other's earnestness, sat in a brown study. His ideas had been shaken. The theory of Skeel's guilt, to which he had clung from the moment of the identification of the fingerprints, had, it must be admitted, not entirely satisfied him, although he had been able to suggest no alternative. Now Vance had categorically repudiated this theory and at the same time had advanced another which, despite its indefiniteness, had nevertheless taken into account all the physical points of the case; and Markham, at first antagonistic, had found himself, almost against his will, becoming more and more sympathetic to this new point of view.

"Damn it, Vance!" he said. "I'm not in the least convinced by your theatrical theory. And yet, I feel a curious undercurrent of plausibility in your analyses. . . . I wonder—"

He turned sharply, and scrutinized the other steadfastly for a moment.

"Look here! Have you anyone in mind as the protagonist of the drama you've outlined?"

"'Pon my word, I haven't the slightest notion as to who killed the lady," Vance assured him. "But if you are ever to find the murderer, you must look for a shrewd, superior man with nerves of iron, who was in imminent danger of being irremediably ruined by the girl—a man of inherent cruelty and vindictiveness; a supreme egoist; a fatalist more or less; and, I'm inclined to believe, something of a madman."

"Mad!"

"Oh, not a lunatic, just a madman, a perfectly normal, logical, calculating madman—same as you and I and Van here. Only, our hobbies are harmless, d' ye see. This chap's mania is outside your preposterously revered law. That's why you're after him. If his aberration were stamp collecting or golf, you wouldn't give him a second thought. But his perfectly rational *penchant* for eliminating *déclassées* ladies who bothered him fills you with horror; it's not *your* hobby. Consequently, you have a hot yearning to flay him alive."

"I'll admit," said Markham coolly, "that a homicidal mania is my idea of madness."

"But he didn't have a homicidal mania, Markham old thing. You miss all the fine distinctions in psychology. This man was annoyed by a certain person, and set to work, masterfully and reasonably, to do away with the source of his annoyance. And he did it with surpassin' cleverness. To be sure, his act was a bit grisly. But when, if ever, you get your hands on him, you'll be amazed to find how normal he is. And able, too—oh, able no end."

Again Markham lapsed into a long, thoughtful silence. At last he spoke.

"The only trouble with your ingenious deductions is that they don't accord with the known circumstances of the case. And facts, my dear Vance, are still regarded by a few of us old-fashioned lawyers as more or less conclusive."

"Why this needless confession of your shortcomings?" inquired Vance whimsically. Then, after a moment: "Let me have the facts which appear to you antagonistic to my deductions."

"Well, there are only four men of the type you describe who could have had any remote reason for murdering the Odell woman. Heath's scouts went into her history pretty thoroughly, and for over two years—that is, since her appearance in the 'Follies'—the only *personæ gratæ* at her apartment have been Mannix, Doctor Lindquist, Pop Cleaver, and, of course, Spotswoode. The Canary was a bit exclusive, it seems; and no other man got near enough to her even to be considered as a possible murderer."

"It appears, then, that you have a complete quartet to draw on." Vance's tone was apathetic. "What do you crave—a regiment?"

"No," answered Markham patiently. "I crave only one logical possibility. But Mannix was through with the girl over a year ago; Cleaver and Spotswoode both have watertight alibis; and that leaves only Doctor Lindquist, whom I can't exactly picture as a strangler and meretricious burglar, despite his irascibility. Moreover, he, too, has an alibi; and it may be a genuine one."

Vance wagged his head. "There's something positively pathetic about the childlike faith of the legal mind."

"It does cling to rationality at times, doesn't it?" observed Markham.

"My dear fellow!" Vance rebuked him. "The presumption implied in that remark is most immodest. If you could distinguish between rationality and irrationality you wouldn't be a lawyer—you'd be a god. . . . No; you're going at this thing the wrong way. The real factors in the case are not what you call the known circumstances, but the unknown quantities—the human *x*'s, so to speak—the personalities, or natures, of your quartet."

He lit a fresh cigarette, and lay back, closing his eyes.

"Tell me what you know of these four *cavalieri serventi*—you say Heath has turned in his report. Who were their mamas? What do they eat for breakfast? Are they susceptible to poison ivy? . . . Let's have Spotswoode's dossier first. Do you know anything about him?"

"In a general way," returned Markham. "Old Puritan stock, I believe—governors, burgomasters, a few successful traders. All Yankee forebears—no intermixture. As a matter of fact, Spotswoode represents the oldest and hardiest of the New England aristocracy—although I imagine the so-called wine of the Puritans has become pretty well diluted by now. His affair with the Odell girl is hardly consonant with the older Puritans' mortification of the flesh."

"It's wholly consonant, though, with the psychological reactions which are apt to follow the inhibitions produced by such mortification," submitted Vance. "But what does he do? Whence cometh his lucre?"

"His father manufactured automobile accessories, made a fortune at it, and left the business to him. He tinkers at it, but not seriously, though I believe he has designed a few appurtenances."

"I do hope the hideous cut-glass olla for holding paper bouquets is not one of them. The man who invented that tonneau decoration is capable of any fiendish crime."

"It couldn't have been Spotswoode, then," said Markham tolerantly, "for he certainly can't qualify as your potential strangler. We know the girl was alive after he left her, and that, during the time she was murdered, he was with

Judge Redfern. . . . Even you, friend Vance, couldn't manipulate those facts to the gentleman's disadvantage."

"On that, at least, we agree," conceded Vance. "And that's all you know of the gentleman?"

"I think that's all, except that he married a well-to-do woman—a daughter of a Southern senator, I believe."

"Doesn't help any. . . . And now, let's have Mannix's history."

Markham referred to a typewritten sheet of paper.

"Both parents immigrants—came over in the steerage. Original name Mannikiewicz, or something like that. Born on the East Side; learned the fur business in his father's retail shop in Hester Street; worked for the Sanfrasco Cloak Company and got to be factory foreman. Saved his money and sweetened the pot by manipulating real estate; then went into the fur business for himself and steadily worked up to his present opulent state. Public school and night commercial college. Married in 1900 and divorced a year later. Lives a gay life—helps support the nightclubs, but never gets drunk. I suppose he comes under the head of a spender and wine opener. Has invested some money in musical comedies and always has a stage beauty in tow. Runs to blondes."

"Not very revealin'," sighed Vance. "The city is full of Mannixes. . . . What did you garner in connection with our bon-ton medico?"

"The city has its quota of Doctor Lindquists, too, I fear. He was brought up in a small Middle-West bailiwick—French and Magyar extraction; took his M.D. from the Ohio State Medical, practiced in Chicago—some shady business there, but never convicted; came to Albany and got in on the X-ray-machine craze; invented a breast pump and formed a stock company—made a small fortune out of it; went to Vienna for two years—"

"Ah, the Freudian motif!"

"—returned to New York and opened a private sanitarium; charged outrageous prices and thereby endeared himself to the *nouveau riche.* Has been at the endearing process ever since. Was defendant in a breach-of-promise suite some years ago, but the case was settled out of court. He's not married."

"He wouldn't be," commented Vance. "Such gentry never are. . . . Interestin' summary, though—yes, decidedly interestin'. I'm tempted to develop a psychoneurosis and let Ambroise treat me. I do so want to know him better. And where—oh, where—was this egregious healer at the moment of our erring sister's demise? Ah, who can tell, my Markham; who knows—who knows?"

"In any event, I don't think he was murdering anyone."

"You're so prejudicial!" said Vance. "But let us move reluctantly on. What's your *portrait parlé* of Cleaver? The fact that he's familiarly called Pop is helpful as a starter. You simply couldn't imagine Beethoven being called Shorty, or Bismarck being referred to as Snookums."

"Cleaver has been a politician all of his life—a Tammany Hall 'regular.' Was a ward boss at twenty-five; ran a Democratic club of some kind in Brooklyn for a time; was an alderman for two terms and practiced general law. Was appointed Tax Commissioner; left politics and raised a small racing stable. Later secured an illegal gambling concession at Saratoga; and now operates a poolroom in Jersey City. He's what you might call a professional sport. Loves his liquor."

"No marriages?"

"None on the records. But see here: Cleaver's out of it. He was ticketed in Boonton that night at half past eleven."

"Is that, by any chance, the watertight alibi you mentioned a moment ago?"

"In any primitive legal way I considered it as such." Markham resented Vance's question. "The summons was handed him at half past eleven; it's so marked and dated. And Boonton is fifty miles from here—a good two hours' motor ride. Therefore, Cleaver unquestionably left New York about half past nine; and even if he'd driven directly back, he couldn't have reached here until long after the time the medical examiner declared the girl was dead. As a matter of routine, I investigated the summons and even spoke by phone to the officer who issued it. It was genuine enough—I ought to know: I had it quashed."

"Did this Boonton Dogberry know Cleaver by sight?"

"No, but he gave me an accurate description of him. And naturally he took the car's number."

Vance looked at Markham with open-eyed sorrow.

"My dear Markham—my very dear Markham—can't you see that all you've actually proved is that a bucolic traffic Nemesis handed a speed-violation summons to a smooth-faced, middle-aged, stout man who was driving Cleaver's car near Boonton at half past eleven on the night of the murder? . . . And, my word! Isn't that exactly the sort of alibi the old boy would arrange if he intended taking the lady's life at midnight or thereabouts?"

"Come, come!" laughed Markham. "That's a bit too far-fetched. You'd give every lawbreaker credit for concocting schemes of the most diabolical cunning."

"So I would," admitted Vance apathetically. "And—d' ye know?—rather fancy that's just the kind of schemes a lawbreaker would concoct, if he was planning a murder, and his own life was at stake. What really amazes me is the naïve assumption of you investigators that a murderer gives no intelligent thought whatever to his future safety. It's rather touchin', y' know."

Markham grunted. "Well, you can take it from me, it was Cleaver himself who got the summons."

"I dare say you're right," Vance conceded. "I merely suggested the possibility of deception, don't y' know. The only point I really insist on is that the fascinatin' Miss Odell was killed by a man of subtle and superior mentality."

"And I, in turn," irritably rejoined Markham, "insist that the only men of that type who touched her life intimately enough to have had any reason to do it are Mannix, Cleaver, Lindquist, and Spotswoode. And I further insist that not one of them can be regarded as a promising possibility."

"I fear I must contradict you, old dear," said Vance serenely. "They're all possibilities—and one of them is guilty."

Markham glared at him derisively.

"Well, well! So the case is settled! Now, if you'll but indicate which is the guilty one, I'll arrest him at once and return to my other duties."

"You're always in such haste," Vance lamented. "Why leap and run? The wisdom of the world's philosophers is against it. *Festina lente,* says Cæsar; or, as Rufus has it, *Festinatio tarda est.* And the Koran says quite frankly that haste is of the Devil. Shakespeare was constantly belittling speed: 'He tires betimes that spurs too fast betimes'; and, 'Wisely, and slow; they stumble that run fast.' Then there was Molière—remember *Sganarelle?*—: *'Le trop de promptitude à l'erreur nous expose.'* Chaucer also held similar views. 'He hasteth wel,' said he, 'that wysely can abyde.' Even God's common people have embalmed the idea in numberless proverbs: 'Good and quickly seldom meet'; and 'Hasty men never want woe——' ' "

Markham rose with a gesture of impatience.

"Hell! I'm going home before you start a bedtime story," he growled.

The ironical aftermath of this remark was that Vance did tell a "bedtime story" that night; but he told it to me in the seclusion of his own library; and the gist of it was this:

"Heath is committed, body and soul, to a belief in Skeel's guilt; and Markham is as effectively strangled with legal red tape as the poor Canary was strangled with powerful hands. *Eheu,* Van! There's nothing left for me but to set forth tomorrow *a cappella,* like Gaboriau's Monsieur Lecoq, and see what can be done in the noble cause of justice. I shall ignore both Heath and Markham, and become as a pelican of the wilderness, an owl of the desert, a sparrow alone upon the housetop. . . . Really, y' know, I'm no avenger of society, but I do detest an unsolved problem."

16
SIGNIFICANT DISCLOSURES

(*Thursday, September 13; forenoon*)

GREATLY TO Currie's astonishment Vance gave instructions to be called at nine o'clock the following morning; and at ten o'clock we were sitting on his little roof garden having breakfast in the mellow mid-September sunshine.

"Van," he said to me, when Currie had brought us our second cup of coffee, "however secretive a woman may be, there's always someone to whom she unburdens her soul. A confidant is an essential to the feminine temperament. It may be a mother, or a lover, or a priest, or a doctor, or, more generally, a girl chum. In the Canary's case we haven't a mother or a priest. Her lover, the elegant Skeel, was a potential enemy; and we're pretty safe in ruling out her doctor—she was too shrewd to confide in such a creature as Lindquist. The girl chum, then, remains. And today we seek her." He lit a cigarette and rose. "But, first, we must visit Mr. Bemjamin Browne of Seventh Avenue."

Benjamin Browne was a well-known photographer of stage celebrities, with galleries in the heart of the city's theatrical district; and as we entered the reception room of his luxurious studio later that morning my curiosity as to the object of our visit was at the breaking point. Vance went straight to the desk, behind which sat a young woman with flaming red hair and mascaro-shaded

eyes, and bowed in his most dignified manner. Then, taking a small un-
mounted photograph from his pocket, he laid it before her.

"I am producing a musical comedy, mademoiselle," he said, "and I wish to
communicate with the young lady who left this picture of herself with me. Unfortunately I've misplaced her card; but as her photograph bore the imprint of
Browne's, I thought you might be good enough to look in your files and tell
me who she is and where I may find her."

He slipped a five-dollar bill under the edge of the blotter, and waited with
an air of innocent expectancy.

The young woman looked at him quizzically, and I thought I detected the
hint of a smile at the corners of her artfully rouged lips. But after a moment
she took the photograph without a word and disappeared through a rear door.
Ten minutes later she returned and handed Vance the picture. On the back of
it she had written a name and address.

"The young lady is Miss Alys La Fosse, and she lives at the Belafield
Hotel." There was now no doubt as to her smile. "You really shouldn't be so
careless with the addresses of your applicants—some poor girl might lose an
engagement." And her smile suddenly turned into soft laughter.

"Mademoiselle," replied Vance, with mock seriousness, "in the future I
shall be guided by your warning." And with another dignified bow, he went
out.

"Good Lord!" he said, as we emerged into Seventh Avenue. "Really, y'
know, I should have disguised myself as an impresario, with a gold-headed
cane, a derby, and a purple shirt. That young woman is thoroughly convinced
that I'm contemplating an intrigue. . . . A jolly smart *tête-rouge*, that."

He turned into a florist's shop at the corner, and selecting a dozen American
Beauties, addressed them to "Benjamin Browne's Receptionist."

"And now," he said, "let us stroll to the Belafield, and seek an audience
with Alys."

As we walked across town Vance explained.

"That first morning, when we were inspecting the Canary's rooms, I was
convinced that the murder would never be solved by the usual elephantine
police methods. It was a subtle and well-planned crime, despite its obvious appearances. No routine investigation would suffice. Intimate information was
needed. Therefore, when I saw this photograph of the xanthous Alys half hidden under the litter of papers on the escritoire, I reflected: 'Ah! A girl friend of
the departed Margaret's. She may know just the things that are needed.' So,
when the Sergeant's broad back was turned, I put the picture in my pocket.
There was no other photograph about the place, and this one bore the usual
sentimental inscription. 'Ever thine,' and was signed 'Alys.' I concluded,
therefore, that Alys had played Anactoria to the Canary's Sappho. Of course I
erased the inscription before presenting the picture to the penetrating sibyl at
Browne's. . . . And here we are at the Belafield, hopin' for a bit of enlightenment."

The Belafield was a small, expensive apartment-hotel in the East Thirties,
which, to judge from the guests to be seen in the Americanized Queen Anne
lobby, catered to the well-off sporting set. Vance sent his card up to Miss La
Fosse, and received the message that she would see him in a few minutes. The
few minutes, however, developed into three-quarters of an hour, and it was

nearly noon when a resplendent bellboy came to escort us to the lady's apartment.

Nature had endowed Miss La Fosse with many of its arts, and those that Nature had omitted, Miss La Fosse herself had supplied. She was slender and blond. Her large blue eyes were heavily lashed, but though she looked at one with a wide-eyed stare, she was unable to disguise their sophistication. Her toilet had been made with elaborate care; and as I looked at her, I could not help thinking what an excellent model she would have been for Chéret's pastel posters.

"So you are Mr. Vance," she cooed. "I've often seen your name in *Town Topics.*"

Vance gave a shudder.

"And this is Mr. Van Dine," he said sweetly, "—a mere attorney, who, thus far, has been denied the pages of that fashionable weekly."

"Won't you sit down?" (I am sure Miss La Fosse had spoken the line in a play; she made of the invitation an impressive ceremonial.) "I really don't know why I should have received you. But I suppose you called on business. Perhaps you wish me to appear at a society bazaar, or something of the kind. But I'm so busy, Mr. Vance. You simply can't imagine how occupied I am with my work. . . . I just love my work," she added, with an ecstatic sigh.

"And I'm sure there are many thousands of others who love it, too," returned Vance, in his best drawing-room manner. "But unfortunately I have no bazaar to be graced by your charming presence. I have come on a much more serious matter. . . . You were a very close friend of Miss Margaret Odell's——"

The mention of the Canary's name brought Miss La Fosse suddenly to her feet. Her ingratiating air of affected elegance had quickly disappeared. Her eyes flashed, and their lids drooped harshly. A sneer distorted the lines of her cupid's-bow mouth, and she tossed her head angrily.

"Say, listen! Who do you think you are? I don't know nothing, and I got nothing to say. So run along—you and your lawyer."

But Vance made no move to obey. He took out his cigarette case and carefully selected a Régie.

"Do you mind if I smoke? And won't you have one? I import them direct from my agent in Constantinople. They're exquisitely blended."

The girl snorted, and gave him a look of cold disdain. The doll-baby had become a virago.

"Get yourself outa my apartment, or I'll call the house detective." She turned to the telephone on the wall at her side.

Vance waited until she had lifted the receiver.

"If you do that, Miss La Fosse, I'll order you taken to the district attorney's office for questioning," he told her indifferently, lighting his cigarette and leaning back in his chair.

Slowly she replaced the receiver and turned. "What's your game, anyway? . . . Suppose I did know Margy—then what? And where do you fit into the picture?"

"Alas! I don't fit in at all." Vance smiled pleasantly. "But, for that matter, nobody seems to fit in. The truth is, they're about to arrest a poor blighter for killing your friend, who wasn't in the tableau, either. I happen to be a friend of the district attorney's; and I know exactly what's being done. The police are scouting round in a perfect frenzy of activity, and it's hard to say what trail they'll strike next. I thought, don't y' know, I might save you a lot of unpleasantness by a friendly little chat. . . . Of course," he added, "if you prefer to have me give your name to the police, I'll do so, and let them hold the audience in their own inimitable but crude fashion. I might say, however, that, as yet, they are blissfully unaware of your relationship with Miss Odell, and that, if you are reasonable, I see no reason why they should be informed of it."

The girl had stood, one hand on the telephone, studying Vance intently. He had spoken carelessly and with a genial inflection; and she at length resumed her seat.

"Now, won't you have one of my cigarettes?" he asked, in a tone of gracious reconciliation.

Mechanically she accepted his offer, keeping her eyes on him all the time, as if attempting to determine how far he was to be trusted.

"Who are they thinking of arresting?" She asked the question with scarcely a movement of her features.

"A johnny named Skeel. Silly idea, isn't it?"

"Him!" Her tone was one of mingled contempt and disgust. "That cheap crook? He hasn't got nerve enough to strangle a cat."

"Precisely. But that's no reason for sending him to the electric chair, what?" Vance leaned forward and smiled engagingly. "Miss La Fosse, if you will talk to me for five minutes, and forget I'm a stranger, I'll give you my word of honor not to let the police or the district attorney know anything about you. I'm not connected with the authorities, but somehow I dislike the idea of seeing the wrong man punished. And I'll promise to forget the source of any information you will be kind enough to give me. If you will trust me, it will be infinitely easier for you in the end."

The girl made no answer for several minutes. She was, I could see, trying to estimate Vance; and evidently she decided that, in any case, she had nothing to lose—now that her friendship with the Canary had been discovered—by talking to this man who had promised her immunity from further annoyance.

"I guess you're all right," she said, with a reservation of dubiety; "but I don't know why I should think so." She paused. "But, look here: I was told to keep out of this. And if I don't keep out of it, I'm apt to be back hoofing it in the chorus again. And that's no life for a sweet young thing like me with extravagant tastes—believe me, my friend!"

"That calamity will never befall you through any lack of discretion on my part," Vance assured her, with good-natured earnestness. . . . "Who told you to keep out of it?"

"My—fiancé." She spoke somewhat coquettishly. "He's very well known and he's afraid there might be scandal if I got mixed up in the case as a witness, or anything like that."

"I can readily understand his feelings." Vance nodded sympathetically. "And who, by the bye, is this luckiest of men?"

"Say! You're good." She complimented him with a coy *moue*. "But I'm not announcing my engagement yet."

"Don't be horrid," begged Vance. "You know perfectly well that I could find out his name by making a few inquiries. And if you drove me to learn the facts elsewhere, then my promise to keep your name a secret would no longer bind me."

Miss La Fosse considered this point.

"I guess you could find out all right . . . so I might as well tell you—only I'm trusting to your word to protect me." She opened her eyes wide and gave Vance a melting look. "I know you wouldn't let me down."

"My dear Miss La Fosse!" His tone was one of pained surprise.

"Well, my fiancé is Mr. Mannix, and he's the head of a big fur-importing house. . . . You see"—she became clingingly confidential—"Louey—that is, Mr. Mannix—used to go round with Margy. That's why he didn't want me to get mixed up in the affair. He said the police might bother him with questions, and his name might get into the papers. And that would hurt his commercial standing."

"I quite understand," murmured Vance. "And do you happen to know where Mr. Mannix was Monday night?"

The girl looked startled.

"Of course I know. He was right here with me from half past ten until two in the morning. We were discussing a new musical show he was interested in; and he wanted me to take the leading role."

"I'm sure it will be a success." Vance spoke with disarming friendliness. "Were you home alone all Monday evening?"

"Hardly." The idea seemed to amuse her. "I went to the *Scandals*—but I came home early. I knew Louey—Mr. Mannix—was coming."

"I trust he appreciated your sacrifice." Vance, I believe, was disappointed by this unexpected alibi of Mannix's. It was, indeed, so final that further interrogation concerning it seemed futile. After a momentary pause, he changed the subject.

"Tell me; what do you know about a Mr. Charles Cleaver? He was a friend of Miss Odell's."

"Oh, Pop's all right." The girl was plainly relieved by this turn in the conversation. "A good scout. He was certainly gone on Margy. Even after she threw him over for Mr. Spotswoode, he was faithful, as you might say—always running after her, sending her flowers and presents. Some men are like that. Poor old Pop! He even phoned me Monday night to call up Margy for him and try to arrange a party. Maybe if I'd done it, she wouldn't be dead now. . . . It's a funny world, isn't it?"

"Oh, no end funny." Vance smoked calmly for a minute; I could not help admiring his self-control. "What time did Mr. Cleaver phone you Monday night—do you recall?" From his voice one would have thought the question of no importance.

"Let me see. . . ." She pursed her lips prettily. "It was just ten minutes to twelve. I remember that the little chime clock on the mantel over there was striking midnight, and at first I couldn't hear Pop very well. You see, I always keep my clock ten minutes fast so I'll never be late for an appointment."

Vance compared the clock with his watch.

"Yes, it's ten minutes fast. And what about the party?"

"Oh, I was too busy talking about the new show, and I had to refuse. Anyway, Mr. Mannix didn't want to have a party that night. . . . It wasn't my fault was it?"

"Not a bit of it," Vance assured her. "Work comes before pleasure—especially work as important as yours. . . . And now, there is one other man I want to ask you about, and then I won't bother you any more.—What was the situation between Miss Odell and Doctor Lindquist?"

Miss La Fosse became genuinely perturbed.

"I was afraid you were going to ask me about him." There was apprehension in her eyes. "I don't know just what to say. He was wildly in love with Margy; and she led him on, too. But she was sorry for it afterward, because he got jealous—like a crazy person. He used to pester the life out of her. And once—do you know!—he threatened to shoot her and then shoot himself. I told Margy to look out for him. But she didn't seem to be afraid. Anyway, I think she was taking awful chances. . . . Oh! Do you think it could have been—do you really think——?"

"And wasn't there anyone else," Vance interrupted, "who might have felt the same way? Anyone Miss Odell had reason to fear?"

"No." Miss La Fosse shook her head. "Margy didn't know many men intimately. She didn't change often, if you know what I mean. There wasn't anybody else outside of those you've mentioned, except, of course, Mr. Spotswoode. He cut Pop out several months ago. She went to dinner with him Monday night, too. I wanted her to go to the *Scandals* with me—that's how I know."

Vance rose and held out his hand.

"You've been very kind. And you have nothing whatever to fear. No one shall ever know of our little visit this morning."

"Who do you think killed Margy?" There was genuine emotion in the girl's voice. "Louey says it was probably some burglar who wanted her jewels."

"I'm too wise to sow discord in this happy ménage by even questioning Mr. Mannix's opinion," said Vance half banteringly. "No one *knows* who's guilty; but the police agree with Mr. Mannix."

For a moment the girl's doubts returned, and she gave Vance a searching look. "Why are you so interested? You didn't know Margy, did you? She never mentioned you."

Vance laughed. "My dear child! I only wish I knew why I am so deuced concerned in this affair. 'Pon my word, I can't give you even the sketchiest explanation. . . . No, I never met Miss Odell. But it would offend my sense of proportion if Mr. Skeel were punished and the real culprit went free. Maybe I'm getting sentimental. A sad fate, what?"

"I guess I'm getting soft, too." She nodded her head, still looking Vance square in the eyes. "I risked my happy home to tell you what I did, because somehow I believed you. . . . Say, you weren't stringing me, by any chance?"

Vance put his hand to his heart, and became serious.

"My dear Miss La Fosse, when I leave here it will be as though I had never entered. Dismiss me and Mr. Van Dine here from your mind."

Something in his manner banished her misgivings, and she bade us a kittenish farewell.

17

CHECKING AN ALIBI

(Thursday, September 13; afternoon)

"MY SLEUTHING goes better," exulted Vance, when we were again in the street. "Fair Alys was a veritable mine of information—eh, what? Only, you should have controlled yourself better when she mentioned her beloved's name—really, you should, Van old thing. I saw you jump and heard you heave. Such emotion is unbecoming in a lawyer."

From a booth in a drugstore near the hotel he telephoned Markham: "I am taking you to lunch. I have numerous confidences I would pour into your ear." A debate ensued, but in the end Vance emerged triumphant; and a moment later a taxicab was driving us downtown.

"Alys is clever—there are brains in that fluffy head," he ruminated. "She's much smarter than Heath; she knew at once that Skeel wasn't guilty. Her characterization of the immaculate Tony was inelegant but how accurate—oh, how accurate! And you noticed, of course, how she trusted me. Touchin', wasn't it? ... It's a knotty problem, Van. Something's amiss somewhere."

He was silent, smoking, for several blocks.

"Mannix. ... Curious he should crop up again. And he issued orders to Alys to keep mum. Now, why? Maybe the reason he gave her was the real one. Who knows? On the other hand, was he with his *chère amie* from half past ten till early morning? Well, well. Again, who knows? Something queer about that business discussion. ... Then Cleaver. He called up just ten minutes before midnight—oh, yes, he called up. That wasn't a fairytale. But how could he telephone from a speeding car? He couldn't. Maybe he really wanted to have a party with his recalcitrant Canary, don't y' know. But, then, why the brummagem alibi? Funk? Maybe. But why the circuitousness? Why didn't he call his lost love direct? Ah, perhaps he did! Someone certainly called her by phone at twenty minutes to twelve. We must look into that, Van. ... Yes, he may have called her, and then when a man answered—who the deuce was that man, anyway?—he may have appealed to Alys. Quite natural, y' know. Anyway, he wasn't in Boonton. Poor Markham! How upset he'll be when he finds out! ... But what really worries me is that story of the doctor. Jealous mania: it squares with Ambroise's character perfectly. He's the kind that does go off his head. I knew his confession of paternalism was a red herring. My word! So the doctor was making threats and flourishing pistols, eh? Bad, bad. I don't like it. With those ears of his, he wouldn't hesitate to pull the trigger. Paranoia—that's it. Delusions of persecution. Probably thought the girl and Pop—or maybe the girl and Spotswoode—were plotting his misery and laughing at him. You can't tell about those chaps. They're deep and they're dangerous. The canny Alys had him sized up—warned the Canary against him. ... Taken by and large, it's a devilish tangle. Anyway, I feel rather bucked. We're moving—oh, undoubtedly we're moving—though in what direction I can't even guess. It's beastly annoyin'."

Markham was waiting for us at the Bankers' Club. He greeted Vance irritably. "What have you got to tell me that's so damned important?"

"Now, don't get ratty." Vance was beaming. "How's your lodestar, Skeel, behaving?"

"So far he's done everything that's pure and refined except join the Christian Endeavor Society."

"Sunday's coming. Give him time.... So you're not happy, Markham dear?"

"Was I dragged away from another engagement to report on my state of mind?"

"No need. Your state of mind's execrable.... Cheerio! I've brought you something to think about."

"Damn it! I've got too much to think about now."

"Here, have some brioche." Vance gave the order for lunch without consulting either of us. "And now for my revelations. *Imprimis:* Pop Cleaver wasn't in Boonton last Monday night. He was very much in the midst of our modern Gomorrah, trying to arrange a midnight party."

"Wonderful!" snorted Markham. "I lave in the font of your wisdom. His alter ego, I take it, was on the road to Hopatcong. The supernatural leaves me cold."

"You may be as pancosmic as you choose. Cleaver was in New York at midnight Monday, craving excitement."

"What about the summons for speeding?"

"That's for you to explain. But if you'll take my advice, you'll send for this Boonton catchpole and let him have a look at Pop. If he says Cleaver is the man he ticketed, I'll humbly do away with myself."

"Well! That makes it worth trying. I'll have the officer at the Stuyvesant Club this afternoon and I'll point out Cleaver to him.... What other staggering revelations have you in store?"

"Mannix will bear looking into."

Markham put down his knife and fork and leaned back. "I'm overcome! Such Himalayan sagacity! With that evidence against him, he should be arrested at once.... Vance, my dear old friend, are you feeling quite normal? No dizzy spells lately? No shooting pains in the head? Knee jerks all right?"

"Furthermore, Doctor Lindquist was wildly infatuated with the Canary, and insanely jealous. Recently threatened to take a pistol and hold a little pogrom of his own."

"That's better." Markham sat up. "Where did you get this information?"

"Ah! That's my secret."

Markham was annoyed.

"Why so mysterious?"

"Needs must, old chap. Gave my word and all that sort of thing. And I'm a bit quixotic, don't y' know—too much Cervantes in my youth." He spoke lightly, but Markham knew him too well to push the question.

In less than five minutes after we had returned to the district attorney's office, Heath came in.

"I got something else on Mannix, sir; thought you might want to add it to the report I turned in yesterday. Burke secured a picture of him and showed it to the phone operators at Odell's house. Both of 'em recognized it. He's been there several times, but it wasn't the Canary he called on. It was the woman in Apartment 2. She's named Frisbee and used to be one of Mannix's fur models. He's been to see her several times during the past six months and has taken her out once or twice; but he hasn't called on her for a month or more. . . . Any good?"

"Can't tell." Markham shot Vance an inquisitive look. "But thanks for the information, Sergeant."

"By the bye," said Vance dulcetly, when Heath had left us, "I'm feeling tophole. No pains in the head; no dizzy spells. Knee jerks perfect."

"Delighted. Still, I can't charge a man with murder because he calls on his fur model."

"You're so hasty! Why should you charge him with murder?" Vance rose and yawned. "Come, Van. I'd rather like to gaze on Perneb's tomb at the Metropolitan this afternoon. Could you bear it?" At the door he paused. "I say, Markham, what about the Boonton bailiff?" Markham rang for Swacker. "I'll see to it at once. Drop in at the club around five, if you feel like it. I'll have the officer there then, as Cleaver is sure to come in before dinner."

When Vance and I returned to the club late that afternoon, Markham was stationed in the lounge room facing the main door of the rotunda; and beside him sat a tall, heavyset, bronzed man of about forty, alert but ill at ease.

"Traffic Officer Phipps arrived from Boonton a little while ago," said Markham, by way of introduction. "Cleaver is expected at any moment now. He has an appointment here at half past five."

Vance drew up a chair.

"I do hope he's a punctual beggar."

"So do I," returned Markham viciously. "I'm looking forward to your *felo-de-se.*"

" 'Our hap is loss, our hope but sad despair,' " murmured Vance.

Less than ten minutes later Cleaver entered the rotunda from the street, paused at the desk, and sauntered into the lounge room. There was no escaping the observation point Markham had chosen; and as he walked by us he paused and exchanged greetings. Markham detained him a moment with a few casual questions; and then Cleaver passed on.

"That the man you ticketed, Officer?" asked Markham, turning to Phipps.

Phipps was scowling perplexedly. "It looks something like him, sir; there's a kind of resemblance. But it ain't him." He shook his head. "No, sir; it ain't him. The fellow I hung a summons on was stouter than this gent and wasn't as tall."

"You're positive?"

"Yes, sir—no mistake. The guy I tagged tried to argue with me and then he tried to slip me a fiver to forget it. I had my headlight on him full."

Phipps was dismissed with a substantial *pourboire.*

"*Væ misero mihi!*" sighed Vance. "My worthless existence is to be prolonged. Sad. But you must try to bear it. . . . I say, Markham, what does Pop Cleaver's brother look like?"

"That's it," nodded Markham. "I've met his brother; he's shorter and stouter. . . . This thing is getting beyond me. I think I'll have it out with Cleaver now."

He started to rise, but Vance forced him back into his seat.

"Don't be impetuous. Cultivate patience. Cleaver's not going to do a bunk; and there are one or two prelimin'ry steps strongly indicated. Mannix and Lindquist still seduce my curiosity."

Markham clung to his point. "Neither Mannix nor Lindquist is here now, and Cleaver is. And I want to know why he lied to me about that summons."

"I can tell you that," said Vance. "He wanted you to think he was in the wilds of New Jersey at midnight Monday. Simple, what?"

"The inference is a credit to your intelligence! But I hope you don't seriously think that Cleaver is guilty. It's possible he knows something; but I certainly cannot picture him as a strangler."

"And why?"

"He's not the type. It's inconceivable—even if there were evidence against him."

"Ah! The psychological judgment! You eliminate Cleaver because you don't think his nature harmonizes with the situation. I say, doesn't that come perilously near being an esoteric hypothesis?—or a metaphysical deduction? . . . However, I don't entirely agree with you in your application of the theory to Cleaver. That fish-eyed gambler has unsuspected potentialities for evil. But with the theory itself I am wholly in accord. And behold, my dear Markham: you yourself apply psychology in its abecedarian implications, yet ridicule my application of it in its higher developments. Consistency may be the hobgoblin of little minds, y' know, but it's nonetheless a priceless jewel. . . . How about a cup of tea?"

We sought the Palm Room and sat down at a table near the entrance. Vance ordered oolong tea, but Markham and I took black coffee. A very capable four-piece orchestra was playing Tchaikovsky's *Casse-Noisette Suite,* and we sat restfully in the comfortable chairs without speaking. Markham was tired and dispirited, and Vance was busy with the problem that had absorbed him continuously since Tuesday morning. Never before had I seen him so preoccupied.

We had, been there perhaps half an hour when Spotswoode strolled in. He stopped and spoke, and Markham asked him to join us. He, too, appeared depressed, and his eyes showed signs of worry.

"I hardly dare ask you, Mr. Markham," he said diffidently, after he had ordered a ginger ale, "but how do my chances stand now of being called as a witness?"

"That fate is certainly no nearer than when I last saw you," Markham replied. "In fact, nothing has happened to change the situation materially."

"And the man you had under suspicion?"

"He's still under suspicion, but no arrest has been made. We're hoping, however, that something will break before long."

"And I suppose you still want me to remain in the city?"

"If you can arrange it—yes."

Spotswoode was silent for a time; then he said, "I don't want to appear to shirk any responsibility—and perhaps it may seem wholly selfish for me even to suggest it—but, in any event, wouldn't the testimony of the telephone operator as to the hour of Miss Odell's return and her calls for help be sufficient to establish the facts, without my corroboration?"

"I have thought of that, of course; and if it is at all possible to prepare the case for the prosecution without summoning you to appear, I assure you it will be done. At the moment, I can see no necessity of your being called as a witness. But one never knows what may turn up. If the defense hinges on a question of exact time, and the operator's testimony is questioned or disqualified for any reason, you may be required to come forward. Otherwise not."

Spotswoode sipped his ginger ale. A little of his depression seemed to have departed.

"You're very generous, Mr. Markham. I wish there was some adequate way of thanking you." He looked up hesitantly. "I presume you are still opposed to my visiting the apartment. . . . I know you think me unreasonable and perhaps sentimental; but the girl represented something in my life that I find very difficult to tear out. I don't expect you to understand it—I hardly understand it myself."

"I think it's easily understandable, don't y' know," remarked Vance, with a sympathy I had rarely seen him manifest. "Your attitude needs no apology. History and fable are filled with the same situation, and the protagonists have always exhibited sentiments similar to yours. Your most famous prototype, of course, was Odysseus on the citron-scented isle of Ogygia with the fascinatin' Calypso. The soft arms of sirens have gone snaking round men's necks ever since the red-haired Lilith worked her devastatin' wiles on the impressionable Adam. We're all sons of that racy old boy."

Spotswoode smiled. "You at least give me an historic background," he said. Then he turned to Markham. "What will become of Miss Odell's possessions—her furniture and so forth?"

"Sergeant Heath heard from an aunt of hers in Seattle," Markham told him. "She's on her way to New York, I believe, to take over what there is of the estate."

"And everything will be kept intact until then?"

"Probably longer, unless something unexpected happens. Anyway, until then."

"There are one or two little trinkets I'd like to keep," Spotswoode confessed, a bit shamefacedly, I thought.

After a few more minutes of desultory talk he rose and, pleading an engagement, bade us good afternoon.

"I hope I can keep his name clear of the case," said Markham, when he had gone.

"Yes; his situation is not an enviable one," concurred Vance. "It's always sad to be found out. The moralist would set it down to retribution."

"In this instance chance was certainly on the side of righteousness. If he hadn't chosen Monday night for the Winter Garden, he might now be in the bosom of his family, with nothing more troublesome to bother him than a guilty conscience."

"It certainly looks that way." Vance glanced at his watch. "And your mention of the Winter Garden reminds me. Do you mind if we dine early? Frivolity beckons me tonight. I'm going to the *Scandals*."

We both looked at him as though he had taken leave of his senses.

"Don't be so horrified, my Markham. Why should I not indulge an impulse? . . . And, incidentally, I hope to have glad tidings for you by lunchtime tomorrow."

18

THE TRAP

(Friday, September 14; noon)

VANCE SLEPT late the following day. I had accompanied him to the *Scandals* the night before, utterly at a loss to understand his strange desire to attend a type of entertainment which I knew he detested. At noon he ordered his car, and instructed the chauffeur to drive to the Belafield Hotel.

"We are about to call again on the allurin' Alys," he said. "I'd bring posies to lay at her shrine, but I fear dear Mannix might question her unduly about them."

Miss La Fosse received us with an air of crestfallen resentment.

"I might've known it!" She nodded her head with sneering perception. "I suppose you've come to tell me the cops found out about me without the slightest assistance from you." Her disdain was almost magnificent. "Did you bring 'em with you? . . . A swell guy *you* are!—But it's my own fault for being a damn fool."

Vance waited unmoved until she had finished her contemptuous tirade. Then he bowed pleasantly.

"Really, y' know, I merely dropped in to pay my respects, and to tell you that the police have turned in their report of Miss Odell's acquaintances, and that your name was not mentioned on it. You seemed a little worried yesterday on that score, and it occurred to me I could set your mind wholly at ease."

The vigilance of her attitude relaxed. "Is that straight? . . . My God! I don't know what would happen if Louey'd find out I'd been blabbing."

"I'm sure he won't find out, unless you choose to tell him. . . . Won't you be generous and ask me to sit down a moment?"

"Of course—I'm so sorry. I'm just having my coffee. Please join me." She rang for two extra services.

Vance had drunk two cups of coffee less than half an hour before, and I marveled at his enthusiasm for this atrocious hotel beverage.

"I was a belated spectator of the *Scandals* last night," he remarked in a negligent, conversational tone. "I missed the revue earlier in the season. How is it you yourself were so late in seeing it?"

"I've been so busy," she confided. "I was rehearsing for 'A Pair of Queens'; but the production's been postponed. Louey couldn't get the theater he wanted."

"Do you like revues?" asked Vance. "I should think they'd be more difficult for the principals than the ordin'ry musical comedy."

"They are." Miss La Fosse adopted a professional air. "And they're unsatisfactory. The individual is lost in them. There's no real scope for one's talent. They're breathless if you know what I mean."

"I should imagine so." Vance bravely sipped his coffee. "And yet, there were several numbers in the *Scandals* that you could have done charmingly; they seemed particularly designed for you. I thought of you doing them, and—d' ye know?—the thought rather spoiled my enjoyment of the young lady who appeared in them."

"You flatter me, Mr. Vance. But, really, I have a good voice. I've studied very hard. And I learned dancing with Professor Markoff."

"Indeed!" (I'm sure Vance had never heard the name before, but his exclamation seemed to imply that he regarded Professor Markoff as one of the world's most renowned ballet masters.) "Then, you certainly should have been starred in the *Scandals*. The young lady I have in mind sang rather indifferently, and her dancing was most inadequate. Moreover, she was many degrees your inferior in personality and attractiveness. . . . Confess: didn't you have just a little desire Monday night to be singing the 'Chinese Lullaby' song?"

"Oh, I don't know." Miss La Fosse carefully considered the suggestion. "They kept the lights awfully low; and I don't look so well in cerise. But the costumes were adorable, weren't they?"

"On you they certainly would have been adorable. . . . What color are you partial to?"

"I love the orchid shades," she told him enthusiastically; "though I don't look at all bad in turquoise blue. But an artist once told me I should always wear white. He wanted to paint my portrait, but the gentleman I was engaged to then didn't like him."

Vance regarded her appraisingly.

"I think your artist friend was right. And, y' know, the St. Moritz scene in the *Scandals* would have suited you perfectly. The little brunette who sang the snow song, all in white, was delightful; but really, now, she should have had golden hair. Dusky beauties belong to the southern climes. And she impressed me as lacking the sparkle and vitality of a Swiss resort in midwinter. You could have supplied those qualities admirably."

"Yes; I'd have liked that better than the Chinese number, I think. White fox is my favorite fur, too. But, even so, in a revue you're on in one number and off in another. When it's all over, you're forgotten." She sighed unhappily.

Vance set down his cup and looked at her with whimsically reproachful eyes. After a moment he said, "My dear, why did you fib to me about the time Mr. Mannix returned to you last Monday night? It wasn't a bit nice of you."

"What do you mean?" Miss La Fosse exclaimed in frightened indignation, drawing herself up into an attitude of withering hauteur.

"You see," explained Vance, "the St. Moritz scene of the *Scandals* doesn't go on until nearly eleven, and it closes the bill. So you couldn't possible have seen it and also received Mr. Mannix here at half past ten. Come. What time did he arrive here Monday night?"

The girl flushed angrily. "You're pretty slick, aren't you? You shoulda been a cop. . . . Well, what if I didn't get home till after the show? Any crime in that?"

"None whatever," answered Vance mildly. "Only a little breach of good faith in telling me you came home early." He bent forward earnestly. "I'm not here to make you trouble. On the contr'ry, I'd like to protect you from any distress or bother. You see, if the police go nosing round, they may run on to you. But if I'm able to give the district attorney accurate information about certain things connected with Monday night, there'll be no danger of the police being sent to look for you."

Miss La Fosse's eyes grew suddenly hard, and her brow crinkled with determination. "Listen! I haven't got anything to hide, and neither has Louey. But if Louey asks me to say he's somewhere at half past ten, I'm going to say it—see? That's my idea of friendship. Louey had some good reason to ask it, too, or he wouldn't have done it. However, since you're so smart, and have accused me of playing unfair, I'm going to tell you that he didn't get in till after midnight. But if anybody else asks me about it, I'll see 'em in hell before I tell 'em anything but the half-past-ten story. Get that?"

Vance bowed. "I get it; and I like you for it."

"But don't go away with the wrong idea," she hurried on, her eyes sparkling with fervor. "Louey may not have got here till after midnight, but if you think he knows anything about Margy's death, you're crazy. He was through with Margy a year ago. Why, he hardly knew she was on earth. And if any fool cop gets the notion in his head that Louey was mixed up in the affair, I'll alibi him—so help me God!—if it's the last thing I do in this world."

"I like you more and more," said Vance; and when she gave him her hand at parting he lifted it to his lips.

As we rode downtown Vance was thoughtful. We were nearly to the Criminal Courts Building before he spoke.

"The primitive Alys rather appeals to me," he said. "She's much too good for the oleaginous Mannix. . . . Women are so shrewd—and so gullible. A woman can read a man with almost magical insight; but, on the other hand, she is inexpressibly blind when it comes to *her* man. Witness sweet Alys's faith in Mannix. He probably told her he was slaving at the office Monday night. Naturally, she doesn't believe it; but she knows—*knows*, mind you—that her Louey just couldn't have been concerned in the Canary's death. Ah, well, let us hope she's right and that Mannix is not apprehended—at least not until her new show is financed. . . . My word! If this being a detective involves many more revues, I shall have to resign. Thank Heaven, though, the lady didn't attend the cinema Monday night!"

When we arrived at the District Attorney's office we found Heath and Markham in consultation. Markham had a pad before him, several pages of which were covered with tabulated and annotated entries. A cloud of cigar smoke enveloped him. Heath sat facing him, his elbows on the table, his chin resting in his hands. He looked pugnacious but disconsolate.

"I'm going over the case with the sergeant," Markham explained, with a brief glance in our direction. "We're trying to get all the salient points down in some kind of order, to see if there are any connecting links we've overlooked. I've told the sergeant about the doctor's infatuation and his threats, and of the failure of Traffic Officer Phipps to identify Cleaver. But the more we learn, the worse, apparently, the jumble grows."

He picked up the sheets of paper and fastened them together with a clip.

"The truth is, we haven't any real evidence against anybody. There are suspicious circumstances connected with Skeel and Doctor Lindquist and Cleaver; and our interview with Mannix didn't precisely allay suspicions in his direction, either. But when we come right down to it, what's the situation! We've got some fingerprints of Skeel, which might have been made late Monday afternoon. Doctor Lindquist goes berserk when we ask him where he was Monday night, and then offers us a weak alibi. He admits a fatherly interest in the girl, whereas he's really in love with her—a perfectly natural bit of mendacity. Cleaver lent his car to his brother and lied about it, so that I'd think he was in Boonton Monday at midnight. And Mannix gives us a number of shifty answers to our questions concerning his relations with the girl. . . . Not an embarrassment of riches."

"I wouldn't say your information was exactly negligent," observed Vance, taking a chair beside the sergeant. "It may all prove devilish valuable if only it could be put together properly. The difficulty, it appears to me, is that certain parts of the puzzle are missing. Find 'em, and I'll warrant everything will fit beautifully—like a mosaic."

"Easy enough to say 'find 'em,' " grumbled Markham. "The trouble is to know where to look."

Heath relighted his dead cigar and made an impatient gesture.

"You can't get away from Skeel. He's the boy that did it, and, if it wasn't for Abe Rubin, I'd sweat the truth outa him. And by the way, Mr. Vance, he had his own private key to the Odell apartment, all right." He glanced at Markham hesitantly. "I don't want to look as if I was criticising, sir, but I got a feeling we're wasting time chasing after these gentlemen friends of Odell—Cleaver and Mannix and this here doctor."

"You may be right." Markham seemed inclined to agree with him. "However, I'd like to know why Lindquist acted the way he did."

"Well, that might help some," Heath compromised. "If the doc was so far gone on Odell as to threaten to shoot her, and if he went off his head when you asked him to alibi himself, maybe he could tell us something. Why not throw a little scare into him? His record ain't any too good, anyway."

"An excellent idea," chimed in Vance.

Markham looked up sharply. Then he consulted his appointment book. "I'm fairly free this afternoon, so suppose you bring him down here, Sergeant. Get a subpœna if you have to—only see that he comes. And make it as soon after lunch as you can." He tapped on the desk irritably. "If I don't do anything else, I'm going to eliminate some of this human flotsam that's cluttering up the case. And Lindquist is as good as any to start with. I'll either develop these various suspicious circumstances into something workable or I'll root them up. Then we'll see where we stand."

Heath shook hands pessimistically and went out.

"Poor hapless man!" sighed Vance, looking after him. "He giveth way to all the pangs and fury of despair."

"And so would you," snapped Markham, "if the newspapers were butchering you for a political holiday. By the way, weren't you to be a harbinger of glad tidings this noon, or something of the sort?"

"I believe I did hold out some such hope." Vance sat looking meditatively out of the window for several minutes. "Markham, this fellow Mannix lures me like a magnet. He irks and whirrets me. He infests my slumbers. He's the raven on my bust of Pallas. He plagues me like a banshee."

"Does this jeremiad come under the head of tidings?"

"I sha'n't rest peacefully," pursued Vance, "until I know where Louey the furrier was between eleven o'clock and midnight Monday. He was somewhere he shouldn't have been. And you, Markham, must find out. Please make Mannix the second offensive in your assault upon the flotsam. He'll parley, with the right amount of pressure. Be brutal, old dear; let him think you suspect him of the throttling. Ask him about the fur model—what's her name?— Frisbee——" He stopped short and knit his brows. "My eye—oh, my eye! I wonder.... Yes, yes, Markham; you must question him about the fur model. Ask him when he saw her last, and try to look wise and mysterious when you're doing it."

"See here, Vance"—Markham was exasperated—"you've been harping on Mannix for three days. What's keeping your nose to that scent?"

"Intuition—sheer intuition. My psychic temperament, don't y' know."

"I'd believe that if I hadn't known you for fifteen years." Markham inspected him shrewdly, then shrugged his shoulders. "I'll have Mannix on the tapis when I'm through with Lindquist."

19

THE DOCTOR EXPLAINS

(*Friday, September 14; 2 P.M.*)

WE LUNCHED in the district attorney's private sanctum; and at two o'clock Doctor Lindquist was announced. Heath accompanied him, and, from the expression on the sergeant's face, it was plain he did not at all like his companion.

The doctor, at Markham's request, seated himself facing the district attorney's desk.

"What is the meaning of this new outrage?" he demanded coldly. "Is it your prerogative to force a citizen to leave his private affairs in order to be bullied?"

"It's my duty to bring murderers to justice," replied Markham, with equal coldness. "And if any citizen considers that giving aid to the authorities is an outrage, that's *his* prerogative. If you have anything to fear by answering my questions, Doctor, you are entitled to have your attorney present. Would you care to phone him to come here now and give you legal protection?"

Doctor Lindquist hesitated. "I need no legal protection, sir. Will you be good enough to tell me at once why I was brought here?"

"Certainly; to explain a few points which have been discovered regarding your relationship with Miss Odell, and to elucidate—if you care to—your reasons for deceiving me, at our last conference, in regard to that relationship."

"You have, I infer, been prying unwarrantably into my private affairs. I had heard that such practices were once common in Russia...."

"If the prying was unwarranted, you can, Doctor Lindquist, easily convince me on that point; and whatever we may have learned concerning you will be instantly forgotten. It is true, is it not, that your interest in Miss Odell went somewhat beyond mere paternal affection?"

"Are not even a man's sacred sentiments respected by the police of this country?" There was insolent scorn in the doctor's tone.

"Under some conditions, yes; under others, no." Markham controlled his fury admirably. "You need not answer me, of course; but, if you choose to be frank, you may possibly save yourself the humiliation of being questioned publicly by the people's attorney in a court of law."

Doctor Lindquist winced and considered the matter at some length. "And if I admit that my affection for Miss Odell was other than paternal—what then?"

Markham accepted the question as an affirmation.

"You were intensely jealous of her, were you not, Doctor?"

"Jealousy," Doctor Lindquist remarked, with an air of ironic professionalism, "is not an unusual accompaniment to an infatuation. Authorities such as Kraft-Ebing, Moll, Freud, Ferenczi, and Adler, I believe, regard it as an intimate psychological corollary of amatory attraction."

"Most instructive." Markham nodded his head appreciatively. "I am to assume, then, that you were infatuated with—or, let us say, amatorily attracted by—Miss Odell, and that on occasions you exhibited the intimate psychological corollary of jealousy?"

"You may assume what you please. But I fail to understand why my emotions are any of your affair."

"Had your emotions not led you to highly questionable and suspicious acts, I would not be interested in them. But I have it on unimpeachable authority that your emotions so reacted on your better judgment that you threatened to take Miss Odell's life and also your own. And, in view of the fact that the young woman has since been murdered, the law naturally—and reasonably—is curious."

The doctor's normally pale face seemed to turn yellow, and his long splay fingers tightened over the arms of his chair; but otherwise he sat immobile and rigidly dignified, his eyes fixed intently on the district attorney.

"I trust," added Markham, "you will not augment my suspicions by any attempt at denial."

Vance was watching the man closely. Presently he leaned forward.

"I say, Doctor, what method of extermination did you threaten Miss Odell with?"

Doctor Lindquist jerked round, thrusting his head toward Vance. He drew in a long rasping breath, and his whole frame became tense. Blood suffused his cheeks; and there was a twitching of the muscles about his mouth and throat. For a moment I was afraid he was going to lose his self-control. But after a moment's effort he steadied himself.

"You think perhaps I threatened to strangle her?" His words were vibrant with the intensity of his passionate anger. "And you would like to turn my threat into a noose to hang me?—Paugh!" He paused, and when he spoke again, his voice had become calmer. "It is quite true I once inadvisedly attempted to frighten Miss Odell with a threat to kill her and to commit suicide. But if your information is as accurate as you would have me believe, you are aware that I threatened her with a revolver. It is the weapon, I believe, that is conventionally mentioned when making empty threats. I certainly would not have threatened her with thuggee, even had I contemplated so abominable an act."

"True," nodded Vance. "And it's a rather good point, don't y' know."

The doctor was evidently encouraged by Vance's attitude. He again faced Markham and elaborated his confession. "A threat, I presume you know, is rarely the forerunner of a violent deed. Even a brief study of the human mind would teach you that a threat is *prima facie* evidence of one's innocence. A threat, generally, is made in anger, and acts as its own safety valve." He shifted his eyes. "I am not a married man; my emotional life has not been stabilized, as it were; and I am constantly coming in close contact with hypersensitive and overwrought people. During a period of abnormal susceptibility I conceived an infatuation for the young woman, an infatuation which she did not reciprocate—certainly not with an ardor commensurate with my own. I suffered deeply; and she made no effort to mitigate my sufferings. Indeed, I suspected her, more than once, of deliberately and perversely torturing me with other men. At any rate, she took no pains to hide her infidelities from me. I confess that once or twice I was almost distracted. And it was in the hope of frightening her into a more amenable and considerate attitude that I threatened her. I trust that you are a sufficiently discerning judge of human nature to believe me."

"Leaving that point for a moment," answered Markham noncommittally, "will you give me more specific information as to your whereabouts Monday night?"

Again I noted a yellow tinge creep over the man's features, and his body stiffened perceptibly. But when he spoke, it was with his habitual suavity.

"I considered that my note to you covered that question satisfactorily. What did I omit?"

"What was the name of the patient on whom you were calling that night?"

"Mrs. Anna Breedon. She is the widow of the late Amos H. Breedon of the Breedon National Bank of Long Branch."

"And you were with her, I believe you stated, from eleven until one?"

"That is correct."

"And was Mrs. Breedon the only witness to your presence at the sanitarium between those hours?"

"I am afraid that is so. You see, after ten o'clock at night I never ring the bell. I let myself in with my own key."

"And I suppose that I may be permitted to question Mrs. Breedon?"

Doctor Lindquist was profoundly regretful. "Mrs. Breedon is a very ill woman. She suffered a tremendous shock at the time of her husband's death last summer, and has been practically in a semiconscious condition ever since. There are times when I even fear for her reason. The slightest disturbance of excitement might produce very serious results."

He took a newspaper cutting from a gold-edged letter case and handed it to Markham.

"You will observe that this obituary notice mentions her prostration and confinement in a private sanitarium. I have been her physician for years."

Markham, after glancing at the cutting, handed it back. There was a short silence broken by a question from Vance.

"By the bye, Doctor, what is the name of the night nurse at your sanitarium?"

Doctor Lindquist looked up quickly.

"My night nurse? Why—what has she to do with it? She was very busy Monday night. I can't understand.... Well, if you want her name I have no objection. It's Finckle—Miss Amelia Finckle."

Vance wrote down the name and, rising, carried the slip of paper to Heath.

"Sergeant, bring Miss Finckle here tomorrow morning at eleven," he said, with a slight lowering of one eyelid.

"I sure will, sir. Good idea." His manner boded no good for Miss Finckle.

A cloud of apprehension spread over Doctor Lindquist's face.

"Forgive me if I say that I am insensible to the sanity of your cavalier methods." His tone betrayed only contempt. "May I hope that for the present your inquisition is ended?"

"I think that will be all, Doctor," returned Markham politely. "May I have a taxicab called for you?"

"Your consideration overwhelms me. But my car is below." And Doctor Lindquist haughtily withdrew.

Markham immediately summoned Swacker and sent him for Tracy. The detective came at once, polishing his pince-nez and bowing affably. One would have taken him for an actor rather than a detective, but his ability in matters requiring delicate handling was a byword in the department.

"I want you to fetch Mr. Louis Mannix again," Markham told him. "Bring him here at once; I'm waiting to see him."

Tracy bowed genially and, adjusting his glasses, departed on his errand.

"And now," said Markham, fixing Vance with a reproachful look, "I want to know what your idea was in putting Lindquist on his guard about the night nurse. Your brain isn't at par this afternoon. Do you think I didn't have the nurse in mind? And now you've warned him. He'll have until eleven tomorrow morning to coach her in her answers. Really, Vance, I can't conceive of anything better calculated to defeat us in our attempt to substantiate the man's alibi."

"I did put a little fright into him, didn't I?" Vance grinned complacently. "Whenever your antagonist begins talking exaggeratedly about the insanity of your notions, he's already deuced hot under the collar. But, Markham old thing, don't burst into tears over my mental shortcomings. If you and I both thought of the nurse, don't you suppose the wily doctor also thought of her? If this Miss Finckle were the type that could be suborned, he would have enlisted her perjurious service two days ago, and she would have been mentioned, along with the comatose Mrs. Breedon, as a witness to his presence at the sanitarium Monday night. The fact that he avoided all reference to the nurse shows that she's not to be wheedled into swearing falsely.... No, Markham. I deliberately put him on his guard. Now he'll have to do something before we question Miss Finckle. And I'm vain enough to think I know what it'll be."

"Let me get this right," put in Heath. "Am I, or am I not, to round up the Finckle woman tomorrow morning?"

"There'll be no need," said Vance. "We are doomed, I fear, not to gaze upon this Florence Nightingale. A meeting between us is about the last thing the doctor would desire."

"That may be true," admitted Markham. "But don't forget that he may have been up to something Monday night wholly unconnected with the murder, that he simply doesn't want known."

"Quite—quite. And yet, nearly everyone who knew the Canary seems to have selected Monday night for the indulgence of *sub rosa* peccadilloes. It's a bit thick, what? Skeel tries to make us believe he was immersed in Khun Khan. Cleaver was—if you take his word for it—touring the countryside in Jersey's lake district. Lindquist wants us to picture him as comforting the afflicted. And Mannix, I happen to know, has gone to some trouble to build up an alibi in case we get nosey. All of 'em, in fact, were doing something they don't want us to know about. Now, what was it? And why did they, of one accord, select the night of the murder for mysterious affairs which they don't dare mention, even to clear themselves of suspicion? Was there an invasion of efreets in the city that night? Was there a curse on the world, driving men to dark bawdy deeds? Was there Black Magic abroad? I think not."

"I'm laying my money on Skeel," declared Heath stubbornly. "I know a professional job when I see it. And you can't get away from those fingerprints and the Professor's report on the chisel."

Markham was sorely perplexed. His belief in Skeel's guilt had, I knew, been undermined in some measure by Vance's theory that the crime was the carefully premeditated act of a shrewd and educated man. But now he seemed to swing irresolutely back to Heath's point of view.

"I'll admit," he said, "that Lindquist and Cleaver and Mannix don't inspire one with a belief in their innocence. But since they're all tarred with the same stick, the force of suspicion against them is somewhat dispersed. After all, Skeel is the only logical aspirant for the role of strangler. He's the only one with a visible motive; and he's the only one against whom there's any evidence."

Vance sighed wearily. "Yes, yes. Fingerprints—chisel marks. You're such a trustin' soul, Markham. Skeel's fingerprints are found in the apartment; therefore, Skeel strangled the lady. So beastly simple. Why bother further? A *chose jugée*—an adjudicated case. Send Skeel to the chair, and that's that! . . . It's effective, y' know, but is it art?"

"In your critical enthusiasm you understate our case against Skeel," Markham reminded him testily.

"Oh, I'll grant that your case against him is ingenious. It's so deuced ingenious I just haven't the heart to reject it. But most popular truth is mere ingenuity—that's why it's so wrong-headed. Your theory would appeal strongly to the popular mind. And yet, y' know, Markham, it isn't true."

The practical Heath was unmoved. He sat stolidly, scowling at the table. I doubt if he had even heard the exchange of opinions between Markham and Vance.

"You know, Mr. Markham," he said, like one unconsciously voicing an obscure line of thought, "if we could show how Skeel got in and out of Odell's apartment, we'd have a better case against him. I can't figure it out—it's got me stopped. So, I've been thinking we oughta get an architect to go over those rooms. The house is an oldtimer—God knows when it was originally built—and there may be some way of getting into it that we haven't discovered yet."

" 'Pon my soul!" Vance stared at him in satirical wonderment. "You're becoming downright romantic! Secret passageways, hidden doors, stairways between the walls. So that's it, is it? Oh, my word! . . . . Sergeant, beware of the cinema. It has ruined many a good man. Try grand opera for a while—it's more borin' but less corruptin'."

"That's all right, Mr. Vance." Apparently Heath himself did not relish the architectural idea particularly. "But as long as we don't know how Skeel got in, it's just as well to make sure of a few ways he didn't get in."

"I agree with you, Sergeant," said Markham. "I'll get an architect on the job at once." He rang for Swacker and gave the necessary instructions.

Vance extended his legs and yawned.

"All we need now is a Favorite of the Harem, a few blackamoors with palm-leaf fans, and some *pizzicato* music."

"You will joke, Mr. Vance." Heath lit a fresh cigar. "But even if the architect don't find anything wrong with the apartment, Skeel's liable to give his hand away 'most any time."

"I'm pinnin' my childish faith on Mannix," said Vance. "I don't know why I should; but he's not a nice man, and he's suppressing something. Markham, don't you dare let him go until he tells you where he was Monday night. And don't forget to hint mysteriously about the fur model."

20

A MIDNIGHT WITNESS

(Friday, September 14; 3:30 P.M.)

IN LESS than half an hour Mannix arrived. Heath relinquished his seat to the newcomer and moved to a large chair beneath the windows. Vance had taken a place at the small table on Markham's right where he was able to face Mannix obliquely.

It was patent that Mannix did not relish the idea of another interview. His little eyes shifted quickly about the office, lingered suspiciously for a moment on Heath, and at last came to rest on the district attorney. He was more vigilant even than during his first visit; and his greeting to Markham, while fulsome, had in it a note of trepidation. Nor was Markham's air calculated to put him at ease. It was an ominous, indomitable Public Prosecutor who motioned him to be seated. Mannix laid his hat and cane on the table and sat down on the edge of his chair, his back as perpendicular as a flagpole.

"I'm not at all satisfied with what you told me Wednesday, Mr. Mannix," Markham began, "and I trust you won't necessitate me to take drastic steps to find out what you know about Miss Odell's death."

"What I know!" Mannix forced a smile intended to be disarming. "Mr. Markham—Mr. Markham!" He seemed oilier than usual as he spread his hands in hopeless appeal. "If I knew anything, believe me, I would tell you— positively I would tell you."

"I'm delighted to hear it. Your willingness makes my task easier. First, then, please tell me where you were at midnight Monday."

Mannix's eyes slowly contracted until they looked like two tiny shining disks, but otherwise the man did not move. After what seemed an interminable pause, he spoke.

"I should tell you where I was Monday? Why should I have to do that? . . . Maybe I'm suspected of the murder—yes?"

"You're not suspected now. But your apparent unwillingness to answer my question is certainly suspicious. Why don't you care to have me know where you were?"

"I got no reason to keep it from you, y' understand." Mannix shrugged. "I got nothing to be ashamed of—absolutely! . . . I had a lot of accounts to go over at the office—winter-season stocks. I was down at the office until ten o'clock—maybe later. Then at half past ten—"

"That'll do!" Vance's voice cut in tartly. "No need to drag anyone else into this thing."

He spoke with a curious significance of emphasis, and Mannix studied him craftily, trying to read what knowledge, if any, lay behind his words. But he received no enlightenment from Vance's features. The warning, however, had been enough to halt him.

"You don't want to know where I was at half past ten?"

"Not particularly," said Vance. "We want to know where you were at midnight. And it won't be necess'ry to mention anyone who saw you at that time. When you tell us the truth, we'll know it." He himself had assumed the air of wisdom and mystery that he had deputed to Markham earlier in the afternoon. Without breaking faith with Alys La Fosse, he had sowed the seeds of doubt in Mannix's mind.

Before the man could frame an answer, Vance stood up and leaned impressively over the district attorney's desk.

"You know a Miss Frisbee. Lives in 71st Street; accurately speaking—at number 184; to be more exact—in the house where Miss Odell lived; to put it precisely—in Apartment Number 2. Miss Frisbee was a former model of yours. Sociable girl: still charitable to the advances of her erstwhile employer—meanin' yourself. When did you see her last, Mr. Mannix? . . . Take your time about answering. You may want to think it over."

Mannix took his time. It was a full minute before he spoke, and then it was to put another question.

"Haven't I got a right to call on a lady—haven't I?"

"Certainly. Therefore, why should a question about so obviously correct and irreproachable an episode make you uneasy?"

"Me uneasy?" Mannix, with considerable effort, produced a grin. "I'm just wondering what you got in your mind, asking me about my private affairs."

"I'll tell you. Miss Odell was murdered at about midnight Monday. No one came or went through the front door of the house, and the side door was locked. The only way any one could have entered her apartment was by way of Apartment 2; and nobody who knew Miss Odell ever visited Apartment 2 except yourself."

At these words Mannix leaned over the table, grasping the edge of it with both hands for support. His eyes were wide and his sensual lips hung open. But it was not fear that one read in his attitude; it was sheer amazement. He sat for a moment staring at Vance, stunned and incredulous.

"That's what you think, is it? No one could've got in or out except by Apartment 2, because the side door was locked?" He gave a short, vicious laugh. "If that side door didn't happen to be locked Monday night, where'd I stand then—huh? Where'd I stand?"

"I rather think you'd stand with us—with the district attorney." Vance was watching him like a cat.

"Sure I would!" spat Mannix. "And let me tell you something, my friend: that's just where I stand—absolutely!" He swung heavily about and faced Markham. "I'm a good fellow, y' understand, but I've kept my mouth shut long enough. . . . *That side door wasn't locked Monday night. And I know who sneaked out of it at five minutes to twelve!*"

"*Ça marche!*" murmured Vance, reseating himself and calmly lighting a cigarette.

Markham was too astonished to speak at once; and Heath sat stock-still, his cigar halfway to his mouth.

At length Markham leaned back and folded his arms.

"I think you'd better tell us the whole story, Mr. Mannix." His voice held a quality which made the request an imperative.

Mannix, too, settled back in his chair.

"Oh, I'm going to tell it—believe me, I'm going to tell it. You had the right idea. I spent the evening with Miss Frisbee. No harm in that, though."

"What time did you go there?"

"After office hours—half past five, quarter to six. Came up in the subway, got off at 72d, and walked over."

"And you entered the house through the front door?"

"No. I walked down the alleyway and went in the side door—like I generally do. It's nobody's business who I call on, and what the telephone operator in the front hall don't know don't hurt him."

"That's all right so far," observed Heath. "The janitor didn't bolt the side door until after six."

"And did you stay the entire evening, Mr. Mannix?" asked Markham.

"Sure—till just before midnight. Miss Frisbee cooked the dinner, and I'd brought along a bottle of wine. Social little party—just the two of us. And I didn't go outside the apartment, understand, until five minutes to twelve. You can get the lady down here and ask her. I'll call her up now and tell her to explain the exact situation about Monday night. I'm not asking you to take my word for it—positively not."

Markham made a gesture dismissing the suggestion.

"What took place at five minutes to twelve?"

Mannix hesitated, as if loath to come to the point.

"I'm a good fellow, y' understand. And a friend's a friend. But—I ask you—is that any reason why I should get in wrong for something I didn't have absolutely nothing to do with?"

He waited for an answer, but receiving none, continued.

"Sure, I'm right. Anyway, here's what happened. As I said, I was calling on the lady. But I had another date for later that night; so a few minutes before midnight I said good-bye and started to go. Just as I opened the door I saw someone sneaking away from the Canary's apartment down the little back hall to the side door. There was a light in the hall, and the door of Apartment

2 faces that side door. I saw the fellow as plain as I see you—positively as plain."

"Who was it?"

"Well, if you got to know, it was Pop Cleaver."

Markham's head jerked slightly.

"What did you do then?"

"Nothing, Mr. Markham—nothing at all. I didn't think much about it, y' understand. I knew Pop was chasing after the Canary, and I just supposed he'd been calling on her. But I didn't want Pop to see me—none of his business where I spend my time. So I waited quietly till he went out—"

"By the side door?"

"Sure. Then I went out the same way. I was going to leave by the front door, because I knew the side door was always locked at night. But when I saw Pop go out that way, I said to myself I'd do the same. No sense giving your business away to a telephone operator if you haven't got to—no sense at all. So I went out the same way I came in. Picked up a taxi on Broadway, and went——"

"That's enough!" Again Vance's command cut him short.

"Oh, all right—all right." Mannix seemed content to end his statement at this point. "Only, y' understand, I don't want you to think—"

"We don't."

Markham was puzzled at these interruptions, but made no comment.

"When you read of Miss Odell's death," he said, "why didn't you come to the police with this highly important information?"

"I should get mixed up in it!" exclaimed Mannix in surprise. "I got enough trouble without looking for it—plenty."

"An exigent course," commented Markham with open disgust. "But you nevertheless suggested to me, after you knew of the murder, that Cleaver was being blackmailed by Miss Odell."

"Sure I did. Don't that go to show I wanted to do the right thing by you— giving you a valuable tip?"

"Did you see anyone else that night in the halls or alleyway?"

"Nobody—absolutely nobody."

"Did you hear anyone in the Odell apartment—anyone speaking or moving about, perhaps?"

"Didn't hear a thing." Mannix shook his head emphatically.

"And you're certain of the time you saw Cleaver go out—five minutes to twelve?"

"Positively. I looked at my watch, and I said to the lady: 'I'm leaving the same day I came; it won't be tomorrow for five minutes yet.' "

Markham went over his story point by point, attempting by various means to make him admit more than he had already told. But Mannix neither added to his statement nor modified it in any detail; and after half an hour's cross-examination he was permitted to go.

"We've found one missing piece of the puzzle, at any rate," commented Vance. "I don't see now just how it fits into the complete pattern, but it's helpful and suggestive. And, I say, how beautifully my intuition about Mannix was verified, don't y' know!"

"Yes, of course—your precious intuition." Markham looked at him sceptically. "Why did you shut him up twice when he was trying to tell me something?"

"*O, tu ne sauras jamais,*" recited Vance. "I simply can't tell you, old dear. Awfully sorry, and all that."

His manner was whimsical, but Markham knew that at such times Vance was at heart most serious, and he did not press the question. I could not help wondering if Miss La Fosse realized just how secure she had been in putting her faith in Vance's integrity.

Heath had been considerably shaken by Mannix's story.

"I don't savvy that side door being unlocked," he complained. "How the hell did it get bolted again on the inside after Mannix went out? And who unbolted it after six o'clock?"

"In God's good time, my sergeant, all things will be revealed," said Vance.

"Maybe—and maybe not. But if we do find out, you can take it from me that the answer'll be Skeel. He's the bird we gotta get the goods on. Cleaver is no expert jimmy artist; and neither is Mannix."

"Just the same, there was a very capable technician on hand that night, and it wasn't your friend the Dude, though he was probably the Donatello who sculptured open the jewel case."

"A pair of 'em, was there? That's your theory, is it, Mr. Vance? You said that once before; and I'm not saying you're wrong. But if we can hang any part of it on Skeel, we'll make him come across as to who his pal was."

"It wasn't a pal, Sergeant. It was more likely a stranger."

Markham sat glowering into space.

"I don't at all like the Cleaver end of this affair," he said. "There's been something damned wrong about him ever since Monday."

"And I say," put in Vance, "doesn't the gentleman's false alibi take on a certain shady significance now, what? You apprehend, I trust, why I restrained you from questioning him about it at the club yesterday. I rather fancied that if you could get Mannix to pour out his heart to you, you'd be in a stronger position to draw a few admissions from Cleaver. And behold? Again the triumph of intuition! With what you now know about him, you can chivvy him most unconscionably—eh, what?"

"And that's precisely what I'm going to do." Markham rang for Swacker. "Get hold of Charles Cleaver," he ordered irritably. "Phone him at the Stuyvesant Club and also his home—he lives round the corner from the club in West 27th Street. And tell him I want him to be here in half an hour, or I'll send a couple of detectives to bring him in handcuffs."

For five minutes Markham stood before the window, smoking agitatedly, while Vance, with a smile of amusement, busied himself with *The Wall Street Journal.* Heath got himself a drink of water, and took a turn up and down the room. Presently Swacker reentered.

"Sorry, Chief, but there's nothing doing. Cleaver's gone into the country somewhere. Won't be back till late tonight."

"Hell! . . . All right—that'll do." Markham turned to Heath. "You have Cleaver rounded up tonight, Sergeant, and bring him in here tomorrow morning at nine."

"He'll be here, sir!" Heath paused in his pacing and faced Markham. "I've been thinking, sir; and there's one thing that keeps coming up in my mind, so to speak. You remember that black document box that was setting on the living room table? It was empty; and what a woman generally keeps in that kind of a box is letters and things like that. Well, now, here's what's been bothering me: that box wasn't jimmied open—it was unlocked with a key. And, anyway, a professional crook don't take letters and documents.... You see what I mean, sir?"

"Sergeant of mine!" exclaimed Vance. "I abase myself before you! I sit at your feet! ... The document box—the tidily opened, empty document box! Of course. Skeel didn't open it—never in this world! That was the other chap's handiwork."

"What was in your mind about that box, Sergeant?" asked Markham.

"Just this, sir. As Mr. Vance has insisted right along, there mighta been someone besides Skeel in that apartment during the night. And you told me that Cleaver admitted to you he'd paid Odell a lot of money last June to get back his letters. But suppose he never paid that money; suppose he went there Monday night and took those letters. Wouldn't he have told you just the story he did about buying 'em back? Maybe that's how Mannix happened to see him there."

"That's not unreasonable," Markham acknowledged. "But where does it lead us?"

"Well, sir, if Cleaver did take 'em Monday night, he mighta held on to 'em. And if any of those letters were dated later than last June, when he says he bought 'em back, then we'd have the goods on him."

"Well?"

"As I say, sir, I've been thinking.... Now, Cleaver is outa town today; and if we could get hold of those letters...."

"It might prove helpful, of course," said Markham coolly, looking the sergeant straight in the eye. "But such a thing is quite out of the question."

"Still and all," mumbled Heath. "Cleaver's been pulling a lot of raw stuff on you, sir."

21

A CONTRADICTION IN DATES

(*Saturday, September 15; 9 A.M.*)

THE NEXT morning Markham and Vance and I breakfasted together at the Prince George, and arrived at the district attorney's office a few minutes past nine. Heath, with Cleaver in tow, was waiting in the reception room.

To judge by Cleaver's manner as he entered, the sergeant had been none too considerate of him. He strode belligerently to the district attorney's desk and fixed a cold, resentful eye on Markham.

"Am I, by any chance, under arrest?" he demanded softly, but it was the rasping, suppressed softness of wrathful indignation.

"Not yet," said Markham curtly. "But if you were, you'd have only yourself to blame. Sit down."

Cleaver hesitated, and took the nearest chair.

"Why was I routed out of bed at seven thirty by this detective of yours"—he jerked his thumb toward Heath—"and threatened with patrol wagons and warrants because I objected to such high-handed and illegal methods?"

"You were merely threatened with legal procedure if you refused to accept my invitation voluntarily. This is my short day at the office; and there was some explaining I wanted from you without delay."

"I'm damned if I'll explain anything to you under these conditions!" For all his nerveless poise, Cleaver was finding it difficult to control himself. "I'm no pickpocket that you can drag in here when it suits your convenience and put through a third degree."

"That's eminently satisfactory to me." Markham spoke ominously. "But since you refuse to do your explaining as a free citizen, I have no other course than to alter your present status." He turned to Heath. "Sergeant, go across the hall and have Ben swear out a warrant for Charles Cleaver. Then lock this gentleman up."

Cleaver gave a start and caught his breath sibilantly. "On what charge?" he demanded.

"The murder of Margaret Odell."

The man sprang to his feet. The color had gone from his face, and the muscles of his jowls worked spasmodically. "Wait! You're giving me a raw deal. And you'll lose out, too. You couldn't make that charge stick in a thousand years."

"Maybe not. But if you don't want to talk here, I'll make you talk in court."

"I'll talk here," Cleaver sat down again. "What do you want to know?"

Markham took out a cigar and lit it with deliberation. "First: why did you tell me you were in Boonton Monday night?"

Cleaver apparently had expected the question. "When I read of the Canary's death, I wanted an alibi; and my brother had just given me the summons he'd been handed in Boonton. It was a ready-made alibi right in my hand. So I used it."

"Why did you need an alibi?"

"I didn't need it; but I thought it might save me trouble. People knew I'd been running round with the Odell girl; and some of them knew she'd been blackmailing me—I'd told 'em, like a damn fool. I told Mannix, for instance. We'd both been stung."

"Is that your only reason for concocting this alibi?" Markham was watching him sharply.

"Wasn't it reason enough? Blackmail would have constituted a motive, wouldn't it?"

"It takes more than a motive to arouse unpleasant suspicion."

"Maybe so. Only I didn't want to be drawn into it. You can't blame me for trying to keep clear of it."

Markham leaned over with a threatening smile. "The fact that Miss Odell had blackmailed you wasn't your only reason for lying about the summons. It wasn't even your main reason."

Cleaver's eyes narrowed, but otherwise he was like a graven image. "You evidently know more about it than I do." He managed to make his words sound casual.

"Not more, Mr. Cleaver," Markham corrected him, "but nearly as much. Where were you between eleven o'clock and midnight Monday?"

"Perhaps that's one of the things you know."

"You're right. You were in Miss Odell's apartment."

Cleaver sneered, but he did not succeed in disguising the shock that Markham's accusation caused him.

"If that's what you think, then it happens you don't know, after all. I haven't put foot in her apartment for two weeks."

"I have the testimony of reliable witnesses to the contrary."

"Witnesses!" The word seemed to force itself from Cleaver's compressed lips.

Markham nodded. "You were seen coming out of Miss Odell's apartment and leaving the house by the side door at five minutes to twelve on Monday night."

Cleaver's jaw sagged slightly, and his labored breathing was quite audible.

"And between half past eleven and twelve o'clock," pursued Markham's relentless voice, "Miss Odell was strangled and robbed. What do you say to that?"

For a long time there was tense silence. Then Cleaver spoke.

"I've got to think this thing out."

Markham waited patiently. After several minutes Cleaver drew himself together and squared his shoulders.

"I'm going to tell you what I did that night, and you can take it or leave it." Again he was the cold, self-contained gambler. "I don't care how many witnesses you've got; it's the only story you'll ever get out of me. I should have told you in the first place, but I didn't see any sense of stepping into hot water if I wasn't pushed in. You might have believed me last Tuesday, but now you've got something in your head, and you want to make an arrest to shut up the newspapers——"

"Tell your story," ordered Markham. "If it's straight, you needn't worry about the newspapers."

Cleaver knew in his heart that this was true. No one, not even his bitterest political enemies, had ever accused Markham of buying kudos with any act of injustice, however small.

"There's not much to tell, as a matter of fact," the man began. "I went to Miss Odell's house a little before midnight, but I didn't enter her apartment; I didn't even ring her bell."

"Is that your customary way of paying visits?"

"Sounds fishy, doesn't it? But it's the truth, nevertheless. I intended to see her—that is, I wanted to—but when I reached her door, something made me change my mind——"

"Just a moment. How did you enter the house?"

"By the side door, the one off the alleyway. I always used it when it was open. Miss Odell requested me to, so that the telephone operator wouldn't see me coming in so often."

"And the door was unlocked at that time Monday night?"

"How else could I have got in by it? A key wouldn't have done me any good, even if I'd had one, for the door locks by a bolt on the inside. I'll say this, though: that's the first time I ever remember finding the door unlocked at night."

"All right. You went in the side entrance. Then what?"

"I walked down the rear hall and listened at the door of Miss Odell's apartment for a minute. I thought there might be someone else with her, and I didn't want to ring unless she was alone...."

"Pardon my interrupting, Mr. Cleaver," interposed Vance. "But what made you think someone else was there?"

The man hesitated.

"Was it," prompted Vance, "because you had telephoned to Miss Odell a little while before, and had been answered by a man's voice?"

Cleaver nodded slowly. "I can't see any particular point in denying it.... Yes, that's the reason."

"What did this man say to you?"

"Damn little. He said 'Hello,' and when I asked to speak to Miss Odell, he informed me she wasn't in, and hung up."

Vance addressed himself to Markham. "That, I think, explains Jessup's report of the brief phone call to the Odell apartment at twenty minutes to twelve."

"Probably." Markham spoke without interest. He was intent on Cleaver's account of what happened later and he took up the interrogation at the point where Vance had interrupted.

"You say you listened at the apartment door. What caused you to refrain from ringing?"

"I heard a man's voice inside."

Markham straightened up.

"A man's voice? You're sure?"

"That's what I said." Cleaver was matter of fact about it. "A man's voice. Otherwise I'd have rung the bell."

"Could you identify the voice?"

"Hardly. It was very indistinct; and it sounded a little hoarse. It wasn't anyone's voice I was familiar with; but I'd be inclined to say it was the same one that answered me over the phone."

"Could you make out anything that was said?"

Cleaver frowned and looked past Markham through the open window.

"I know what the words sounded like," he said slowly. "I didn't think anything of them at the time. But after reading the papers the next day, those words came back to me——"

"What were the words?" Markham cut in impatiently.

"Well, as near as I could make out, they were: 'Oh, my God! Oh, my God!'—repeated two or three times."

This statement seemed to bring a sense of horror into the dreary old office—a horror all the more potent because of the casual, phlegmatic way in which Cleaver repeated that cry of anguish. After a brief pause Markham asked, "When you heard this man's voice, what did you do?"

"I walked softly back down the rear hall and went out again through the side door. Then I went home."

A short silence ensued. Cleaver's testimony had been in the nature of a surprise; but it fitted perfectly with Mannix's statement.

Presently Vance lifted himself out of the depths of his chair. "I say, Mr. Cleaver, what were you doing between twenty minutes to twelve, when you

phoned Miss Odell, and five minutes to twelve, when you entered the side
door of her apartment house?"

"I was riding uptown in the subway from 23d Street," came the answer after
a short pause.

"Strange—very strange." Vance inspected the tip of his cigarette. "Then
you couldn't possibly have phoned to anyone during that fifteen minutes—eh,
what?"

I suddenly remembered Alys La Fosse's statement that Cleaver had telephoned to her on Monday night at ten minutes to twelve. Vance, by his question, had, without revealing his own knowledge, created a state of uncertainty
in the other's mind. Afraid to commit himself too emphatically, Cleaver resorted to an evasion.

"It's possible, is it not, that I could have phoned someone after leaving the
subway at 72d Street and before I walked the block to Miss Odell's house?"

"Oh, quite," murmured Vance. "Still, looking at it mathematically, if you
phoned Miss Odell at twenty minutes to twelve, and then entered the subway,
rode to 72d Street, walked a block to 71st, went into the building, listened at
her door, and departed at five minutes to twelve—making the total time consumed only fifteen minutes—you'd scarcely have sufficient leeway to stop en
route and phone to anyone. However, I sha'n't press the point. But I'd really
like to know what you did between eleven o'clock and twenty minutes to
twelve, when you phoned to Miss Odell."

Cleaver studied Vance intently for a moment. "To tell you the truth, I was
upset that night. I knew Miss Odell was out with another man—she'd broken
an appointment with me—and I walked the streets for an hour or more, fuming and fretting."

"Walked the streets?" Vance frowned.

"That's what I said." Cleaver spoke with animus. Then, turning, he gave
Markham a long, calculating look. "You remember I once suggested to you
that you might learn something from a Doctor Lindquist. . . . Did you ever get
after him?"

Before Markham could answer, Vance broke in. "Ah! That's it!—Doctor
Lindquist! Well, well—of course! . . . So, Mr. Cleaver, you were walking the
streets? The *streets,* mind you! Precisely! You state the fact, and I echo the
word *streets.* And you—apparently out of a clear sky—ask about Doctor
Lindquist. Why Doctor Lindquist? No one has mentioned him. But that word
streets—that's the connection. The streets and Doctor Lindquist are one—
same as Paris and springtime are one. Neat, very neat. . . . And now I've got
another piece to the puzzle."

Markham and Heath looked at him as if he had suddenly gone mad. He
calmly selected a Régie from his case and proceeded to light it. Then he
smiled beguilingly at Cleaver.

"The time has come, my dear sir, for you to tell us when and where you met
Doctor Lindquist while roaming the streets Monday night. If you don't, 'pon
my word, I'll come pretty close to doing it for you."

A full minute passed before Cleaver spoke; and during that time his cold,
staring eyes never moved from the district attorney's face.

"I've already told most of the story; so here's the rest." He gave a soft
mirthless laugh. "I went to Miss Odell's house a little before half past

eleven—thought she might be home by that time. There I ran into Doctor Lindquist standing in the entrance to the alleyway. He spoke to me and told me someone was with Miss Odell in her apartment. Then I walked round the corner to the Ansonia Hotel. After ten minutes or so I telephoned Miss Odell, and, as I said, a man answered. I waited another ten minutes and phoned a friend of Miss Odell's, hoping to arrange a party; but, failing, I walked back to the house. The doctor had disappeared, and I went down the alleyway and in the side door. After listening a minute, as I told you, and hearing a man's voice, I came away and went home. . . . That's everything."

At that moment Swacker came in and whispered something to Heath. The sergeant rose with alacrity and followed the secretary out of the room. Almost at once he returned, bearing a bulging manila folder. Handing it to Markham, he said something in a low voice inaudible to the rest of us. Markham appeared both astonished and displeased. Waving the sergeant back to his seat, he turned to Cleaver.

"I'll have to ask you to wait in the reception room for a few minutes. Another urgent matter has just arisen."

Cleaver went out without a word, and Markham opened the folder. "I don't like this sort of thing, Sergeant. I told you so yesterday when you suggested it."

"I understand, sir." Heath, I felt, was not as contrite as his tone indicated. "But if those letters and things are all right, and Cleaver hasn't been lying to us about 'em, I'll have my man put 'em back so's no one'll ever know they were taken. And if they do make Cleaver out a liar, then we've got a good excuse for grabbing 'em."

Markham did not argue the point. With a gesture of distaste he began running through the letters, looking particularly at the dates. Two photographs he put back after a cursory glance; and one piece of paper, which appeared to contain a pen-and-ink sketch of some kind, he tore up with disgust and threw into the wastebasket. Three letters, I noticed, he placed to one side. After five minutes' inspection of the others, he returned them to the folder. Then he nodded to Heath.

"Bring Cleaver back." He rose and, turning, gazed out of the window.

As soon as Cleaver was again seated before the desk, Markham said, without looking round, "You told me it was last June that you bought your letters back from Miss Odell. Do you recall the date?"

"Not exactly," said Cleaver easily. "It was early in the month, though—during the first week, I think."

Markham now spun about and pointed to the three letters he had segregated.

"How, then, do you happen to have in your possession compromising letters which you wrote to Miss Odell from the Adirondacks late in July?"

Cleaver's self-control was perfect. After a moment's stoical silence, he merely said in a mild, quiet voice, "You of course came by those letters legally."

Markham was stung, but he was also exasperated by the other's persistent deceptions.

"I regret to confess," he said, "that they were taken from your apartment—though, I assure you, it was against my instructions. But since they have come unexpectedly into my possession, the wisest thing you can do is to explain them. There was an empty document box in Miss Odell's apartment the morning her body was found, and, from all appearances, it had been opened Monday night."

"I see." Cleaver laughed harshly. "Very well. The fact is—though I frankly don't expect you to believe me—I didn't pay my blackmail to Miss Odell until the middle of August, about three weeks ago. That's when all my letters were returned. I told you it was June in order to set back the date as far as possible. The older the affair was, I figured, the less likelihood there'd be of your suspecting me."

Markham stood fingering the letters undecidedly. It was Vance who put an end to his irresolution.

"I rather think, don't y' know," he said, "that you'd be safe in accepting Mr. Cleaver's explanation and returning his billets-doux."

Markham, after a momentary hesitation, picked up the manila folder and, replacing the three letters, handed it to Cleaver.

"I wish you to understand that I did not sanction the appropriating of this correspondence. You'd better take it home and destroy it—I won't detain you any longer now. But please arrange to remain where I can reach you if necessary."

"I'm not going to run away," said Cleaver; and Heath directed him to the elevator.

22

A TELEPHONE CALL

(*Saturday, September 15; 10 A.M.*)

HEATH RETURNED to the office, shaking his head hopelessly. "There musta been a regular wake at Odell's Monday night."

"Quite," agreed Vance. "A midnight conclave of the lady's admirers. Mannix was there, unquestionably; and he saw Cleaver; and Cleaver saw Lindquist; and Lindquist saw Spotswoode——"

"Humph! But nobody saw Skeel."

"The trouble is," said Markham, "we don't know how much of Cleaver's story is true. And, by the way, Vance, do you believe he really bought his letters back in August?"

"If only we knew! Dashed confusin', ain't it?"

"Anyway," argued Heath, "Cleaver's statement about phoning Odell at twenty minutes to twelve, and a man answering, is verified by Jessup's testimony. And I guess Cleaver saw Lindquist all right that night, for it was him who first tipped us off about the doc. He took a chance doing it, because the doc was liable to tell us he saw Cleaver."

"But if Cleaver had an allurin' alibi," said Vance, "he could simply have said the doctor was lying. However, whether you accept Cleaver's absorbin' legend or not, you can take my word for it there was a visitor, other than Skeel, in the Odell apartment that night."

"That's all right, too," conceded Heath reluctantly. "But, even so, this other fellow is only valuable to us as a possible source of evidence against Skeel."

"That may be true, Sergeant." Markham frowned perplexedly. "Only, I'd like to know how that side door was unbolted and then rebolted on the inside. We know now that it was open around midnight, and that Mannix and Cleaver both used it."

"You worry so over trifles," said Vance negligently. "The door problem will solve itself once we discover who was keeping company with Skeel in the Canary's gilded cage."

"I should say it boils down to Mannix, Cleaver, and Lindquist. They were the only three at all likely to be present; and if we accept Cleaver's story in its essentials, each of them had an opportunity of getting into the apartment between half past eleven and midnight."

"True. But you have only Cleaver's word that Lindquist was in the neighborhood. And that evidence, uncorroborated, can't be accepted as the lily-white truth."

Heath stirred suddenly and looked at the clock. "Say, what about that nurse you wanted at eleven o'clock?"

"I've been worrying horribly about her for an hour." Vance appeared actually troubled. "Really, y' know, I haven't the slightest desire to meet the lady. I'm hoping for a revelation, don't y' know. Let's wait for the doctor until half past ten, Sergeant."

He had scarcely finished speaking when Swacker informed Markham that Doctor Lindquist had arrived on a mission of great urgency. It was an amusing situation. Markham laughed outright, while Heath stared at Vance with uncomprehending astonishment.

"It's not necromancy, Sergeant," smiled Vance. "The doctor realized yesterday that we were about to catch him in a falsehood; so he decided to forestall us by explaining personally. Simple, what?"

"Sure." Heath's look of wonderment disappeared.

As Doctor Lindquist entered the room I noted that his habitual urbanity had deserted him. His air was at once apologetic and apprehensive. That he was laboring under some great strain was evident.

"I've come, sir," he announced, taking the chair Markham indicated, "to tell you the truth about Monday night."

"The truth is always welcome, Doctor," said Markham encouragingly.

Doctor Lindquist bowed agreement.

"I deeply regret that I did not follow that course at our first interview. But at that time I had not weighed the matter sufficiently; and, having once committed myself to a false statement, I felt I had no option but to abide by it. However, after more mature consideration, I have come to the conclusion that frankness is the wiser course. The fact is, sir, I was not with Mrs. Breedon Monday night between the hours I mentioned. I remained at home until about half past ten. Then I went to Miss Odell's house, arriving a little before eleven. I stood outside in the street until half past eleven; then I returned home."

"Such a bare statement needs considerable amplification."

"I realize it, sir; and I am prepared to amplify it." Doctor Lindquist hesitated, and a strained look came into his white face. His hands were tightly clenched. "I had learned that Miss Odell was going to dinner and the theater with a man named Spotswoode; and the thought of it began to prey on my mind. It was Spotswoode to whom I owed the alienation of Miss Odell's affections; and it was his interference that had driven me to my threat against the young woman. As I sat at home that night, letting my mind dwell morbidly on the situation, I was seized by the impulse to carry out that threat. Why not, I asked myself, end the intolerable situation at once? And why not include Spotswoode in the debacle? . . ."

As he talked he became more and more agitated. The nerves about his eyes had begun to twitch, and his shoulders jerked like those of a man attempting vainly to control a chill.

"Remember, sir, I was suffering agonies, and my hatred of Spotswoode seemed to cloud my reason. Scarcely realizing what I was doing, and yet operating under an irresistible determination, I put my automatic in my pocket and hurried out of the house. I thought Miss Odell and Spotswoode would be returning from the theater soon, and I intended to force my way into the apartment and perform the act I had planned. . . . From across the street I saw them enter the house—it was about eleven then—but, when I came face to face with the actuality, I hesitated. I delayed my revenge; I—I played with the idea, getting a kind of insane satisfaction out of it—knowing they were now at my mercy. . . ."

His hands were shaking as with a coarse tremor; and the twitching about his eyes had increased.

"For half an hour I waited, gloating. Then, as I was about to go in and have it over with, a man named Cleaver came along and saw me. He stopped and spoke. I thought he might be going to call on Miss Odell, so I told him she already had a visitor. He then went on toward Broadway, and while I was waiting for him to turn the corner, Spotswoode came out of the house and jumped into a taxicab that had just driven up. . . . My plan had been thwarted—I had waited too long. Suddenly I seemed to awake as from some terrible nightmare. I was almost in a state of collapse, but I managed to get home. . . . That's what happened—so help me God!"

He sank back weakly in his chair. The suppressed nervous excitement that had fired him while he spoke had died out, and he appeared listless and indifferent. He sat several minutes breathing stertorously, and twice he passed his hand vaguely across his forehead. He was in no condition to be questioned, and finally Markham sent for Tracy and gave orders that he was to be taken to his home.

"Temporary exhaustion from hysteria," commented Vance indifferently. "All these paranoia lads are hyperneurasthenic. He'll be in a psychopathic ward in another year."

"That's as may be, Mr. Vance," said Heath, with an impatience that repudiated all enthusiasm for the subject of abnormal psychology. "What interests me just now is the way all these fellows' stories hang together."

"Yes," nodded Markham. "There is undeniably a groundwork of truth in their statements."

"But please observe," Vance pointed out, "that their stories do not eliminate any one of them as a possible culprit. Their tales, as you say, synchronize perfectly; and yet, despite all that neat coordination, any one of the three could have got into the Odell apartment that night. For instance: Mannix could have entered from Apartment 2 before Cleaver came along and listened; and he could have seen Cleaver going away when he himself was leaving the Odell apartment. Cleaver could have spoken to the doctor at half past eleven, walked to the Ansonia, returned a little before twelve, gone into the lady's apartment, and come out just as Mannix opened Miss Frisbee's door. Again, the excitable doctor may have gone in after Spotswoode came out at half past eleven, stayed twenty minutes or so, and departed before Cleaver returned from the Ansonia.... No; the fact that their stories dovetail doesn't in the least tend to exculpate any one of them."

"And," supplemented Markham, "that cry of 'Oh, my God!' might have been made by either Mannix or Lindquist—provided Cleaver really heard it."

"He heard it unquestionably," said Vance. "Someone in the apartment was invoking the Deity around midnight. Cleaver hasn't sufficient sense of the dramatic to fabricate such a thrillin' *bonne-bouche.*"

"But if Cleaver actually heard that voice," protested Markham, "then, he is automatically eliminated as a suspect."

"Not at all, old dear. He may have heard it after he had come out of the apartment, and realized then, for the first time, that someone had been hidden in the place during his visit."

"Your man in the clothes closet, I presume you mean."

"Yes—of course. . . . You know, Markham, it might have been the horrified Skeel, emerging from his hiding place upon a scene of tragic wreckage, who let out that evangelical invocation."

"Except," commented Markham, with sarcasm, "Skeel doesn't impress me as particularly religious."

"Oh, that?" Vance shrugged. "A point in substantiation. Irreligious persons call on God much more than Christians. The only true and consistent theologians, don't y' know, are the atheists."

Heath, who had been sitting in gloomy meditation, took his cigar from his mouth and heaved a heavy sigh.

"Yes," he rumbled, "I'm willing to admit somebody besides Skeel got into Odell's apartment, and that the Dude hid in the clothes closet. But, if that's so, then, this other fellow didn't see Skeel; and it's not going to do us a whole lot of good even if we identify him."

"Don't fret on that point, Sergeant," Vance counselled him cheerfully. "When you've identified this other mysterious visitor, you'll be positively amazed how black care will desert you. You'll rubricate the hour you find him. You'll leap gladsomely in the air. You'll sing a roundelay."

"The hell I will!" said Heath.

Swacker came in with a typewritten memorandum and put it on the district attorney's desk. "The architect just phoned in this report."

Markham glanced it over; it was very brief. "No help here," he said. "Walls solid. No waste space. No hidden entrances."

"Too bad, Sergeant," sighed Vance. "You'll have to drop the cinema idea. . . . Sad."

Heath grunted and looked disconsolate. "Even without no other way of getting in or out except that side door," he said to Markham, "couldn't we get an indictment against Skeel, now that we know the door was unlocked Monday night?"

"We might, Sergeant. But our chief snag would be to show how it was originally unlocked and then rebolted after Skeel left. And Abe Rubin would concentrate on that point. No, we'd better wait awhile and see what develops."

Something "developed" at once. Swacker entered and informed the sergeant that Snitkin wanted to see him immediately.

Snitkin came in, visibly agitated, accompanied by a wizened, shabbily dressed little man of about sixty, who appeared awed and terrified. In the detective's hand was a small parcel wrapped in newspaper, which he laid on the district attorney's desk with an air of triumph.

"The Canary's jewelry," he announced. "I've checked it up from the list the maid gave me, and it's all there."

Heath sprang forward, but Markham was already untying the package with nervous fingers. When the paper had been opened, there lay before us a small heap of dazzling trinkets—several rings of exquisite workmanship, three magnificent bracelets, a sparkling sunburst, and a delicately wrought lorgnette. The stones were all large and of unconventional cut.

Markham looked up from them inquisitively, and Snitkin, not waiting for the inevitable question, explained.

"This man Potts found 'em. He's a street cleaner, and he says they were in one of the D. S. C. cans at 23d Street near the Flatiron Building. He found 'em yesterday afternoon, so he says, and took 'em home. Then he got scared and brought 'em to Police Headquarters this morning."

Mr. Potts, the "white-wing," was trembling visibly.

"Thass right, sir—thass right," he assured Markham, with frightened eagerness. "I allus look into any bundles I find. I didn't mean no harm takin' 'em home, sir. I wasn't gonna keep 'em. I laid awake worryin' all night, an' this mornin', as soon as I got a chance, I took 'em to the p'lice." He shook so violently I was afraid he was going to break down completely.

"That's all right, Potts," Markham told him in a kindly voice. Then to Snitkin: "Let the man go—only get his full name and address."

Vance had been studying the newspaper in which the jewels had been wrapped.

"I say, my man," he asked, "is this the original paper you found them in?"

"Yes, sir—the same. I ain't touched nothin'."

"Right-o."

Mr. Potts, greatly relieved, shambled out, followed by Snitkin.

"The Flatiron Building is directly across Madison Square from the Stuyvesant Club," observed Markham, frowning.

"So it is." Vance then pointed to the left-hand margin of the newspaper that held the jewels. "And you'll notice that this *Herald* of yesterday has three punctures evidently made by the pins of a wooden holder such as is generally used in a club's reading room."

"You got a good eye, Mr. Vance." Heath nodded, inspecting the newspaper.

"I'll see about this." Markham viciously pressed a button. "They keep their papers on file for a week at the Stuyvesant Club."

When Swacker appeared, he asked that the club's steward be got immediately on the telephone. After a short delay, the connection was made. At the end of five minutes' conversation Markham hung up the receiver and gave Heath a baffled look.

"The club takes two *Heralds*. Both of yesterday's copies are there, on the rack."

"Didn't Cleaver once tell us he read nothing but *The Herald*—that and some racing sheet at night?" Vance put the question offhandedly.

"I believe he did." Markham considered the suggestion. "Still, both the club *Heralds* are accounted for." He turned to Heath. "When you were checking up on Mannix, did you find out what clubs he belonged to?"

"Sure." The sergeant took out his notebook and riffled the pages for a minute or two. "He's a member of the Furriers' and the Cosmopolis."

Markham pushed the telephone toward him.

"See what you can find out."

Heath was fifteen minutes at the task. "A blank," he announced finally. "The Furriers' don't use holders, and the Cosmopolis don't keep any back numbers."

"What about Mr. Skeel's clubs, Sergeant?" asked Vance, smiling.

"Oh, I know the finding of that jewelry gums up my theory about Skeel," said Heath, with surly ill nature. "But what's the good of rubbing it in? Still, if you think I'm going to give that bird a clean bill of health just because the Odell swag was found in a trashcan, you're mighty mistaken. Don't forget we're watching the Dude pretty close. He may have got leery, and tipped off some pal he'd cached the jewels with."

"I rather fancy the experienced Skeel would have turned his booty over to a professional receiver. But even had he passed it on to a friend, would this friend have been likely to throw it away because Skeel was worried?"

"Maybe not. But there's some explanation for those jewels being found, and when we get hold of it, it won't eliminate Skeel."

"No; the explanation won't eliminate Skeel," said Vance; "but—my word!—how it'll change his *locus standi.*"

Heath contemplated him with shrewdly appraising eyes. Something in Vance's tone had apparently piqued his curiosity and set him to wondering. Vance had too often been right in his diagnoses of persons and things for the sergeant to ignore his opinions wholly.

But before he could answer, Swacker stepped alertly into the room, his eyes animated.

"Tony Skeel's on the wire, Chief, and wants to speak to you."

Markham, despite his habitual reserve, gave a start. "Here, Sergeant," he said quickly. "Take that extension phone on the table and listen in." He nodded curtly to Swacker, who disappeared to make the connection. Then he took up the receiver of his own telephone and spoke to Skeel.

For a minute or so he listened. Then, after a brief argument, he concurred with some suggestion that had evidently been made; and the conversation ended.

"Skeel craves an audience, I gather," said Vance. "I've rather been expecting it, y' know."

"Yes. He's coming here tomorrow at ten."

"And he hinted that he knew who slew the Canary—eh, what?"

"That's just what he did say. He promised to tell me the whole story tomorrow morning."

"He's the lad that's in a position to do it," murmured Vance.

"But, Mr. Markham," said Heath, who still sat with his hand on the telephone, gazing at the instrument with dazed incredulity, "I don't see why you don't have him brought here today."

"As you heard, Sergeant, Skeel insisted on tomorrow and threatened to say nothing if I forced the issue. It's just as well not to antagonize him. We might spoil a good chance of getting some light on this case if I ordered him brought here and used pressure. And tomorrow suits me. It'll be quiet around here then. Moreover, your man's watching Skeel, and he won't get away."

"I guess you're right, sir. The Dude's touchy and he can give a swell imitation of an oyster when he feels like it." The sergeant spoke with feeling.

"I'll have Swacker here tomorrow to take down his statement," Markham went on; "and you'd better put one of your men on the elevator. The regular operator is off Sundays. Also, plant a man in the hall outside and put another one in Swacker's office."

Vance stretched himself luxuriously and rose.

"Most considerate of the gentleman to call up at this time, don't y' know. I had a longing to see the Monets at Durand-Ruel's this afternoon, and I was afraid I wasn't going to be able to drag myself away from this fascinatin' case. Now that the apocalypse has been definitely scheduled for tomorrow, I'll indulge my taste for Impressionism. . . . *A demain*, Markham. Bye-bye, Sergeant."

23

THE TEN-O'CLOCK APPOINTMENT

(*Sunday, September 16; 10 A.M.*)

A FINE drizzle was falling the next morning when we rose; and a chill—the first forerunner of winter—was in the air. We had breakfast in the library at half past eight, and at nine o'clock Vance's car, which had been ordered the night before, called for us. We rode down Fifth Avenue, now almost deserted in its thick blanket of yellow fog, and called for Markham at his apartment in West 12th Street. He was waiting for us in front of the house and stepped quickly into the car with scarcely a word of greeting. From his anxious, preoccupied look I knew that he was depending a good deal on what Skeel had to tell him.

We had turned into West Broadway beneath the Elevated tracks before any of us spoke. Then Markham voiced a doubt which was plainly an articulation of his troubled ruminations.

"I'm wondering if, after all, this fellow Skeel can have any important information to give us. His phone call was very strange. Yet he spoke confidently enough regarding his knowledge. No dramatics, no request for immunity—

just a plain, assured statement that he knew who murdered the Odell girl, and had decided to come clean."

"It's certain he himself didn't strangle the lady," pronounced Vance. "My theory, as you know, is that he was hiding in the clothes press when the shady business was being enacted; and all along I've clung lovingly to the idea that he was *au secret* to the entire proceedings. The keyhole of that closet door is on a direct line with the end of the davenport where the lady was strangled; and if a rival was operating at the time of his concealment, it's not unreasonable to assume that he peered forth—eh, what? I questioned him on this point, you remember; and he didn't like it a bit."

"But, in that case——"

"Oh, I know. There are all kinds of erudite objections to my wild dream. Why didn't he give the alarm? Why didn't he tell us about it before? Why this? and why that? . . . I make no claim to omniscience, y' know; I don't even pretend to have a logical explanation for the various *traits d'union* of my vagary. My theory is only sketched in, as it were. But I'm convinced, nevertheless, that the modish Tony knows who killed his *bona roba* and looted her apartment."

"But of the three persons who possibly could have got into the Odell apartment that night—namely, Mannix, Cleaver, and Lindquist—Skeel evidently knows only one—Mannix."

"Yes, to be sure. And Mannix, it would seem, is the only one of the trio who knows Skeel. . . . An interestin' point."

Heath met us at the Franklin Street entrance to the Criminal Courts Building. He, too, was anxious and subdued and he shook hands with us in a detached manner devoid of his usual heartiness.

"I've got Snitkin running the elevator," he said, after the briefest of salutations. "Burke's in the hall upstairs, and Emery is with him, waiting to be let into Swacker's office."

We entered the deserted and almost silent building and rode up to the fourth floor. Markham unlocked his office door and we passed in.

"Guilfoyle, the man who's tailing Skeel," Heath explained, when we were seated, "is to report by phone to the Homicide Bureau as soon as the Dude leaves his rooms."

It was now twenty minutes to ten. Five minutes later Swacker arrived. Taking his stenographic notebook, he stationed himself just inside of the swinging door of Markham's private sanctum, where he could hear all that was said without being seen. Markham lit a cigar, and Heath followed suit. Vance was already smoking placidly. He was the calmest person in the room, and lay back languorously in one of the great leather chairs as though immune to all cares and vicissitudes. But I could tell by the overdeliberate way he flicked his ashes into the receiver that he, too, was uneasy.

Five or six minutes passed in complete silence. Then the sergeant gave a grunt of annoyance. "No, sir," he said, as if completing some unspoken thought, "I can't get a slant on this business. The finding of that jewelry, now, all nicely wrapped up . . . and then the Dude offering to squeal. . . . There's no sense to it."

"It's tryin', I know, Sergeant; but it's not altogether senseless." Vance was gazing lazily at the ceiling. "The chap who confiscated those baubles didn't have any use for them. He didn't want them, in fact—they worried him abominably."

The point was too complex for Heath. The previous day's developments had shaken the foundation of all his arguments; and he lapsed again into brooding silence.

At ten o'clock he rose impatiently and, going to the hall door, looked out. Returning, he compared his watch with the office clock and began pacing restlessly. Markham was attempting to sort some papers on his desk, but presently he pushed them aside with an impatient gesture.

"He ought to be coming along now," he remarked, with an effort at cheerfulness.

"He'll come," growled Heath, "or he'll get a free ride." And he continued his pacing.

A few minutes later he turned abruptly and went out into the hall. We could hear him calling to Snitkin down the elevator shaft, but when he came back into the office, his expression told us that as yet there was no news of Skeel.

"I'll call up the bureau," he decided, "and see what Guilfoyle had to report. At least we'll know then when the Dude left his house."

But when the sergeant had been connected with police headquarters, he was informed that Guilfoyle had as yet made no report.

"That's damn funny," he commented, hanging up the receiver.

It was now twenty minutes past ten. Markham was growing restive. The tenacity with which the Canary murder case had resisted all his efforts toward a solution had filled him with discouragement; and he had hoped, almost desperately, that this morning's interview with Skeel would clear up the mystery, or at least supply him with information on which definite action could be taken. Now, with Skeel late for this all-important appointment, the strain was becoming tense.

He pushed back his chair nervously and, going to the window, gazed out into the dark haze of fine rain. When he returned to his desk his face was set.

"I'll give our friend until half past ten," he said grimly. "If he isn't here then, Sergeant, you'd better call up the local station house and have them send a patrol wagon for him."

There was another few minutes of silence. Vance lolled in his chair with half-closed eyes, but I noticed that, though he still held his cigarette, he was not smoking. His forehead was puckered by a frown, and he was very quiet. I knew that some unusual problem was occupying him. His lethargy had in it a quality of intentness and concentration.

As I watched him he suddenly sat up straight, his eyes open and alert. He tossed his dead cigarette into the receiver with a jerky movement that attested to some inner excitation.

"Oh, my word!" he exclaimed. "It really can't be, y' know! And yet"—his face darkened—"and yet, by Jove, that's it! . . . What an ass I've been—what an unutterable ass! . . . Oh!"

He sprang to his feet, then stood looking down at the floor like a man dazed, afraid of his own thoughts.

"Markham, I don't like it—I don't like it at all." He spoke almost as if he were frightened. "I tell you, there's something terrible going on—something uncanny. The thought of it makes my flesh creep. . . . I must be getting old and sentimental," he added, with an effort at lightness; but the look in his eyes belied his tone. "Why didn't I see this thing yesterday? . . . But I let it go on. . . ."

We were all staring at him in amazement. I had never seen him affected in this way before, and the fact that he was habitually so cynical and aloof, so adamant to emotion and impervious to outside influences, gave his words and actions an impelling and impressive quality.

After a moment he shook himself slightly, as if to throw off the pall of horror that had descended upon him, and, stepping to Markham's desk, he leaned over, resting on both hands.

"Don't you see?" he asked. "Skeel's not coming. No use to wait—no use of our having come here in the first place. We have to go to him. He's waiting for us. . . . Come! Get your hat."

Markham had risen, and Vance took him firmly by the arm.

"You needn't argue," he persisted. "You'll have to go to him sooner or later. You might as well go now, don't y' know. My word! What a situation!"

He had led Markham, astonished and but mildly protesting, into the middle of the room, and he now beckoned to Heath with his free hand.

"You, too, Sergeant. Sorry you had all this trouble. My fault. I should have foreseen this thing. A devilish shame; but my mind was on Monets all yesterday afternoon. . . . You know where Skeel lives?"

Heath nodded mechanically. He had fallen under the spell of Vance's strange and dynamic importunities.

"Then, don't wait. And, Sergeant! You'd better bring Burke or Snitkin along. They won't be needed here—nobody'll be needed here any more today."

Heath looked inquiringly to Markham for counsel; his bewilderment had thrown him into a state of mute indecision. Markham nodded his approval of Vance's suggestions, and, without a word, slipped into his raincoat. A few minutes later the four of us, accompanied by Snitkin, had entered Vance's car and were lurching uptown. Swacker had been sent home; the office had been locked up; and Burke and Emery had departed for the Homicide Bureau to await further instructions.

Skeel lived in 35th Street, near the East River, in a dingy, but once pretentious, house which formerly had been the residence of some old family of the better class. It now had an air of dilapidation and decay; there was rubbish in the areaway; and a large sign announcing rooms for rent was posted in one of the ground-floor windows.

As we drew up before it Heath sprang to the street and looked sharply about him. Presently he espied an unkempt man slouching in the doorway of a grocery store diagonally opposite, and beckoned to him. The man shambled over furtively.

"It's all right, Guilfoyle," the sergeant told him. "We're paying the Dude a social visit. What's the trouble? Why didn't you report?"

Guilfoyle looked surprised. "I was told to phone in when he left the house, sir. But he ain't left yet. Mallory tailed him home last night round ten o'clock, and I relieved Mallory at nine this morning. The Dude's still inside."

"Of course he's still inside, Sergeant," said Vance, a bit impatiently.

"Where's his room situated, Guilfoyle?" asked Heath.

"Second floor, at the back."

"Right. We're going in. Stand by."

"Look out for him," admonished Guilfoyle. "He's got a gat."

Heath took the lead up the worn steps which led from the pavement to the little vestibule. Without ringing, he roughly grasped the doorknob and shook it. The door was unlocked, and we stepped into the stuffy lower hallway.

A bedraggled woman of about forty, in a disreputable dressing gown, and with hair hanging in strings over her shoulders, emerged suddenly from a rear door and came toward us unsteadily, her bleary eyes focused on us with menacing resentment.

"Say!" she burst out, in a rasping voice. "What do youse mean by bustin' in like this on a respectable lady?" And she launched forth upon a stream of profane epithets.

Heath, who was nearest her, placed his large hand over her face, and gave her a gentle but firm shove backward.

"You keep outa this, Cleopatra!" he advised her, and began to ascend the stairs.

The second-floor hallway was dimly lighted by a small flickering gas jet, and at the rear we could distinguish the outlines of a single door set in the middle of the wall.

"That'll be Mr. Skeel's abode," observed Heath.

He walked up to it and, dropping one hand in his right coat pocket, turned the knob. But the door was locked. He then knocked violently upon it and, placing his ear to the jamb, listened. Snitkin stood directly behind him, his hand also in his pocket. The rest of us remained a little in the rear.

Heath had knocked a second time when Vance's voice spoke up from the semidarkness. "I say, Sergeant, you're wasting time with all that formality."

"I guess you're right," came the answer after a moment of what seemed unbearable silence.

Heath bent down and looked at the lock. Then he took some instrument from his pocket and inserted it into the keyhole.

"You're right," he repeated. "The key's gone."

He stepped back and, balancing on his toes like a sprinter, sent his shoulders crashing against the panel directly over the knob. But the lock held.

"Come on, Snitkin," he ordered.

The two detectives hurled themselves against the door. At the third onslaught there was a splintering of wood and a tearing of the lock's bolt through the molding. The door swung drunkenly inward.

The room was in almost complete darkness. We all hesitated on the threshold, while Snitkin crossed warily to one of the windows and sent the shade clattering up. The yellow-gray light filtered in, and the objects of the room at once took definable form. A large, old-fashioned bed projected from the wall on the right.

"Look!" cried Snitkin, pointing; and something in his voice sent a shiver over me.

We pressed forward. On the foot of the bed, at the side toward the door, sprawled the crumpled body of Skeel. Like the Canary, he had been strangled. His head hung back over the footboard, his face a hideous distortion. His arms were outstretched, and one leg trailed over the edge of the mattress, resting on the floor.

"Thuggee," murmured Vance. "Lindquist mentioned it. Curious!"

Heath stood staring fixedly at the body, his shoulders hunched. His normal ruddiness of complexion was gone, and he seemed like a man hypnotized.

"Mother o' God!" he breathed, awestricken. And, with an involuntary motion, he crossed himself.

Markham was shaken also. He set his jaw rigidly.

"You're right, Vance." His voice was strained and unnatural. "Something sinister and terrible has been going on here. . . . There's a fiend loose in this town—a werewolf."

"I wouldn't say that, old man." Vance regarded the murdered Skeel critically. "No, I wouldn't say that. Not a werewolf. Just a desperate human being. A man of extremes, perhaps, but quite rational, and logical—oh, how deuced logical!"

24

AN ARREST

(*Sunday, P.M., Monday, A.M.; September 16–17*)

THE INVESTIGATION into Skeel's death was pushed with great vigor by the authorities. Doctor Doremus, the medical examiner, arrived promptly and declared that the crime had taken place between ten o'clock and midnight. Immediately Vance insisted that all the men who were known to have been intimately acquainted with the Odell girl—Mannix, Lindquist, Cleaver, and Spotswoode—be interviewed at once and made to explain where they were during these two hours. Markham agreed without hesitation and gave the order to Heath, who at once put four of his men on the task.

Mallory, the detective who had shadowed Skeel the previous night, was questioned regarding possible visitors; but inasmuch as the house where Skeel lived accommodated over twenty roomers, who were constantly coming and going at all hours, no information could be gained through that channel. All that Mallory could say definitely was that Skeel had returned home at about ten o'clock, and had not come out again. The landlady, sobered and subdued by the tragedy, repudiated all knowledge of the affair. She explained that she had been "ill" in her room from dinnertime until we had disturbed her recuperation the next morning. The front door, it seemed, was never locked, since her tenants objected to such an unnecessary inconvenience. The tenants themselves were questioned, but without result; they were not of a class likely to give information to the police, even had they possessed any.

The fingerprint experts made a careful examination of the room but failed to find any marks except Skeel's own. A thorough search through the murdered man's effects occupied several hours; but nothing was discovered that gave any hint of the murderer's identity. A .38 Colt automatic, fully loaded, was found under one of the pillows on the bed; and eleven hundred dollars, in bills of large denomination, was taken from a hollow brass curtain rod. Also, under a loose board in the hall, the missing steel chisel, with the fissure in the blade, was found. But these items were of no value in solving the mystery of Skeel's death; and at four o'clock in the afternoon the room was closed with an emergency padlock and put under guard.

Markham and Vance and I had remained several hours after our discovery of the body. Markham had taken immediate charge of the case and had conducted the interrogation of the tenants. Vance had watched the routine activities of the police with unwonted intentness, and had even taken part in the search. He had seemed particularly interested in Skeel's evening clothes, and had examined them garment by garment. Heath had looked at him from time to time, but there had been neither contempt nor amusement in the sergeant's glances.

At half past two Markham departed, after informing Heath that he would be at the Stuyvesant Club during the remainder of the day; and Vance and I went with him. We had a belated luncheon in the empty grill.

"This Skeel episode rather knocks the foundation from under everything," Markham said dispiritedly, as our coffee was served.

"Oh, no—not that," Vance answered. "Rather, let us say that it has added a new column to the edifice of my giddy theory."

"Your theory—yes. It's about all that's left to go on." Markham sighed. "It has certainly received substantiation this morning. . . . Remarkable how you called the turn when Skeel failed to show up."

Again Vance contradicted him.

"You overestimate my little flutter in forensics, Markham dear. You see, I assumed that the lady's strangler knew of Skeel's offer to you. That offer was probably a threat of some kind on Skeel's part; otherwise he wouldn't have set the appointment a day ahead. He no doubt hoped the victim of his threat would become amenable in the meantime. And that money hidden in the curtain rod leads me to think he was blackmailing the Canary's murderer and had been refused a further donation just before he phoned you yesterday. That would account, too, for his having kept his guilty knowledge to himself all this time."

"You may be right. But now we're worse off than ever, for we haven't even Skeel to guide us."

"At least we've forced our elusive culprit to commit a second crime to cover up his first, don't y' know. And when we have learned what the Canary's various amorists were doing last night between ten and twelve, we may have something suggestive on which to work. By the bye, when may we expect this thrillin' information?"

"It depends upon what luck Heath's men have. Tonight sometime, if everything goes well."

It was, in fact, about half past eight when Heath telephoned the reports. But here again Markham seemed to have drawn a blank. A less satisfactory account could scarcely be imagined. Doctor Lindquist had suffered a "nervous stroke" the preceding afternoon, and had been taken to the Episcopal Hospital. He was still there under the care of two eminent physicians whose word it was impossible to doubt; and it would be a week at least before he would be able to resume his work. This report was the only definite one of the four, and it completely exonerated the doctor from any participation in the previous night's crime.

By a curious coincidence neither Mannix, nor Cleaver, nor Spotswoode could furnish a satisfactory alibi. All three of them, according to their statements, had remained at home the night before. The weather had been inclement; and though Mannix and Spotswoode admitted to having been out earlier in the evening, they stated that they had returned home before ten o'clock. Mannix lived in an apartment hotel, and, as it was Saturday night, the lobby was crowded, so that no one would have been likely to see him come in. Cleaver lived in a small private apartment house without a doorman or hallboys to observe his movements. Spotswoode was staying at the Stuyvesant Club, and since his rooms were on the third floor, he rarely used the elevator. Moreover, there had been a political reception and dance at the club the previous night, and he might have walked in and out at random a dozen times without being noticed.

"Not what you'd call illuminatin'," said Vance, when Markham had given him this information.

"It eliminates Lindquist, at any rate."

"Quite. And, automatically, it eliminates him as an object of suspicion in the Canary's death also; for these two crimes are part of a whole—integers of the same problem. They complement each other. The latter was conceived in relation to the first—was, in fact, a logical outgrowth of it."

Markham nodded.

"That's reasonable enough. Anyway, I've passed the combative stage. I think I'll drift for a while on the stream of your theory and see what happens."

"What irks me is the disquietin' feeling that positively nothing will happen unless we force the issue. The lad who maneuvered those two obits had real bean in him."

As he spoke Spotswoode entered the room and looked about as if searching for someone. Catching sight of Markham, he came briskly forward, with a look of inquisitive perplexity.

"Forgive me for intruding, sir," he apologized, nodding pleasantly to Vance and me, "but a police officer was here this afternoon inquiring as to my whereabouts last night. It struck me as strange, but I thought little of it until I happened to see the name of Tony Skeel in the headlines of a 'special' tonight and read he had been strangled. I remember you asked me regarding such a man in connection with Miss Odell, and I wondered if, by any chance, there could be any connection between the two murders, and if I was, after all, to be drawn into the affair."

"No, I think not," said Markham. "There seemed a possibility that the two crimes were related; and, as a matter of routine, the police questioned all the close friends of Miss Odell in the hope of turning up something suggestive. You may dismiss the matter from your mind. I trust," he added, "the officer was not unpleasantly importunate."

"Not at all." Spotswoode's look of anxiety disappeared. "He was extremely courteous but a bit mysterious. Who was this man Skeel?"

"A half-world character and ex-burglar. He had some hold on Miss Odell, and, I believe, extorted money from her."

A cloud of angry disgust passed over Spotswoode's face. "A creature like that deserves the fate that overtook him."

We chatted on various matters until ten o'clock, when Vance rose and gave Markham a reproachful look.

"I'm going to try to recover some lost sleep. I'm temperamentally unfitted for a policeman's life."

Despite this complaint, however, nine o'clock the next morning found him at the district attorney's office. He had brought several newspapers with him, and was reading, with much amusement, the first complete accounts of Skeel's murder. Monday was generally a busy day for Markham and he arrived at the office before half past eight in an effort to clean up some pressing routine matters before proceeding with his investigation of the Odell case. Heath, I knew, was to come for a conference at ten o'clock. In the meantime there was nothing for Vance to do but read the newspapers; and I occupied myself in like manner.

Punctually at ten Heath arrived, and from his manner it was plain that something had happened to cheer him immeasurably. He was almost jaunty, and his formal, self-satisfied salutation to Vance was like that of a conqueror to a vanquished adversary. He shook hands with Markham with more than his customary punctility.

"Our troubles are over, sir," he said, and paused to light his cigar. "I've arrested Jessup."

It was Vance who broke the dramatic silence following this astounding announcement.

"In the name of Heaven—what for?"

Heath turned deliberately, in no wise abashed by the other's tone.

"For the murder of Margaret Odell and Tony Skeel."

"Oh, my aunt! Oh, my precious aunt!" Vance sat up and stared at him in amazement. "Sweet angels of Heaven, come down and solace me!"

Heath's complacency was unshaken. "You won't need no angels, or aunts either, when you hear what I've found out about this fellow. I've got him tied up in a sack, ready to hand to the jury."

The first wave of Markham's astonishment had subsided. "Let's have the story, Sergeant."

Heath settled himself in a chair. He took a few moments to arrange his thoughts.

"It's like this, sir. Yesterday afternoon I got to thinking. Here was Skeel murdered, same like Odell, after he'd promised to squeal; and it certainly looked as though the same guy had strangled both of 'em. Therefore, I concluded that there musta been two guys in the apartment Monday night—the Dude and the murderer—just like Mr. Vance has been saying all along. Then I figured that they knew each other pretty well, because not only did the other fellow know where the Dude lived, but he musta been wise to the fact that the Dude was going to squeal yesterday. It looked to me, sir, like they had pulled the Odell job together—which is why the Dude didn't squeal in the first place. But after the other fellow lost his nerve and threw the jewelry away, Skeel thought he'd play safe by turning state's evidence, so he phoned you."

The sergeant smoked a moment.

"I never put much stock in Mannix and Cleaver and the doc. They weren't the kind to do a job like that, and they certainly weren't the kind that would be mixed up with a jailbird like Skeel. So I stood all three of 'em to one side and began looking around for a bad egg—somebody who'd have been likely to be Skeel's accomplice. But first I tried to figure out what you might call the physical obstacles in the case—that is, the snags we were up against in our reconstruction of the crime."

Again he paused.

"Now, the thing that's been bothering us most is that side door. How did it get unbolted after six o'clock? And who bolted it again after the crime? Skeel musta come in by it before eleven, because he was in the apartment when Spotswoode and Odell returned from the theater; and he probably went out by it after Cleaver had come to the apartment at about midnight. But that wasn't explaining how it got bolted again on the inside. Well, sir, I studied over this for a long time yesterday and then I went up to the house and took another look at the door. Young Spively was running the switchboard, and I asked him where Jessup was, for I wanted to ask him some questions. And Spively told me he'd quit his job the day before—Saturday afternoon!"

Heath waited to let this fact sink in.

"I was on my way downtown before the idea came to me. Then it hit me sudden-like; and the whole case broke wide open. Mr. Markham, nobody but Jessup coulda opened that side door and locked it again—nobody. Figure it out for yourself, sir—though I guess you've pretty well done it already. Skeel couldn't've done it. And there wasn't nobody else to do it."

Markham had become interested and leaned forward.

"After this idea had hit me," Heath continued, "I decided to take a chance; so I got outa the subway at the Penn Station and phoned Spively for Jessup's address. Then I got my first good news: Jessup lived on Second Avenue, right around the corner from Skeel! I picked up a coupla men from the local station and went to his house. We found him packing up his things, getting ready to go to Detroit. We locked him up, and I took his fingerprints and sent 'em to Dubois. I thought I might get a line on him that way, because crooks don't generally begin with a job as big as the Canary prowl."

Heath permitted himself a grin of satisfaction.

"Well, sir, Dubois nailed him up! His name ain't Jessup at all. The William part is all right, but his real moniker is Benton. He was convicted of assault and battery in Oakland in 1909 and served a year in San Quentin when Skeel was a prisoner there. He was also grabbed as a lookout in a bank robbery in Brooklyn in 1914, but didn't come to trial—that's how we happen to have his fingerprints at Headquarters. When we put him on the grill last night, he said he changed his name after the Brooklyn racket and enlisted in the army. That's all we could get outa him; but we didn't need any more. Now, here are the facts: Jessup has served time for assault and battery. He was mixed up in a bank robbery. Skeel was a fellow prisoner of his. He's got no alibi for Saturday night when Skeel was killed and he lives round the corner. He quit his job suddenly Saturday afternoon. He's husky and strong and could easily have done the business. He was planning his getaway when we nabbed him. And— he's the only person who could've unbolted and rebolted that side door Monday night. . . . Is that a case, or ain't it, Mr. Markham?"

Markham sat several minutes in thought.

"It's a good case as far as it goes," he said slowly. "But what was his motive in strangling the girl?"

"That's easy. Mr. Vance here suggested it the first day. You remember he asked Jessup about his feelings for Odell; and Jessup turned red and got nervous."

"Oh, Lord!" exclaimed Vance. "Am I to be made responsible for any part of this priceless lunacy? . . . True, I pried into the chap's emotions toward the lady; but that was before anything had come to light. I was bein' careful—tryin' to test each possibility as it arose."

"Well, that was a lucky question of yours, just the same." Heath turned back to Markham. "As I see it: Jessup was stuck on Odell, and she told him to trot along and sell his papers. He got all worked up over it, sitting there night after night, seeing these other guys calling on her. Then Skeel comes along, and, recognizing him, suggests burglarizing Odell's apartment. Skeel can't do the job without help, for he has to pass the phone operator coming and going; and as he's been there before, he'd be recognized. Jessup sees a chance of getting even with Odell and putting the blame on someone else; so the two of 'em cook up the job for Monday night. When Odell goes out, Jessup unlocks the side door, and the Dude lets himself into the apartment with his own key. Then Odell and Spotswoode arrive unexpectedly. Skeel hides in the closet, and after Spotswoode has gone, he accidentally makes a noise, and Odell screams. He steps out, and when she sees who he is, she tells Spotswoode it's a mistake. Jessup now knows Skeel has been discovered, and decides to make use of the fact. Soon after Spotswoode has gone, he enters the apartment with a passkey. Skeel, thinking it's somebody else, hides again in the closet; and then Jessup grabs the girl and strangles her, intending to let Skeel get the credit for it. But Skeel comes out of hiding and they talk it over. Finally they come to an agreement, and proceed with their original plan to loot the place. Jessup tries to open the jewel case with the poker, and Skeel finishes the job with his chisel. Then they go out. Skeel leaves by the side door, and Jessup rebolts it. The next day Skeel hands the swag to Jessup to keep till things blow over; and Jessup gets scared and throws it away. Then they have a row. Skeel decides to tell everything, so he can get out from under; and Jessup, suspecting he's going to do it, goes round to his house Saturday night and strangles him like he did Odell."

Heath made a gesture of finality and sank back in his chair.

"Clever—deuced clever," murmured Vance. "Sergeant, I apologize for my little outburst a moment ago. Your logic is irreproachable. You've reconstructed the crime beautifully. You've solved the case. . . . It's wonderful—simply wonderful. But it's wrong."

"It's right enough to send Mr. Jessup to the chair."

"That's the terrible thing about logic," said Vance. "It so often leads one irresistably to a false conclusion."

He stood up and walked across the room and back, his hands in his coat pockets. When he came abreast of Heath he halted.

"I say, Sergeant; if somebody else could have unlocked that side door and then rebolted it again after the crime, you'd be willing to admit that it would weaken your case against Jessup—eh, what?"

Heath was in a generous mood.

"Sure. Show me someone else who coulda done that, and I'll admit that maybe I'm wrong."

"Skeel could have done it, Sergeant. And he did do it—without anyone knowing it."

"Skeel! This ain't the age of miracles, Mr. Vance."

Vance swung about and faced Markham. "Listen! I'm telling you Jessup's innocent." He spoke with a fervor that amazed me. "And I'm going to prove it to you—some way. My theory is pretty complete; it's deficient only in one or two small points; and, I'll confess, I haven't yet been able to put a name to the culprit. But it's the right theory, Markham, and it's diametrically opposed to the sergeant's. Therefore, you've got to give me an opportunity to demonstrate it before you proceed against Jessup. Now, I can't demonstrate it here; so you and Heath must come over with me to the Odell house. It won't take over an hour. But if it took a week, you'd have to come just the same."

He stepped nearer to the desk.

"I know that it was Skeel, and not Jessup, who unbolted that door before the crime and rebolted it afterward."

Markham was impressed.

"You know this—you know it for a fact?"

"Yes! And I know how he did it!"

25

VANCE DEMONSTRATES

(*Monday, September 17; 11:30 A.M.*)

HALF AN HOUR later we entered the little apartment house in 71st Street. Despite the plausibility of Heath's case against Jessup, Markham was not entirely satisfied with the arrest; and Vance's attitude had sown further seeds of doubt in his mind. The strongest point against Jessup was that relating to the bolting and unbolting of the side door; and when Vance had asserted that he was able to demonstrate how Skeel could have manipulated his own entrance and exit, Markham, though only partly convinced, had agreed to accompany him. Heath, too, was interested, and, though supercilious, had expressed a willingness to go along.

Spively, scintillant in his chocolate-colored suit, was at the switchboard and stared at us apprehensively. But when Vance suggested pleasantly that he take a ten-minute walk round the block, he appeared greatly relieved and lost no time in complying.

The officer on guard outside of the Odell apartment came forward and saluted.

"How goes it?" asked Heath. "Any visitors?"

"Only one—a toff who said he'd known the Canary and wanted to see the apartment. I told him to get an order from you or the district attorney."

"That was correct, Officer," said Markham; then, turning to Vance: "Probably Spotswoode, poor devil."

"Quite," murmured Vance. "So persistent! Rosemary and all that. . . . Touchin'."

Heath told the officer to go for a half-hour's stroll; and we were left alone.

"And now, Sergeant," said Vance cheerfully, "I'm sure you know how to operate a switchboard. Be so kind as to act as Spively's understudy for a few minutes—there's a good fellow. . . . But, first, please bolt the side door—and be sure that you bolt it securely, just as it was on the fatal night."

Heath grinned good-naturedly.

"Sure thing." He put his forefinger to his lips mysteriously, and crouching, tiptoed down the hall like a burlesque detective in a farce. After a few moments he came tiptoeing back to the switchboard, his finger still on his lips. Then, glancing surreptitiously about him with globular eyes, he put his mouth to Vance's ear.

"His-s-st!" he whispered. "The door's bolted. Gr-r-r. . . ." He sat down at the switchboard. "When does the curtain go up, Mr. Vance?"

"It's up, Sergeant." Vance fell in with Heath's jocular mood. "Behold! The hour is half past nine on Monday night. You are Spively—not nearly so elegant; and you forgot the moustache—but still Spively. And I am the bedizened Skeel. For the sake of realism, please try to imagine me in chamois gloves and a pleated silk shirt. Mr. Markham and Mr. Van Dine here represent 'the many-headed monster of the pit.'—And, by the bye, Sergeant, let me have the key to the Odell apartment; Skeel had one, don't y' know."

Heath produced the key and handed it over, still grinning.

"A word of stage direction," Vance continued. "When I have departed by the front door, you are to wait exactly three minutes, and then knock at the late Canary's apartment."

He sauntered to the front door and, turning, walked back toward the switchboard. Markham and I stood behind Heath in the little alcove, facing the front of the building.

"Enter Mr. Skeel!" announced Vance. "Remember, it's half past nine." Then, as he came abreast of the switchboard: "Dash it all! You forgot your lines, Sergeant. You should have told me that Miss Odell was out. But it doesn't matter. . . . Mr. Skeel continues to the lady's door . . . thus."

He walked past us, and we heard him ring the apartment bell. After a brief pause, he knocked on the door. Then he came back down the hall.

"I guess you were right," he said, quoting the words of Skeel as reported by Spively; and went on to the front door. Stepping out into the street, he turned toward Broadway.

For exactly three minutes we waited. None of us spoke. Heath had become serious, and his accelerated puffing on his cigar bore evidence of his state of expectancy. Markham was frowning stoically. At the end of the three minutes Heath rose and hurried up the hall, with Markham and me at his heels. In answer to his knock, the apartment door was opened from the inside. Vance was standing in the little foyer.

"The end of the first act," he greeted us airly. "Thus did Mr. Skeel enter the lady's boudoir Monday night after the side door had been bolted, without the operator's seeing him."

Heath narrowed his eyes but said nothing. Then he suddenly swung round and looked down the rear passageway to the oak door at the end. The handle of the bolt was in a vertical position, showing that the catch had been turned and that the door was unbolted. Heath regarded it for several moments; then he turned his eyes toward the switchboard. Presently he let out a gleeful whoop.

"Very good, Mr. Vance—very good!" he proclaimed, nodding his head knowingly. "That was easy, though. And it don't take psychology to explain it. After you rang the apartment bell, you ran down this rear hallway and unbolted the door. Then you ran back and knocked. After that you went out the front entrance, turned toward Broadway, swung round across the street, came in the alley, walked in the side door, and quietly let yourself into the apartment behind our backs."

"Simple, wasn't it?" agreed Vance.

"Sure." The sergeant was almost contemptuous. "But that don't get you nowhere. Anybody coulda figured it out if that had been the only problem connected with Monday night's operations. But it's the rebolting of that side door, after Skeel had gone, that's been occupying my mind. Skeel might've—*might*'ve, mind you—got in the way you did. But he couldn't have got out that way, because the door was bolted the next morning. And if there was someone here to bolt the door after him, then that same person could've unbolted the door for him earlier, without his doing the ten-foot dash down the rear hall to unbolt the door himself at half past nine. So I don't see that your interesting little drama helps Jessup out any."

"Oh, but the drama isn't over," Vance replied. "The curtain is about to go up on the next act."

Heath lifted his eyes sharply.

"Yeah?" His tone was one of almost jeering incredulity, but his expression was searching and dubious. "And you're going to show us how Skeel got out and bolted the door on the inside without Jessup's help?"

"That is precisely what I intend to do, my sergeant."

Heath opened his mouth to speak but thought better of it. Instead, he merely shrugged his shoulders and gave Markham a sly look.

"Let us repair to the public atrium," proceeded Vance; and he led us into the little reception room diagonally opposite to the switchboard. This room as I have explained, was just beyond the staircase, and along its rear wall ran the little passageway to the side door. (A glance at the accompanying diagram will clarify the arrangement.)

Vance shepherded us ceremoniously to chairs and cocked his eye at the sergeant.

"You will be so good as to rest here until you hear me knock at the side door. Then come and open it for me." He went toward the archway. "Once more I personate the departed Mr. Skeel; so picture me again *en grande tenue*—sartorially radiant. . . . The curtain ascends."

He bowed and, stepping from the reception room into the main hall, disappeared round the corner into the rear passageway.

Heath shifted his position restlessly and gave Markham a questioning troubled look. "Will he pull it off, sir, do you think?" All jocularity had gone out of his tone.

"I can't see how." Markham was scowling. "If he does, though, it will knock the chief underpinning from your theory of Jessup's guilt."

"I'm not worrying," declared Heath. "Mr. Vance knows a lot; he's got ideas. But how in hell——?"

He was interrupted by a loud knocking on the side door. The three of us sprang up simultaneously and hurried round the corner of the main hall. The

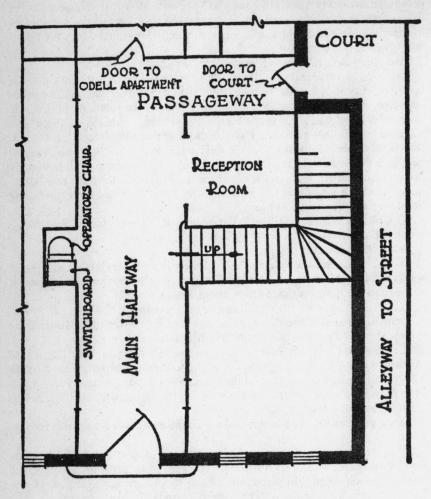

COURT

DOOR TO
ODELL APARTMENT

DOOR TO
COURT

PASSAGEWAY

RECEPTION
ROOM

OPERATOR'S CHAIR

SWITCHBOARD

MAIN HALLWAY

UP

ALLEYWAY TO STREET

WEST SEVENTY-FIRST STREET

rear passageway was empty. There was no door or aperture of any kind on either side of it. It consisted of two blank walls; and at the end, occupying almost its entire width, was the oak door which led to the court. Vance could have disappeared only through that oak door. And the thing we all noticed at once—for our eyes had immediately sought it—was the horizontal position of the bolt handle. This meant that the door was bolted.

Heath was not merely astonished—he was dumbfounded. Markham had halted abruptly, and stood staring down the empty passageway as if he saw a ghost. After a momentary hesitation Heath walked rapidly to the door. But he did not open it at once. He went down on his knees before the lock and scrutinized the bolt carefully. Then he took out his pocket knife and inserted the blade into the crack between the door and the casing. The point halted against the inner moulding, and the edge of the blade scraped upon the circular bolt. There was no question that the heavy oak casings and mouldings of the door were solid and well fitted, and that the bolt had been securely thrown from the inside. Heath, however, was still suspicious and, grasping the doorknob, he tugged at it violently. But the door held firmly. At length he threw the bolt handle to a vertical position and opened the door. Vance was standing in the court, placidly smoking and inspecting the brickwork of the alley wall.

"I say, Markham," he remarked, "here's a curious thing. This wall, d' ye know, must be very old. It wasn't built in these latter days of breathless efficiency. The beauty-loving mason who erected it laid the bricks in Flemish bond instead of the Running—or Stretcher—bond of our own restless age. And up there a bit"—he pointed toward the rear yard—"is a Rowlock and Checkerboard pattern. Very neat and very pretty—more pleasing even than the popular English Cross bond. And the mortar joints are all V-tooled. . . . Fancy!"

Markham was fuming. "Damn it, Vance! I'm not building brick walls. What I want to know is how you got out here and left the door bolted on the inside."

"Oh, that!" Vance crushed out his cigarette and reentered the building. "I merely made use of a bit of clever criminal mechanism. It's very simple, like all truly effective appliances—oh, simple beyond words. I blush at its simplicity. . . . Observe!"

He took from his pocket a tiny pair of tweezers to the end of which was tied

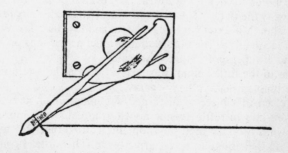

a piece of purple twine about four feet long. Placing the tweezers over the vertical bolt handle, he turned them at a very slight angle to the left and then ran the twine under the door so that about a foot of it projected over the sill. Stepping into the court, he closed the door. The tweezers still held the bolt handle as in a vise, and the string extended straight to the floor and disappeared under the door into the court. The three of us stood watching the bolt with fascinated attention. Slowly the string became taut, as Vance gently pulled upon the loose end outside, and then the downward tug began slowly but surely to turn the bolt handle. When the bolt had been thrown and the handle was in a horizontal position, there came a slight jerk on the string. The tweezers were disengaged from the bolt handle and fell noiselessly to the carpeted floor. Then as the string was pulled from without, the tweezers disappeared under the crack between the bottom of the door and the sill.

"Childish, what?" commented Vance, when Heath had let him in. "Silly, too, isn't it? And yet, Sergeant dear, that's how the deceased Tony left these premises last Monday night. . . . But let's go into the lady's apartment, and I'll tell you a story. I see that Mr. Spively has returned from his promenade; so he can resume his telephonic duties and leave us free for a *causerie.*"

"When did you think up that hocus-pocus with the tweezers and string?" demanded Markham irritably, when we were seated in the Odell living room.

"I didn't think it up at all, don't y' know," Vance told him carelessly, selecting a cigarette with annoying deliberation. "It was Mr. Skeel's idea. Ingenious lad—eh, what?"

"Come, come!" Markham's equanimity was at last shaken. "How can you possibly know that Skeel used this means of locking himself out?"

"I found the little apparatus in his evening clothes yesterday morning."

"What!" cried Heath belligerently. "You took that outa Skeel's room yesterday during the search without saying anything about it?"

"Oh, only after your ferrets had passed it by. In fact, I didn't even look at the gentleman's clothes until your experienced searchers had inspected them and relocked the wardrobe door. Y' see, Sergeant, this little thingumbob was stuffed away in one of the pockets of Skeel's dress waistcoat, under the silver cigarette case. I'll admit I went over his evening suit rather lovin'ly. He wore it, y' know, on the night the lady departed this life, and I hoped to find some slight indication of his collaboration in the event. When I found this little eyebrow plucker, I hadn't the slightest inkling of its significance. And the purple twine attached to it bothered me frightfully, don't y' know. I could see that Mr. Skeel didn't pluck his eyebrows; and even if he had been addicted to the practice, why the twine? The tweezers are a delicate little gold affair—just what the ravishin' Margaret might have used; and last Tuesday morning I noticed a small lacquer tray containing similar toilet accessories on her dressing table near the jewel case. But that wasn't all."

He pointed to the little vellum wastebasket beside the escritoire, in which lay a large crumpled mass of heavy paper.

"I also noticed that piece of discarded wrapping-paper stamped with the name of a well-known Fifth Avenue novelty shop; and this morning, on my way downtown, I dropped in at the shop and learned that they make a practice of tying up their bundles with purple twine. Therefore, I concluded that Skeel had taken the tweezers and the twine from this apartment during his visit here that eventful night. . . . Now, the question was: Why should he have spent his time tying strings to eyebrow pluckers? I confess, with maidenly modesty, that I couldn't find an answer. But this morning when you told of arresting Jessup and emphasized the rebolting of the side door after Skeel's departure, the fog lifted, the sun shone, the birds began to sing. I became suddenly mediumistic; I had a psychic seizure. The whole *modus operandi* came to me—as they say—in a flash. . . . I told you, Markham old thing, it would take spiritualism to solve this case."

26

RECONSTRUCTING THE CRIME

(*Monday, September 17; noon*)

WHEN VANCE finished speaking, there was several minutes' silence. Markham sat deep in his chair glaring into space. Heath, however, was watching Vance with a kind of grudging admiration. The cornerstone in the foundation of his case against Jessup had been knocked out, and the structure he had built was tottering precariously. Markham realized this, and the fact played havoc with his hopes.

"I wish your inspirations were more helpful," he grumbled, turning his gaze upon Vance. "This latest revelation of yours puts us back almost to where we started from."

"Oh, don't be pessimistic. Let us face the future with a bright eye. . . . Want to hear my theory?—it's fairly bulging with possibilities." He arranged himself comfortably in his chair. "Skeel needed money—no doubt his silk shirts were running low—and after his unsuccessful attempt to extort it from the lady a week before her demise, he came here last Monday night. He had learned she would be out, and he intended to wait for her; for she had probably refused to receive him in the custom'ry social way. He knew the side door was bolted at night, and, as he didn't want to be seen entering the apartment, he devised the little scheme of unbolting the door for himself under cover of a futile call at half past nine. The unbolting accomplished, he returned via the alleyway, and let himself into the apartment at some time before eleven. When the lady returned with an escort, he quickly hid in the clothes closet, and remained there until the escort had departed. Then he came forth, and the lady, startled by his sudden appearance, screamed. But, on recognizing him, she told Spotswoode, who was now hammering at the door, that it was all a mistake. So Spotswoode ran along and played poker. A financial discussion between Skeel and the lady—probably a highly acrimonious tiff—ensued. In the midst of it the telephone rang, and Skeel snatched off the receiver and said the Canary was out. The tiff was resumed; but presently another suitor appeared on the scene. Whether he rang the bell or let himself in with a key I can't say—probably the latter, for the phone operator was unaware of his visit. Skeel hid himself a second time in the closet and luckily took the precaution of locking himself in.

Also, he quite naturally put his eye to the keyhole to see who the second intruder was."

Vance pointed to the closet door.

"The keyhole, you will observe, is on a line with the davenport; and as Skeel peered out into the room he saw a sight that froze his blood. The new arrival—in the midst, perhaps, of some endearing sentence—seized the lady by the throat and proceeded to throttle her. . . . Imagine Skeel's emotions, my dear Markham. There he was, crouching in a dark closet, and a few feet from him stood a murderer in the act of strangling a lady! *Pauvre Antoine!* I don't wonder he was petrified and speechless. He saw what he imagined to be maniacal fury in the strangler's eyes; and the strangler must have been a fairly powerful creature, whereas Skeel was slender and almost undersized. . . . No, *merci.* Skeel wasn't having any. He lay doggo. And I can't say that I blame the beggar, what?"

He made a gesture of interrogation.

"What did the strangler do next? Well, well; we'll probably never know, now that Skeel, the horrified witness, has gone to his Maker. But I rather imagine he got out that black document box, opened it with a key he had taken from the lady's handbag, and extracted a goodly number of incriminating documents. Then, I fancy, the fireworks began. The gentleman proceeded to wreck the apartment in order to give the effect of a professional burglary. He tore the lace on the lady's gown and severed the shoulder strap; snatched her orchid corsage and threw it in her lap; stripped off her rings and bracelets; and tore the pendant from its chain. After that he upset the lamp, rifled the escritoire, ransacked the Boule cabinet, broke the mirror, overturned the chairs, tore the draperies. . . . And all the time Skeel kept his eye glued to the keyhole with fascinated horror, afraid to move, terrified lest he be discovered and sent to join his erstwhile *inamorata,* for by now he was no doubt thoroughly convinced that the man outside was a raving lunatic. I can't say that I envy Skeel his predicament; it was ticklish, y' know. Rather! And the devastation went on. He could hear it even when the operations had passed from out his radius of vision. And he himself was caught like a rat in a trap, with no means of escape. A harrowin' situation—my word!"

Vance smoked a moment and then shifted his position slightly.

"Y' know, Markham, I imagine that the worst moment in the whole of Skeel's checkered career came when that mysterious wrecker tried to open the closet door behind which he was crouching. Fancy! There he was cornered, and not two inches from him stood, apparently, a homicidal maniac trying to get to him, rattling that thin barricade of white pine. . . . Can you picture the blighter's relief when the murderer finally released the knob and turned away? It's a wonder he didn't collapse from the reaction. But he didn't. He listened and watched in a sort of hypnotic panic, until he heard the invader leave the apartment. Then, weak-kneed and in a cold sweat, he came forth and surveyed the battlefield."

Vance glanced about him.

"Not a pretty sight—eh, what? And there on the davenport reclined the lady's strangled body. That corpse was Skeel's dominant horror. He staggered to the table to look at it, and steadied himself with his right hand—that's how you got your fingerprints, Sergeant. Then the realization of his own position suddenly smote him. Here he was alone with a murdered person. He was known to have been intimate with the lady; and he was a burglar with a record. Who would believe that he was innocent? And though he had probably recognized the man who had negotiated the business, he was in no position to tell his story. Everything was against him—his sneaking in, his presence in the house at half past nine, his relations with the girl, his profession, his reputation. He hadn't a chance in the world. . . . I say, Markham, would *you* have credited his tale?"

"Never mind that," retorted Markham. "Go on with your theory." He and Heath had been listening with rapt interest.

"My theory from this point on," resumed Vance, "is what you might term self-developing. It proceeds on its own inertia, so to speak.—Skeel was confronted by the urgent problem of getting away and covering up his tracks. His mind in this emergency became keen and highly active; his life was forfeit if he didn't succeed. He began to think furiously. He could have left by the side door at once without being seen; but then, the door would have been unbolted. And this fact, taken in connection with his earlier visit that night, would have suggested his manner of unbolting the door. . . . No, that method of escape wouldn't do—decidedly it wouldn't do. He knew he was likely, in any event, to be suspected of the murder, in view of his shady association with the lady and his general character. Motive, place, opportunity, time, means, conduct, and his own record—all were against him. Either he must cover up his tracks, don't y' know, or else his career as a Lothario was at an end. A sweet dilemma! He realized, of course, that if he could get out and leave that side door bolted on the inside, he'd be comparatively safe. No one could then explain how he had come in or gone out. It would establish his only possible alibi—a negative one, to be sure; but, with a good lawyer, he could probably make it hold. Doubtless he searched for other means of escape, but found himself confronted with obstacles on every hand. The side door was his only hope. How could it be worked?"

Vance rose and yawned.

"That's my caressin' theory. Skeel was caught in a trap, and with his shrewd, tricky brain he figured his way out. He may have roamed up and down these two rooms for hours before he hit on his plan; and it's not unlikely that he appealed to the Deity with an occasional 'Oh, my God!' As for his using the tweezers, I'm inclined to think the mechanism of the idea came to him almost immediately—Y' know, Sergeant, this locking of a door on the inside is an old trick. There are any number of recorded cases of it in the criminal literature of Europe. Indeed, in Professor Hans Gross's handbook of criminology there's a whole chapter on the devices used by burglars for illegal entries and exits.* But all such devices have had to do with the locking, not the bolting, of doors. The principle, of course, is the same, but the technic is different. To lock a door on the inside, a needle, or strong slender pin, is inserted through the bow of the key and pulled downward with a string. But on the side door of this house there is no lock and key; nor is there a bow in the bolt handle.—Now, the resourceful Skeel, while pacing nervously about, looking

* The treatise referred to by Vance was *Handbuch für Untersuchungsrichter als System der Kriminalistik.*

for something that might offer a suggestion, probably espied the tweezers on the lady's dressing table—no lady nowadays is without these little eyebrow pluckers, don't y' know—and immediately his problem was solved. It remained only to test the device. Before departing, however, he chiseled open the jewel case which the other chap had merely dented, and found the solitaire diamond ring that he later attempted to pawn. Then he erased, as he thought, all his fingerprints, forgetting to wipe off the inside doorknob of the closet and overlooking the hand mark on the table. After that he let himself out quietly and rebolted the side door the same as I did, stuffing the tweezers in his waistcoat pocket and forgetting them."

Heath nodded his head oracularly.

"A crook, no matter how clever he is, always overlooks something."

"Why single out crooks for your criticism, Sergeant?" asked Vance lazily. "Do you know of anybody in this imperfect world who doesn't always overlook something?" He gave Heath a benignant smile. "Even the police, don't y' know, overlooked the tweezers."

Heath grunted. His cigar had gone out, and he relighted it slowly and thoroughly. "What do you think, Mr. Markham?"

"The situation doesn't become much clearer," was Markham's gloomy comment.

"My theory isn't exactly a blindin' illumination," said Vance. "Yet I wouldn't say that it left things in pristine darkness. There are certain inferences to be drawn from my vagaries. To wit: Skeel either knew or recognized the murderer; and once he had made good his escape from the apartment and had regained a modicum of self-confidence, he undoubtedly blackmailed his homicidal confrere. His death was merely another manifestation of our *inconnu's* bent for ridding himself of persons who annoyed him. Furthermore, my theory accounts for the chiseled jewel case, the fingerprints, the unmolested closet, the finding of the gems in the refuse tin—the person who took them really didn't want them, y' know—and Skeel's silence. It also explains the unbolting and bolting of the side door."

"Yes," sighed Markham. "It seems to clarify everything but the one all-important point—the identity of the murderer."

"Exactly," said Vance. "Let's go to lunch."

Heath, morose and confused, departed for police headquarters; and Markham, Vance, and I rode to Delmonico's, where we chose the main dining room in preference to the grill.

"The case now would seem to center in Cleaver and Mannix," said Markham, when we had finished our luncheon. "If your theory that the same man killed both Skeel and the Canary is correct, then Lindquist is out of it, for he certainly was in the Episcopal Hospital Saturday night."

"Quite," agreed Vance. "The doctor is unquestionably eliminated. . . . Yes; Cleaver and Mannix—they're the allurin' twins. Don't see any way to go beyond them." He frowned and sipped his coffee. "My original quartet is dwindling, and I don't like it. It narrows the thing down too much—there's no scope for the mind, as it were, in only two choices. What if we should succeed in eliminating Cleaver and Mannix? Where would we be—eh, what? Nowhere—simply nowhere. And yet, one of the quartet is guilty; let's cling to that consolin' fact. It can't be Spotswoode and it can't be Lindquist. Cleaver and Mannix remain: two from four leaves two. Simple arithmetic, what? The only trouble is, this case isn't simple. Lord, no!—I say, how would the equation work out if we used algebra, or spherical trigonometry, or differential calculus? Let's cast it in the fourth dimension—or the fifth, or the sixth. . . ." He held his temples in both hands. "Oh, promise, Markham—promise me that you'll hire a kind, gentle keeper for me."

"I know how you feel. I've been in the same mental state for a week."

"It's the quartet idea that's driving me mad," moaned Vance. "It wrings me to have my tetrad lopped off in such brutal fashion. I'd set my young trustin' heart on that quartet, and now it's only a pair. My sense of order and proportion has been outraged. . . . I want my quartet."

"I'm afraid you'll have to be satisfied with two of them," Markham returned wearily. "One of them can't qualify, and one is in bed. You might send some flowers to the hospital if it would cheer you any."

"One is in bed—one is in bed," repeated Vance. "Well, well—to be sure! And one from four leaves three. More arithmetic. Three! . . . On the other hand, there is no such thing as a straight line. All lines are curved; they transcribe circles in space. They look straight, but they're not. Appearances, y' know—so deceptive! . . . Let's enter the silence, and substitute mentation for sight."

He gazed up out of the great windows into Fifth Avenue. For several moments he sat smoking thoughtfully. When he spoke again, it was in an even, deliberate voice.

"Markham, would it be difficult for you to invite Mannix and Cleaver and Spotswoode to spend an evening—this evening, let us say—in your apartment?"

Markham set down his cup with a clatter and regarded Vance narrowly. "What new harlequinade is this?"

"Fie on you! Answer my question."

"Well, of course, I might arrange it," replied Markham hesitantly. "They're all more or less under my jurisdiction at present."

"So that such an invitation would be rather in line with the situation—eh, what? And they wouldn't be likely to refuse you, old dear—would they?"

"No, I hardly think so. . . ."

"And if, when they had assembled in your quarters, you should propose a few hands of poker, they'd probably accept, without thinking the suggestion strange?"

"Probably," said Markham, nonplussed at Vance's amazing request. "Cleaver and Spotswoode both play, I know; and Mannix doubtless knows the game. But why poker? Are you serious, or has your threatened dementia already overtaken you?"

"Oh, I'm deuced serious." Vance's tone left no doubt as to the fact. "The game of poker, d' ye see, is the crux of the matter. I knew Cleaver was an old hand at the game; and Spotswoode, of course, played with Judge Redfern last Monday night. So that gave me a basis for my plan. Mannix, we'll assume, also plays."

He leaned forward, speaking earnestly.

"Nine-tenths of poker, Markham, is psychology; and if one understands the game, one can learn more of a man's inner nature at a poker table in an hour than during a year's casual association with him. You rallied me once when I said I could lead you to the perpetrator of any crime by examining the factors of the crime itself. But naturally I must know the man to whom I am to lead you; otherwise I cannot relate the psychological indications of the crime to the culprit's nature. In the present case, I know the kind of man who committed the crime; but I am not sufficiently acquainted with the suspects to point out the guilty one. However, after our game of poker I hope to be able to tell you who planned and carried out the Canary's murder."*

Markham gazed at him in blank astonishment. He knew that Vance played poker with amazing skill and that he possessed an uncanny knowledge of the psychological elements in the game; but he was unprepared for the latter's statement that he might be able to solve the Odell murder by means of it. Yet Vance had spoken with such undoubted earnestness that Markham was impressed. I knew what was passing in his mind almost as well as if he had voiced his thoughts. He was recalling the way in which Vance had, in a former murder case, put his finger unerringly on the guilty man by a similar process of psychological deduction. And he was also telling himself that, however incomprehensible and seemingly extravagant Vance's requests were, there was always a fundamentally sound reason behind them.

"Damn it!" he muttered at last. "The whole scheme seems idiotic. . . . And yet, if you really want a game of poker with these men, I've no special objection. It'll get you nowhere—I'll tell you that beforehand. It's stark nonsense to suppose that you can find the guilty man by such fantastic means."

"Ah, well," sighed Vance, "a little futile recreation will do us no harm."

"But why do you include Spotswoode?"

"Really, y' know, I haven't the slightest notion—except, of course, that he's one of my quartet. And we'll need an extra hand."

"Well, don't tell me afterwards that I'm to lock him up for murder. I'd have to draw the line. Strange as it may seem to your layman's mind, I wouldn't care to prosecute a man, knowing that it was physically impossible for him to have committed the crime."

"As to that," drawled Vance, "the only obstacles that stand in the way of physical impossibilities are material facts. And material facts are notoriously deceivin'. Really, y' know, you lawyers would do better if you ignored them entirely."

Markham did not deign to answer such heresy, but the look he gave Vance was most expressive.

---

* Recently I ran across an article by Doctor George A. Dorsey, professor of anthropology at the University of Chicago, and author of "Why We Behave Like Human Beings," which bore intimate testimony to the scientific accuracy of Vance's theory. In it Doctor Dorsey said: "Poker is a cross-section of life. The way a man behaves in a poker game is the way he behaves in life. . . . His success or failure lies in the way his physical organism responds to the stimuli supplied by the game. . . . I have studied humanity all my life from the anthropologic and psychological viewpoint. And I have yet to find a better laboratory exercise than to observe the manners of men as they see my raise and come back at me. . . . The psychologist's verbalized, visceral, and manual behaviors are functioning at their highest in a poker game. . . . I can truthfully say that I learned about men from poker."

27

A GAME OF POKER

(Monday, September 17; 9 P.M.)

VANCE AND I went home after lunch, and at about four o'clock Markham telephoned to say that he had made the necessary arrangements for the evening with Spotswoode, Mannix, and Cleaver. Immediately following this confirmation Vance left the house and did not return until nearly eight o'clock. Though I was filled with curiosity at so unusual a proceeding, he refused to enlighten me. But when, at a quarter to nine, we went downstairs to the waiting car, there was a man I did not know in the tonneau; and I at once connected him with Vance's mysterious absence.

"I've asked Mr. Allen to join us tonight," Vance vouchsafed, when he had introduced us. "You don't play poker, and we really need another hand to make the game interestin', y' know. Mr. Allen, by the bye, is an old antagonist of mine."

The fact that Vance would, apparently without permission, bring an uninvited guest to Markham's apartment amazed me but little more than the appearance of the man himself. He was rather short, with sharp, shrewd features; and what I saw of his hair beneath his jauntily tipped hat was black and sleek, like the painted hair on Japanese dolls. I noted, too, that his evening tie was enlivened by a design of tiny white forget-me-nots, and that his shirtfront was adorned with diamond studs.

The contrast between him and the immaculately stylish and meticulously correct Vance was aggressively evident. I wondered what could be the relationship between them. Obviously it was neither social nor intellectual.

Cleaver and Mannix were already on hand when we were ushered into Markham's drawing room, and a few minutes later Spotswoode arrived. The amenities of introduction over, we were soon seated comfortably about the open log fire, smoking, and sipping very excellent Scotch highballs. Markham had, of course, accepted the unexpected Mr. Allen cordially, but his occasional glances in the latter's direction told me he was having some difficulty in reconciling the man's appearance with Vance's sponsorship.

A tense atmosphere lay beneath the spurious and affected affability of the little gathering. Indeed, the situation was scarcely conducive to spontaneity. Here were three men each of whom was known to the others to have been interested in the same woman; and the reason for their having been brought together was the fact that this woman had been murdered. Markham, however, handled the situation with such tact that he largely succeeded in giving each one the feeling of being a disinterested spectator summoned to discuss an abstract problem. He explained at the outset that the "conference" had been actuated by his failure to find any approach to the problem of the murder. He hoped, he said, by a purely informal discussion, divested of all officialism and coercion, to turn up some suggestion that might lead to a fruitful line of inquiry. His manner was one of friendly appeal, and when he finished speaking, the general tension had been noticeably relaxed.

During the discussion that followed I was interested in the various attitudes of the men concerned. Cleaver spoke bitterly of his part in the affair, and was more self-condemnatory than suggestive. Mannix was voluble and pretentiously candid, but beneath his comments ran a strain of apologetic wariness. Spotswoode, unlike Mannix, seemed loath to discuss the matter and maintained a consistently reticent attitude. He responded politely to Markham's questions, but he did not succeed entirely in hiding his resentment at thus being dragged into a general discussion. Vance had little to say, limiting himself to occasional remarks directed always to Markham. Allen did not speak but sat contemplating the others with a sort of canny amusement.

The entire conversation struck me as utterly futile. Had Markham really hoped to garner information from it, he would have been woefully disappointed. I realized, though, that he was merely endeavoring to justify himself for having taken so unusual a step and to pave the way for the game of poker which Vance had requested. When the time came to broach the subject, however, there was no difficulty about it.

It was exactly eleven o'clock when he made the suggestion. His tone was gracious and unassuming; but by couching his invitation in terms of a personal request, he practically precluded declination. But his verbal strategy, I felt, was unnecessary. Both Cleaver and Spotswoode seemed genuinely to welcome the opportunity of dropping a distasteful discussion in favor of playing cards; and Vance and Allen, of course, concurred instantly. Mannix alone declined. He explained that he knew the game only slightly and disliked it; though he expressed an enthusiastic desire to watch the others. Vance urged him to reconsider but without success; and Markham finally ordered his man to arrange the table for five.

I noticed that Vance waited until Allen had taken his place, and then dropped into the chair at his right. Cleaver took the seat at Allen's left. Spotswoode sat at Vance's right; and then came Markham. Mannix drew up his chair midway behind Markham and Cleaver. Thus:

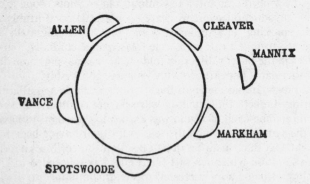

Cleaver first named a rather moderate limit, but Spotswoode at once suggested much larger stakes. Then Vance went still higher, and as both Markham and Allen signified their agreement, his figure was accepted. The prices placed on the chips somewhat took my breath away, and even Mannix whistled softly.

That all five men at the table were excellent players became obvious before the game had progressed ten minutes. For the first time that night Vance's friend Allen seemed to have found his milieu and to be wholly at ease.

Allen won the first two hands, and Vance the third and fourth. Spotswoode then had a short run of good luck, and a little later Markham took a large jackpot, which put him slightly in the lead. Cleaver was the only loser thus far; but in another half-hour he had succeeded in recovering a large portion of his losses. After that Vance forged steadily ahead, only to relinquish his winning streak to Allen. Then for a while the fortunes of the game were rather evenly distributed. But later on both Cleaver and Spotswoode began to lose heavily. By half past twelve a grim atmosphere had settled over the party; for so high were the stakes, and so rapidly did the betting pyramid, that even for men of means—such as all these players undoubtedly were—the amounts which continually changed hands represented very considerable items.

Just before one o'clock, when the fever of the game had reached a high point, I saw Vance glance quickly at Allen and pass his handkerchief across his forehead. To a stranger the gesture would have appeared perfectly natural; but, so familiar was I with Vance's mannerisms, I immediately recognized its artificiality. And simultaneously I noticed that it was Allen who was shuffling the cards preparatory to dealing. Some smoke from his cigar evidently went into his eye at that moment, for he blinked, and one of the cards fell to the floor. Quickly retrieving it, he reshuffled the deck and placed it before Vance to cut.

The hand was a jackpot, and there was a small fortune in chips already on the table. Cleaver, Markham, and Spotswoode passed. The decision thus reached Vance, and he opened for an unusually large amount. Allen at once laid down his hand, but Cleaver stayed. Then Markham and Spotswoode both dropped out, leaving the entire play between Vance and Cleaver. Cleaver drew one card, and Vance, who had opened, drew two. Vance made a nominal wager, and Cleaver raised it substantially. Vance in turn raised Cleaver, but only for a small amount; and Cleaver again raised Vance—this time for an even larger sum than before. Vance hesitated, and called him. Cleaver exposed his hand triumphantly.

"Straight flush—jack high," he announced. "Can you beat that?"

"Not on a two-card draw," said Vance ruefully. He put his cards down to show his openers. He had four kings.

About half an hour later Vance again took out his handkerchief and passed it across his forehead. As before, I noted that it was Allen's deal, and also that the hand was a jackpot which had been twice sweetened. Allen paused to take a drink of his highball and to light his cigar. Then, after Vance had cut the cards, he dealt them.

Cleaver, Markham, and Spotswoode passed, and again Vance opened, for the full amount of the pot. No one stayed except Spotswoode; and this time it was a struggle solely between him and Vance. Spotswoode asked for one card; and Vance stood pat. Then there followed a moment of almost breathless silence. The atmosphere seemed to me to be electrically charged, and I think the others sensed it too, for they were watching the play with a curiously strained intentness. Vance and Spotswoode, however, appeared frozen in attitudes of

superlative calm. I watched them closely, but neither revealed the slightest indication of any emotion.

It was Vance's first bet. Without speaking he moved a stack of yellow chips
to the center of the table—it was by far the largest wager that had been made
during the game. But immediately Spotswoode measured another stack
alongside of it. Then he coolly and deftly counted the remainder of his chips,
and pushed them forward with the palm of his hand, saying quietly, "The
limit."

Vance shrugged almost imperceptibly.

"The pot, sir, is yours." He smiled pleasantly at Spotswoode and put down
his hand face up, to establish his openers. He had held four aces!

"Gad! That's poker!" exclaimed Allen, chuckling.

"Poker?" echoed Markham. "To lay down four aces with all that money at
stake?"

Cleaver also grunted his astonishment, and Mannix pursed his lips disgustedly.

"I don't mean any offense, y' understand, Mr. Vance," he said. "But looking
at that play from a strictly business standpoint, I'd say you quit too soon."

Spotswoode glanced up.

"You gentlemen wrong Mr. Vance," he said. "He played his hand perfectly.
His withdrawal, even with four aces, was scientifically correct."

"Sure it was," agreed Allen. "Oh, boy! What a battle that was!"

Spotswoode nodded and, turning to Vance, said, "Since the exact situation
is never likely to occur again, the least I can do, by way of showing my appreciation of your remarkable perception, is to gratify your curiosity. I held
nothing."

Spotswoode put down his hand and extended his fingers gracefully toward
the upturned cards. There were revealed a five, six, seven, and eight of clubs,
and a knave of hearts.

"I can't say that I follow your reasoning, Mr. Spotswoode," Markham confessed. "Mr. Vance had you beaten—and he quit."

"Consider the situation," Spotswoode replied, in a suave, even voice. "I
most certainly would have opened so rich a pot, had I been able to, after Mr.
Cleaver and you had passed. But since I nevertheless stayed after Mr. Vance
had opened for so large an amount, it goes without saying that I must have
had either a four-straight, a four-flush, or a four-straight-flush. I believe I may
state without immodesty that I am too good a player to have stayed otherwise. . . ."

"And I assure you, Markham," interrupted Vance, "that Mr. Spotswoode is
too good a player to have stayed unless he had actually had a four-straight-
flush. That is the only hand he would have been justified in backing at the
betting odds of two to one. You see, I had opened for the amount in the pot,
and Mr. Spotswoode had to put up half the amount of the money on the table
in order to stay—making it a two-to-one bet. Now, these odds are not high,
and any nonopening hand smaller than a four-straight-flush would not have
warranted the risk. As it was, he had, with a one-card draw, two chances in
forty-seven of making a straight-flush, nine chances in forty-seven of making a
flush, and eight chances in forty-seven of making a straight; so that he had
nineteen chances in forty-seven—or more than one chance in three—

of strengthening his hand into either a straight-flush, a flush, or a straight."

"Exactly," assented Spotswoode. "However, after I had drawn my one card, the only possible question in Mr. Vance's mind was whether or not I had made my straight-flush. If I had not made it—or had merely drawn a straight or a flush—Mr. Vance figured, and figured rightly, that I would not have seen his large bet and also have raised it the limit. To have done so, in those circumstances, would have been irrational poker. Not one player in a thousand would have taken such a risk on a mere bluff. Therefore, had Mr. Vance not laid down his four aces when I raised him, he would have been foolhardy in the extreme. It turned out, of course, that I was actually bluffing; but that does not alter the fact that the correct and logical thing was for Mr. Vance to quit."

"Quite true," Vance agreed. "As Mr. Spotswoode says, not one player in a thousand would have wagered the limit without having filled his straight-flush, knowing I had a pat hand. Indeed, one might also say that Mr. Spotswoode, by doing so, has added another decimal point to the psychological subtleties of the game; for, as you see, he analyzed my reasoning, and carried his own reasoning a step further."

Spotswoode acknowledged the compliment with a slight bow; and Cleaver reached for the cards and began to shuffle them. But the tension had been broken, and the game was not resumed.

Something, however, seemed to have gone wrong with Vance. For a long while he sat frowning at his cigarette and sipping his highball in troubled abstraction. At last he rose and walked to the mantel, where he stood studying a Cézanne watercolor he had given Markham years before. His action was a typical indication of his inner puzzlement.

Presently, when there came a lull in the conversation, he turned sharply and looked at Mannix.

"I say, Mr. Mannix"—he spoke with only casual curiosity—"how does it happen you've never acquired a taste for poker? All good businessmen are gamblers at heart."

"Sure they are," Mannix replied, with pensive deliberation. "But poker, now, isn't my idea of gambling—positively not. It's got too much science. And it ain't quick enough for me—it hasn't got the kick in it, if you know what I mean. Roulette's my speed. When I was in Monte Carlo last summer, I dropped more money in ten minutes than you gentlemen lost here this whole evening. But I got action for my money."

"I take it, then, you don't care for cards at all."

"Not to play games with." Mannix had become expansive. "I don't mind betting money on the draw of a card, for instance. But no two out of three, y' understand. I want my pleasures to come rapid." And he snapped his thick fingers several times in quick succession to demonstrate the rapidity with which he desired to have his pleasures come.

Vance sauntered to the table and carelessly picked up a deck of cards. "What do you say to cutting once for a thousand dollars?"

Mannix rose instantly. "You're on!"

Vance handed the cards over, and Mannix shuffled them. Then he put them down and cut. He turned up a ten. Vance cut and showed a king.

"A thousand I owe you," said Mannix, with no more concern than if it had been ten cents.

Vance waited without speaking, and Mannix eyed him craftily.

"I'll cut with you again—two thousand this time. Yes?"

Vance raised his eyebrows. "Double? . . . By all means." He shuffled the cards and cut a seven.

Mannix's hand swooped down and turned a five.

"Well, that's three thousand I owe you," he said. His little eyes had now narrowed into slits, and he held his cigar clamped tightly between his teeth.

"Like to double it again—eh, what?" Vance asked. "Four thousand this time?"

Markham looked at Vance in amazement, and over Allen's face there came an expression of almost ludicrous consternation. Everyone present, I believe, was astonished at the offer, for obviously Vance knew that he was giving Mannix tremendous odds by permitting successive doubling. In the end he was sure to lose. I believe Markham would have protested if at that moment Mannix had not snatched the cards from the table and begun to shuffle them.

"Four thousand it is!" he announced, putting down the deck and cutting. He turned up the queen of diamonds. "You can't beat the lady—positively not!" He was suddenly jovial.

"I fancy you're right," murmured Vance; and he cut a trey.

"Want some more?" asked Mannix, with good-natured aggressiveness.

"That's enough." Vance seemed bored. "Far too excitin'. I haven't your rugged constitution, don't y' know."

He went to the desk and made out a check to Mannix for a thousand dollars. Then he turned to Markham and held out his hand. "Had a jolly evening and all that sort of thing. . . . And, don't forget: we lunch together tomorrow. One o'clock at the club, what?"

Markham hesitated. "If nothing interferes."

"But really, y' know, it mustn't," insisted Vance. "You've no idea how eager you are to see me."

He was unusually silent and thoughtful during the ride home. Not one explanatory word could I get out of him. But when he bade me good night he said, "There's a vital part of the puzzle still missing, and until it's found, none of it has any meaning."

28

THE GUILTY MAN

(*Tuesday, September 18; 1 P.M.*)

VANCE SLEPT late the following morning and spent the hour or so before lunch checking a catalog of ceramics which were to be auctioned next day at the Anderson Galleries. At one o'clock we entered the Stuyvesant Club and joined Markham in the grill.

"The lunch is on you, old thing," said Vance. "But I'll make it easy. All I want is a rasher of English bacon, a cup of coffee, and a croissant."

Markham gave him a mocking smile.

"I don't wonder you're economizing after your bad luck of last night."

Vance's eyebrows went up. "I rather fancied my luck was most extr'ordin'ry."

"You held four of a kind twice and lost both hands."

"But, y' see," blandly confessed Vance, "I happened to know both times exactly what cards my opponents held."

Markham stared at him in amazement.

"Quite so," Vance assured him. "I had arranged before the game, d' ye see, to have those particular hands dealt." He smiled benignly. "I can't tell you, old chap, how I admire your delicacy in not referring to my rather unique guest, Mr. Allen, whom I had the bad taste to introduce so unceremoniously into your party. I owe you an explanation and an apology. Mr. Allen is not what one would call a charming companion. He is deficient in the patrician elegancies, and his display of jewelry was a bit vulgar—though I infinitely preferred his diamond studs to his piebald tie. But Mr. Allen has his points—decidedly he has his points. He ranks with Andy Blakely, Canfield, and Honest John Kelly as an indoor soldier of fortune. In fact, our Mr. Allen is none other than Doc Wiley Allen, of fragrant memory."

"Doc Allen! Not the notorious old crook who ran the Eldorado Club?"

"The same. And, incidentally, one of the cleverest card manipulators in a once lucrative but shady profession."

"You mean this fellow Allen stacked the cards last night?" Markham was indignant.

"Only for the two hands you mentioned. Allen, if you happen to remember, was the dealer both times. I, who purposely sat on his right, was careful to cut the cards in accordance with his instructions. And you really must admit that no stricture can possibly attach to my deception, inasmuch as the only beneficiaries of Allen's manipulations were Cleaver and Spotswoode. Although Allen did deal me four of a kind on each occasion, I lost heavily both times."

Markham regarded Vance for a moment in puzzled silence and then laughed good-naturedly. "You appear to have been in a philanthropic mood last night. You practically gave Mannix a thousand dollars by permitting him to double the stakes on each draw. A rather quixotic procedure, I should say."

"It all depends on one's point of view, don't y' know. Despite my financial losses—which, by the bye, I have every intention of charging up to your office budget—the game was most successful. . . . Y' see, I attained the main object of my evening's entertainment."

"Oh, I remember!" said Markham vaguely, as if the matter, being of slight importance, had for the moment eluded his memory. "I believe you were going to ascertain who murdered the Odell girl."

"Amazin' memory! . . . Yes, I let fall the hint that I might be able to clarify the situation today."

"And whom am I to arrest?"

Vance took a drink of coffee and slowly lit a cigarette.

"I'm quite convinced, y' know, that you won't believe me," he returned in an even, matter-of-fact voice. "But it was Spotswoode who killed the girl."

"You don't tell me!" Markham spoke with undisguised irony. "So it was Spotswoode! My dear Vance, you positively bowl me over. I would telephone Heath at once to polish up his handcuffs, but, unfortunately, miracles—such as strangling persons from across town—are not recognized possibilities in this day and age. . . . Do let me order you another croissant."

Vance extended his hands in a theatrical gesture of exasperated despair. "For an educated, civilized man, Markham, there's something downright primitive about the way you cling to optical illusions. I say, y' know, you're exactly like an infant who really believes that the magician generates a rabbit in a silk hat, simply because he sees it done."

"Now you're becoming insulting."

"Rather!" Vance pleasantly agreed. "But something drastic must be done to disentangle you from the Lorelei of legal facts. You're so deficient in imagination, old thing."

"I take it that you would have me close my eyes and picture Spotswoode sitting upstairs here in the Stuyvesant Club and extending his arms to 71st Street. But I simply couldn't do it. I'm a commonplace chap. Such a vision would strike me as ludicrous; it would smack of a hasheesh dream. . . . You yourself don't use *Cannabis indica,* do you?"

"Put that way, the idea does sound a bit supernatural. And yet: *Certum est quia impossibile est.* I rather like that maxim, don't y' know; for, in the present case, the impossible is true. Oh, Spotswoode's guilty—no doubt about it. And I'm going to cling tenaciously to that apparent hallucination. Moreover, I'm going to try to lure you into its toils; for your own—as we absurdly say—good name is at stake. As it happens, Markham, you are at this moment shielding the real murderer from publicity."

Vance had spoken with the easy assurance that precludes argument; and from the altered expression on Markham's face I could see he was moved.

"Tell me," he said, "how you arrived at your fantastic belief in Spotswoode's guilt."

Vance crushed out his cigarette and folded his arms on the table.

"We begin with my quartet of possibilities—Mannix, Cleaver, Lindquist, and Spotswoode. Realizing, as I did, that the crime was carefully planned with the sole object of murder, I knew that only someone hopelessly ensnared in the lady's net could have done it. And no suitor outside of my quartet could have been thus enmeshed, or we would have learned of him. Therefore, one of the four was guilty. Now, Lindquist was eliminated when we found out that he was bedridden in a hospital at the time of Skeel's murder; for obviously the same person committed both crimes——"

"But," interrupted Markham, "Spotswoode had an equally good alibi for the night of the Canary's murder. Why eliminate one and not the other?"

"Sorry, but I can't agree with you. Being prostrated at a known place surrounded by incorruptible and disinterested witnesses, both preceding and during an event, is one thing; but being actually on the ground, as Spotswoode was that fatal evening, within a few minutes of the time the lady was murdered, and then being alone in a taxiab for fifteen minutes or so following the event—that is another thing. No one, as far as we know, actually saw the lady alive after Spotswoode took his departure."

"But the proof of her having been alive and spoken to him is incontestable."

"Granted. I admit that a dead woman doesn't scream and call for help and then converse with her murderer."

"I see." Markham spoke with sarcasm. "You think it was Skeel, disguising his voice."

"Lord no! What a priceless notion! Skeel didn't want anyone to know he was there. Why should he have staged such a masterpiece of idiocy? That certainly isn't the explanation. When we find the answer it will be reasonable and simple."

"That's encouraging," smiled Markham. "But proceed with your reason for Spotswoode's guilt."

"Three of my quartet, then, were potential murderers," Vance resumed. "Accordingly, I requested an evening of social relaxation, that I might put them under the psychological microscope, as it were. Although Spotswoode's ancestry was wholly consistent with his having been the guilty one, nevertheless I confess I thought that Cleaver or Mannix had committed the crime; for, by their own statements, either of them could have done it without contradicting any of the known circumstances of the situation. Therefore, when Mannix declined your invitation to play poker last night, I put Cleaver to the first test. I wig-wagged to Mr. Allen, and he straightway proceeded to perform his first feat of prestidigitation."

Vance paused and looked up.

"You perhaps recall the circumstances? It was a jackpot. Allen dealt Cleaver a four-straight-flush and gave me three kings. The other hands were so poor that everyone else was compelled to drop out. I opened, and Cleaver stayed. On the draw, Allen gave me another king, and gave Cleaver the card he needed to complete his straight-flush. Twice I bet a small amount, and each time Cleaver raised me. Finally I called him, and, of course, he won. He couldn't help but win d' ye see. He was betting on a sure thing. Since I opened the pot and drew two cards, the highest hand I could possibly have held would have been four of a 'kind. Cleaver knew this, and having a straight-flush, he also knew, before he raised my bet, that he had me beaten. At once I realized that he was not the man I was after."

"By what reasoning?"

"A poker player, Markham, who would bet on a sure thing is one who lacks the egotistical self-confidence of the highly subtle and supremely capable gambler. He is not a man who will take hazardous chances and tremendous risks, for he possesses, to some degree, what the psychoanalysts call an inferiority complex, and instinctively he grasps at every possible opportunity of protecting and bettering himself. In short, he is not the ultimate, unadulterated gambler. And the man who killed the Odell girl was a supreme gambler who would stake everything on a single turn of the wheel, for, in killing her, that is exactly what he did. And only a gambler whose paramount self-confidence would make him scorn, through sheer egotism, to bet on a sure thing, could have committed such a crime. Therefore, Cleaver was eliminated as a suspect."

Markham was now listening intently.

"The test to which I put Spotswoode a little later," Vance went on, "had originally been intended for Mannix, but he was out of the game. That didn't matter, however, for, had I been able to eliminate both Cleaver and Spotswoode, then Mannix would undoubtedly have been the guilty man. Of course I would have planned something else to substantiate the fact; but, as it was, that wasn't necessary. . . . The test I applied to Spotswoode was pretty well explained by the gentleman himself. As he said, not one player in a thousand would have wagered the limit against a pat hand, when he himself held nothing. It was tremendous—superb! It was probably the most remarkable bluff ever made in a game of poker. I couldn't help admiring him when he calmly shoved forward all his chips, knowing, as I did, that he held nothing. He staked everything, d' ye see, wholly on his conviction that he could follow my reasoning step by step and, in the last analysis, outwit me. It took courage and daring to do that. And it also took a degree of self-confidence which would never have permitted him to bet on a sure thing. The psychological principles involved in that hand were identical with those of the Odell crime. I threatened Spotswoode with a powerful hand—a pat hand—just as the girl, no doubt, threatened him; and instead of compromising—instead of calling me or laying down—he outreached me; he resorted to one supreme coup, though it meant risking everything. . . . My word, Markham! Can't you see how the man's character, as revealed in that amazing gesture, dovetails with the psychology of the crime?"

Markham was silent for a while; he appeared to be pondering the matter.

"But you yourself, Vance, were not satisfied at the time," he submitted at length. "In fast, you looked doubtful and worried."

"True, old dear. I was no end worried. The psychological proof of Spotswoode's guilt came so dashed unexpectedly—I wasn't looking for it, don't y' know. After eliminating Cleaver I had a *parti pris,* so to speak, in regard to Mannix; for all the material evidence in favor of Spotswoode's innocence— that is, the seeming physical impossibility of his having strangled the lady— had, I admit, impressed me. I'm not perfect, don't y' know. Being unfortunately human, I'm still susceptible to the malicious animal magnetism about facts and appearances, which you lawyer chaps are continuously exuding over the earth like some vast asphyxiating effluvium. And even when I found that Spotswoode's psychological nature fitted perfectly with all the factors of the crime, I still harbored a doubt in regard to Mannix. It was barely possible that he would have played the hand just as Spotswoode played it. That is why, after the game was over, I tackled him on the subject of gambling. I wanted to check his psychological reactions."

"Still, he staked everything on one turn of the wheel, as you put it."

"Ah! But not in the same sense that Spotswoode did. Mannix is a cautious and timid gambler as compared with Spotswoode. To begin with, he had an equal chance and an even bet, whereas Spotswoode had no chance at all—his hand was worthless. And yet Spotswoode wagered the limit on a pure bit of mental calculation. That was gambling in the higher ether. On the other hand, Mannix was merely tossing a coin, with an even chance of winning. Furthermore, no calculation of any kind entered into it; there was no planning, no figuring, no daring. And, as I have told you from the start, the Odell murder was premeditated and carefully worked out with shrewd calculation and supreme daring. . . . And what true gambler would ask an adversary to double a bet on the second flip of the coin, and then accept an offer to redouble on the third flip? I purposely tested Mannix in that way, so as to preclude any possibility of error. Thus I not only eliminated him, I expunged him, eradicated him, wiped him out utterly. It cost me a thousand dollars, but it purged my mind of any lingering doubt. I then knew, despite all the contr'ry material indications, that Spotswoode had done away with the lady."

"You make your case theoretically plausible. But, practically, I'm afraid I can't accept it." Markham was more impressed, I felt, than he cared to admit. "Damn it, man!" he exploded after a moment. "Your conclusion demolishes all the established landmarks of rationality and sane credibility.—Just consider the facts." He had now reached the argumentative stage of his doubt. "You say Spotswoode is guilty. Yet we know, on irrefutable evidence, that five minutes after he came out of the apartment, the girl screamed and called for help. He was standing by the switchboard, and, accompanied by Jessup, he went to the door and carried on a brief conversation with her. She was certainly alive then. Then he went out the front door, entered a taxicab, and drove away. Fifteen minutes later he was joined by Judge Redfern as he alighted from the taxicab in front of the club here—nearly forty blocks away from the apartment house! It would have been impossible for him to have made the trip in less time; and, moreover, we have the chauffeur's record. Spotswoode simply did not have either the opportunity or the time to commit the murder between half past eleven and ten minutes of twelve, when Judge Redfern met him. And, remember, he played poker in the club here until three in the morning—hours after the murder took place."

Markham shook his head with emphasis.

"Vance, there's no human way to get round those facts. They're firmly established; and they preclude Spotswoode's guilt as effectively and finally as though he had been at the North Pole that night."

Vance was unmoved.

"I admit everything you say," he rejoined. "But as I have stated before, when material facts and psychological facts conflict, the material facts are wrong. In this case, they may not actually be wrong, but they're deceptive."

"Very well, *magnus Apollo!*" The situation was too much for Markham's exacerbated nerves. "Show me how Spotswoode could have strangled the girl and ransacked the apartment, and I'll order Heath to arrest him."

" 'Pon my word, I can't do it," expostulated Vance. "Omniscience was denied me. But—deuce take it!—I think I've done rather well in pointing out the culprit. I never agreed to expound his technic, don't y' know."

"So! Your vaunted penetration amounts only to that, does it? Well, well! Here and now I become a professor of the higher mental sciences, and I pronounce solemnly that Doctor Crippen murdered the Odell girl. To be sure, Crippen's dead; but that fact doesn't interfere with my newly adopted psychological means of deduction. Crippen's nature, you see, fits perfectly with all the esoteric and recondite indications of the crime. Tomorrow I'll apply for an order of exhumation."

Vance looked at him with waggish reproachfulness and sighed. "Recognition of my transcendent genius, I see, is destined to be posthumous. *Omnia post obitum fingit majora vetustas.* In the meantime I bear the taunts and jeers of the multitude with a stout heart. 'My head is bloody, but unbowed.' "

He looked at his watch and then seemed to become absorbed with some line of thought.

"Markham," he said, after several minutes, "I've a concert at three o'clock, but there's an hour to spare. I want to take another look at that apartment and its various approaches. Spotswoode's trick—and I'm convinced it was nothing more than a trick—was enacted there; and if we are ever to find the explanation, we shall have to look for it on the scene."

I had got the impression that Markham, despite his emphatic denial of the possibility of Spotswoode's guilt, was not entirely unconvinced. Therefore, I was not surprised when, with only a halfhearted protest, he assented to Vance's proposal to revisit the Odell apartment.

29

BEETHOVEN'S "ANDANTE"

(*Tuesday, September 18; 2 P.M.*)

LESS THAN half an hour later we again entered the main hall of the little apartment building in 71st Street. Spively, as usual, was on duty at the switchboard. Just inside the public reception room the officer on guard reclined in an easy chair, a cigar in his mouth. On seeing the district attorney, he rose with forced alacrity.

"When you going to open things up, Mr. Markham?" he asked. "This rest cure is ruinin' my health."

"Very soon, I hope, Officer," Markham told him. "Any more visitors?"

"Nobody, sir." The man stifled a yawn.

"Let's have your key to the apartment. Have you been inside?"

"No, sir. Orders were to stay out here."

We passed into the dead girl's living room. The shades were still up, and the sunlight of midday was pouring in. Nothing apparently had been touched; not even the overturned chairs had been righted. Markham went to the window and stood, his hands behind him, surveying the scene despondently. He was laboring under a growing uncertainty, and he watched Vance with a cynical amusement which was far from spontaneous.

Vance, after lighting a cigarette, proceeded to inspect the two rooms, letting his eyes rest searchingly on the various disordered objects. Presently he went into the bathroom and remained several minutes. When he came out he carried a towel with several dark smudges on it.

"This is what Skeel used to erase his fingerprints," he said, tossing the towel on the bed.

"Marvelous!" Markham rallied him. "That, of course, convicts Spotswoode."

"Tut, tut! But it helps substantiate my theory of the crime." He walked to the dressing table and sniffed at a tiny silver atomizer. "The lady used Coty's Chypre," he murmured. "Why *will* they all do it?"

"And just what does that help substantiate?"

"Markham dear, I'm absorbing atmosphere. I'm attuning my soul to the apartment's vibrations. Do let me attune in peace. I may have a visitation at any moment—a revelation from Sinai, as it were."

He continued his round of investigation and at last passed out into the main hall, where he stood, one foot holding open the door, looking about him with curious intentness. When he returned to the living room, he sat down on the edge of the rosewood table and surrendered himself to gloomy contemplation. After several minutes he gave Markham a sardonic grin.

"I say! This *is* a problem. Dash it all, it's uncanny!"

"I had an idea," scoffed Markham, "that sooner or later you'd revise your deductions in regard to Spotswoode."

Vance stared idly at the ceiling.

"You're devilish stubborn, don't y' know. Here I am trying to extricate you from a deuced unpleasant predicament, and all you do is to indulge in caustic observations calculated to damp my youthful ardor."

Markham left the window and seated himself on the arm of the davenport facing Vance. His eyes held a worried look.

"Vance, don't get me wrong. Spotswoode means nothing in my life. If he did this thing, I'd like to know it. Unless this case is cleared up, I'm in for an ungodly walloping by the newspapers. It's not to my interests to discourage any possibility of a solution. But your conclusion about Spotswoode is impossible. There are too many contradictory facts."

"That's just it, don't y' know. The contradic'try indications are far too perfect. They fit together too beautifully; they're almost as fine as the forms in a Michelangelo statue. They're too carefully coordinated, d' ye see, to have been merely a haphazard concatenation of circumstances. They signify conscious design."

Markham rose and, slowly returning to the window, stood looking out into the little rear yard.

"If I could grant your premise that Spotswoode killed the girl," he said, "I could follow your syllogism. But I can't very well convict a man on the grounds that his defense is too perfect."

"What we need, Markham, is inspiration. The mere contortions of the sibyl are not enough." Vance took a turn up and down the room. "What really infuriates me is that I've been outwitted. And by a manufacturer of automobile access'ries! . . . It's most humiliatin'."

He sat down at the piano and played the opening bars of Brahms's Capriccio No. 1. "Needs tuning," he muttered; and, sauntering to the Boule cabinet, he ran his finger over the marquetry. "Pretty and all that," he said, "but a bit fussy. Good example, though. The deceased's aunt from Seattle should get a very fair price for it." He regarded a pendent girandole at the side of the cabinet. "Rather nice, that, if the original candles hadn't been supplanted with modern frosted bulbs." He paused before the little china clock on the mantel. "Gingerbread. I'm sure it kept atrocious time." Passing on to the escritoire, he examined it critically. "Imitation French Renaissance. But rather dainty, what?" Then his eye fell on the wastepaper basket, and he picked it up. "Silly idea," he commented, "—making a basket out of vellum. The artistic triumph of some lady interior decorator, I'll wager. Enough vellum here to bind a set of Epictetus. But why ruin the effect with hand-painted garlands? The æsthetic instinct has not as yet invaded these fair States—decidedly not."

Setting the basket down, he studied it meditatively for a moment. Then he leaned over and took from it the piece of crumpled wrapping paper to which he had referred the previous day.

"This doubtless contained the lady's last purchase on earth," he mused. "Very touchin'. Are you sentimental about such trifles, Markham? Anyway, the purple string round it was a godsend to Skeel. . . . What knickknack, do you suppose, paved the way for the frantic Tony's escape?"

He opened the paper, revealing a broken piece of corrugated cardboard and a large square dark-brown envelope.

"Ah, to be sure! Phonograph records." He glanced about the apartment. "But, I say, where did the lady keep the bally machine?"

"You'll find it in the foyer," said Markham wearily, without turning. He knew that Vance's chatter was only the outward manifestation of serious and perplexed thinking; and he was waiting with what patience he could muster.

Vance sauntered idly through the glass doors into the little reception hall, and stood gazing abstractedly at a console phonograph of Chinese Chippendale design which stood against the wall at one end. The squat cabinet was partly covered with a prayer rug, and upon it sat a polished bronze flower bowl.

"At any rate, it doesn't look phonographic," he remarked. "But why the prayer rug?" He examined it casually. "Anatolian—probably called a Cæsarian for sale purposes. Not very valuable—too much on the Oushak type. . . . Wonder what the lady's taste in music was. Victor Herbert, doubtless." He turned back the rug and lifted the lid of the cabinet. There was a record already on the machine, and he leaned over and looked at it.

"My word! The Andante from Beethoven's C-Minor Symphony!" he exclaimed cheerfully. "You know the movement, of course, Markham. The most perfect Andante ever written." He wound up the machine. "I think a little music might clear the atmosphere and volatilize our perturbation, what?"

Markham paid no attention to his banter; he was still gazing dejectedly out of the window.

Vance started the motor, and placing the needle on the record, returned to the living room. He stood staring at the davenport, concentrating on the problem in hand. I sat in the wicker chair by the door waiting for the music. The situation was getting on my nerves, and I began to feel fidgety. A minute or two passed, but the only sound which came from the phonograph was a faint scratching. Vance looked up with mild curiosity, and walked back to the machine. Inspecting it cursorily, he once more set it in operation. But though he waited several minutes, no music came forth.

"I say! That's deuced queer, y' know," he grumbled, as he changed the needle and rewound the motor.

Markham had now left the window and stood watching him with good-natured tolerance. The turntable of the phonograph was spinning, and the needle was tracing its concentric revolutions; but still the instrument refused to play. Vance, with both hands on the cabinet, was leaning forward, his eyes fixed on the silently revolving record with an expression of amused bewilderment.

"The sound box is probably broken," he said. "Silly machines, anyway."

"The difficulty, I imagine," Markham chided him, "lies in your patrician ignorance of so vulgar and democratic a mechanism. Permit me to assist you."

He moved to Vance's side, and I stood looking curiously over his shoulder. Everything appeared to be in order, and the needle had now almost reached the end of the record. But only a faint scratching was audible.

Markham stretched forth his hand to lift the sound box. But his movement was never completed.

At that moment the little apartment was filled with several terrifying treble screams, followed by two shrill calls for help. A cold chill swept my body, and there was a tingling at the roots of my hair.

After a short silence, during which the three of us remained speechless, the same feminine voice said in a loud, distinct tone: *"No; nothing is the matter. I'm sorry.... Everything is all right.... Please go home, and don't worry."*

The needle had come to the end of the record. There was a slight click, and the automatic device shut off the motor. The almost terrifying silence that followed was broken by a sardonic chuckle from Vance.

"Well, old dear," he remarked languidly, as he strolled back into the living room, "so much for your irrefutable facts!"

There came a loud knocking on the door, and the officer on duty outside looked in with a startled face.

"It's all right," Markham informed him in a husky voice. "I'll call you when I want you."

Vance lay down on the davenport and took out another cigarette. Having lighted it, he stretched his arms far over his head and extended his legs, like a man in whom a powerful physical tension had suddenly relaxed.

" 'Pon my soul, Markham, we've all been babes in the woods," he drawled. "An incontrovertible alibi—my word! If the law supposes that, as Mr. Bumble said, the law is a ass, a idiot.—Oh, Sammy, Sammy, vy worn't there a alleybi! ... Markham, I blush to admit it, but it's you and I who've been the unutterable asses."

Markham had been standing by the instrument like a man dazed, his eyes riveted hypnotically on the telltale record. Slowly he came into the room and threw himself wearily into a chair.

"Those precious facts of yours!" continued Vance. "Stripped of their carefully disguised appearance, what are they?—Spotswoode prepared a phonograph record—a simple enough task. Everyone makes 'em nowadays——"

"Yes. He told me he had a workshop at his home on Long Island where he tinkered a bit."

"He really didn't need it, y' know. But it facilitated things, no doubt. The voice on the record is merely his own in falsetto—better for the purpose than a woman's, for it's stronger and more penetrating. As for the label, he simply soaked it off an ordin'ry record, and pasted it on his own. He brought the lady several new records that night, and concealed this one among them. After the theater he enacted his gruesome little drama and then carefully set the stage so that the police would think it was a typical burglar's performance. When this had been done, he placed the record on the machine, set it going, and calmly walked out. He had placed the prayer rug and bronze bowl on the cabinet of the machine to give the impression that the phonograph was rarely used. And the precaution worked, for no one thought of looking into it. Why should they? ... Then he asked Jessup to call a taxicab—everything quite natural, y' see. While he was waiting for the car the needle reached the recorded screams. They were heard plainly: it was night, and the sounds carried distinctly. Moreover, being filtered through a wooden door, their phonographic timbre was well disguised. And, if you'll note, the enclosed horn is directed toward the door, not three feet away."

"But the synchronization of his questions and the answers on the record. . . ?"

"The simplest part of it. You remember Jessup told us that Spotswoode was standing with one arm on the switchboard when the screams were heard. He merely had his eye on his wristwatch. The moment he heard the cry, he calculated the intermission on the record and put his question to the imagin'ry lady at just the right moment to receive the record's response. It was all carefully figured out beforehand; he no doubt rehearsed it in his laborat'ry. It was deuced simple, and practically proof against failure. The record is a large one—twelve-inch diameter, I should say—and it requires about five minutes for the needle to traverse it. By putting the screams at the end, he allowed himself ample time to get out and order a taxicab. When the car at last came, he rode direct to the Stuyvesant Club, where he met Judge Redfern and played poker till three. If he hadn't met the judge, rest assured he would have impressed his presence on someone else so as to have established an alibi."

Markham shook his head gravely.

"Good God! No wonder he importuned me on every possible occasion to let him visit this apartment again. Such a damning piece of evidence as that record must have kept him awake at night."

"Still, I rather fancy that if I hadn't discovered it, he would have succeeded in getting possession of it as soon as your *sergent-de-ville* was removed. It was annoyin' to be unexpectedly barred from the apartment, but I doubt if it worried him much. He would have been on hand when the Canary's aunt took possession, and the retrieving of the record would have been comparatively easy. Of course the record constituted a hazard, but Spotswoode isn't the type who'd shy at a low bunker of that kind. No; the thing was planned scientifically enough. He was defeated by sheer accident."

"And Skeel?"

"He was another unfortunate circumstance. He was hiding in the closet there when Spotswoode and the lady came in at eleven. It was Spotswoode whom he saw strangle his erstwhile *amoureuse* and rifle the apartment. Then, when Spotswoode went out, he came forth from hiding. He was probably looking down at the girl when the phonograph emitted its blood-chilling wails. . . . My word! Fancy being in a cold funk, gazing at a murdered woman, and then hearing piercing screams behind you! It was a bit too much even for the hardened Tony. I don't wonder he forgot all caution and put his hand on the table to steady himself. . . . And then came Spotswoode's voice through the door, and the record's answer. This must have puzzled Skeel. I imagine he thought for a moment he'd lost his reason. But pretty soon the significance of it dawned on him; and I can see him grinning to himself. Obviously he knew who the murderer was—it would not have been in keeping with his character had he failed to learn the identities of the Canary's admirers. And now there had fallen into his lap, like manna from heaven, the most perfect opportunity for blackmail that any such charmin' young gentleman could desire. He doubtless indulged himself with roseate visions of a life of opulence and ease at Spotswoode's expense. When Cleaver phoned a few minutes later, he merely said the lady was out, and then set to work planning his own departure."

"But I don't see why he didn't take the record with him."

"And remove from the scene of the crime the one piece of unanswerable evidence? . . . Bad strategy, Markham. If he himself had produced the record later, Spotswoode would simply have denied all knowledge of it, and accused the blackmailer of a plot. Oh, no; Skeel's only course was to leave it and apply for an enormous settlement from Spotswoode at once. And I imagine that's what he did. Spotswoode no doubt gave him something on account and promised him the rest anon, hoping in the meantime to retrieve the record. When he failed to pay, Skeel phoned you and threatened to tell everything, thinking to spur Spotswoode to action. . . . Well, he spurred him—but not to the action desired. Spotswoode probably met him by appointment last Saturday night, ostensibly to hand over the money, but instead, throttled the chap. Quite in keeping with his nature, don't y' know. . . . Stout fella, Spotswoode."

"The whole thing . . . it's amazing."

"I shouldn't say that, now. Spotswoode had an unpleasant task to perform and he set about it in a cool, logical, forthright, businesslike manner. He had decided that his little Canary must die for his peace of mind; she'd probably made herself most annoyin'. So he arranged the date—like any judge passing sentence on a prisoner at the bar—and then proceeded to fabricate an alibi. Being something of a mechanic, he arranged a mechanical alibi. The device he chose was simple and obvious enough—no tortuosities or complications. And it would have succeeded but for what the insurance companies piously call an act of God. No one can foresee accidents, Markham; they wouldn't be accidental if one could. But Spotswoode certainly took every precaution that was humanly possible. It never occurred to him that you would thwart his every effort to return here and confiscate the record; and he couldn't anticipate my taste in music, nor know that I would seek solace in the tonal art. Furthermore, when one calls on a lady, one doesn't expect that another suitor is going to hide himself in the clothes press. It isn't done, don't y' know. . . . All in all, the poor johnny was beaten by a run of abominable luck."

"You overlook the fiendishness of the crime," Markham reproached him tartly.

"Don't be so confoundedly moral, old thing. Everyone's a murderer at heart. The person who has never felt a passionate hankering to kill someone is without emotions. And do you think it's ethics or theology that stays the average person from homicide? Dear no! It's lack of courage—the fear of being found out, or haunted, or cursed with remorse. Observe with what delight the people *en masse*—to wit, the state—put men to death and then gloat over it in the newspapers. Nations declare war against one another on the slightest provocation, so they can, with immunity, vent their lust for slaughter. Spotswoode, I'd say, is merely a rational animal with the courage of his convictions."

"Society unfortunately isn't ready for your nihilistic philosophy just yet," said Markham. "And during the intervening transition human life must be protected."

He rose resolutely and, going to the telephone, called up Heath.

"Sergeant," he ordered, "get a John-Doe warrant and meet me immediately at the Stuyvesant Club. Bring a man with you—there's an arrest to be made."

"At last the law has evidence after its own heart," chirped Vance, as he lazily donned his topcoat and picked up his hat and stick. "What a grotesque affair your legal procedure is, Markham! Scientific knowledge—the facts of psychology—mean nothing to you learned Solons. But a phonograph record—ah! There, now, is something convincing, irrefragable, final, what?"

On our way out Markham beckoned to the officer on guard. "Under no conditions," he said, "is anyone to enter this apartment until I return—not even with a signed permit."

When we had entered the taxicab, he directed the chauffeur to the club.

"So the newspapers want action, do they? Well, they're going to get it. . . . You've helped me out of a nasty hole, old man."

As he spoke, his eyes turned to Vance. And that look conveyed a profounder gratitude than any words could have expressed.

30

THE END

(*Tuesday, September 18; 3:30 P.M.*)

IT WAS exactly half past three when we entered the rotunda of the Stuyvesant Club. Markham at once sent for the manager and held a few words of private conversation with him. The manager then hastened away and was gone about five minutes.

"Mr. Spotswoode is in his rooms," he informed Markham, on returning. "I sent the electrician up to test the light bulbs. He reports that the gentleman is alone, writing at his desk."

"And the room number?"

"Three forty-one." The manager appeared perturbed. "There won't be any fuss, will there, Mr. Markham?"

"I don't look for any." Markham's tone was chilly. "However, the present matter is considerably more important than your club."

"What an exaggerated point of view!" sighed Vance when the manager had left us. "The arrest of Spotswoode, I'd say, was the acme of futility. The man isn't a criminal, don't y' know; he has nothing in common with Lombroso's *Uomo Delinquente.* He's what one might term a philosophic behaviorist."

Markham grunted but did not answer. He began pacing up and down agitatedly, keeping his eyes expectantly on the main entrance. Vance sought a comfortable chair and settled himself in it with placid unconcern.

Ten minutes later Heath and Snitkin arrived. Markham at once led them into an alcove and briefly explained his reason for summoning them.

"Spotswoode's upstairs now," he said. "I want the arrest made as quietly as possible."

"Spotswoode!" Heath repeated the name in astonishment. "I don't see——"

"You don't have to see—yet," Markham cut in sharply. "I'm taking all responsibility for the arrest. And you're getting the credit—if you want it. That suit you?"

Heath shrugged his shoulders. "It's all right with me . . . anything you say, sir." He shook his head uncomprehendingly. "But what about Jessup?"

"We'll keep him locked up. Material witness."

We ascended in the elevator and emerged at the third floor. Spotswoode's rooms were at the end of the hall, facing the Square. Markham, his face set grimly, led the way.

In answer to his knock Spotswoode opened the door and, greeting us pleasantly, stepped aside for us to enter.

"Any news yet?" he asked, moving a chair forward.

At this moment he got a clear view of Markham's face in the light, and at once he sensed the minatory nature of our visit. Though his expression did not alter, I saw his body suddenly go taut. His cold, indecipherable eyes moved slowly from Markham's face to Heath and Snitkin. Then his gaze fell on Vance and me, who were standing a little behind the others, and he nodded stiffly.

No one spoke; yet I felt that an entire tragedy was somehow being enacted, and that each actor heard and understood every word.

Markham remained standing, as if reluctant to proceed. Of all the duties of his office, I knew that the arrest of malefactors was the most distasteful to him. He was a worldly man, with the worldly man's tolerance for the misfortunes of evil. Heath and Snitkin had stepped forward and now waited with passive alertness for the district attorney's order to serve the warrant.

Spotswoode's eyes were again on Markham. "What can I do for you, sir?" His voice was calm and without the faintest quaver.

"You can accompany these officers, Mr. Spotswoode," Markham told him quietly, with a slight inclination of his head toward the two imperturbable figures at his side. "I arrest you for the murder of Margaret Odell."

"Ah!" Spotswoode's eyebrows lifted mildly. "Then you have—discovered something?"

"The Beethoven Andante."

Not a muscle of Spotswoode's face moved; but after a short pause he made a barely perceptible gesture of resignation. "I can't say that it was wholly unexpected," he said evenly, with the tragic suggestion of a smile; "especially as you thwarted every effort of mine to secure the record. But then . . . the fortunes of the game are always uncertain." His smile faded, and his manner became grave. "You have acted generously toward me, Mr. Markham, in shielding me from the *canaille;* and because I appreciate that courtesy I should like you to know that the game I played was one in which I had no alternative."

"Your motive, however powerful," said Markham, "cannot extenuate your crime."

"Do you think I seek extenuation?" Spotswoode dismissed the imputation with a contemptuous gesture. "I'm not a schoolboy. I calculated the consequences of my course of action and, after weighing the various factors involved, decided to risk it. It was a gamble, to be sure; but it's not my habit to complain about the misfortunes of a deliberately planned risk. Furthermore, the choice was practically forced upon me. Had I not gambled in this instance, I stood to lose heavily nevertheless."

His face grew bitter.

"This woman, Mr. Markham, had demanded the impossible of me. Not content with bleeding me financially, she demanded legal protection, position, social prestige—such things as only my name could give her. She informed me

I must divorce my wife and marry her. I wonder if you apprehend the enormity of that demand? . . . You see, Mr. Markham, I love my wife, and I have children whom I love. I will not insult your intelligence by explaining how, despite my conduct, such a thing is entirely possible. . . . And yet, this woman commanded me to wreck my life and crush utterly those I held dear, solely to gratify her petty, ridiculous ambition! When I refused, she threatened to expose our relations to my wife, to send her copies of the letters I had written, to sue me publicly—in fine, to create such a scandal that, in any event, my life would be ruined, my family disgraced, my home destroyed."

He paused and drew a deep inspiration.

"I have never been partial to halfway measures," he continued impassively. "I have no talent for compromise. Perhaps I am a victim of my heritage. But my instinct is to play out a hand to the last chip—to force whatever danger threatens. And for just five minutes, a week ago, I understood how the fanatics of old could, with a calm mind and a sense of righteousness, torture their enemies who threatened them with spiritual destruction. . . . I chose the only course which might save those I love from disgrace and suffering. It meant taking a desperate risk. But the blood within me was such that I did not hesitate, and I was fired by the agony of a tremendous hate. I staked my life against a living death, on the remote chance of attaining peace. And I lost."

Again he smiled faintly.

"Yes—the fortunes of the game. . . . But don't think for a minute that I am complaining or seeking sympathy. I have lied to others perhaps, but not to myself. I detest a whiner—a self-excuser. I want you to understand that."

He reached to the table at his side and took up a small limp-leather volume.

"Only last night I was reading Wilde's 'De Profundis.' Had I been gifted with words, I might have made a similar confession. Let me show you what I mean so that, at least, you won't attribute to me the final infamy of cravenness."

He opened the book, and began reading in a voice whose very fervor held us all silent:

" 'I brought about my own downfall. No one, be he high or low, need be ruined by any other hand than his own. Readily as I confess this, there are many who will, at this time at least, receive the confession sceptically. And although I thus mercilessly accuse myself, bear in mind that I do so without offering any excuse. Terrible as is the punishment inflicted upon me by the world, more terrible is the ruin I have brought upon myself. . . . In the dawn of manhood I recognized my position. . . . I enjoyed an honored name, an eminent social position. . . . Then came the turning-point. I had become tired of dwelling on the heights—and descended by my own will into the depths. . . . I satisfied my desires wherever it suited me, and passed on. I forgot that every act, even the most insignificant act of daily life, in some degree, makes or unmakes the character; and every occurrence which transpires in the seclusion of the chamber will some day be proclaimed from the housetops. I lost control of myself. I was no longer at the helm, and knew it not. I had become a slave to pleasure. . . . One thing only is left to me—complete humility.' "

He tossed the book aside.

"You understand now, Mr. Markham?"

Markham did not speak for several moments.

"Do you care to tell me about Skeel?" he at length asked.

"That swine!" Spotswoode sneered his disgust. "I could murder such creatures every day and regard myself as a benefactor of society.... Yes, I strangled him, and I would have done it before, only the opportunity did not offer.... It was Skeel who was hiding in the closet when I returned to the apartment after the theater, and he must have seen me kill the woman. Had I known he was behind that locked closet door, I would have broken it down and wiped him out then. But how was I to know? It seemed natural that the closet might have been kept locked—I didn't give it a second thought.... And the next night he telephoned me to the club here. He had first called my home on Long Island and learned that I was staying here. I had never seen him before—didn't know of his existence. But, it seems, he had equipped himself with a knowledge of my identity—probably some of the money I gave to the woman went to him. What a muck heap I had fallen into!... When he phoned, he mentioned the phonograph, and I knew he had found out something. I met him in the Waldorf lobby, and he told me the truth: there was no doubting his word. When he saw I was convinced, he demanded so enormous a sum that I was staggered."

Spotswoode lit a cigarette with steady fingers.

"Mr. Markham, I am no longer a rich man. The truth is, I am on the verge of bankruptcy. The business my father left me has been in a receiver's hands for nearly a year. The Long Island estate on which I live belongs to my wife. Few people know these things, but unfortunately they are true. It would have been utterly impossible for me to raise the amount Skeel demanded, even had I been inclined to play the coward. I did, however, give him a small sum to keep him quiet for a few days, promising him all he asked as soon as I could convert some of my holdings. I hoped in the interim to get possession of the record and thus spike his guns. But in that I failed; and so, when he threatened to tell you everything, I agreed to bring the money to his home late Saturday night. I kept the appointment, with the full intention of killing him. I was careful about entering, but he had helped me by explaining when and how I could get in without being seen. Once there, I wasted no time. The first moment he was off his guard I seized him—and gloried in the act. Then, locking the door and taking the key, I walked out of the house quite openly, and returned here to the club.—That's all, I think."

Vance was watching him musingly.

"So when you raised my bet last night," he said, "the amount represented a highly important item in your exchequer."

Spotswoode smiled faintly. "It represented practically every cent I had in the world."

"Astonishin'!... And would you mind if I asked you why you selected the label of Beethoven's Andante for your record?"

"Another miscalculation," the man said wearily. "It occurred to me that if anyone should, by any chance, open the phonograph before I could return and destroy the record, he wouldn't be as likely to want to hear the classics as he would a more popular selection."

"And one who detests popular music had to find it! I fear, Mr. Spotswoode, that an unkind fate sat in at your game."

"Yes. . . . If I were religiously inclined, I might talk poppycock about retribution and divine punishment."

"I'd like to ask you about the jewelry," said Markham. "It's not sportsmanlike to do it, and I wouldn't suggest it, except that you've already confessed voluntarily to the main points at issue."

"I shall take no offense at any question you desire to ask, sir," Spotswoode answered. "After I had recovered my letters from the document box, I turned the rooms upside down to give the impression of a burglary—being careful to use gloves, of course. And I took the woman's jewelry for the same reason. Parenthetically, I had paid for most of it. I offered it as a sop to Skeel, but he was afraid to accept it; and finally I decided to rid myself of it. I wrapped it in one of the club newspapers and threw it in a wastebin near the Flatiron Building."

"You wrapped it in the morning *Herald,*" put in Heath. "Did you know that Pop Cleaver reads nothing but the *Herald?*"

"Sergeant!" Vance's voice was a cutting reprimand. "Certainly Mr. Spotswoode was not aware of that fact—else he would not have selected the *Herald.*"

Spotswoode smiled at Heath with pitying contempt. Then, with an appreciative glance at Vance, he turned back to Markham.

"An hour or so after I had disposed of the jewels, I was assailed by the fear that the package might be found and the paper traced. So I bought another *Herald* and put it on the rack." He paused. "Is that all?"

Markham nodded.

"Thank you—that's all; except that I must now ask you to go with these officers."

"In that case," said Spotswoode quietly, "there's a small favor I have to ask of you, Mr. Markham. Now that the blow has fallen, I wish to write a certain note—to my wife. But I want to be alone when I write it. Surely you understand that desire. It will take but a few moments. Your men may stand at the door—I can't very well escape. . . . The victor can afford to be generous to that extent."

Before Markham had time to reply, Vance stepped forward and touched his arm.

"I trust," he interposed, "that you won't deem it necess'ry to refuse Mr. Spotswoode's request."

Markham looked at him hesitantly.

"I guess you've pretty well earned the right to dictate, Vance," he acquiesced.

Then he ordered Heath and Snitkin to wait outside in the hall, and he and Vance and I went into the adjoining room. Markham stood, as if on guard, near the door; but Vance, with an ironical smile, sauntered to the window and gazed out into Madison Square.

"My word, Markham!" he declared. "There's something rather colossal about that chap. Y' know, one can't help admiring him. He's so eminently sane and logical."

Markham made no response. The drone of the city's midafternoon noises, muffled by the closed windows, seemed to intensify the ominous silence of the little bedchamber where we waited.

Then came a sharp report from the other room.

Markham flung open the door. Heath and Snitkin were already rushing toward Spotswoode's prostrate body, and were bending over it when Markham entered. Immediately he wheeled about and glared at Vance, who now appeared in the doorway.

"He's shot himself!"

"Fancy that," said Vance.

"You—you knew he was going to do that?" Markham spluttered.

"It was rather obvious, don't y' know."

Markham's eyes flashed angrily.

"And you deliberately interceded for him—to give him the opportunity?"

"Tut, tut, my dear fellow!" Vance reproached him. "Pray don't give way to conventional moral indignation. However unethical—theoretically—it may be to take another's life, a man's own life is certainly his to do with as he chooses. Suicide is his inalienable right. And under the paternal tyranny of our modern democracy, I'm rather inclined to think it's about the only right he has left, what?"

He glanced at his watch and frowned.

"D' ye know, I've missed my concert, bothering with your beastly affairs," he complained amiably, giving Markham an engaging smile; "and now you're actually scolding me. 'Pon my word, old fellow, you're deuced ungrateful!"

The Bishop Murder Case

The Earth is a Temple where there is going on a Mystery Play, childish and poignant, ridiculous and awful enough in all conscience.

—*Conrad*

CHARACTERS OF THE BOOK

PHILO VANCE

JOHN F.-X. MARKHAM
District Attorney of New York County.

ERNEST HEATH
Sergeant of the Homicide Bureau.

PROFESSOR BERTRAND DILLARD
A famous physicist.

BELLE DILLARD
His niece.

SIGURD ARNESSON
His adopted son: an associate professor of mathematics.

PYNE
The Dillard butler.

BEEDLE
The Dillard cook.

ADOLPH DRUKKER
Scientist and author.

MRS. OTTO DRUKKER
His mother.

GRETE MENZEL
The Drukker cook.

JOHN PARDEE
Mathematician and chess expert: inventor of the Pardee gambit.

J. C. ROBIN
Sportsman and champion archer.

RAYMOND SPERLING
Civil Engineer.

JOHN E. SPRIGG
Senior at Columbia University.

DR. WHITNEY BARSTEAD
An eminent neurologist.

QUINAN
Police Reporter of the *World*.

MADELEINE MOFFAT
CHIEF INSPECTOR O'BRIEN
    Of the Police Department of New York City.
WILLIAM M. MORAN
    Commanding Officer of the Detective Bureau.
CAPTAIN PITTS
    Of the Homicide Bureau.
GUILFOYLE
    Detective of the Homicide Bureau.
SNITKIN
    Detective of the Homicide Bureau.
HENNESSEY
    Detective of the Homicide Bureau.
EMERY
    Detective of the Homicide Bureau.
BURKE
    Detective of the Homicide Bureau.
CAPTAIN DUBOIS
    Finger-print expert.
DR. EMANUEL DOREMUS
    Medical Examiner.
SWACKER
    Secretary of the District Attorney.
CURRIE
    Vance's valet.

1

"WHO KILLED COCK ROBIN?"

(Saturday, April 2; noon)

OF ALL the criminal cases in which Philo Vance participated as an unofficial investigator, the most sinister, the most bizarre, the seemingly most incomprehensible, and certainly the most terrifying, was the one that followed the famous Greene murders.* The orgy of horror at the old Greene mansion had been brought to its astounding close in December; and after the Christmas holidays Vance had gone to Switzerland for the winter sports. Returning to New York at the end of February he had thrown himself into some literary work he had long had in mind—the uniform translation of the principal fragments of Menander found in the Egyptian papyri during the early years of the present century; and for over a month he had devoted himself sedulously to this thankless task.

Whether or not he would have completed the translations, even had his labors not been interrupted, I do not know; for Vance was a man of cultural ardencies, in whom the spirit of research and intellectual adventure was constantly at odds with the drudgery necessary to scholastic creation. I remember that only the preceding year he had begun writing a life of Xenophon— the result of an enthusiasm inherited from his university days when he had first read the *Anabasis* and the *Memorabilia*—and had lost interest in it at the point where Xenophon's historic march led the Ten Thousand back to the sea. However, the fact remains that Vance's translation of Menander was rudely interrupted in early April; and for weeks he became absorbed in a criminal mystery which threw the entire country into a state of gruesome excitement.

This new criminal investigation, in which he acted as a kind of *amicus curiæ* for John F.-X. Markham, the District Attorney of New York, at once became known as the Bishop murder case. The designation—the result of our journalistic instinct to attach labels to every *cause célèbre*—was, in a sense, a misnomer. There was nothing ecclesiastical about that ghoulish saturnalia of crime which set an entire community to reading the "Mother Goose Melodies" with fearful apprehension;* and no one of the name of Bishop was, as

* "The Greene Murder Case."

341

far as I know, even remotely connected with the monstrous events which bore
that appellation. But, withal, the word "Bishop" was appropriate, for it was an
alias used by the murderer for the grimmest of purposes. Incidentally it was
this name that eventually led Vance to the almost incredible truth, and ended
one of the most ghastly multiple crimes in police history.

The series of uncanny and apparently unrelated events which constituted
the Bishop murder case and drove all thought of Menander and Greek mono-
stichs from Vance's mind, began on the morning of April 2, less than five
months after the double shooting of Julia and Ada Greene. It was one of those
warm luxurious spring days which sometimes bless New York in early April;
and Vance was breakfasting in his little roof garden atop his apartment in East
38th Street. It was nearly noon—for Vance worked or read until all hours, and
was a late riser—and the sun, beating down from a clear blue sky, cast a man-
tle of introspective lethargy over the city. Vance sprawled in an easy chair, his
breakfast on a low table beside him, gazing with cynical, regretful eyes down
at the treetops in the rear yard.

I knew what was in his mind. It was his custom each spring to go to France;
and it had long since come to him to think, as it came to George Moore, that
Paris and May were one. But the great trek of the post-war American *nou-
veaux riches* to Paris had spoiled his pleasure in this annual pilgrimage; and,
only the day before, he had informed me that we were to remain in New York
for the summer.

For years I had been Vance's friend and legal adviser—a kind of monetary
steward and agent-companion. I had quitted my father's law firm of Van
Dine, Davis & Van Dine to devote myself wholly to his interests—a post I
found far more congenial than that of general attorney in a stuffy office—and
though my own bachelor quarters were in a hotel on the West Side, I spent
most of my time at Vance's apartment.

I had arrived early that morning, long before Vance was up, and, having
gone over the first-of-the-month accounts, now sat smoking my pipe idly as he
breakfasted.

"Y' know, Van," he said to me, in his emotionless drawl; "the prospect
of spring and summer in New York is neither excitin' nor romantic. It's going to be a beastly bore. But it'll be less annoyin' than travelin' in Europe
with the vulgar hordes of tourists jostlin' one at every turn. . . . It's very
distressin'."

Little did he suspect what the next few weeks held in store for him. Had he
known I doubt if even the prospect of an old pre-war spring in Paris would
have taken him away; for his insatiable mind liked nothing better than a complicated problem; and even as he spoke to me that morning the gods that pre-
sided over his destiny were preparing for him a strange and fascinating
enigma—one which was to stir the nation deeply and add a new and terrible
chapter to the annals of crime.

Vance had scarcely poured his second cup of coffee when Currie, his old

* Mr. Joseph A. Margolies of Brentano's told me that for a period of several weeks
during the Bishop murder case more copies of "Mother Goose Melodies" were sold than
of any current novel. And one of the smaller publishing houses reprinted and completely
sold out an entire edition of those famous old nursery rhymes.

English butler and general factotum, appeared at the French doors bearing a portable telephone.

"It's Mr. Markham, sir," the old man said apologetically. "As he seemed rather urgent, I took the liberty of informing him you were in." He plugged the telephone into a baseboard switch, and set the instrument on the breakfast table.

"Quite right, Currie," Vance murmured, taking off the receiver. "Anything to break this deuced monotony." Then he spoke to Markham. "I say, old man, don't you ever sleep? I'm in the midst of an *omelette aux fines herbes.* Will you join me? Or do you merely crave the music of my voice————?"

He broke off abruptly, and the bantering look on his lean features disappeared. Vance was a marked Nordic type, with a long, sharply chiselled face; gray, wide-set eyes; a narrow aquiline nose; and a straight oval chin. His mouth, too, was firm and clean-cut, but it held a look of cynical cruelty which was more Mediterranean than Nordic. His face was strong and attractive, though not exactly handsome. It was the face of a thinker and recluse; and its very severity—at once studious and introspective—acted as a barrier between him and his fellows.

Though he was immobile by nature and sedulously schooled in the repression of his emotions, I noticed that, as he listened to Markham on the phone that morning, he could not entirely disguise his eager interest in what was being told him. A slight frown ruffled his brow; and his eyes reflected his inner amazement. From time to time he gave vent to a murmured "Amazin'!" or "My word!" or "Most extr'ordin'ry!"—his favorite expletives—and when at the end of several minutes he spoke to Markham, a curious excitement marked his manner.

"Oh, by all means!" he said. "I shouldn't miss it for all the lost comedies of Menander. . . . It sounds mad. . . . I'll don fitting raiment immediately. . . . *Au revoir.*"

Replacing the receiver, he rang for Currie.

"My gray tweeds," he ordered. "A sombre tie, and my black Homburg hat." Then he returned to his omelet with a preoccupied air.

After a few moments he looked at me quizzically.

"What might you know of archery, Van?" he asked.

I knew nothing of archery, save that it consisted of shooting arrows at targets, and I confessed as much.

"You're not exactly revealin', don't y' know." He lighted one of his *Régie* cigarettes indolently. "However, we're in for a little flutter of toxophily, it seems. I'm no leading authority on the subject myself, but I did a bit of potting with the bow at Oxford. It's not a passionately excitin' pastime—much duller than golf and fully as complicated." He smoked a while dreamily. "I say, Van; fetch me Doctor Elmer's tome on archery from the library—there's a good chap."*

I brought the book, and for nearly half an hour he dipped into it, tarrying over the chapters on archery associations, tournaments and matches, and scanning the long tabulation of the best American scores. At length he settled

---

* The book Vance referred to was that excellent and comprehensive treatise, "Archery," by Robert P. Elmer, M.D.

back in his chair. It was obvious he had found something that caused him troubled concern and set his sensitive mind to work.

"It's quite mad, Van," he remarked, his eyes in space. "A mediæval tragedy in modern New York! We don't wear buskins and leathern doublets, and yet—*By Jove!*" He suddenly sat upright. "No—no! It's absurd. I'm letting the insanity of Markham's news affect me. . . ." He drank some more coffee, but his expression told me that he could not rid himself of the idea that had taken possession of him.

"One more favor, Van," he said at length. "Fetch me my German diction'ry and Burton E. Stevenson's 'Home Book of Verse.' "

When I had brought the volumes, he glanced at one word in the dictionary, and pushed the book from him.

"That's that, unfortunately—though I knew it all the time."

Then he turned to the section in Stevenson's gigantic anthology which included the rhymes of the nursery and of childhood. After several minutes he closed that book, too, and, stretching himself out in his chair, blew a long ribbon of smoke toward the awning overhead.

"It can't be true," he protested, as if to himself. "It's too fantastic, too fiendish, too utterly distorted. A fairy tale in terms of blood—a world in anamorphosis—a perversion of all rationality. . . . It's unthinkable, senseless, like black magic and sorcery and thaumaturgy. It's downright demented."

He glanced at his watch and, rising, went indoors, leaving me to speculate vaguely on the cause of his unwonted perturbation. A treatise on archery, a German dictionary, a collection of children's verses, and Vance's incomprehensible utterances regarding insanity and fantasy—what possible connection could these things have? I attempted to find a least common denominator, but without the slightest success. And it was no wonder I failed. Even the truth, when it came out weeks later bolstered up by an array of incontestable evidence, seemed too incredible and too wicked for acceptance by the normal mind of man.

Vance shortly broke in on my futile speculations. He was dressed for the street, and seemed impatient at Markham's delay in arriving.

"Y' know, I wanted something to interest me—a nice fascinatin' crime, for instance," he remarked; "but—my word!—I wasn't exactly longin' for a nightmare. If I didn't know Markham so well I'd suspect him of spoofing."

When Markham stepped into the roof garden a few minutes later it was only too plain that he had been in deadly earnest. His expression was sombre and troubled, and his usual cordial greeting he reduced to the merest curt formality. Markham and Vance had been intimate friends for fifteen years. Though of antipodal natures—the one sternly aggressive, brusque, forthright, and almost ponderously serious; the other whimsical, cynical, debonair, and aloof from the transient concerns of life—they found in each other that attraction of complementaries which so often forms the basis of an inseparable and enduring companionship.

During Markham's year and four months as District Attorney of New York he had often called Vance into conference on matters of grave importance, and in every instance Vance had justified the confidence placed in his judgments. Indeed, to Vance almost entirely belongs the credit for solving the large number of major crimes which occurred during Markham's four years' incumbency. His knowledge of human nature, his wide reading and cultural attainments, his shrewd sense of logic, and his *flair* for the hidden truth beneath misleading exteriors, all fitted him for the task of criminal investigator—a task which he fulfilled unofficially in connection with the cases which came under Markham's jurisdiction.

Vance's first case, it will be remembered, had to do with the murder of Alvin Benson;* and had it not been for his participation in that affair I doubt if the truth concerning it would ever have come to light. Then followed the notorious strangling of Margaret Odell†—a murder mystery in which the ordinary methods of police detection would inevitably have failed. And last year the astounding Greene murders (to which I have already referred) would undoubtedly have succeeded had not Vance been able to frustrate their final intent.

It was not surprising, therefore, that Markham should have turned to Vance at the very beginning of the Bishop murder case. More and more, I had noticed, he had come to rely on the other's help in his criminal investigations; and in the present instance it was particularly fortunate that he appealed to Vance, for only through an intimate knowledge of the abnormal psychological manifestations of the human mind, such as Vance possessed, could that black, insensate plot have been contravened and the perpetrator unearthed.

"This whole thing may be a mare's-nest," said Markham, without conviction. "But I thought you might want to come along. . . ."

"Oh, quite!" Vance gave Markham a sardonic smile. "Sit down a moment and tell me the tale coherently. The corpse won't run away. And it's best to get our facts in some kind of order before we view the remains.—Who are the parties of the first part, for instance? And why the projection of the District Attorney's office into a murder case within an hour of the deceased's passing? All that you've told me so far resolves itself into the utterest nonsense."

Markham sat down gloomily on the edge of a chair and inspected the end of his cigar.

"Damn it, Vance! Don't start in with a mysteries-of-Udolpho attitude. The crime—if it is a crime—seems clear-cut enough. It's an unusual method of murder, I'll admit; but it's certainly not senseless. Archery has become quite a fad of late. Bows and arrows are in use to-day in practically every city and college in America."

"Granted. But it's been a long time since they were used to kill persons named Robin."

Markham's eyes narrowed, and he looked at Vance searchingly.

"That idea occurred to you, too, did it?"

"Occurred to me? It leapt to my brain the moment you mentioned the victim's name." Vance puffed a moment on his cigarette. " 'Who Killed Cock Robin?' And with a bow and arrow! . . . Queer how the doggerel learned in childhood clings to the memory.—By the by, what was the unfortunate Mr. Robin's first name?"

"Joseph, I believe."

"Neither edifyin' nor suggestive. . . . Any middle name?"

* "The Benson Murder Case."
† "The 'Canary' Murder Case."

"See here, Vance!" Markham rose irritably. "What has the murdered man's middle name to do with the case?"

"I haven't the groggiest. Only, as long as we're going insane we may as well go the whole way. A mere shred of sanity is of no value."

He rang for Currie and sent him for the telephone directory. Markham protested, but Vance pretended not to hear; and when the directory arrived he thumbed its pages for several moments.

"Did the departed live on Riverside Drive?" he asked finally, holding his finger on a name he had found.

"I think he did."

"Well, well." Vance closed the book, and fixed a quizzically triumphant gaze on the District Attorney. "Markham," he said slowly, "there's only one Joseph Robin listed in the telephone direct'ry. He lives on Riverside Drive, and his middle name is—Cochrane!"

"What rot is this?" Markham's tone was almost ferocious. "Suppose his name *was* Cochrane: are you seriously suggesting that the fact had anything to do with his being murdered?"

" 'Pon my word, old man, I'm suggesting nothing." Vance shrugged his shoulders slightly. "I'm merely jotting down, so to speak, a few facts in connection with the case. As the matter stands now: a Mr. Joseph Cochrane Robin—to wit: Cock Robin—has been killed by a bow and arrow.—Doesn't that strike even your legal mind as deuced queer?"

"No!" Markham fairly spat the negative. "The name of the dead man is certainly common enough; and it's a wonder more people haven't been killed or injured with all this revival of archery throughout the country. Moreover, it's wholly possible that Robin's death was the result of an accident."

"Oh, my aunt!" Vance wagged his head reprovingly. "That fact, even were it true, wouldn't help the situation any. It would only make it queerer. Of the thousands of archery enthusiasts in these fair states, the one with the name of Cock Robin should be accidentally killed with an arrow! Such a supposition would lead us into spiritism and demonology and whatnot. Do you, by any chance, believe in Eblises and Azazels and jinn who go about playing Satanic jokes on mankind?"

"Must I be a Mohammedan mythologist to admit coincidences?" returned Markham tartly.

"My dear fellow! The proverbial long arm of coincidence doesn't extend to infinity. There are, after all, laws of probability, based on quite definite mathematical formulas. It would make me sad to think that such men as Laplace* and Czuber and von Kries had lived in vain.—The present situation, however, is even more complicated than you suspect. For instance, you mentioned over the phone that the last person known to have been with Robin before his death is named Sperling."

"And what esoteric significance lies in that fact?"

"Perhaps you know what *Sperling* means in German," suggested Vance dulcetly.

---

* Though Laplace is best known for his "Méchanique Céleste," Vance was here referring to his masterly work, "Théorie Analytique des Probabilités," which Herschel called "the ne plus ultra of mathematical skill and power."

"I've been to High School," retorted Markham. Then his eyes opened slightly, and his body became tense.

Vance pushed the German dictionary toward him.

"Well, anyway, look up the word. We might as well be thorough. I looked it up myself. I was afraid my imagination was playing tricks on me, and I had a yearnin' to see the word in black and white."

Markham opened the book in silence, and let his eye run down the page. After staring at the word for several moments he drew himself up resolutely, as if fighting off a spell. When he spoke his voice was defiantly belligerent.

"*Sperling* means 'sparrow.' Any school boy knows that. What of it?"

"Oh, to be sure." Vance lit another cigarette languidly. "And any school boy knows the old nursery rhyme entitled 'The Death and Burial of Cock Robin,' what?" He glanced tantalizingly at Markham, who stood immobile, staring out into the spring sunshine. "Since you pretend to be unfamiliar with that childhood classic, permit me to recite the first stanza."

A chill, as of some unseen spectral presence, passed over me as Vance repeated those old familiar lines:

> "Who killed Cock Robin?
> 'I,' said the sparrow,
> 'With my bow and arrow.
> I killed Cock Robin.' "

2

ON THE ARCHERY RANGE

(*Saturday, April 2; 12:30 P.M.*)

SLOWLY MARKHAM brought his eyes back to Vance.

"It's mad," he remarked, like a man confronted with something at once inexplicable and terrifying.

"Tut, tut!" Vance waved his hand airily. "That's plagiarism. I said it first." (He was striving to overcome his own sense of perplexity by a lightness of attitude.) "And now there really should be an *inamorata* to bewail Mr. Robin's passing. You recall, perhaps, the stanza:

> "Who'll be chief mourner?
> 'I,' said the dove,
> 'I mourn my lost love;
> I'll be chief mourner.' "

Markham's head jerked slightly, and his fingers beat a nervous tattoo on the table.

"Good God, Vance! There *is* a girl in the case. And there's a possibility that jealousy lies at the bottom of this thing."

"Fancy that, now! I'm afraid the affair is going to develop into a kind of *tableau-vivant* for grown-up kindergartners, what? But that'll make our task easier. All we'll have to do is to find the fly."

"The fly?"

"The *Musca domestica,* to speak pedantically. . . . My dear Markham, have you forgotten?———

> "Who saw him die?
> 'I,' said the fly,
> 'With my little eye;
> I saw him die.' "

"Come down to earth!" Markham spoke with acerbity. "This isn't a child's game. It's damned serious business."

Vance nodded abstractedly.

"A child's game is sometimes the most serious business in life." His words held a curious, far-away tone. "I don't like this thing—I don't at all like it. There's too much of the child in it—the child born old and with a diseased mind. It's like some hideous perversion." He took a deep inhalation on his cigarette, and made a slight gesture of repugnance. "Give me the details. Let's find out where we stand in this topsy-turvy land."

Markham again seated himself.

"I haven't many details. I told you practically everything I know of the case over the phone. Old Professor Dillard called me shortly before I communicated with you———"

"Dillard? By any chance, Professor Bertrand Dillard?"

"Yes. The tragedy took place at his house.—You know him?"

"Not personally. I know him only as the world of science knows him—as one of the greatest living mathematical physicists. I have most of his books.—How did he happen to call you?"

"I've known him for nearly twenty years. I had mathematics under him at Columbia, and later did some legal work for him. When Robin's body was found he phoned me at once—about half past eleven. I called up Sergeant Heath at the Homicide Bureau and turned the case over to him—although I told him I'd come along personally later on. Then I phoned you. The Sergeant and his men are waiting for me now at the Dillard home."

"What's the domestic situation there?"

"The professor, as you probably know, resigned his chair some ten years ago. Since then he's been living in West 75th Street, near the Drive. He took his brother's child—a girl of fifteen—to live with him. She's around twenty-five now. Then there's his protégé, Sigurd Arnesson, who was a classmate of mine at college. The professor adopted him during his junior year. Arnesson is now about forty, an instructor in mathematics at Columbia. He came to this country from Norway when he was three, and was left an orphan five years later. He's something of a mathematical genius, and Dillard evidently saw the makings of a great physicist in him and adopted him."

"I've heard of Arnesson," nodded Vance. "He recently published some modifications of Mie's theory on the electrodynamics of moving bodies. . . . And do these three—Dillard, Arnesson and the girl—live alone?"

"With two servants. Dillard appears to have a very comfortable income. They're not very much alone, however. The house is a kind of shrine for mathematicians, and quite a *cénacle* has developed. Moreover, the girl, who has always gone in for outdoor sports, has her own little social set. I've been at the house several times, and there have always been visitors about—either a serious student or two of the abstract sciences up-stairs in the library, or some noisy young people in the drawing-room below."

"And Robin?"

"He belonged to Belle Dillard's set—an oldish young society man who held several archery records. . . ."

"Yes, I know. I just looked up the name in this book on archery. A Mr. J. C. Robin seems to have made the high scores in several recent championship meets. And I noted, too, that a Mr. Sperling has been the runner-up in several large archery tournaments.—Is Miss Dillard an archer as well?"

"Yes, quite an enthusiast. In fact, she organized the Riverside Archery Club. Its permanent ranges are at Sperling's home in Scarsdale; but Miss Dillard has rigged up a practice range in the side yard of the professor's 75th-Street house. It was on this range that Robin was killed."

"Ah! And, as you say, the last person known to have been with him was Sperling. Where is our sparrow now?"

"I don't know. He was with Robin shortly before the tragedy; but when the body was found he had disappeared. I imagine Heath will have news on that point."

"And wherein lies the possible motive of jealousy you referred to?" Vance's eyelids had drooped lazily, and he smoked with leisurely but precise deliberation—a sign of his intense interest in what was being told him.

"Professor Dillard mentioned an attachment between his niece and Robin; and when I asked him who Sperling was and what his status was at the Dillard house, he intimated that Sperling was also a suitor for the girl's hand. I didn't go into the situation over the phone, but the impression I got was that Robin and Sperling were rivals, and that Robin had the better of it."

"And so the sparrow killed Cock Robin." Vance shook his head dubiously. "It won't do. It's too dashed simple; and it doesn't account for the fiendishly perfect reconstruction of the Cock-Robin rhyme. There's something deeper—something darker and more horrible—in this grotesque business.—Who, by the by, found Robin?"

"Dillard himself. He had stepped out on the little balcony at the rear of the house, and saw Robin lying below on the practice range, with an arrow through his heart. He went down-stairs immediately—with considerable difficulty, for the old man suffers abominably from gout—and, seeing that the man was dead, phoned me.—That's all the advance information I have."

"Not what you'd call a blindin' illumination, but still a bit suggestive." Vance got up. "Markham old dear, prepare for something rather bizarre—and damnable. We can rule out accidents and coincidence. While it's true that ordin'ry target arrows—which are made of soft wood and fitted with little bevelled piles—could easily penetrate a person's clothing and chest wall, even when driven with a medium weight bow, the fact that a man named 'Sparrow' should kill a man named Cochrane Robin, *with a bow and arrow*, precludes any haphazard concatenation of circumstances. Indeed, this incredible set of events proves conclusively that there has been a subtle, diabolical intent beneath the whole affair." He moved toward the door. "Come, let us find out something more about it at what the Austrian police officials eruditely call the *situs criminis.*"

We left the house at once and drove up-town in Markham's car. Entering Central Park at Fifth Avenue we emerged through the 72nd-Street gate, and a few minutes later were turning off of West End Avenue into 75th Street. The Dillard house—number 391—was on our right, far down the block toward the river. Between it and the Drive, occupying the entire corner, was a large fifteen-story apartment house. The professor's home seemed to nestle, as if for protection, in the shadow of this huge structure.

The Dillard house was of gray, weather-darkened limestone, and belonged to the days when homes were built for permanency and comfort. The lot on which it stood had a thirty-five-foot frontage, and the house itself was fully twenty-five feet across. The other ten feet of the lot, which formed an areaway separating the house from the apartment structure, was shut off from the street by a ten-foot stone wall with a large iron door in the centre.

The house was of modified Colonial architecture. A short flight of shallow steps led from the street to a narrow brick-lined porch adorned with four white Corinthian pillars. On the second floor a series of casement windows, paned with rectangular leaded glass, extended across the entire width of the house. (These, I learned later, were the windows of the library.) There was something restful and distinctly old-fashioned about the place: it appeared like anything but the scene of a gruesome murder.

Two police cars were parked near the entrance when we drove up, and a dozen or so curious onlookers had gathered in the street. A patrolman lounged against one of the fluted columns of the porch, gazing at the crowd before him with bored disdain.

An old butler admitted us and led us into the drawing-room on the left of the entrance hall, where we found Sergeant Ernest Heath and two other men from the Homicide Bureau. The Sergeant, who was standing beside the centre-table smoking, his thumbs hooked in the armholes of his waistcoat, came forward and extended his hand in a friendly greeting to Markham.

"I'm glad you got here, sir," he said; and the worried look in his cold blue eyes seemed to relax a bit. "I've been waiting for you. There's something damn fishy about this case."

He caught sight of Vance, who had paused in the background, and his broad pugnacious features crinkled in a good-natured grin.

"Howdy, Mr. Vance. I had a sneaking idea you'd be lured into this case. What you been up to these many moons?" I could not help comparing this genuine friendliness of the Sergeant's attitude with the hostility of his first meeting with Vance at the time of the Benson case. But much water had run under the bridge since that first encounter in the murdered Alvin's garish living-room; and between Heath and Vance there had grown up a warm attachment, based on a mutual respect and a frank admiration for each other's capabilities.

Vance held out his hand, and a smile played about the corners of his mouth.

"The truth is, Sergeant, I've been endeavorin' to discover the lost glories of an Athenian named Menander, a dramatic rival of Philemon's. Silly, what?"

Heath grunted disdainfully.

"Well, anyhow, if you're as good at it is as you are at discovering crooks, you'll probably get a conviction." It was the first compliment I had ever heard pass his lips, and it attested not only to his deep-seated admiration for Vance, but also to his own troubled and uncertain state of mind.

Markham sensed the Sergeant's mental insecurity, and asked somewhat abruptly: "Just what seems to be the difficulty in the present case?"

"I didn't say there was any difficulty, sir," Heath replied. "It looks as though we had the bird who did it dead to rights. But I ain't satisfied, and—oh, hell! Mr. Markham . . . it ain't natural; it don't make sense."

"I think I understand what you mean." Markham regarded the Sergeant appraisingly. "You're inclined to think that Sperling's guilty?"

"Sure, he's guilty," declared Heath with over-emphasis. "But that's not what's worrying me. To tell you the truth, I don't like the name of this guy who was croaked—especially as he was croaked with a bow and arrow. . . ." He hesitated, a bit shame-faced. "Don't it strike you as peculiar, sir?"

Markham nodded perplexedly.

"I see that you, too, remember your nursery rhymes," he said, and turned away.

Vance fixed a waggish look on Heath.

"You referred to Mr. Sperling just now as a 'bird,' Sergeant. The designation was most apt. *Sperling,* d'ye see, means 'sparrow' in German. And it was a sparrow, you recall, who killed Cock Robin with an arrow. . . . A fascinatin' situation—eh, what?"

The Sergeant's eyes bulged slightly, and his lips fell apart. He stared at Vance with almost ludicrous bewilderment.

"I said this here business was fishy!"

"I'd say, rather, it was avian, don't y' know."

"You *would* call it something nobody'd understand," Heath retorted truculently. It was his wont to become bellicose when confronted with the inexplicable.

Markham intervened diplomatically.

"Let's have the details of the case, Sergeant. I take it you've questioned the occupants of the house."

"Only in a general way, sir." Heath flung one leg over the corner of the centre-table and relit his dead cigar. "I've been waiting for you to show up. I knew you were acquainted with the old gentleman up-stairs; so I just did the routine things. I put a man out in the alley to see that nobody touches the body till Doc Doremus arrives,*—he'll be here when he finishes lunch.—I phoned the finger-print men before I left the office, and they oughta be on the job any minute now; though I don't see what good they can do. . . ."

"What about the bow that fired the arrow?" put in Vance.

"That was our one best bet; but old Mr. Dillard said he picked it up from the alley and brought it in the house. He probably gummed up any prints it mighta had."

"What have you done about Sperling?" asked Markham.

"I got his address—he lives in a country house up Westchester way—and set a coupla men to bring him here as soon as they could lay hands on him.

* Heath was referring to Doctor Emanuel Doremus, the Chief Medical Examiner of New York.

Then I talked to the two servants—the old fellow that let you in, and his daughter, a middle-aged woman who does the cooking. But neither of 'em seemed to know anything, or else they're acting dumb.—After that I tried to question the young lady of the house." The Sergeant raised his hands in a gesture of irritated despair. "But she was all broke up and crying; so I thought I'd let *you* have the pleasure of interviewing her.—Snitkin and Burke"—he jerked his thumb toward the two detectives by the front window—"went over the basement and the alley and back yard trying to pick up something; but drew a blank.—And that's all I know so far. As soon as Doremus and the finger-print men get here, and after I've had a heart-to-heart talk with Sperling, then I'll get the ball to rolling and clean up the works."

Vance heaved an audible sigh.

"You're so sanguine, Sergeant! Don't be disappointed if your ball turns out to be a parallelopiped that won't roll. There's something deuced oddish about this nursery extravaganza; and, unless all the omens deceive me, you'll be playing blind-man's-bluff for a long time to come."

"Yeh?" Heath gave Vance a look of despondent shrewdness. It was evident he was more or less of the same opinion.

"Don't let Mr. Vance dishearten you, Sergeant," Markham rallied him. "He's permitting his imagination to run away with him." Then with an impatient gesture he turned toward the door. "Let's look over the ground before the others arrive. Later I'll have a talk with Professor Dillard and the other members of the household. And, by the way, Sergeant, you didn't mention Mr. Arnesson. Isn't he at home?"

"He's at the university; but he's expected to return soon."

Markham nodded and followed the Sergeant into the main hall. As we passed down the heavily-carpeted passage to the rear, there was a sound on the staircase, and a clear but somewhat tremulous woman's voice spoke from the semi-darkness above.

"Is that you, Mr. Markham? Uncle thought he recognized your voice. He's waiting for you in the library."

"I'll join your uncle in a very few minutes, Miss Dillard." Markham's tone was paternal and sympathetic. "And please wait with him, for I want to see you, too."

With a murmured acquiescence, the girl disappeared round the head of the stairs.

We moved on to the rear door of the lower hall. Beyond was a narrow passageway terminating in a flight of wooden steps which led to the basement. At the foot of these steps we came into a large, low-ceilinged room with a door giving directly upon the areaway at the west side of the house. This door was slightly ajar, and in the opening stood the man from the Homicide Bureau whom Heath had set to guard the body.

The room had obviously once been a basement storage; but it had been altered and redecorated, and now served as a sort of club-room. The cement floor was covered with fibre rugs, and one entire wall was painted with a panorama of archers throughout the ages. In an oblong panel on the left was a huge illustrated reproduction of an archery range labelled "Ayme for Finsburie Archers—London 1594," showing Bloody House Ridge in one corner, Westminster Hall in the centre, and Welsh Hall in the foreground. There were a piano and a phonograph in the room; numerous comfortable wicker chairs; a varicolored divan; an enormous wicker centre-table littered with all manner of sports magazines; and a small bookcase filled with works on archery. Several targets rested in one corner, their gold discs and concentric chromatic rings making brilliant splashes of color in the sunlight which flooded in from the two rear windows. One wall space near the door was hung with long bows of varying sizes and weights; and near them was a large old-fashioned tool-chest. Above it was suspended a small cupboard, or ascham, strewn with various odds and ends of tackle, such as bracers, shooting-gloves, piles, points of aim, and bow strings. A large oak panel between the door and the west window contained a display of one of the most interesting and varied collections of arrows I had ever seen.

This panel attracted Vance particularly, and adjusting his monocle carefully, he strolled over to it.

"Hunting and war arrows," he remarked. "Most inveiglin'. . . . *Ah!* One of the trophies seems to have disappeared. Taken down with considerable haste, too. The little brass brad that held it in place is shockingly bent."

On the floor stood several quivers filled with target arrows. He leaned over and, withdrawing one, extended it to Markham.

"This frail shaft may not look as if it would penetrate the human breast; but target arrows will drive entirely through a deer at eighty yards. . . . Why, then, the missing hunting arrow from the panel? An interestin' point."

Markham frowned and compressed his lips; and I realized that he had been clinging to the forlorn hope that the tragedy might have been an accident. He tossed the arrow hopelessly on a chair, and walked toward the outer door.

"Let's take a look at the body and the lie of the land," he said gruffly.

As we emerged into the warm spring sunlight a sense of isolation came over me. The narrow paved areaway in which we stood seemed like a canyon between steep stone walls. It was four or five feet below the street level, which was reached by a short flight of steps leading to the gate in the wall. The blank, windowless rear wall of the apartment house opposite extended upwards for 150 feet; and the Dillard house itself, though only four stories high, was the equivalent of six stories gauged by the architectural measurements of to-day. Though we were standing out of doors in the heart of New York, no one could see us except from the few side windows of the Dillard house and from a single bay window of the house on 76th Street, whose rear yard adjoined that of the Dillard grounds.

This other house, we were soon to learn, was owned by a Mrs. Drukker; and it was destined to play a vital and tragic part in the solution of Robin's murder. Several tall willow trees acted as a mask to its rear windows; and only the bay window at the side of the house had an unobstructed view of that part of the areaway in which we stood.

I noticed that Vance had his eye on this bay window, and as he studied it I saw a flicker of interest cross his face. It was not until much later that afternoon that I was able to guess what had caught and held his attention.

The archery range extended from the wall of the Dillard lot on 75th Street all the way to a similar street wall of the Drukker lot on 76th Street, where a butt of hay bales had been erected on a shallow bed of sand. The distance between the two walls was 200 feet, which, as I learned later, made possible a sixty-yard range, thus permitting target practice for all the standard archery events, with the one exception of the York Round for men.

The Dillard lot was 135 feet deep, the depth of the Drukker lot therefore being sixty-five feet. A section of the tall ironwork fence that separated the two rear yards had been removed where it had once transected the space now used for the archery range. At the further end of the range, backing against the western line of the Drukker property, was another tall apartment house occupying the corner of 76th Street and Riverside Drive. Between these two gigantic buildings ran a narrow alleyway, the range end of which was closed with a high board fence in which had been set a small door with a lock.

For purposes of clarity I am incorporating in this record a diagram of the entire scene; for the arrangement of the various topographical and architectural details had a very important bearing on the solution of the crime. I would call attention particularly to the following points:—first, to the little second-story balcony at the rear of the Dillard house, which projects slightly over the archery range; secondly, to the bay window (on the second floor) of the Drukker house, whose southern angle has a view of the entire archery range toward 75th Street; and thirdly, to the alleyway between the two apartment houses, which leads from Riverside Drive into the Dillard rear yard.

The body of Robin lay almost directly outside of the archery-room door. It was on its back, the arms extended, the legs slightly drawn up, the head pointing toward the 76th-Street end of the range. Robin had been a man of perhaps thirty-five, of medium height, and with an incipient corpulency. There was a rotund puffiness to his face, which was smooth-shaven except for a narrow blond moustache. He was clothed in a two-piece sport suit of light gray flannel, a pale-blue silk shirt, and then Oxfords with thick rubber soles. His hat—a pearl-colored felt fedora—was lying near his feet.

Beside the body was a large pool of coagulated blood which had formed in the shape of a huge pointing hand. But the thing which held us all in a spell of fascinated horror was the slender shaft that extended vertically from the left side of the dead man's breast. The arrow protruded perhaps twenty inches, and where it had entered the body there was the large dark stain of the hemorrhage. What made this strange murder seem even more incongruous were the beautifully fletched feathers on the arrow. They had been dyed a bright red; and about the shaftment were two stripes of turquoise blue—giving the arrow a gala appearance. I had a feeling of unreality about the tragedy, as though I were witnessing a scene in a sylvan play for children.

Vance stood looking down at the body with half-closed eyes, his hands in his coat pockets. Despite the apparent indolence of his attitude I could tell that he was keenly alert, and that his mind was busy co-ordinating the factors of the scene before him.

"Dashed queer, that arrow," he commented. "Designed for big game; . . . undoubtedly belongs to that ethnological exhibit we just saw. And a clean hit—directly into the vital spot, between the ribs and without the slightest deflection. Extr'ordin'ry! . . . I say, Markham; such marksmanship isn't human. A chance shot might have done it; but the slayer of this johnny wasn't leaving anything to chance. That powerful hunting arrow, which was obviously wrenched from the panel inside, shows premeditation and design———"

Suddenly he bent over the body. "Ah! Very interestin'. The nock of the arrow

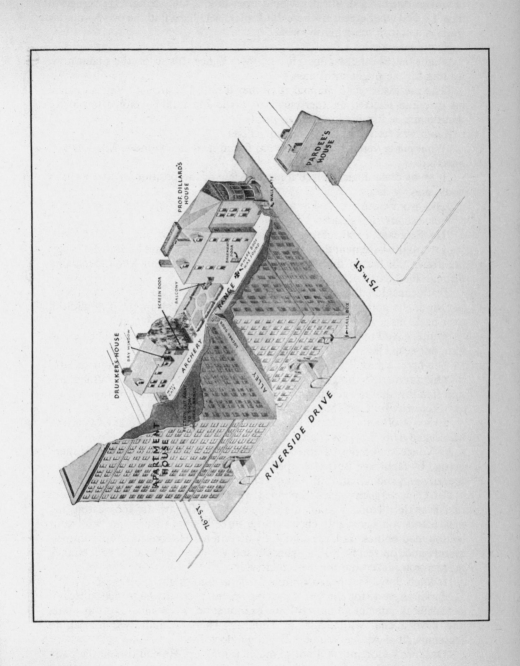

is broken down,—I doubt if it would even hold a taut string." He turned to Heath. "Tell me, Sergeant: where did Professor Dillard find the bow?—not far from that club-room window, what?"

Heath gave a start.

"Right outside the window, in fact, Mr. Vance. It's in on the piano now, waiting for the finger-print men."

"The professor's sign-manual is all they'll find, I'm afraid." Vance opened his case and selected another cigarette. "And I'm rather inclined to believe that the arrow itself is innocent of prints."

Heath was scrutinizing Vance inquisitively.

"What made you think the bow was found near the window, Mr. Vance?" he asked.

"It seemed the logical place for it, in view of the position of Mr. Robin's body, don't y' know."

"Shot from close range, you mean?"

Vance shook his head.

"No, Sergeant. I was referring to the fact that the deceased's feet are pointing toward the basement door, and that, though his arms are extended, his legs are drawn up. Is that the way you'd say a man would fall who'd been shot through the heart?"

Heath considered the point.

"No-o," he admitted. "He'd likely be more crumpled up; or, if he did fall over back, his legs would be straight out and his arms drawn in."

"Quite.—And regard his hat. If he had fallen backwards it would be behind him, not at his feet."

"See here, Vance," Markham demanded sharply; "what's in your mind?"

"Oh, numberless things. But they all boil down to the wholly irrational notion that this defunct gentleman wasn't shot with a bow and arrow at all."

"Then why, in God's name————"

"Exactly! Why the utter insanity of the elaborate stage-setting?—My word, Markham! This business is ghastly."

As Vance spoke the basement door opened, and Doctor Doremus, shepherded by Detective Burke, stepped jauntily into the areaway. He greeted us breezily and shook hands all round. Then he fixed a fretful eye on Heath.

"By Gad, Sergeant!" he complained, pulling his hat down to an even more rakish angle. "I only spend three hours out of the twenty-four eating my meals; and you invariably choose those three hours to worry me with your confounded bodies. You're ruining my digestion." He looked about him petulantly and, on seeing Robin, whistled softly. "For Gad's sake! A nice fancy murder you picked out for me this time!"

He knelt down and began running his practised fingers over the body.

Markham stood for a moment looking on, but presently he turned to Heath.

"While the doctor's busy with his examination, Sergeant, I'll go up-stairs and have a chat with Professor Dillard." Then he addressed himself to Doremus. "Let me see you before you go, doctor."

"Oh, sure." Doremus did not so much as look up. He had turned the body on one side, and was feeling the base of the skull.

3

A PROPHECY RECALLED

(*Saturday, April 2; 1:30 P.M.*)

WHEN WE reached the main hall Captain Dubois and Detective Bellamy, the finger-print experts from Headquarters, were just arriving. Detective Snitkin, who had evidently been watching for them, led them at once toward the base-ment stairs, and Markham, Vance and I went up to the second floor.

The library was a large, luxurious room at least twenty feet deep, occupying the entire width of the building. Two sides of it were lined to the ceiling with great embayed bookcases; and in the centre of the west wall rose a massive bronze Empire fireplace. By the door stood an elaborate Jacobean side-board, and opposite, near the windows which faced on 75th Street, was an enormous carved table-desk, strewn with papers and pamphlets. There were many inter-esting *objets-d'art* in the room; and two diagrammatic Dürers looked down on us from the tapestried panels beside the mantel. All the chairs were spacious and covered with the dark leather.

Professor Dillard sat before the desk, one foot resting on a small tufted ot-toman; and in a corner near the windows, huddled in a sprawling armchair, was his niece, a vigorous, severely tailored girl with strong, chiselled features of classic cast. The old professor did not rise to greet us, and made no apology for the omission. He appeared to take it for granted that we were aware of his disability. The introductions were perfunctory, though Markham gave a brief explanation of Vance's and my presence there.

"I regret, Markham," the professor said, when we had settled ourselves, "that a tragedy should be the reason for this meeting; but it's always good to see you.—I suppose you will want to cross-examine Belle and me. Well, ask anything you care to."

Professor Bertrand Dillard was a man in his sixties, slightly stooped from a sedentary studious life: clean-shaven, and with a marked brachycephalic head surmounted with thick white hair combed pompadour. His eyes, though small, were remarkably intense and penetrating; and the wrinkles about his mouth held that grim pursed expression which often comes with years of con-centration on difficult problems. His features were those of the dreamer and scientist; and, as the world knows, this man's wild dreams of space and time and motion had been actualized into a new foundation of scientific fact. Even now his face reflected an introspective abstraction, as if the death of Robin were but an intrusion upon the inner drama of his thoughts.

Markham hesitated a moment before answering. Then he said with marked deference:

"Suppose, sir, you tell me just what you know of the tragedy. Then I'll put whatever questions I deem essential."

Professor Dillard reached for an old meerschaum pipe on the stand beside him. When he had filled and lighted it he shifted himself more comfortably in his chair.

"I told you practically everything I know over the telephone. Robin and

357

Sperling called this morning about ten o'clock to see Belle. But she had gone to the courts to play tennis, so they waited in the drawing-room down-stairs. I heard them talking there together for half an hour or so before they went to the basement club-room. I remained here reading for perhaps an hour, and then, as the sunshine looked so pleasant, I decided to step out on the balcony at the rear of the house. I had been there about five minutes, I should say, when I chanced to look down on the archery range; and to my horrified amazement I saw Robin lying on his back with an arrowshaft protruding from his breast. I hastened down as quickly as my gout would permit, but I could see at once that the poor fellow was dead; so I immediately telephoned to you. There was no one in the house at the time but old Pyne—the butler—and myself. The cook had gone marketing; Arnesson had left for the university at nine o'clock; and Belle was still out playing tennis. I sent Pyne to look for Sperling, but he was nowhere about; and I came back to the library here to wait for you. Belle returned shortly before your men arrived, and the cook came in a little later. Arnesson won't be back until after two."

"There was no one else here this morning—no strangers or visitors?"

The professor shook his head.

"Only Drukker,—I believe you met him here once. He lives in the house at our rear. He often drops in—mostly, however, to see Arnesson: they have much in common. He's written a book on 'World Lines in Multidimensional Continua.' The man's quite a genius in his way; has the true scientific mind. . . . But when he found that Arnesson was out he sat for a while with me discussing the Brazilian expedition of the Royal Astronomical Society. Then he went home."

"What time was this?"

"About half past nine. Drukker had already gone when Robin and Sperling called."

"Was it unusual, Professor Dillard," asked Vance, "for Mr. Arnesson to be away on Saturday mornings?"

The old professor looked up sharply, and there was a brief hesitation before he answered.

"Not unusual exactly; although he's generally here on Saturdays. But this morning he had some important research work to do for me in the faculty library. . . . Arnesson," he added, "is working with me on my next book."*

There was a short silence; then Markham spoke.

"You said this morning that both Robin and Sperling were suitors for Miss Dillard's hand. . . ."

"Uncle!" The girl sat upright in her chair and turned angry, reproachful eyes upon the old professor. "That wasn't fair."

"But it was true, my dear." His voice was noticeably tender.

"It was true—in a way," she admitted. "But there was no need of mentioning it. You know, as well as they did, how I regarded them. We were good friends—that was all. Only last night, when they were here together, I told

---

* The book referred to by Professor Dillard was the great work which appeared two years later, "The Atomic Structure of Radiant Energy," a mathematical emendation of Planck's quantum theory refuting the classical axiom of the continuity of all physical processes, as contained in Maximus Tyrius' Οὐδὲ ἐνταῦθα ἡ φύσις μοταπῆὸφ δθρόως.

them—quite plainly—that I wouldn't listen to any more silly talk of marriage from either of them. They were only boys . . . and now one of them's gone. . . . Poor Cock Robin!" She strove bravely to stifle her emotion.

Vance raised his eyebrows and leaned forward.

" 'Cock Robin'?"

"Oh, we all called him that. We did it to tease him, because he didn't like the nickname."

"The sobriquet was inevitable," Vance observed sympathetically. "And it was rather a nice nickname, don't y' know. The original Cock Robin was loved by 'all the birds of the air,' and they all mourned his passing." He watched the girl closely as he spoke.

"I know," she nodded. "I told him that once.—And every one liked Joseph, too. You couldn't help liking him. He was so—so goodhearted and kind."

Vance again settled back in his chair; and Markham continued his questioning.

"You mentioned, professor, that you heard Robin and Sperling talking in the drawing-room. Could you hear any of their conversation?"

The old man shot a sidelong glance at his niece.

"Does that question really matter, Markham?" he asked, after a moment's hesitation.

"It may have some very vital bearing on the situation."

"Perhaps." The professor drew on his pipe thoughtfully. "On the other hand, if I answer it I may give an erroneous impression, and do a grave injustice to the living."

"Can you not trust me to judge that point?" Markham's voice had become at once grave and urgent.

There was another short silence, broken by the girl.

"Why don't you tell Mr. Markham what you heard, uncle? What harm can it do?"

"I was thinking of you, Belle," the professor answered softly. "But perhaps you are right." He looked up reluctantly. "The fact is, Markham, Robin and Sperling were having some angry words over Belle. I heard only a little, but I gathered that each regarded the other as being guilty of playing unfair—of standing in each other's way. . . ."

"Oh! They didn't mean it," Miss Dillard interpolated vehemently. "They were always ragging each other. There *was* a little jealousy between them but I wasn't the real cause of it. It was their archery records. You see, Raymond—Mr. Sperling—used to be the better shot; but this last year Joseph beat him at several meets, and at our last annual tournament he became the club's Champion Archer."

"And Sperling thought, perhaps," added Markham, "that he had correspondingly fallen in your estimation."

"That's absurd!" the girl retorted hotly.

"I think, my dear, we can leave the matter safely in Mr. Markham's hands," Professor Dillard said mollifyingly. Then to Markham: "Were there any other questions you cared to ask?"

"I'd like to know anything you can tell me about Robin and Sperling—who they are; their associations; and how long you have known them."

"I think that Belle can enlighten you better than I. Both boys belonged to her set. I saw them only occasionally."

Markham turned inquiringly to the girl.

"I've known both of them for years," she said promptly. "Joseph was eight or ten years older than Raymond, and lived in England up to five years ago, when his father and mother both died. He came to America, and took bachelor quarters on the Drive. He had considerable money, and lived idly, devoting himself to fishing and hunting and other outdoor sports. He went about in society a little, and was a nice, comfortable friend who'd always fill in at a dinner or make a fourth hand at bridge. There was nothing really much to him—in an intellectual way, you understand. . . ."

She paused, as if her remarks were in some way disloyal to the dead, and Markham, sensing her feelings, asked simply:

"And Sperling?"

"He's the son of a wealthy manufacturer of something or other—retired now. They live in Scarsdale in a beautiful country home,—our archery club has its regular ranges there,—and Raymond is a consulting engineer for some firm down-town; though I imagine he works merely to placate his father, for he only goes to the office two or three days a week. He's a graduate of Boston Tech, and I met him when he was a sophomore, home on vacation. Raymond will never set the world afire, Mr. Markham; but he's really an awfully fine type of American young man—sincere, jolly, a little bashful, and perfectly straight."

It was easy to picture both Robin and Sperling from the girl's brief descriptions; and it was correspondingly difficult to connect either of them with the sinister tragedy that had brought us to the house.

Markham sat frowning for a while. Finally he lifted his head and looked straight at the girl.

"Tell me, Miss Dillard: have you any theory or explanation that might, in any way, account for the death of Mr. Robin?"

"No!" The word fairly burst from her. "Who could want to kill Cock Robin? He hadn't an enemy in the world. The whole thing is incredible. I couldn't believe it had happened until I went and—and saw for myself. Even then it didn't seem real."

"Still, my dear child," put in Professor Dillard, "the man was killed; so there must have been something in his life that you didn't know or suspect. We're constantly finding new stars that the old-time astronomers didn't believe existed."

"I can't believe Joseph had an enemy," she retorted. "I won't believe it. It's too utterly absurd."

"You think then," asked Markham, "that it's unlikely Sperling was in any way responsible for Robin's death?"

"Unlikely?" The girls' eyes flashed. "It's impossible!"

"And yet, y' know, Miss Dillard,"—it was Vance who now spoke in his lazy casual tone—"*Sperling* means 'sparrow'."

The girl sat immobile. Her face had gone deathly pale, and her hands tightened over the arms of the chair. Then slowly, and as if with great difficulty, she nodded, and her breast began to rise and fall with her labored breathing. Suddenly she shuddered and pressed her handkerchief to her face.

"I'm afraid!" she whispered.

Vance rose and, going to her, touched her comfortingly on the shoulder.

"Why are you afraid?"

She looked up and met his eyes. They seemed to reassure her, for she forced a pitiful smile.

"Only the other day," she said, in a strained voice, "we were all on the archery range down-stairs; and Raymond was just preparing to shoot a single American Round, when Joseph opened the basement door and stepped out on the range. There really wasn't any danger, but Sigurd—Mr. Arnesson, you know—was sitting on the little rear balcony watching us; and when I cried 'He! He!' jokingly to Joseph, Sigurd leaned over and said: 'You don't know what a chance you're running, young man. You're a Cock Robin, and that archer's a sparrow; and you remember what happened to your namesake when a Mr. Sparrow wielded the bow and arrow'—or something like that. No one paid much attention to it at the time. But now! . . ." Her voice trailed off into an awed murmur.

"Come, Belle; don't be morbid." Professor Dillard spoke consolingly, but not without impatience. "It was merely one of Sigurd's ill-timed witticisms. You know he's continually sneering and jesting at realities: it's about the only outlet he has from his constant application to abstractions."

"I suppose so," the girl answered. "Of course, it was only a joke. But now it seems like some terrible prophecy.—Only," she hastened to add, "Raymond *couldn't* have done it."

As she spoke the library door opened suddenly, and a tall gaunt figure appeared on the threshold.

"Sigurd!" Belle Dillard's startled exclamation held an undeniable note of relief.

Sigurd Arnesson, Professor Dillard's protégé and adopted son, was a man of striking appearance—over six feet tall, wiry and erect, with a head which, at first view, appeared too large for his body. His almost yellow hair was unkempt, like a schoolboy's; his nose was aquiline; and his jowls were lean and muscular. Though he could not have been over forty, there was a net-work of lines in his face. His expression was sardonically puckish; but the intense intellectual passion that lighted his blue-gray eyes belied any superficiality of nature. My initial reaction to his personality was one of liking and respect. There were depths in the man—powerful potentialities and high capabilities.

As he entered the room that afternoon, his searching eyes took us all in with a swift, inquisitive glance. He nodded jerkily to Miss Dillard, and then fixed the old professor with a look of dry amusement.

"What, pray, has happened in this three-dimensional house? Wagons and populace without: a guardian at the portals . . . and when I finally overcame the Cerberus and was admitted by Pyne, two plainclothes men hustled me up here without ceremony or explanation. Very amusing, but disconcerting. . . . Ah! I seem to recognize the District Attorney. Good morning—or rather, afternoon—, Mr. Markham."

Before Markham could return this belated greeting Belle Dillard spoke.

"Sigurd, please be serious.—Mr. Robin has been killed."

" 'Cock Robin,' you mean. Well, well! With such a name what could the beggar expect?" He appeared wholly unmoved by the news. "Who, or what, returned him to the elements?"

"As to who it was, we don't know." It was Markham who answered, in a tone of reproach for the other's levity. "But Mr. Robin was killed with an arrow through the heart."

"Most fitting." Arnesson sat down on the arm of a chair and extended his long legs. "What could be more appropriate than that Cock Robin should die from an arrow shot from the bow of———"

"Sigurd!" Belle Dillard cut him short. "Haven't you joked enough about that? You *know* that Raymond didn't do it."

"Of course, sis." The man looked at her somewhat wistfully. "I was thinking of Mr. Robin's ornithological progenitor." He turned slowly to Markham. "So it's a real murder mystery, is it—with a corpse, and clews, and all the trappings? May I be entrusted with the tale?"

Markham gave him a brief outline of the situation, to which he listened with rapt interest. When the account was ended he asked:

"Was there no bow found on the range?"

"Ah!" Vance, for the first time since the man's arrival, roused himself from seeming lethargy, and answered for Markham. "A most pertinent question, Mr. Arnesson.—Yes, a bow was found just outside of the basement window, barely ten feet from the body."

"That of course simplifies matters," said Arnesson, with a note of disappointment. "It's only a question now of taking the finger-prints."

"Unfortunately the bow has been handled," explained Markham. "Professor Dillard picked it up and brought it into the house."

Arnesson turned to the older man curiously.

"What impulse, sir, directed you to do that?"

"Impulse? My dear Sigurd, I didn't analyze my emotions. But it struck me that the bow was a vital piece of evidence, and I placed it in the basement as a precautionary measure until the police arrived."

Arnesson made a wry face and cocked one eye humorously.

"That sounds like what our psychoanalytic friends would call a suppression-censor explanation. I wonder what submerged idea was actually in your mind. . . ."

There was a knock at the door, and Burke put his head inside.

"Doc Doremus is waiting for you down-stairs, Chief. He's finished his examination."

Markham rose and excused himself.

"I sha'n't bother you people any more just at present. There's considerable preliminary routine work to be done. But I must ask you to remain upstairs for the time being. I'll see you again before I go."

Doremus was teetering impatiently on his toes when we joined him in the drawing-room.

"Nothing complicated about it," he began, before Markham had a chance to speak. "Our sporty friend was killed by an arrow with a mighty sharp point entering his heart through the fourth intercostal space. Lot of force behind it. Plenty of hemorrhage inside and out. He's been dead about two hours, I should say, making the time of his death around half past eleven. That's only guesswork, however. No signs of a struggle—no marks on his clothes or abrasions on his hands. Death supervened most likely without his knowing what it was all about. He got a nasty bump, though, where his head hit the rough cement when he fell. . . ."

"Now, that's very interestin'." Vance's drawling voice cut in on the Medical Examiner's staccato report. "How serious a 'bump' was it, Doctor?"

Doremus blinked and eyed Vance with some astonishment.

"Bad enough to fracture the skull. I couldn't feel it, of course; but there was a large hæmatoma over the occipital region, dried blood in the nostrils and the ears, and unequal pupils, indicating a fracture of the vault. I'll know more about it after the autopsy." He turned back to the District Attorney. "Anything else?"

"I think not, Doctor. Only let us have your *post-mortem* report as soon as possible."

"You'll have it to-night. The Sergeant's already phoned for the wagon." And shaking hands with all of us, he hurried away.

Heath had stood glowering on the background.

"Well, that don't get us anywheres, sir," he complained, chewing viciously on his cigar.

"Don't be downhearted, Sergeant," Vance chided him. "That blow on the back of the head is worthy of your profoundest consideration. I'm of the opinion it wasn't entirely due to the fall, don't y' know."

The Sergeant was unimpressed by this observation.

"What's more, Mr. Markham," he went on, "there wasn't any finger-prints on either the bow or the arrow. Dubois says they looked as though they'd both been wiped clean. There were a few smears on the end of the bow where the old gentleman picked it up; but not another sign of a print."

Markham smoked a while in gloomy silence.

"What about the handle on the gate leading to the street? And the knob on the door to the alley between the apartment houses?"

"Nothing!" Heath snorted his disgust. "Both of rough, rusty iron that wouldn't take a print."

"I say, Markham," observed Vance; "you're going at this thing the wrong way. Naturally there'd be no finger-prints. Really, y' know, one doesn't carefully produce a playlet and then leave all the stage props in full view of the audience. What we've got to learn is why this particular impresario decided to indulge in silly theatricals."

"It ain't as easy as all that, Mr. Vance," submitted Heath bitterly.

"Did I intimate it was easy? No, Sergeant; it's deucedly difficult. And it's worse than difficult: it's subtle and obscure and . . . fiendish."

4

A MYSTERIOUS NOTE

(*Saturday, April 2; 2 P.M.*)

MARKHAM SAT down resolutely before the centre-table.

"Suppose, Sergeant, we overhaul the two servants now."

Heath stepped into the hall and gave an order to one of his men. A few moments later a tall, sombre, disjointed man entered and stood at respectful attention.

"This is the butler, sir," explained the Sergeant. "Named Pyne."

Markham studied the man appraisingly. He was perhaps sixty years old. His features were markedly acromegalic; and this distortion extended to his entire figure. His hands were large, and his feet broad and misshapen. His clothes, though neatly pressed, fitted him badly; and his high clerical collar was several sizes too large for him. His eyes, beneath gray, bushy eyebrows, were pale and watery, and his mouth was a mere slit in an unhealthily puffy face. Despite his utter lack of physical prepossession, however, he gave one the impression of shrewd competency.

"So you are the Dillard butler," mused Markham. "How long have you been with the family, Pyne?"

"Going on ten years, sir."

"You came, then, just after Professor Dillard resigned his chair at the university?"

"I believe so, sir." The man's voice was deep and rumbling.

"What do you know of the tragedy that occurred here this morning?" Though Markham put the question suddenly, in the hope, I imagine, of surprising some admission, Pyne received it with the utmost stoicism.

"Nothing whatever, sir. I was unaware that anything had happened until Professor Dillard called to me from the library and asked me to look for Mr. Sperling."

"He told you of the tragedy then?"

"He said: 'Mr. Robin has been murdered, and I wish you'd find Mr. Sperling for me.'—That was all, sir."

"You're sure he said 'murdered,' Pyne?" interjected Vance.

For the first time the butler hesitated, and an added astuteness crept into his look.

"Yes, sir—I'm sure he did. 'Murdered' is what he said."

"And did you see the body of Mr. Robin when you pushed your search?" pursued Vance, his eyes idly tracing a design on the wall.

Again there was a brief hesitation.

"Yes, sir. I opened the basement door to look out on the archery range, and there I saw the poor young gentleman. . . ."

"A great shock it must have given you, Pyne," Vance observed drily. "Did you, by any hap, touch the poor young gentleman's body?—or the arrow, perhaps?—or the bow?"

Pyne's watery eyes glistened for a moment.

"No—of course not, sir. . . . Why should I, sir?"

"Why, indeed?" Vance sighed wearily. "But you saw the bow?"

The man squinted, as if for purposes of mental visualization.

"I couldn't say, sir. Perhaps, yes; perhaps, no. I don't recall."

Vance seemed to lose all interest in him; and Markham resumed the interrogation.

"I understand, Pyne, that Mr. Drukker called here this morning about half past nine. Did you see him?"

"Yes, sir. He always uses the basement door; and he said good-morning to me as he passed the butler's pantry at the head of the steps."

"He returned the same way he came?"

"I suppose so, sir—though I was up-stairs when he went. He lives in the house at the rear————"

"I know." Markham leaned forward. "I presume it was you who admitted Mr. Robin and Mr. Sperling this morning."

"Yes, sir. At about ten o'clock."

"Did you see them again, or overhear any of their remarks while they waited here in the drawingroom?"

"No, sir. I was busy in Mr. Arnesson's quarters most of the morning."

"Ah!" Vance turned his eyes on the man. "That would be on the second floor rear, wouldn't it?—the room with the balcony?"

"Yes, sir."

"Most interestin'. . . . And it was from that balcony that Professor Dillard first saw Mr. Robin's body.—How could he have entered the room without your knowing it? You said, I believe, that your first intimation of the tragedy was when the professor called you from the library and told you to seek Mr. Sperling."

The butler's face turned a pasty white, and I noticed that his fingers twitched nervously.

"I might have stepped out of Mr. Arnesson's room for a moment," he explained, with effort. "Yes—it's quite likely. In fact, sir, I recall going to the linen closet. . . ."

"Oh, to be sure." Vance lapsed into lethargy.

Markham smoked a while, his gaze concentrated on the table-top.

"Did any one else call at the house this morning, Pyne?" he asked presently.

"No one, sir."

"And you can suggest no explanation for what happened here?"

The man shook his head heavily, his watery eyes in space.

"No, sir. Mr. Robin seemed a pleasant, well-liked young man. He wasn't the kind to inspire murder—if you understand what I mean."

Vance looked up.

"I can't say that I, personally, understand exactly what you mean, Pyne. How do you know it wasn't an accident?"

"I don't, sir," was the unperturbed answer. "But I know a bit about archery—if you'll pardon my saying so—and I saw right away that Mr. Robin had been killed by a hunting arrow."

"You're very observin', Pyne," nodded Vance. "And quite correct."

It was plain that no direct information was to be got from the butler, and Markham dismissed him abruptly, at the same time ordering Heath to send in the cook.

When she entered I noticed at once a resemblance between father and daughter. She was a slatternly woman of about forty, also tall and angular, with a thin, elongated face and large hands and feet. Hyperpituitarism evidently ran in the Pyne family.

A few preliminary questions brought out the information that she was a widow, named Beedle, and had, at the death of her husband five years before, come to Professor Dillard as the result of Pyne's recommendation.

"What time did you leave the house this morning, Beedle?" Markham asked her.

"Right after half past ten." She seemed uneasy and on the alert, and her voice was defensively belligerent.

"And what time did you return?"

"About half past twelve. That man let me in"—she looked viciously at Heath—"and treated me like I'd been a criminal."

Heath grinned. "The time's O. K., Mr. Markham. She got sore because I wouldn't let her go down-stairs."

Markham nodded non-committally.

"Do you know anything of what took place here this morning?" he went on, studying the woman closely.

"How should I know? I was at Jefferson market."

"Did you see either Mr. Robin or Mr. Sperling?"

"They went down-stairs to the archery-room past the kitchen a little while before I went out."

"Did you overhear anything they said?"

"I don't listen at keyholes."

Markham set his jaw angrily and was about to speak when Vance addressed the woman suavely.

"The District Attorney thought that perhaps the door was open, and that you might have overheard some of their conversation despite your commendable effort not to listen."

"The door might've been open, but I didn't hear anything," she answered sullenly.

"Then you couldn't tell us if there was any one else in the archery-room."

Beedle narrowed her eyes and gave Vance a calculating look.

"Maybe there was some one else," she said slowly. "In fact, I thought I heard Mr. Drukker." A note of venom came into her voice, and the shadow of a hard smile passed over her thin lips. "He was here to call on Mr. Arnesson early this morning."

"Oh, was he, now?" Vance appeared surprised at this news. "You saw him perhaps?"

"I saw him come in, but I didn't see him go out—anyway, I didn't notice. He sneaks in and out at all hours."

"Sneaks, eh? Fancy that! . . . By the by, which door did you use when you went a-marketing?"

"The front door. Since Miss Belle made a clubroom out of the basement, I always use the front door."

"Then you didn't enter the archery-room this morning?"

"No."

Vance raised himself in his chair.

"Thanks for your help, Beedle. We won't need you any more now."

When the woman had left us Vance rose and walked to the window.

"We're expending too much zeal in irrelevant channels, Markham," he said. "We'll never get anywhere by ballyragging servants and questioning members of the household. There's a psychological wall to be battered down before we can begin storming the enemy's trenches. Everybody in this ménage has some pet privacy that he's afraid will leak out. Each person so far has told us either less or more than he knows. Disheartenin', but true. Nothing that we've learned dovetails with anything else; and when chronological events don't fit together, you may rest assured that the serrated points of contact have been deliberately distorted. I haven't found one clean joinder in all the tales that have been poured into our ears."

"It's more likely the connections are missing," Markham argued; "and we'll never find them if we don't pursue our questionings."

"You're much too trustin'." Vance walked back to the centre-table. "The more questions we ask the farther afield we'll be taken. Even Professor Dillard didn't give us a wholly honest account. There's something he's keeping back—some suspicion he won't voice. Why did he bring that bow indoors? Arnesson put his finger on a vital spot when he asked the same question. Shrewd fella, Arnesson.—Then there's our athletic young lady with the muscular calves. She's entangled in various amat'ry meshes, and is endeavoring to extricate herself and her whole coterie without leaving a blemish on any one. A praiseworthy aim, but not one conducive to the un-adulterated truth.—Pyne has ideas, too. That flabby facial mask of his cur-tains many an entrancin' thought. But we'll never probe his cortex by chivyin' him with questions. Somethin' rum, too, about his matutinal labors. He says he was in Arnesson's room all morning; but he obviously didn't know that the professor took a sunnin' on Arnesson's verandah. And that linen-closet alibi—much too specious.—Also, Markham, let your mind flutter about the widowed Beedle's tale. She doesn't like the over-sociable Mr. Drukker; and when she saw a chance to involve him, she did so. She 'thought' she heard his voice in the archery-room. But did she? Who knows? True, he might have tarried among the slings and javelins on his way home and been joined later by Robin and Sperling. . . . Yes, it's a point we must investigate. In fact, a bit of polite converse with Mr. Drukker is strongly indicated. . . ."

Footsteps were heard descending the front stairs, and Arnesson appeared in the archway of the livingroom.

"Well, who killed Cock Robin?" he asked, with a satyr-like grin.

Markham rose, annoyed, and was about to protest at the intrusion; but Ar-nesson held up his hand.

"One moment, please. I'm here to offer my exalted services in the noble cause of justice—mundane justice, I would have you understand. Philosophi-cally, of course, there's no such thing as justice. If there really were justice we'd all be in for a shingling in the cosmic wood-shed." He sat down facing Markham and chuckled cynically. "The fact is, the sad and precipitate depar-ture of Mr. Robin appeals to my scientific nature. It makes a nice, orderly problem. It has a decidedly mathematical flavor—no undistributed terms, you understand; clear-cut integers with certain unknown quantities to be deter-mined.—Well, I'm the genius to solve it."

"What would be your solution, Arnesson?" Markham knew and respected the man's intelligence, and seemed at once to sense a serious purpose beneath his attitude of sneering flippancy.

"Ah! As yet I haven't tackled the equation." Arnesson drew out an old briar pipe and fingered it affectionately. "But I've always wanted to do a little de-tective work on a purely earthly plane—the insatiable curiosity and natural inquisitiveness of the physicist, you understand. And I've long had a theory that the science of mathematics can be advantageously applied to the trivialities of our life on this unimportant planet. There's nothing but law in the universe—unless Eddington is right and there's no law at all—and I see no sufficient reason why the identity and position of a criminal can't be determined just as Leverrier calculated the mass and ephemeris of Neptune from the observed deviations in the orbit of Uranus. You remember how, after his computations, he told Galle, the Berlin astronomer, to look for the planet in a specified longitude of the ecliptic."

Arnesson paused and filled his pipe.

"Now, Mr. Markham," he went on; and I tried to decide whether or not the man was in earnest, "I'd like the opportunity of applying to this absurd muddle the purely rational means used by Leverrier in discovering Neptune. But I've got to have the data on the perturbations of Uranus's orbit, so to speak—that is, I must know all the varying factors in the equation. The favor I've come here to ask is that you take me into your confidence and tell me all the facts. A sort of intellectual partnership. I'll figure out this problem for you along scientific lines. It'll be bully sport; and incidentally I'd like to prove my theory that mathematics is the basis of all truth however far removed from scholastic abstractions." He at last got his pipe going, and sank back in his chair. "Is it a bargain?"

"I'll be glad to tell you whatever we know, Arnesson," Markham replied after a brief pause. "But I can't promise to reveal everything that may arise from now on. It might work against the ends of justice and embarrass our investigation."

Vance had sat with half-closed eyes, apparently bored by Arnesson's astonishing request; but now he turned to Markham with a considerable show of animation.

"I say, y' know; there's really no reason why we shouldn't give Mr. Arnesson a chance to translate this crime into the realm of applied mathematics. I'm sure he'd be discreet and use our information only for scientific purposes. And—one never knows, does one?—we may need his highly trained assistance before we're through with this fascinatin' affair."

Markham knew Vance well enough to realize that his suggestion had not been made thoughtlessly; and I was in no wise astonished when he faced Arnesson and said:

"Very well, then. We'll give you whatever data you need to work out your mathematical formula. Anything special you want to know now?"

"Oh, no. I know the details thus far as well as you; and I'll strip Beedle and old Pyne of their contributions when you're gone. But if I solve this problem and determine the exact position of the criminal, don't pigeon-hole my findings as Sir George Airy did those of poor Adams when he submitted his Neptunean calculations prior to Leverrier's. . . ."

At this moment the front door opened, and the uniformed officer stationed on the porch came in, followed by a stranger.

"This gent here says he wants to see the professor," he announced with radiating suspicion; and turning to the man he indicated Markham with a gesture of the head. "That's the District Attorney. Tell him your troubles."

The newcomer seemed somewhat embarrassed. He was a slender, well-groomed man with an unmistakable air of refinement. His age, I should say, was fifty, though his face held a perennially youthful look. His hair was thin and graying, his nose a trifle sharp, and his chin small but in no way weak. His eyes, surmounted by a high broad forehead, were his most striking characteristic. They were the eyes of a disappointed and disillusioned dreamer—half sad, half resentful, as if life had tricked him and left him unhappy and bitter.

He was about to address Markham when he caught sight of Arnesson.

"Oh, good-morning, Arnesson," he said, in a quiet, well-modulated voice. "I hope there's nothing seriously wrong."

"A mere death, Pardee," the other replied carelessly. "The proverbial tempest in a teapot."

Markham was annoyed at the interruption.

"What can I do for you, sir?" he asked.

"I trust I am not intruding," the man apologized. "I am a friend of the family,—I live just across the street; and I perceived that something unusual had happened here. It occurred to me I might be of some service."

Arnesson chuckled. "My dear Pardee! Why clothe your natural curiosity in the habiliments of rhetoric?"

Pardee blushed.

"I assure you, Arnesson————" he began; but Vance interrupted him.

"You say you live opposite, Mr. Pardee. You have perhaps been observing this house during the forenoon?"

"Hardly that, sir. My study, however, overlooks 75th Street, and it's true I was sitting at the window most of the morning. But I was busy writing. When I returned to my work from lunch I noticed the crowd and the police cars and also the officer in uniform at the door."

Vance had been studying him from the corner of his eye.

"Did you happen to see any one enter or leave this house this morning, Mr. Pardee?" he asked.

The man shook his head slowly.

"No one in particular. I noticed two young men—friends of Miss Dillard—call at about ten o'clock; and I saw Beedle go out with her market basket. But that's all I recall."

"Did you see either of these young men depart?"

"I don't remember." Pardee knit his brows. "And yet it seems to me one of them left by the range gate. But it's only an impression."

"What time would that have been?"

"Really, I couldn't say. Perhaps an hour or so after his arrival. I wouldn't care to be more specific."

"You recall no other person whatever either coming or going from the house this morning?"

"I saw Miss Dillard return from the tennis courts about half past twelve, just as I was called to lunch. In fact, she waved her racket to me."

"And no one else?"

"I'm afraid not." There was unmistakable regret in his quiet response.

"One of the young men you saw enter here has been killed," Vance told him.

"Mr. Robin—*alias* Cock Robin," supplemented Arnesson, with a comic grimace which affected me unpleasantly.

"Good Heavens! How unfortunate!" Pardee appeared genuinely shocked. "Robin? Wasn't he the Champion Archer of Belle's club?"

"His one claim to immortality.—That's the chap."

"Poor Belle!" Something in the man's manner caused Vance to regard him sharply. "I hope she's not too greatly upset by the tragedy."

"She's dramatizing it, naturally," Arnesson returned. "So are the police, for that matter. Awful pother about nothing in particular. The earth is covered with 'small crawling masses of impure carbohydrates' like Robin—referred to in the aggregate as humanity."

Pardee smiled with tolerant sadness,—he was obviously familiar with Arnesson's cynicisms. Then he appealed to Markham.

"May I be permitted to see Miss Dillard and her uncle?"

"Oh, by all means." It was Vance who answered before Markham could reach a decision. "You'll find them in the library, Mr. Pardee."

The man left the room with a polite murmur of thanks.

"Queer fellow," commented Arnesson, when Pardee was out of hearing. "Cursed with money. Leads an indolent life. His one passion is solving chess problems. . . ."

"Chess?" Vance looked up with interest. "Is he, by any chance, John Pardee, the inventor of the famous Pardee gambit?"

"The same." Arnesson's face crinkled humorously. "Spent twenty years developing a cast-iron offensive that was to add new decimal points to the game. Wrote a book about it. Then went forth proselytizing like a crusader before the gates of Damascus. He's always been a great patron of chess, contributing to tournaments, and scurrying round the world to attend the various chess jousting-bouts. Consequently was able to get his gambit tested. It made a great stir among the infra-champions of the Manhattan Chess Club. Then poor Pardee organized a series of Masters Tournaments. Paid all the expenses himself. Cost him a fortune, by the way. And of course he stipulated that the Pardee gambit be played exclusively. Well, well, it was very sad. When men like Doctor Lasker and Capablanca and Rubinstein and Finn got to combating it, it went to pieces. Almost every player who used it lost. It was disqualified—even worse than the ill-fated Rice gambit. Terrible blow for Pardee. It put snow in his hair, and took all the rubber out of his muscles. Aged him, in short. He's a broken man."

"I know the history of the gambit," murmured Vance, his eyes resting pensively on the ceiling. "I've used it myself. Edward Lasker* taught it to me. . . ."

The uniformed officer again appeared in the archway and beckoned to Heath. The Sergeant rose with alacrity—the ramifications of chess obviously bored him—and went into the hall. A moment later he returned bearing a small sheet of paper.

"Here's a funny one, sir," he said, handing it to Markham. "The officer outside happened to see it sticking outa the mail-box just now, and thought he'd take a peep at it.—What do you make of it, sir?"

Markham studied it with puzzled amazement, and then without a word handed it to Vance. I rose and looked over his shoulder. The paper was of the conventional typewriter size, and had been folded to fit into the mail-box. It contained several lines of typing done on a machine with élite characters and a faded blue ribbon.

---

* The American chess master—sometimes confused with Doctor Emanuel Lasker, the former world champion.

The first line read:

Joseph Cochrane Robin is dead.

The second line asked:

Who Killed Cock Robin?

Underneath was typed:

Sperling means sparrow.

And in the lower right-hand corner—the place of the signature—were the two words, in capitals:

THE BISHOP.

5

A WOMAN'S SCREAM

(Saturday, April 2; 2:30 P.M.)

VANCE, AFTER glancing at the strange message with its even stranger signature, reached for his monocle with that slow deliberation which I knew indicated a keen suppressed interest. Having adjusted the glass he studied the paper intently. Then he handed it to Arnesson.

"Here's a valuable factor for your equation." His eyes were fixed banteringly on the man.

Arnesson regarded the note superciliously, and with a wry grimace laid it on the table.

"I trust the clergy are not involved in this problem. They're notoriously unscientific. One can't attack them with mathematics. 'The Bishop' . . . ," he mused. "I'm unacquainted with any gentlemen of the cloth.—I think I'll rule out this abracadabra when making my calculations."

"If you do, Mr. Arnesson," replied Vance seriously, "your equation, I fear, will fall to pieces. That cryptic epistle strikes me as rather significant. Indeed—if you will pardon a mere lay opinion—I believe it is the most mathematical thing that has appeared thus far in the case. It relieves the situation of all haphazardness or accident. It's the g, so to speak—the gravitational constant which will govern all our equations."

Heath had stood looking down on the typewritten paper with solemn disgust.

"Some crank wrote this, Mr. Vance," he declared.

"Undoubtedly a crank, Sergeant," agreed Vance. "But don't overlook the fact that this particular crank must have known many interestin' and intimate details—to wit, that Mr. Robin's middle name was Cochrane; that the gentleman had been killed with a bow and arrow; and that Mr. Sperling was in the vicinity at the time of the Robin's passing. Moreover, this well-informed crank must have had what amounted to foreknowledge regarding the murder; for the note was obviously typed and inserted in the letter-box before you and your men arrived on the scene."

"Unless," countered Heath doggedly, "he's one of those bimboes out in the street, who got wise to what had happened and then stuck this paper in the box when the officer's back was turned."

"Having first run home and carefully typewritten his communication—eh, what?" Vance shook his head with a rueful smile. "No, Sergeant, I'm afraid your theory won't do."

"Then what in hell does it mean?" Heath demanded truculently.

"I haven't the foggiest idea." Vance yawned and rose. "Come, Markham, let's while away a few brief moments with this Mr. Drukker whom Beedle abhors."

"Drukker!" exclaimed Arnesson, with considerable surprise. "Where does he fit in?"

"Mr. Drukker," explained Markham, "called here this morning to see you; and it's barely possible he met Robin and Sperling before he returned home." He hesitated. "Would you care to accompany us?"

"No, thanks." Arnesson knocked out his pipe and got up. "I've a pile of class papers to look over.—It might be as well, however, to take Belle along. Lady Mae's a bit peculiar. . . ."

"Lady Mae?"

"My mistake. Forgot you didn't know her. We all call her Lady Mae. Courtesy title. Pleases the poor old soul. I'm referring to Drukker's mother. Odd character." He tapped his forehead significantly. "Bit touched. Oh, perfectly harmless. Bright as a whistle, but monominded, as it were. Thinks the sun rises and sets in Drukker. Mothers him as if he were an infant. Sad situation. . . . Yes, you'd better take Belle along. Lady Mae likes Belle."

"A good suggestion, Mr. Arnesson," said Vance. "Will you ask Miss Dillard if she'll be good enough to accompany us?"

"Oh, certainly." Arnesson gave us an inclusive smile of farewell—a smile which seemed at once patronizing and satirical—and went up-stairs. A few moments later Miss Dillard joined us.

"Sigurd tells me you want to see Adolph. He, of course, won't mind; but poor Lady Mae gets so upset over even the littlest things. . . ."

"We sha'n't upset her, I hope." Vance spoke reassuringly. "But Mr. Drukker was here this morning, d' ye see; and the cook says she thought she heard him speaking to Mr. Robin and Mr. Sperling in the archery-room. He may be able to help us."

"I'm sure he will if he can," the girl answered with emphasis. "But be very careful with Lady Mae, won't you?"

There was a pleading, protective note in her voice, and Vance regarded her curiously.

"Tell us something of Mrs. Drukker—or Lady Mae—before we visit her. Why should we be so careful?"

"She's had such a tragic life," the girl explained. "She was once a great singer—oh, not just a second-rate artist, but a prima donna with a marvelous career before her.* She married a leading critic of Vienna—Otto

---

* Mae Brenner will still be remembered by Continental music lovers. Her début was made at the unprecedented age of twenty-three as *Sulamith* in "Die Königin von Saba" at the Imperial Opera House in Vienna; although her greatest success was perhaps her *Desdemona* in "Otello"—the last rôle she sang before her retirement.

Drucker*—and four years later Adolph was born. Then one day in the Wiener Prater, when the baby was two years old, she let him fall; and from that moment on her entire life was changed. Adolph's spine was injured, and he became a cripple. Lady Mae was heartbroken. She held herself to blame for his injury, and gave up her career to devote herself to his care. When her husband died a year later she brought Adolph to America, where she had spent some of her girlhood, and bought the house where she now lives. Her whole life has been centred on Adolph, who grew up a hunchback. She has sacrificed everything for him, and cares for him as though he were a baby...." A shadow crossed her face. "Sometimes I think—we all think—that she still imagines he's only a child. She has become—well, morbid about it. But it's the sweet, terrible morbidity of a tremendous motherlove—a sort of insanity of tenderness, uncle calls it. During the past few months she has grown very strange—and peculiar. I've often found her crooning old German lullabies and kindergarten songs, with her arms crossed on her breast, as if—oh, it seems so sacred and so terrible!—as if she were holding a baby.... And she has become frightfully jealous of Adolph. She's resentful of all other men. Only last week I took Mr. Sperling to see her—we often drop in to call on her: she seems so lonely and unhappy—and she looked at him almost fiercely, and said: 'Why weren't you a cripple, too?' ..."

The girl paused and searched our faces.

"Now don't you understand why I asked you to be careful? ... Lady Mae may think we have come to harm Adolph."

"We sha'n't add unnecessarily to her suffering," Vance assured her sympathetically. Then, as we moved toward the hall, he asked her a question which recalled to my mind his brief intent scrutiny of the Drukker house earlier that afternoon. "Where is Mrs. Drukker's room situated?"

The girl shot him a startled look, but answered promptly:

"On the west side of the house—its bay window overlooks the archery range."

"Ah!" Vance took out his cigarette case, and carefully selected a *Régie.* "Does she sit much at this window?"

"A great deal. Lady Mae always watches us at archery practice—why I don't know. I'm sure it pains her to see us, for Adolph isn't strong enough to shoot. He's tried it several times, but it tired him so he had to give it up."

"She may watch you practising for the very reason that it does torture her—a kind of self-immolation, y' know. Those situations are very distressing." Vance spoke almost with tenderness—which, to one who did not know his real nature, would have sounded strange. "Perhaps," he added, as we emerged into the archery range through the basement door, "it would be best if we saw Mrs. Drukker first for a moment. It might tend to allay any apprehensions our visit might cause her. Could we reach her room without Mr. Drukker's knowledge?"

"Oh, yes." The girl was pleased at the idea. "We can go in the rear way. Adolph's study, where he does his writing, is at the front of the house."

We found Mrs. Drukker sitting in the great bay window on a sprawling

---

* The name was, of course, originally spelled Drucker. The change—possibly some vague attempt at Americanization—was made by Mrs. Drukker when she settled in this country.

old-fashioned chaise-longue, propped up with pillows. Miss Dillard greeted her filially and, bending over her with tender concern, kissed her forehead.

"Something rather awful has happened at our house this morning, Lady Mae," she said; "and these gentlemen wanted to see you. I offered to bring them over. You don't mind, do you?"

Mrs. Drukker's pale, tragic face had been turned away from the door as we entered, but now she stared at us with fixed horror. She was a tall woman, slender to the point of emaciation; and her hands, which lay slightly flexed on the arms of the chair, were sinewy and wrinkled like the talons of fabulous birdwomen. Her face, too, was thin and deeply seamed; but it was not an unattractive face. The eyes were clear and alive, and the nose was straight and dominant. Though she must have been well past sixty, her hair was luxuriant and brown.

For several minutes she neither moved nor spoke. Then her hands closed slowly, and her lips parted.

"What do you want?" she asked in a low resonant voice.

"Mrs. Drukker,"—it was Vance who answered—"as Miss Dillard has told you, a tragedy occurred next door this morning, and since your window is the only one directly overlooking the archery range, we thought that you might have seen something that would aid us in our investigation."

The woman's vigilance relaxed perceptibly, but it was a moment or two before she spoke.

"And what did take place?"

"A Mr. Robin was killed.—You knew him perhaps?"

"The archer—Belle's Champion Archer? ... Yes, I knew him. A strong healthy child who could pull a heavy bow and not get tired.—Who killed him?"

"We don't know." Vance, despite his negligent air, was watching her astutely. "But inasmuch as he was killed on the range, within sight of your window, we hoped you might be able to help us."

Mrs. Drukker's eyelids drooped craftily, and she clasped her hands with a kind of deliberate satisfaction.

"You are sure he was killed on the range?"

"We found him on the range," Vance returned non-committally.

"I see. ... But what can I do to help you?" She lay back relaxed.

"Did you notice any one on the range this morning?" asked Vance.

"No!" The denial was swift and emphatic. "I saw no one. I haven't looked out on the range all day."

Vance met the woman's gaze steadily, and sighed.

"It's most unfortunate," he murmured. "Had you been looking out of the window this morning, it's wholly possible you might have seen the tragedy. ... Mr. Robin was killed with a bow and arrow, and there seems to have been no motive whatever for the act."

"You know he was killed with a bow and arrow?" she asked, a tinge of color coming into her ashen cheeks.

"That was the Medical Examiner's report. There was an arrow through his heart when we found him."

"Of course. That seems perfectly natural, doesn't it? ... An arrow through the Robin's heart!" She spoke with vague aloofness, a distant, fascinated look in her eyes.

There was a strained silence, and Vance moved toward the window.

"Do you mind if I look out?"

With difficulty the woman brought herself back from some far train of thought.

"Oh, no. It isn't much of a view, though. I can see the trees of 76th Street toward the north, and a part of the Dillard yard to the south. But that brick wall opposite is very depressing. Before the apartment house was built I had a beautiful view of the river."

Vance looked for a while down into the archery range.

"Yes," he observed; "if only you had been at the window this morning you might have seen what happened. Your view of the range and the basement door of the Dillards' is very clear. . . . Too bad." He glanced at his watch. "Is your son in, Mrs. Drukker?"

"My son! My baby! What do you want with him?" Her voice rose pitifully, and her eyes fastened on Vance with venomous hatred.

"Nothing important," he said pacifying. "Only, he may have seen some one on the range———"

"He saw no one! He couldn't have seen any one, for he wasn't here. He went out early this morning, and hasn't returned."

Vance looked with pity at the woman.

"He was away all morning?—Do you know where he was?"

"I always know where he is," Mrs. Drukker answered proudly. "He tells me everything."

"And he told you where he was going this morning?" persisted Vance gently.

"Certainly. But I forget for the moment. Let me think. . . ." Her long fingers tapped on the arm of the chair, and her eyes shifted uneasily. "I can't recall. But I'll ask him the moment he returns."

Miss Dillard had stood watching the woman with growing perplexity.

"But, Lady Mae, Adolph was at our house this morning. He came to see Sigurd———"

Mrs. Drukker drew herself up.

"Nothing of the kind!" she snapped, eyeing the girl almost viciously. "Adolph had to go—downtown somewhere. He wasn't near your house— I *know* he wasn't." Her eyes flashed, and she turned a defiant glare on Vance.

It was an embarrassing moment; but what followed was even more painful.

The door opened softly, and suddenly Mrs. Drukker's arms went out.

"My little boy—my baby!" she cried. "Come here, dear."

But the man at the door did not come forward. He stood blinking his beady little eyes at us, like a person waking in strange surroundings. Adolph Drukker was scarcely five feet tall. He had the typical congested appearance of the hunchback. His legs were spindling, and the size of his bulging, distorted torso seemed exaggerated by his huge, domelike head. But there was intellectuality in the man's face—a terrific passionate power which held one's attention. Professor Dillard had called him a mathematical genius; and one could have no doubts as to his erudition.*

---

* He gave me very much the same impression as did General Homer Lee when I visited him at Santa Monica shortly before his death.

"What does all this mean?" he demanded in a high-pitched, tremulous voice, looking toward Miss Dillard. "Are these friends of yours, Belle?"

The girl started to speak, but Vance halted her with a gesture.

"The truth is, Mr. Drukker," he explained sombrely, "there has been a tragedy next door. This is Mr. Markham, the District Attorney, and Sergeant Heath of the Police Department; and at our request Miss Dillard brought us here that we might ask your mother whether or not she had noticed anything unusual on the archery range this morning. The tragedy occurred just outside the basement door of the Dillard house."

Drukker thrust his chin forward and squinted.

"A tragedy, eh? What kind of tragedy?"

"A Mr. Robin was killed—with a bow and arrow."

The man's face began to twitch spasmodically.

"Robin killed? *Killed?* . . . What time?"

"Some time between eleven and twelve probably."

"Between eleven and twelve?" Quickly Drukker's gaze shifted to his mother. He seemed to grow excited, and his huge splay fingers worried the hem of his smoking-jacket. "What did you see?" His eyes glinted as he focussed them on the woman.

"What do you mean, son?" The retort was a panic-stricken whisper.

Drukker's face became hard, and the suggestion of a sneer twisted his lips.

"I mean that it was about that time when I heard a scream in this room."

"You didn't! No—no!" She caught her breath, and wagged her head jerkily. "You're mistaken, son. I didn't scream this morning."

"Well, some one did." There was a cold relentlessness in the man's tone. Then, after a pause, he added: "The fact is, I came up-stairs after I heard the scream, and listened at the door here. But you were walking about humming "Eia Popeia,' so I went back to my work."

Mrs. Drukker pressed a handkerchief to her face, and her eyes closed momentarily.

"You were at your work between eleven and twelve?" Her voice now rang with subdued eagerness. "But I called you several times————"

"I heard you. But I didn't answer. I was too busy."

"So that was it." She turned slowly toward the window. "I thought you were out. Didn't you tell me————?"

"I told you I was going to the Dillards'. But Sigurd wasn't there, and I came back a little before eleven."

"I didn't see you come in." The woman's energy was spent, and she lay back listlessly, her eyes on the brick wall opposite. "And when I called and you didn't answer I naturally thought you were still out."

"I left the Dillards' by the street gate, and took a walk in the park." Drukker's voice was irritable. "Then I let myself in by the front door."

"And you say you heard me scream. . . . But why should I scream, son? I've had no pains in my back this morning."

Drukker frowned, and his little eyes moved swiftly from Vance to Markham.

"I heard some one scream—a woman—in this room," he iterated stubbornly. "About half past eleven." Then he sank into a chair and gazed moodily at the floor.

This perplexing verbal intercourse between mother and son had held us all spellbound. Though Vance had stood before an old eighteenth-century print near the door, regarding it with apparent absorption, I knew that no word or inflection had escaped him. Now he swung about and, giving Markham a signal not to interfere, approached Mrs. Drukker.

"We're very sorry, madam, that we've had to trouble you. Forgive us, if you can."

He bowed and turned to Miss Dillard.

"Do you care to pilot us back? Or shall we find our own way down?"

"I'll come with you," the girl said; and going to Mrs. Drukker she put her arm about her. "I'm so sorry, Lady Mae."

As we were passing out into the hall Vance, as if on second thought, paused and looked back at Drukker.

"You'd better come with us, sir," he said, in a casual yet urgent tone. "You knew Mr. Robin, and you may be able to suggest something————"

"Don't go with them, son!" cried Mrs. Drukker. She was sitting upright now, her face contorted with anguish and fear. "Don't go! They're the enemy. They want to hurt you. . . ."

Drukker had risen.

"Why shouldn't I go with them?" he retorted petulantly. "I want to find out about this affair. Maybe—as they say—I can help them." And with a gesture of impatience he joined us.

6

" 'I,' SAID THE SPARROW"

(Saturday, April 2; 3 P.M.)

WHEN WE were again in the Dillard drawing-room and Miss Dillard had left us to rejoin her uncle in the library, Vance, without preliminaries, proceeded to the business in hand.

"I didn't care to worry your mother, Mr. Drukker, by questioning you in front of her, but inasmuch as you called here this morning shortly before Mr. Robin's death, it is necessary—as a mere routine procedure—that we seek whatever information you can give us."

Drukker had seated himself near the fireplace. He now drew in his head cautiously, but made no answer.

"You came here," continued Vance, "about half past nine, I believe, to call on Mr. Arnesson."

"Yes."

"By way of the archery range and the basement door?"

"I always come that way. Why walk around the block?"

"But Mr. Arnesson was out this morning."

Drukker nodded. "At the university."

"And, finding Mr. Arnesson away, you sat for a while in the library with

Professor Dillard, I understand, discussing an astronomical expedition to South America."

"The expedition of the Royal Astronomical Society to Sobral to test the Einsteinian deflection," amplified Drukker.

"How long were you in the library?"

"Less than half an hour."

"And then?"

"I went down to the archery-room, and glanced at one of the magazines. There was a chess problem in it—a *Zugszwang* end-game that came up recently between Shapiro and Marshall—and I sat down and worked it out. . . ."

"Just a moment, Mr. Drukker." A note of suppressed interest came into Vance's voice. "You're interested in chess?"

"To a certain extent. I don't spend much time at it, however. The game is not purely mathematical; and it's insufficiently speculative to appeal to a wholly scientific mind."

"Did you find the Shapiro-Marshall position difficult?"

"Not so difficult as tricky." Drukker was watching Vance shrewdly. "As soon as I discovered that an apparently useless pawn move was the key to the impasse, the solution was simple."

"How long did it take you?"

"Half an hour or so."

"Until about half past ten, shall we say?"

"That would be about right." Drukker settled deeper into his chair, but his covert alertness did not relax.

"Then you must have been in the archery-room when Mr. Robin and Mr. Sperling came there."

The man did not answer at once, and Vance, pretending not to notice his hesitancy, added: "Professor Dillard said they called at the house about ten and after waiting a while in the drawing-room here, went down to the basement."

"Where's Sperling now, by the way?" Drukker's eyes darted suspiciously from one to the other of us.

"We expect him here any minute," Vance replied. "Sergeant Heath has sent two of his men to fetch him."

The hunchback's eyebrows lifted. "Ah! So Sperling is being forcibly brought back." He pyramided his spatulate fingers and inspected them musingly. Then he slowly lifted his eyes to Vance. "You asked me if I saw Robin and Sperling in the archery-room.—Yes; they came down-stairs just as I was going."

Vance leaned back and stretched his legs before him.

"Did you get the impression, Mr. Drukker, that they had—as we euphemistically say—been having words?"

The man considered this question for several moments.

"Now that you mention it," he said at length, "I do recall that there seemed to be a coolness between them. I wouldn't, however, care to be too categorical on that point. You see, I left the room almost immediately after they entered."

"You went out the basement door, I think you said, and thence through the wall gate into 75th Street. Is that correct?"

For a moment Drukker seemed loath to answer; but he replied with an effort at unconcern.

"Quite. I thought I'd take a stroll along the river before going back to work. I went to the Drive, then up the bridle path, and turned into the park at 79th Street."

Heath, with his habitual suspicion of all statements made to the police, put the next question.

"Did you meet any one you knew?"

Drukker turned angrily, but Vance quickly stepped into the breach.

"It really doesn't matter, Sergeant. If it's necess'ry later on to ascertain that point, we can take the matter up again." Then to Drukker: "You returned from your walk a little before eleven, I think you said, and entered your house by the front door."

"That's right."

"You saw nothing, by the by, that was in the least extr'ordin'ry when you were here this morning?"

"I saw nothing except what I've told you."

"And you're quite sure you heard your mother scream at about half past eleven?"

Vance did not move as he asked this question; but a slightly different note had crept into his voice, and it acted on Drukker in a startling manner. He heaved his squat body out of his chair, and stood glaring down on Vance with menacing fury. His tiny round eyes flashed, and his lips worked convulsively. His hands, dangling before him, flexed and unflexed like those of a man in a paroxysm.

"What are you driving at?" he demanded, his voice a shrill falsetto. "I tell you I heard her scream. I don't care a damn whether she admits it or not. Moreover, I heard her walking in her room. *She was in her room,* understand, *and I was in my room,* between eleven and twelve. And you can't prove anything different. Furthermore, I'm not going to be cross-examined by you or any one else as to what I was doing or where I was. It's none of your damned business—do you hear me? . . ."

So insensate was his wrath that I expected any minute to see him hurl himself on Vance. Heath had risen and stepped forward, sensing the potential danger of the man. Vance, however, did not move. He continued to smoke languidly, and when the other's fury had been spent, he said quietly and without a trace of emotion:

"There's nothing more we have to ask you, Mr. Drukker. And really, y' know, there's no need to work yourself up. It merely occurred to me that your mother's scream might help to establish the exact time of the murder."

"What could her scream have to do with the time of Robin's death? Didn't she tell you she saw nothing?" Drukker appeared exhausted, and leaned heavily against the table.

At this moment Professor Dillard appeared in the archway. Behind him stood Arnesson.

"What seems to be the matter?" the professor asked. "I heard the noise here, and came down." He regarded Drukker coldly. "Hasn't Belle been through enough to-day without your frightening her this way?"

Vance had risen, but before he could speak Arnesson came forward and shook his finger in mock reprimand at Drukker.

"You really should learn control, Adolph. You take life with such abominable seriousness. You've worked in interstellar spatial magnitudes long enough to have some sense of proportion. Why attach so much importance to this pin-point of life on earth?"

Drukker was breathing stertorously.

"These swine————" he began.

"Oh, my dear Adolph!" Arnesson cut him short. "The entire human race are swine. Why particularize? . . . Come along. I'll see you home." And he took Drukker's arm firmly and led him downstairs.

"We're very sorry we disturbed you, sir," Markham apologized to Professor Dillard. "The man flew off the handle for some unknown reason. These investigations are not the pleasantest things in the world; but we hope to be through before long."

"Well, make it as brief as you can, Markham. And do try to spare Belle as much as possible.—Let me see you before you go."

When Professor Dillard had returned up-stairs, Markham took a turn up and down the room, his brows knit, his hands clasped behind him.

"What do you make of Drukker?" he asked, halting before Vance.

"Decidedly not a pleasant character. Diseased physically and mentally. A congenital liar. But canny—oh, deuced canny. An abnormal brain—you often find it in cripples of his type. Sometimes it runs to real constructive genius, as with Steinmetz; but too often it takes to abstruse speculation along impractical lines, as with Drukker. Still, our little verbal give-and-take has not been without fruit. He's hiding something that he'd like to tell but doesn't dare."

"That's possible, of course," returned Markham doubtfully. "He's touchy on the subject of that hour between eleven and noon. And he was watching you all the time like a cat."

"A weasel," Vance corrected him. "Yes, I was aware of his flatterin' scrutiny."

"Anyway, I can't see that he's helped us very much."

"No," agreed Vance. "We're not exactly forrader. But we're at least getting some luggage aboard. Our excitable mathematical wizard has opened up some very interestin' lines of speculation. And Mrs. Drukker is fairly teemin' with possibilities. If we knew what both of 'em together know we might find the key to this silly business."

Heath had been sullen for the past hour, and had looked on at the proceedings with bored disdain. But now he drew himself up combatively.

"I'm here to tell you, Mr. Markham, that we're wasting our time. What's the good of all these parleys? Sperling's the boy we want, and when my men bring him in and put him through a little sweating, we'll have enough material for an indictment. He was in love with the Dillard girl and was jealous of Robin—not only on account of the girl, but because Robin could shoot those red sticks straighter than he could. He had a scrap with Robin in this here room—the professor heard 'em at it; and he was down-stairs with Robin, according to the evidence, a few minutes before the murder. . . ."

"And," added Vance ironically, "his name means 'sparrow.' *Quod erat demonstrandum.*—No, Sergeant; it's much too easy. It works out like a game of Canfield with the cards stacked; whereas this thing was planned much too carefully for suspicion to fall directly on the guilty person."

"I can't see any careful planning about it," persisted Heath. "This Sperling gets sore, picks up a bow, grabs an arrow off of the wall, follows Robin outside, shoots him through the heart, and beats it."

Vance sighed.

"You're far too forthright for this wicked world, Sergeant. If only things happened with such naïve dispatch, life would be very simple—and depressin'. But such was not the *modus operandi* of the Robin's murder. First, no archer could shoot at a moving human target and strike just between the ribs over the vital spot of the heart. Secondly, there's that fracture of Robin's skull. He may have acquired it in falling, but it's not likely. Thirdly, his hat was at his feet, where it wouldn't have been if he had fallen naturally. Fourthly, the nock on the arrow is so bruised that I doubt if it would hold a string. Fifthly, Robin was facing the arrow, and during the drawing and aiming of the bow he would have had time to call out and cover himself. Sixthly. . . ."

Vance paused in the act of lighting a cigarette.

"*By Jove,* Sergeant! I've overlooked something. When a man's stabbed in the heart there's sure to be an immediate flow of blood, especially when the end of the weapon is larger than the shaft and there's no adequate plug for the hole. I say! It's quite possible that you'll find some blood spots on the floor of the archery-room—somewhere near the door most likely."

Heath hesitated, but only momentarily. Experience had long since taught him that Vance's suggestions were not to be treated cavalierly; and with a good-natured grunt he got up and disappeared toward the rear of the house.

"I think, Vance, I begin to see what you mean," observed Markham, with a troubled look. "But, good God! If Robin's apparent death with a bow and arrow was merely an *ex-post-facto* stage-setting, then we're confronted by something almost too diabolical to contemplate."

"It was the work of a maniac," declared Vance, with unwonted sobriety. "Oh, not the conventional maniac who imagines he's Napoleon, but a madman with a brain so colossal that he has carried sanity to a, humanly speaking, *reductio ad absurdum*—to a point, that is, where humor itself becomes a formula in four dimensions."

Markham smoked vigorously, lost in speculation.

"I hope Heath doesn't find anything," he said at length.

"Why—in Heaven's name?" returned Vance. "If there's no material evidence that Robin met his end in the archery-room, it'll only make the problem more difficult legally."

But the material evidence was forthcoming. The Sergeant returned a few minutes later, crestfallen but excited.

"Damn it, Mr. Vance!" he blurted. "You had the dope all right." He made no attempt to keep the admiration out of his look. "There isn't any actual blood on the floor; but there's a dark place on the cement where somebody's scrubbed it with a wet rag to-day some time. It ain't dry yet; and the place is right near the door, where you said. And what makes it more suspicious is that one of those rugs has been pulled over it.—But that don't let Sperling out altogether," he added pugnaciously. "He mighta shot Robin indoors."

"And then cleaned up the blood, wiped off the bow and arrow, and placed the body and the bow on the range, before making his departure? . . . Why? . . . Archery, to begin with, isn't an indoor sport, Sergeant. And Sperling knows too much about it to attempt murder with a bow and arrow. A hit such as the one that ended Robin's uneventful career would have been a pure fluke. Teucer himself couldn't have achieved it with any degree of certainty—and, according to Homer, Teucer was the champion archer of the Greeks."

As he spoke Pardee passed down the hall on his way out. He had nearly reached the front door when Vance rose suddenly and went to the archway.

"Oh, I say, Mr. Pardee. Just a moment, please."

The man turned with an air of gracious compliance.

"There is one other question we'd like to ask you," said Vance. "You mentioned seeing Mr. Sperling and Beedle leave here this morning by the wall gate. Are you sure you saw no one else use the gate?"

"Quite sure. That is, I don't recall any one else."

"I was thinking particularly of Mr. Drukker."

"Oh, Drukker?" Pardee shook his head with mild emphasis. "No, I would have remembered him. But you realize a dozen people might have entered and left this house without my noticing them."

"Quite—quite," Vance murmured indifferently. "How good a chess player, by the by, is Mr. Drukker?"

Pardee showed a flicker of surprise.

"He's not a player in the practical sense at all," he explained with careful precision. "He's an excellent analyst, however, and understands the theory of the game amazingly well. But he's had little practice at actual over-the-board play."

When Pardee had gone Heath cocked a triumphant eye at Vance.

"I notice, sir," he remarked good-naturedly, "that I'm not the only one who'd like to check the hunchback's alibi."

"Ah, but there's a difference between checking an alibi, and demanding that the person himself prove it."

At this moment the front door was thrown open. There were heavy footsteps in the hall, and three men appeared in the archway. Two were obviously detectives, and between them stood a tall, clean-cut youth of about thirty.

"We got him, Sergeant," announced one of the detectives, with a grin of vicious satisfaction. "He beat it straight home from here, and was packing up when we walked in on him."

Sperling's eyes swept the room with angry apprehension. Heath had planted himself before the man, and stood looking him up and down triumphantly.

"Well, young fella, you thought you'd get away, did you?" The Sergeant's cigar bobbed up and down between his lips as he spoke.

The color mounted to Sperling's cheeks, and he set his mouth stubbornly.

"So! You've got nothing to say?" Heath went on, squaring his jaw ferociously. "You're one of these silent lads, are you? Well, we'll make you talk." He turned to Markham. "How about it, sir? Shall I take him to Headquarters?"

"Perhaps Mr. Sperling will not object to answering a few questions here," said Markham quietly.

Sperling studied the District Attorney a moment; then his gaze moved to Vance, who nodded to him encouragingly.

"Answer questions about what?" he asked, with an obvious effort at self-control. "I was preparing to go away for the week-end when these ruffians forced their way into my room; and I was brought here without a word of explanation or even an opportunity to communicate with my family. Now you talk of taking me to Police Headquarters." He gave Heath a defiant glare.

"All right, take me to Police Headquarters—and be damned to you!"

"What time did you leave here this morning, Mr. Sperling?" Vance's tone was soft and ingratiating, and his manner reassuring.

"About a quarter past eleven," the man answered. "In time to catch the 11.40 Scarsdale train from Grand Central."

"And Mr. Robin?"

"I don't know what time Robin went. He said he was going to wait for Belle—Miss Dillard. I left him in the archery-room."

"You saw Mr. Drukker?"

"For a minute—yes. He was in the archery-room when Robin and I went down-stairs; but he left immediately."

"Through the wall gate? Or did he walk down the range?"

"I don't remember—in fact, I didn't notice. . . . Say, look here: what's all this about anyway?"

"Mr. Robin was killed this morning," said Vance, "—at some time near eleven o'clock."

Sperling's eyes seemed to start from his head.

"Robin killed? My God! . . . Who—who killed him?" The man's lips were dry, and he wetted them with his tongue.

"We don't know yet," Vance answered. "He was shot through the heart with an arrow."

This news left Sperling stunned. His eyes traveled vaguely from side to side, and he fumbled in his pocket for a cigarette.

Heath stepped nearer to him, and thrust out his chin.

"Maybe *you* can tell us who killed him—*with a bow and arrow!*"

"Why—why do you—think I know?" Sperling managed to stammer.

"Well," returned the Sergeant relentlessly, "you were jealous of Robin, weren't you? You had a hot argument with him about the girl, right in this room, didn't you? And you were alone with him just before he was croaked, weren't you? And you're a pretty good shot with the bow and arrow, aren't you?—That's why I think that maybe you know something." He narrowed his eyes and drew his upper lip over his teeth. "Say! Come clean. Nobody else but you coulda done it. You had a fight with him over the girl, and you were the last person seen with him—*only a few minutes before he was killed.* And who else woulda shot him with a bow and arrow except a champeen archer—huh? . . . Make it easy for yourself, and spill the story. We've got you."

A strange light had gathered in Sperling's eyes, and his body became rigid.

"Tell me,"—he spoke in a strained, unnatural voice—"did you find the bow?"

"Sure we found it." Heath laughed unpleasantly. "Right where you left it—in the alley."

"What kind of a bow was it?" Sperling's gaze had not moved from some distant point.

"What kind of a bow?" repeated Heath. "A regular bow————"

Vance, who had been watching the youth closely, interrupted.

"I think I understand the question, Sergeant.—It was a woman's bow, Mr. Sperling. About five-feet-six, and rather light—under thirty pounds, I should say."

Sperling drew a slow, deep breath, like a man steeling himself for some bitter resolution. Then his lips parted in a faint, grim smile.

"What's the use?" he asked listlessly. "I thought I'd have time to get away.... Yes, I killed him."

Heath grunted with satisfaction, and his belligerent manner at once disappeared.

"You got more sense than I thought you had," he said, in an almost paternal tone, nodding in a businesslike manner to the two detectives. "Take him along, boys. Use my buggy—it's outside. And lock him up without booking him. I'll prefer the charge when I get to the office."

"Come along, bo," ordered one of the detectives, turning toward the hall. But Sperling did not at once obey. Instead he looked appealingly at Vance.

"Could I—might I———" he began.

Vance shook his head.

"No, Mr. Sperling. It would be best if you didn't see Miss Dillard. No use of harrowin' her feelings just now.... Cheerio."

The man turned without another word and went out between his captors.

7

VANCE REACHES A CONCLUSION

(*Saturday, April 2; 3:30 P.M.*)

WHEN WE were again alone in the drawing-room Vance rose and, stretching himself, went to the window. The scene that had just been enacted, with its startling climax, had left us all somewhat dazed. Our minds were busy, I think, with the same idea; and when Vance spoke it was as if he were voicing our thoughts.

"We're back in the nursery, it seems....

> " 'I,' said the Sparrow,
> 'With my bow and arrow,
> I killed Cock Robin.' ...

I say, Markham; this is getting a bit thick."

He came slowly back to the centre-table and crushed out his cigarette. From the corner of his eye he looked at Heath.

"Why so pensive, Sergeant? You should be singing roundelays and doing a joyous tarantella. Has not your villain confessed to the dark deed? Does it not fill you with gladness to know that the culprit will soon be languishin' in an oubliette?"

"To tell you the truth, Mr. Vance," Heath admitted sullenly, "I'm not satisfied. That confession came too easy, and—well, I've seen a lot of guys come across, but this one somehow didn't act like he was guilty. And that's a fact, sir."

"At any rate," submitted Markham hopefully, "his preposterous confession will damp the newspapers' curiosity and give us a free field to push our investigation. This case is going to make an ungodly noise; but as long as the reporters think the guilty person is jailed, they won't be bothering us for news of 'developments.' "

"I'm not saying he ain't guilty," asserted Heath pugnaciously, obviously arguing against his own convictions. "We certainly had the goods on him, and he mighta realized it and spilled the works, thinking it would go easier with him at the trial. Maybe he's not so dumb, after all."

"It won't do, Sergeant," said Vance. "The lad's mental workin's were deucedly simple. He knew Robin was waiting to see Miss Dillard, and he also knew she'd non-suited him, so to speak, last night. Sperling evidently didn't have a high opinion of Robin; and when he heard of the gentleman's death at the hands of some one who wielded a short, light bow, he jumped to the conclusion that Robin had overstepped the bounds of propriety in his wooing, and received a righteous shaft through the heart. There was then nothing for our noble, mid-Victorian sparrow to do but slap his own manly bosom and proclaim: *'Ecce homo!'* . . . It's most distressin'."

"Well, anyhow," grumbled Heath, "I'm not going to turn him loose. If Mr. Markham don't want to prosecute, that's up to him."

Markham looked at the Sergeant tolerantly. He realized the strain the man was under, and it was in keeping with his bigness of nature that he took no offence at the other's words.

"Perhaps, however, Sergeant," he said kindly, "you'll not object to continuing the investigation with me, even if I don't decide to prosecute Sperling."

Heath was at once contrite. He got up briskly and, going to Markham, held out his hand.

"You know it, sir!"

Markham took the offered hand, and rose with a gracious smile.

"I'll leave things with you, then, for the time being. I've some work to do at the office, and I told Swacker to wait for me."* He moved dispiritedly toward the hall. "I'll explain the situation to Miss Dillard and the professor before I go.—Anything special in mind, Sergeant?"

"Well, sir, I think I'll take a good look for that rag that was used to wipe up the floor down-stairs. And while I'm at it I'll go over the archery-room with a fine-tooth comb. Also, I'll put the screws to the cook and the butler again—especially the cook. She musta been mighty close at hand when the dirty work was going on. . . . Then the regular routine stuff—inquiries in the neighborhood and that sorta thing."

"Let me know the results. I'll be at the Stuyvesant Club later to-day and to-morrow afternoon."

Vance had joined Markham in the archway.

"I say, old man," he remarked, as we went toward the stairs; "don't minimize the importance of that cryptic note left in the mail-box. I've a strong psychic suspicion that it may be the key to the nursery. You'd better ask Professor Dillard and his niece if 'Bishop' has any provocative significance for them. That diocesan signature has a meaning."

---

* Saturday was a "half day" at the District Attorney's office. Swacker was Markham's secretary.

"I'm not so sure," returned Markham dubiously. "It appears utterly meaningless to me. But I'll follow your suggestion."

Neither the professor nor Miss Dillard, however, could recall any personal association with the word *Bishop;* and the professor was inclined to agree with Markham that the note was without any significant bearing on the case.

"It strikes me," he said, "as a piece of juvenile melodrama. It isn't likely that the person who killed Robin would adopt a vague pseudonym and write notes about his crime. I'm not acquainted with criminals, but such conduct doesn't impress me as logical."

"But the crime itself was illogical," ventured Vance pleasantly.

"One can't speak of a thing being illogical, sir," returned the professor tartly, "when one is ignorant of the very premises of a syllogism."

"Exactly." Vance's tone was studiously courteous. "Therefore, the note itself may not be without logic."

Markham tactfully changed the subject.

"What I came particularly to tell you, professor, is that Mr. Sperling called a short time ago and, when informed of Mr. Robin's death, confessed to having done it himself. . . ."

"Raymond confessed!" gasped Miss Dillard.

Markham looked at the girl sympathetically.

"To be quite frank, I didn't believe Mr. Sperling. Some mistaken idea of chivalry undoubtedly led him to admit the crime."

" 'Chivalry'?" she repeated, leaning forward tensely. "What exactly do you mean by that, Mr. Markham?"

It was Vance who answered.

"The bow that was found on the range was a woman's bow."

"Oh!" The girl covered her face with her hands, and her body shook with sobs.

Professor Dillard regarded her helplessly; and his impotency took the form of irritation.

"What flummery is this, Markham?" he demanded. "Any archer can shoot with a woman's bow. . . . That unutterable young idiot! Why should he make Belle miserable by his preposterous confession! . . . Markham, my friend, do what you can for the boy."

Markham gave his assurances, and we rose to go.

"By the by, Professor Dillard," said Vance, pausing at the door; "I trust you won't misunderstand me, but there's a bare possibility that it was some one with access to this house who indulged in the practical joke of typing that note. Is there, by any chance, a typewriter on the premises?"

It was patent that the professor resented Vance's question, but he answered civilly enough.

"No,—nor has there ever been one to my knowledge. I threw my own machine away ten years ago when I left the university. An agency does whatever typing I need."

"And Mr. Arnesson?"

"He never uses a typewriter."

As we descended the stairs we met Arnesson returning from Drukker's.

"I've placated our local Leipnitz," he announced, with an exaggerated sigh. "Poor old Adolph! The world is too much with him. When he's wallowing in the relativist formulas of Lorentz and Einstein he's serene. But when he's dragged down to actuality he disintegrates."

"It may interest you to know," said Vance casually, "that Sperling has just confessed to the murder."

"Ha!" Arnesson chuckled. "Quite in keeping. 'I,' said the Sparrow. . . . Very neat. Still, I don't know how it'll work out mathematically."

"And, since we agreed to keep you posted," continued Vance, "it may help your calculations to know that we have reason to believe that Robin was killed in the archery-room and placed on the range afterwards."

"Glad to know it." Arnesson became momentarily serious. "Yes, that may affect my problem." He walked with us to the front door. "If there's any way I can be of service to you, call on me."

Vance had paused to light a cigarette, but I knew, by the languid look in his eyes, that he was making a decision. Slowly he turned to Arnesson.

"Do you know if Mr. Drukker or Mr. Pardee has a typewriter?"

Arnesson gave a slight start, and his eyes twinkled shrewdly.

"Aha! That Bishop note. . . . I see. Merely a matter of being thorough. Quite right." He nodded with satisfaction. "Yes; both have typewriters. Drukker types incessantly—thinks to the keyboard, so he says. And Pardee's chess correspondence is as voluminous as a movie hero's. Types it all himself, too."

"Would it be any great trouble to you," asked Vance, "to secure a specimen of the typing of each machine, and also a sample of the paper these two gentlemen use?"

"None whatever." Arnesson appeared delighted with the commission. "Have them for you this afternoon. Where'll you be?"

"Mr. Markham will be at the Stuyvesant Club. You might phone him there, and he can arrange———"

"Why bother to arrange anything? I'll bring my findings to Mr. Markham personally. Only too glad. Fascinating game, being a sleuth."

Vance and I returned home in the District Attorney's car, and Markham continued to the office. At seven o'clock that night the three of us met at the Stuyvesant Club for dinner; and at half past eight we were sitting in Markham's favorite corner of the lounge-room smoking and having our coffee.

During the meal no mention of the case had been made. The late editions of the afternoon papers had carried brief accounts of Robin's death. Heath had evidently succeeded in curbing the reporters' curiosity and clipping the wings of their imagination. The District Attorney's office being closed, the newspaper men were unable to bombard Markham with questions, and so the late press was inadequately supplied with information. The Sergeant had guarded the Dillard house well, for the reporters had not succeeded in reaching any member of the household.

Markham had picked up a late *Sun* on his way from the dining-room, and glanced through it carefully as he sipped his coffee.

"This is the first faint echo," he commented ruefully. "I shudder to think what the morning papers will contain."

"There's nothing to do but bear it," smiled Vance unfeelingly. "The moment some bright journalistic lad awakes to the robin-sparrow-arrow combination the city editors will go mad with joy, and every front page in the country will look like a Mother-Goose hoarding."

Markham lapsed into despondency. Finally he struck the arm of his chair angrily with his fist.

"Damn it, Vance! I won't let you inflame my imagination with this idiocy about nursery rhymes." Then he added, with the ferocity of uncertainty: "It's a sheer coincidence, I tell you. There simply couldn't be anything in it."

Vance sighed. "Convince yourself against your will; you're of the same opinion still—to paraphrase Butler." He reached into his pocket and took out a sheet of paper. "Putting all juvenilia to one side *pro tempore,* here's an edifyin' chronology I drew up before dinner. . . . Edifyin'? Well, it might be if we knew how to interpret it."

Markham studied the paper for several minutes. What Vance had written down was this:

> 9.00 A.M. Arnesson left house to go to university library.
> 9.15 A.M. Belle Dillard left house for the tennis courts.
> 9.30 A.M. Drukker called at house to see Arnesson.
> 9.50 A.M. Drukker went down-stairs to archery-room.
> 10.00 A.M. Robin and Sperling called at house and remained in drawing-room for half an hour.
> 10.30 A.M. Robin and Sperling went down to archery-room.
> 10.32 A.M. Drukker says he went out for a walk, by the wall gate.
> 10.35 A.M. Beedle went marketing.
> 10.55 A.M. Drukker says he returned to his own house.
> 11.15 A.M. Sperling went away by wall gate.
> 11.30 A.M. Drukker says he heard a scream in his mother's room.
> 11.35 A.M. Professor Dillard went on balcony of Arnesson's room.
> 11.40 A.M. Professor Dillard saw Robin's body on archery range.
> 11.45 A.M. Professor Dillard telephoned to District Attorney's office.
> 12.25 P.M. Belle Dillard returned from tennis.
> 12.30 P.M. Police arrived at Dillard house.
> 12.35 P.M. Beedle returned from market.
> 2.00 P.M. Arnesson returned from university.

Ergo: Robin was killed at some time between 11.15 (when Sperling departed) and 11.40 (when Professor Dillard discovered body).

The only other persons known to have been in the house during this time were Pyne and Professor Dillard.

The disposition of all other persons connected in any way with the murder was as follows (according to statements and evidence now in hand):

1. Arnesson was at the univesity library between 9 A.M. and 2 P.M.
2. Belle Dillard was at the tennis courts between 9.15 A.M. and 12.25 P.M.
3. Drukker was walking in the park between 10.32 A.M. and 10.55 A.M.; and was in his study from 10.55 A.M. on.
4. Pardee was in his house the entire morning.

5. Mrs. Drukker was in her room the entire morning.
6. Beedle was marketing between 10.35 A.M. and 12.35 P.M.
7. Sperling was on his way to the Grand Central Station between 11.15 A.M. and 11.40 A.M., at which hour he took a train for Scarsdale.

Conclusion: Unless at least one of these seven alibis is shaken, the whole weight of suspicion, and indeed the actual culpability, must rest upon either Pyne or Professor Dillard.

When Markham finished reading the paper, he made a geture of exasperation.

"Your entire implication is preposterous," he said irritably; "and your conclusion is a *non-sequitur.* The chronology helps set the time of Robin's death, but your assumption that one of the person's we've seen to-day is necessarily guilty is arrant nonsense. You completely ignore the possibility that any outsider could have committed the crime. There were three ways of reaching the range and the archery-room without entering the house—the wall gate on 75th Street, the other wall gate on 76th Street, and the alleyway between the two apartment houses, leading to Riverside Drive."

"Oh, it's highly probable that one of these three entrances was used," returned Vance. "But don't overlook the fact that the most secluded, and therefore the most likely, of these three means of entry—to wit, the alleyway—is guarded by a locked door to which no one would be apt to have a key except some member of the Dillard household. I can't picture a murderer walking into the range from either of the street gates: he would be taking too many chances of being seen."

Vance leaned forward seriously.

"And, Markham, there are other reasons why we may eliminate strangers or casual prowlers. The person who sent Robin to his Maker must have been privy to the exact state of affairs in the Dillard house this morning between a quarter past eleven and twenty minutes to twelve. He knew that Pyne and the old professor were alone there. He knew that Belle Dillard was not roaming about the premises. He knew that Beedle was away and could neither hear him nor surprise him. He knew that Robin—his victim—was there, and that Sperling had departed. Moreover, he knew something of the lie of the land— the situation of the archery-room, for instance; for it's only too plain that Robin was killed in that room. No one who wasn't familiar with all these details would have dared enter the grounds and staged a spectacular murder. I tell you, Markham, it was some one very close to the Dillard ménage—some one who was able to find out just what conditions obtained in that household this morning."

"What about that scream of Mrs. Drukker's?"

"Ah, what about it, indeed? Mrs. Drukker's window may have been a factor that the murderer overlooked. Or perhaps he knew about it and decided to take that one chance of being seen. On the other hand, we don't know whether the lady screamed or not. She says No; Drukker says Yes. They both have an ulterior motive for what they poured into our trustin' ears. Drukker may have told of the scream by way of proving he was at home between eleven and twelve; and Mrs. Drukker may have denied it for fear he wasn't home. It's very much of an *olla podrida*. But it doesn't matter. The main point I'm trying to make is that only an intimate of the Dillard house could have done this devilish business."

"We have too few facts to warrant that conclusion," asserted Markham. "Chance may have played a part————"

"Oh, I say, old man! Chance may work out to a few permutations, but not to twenty.—And there is that note left in the mail-box. The murderer even knew Robin's middle name."

"Assuming, of course, that the murderer wrote the note."

"Do you prefer to assume that some balmy joker found out about the crime through telepathy or crystal-gazing, hied to a typewriter, composed a dithyramb, returned hot-footed to the house, and, for no good reason, took the terrific risk of being seen putting the paper in the mail-box?"

Before Markham could answer Heath entered the lounge room and hurried to our corner. That he was worried and uneasy was obvious. With scarcely a word of greeting he handed a typewritten envelope to Markham.

"That was received by the *World* in the late afternoon mail. Quinan, the police reporter of the *World,* brought it to me a little while ago; and he says that the *Times* and the *Herald* also got copies of it. The letters were stamped at one o'clock to-day, so they were probably posted between eleven and twelve. What's more, Mr. Markham, they were mailed in the neighborhood of the Dillard house, for they went through Post Office Station 'N' on West 69th Street."

Markham withdrew the enclosure from the envelope. Suddenly his eyes opened wide, and the muscles about his mouth tightened. Without looking up he handed the letter to Vance. It consisted of a single sheet of typewriting paper, and the words printed on it were identical to those on the note left in the Dillard mail-box. Indeed, the communication was an exact duplicate of the other:—"Joseph Cochrane Robin is dead. Who Killed Cock Robin? Sperling means sparrow.—THE BISHOP."

Vance scarcely glanced at the paper.

"Quite in keeping, don't y' know," he said indifferently. "The Bishop was afraid the public might miss the point of his joke; so he explained it to the press."

"Joke, did you say, Mr. Vance?" asked Heath bitterly. "It ain't the kind of joke I'm used to. This case gets crazier————"

"Exactly, Sergeant. A crazy joke."

A uniformed boy stepped up to the District Attorney and, bending over his shoulder discreetly, whispered something.

"Bring him here right away," ordered Markham. Then to us: "It's Arnesson. He'll probably have those specimens of typing." A shadow had settled on his face; and he glanced again at the note Heath had brought him. "Vance," he said in a low voice, "I'm beginning to believe that this case may turn out to be as terrible as you think. I wonder if the typing will correspond. . . ."

But when the note was compared with the specimens Arnesson brought, no similarity whatever could be discerned. Not only were the typing and the ink different from those of either Pardee's or Drukker's machine, but the paper did not match any one of the samples that Arnesson had secured.

8

ACT TWO

(*Monday, April 11; 11:30 A.M.*)

THERE IS no need to recall here the nation-wide sensation caused by Robin's murder. Every one remembers how that startling tragedy was featured in the country's press. It was referred to by various designations. Some newspapers called it the Cock Robin murder. Others, more alliterative but less accurate,* termed it the Mother Goose murder. But the signature of the typewritten notes appealed strongly to the journalistic sense of mystery; and in time the killing of Robin came to be known as the Bishop murder case. Its strange and fearful combination of horror and nursery jargon inflamed the public's imagination; and the sinister and insane implications of its details affected the entire country like some grotesque nightmare whose atmosphere could not be shaken off.

During the week following the discovery of Robin's body, the detectives of the Homicide Bureau, as well as the detectives connected with the District Attorney's office, were busy night and day pushing their inquiries. The receipt of the duplicate Bishop notes by the leading New York morning papers had dissipated whatever ideas Heath may have held as to Sperling's guilt; and though he refused to put his official imprimatur on the young man's innocence he threw himself, with his usual gusto and pertinacity, into the task of finding another and more plausible culprit. The investigation which he organized and superintended was as complete as had been that of the Greene murder case. No avenue which held the meagrest hope of results was overlooked; and the report he drew up would have given joy even to those meticulous criminologists of the University of Lausanne.

On the afternoon of the day of the murder he and his men had searched for the cloth that had been used to wipe up the blood in the archery-room; but no trace of it was found. Also, a thorough examination of the Dillard basement was made in the hope of finding other clews; but although Heath had put the task in the hands of experts, the result was negative. The only point brought to light was that the fibre rug near the door had recently been moved so as to cover the cleansed spot on the cement floor. This fact, however, merely substantiated the Sergeant's earlier observation.

The *post-mortem* report of Doctor Doremus lent color to the now officially accepted theory that Robin had been killed in the archery-room and then placed on the range. The autopsy showed that the blow on the back of his skull had been a particularly violent one and had been made with a heavy rounded instrument, resulting in a depressed fracture quite different from the fissured fracture caused by striking a flat surface. A search was instituted for the weapon with which the blow had been dealt; but no likely instrument was turned up.

* The old anonymous nursery rhyme, "The Death and Burial of Cock Robin," is not, as is commonly supposed, one of the original "Mother Goose Melodies," although it has often been included in modern editions of that famous work.

Though Beedle and Pyne were questioned by Heath several times, nothing new was learned from them. Pyne insisted that he had been up-stairs the entire morning in Arnesson's room, except for a few brief absences to the linen-closet and the front door, and clung tenaciously to his denial that he had touched either the body or the bow when sent by Professor Dillard to find Sperling. The Sergeant, however, was not entirely satisfied with the man's testimony.

"That bleary-eyed old cormorant has got something up his sleeve," he told Markham disgustedly. "But it would take the rubber hose and the water cure to make him spill it."

A canvass of all the houses in 75th Street between West End Avenue and Riverside Drive was made in the hope of finding a tenant who had noticed some one entering or emerging from the Dillard wall gate during the forenoon. But nothing was gained by this tedious campaign. Pardee, it seemed, was the only resident within view of the Dillard house who had observed any one in the neighborhood that morning. In fact, after several days of arduous inquiries along this line the Sergeant realized that he would have to proceed without any outside or fortuitous assitance.

The various alibis of the seven persons whom Vance had tabulated in his notation for Markham, were gone into as thoroughly as circumstances would permit. It was obviously impossible to check them completely, for, in the main, they were based solely on the statements of the individuals involved. Moreover the investigation had to be made with the utmost care lest suspicion be aroused. The results of these inquiries were as follows:

1. Arnesson had been seen in the university library by various people, including an assistant librarian and two students. But the time covered by their evidence was neither consecutive nor specific as to the hour.
2. Belle Dillard had played several sets of tennis at the public courts at 119th Street and Riverside Drive, but because there had been more than four in her party she had twice relinquished her place to a friend; and none of the players could state positively that she had remained at the courts during these periods.
3. The time that Drukker departed from the archery-room was definitely determined by Sperling; but no one could be found who had seen him thereafter. He admitted he had met no one he knew in the park, but insisted he had stopped for a few minutes to play with some strange children.
4. Pardee had been alone in his study. His old cook and his Japanese valet had been in the rear of the house, and had not seen him until lunch time. His alibi therefore was purely a negative one.
5. Mrs. Drukker's word had to be accepted as to her whereabouts that morning, for no one had seen her between nine-thirty, when Drukker went to call on Arnesson, and one o'clock, when the cook brought up her luncheon.
6. Beedle's alibi was checked with fairly satisfactory completeness. Pardee had seen her leave the house at 10.35; and she was remembered by several of the hucksters at the Jefferson Market between eleven and twelve.
7. The fact that Sperling had taken the 11.40 train to Scarsdale was veri-

fied; therefore he would have had to leave the Dillard house at the time he stated—namely: 11.15. The determination of this point, however, was merely a matter of routine, for he had been practically eliminated from the case. But if, as Heath explained, it had been found that he had not taken the 11.40 train, he would have again become an important possibility.

Pursuing his investigations along more general lines, the Sergeant went into the histories and associations of the various persons involved. The task was not a difficult one. All were well known, and information concerning them was readily accessible; but not one item was unearthed that could be regarded as even remotely throwing any light on Robin's murder. Nothing transpired to give so much as a hint to the motive for the crime; and after a week's intensive inquiry and speculation the case was still cloaked in seemingly impenetrable mystery.

Sperling had not been released. The *prima facie* evidence against him, combined with his absurd confession, made impossible such a step on the part of the authorities. Markham, however, had held an unofficial conference with the attorneys whom Sperling's father had engaged to handle the case, and some sort of a "gentleman's agreement" had, I imagine, been reached; for although the State made no move to apply for an indictment (despite the fact that the Grand Jury was sitting at the time), the defense lawyers did not institute *habeas corpus* proceedings. All the indications pointed to the supposition that both Markham and Sperling's attorneys were waiting for the real culprit to be apprehended.

Markham had had several interviews with the members of the Dillard household, in a persistent effort to bring out some trivial point that might lead to a fruitful line of inquiry; and Pardee had been summoned to the District Attorney's office to make an affidavit as to what he had observed from his window on the morning of the tragedy. Mrs. Drukker had been interrogated again; but not only did she emphatically deny having looked out of her window that morning, but she scoffed at the idea that she had screamed.

Drukker, when re-questioned, modified somewhat his former testimony. He explained that he might have been mistaken as to the source of the scream, and suggested that it could have come from the street or from one of the court windows of the apartment house. In fact, he said, it was highly unlikely that his mother had uttered the scream, for when he went to her door a moment later she was humming an old German nursery song from Humperdinck's "Hänsel und Gretel." Markham, convinced that nothing further was to be learned from either him or Mrs. Drukker, finally concentrated on the Dillard house itself.

Arnesson attended the informal conferences held in Markham's office; but for all his voluble and cynical observations, he appeared to be as much at sea as the rest of us. Vance chaffed him good-naturedly about the mathematical formula that was to solve the case, but Arnesson insisted that a formula could not be worked out until all the factors of the theorem were available. He appeared to regard the entire affair as a kind of Juvenalian lark; and Markham on several occasions gave vent to his exasperation. He reproached Vance for having made Arnesson an unofficial confrère in the investigation, but Vance defended himself on the ground that sooner or later Arnesson would supply some piece of seemingly irrelevant information that could be used as an advantageous *point de départ*.

"His crimino-mathematical theory is of course rubbish," said Vance. "Psychology—not abstract science—will eventually reduce this conundrum to its elements. But we need material to go on, and Arnesson knows the inwardness of the Dillard home better than we can ever know it. He knows the Drukkers, and he knows Pardee; and it goes without saying that a man who has had the academic honors heaped on him that he has, possesses an unusually keen mind. As long as he gives his thought and attention to the case, there's the chance that he'll hit upon something of vital importance to us."

"You may be right," grumbled Markham. "But the man's derisive attitude gets on my nerves."

"Be more catholic," urged Vance. "Consider his ironies in relation to his scientific speculations. What could be more natural than that a man who projects his mind constantly into the vast interplanet'ry reaches, and deals with light-years and infinities and hyperphysical dimensions, should sniff derisively at the infinitesimals of this life? . . . Stout fella, Arnesson. Not homey and comfortable perhaps, but dashed interestin'."

Vance himself had taken the case with unwonted seriousness. His Menander translations had been definitely put aside. He became moody and waspish—a sure sign that his mind was busy with an absorbing problem. After dinner each night he went into his library and read for hours—not the classic and æsthetic volumes on which he generally spent his time, but such books as Bernard Hart's "The Psychology of Insanity," Freud's "Der Witz und seine Beziehung zum Unbewussten," Coriat's "Abnormal Psychology" and "Repressed Emotions," Lippo's "Komik und Humor," Daniel A. Huebsch's "The Murder Complex," Janet's "Les Obsessions et la Psychasthènie," Donath's "Über Arithmomanie," Riklin's "Wish Fulfillment and Fairy Tales," Leppman's "Die forensische Bedeutung der Zwangsvorstellungen," Kuno Fischer's "Über den Witz," Erich Wulffen's "Krimanalpsychologie," Hollenden's "The Insanity of Genius," and Groos's "Die Spiele des Menschen."

He spent hours going over the police reports. He called twice at the Dillards', and on one occasion visited Mrs. Drukker in company with Belle Dillard. He had a long discussion one night with Drukker and Arnesson on de Sitter's conception of physical space as a Lobatchewskian pseudosphere, his object being, I surmised, to acquaint himself with Drukker's mentality. He read Drukker's book, "World Lines in Multidimensional Continua"; and spent nearly an entire day studying Janowski's and Tarrasch's analyses of the Pardee gambit.

On Sunday—eight days after the murder of Robin—he said to me:

"*Eheu*, Van! This problem is unbelievedly subtle. No ordin'ry investigation will ever probe it. It lies in a strange territ'ry of the brain; and its superficial childishness is its most terrible and bafflin' aspect. Nor is the perpetrator going to be content with a single coup. Cock Robin's death serves no definitive end. The perverted imagination that concocted this beastly crime is insatiable; and unless we can expose the abnormal psychological mechanism back of it there will be more grim jokes to contend with. . . ."

The very next morning his prognostication was verified. We went to Markham's office at eleven o'clock to hear Heath's report and to discuss further lines of action. Though nine days had passed since Robin had been found murdered, no progress had been made in the case, and the newspapers had grown bitter in their criticisms of the police and the District Attorney's office. It was therefore with considerable depression that Markham greeted us that Monday morning. Heath had not yet arrived; but when he came a few minutes later it was obvious that he, too, was discouraged.

"We run up against a brick wall, sir, every way we turn," he repined, when he had outlined the results of his men's activities. "There ain't a sign of a motive, and outside of Sperling there's nobody on the landscape that we can hang anything on. I'm coming to the conclusion that it was some stick-up man who ambled into the archery-room that morning and messed things up."

" 'Stick-up' men, Sergeant," countered Vance, "are deuced unimaginative, and they're without a sense of humor; whereas the johnny who sent Robin on the long, long trail had both imagination and humor. He wasn't content merely to kill Robin: he had to turn the act into an insane joke. Then, lest the public wouldn't see the point, he wrote explanat'ry letters to the press.—Does that sound like the procedure of an itinerant thug?"

Heath smoked unhappily for several minutes without speaking, and at length turned a gaze of exasperated dismay upon Markham.

"There's no sense in anything that's breaking round this town lately," he complained. "Just this morning a guy named Sprigg was shot in Riverside Park, up near 84th Street. Money in his pocket—nothing taken. Just shot. Young fella—student at Columbia. Lived with his parents; no enemies. Went out to take his usual walk before going to class. Found dead half an hour later by a bricklayer." The Sergeant chewed viciously on his cigar. "Now we got that homicide to worry about; and we'll probably get hell from the newspapers if we don't clear it up *pronto*. And there's nothing—absolutely nothing—to go on."

"Still, Sergeant," said Vance consolingly, "shooting a man is an ordin'ry event. There are numerous commonplace reasons for that sort of crime. It's the scenic and dramatic appurtenances of Robin's murder that play havoc with all our processes of deduction. If only it wasn't a nursery affair————"

Suddenly he stopped speaking, and his eyelids drooped slightly. Leaning forward he very deliberately crushed out his cigarette.

"Did you say, Sergeant, that this chap's name was Sprigg?"

Heath nodded gloomily.

"And I say,"—despite Vance's effort, there was a note of eagerness in his tone—"what was his first name?"

Heath gave Vance a look of puzzled surprise; but after a brief pause he drew forth his battered notebook and riffled the pages.

"John Sprigg," he answered. "John E. Sprigg."

Vance took out another cigarette, and lighted it with great care.

"And tell me: was he shot with a .32?"

"Huh?" Heath's eyes rounded, and his chin shot forward. "Yes, a .32. . . ."

"And was he shot through the top of his head?"

The Sergeant sprang to his feet, and stared at Vance with ludicrous bewilderment. Slowly his head moved up and down.

"That's right.—But how in hell, sir————?"

Vance held up a silencing hand. It was, however, the look on his face, rather than his gesture, that cut short the query.

"Oh, my precious aunt!" He rose like a man in a daze and gazed fixedly before him. Had I not known him so well I would have sworn he was frightened. Then going to the tall window behind Markham's desk he stood looking down on the gray stone walls of the Tombs.

"I can't credit it," he murmured. "It's too ghastly.... But of course it's so!..."

Markham's impatient voice sounded.

"What's all this mumbling about, Vance? Don't be so damned mysterious! How did you happen to know that Sprigg was shot through the crown with a .32? And what's the point, anyway?"

Vance turned and met Markham's eyes.

"Don't you see?" he asked softly. "It's the second act of this devilish parody!... Have you forgotten your 'Mother-Goose'?" And in a hushed voice that brought a sense of unutterable horror into that dingy old office he recited:

> " 'There was a little man,
>   And he had a little gun,
> And his bullets were made of lead, lead, lead;
>   He shot Johnny Sprig
>   Through the middle of his wig,
> And knocked it right off of his head, head, head.' "

9

THE TENSOR FORMULA

(*Monday, April 11; 11:30 A.M.*)

MARKHAM SAT staring at Vance like a man hyponotized. Heath stood rigid, his mouth partly open, his cigar held a few inches from his lips. There was something almost comic in the Sergeant's attitude, and I had a nervous inclination to laugh; but for the moment my blood seemed frozen, and all muscular movement was impossible.

Markham was the first to speak. Jerking his head backward, he brought his hand down violently on the desk-top.

"What new lunacy of yours is this?" He was fighting desperately against Vance's dumbfounding suggestion. "I'm beginning to think the Robin case has affected your mind. Can't a man with the commonplace name of Sprigg be shot without your trying to turn it into some grotesque hocus-pocus?"

"Still, you must admit, Markham old dear," returned Vance mildly, "this particular Johnny Sprigg was shot with 'a little gun', through 'the middle of his wig', so to speak."

"What if he was?" A dull flush had crept into Markham's face. "Is that any reason for your going about babbling Mother-Goose rhymes?"

"Oh, I say! I never babble, don't y' know." Vance had dropped into a chair facing the District Attorney's desk. "I may not be a thrillin' elocutionist; but really, now, I don't babble." He gave Heath an ingratiating smile. "Do I, Sergeant?"

But Heath had no opinion to express. He still held his astonished pose, though his eyes had now become mere slits in his broad, pugnacious face.

"Are you seriously suggesting———?" began Markham; but Vance interrupted him.

"Yes! I'm seriously suggesting that the person who killed Cock Robin with an arrow has vented his grim humor upon the hapless Sprigg. Coincidence is out of the question. Such repetitive parallels would knock the entire foundation out from all sanity and reason. 'Pon my soul, the world is mad enough; but such madness would dissipate all science and rational thinking. Sprigg's death is rather hideous; but it must be faced. And however much you may force yourself to protest against its incredible implications you'll eventually have to accept them."

Markham had risen, and was pacing nervously up and down.

"I'll grant there are inexplicable elements in this new crime." His combativeness had gone, and his tone had moderated. "But if we assume, even tentatively, that some maniac is at large reconstructing the rhymes of his nursery days, I can't see how it will help us. It would practically close all routine lines of investigation."

"I shouldn't say that, don't y' know." Vance was smoking meditatively. "I'm inclined to think that such an assumption would supply us with a definite basis of inquiry."

"Sure!" snapped Heath with ponderous sarcasm. "All we gotta do is to go out and find one bug among six million people. A cinch!"

"Don't let the fumes of discouragement overcome you, Sergeant. Our elusive jester is a rather distinctive entomological specimen. Moreover, we have certain clews as to his exact habitat. . . ."

Markham swung round. "What do you mean by that?"

"Merely that this second crime is related to the first not only psychologically, but geographically. Both murders were committed within a few blocks of each other,—our destructive demon at least has a weakness for the neighborhood in which the Dillard house is situated. Furthermore, the very factors of the two murders preclude the possibility of his having come from afar to give rein to his distorted humor in unfamiliar surroundings. As I learnedly pointed out to you, Robin was translated into the Beyond by some one who knew all the conditions obtaining at the Dillard house at the exact hour the grisly drama was performed; and surely it's obvious that this second crime could not have been so tidily staged had not the impresario been acquainted with Sprigg's ambulat'ry intentions this morning. Indeed, the entire mechanism of these weird playlets proves that the operator was intimately cognizant of all the circumstances surrounding his victims."

The heavy silence that followed was broken by Heath.

"If you're right, Mr. Vance, then that lets Sperling out." The Sergeant made even this qualified admission reluctantly; but it showed that Vance's argument had not been without its effect on him. He turned desperately to the District Attorney. "What do you think we'd better do, sir?"

Markham was still battling against the acceptance of Vance's theory, and he did not answer. Presently, however, he reseated himself at his desk and drummed with his fingers upon the blotter. Then, without looking up, he asked:

"Who's in charge of the Sprigg case, Sergeant?"

"Captain Pitts. The local men at the 68th-Street Station grabbed it first; but when the news was relayed to the Bureau, Pitts and a couple of our boys went up to look into it. Pitts got back just before I came over here. Says it's a wash-out. But Inspector Moran* told him to stay with it."

Markham pressed the buzzer beneath the edge of his desk, and Swacker, his youthful secretary, appeared at the swinging door that led to the clerical room between the District Attorney's private office and the main waiting-room.

"Get Inspector Moran on the wire," he ordered.

When the connection had been made he drew the telephone toward him and spoke for several minutes. When he had replaced the receiver, he gave Heath a weary smile.

"You're now officially handling the Sprigg case, Sergeant. Captain Pitts will be here presently, and then we'll know where we stand." He began looking through a pile of papers before him. "I've got to be convinced," he added half-heartedly, "that Sprigg and Robin are tied up in the same sack."

Pitts, a short, stocky man, with a lean, hard face and a black tooth-brush moustache, arrived ten minutes later. He was, I learned afterwards, one of the most competent men in the Detective Division. His specialty was "white-collar" gangsters. He shook hands with Markham and gave Heath a companionable leer. When introduced to Vance and me he focussed suspicious eyes on us and bowed grudgingly. But as he was about to turn away his expression suddenly changed.

"Mr. Philo Vance, is it?" he asked.

"Alas! So it seems, Captain," Vance sighed.

Pitts grinned and, stepping forward, held out his hand.

"Glad to meet you, sir. Heard the Sergeant speak of you often."

"Mr. Vance is helping us unofficially with the Robin case, Captain," explained Markham; "and since this man Sprigg was killed in the same neighborhood we thought we'd like to hear your preliminary report on the affair." He took out a box of Corona *Perfectos,* and pushed it across the desk.

"You needn't put the request that way, sir." The Captain smiled, and selecting a cigar held it to his nose with a kind of voluptuous satisfaction. "The Inspector told me you had some ideas about this new case, and wanted to take it on. To tell you the truth, I'm glad to get rid of it." He sat down leisurely, and lighted his cigar. "What would you like to know, sir?"

"Let us have the whole story," said Markham.

Pitts settled himself comfortably.

"Well, I happened to be on hand when the case came through—a little after eight this morning—and I took a couple of the boys and beat it up-town. The local men were on the job, and an assistant Medical Examiner arrived the same time I did...."

---

* Inspector William M. Moran, who died two years ago, was, at the time of the Bishop case, the Commanding Officer of the Detective Bureau.

"Did you hear his report, Captain?" asked Vance.

"Sure. Sprigg was shot through the top of the head with a .32. No signs of a struggle—no bruises or anything. Nothing fancy. Just a straight shooting."

"Was he lying on his back when found?"

"That's right. Stretched out nice and pretty, right in the middle of the walk."

"And wasn't his skull fractured where he'd fallen on the asphalt?" The question was put negligently.

Pitts took his cigar from his mouth and gave Vance a sly look.

"I guess maybe you fellows over here do know something about this case." He nodded his head sagaciously. "Yes, the back of the guy's skull was all bashed in. He sure had a tough fall. But I guess he didn't feel it—not with that bullet in his brain. . . ."

"Speaking of the shot, Captain, didn't anything about it strike you as peculiar?"

"Well . . . yes," Pitts admitted, rolling his cigar meditatively between his thumb and forefinger. "The top of a guy's head isn't where I'd ordinarily look for a bullet-hole. And his hat wasn't touched,—it must have fallen off before he was potted. You might call those facts peculiar, Mr. Vance."

"Yes, Captain, they're dashed peculiar. . . . And I take it the pistol was held at close range."

"Not more'n a couple of inches away. The hair was singed round the hole." He made a broad gesture of inconsequence. "Still and all, the guy might have seen the other fellow draw the gun, and ducked forward, spilling his hat. That would account for his getting the shot at close range in the top of the head."

"Quite, quite. Except that, in that case, he wouldn't have fallen over back, but would have pitched forward on his face. . . . But go on with the story, Captain."

Pitts gave Vance a look of crafty agreement, and continued.

"The first thing I did was to go through the fellow's pockets. He had a good gold watch on him and about fifteen dollars in bills and silver. So it didn't look like a robbery—unless the guy that shot him got panicky and beat it. But that didn't seem likely, for there's never any one round that part of the park early in the morning; and the walk there dips under a stone bluff, so that the view is cut off. The bird that did the job certainly picked a swell place for it. . . . Anyhow, I left a couple of men to guard the body till the wagon came for it, and went up to Sprigg's house in 93rd Street,—I'd got his name and address from a couple of letters in his pocket. I found out he was a student at Columbia, living with his parents, and that it was his habit to take a walk in the park after breakfast. He left home this morning about half past seven. . . ."

"Ah! It was his habit to promenade in the park each morning," murmured Vance. "Most interestin'."

"Even so, that don't get us anywhere," returned Pitts. "Plenty of fellows take an early constitutional. And there was nothing unusual about Sprigg this morning. He wasn't worried about anything, his folks told me; and was cheerful enough when he said good-bye to 'em.—After that I hopped up to the university and made inquiries; talked to a couple of the students that knew him, and also to one of the instructors. Sprigg was a quiet sort of chap. Didn't make friends and kept pretty much to himself. Serious bird—always working at his studies. Stood high in his classes, and was never seen going around with Janes. Didn't like women, in fact. Wasn't what you'd call sociable. From all reports he was the last man to get in a mess of any kind. That's why I can't see anything special in his getting shot. It must have been an accident of some kind. Might have been taken for somebody else."

"And he was found at what time?"

"About quarter of eight. A bricklayer on the new 79th-Street dock was cutting across the embankment toward the railway tracks, and saw him. He notified one of the post officers on the Drive, who phoned in to the local station."

"And Sprigg left his home in 93rd Street at half past seven." Vance gazed at the ceiling meditatively. "Therefore he would have had just enough time to reach this point in the park before being killed. It looks as if some one who knew his habits was waiting for him. Neatness and dispatch, what? ... It doesn't appear exactly fortuitous, does it, Markham?"

Ignoring the jibe Markham addressed Pitts.

"Was there nothing found that could possibly be used as a lead?"

"No, sir. My men combed the spot pretty thoroughly, but nothing showed up."

"And in Sprigg's pockets—among his papers. . . ?"

"Not a thing. I've got all the stuff at the Bureau—a couple of ordinary letters, a few odds and ends of the usual kind. . . ." He paused as if suddenly remembering something, and pulled out a dog-eared note-book. "There was this," he said unenthusiastically, handing a torn, triangular scrap of paper to Markham. "It was found under the fellow's body. It don't mean anything, but I stuck it in my pocket—force of habit."

$$\text{Bikst} = \frac{\lambda}{3} \, (\text{gik gst} - \text{gis gkt})$$

$$\text{Bikst} = 0 \quad (\text{flat at } \infty)$$

The paper was not more than four inches long, and appeared to have been torn from the corner of an ordinary sheet of unruled stationery. It contained part of a typewritten mathematical formula, with the lambda, the equals and the infinity sign marked in with pencil. I reproduce the paper here, for, despite its seeming irrelevancy, it was to play a sinister and amazing part in the investigation of Sprigg's death.

Vance glanced only casually at the exhibit, but Markham held it in his hand frowning at it for several moments. He was about to make some comment when he caught Vance's eye; and, instead, he tossed the paper to the desk carelessly with a slight shrug.

"Is this everything you found?"

"That's all, sir."

Markham rose.

"We're very grateful to you, Captain. I don't know what we'll be able to make out of this Sprigg case, but we'll look into it." He pointed to the box of *Perfectos.* "Put a couple in your pocket before you go."

"Much obliged, sir." Pitts selected the cigars, and placing them tenderly in his waistcoast pocket, shook hands with all of us.

When he had gone Vance got up with alacrity, and bent over the scrap of paper on Markham's desk.

"My word!" He took out his monocle and studied the symbols for several moments. "Most allurin'. Now where have I seen that formula recently? . . . Ah! The Riemann-Christoffel tensor—of course! Drukker uses it in his book for determining the Gaussian curvature of spherical and homaloidal space. . . . But what was Sprigg doing with it? The formula is considerably beyond the college curricula. . . ." He held the paper up to the light. "It's the same stock as that on which the Bishop notes are written. And you probably observed that the typing is also similar."

Heath had stepped forward, and now scrutinized the paper.

"It's the same, all right." The fact seemed to nonplus him. "That's a link anyway between the two crimes."

Vance's eyes took on a puzzled look.

"A link—yes. But the presence of the formula under Sprigg's body appears as irrational as the murder itself. . . ."

Markham moved uneasily.

"You say it is a formula that Drukker uses in his book?"

"Yes. But the fact doesn't necessarily involve him. The tensor is known to all advanced mathematicians. It is one of the technical expressions used in non-Euclidean geometry; and though it was discovered by Riemann in connection with a concrete problem in physics,* it has now become of widespread importance in the mathematics of relativity. It's highly scientific in the abstract sense, and can have no direct bearing on Sprigg's murder." He sat down again. "Arnesson will be delighted with the find. He may be able to work out some astonishing conclusion from it."

"I see no reason," protested Markham, "to inform Arnesson of this new case. My idea would be to keep it under cover as much as possible."

---

* This expression was actually developed by Christoffel for a problem on the conductivity of heat, and published by him in 1869 in the "Crelle Journal für reine und angewandte Mathematik."

"The Bishop won't let you, I fear," returned Vance.

Markham set his jaw.

"Good God!" he burst out. "What damnable sort of thing are we facing? I expect every minute to wake up and discover I've been living a nightmare."

"No such luck, sir," growled Heath. He took a resolute breath like a man preparing for combat. "What's in the cards? Where do we go from here? I need action."

Markham appealed to Vance.

"You seem to have some idea about this affair. What's your suggestion? I frankly admit I'm floundering about in a black chaos."

Vance inhaled deeply on his cigarette. Then he leaned forward as if to give emphasis to his words.

"Markham old man, there's only one conclusion to be drawn. These two murders were engineered by the same brain: both sprang from the same grotesque impulse; and since the first of them was committed by some one intimately familiar with conditions inside the Dillard house, it follows that we must now look for a person who, in addition to that knowledge, had definite information that a man named John Sprigg was in the habit of taking a walk each morning in a certain part of Riverside Park. Having found such a person, we must check up on the points of time, place, opportunity, and possible motive. There's some interrelation between Sprigg and the Dillards. What it is I don't know. But our first move should be to find out. What better starting-point than the Dillard house itself?"

"We'll get some lunch first," said Markham wearily. "Then we'll run out there."

10

A REFUSAL OF AID

(*Monday, April 11; 2 P.M.*)

IT WAS shortly after two o'clock when we reached the Dillard house. Pyne answered our ring; and if our visit caused him any surprise he succeeded admirably in hiding it. In the look he gave Heath, however, I detected a certain uneasiness; but when he spoke his voice had the flat, unctuous quality of the well-trained servant.

"Mr. Arnesson has not returned from the university," he informed us.

"Mind-reading, I see," said Vance, "is not your *forte,* Pyne. We called to see you and Professor Dillard."

The man looked ill at ease; but before he could answer Miss Dillard appeared in the archway of the drawing-room.

"I thought I recognized your voice, Mr. Vance." She included us all in a smile of wistful welcome. "Please come in. . . . Lady Mae dropped in for a few minutes,—we're going riding together this afternoon," she explained, as we entered the room.

Mrs. Drukker stood by the centre-table, one bony hand on the back of the chair from which she had evidently just risen. There was fear in her eyes as she stared at us unblinkingly; and her lean features seemed almost contorted. She made no effort to speak, but stood rigidly as if waiting for some dread pronouncement, like a convicted prisoner at the bar about to receive sentence.

Belle Dillard's pleasant voice relieved the tensity of the situation.

"I'll run up and tell uncle you're here."

She had no sooner quitted the room than Mrs. Drukker leaned over the table and said to Markham in a sepulchral, awe-stricken whisper: "I know why you've come! It's about that fine young man who was shot in the park this morning."

So amazing and unexpected were her words that Markham could make no immediate answer; and it was Vance who replied.

"You have heard of the tragedy, then, Mrs. Drukker? How could the news have come to you so soon?"

A look of canniness came into the woman's expression, giving her the appearance of an evil old witch.

"Every one is talking about it in the neighborhood," she answered evasively.

"Indeed? That's most unfortunate. But why do you assume we have come here to make inquiries about it?"

"Wasn't the young man's name Johnny Sprigg?" A faint, terrible smile accompanied the question.

"So it was. John E. Sprigg. Still, that does not explain his connection with the Dillards."

"Ah, but it does!" Her head moved up and down with a sort of horrible satisfaction. "It's a game—a child's game. First Cock Robin . . . then Johnny Sprig. Children must play—all healthy children must play." Her mood suddenly changed. A softness shone on her face, and her eyes grew sad.

"It's a rather diabolical game, don't you think, Mrs. Drukker?"

"And why not? Isn't life itself diabolical?"

"For some of us—yes." A curious sympathy informed Vance's words as he gazed at this strange tragic creature before us. "Tell me," he went on quickly, in an altered tone; "do you know who the Bishop is?"

"The Bishop?" She frowned perplexedly. "No, I don't know him. Is that another child's game?"

"Something of that kind, I imagine. At any rate, the Bishop is interested in Cock Robin and Johnny Sprig. In fact, he may be the person who is making up these fantastic games. And we're looking for him, Mrs. Drukker. We hope to learn the truth from him."

The woman shook her head vaguely. "I don't know him." Then she glared vindictively at Markham. "But it's not going to do you any good to try to find out who killed Cock Robin and shot Johnny Sprig through the middle of his wig. You'll never learn—never—*never*. . . ." Her voice had risen excitedly, and a fit of trembling seized her.

At this moment Belle Dillard re-entered the room, and going quickly to Mrs. Drukker put her arm about her.

"Come," she said soothingly; "we'll have a long drive in the country, Lady Mae." Reproachfully she turned to Markham, and said coldly: "Uncle wishes you to come to the library." With that she led Mrs. Drukker from the room and down the hall.

"Now that's a queer one, sir," commented Heath, who had stood looking on with bewildered amazement. "She had the dope on this Johnny-Sprig stuff all the time!"

Vance nodded.

"And our appearance here frightened her. Still, her mind is morbid and sensitive, Sergeant; and dwelling as she does constantly on her son's deformity and the early days when he was like other children, it's quite possible she merely hit accidentally upon the Mother-Goose significance of Robin's and Sprigg's death. . . . I wonder." He looked toward Markham. "There are strange undercurrents in this case—incredible and terrifying implications. It's like being lost in the Dovrë-Troll caverns of Ibsen's 'Peer Gynt,' where only monstrosities and abnormalities exist." He shrugged his shoulders, though I knew he had not wholly escaped the pall of horror cast on us by Mrs. Drukker's words. "Perhaps we can find a little solid footing with Professor Dillard."

The professor received us without enthusiasm and with but scant cordiality. His desk was littered with papers, and it was obvious that we had disturbed him in the midst of his labors.

"Why this unexpected visit, Markham?" he asked, after we had seated ourselves. "Have you something to report on Robin's death?" He marked a page in Weyl's "Space, Time and Matter" and, settling back reluctantly, regarded us with impatience. "I'm very busy working on a problem of Mach's mechanics. . . ."

"I regret," said Markham, "I have nothing to report on the Robin case. But there has been another murder in this neighborhood to-day, and we have reason to believe that it may be connected with Robin's death. What I wanted particularly to ask you, sir, is whether or not the name of John E. Sprigg is familiar to you."

Professor Dillard's expression of annoyance changed quickly.

"Is that the name of the man who was killed?" There was no longer any lack of interest in his attitude.

"Yes. A man named John E. Sprigg was shot in Riverside Park, near 84th Street, this morning shortly after half past seven."

The professor's eyes wandered to the mantelpiece, and he was silent for several moments. He seemed to be debating inwardly some point that troubled him.

"Yes," he said at length, "I—we—do know a young man of that name—though it's wholly unlikely he's the same one."

"Who is he?" Markham's voice was eagerly insistent.

Again the professor hesitated.

"The lad I have in mind is Arnesson's prize student in mathematics—what they'd call at Cambridge a senior wrangler."

"How do you happen to know him, sir?"

"Arnesson has brought him to the house here several times. Wanted me to see him and talk to him. Arnesson was quite proud of the boy; and I must admit he showed unusual talent."

"Then he was known to all the members of the household?"

"Yes. Belle met him, I think. And if by 'the household' you include Pyne and Beedle, I should say the name was probably familiar to them too."

Vance asked the next question.

"Did the Drukkers know Sprigg, Professor Dillard?"

"It's quite possible. Arnesson and Drukker see each other a great deal. . . . Come to think of it, I believe Drukker was here one night when Sprigg called."

"And Pardee: did he also know Sprigg?"

"As to that I couldn't say." The professor tapped impatiently on the arm of his chair, and turned back to Markham. "See here"—his voice held a worried petulance—"what's the point of these questions? What has our knowing a student named Sprigg to do with this morning's affair? Surely you don't mean to tell me that the man who was killed was Arnesson's pupil."

"I'm afraid it's true," said Markham.

There was a note of anxiety—of fear almost, I thought—in the professor's voice when he next spoke.

"Even so, what can that fact have to do with us? And how can you possibly connect his death with Robin's?"

"I admit we have nothing definite to go on," Markham told him. "But the purposelessness of both crimes—the total lack of any motive in either case—seems to give them a curious unity of aspect."

"You mean, of course, that you have found no motive. But if all crimes without apparent motive were assumed to be connected——"

"Also there are the elements of time and proximity in these two cases," Markham amplified.

"Is that the basis of your assumption?" The professor's manner was benevolently contemptuous. "You never were a good mathematician, Markham, but at least you should know that no hypothesis can be built on such a flimsy premise."

"Both names," interposed Vance, "—Cock Robin and Johnny Sprig—are the subjects of well-known nursery rhymes."

The old man stared at him with undisguised astonishment; and gradually an angry flush mounted to his face.

"Your humor, sir, is out of place."

"It is not *my* humor, alas!" replied Vance sadly. "The jest is the Bishop's."

"The Bishop?" Professor Dillard strove to curb his irritation. "Look here, Markham; I won't be played with. That's the second mention of a mysterious Bishop that's been made in this room; and I want to know the meaning of it. Even if a crank did write an insane letter to the papers in connection with Robin's death, what has this Bishop to do with Sprigg?"

"A paper was found beneath Sprigg's body bearing a mathematical formula typed on the same machine as the Bishop notes."

"What!" The professor bent forward. "The same machine, you say? And a mathematical formula? . . . What was the formula?"

Markham opened his pocketbook, and held out the triangular scrap of paper that Pitts had given him.

"The Riemann-Christoffel tensor. . . ." Professor Dillard sat for a long time gazing at the paper; then he handed it back to Markham. He seemed suddenly to have grown older; and there was a weary look in his eyes as he lifted them to us. "I don't see any light in this matter." His tone was one of hopeless resignation. "But perhaps you are right in following your present course.—What do you want of me?"

Markham was plainly puzzled by the other's altered attitude.

"I came to you primarily to ascertain if there was any link between Sprigg and this house; but, to be quite candid, I don't see how that link, now that I have it, fits into the chain.—I would, however, like your permission to question Pyne and Beedle in whatever way I think advisable."

"Ask them anything you like, Markham. You shall never be able to accuse me of having stood in your way." He glanced up appealingly. "But you will, I hope, advise me before you take any drastic steps."

"That I can promise you, sir." Markham rose. "But I fear we are a long way from any drastic measures at present." He held out his hand, and from his manner it was evident he had sensed some hidden anxiety in the old man and wanted to express his sympathy without voicing his feelings.

The professor walked with us to the door.

"I can't understand that typed tensor," he murmured, shaking his head. "But if there's anything I can do. . . ."

"There *is* something you can do for us, Professor Dillard," said Vance, pausing at the door. "On the morning Robin was killed we interviewed Mrs. Drukker————"

"Ah!"

"And though she denied having sat at her window during the forenoon there is a possibility she saw something happen on the archery range between eleven and twelve."

"She gave you that impression?" There was an undertone of suppressed interest in the professor's question.

"Only in a remote way. It was Drukker's statement that he had heard his mother scream, and her denial of having screamed, that led me to believe that she might have seen something she preferred to keep from us. And it occurred to me that you would probably have more influence with her than any one else, and that, if she did indeed witness anything, you might prevail upon her to speak."

"No!" Professor Dillard spoke almost harshly; but he immediately placed his hand on Markham's arm, and his tone changed. "There are some things you must not ask me to do for you. If that poor harassed woman saw anything from her window that morning, you must find it out for yourself. I'll have no hand in torturing her; and I sincerely hope you'll not worry her either. There are other ways of finding out what you want to know." He looked straight into Markham's eyes. "*She* must not be the one to tell you. You yourself would be sorry afterwards."

"We must find out what we can," Markham answered resolutely but with kindliness. "There's a fiend loose in this city, and I cannot stay my hand to save any one from suffering—however tragic that suffering may be. But I assure you I shall not unnecessarily torture any one."

"Have you thought," asked Professor Dillard quietly, "that the truth you seek may be more frightful even than the crimes themselves?"

"That I shall have to risk. But even if I know it to be a fact, it would not deter me in any degree."

"Certainly not. But, Markham, I'm much older than you. I had gray hair when you were a lad struggling with your logs and antilogs; and when one gets old one learns the true proportions in the universe. The ratios all change. The estimates we once placed on things lose their meaning. That's why the old are more forgiving: they know that no man-made values are of any importance."

"But as long as we must live by human values," argued Markham, "it is my duty to uphold them. And I cannot, through any personal sense of sympathy, refuse to take any avenue that may lead to the truth."

"You are perhaps right," the professor sighed. "But you must not ask me to help you in this instance. If you learn the truth, be charitable. Be sure your culprit is accountable before you demand that he be sent to the electric chair. There are diseased minds as well as diseased bodies; and often the two go together."

When we had returned to the drawing-room Vance lighted a cigarette with more than his usual care.

"The professor," he said, "is not at all happy about Sprigg's death; and, though he won't admit it, that tensor formula convinced him that Sprigg and Robin belong to the same equation. But he was convinced dashed easily. Now, why?—Moreover, he didn't care to admit that Sprigg was known hereabouts. I don't say he has suspicions, but he has fears. . . . Deuced funny, his attitude. He apparently doesn't want to obstruct the legal justice which you uphold with such touchin' zeal, Markham; but he most decidedly doesn't care to abet your crusade where the Drukkers are concerned. I wonder what's back of his consideration for Mrs. Drukker. I shouldn't say, offhand, that the professor was of a sentimental nature.—And what was that platitude about a diseased mind and a diseased body? Sounded like a prospectus for a physical culture class, what? . . . Lackaday! Let's put a few questions to Pyne and kin."

Markham sat smoking moodily. I had rarely seen him so despondent.

"I don't see what we can hope for from them," he commented. "However, Sergeant, get Pyne in here."

When Heath had stepped out Vance gave Markham a waggish look.

"Really, y' know, you shouldn't repine. Let Terence console you:—*Nil tam difficile est, quin quærendo investigari possit.* And, 'pon my soul, this is a difficult problem. . . ." He became suddenly sober. "We're dealing with unknown quantities here. We're pitted against some strange, abnormal force that doesn't operate according to the accepted laws of conduct. It's at once subtle—oh, no end subtle—and unfamiliar. But at least we know that it emanates from somewhere in the environs of this old house; and we must search in every psychological nook and cranny. Somewhere about us lies the invisible dragon. So don't be shocked at the questions I shall put to Pyne. We must look in the most unlikely places. . . ."

Footsteps were heard approaching the archway, and a moment later Heath entered with the old butler in tow.

11

THE STOLEN REVOLVER

(*Monday, April 11; 3 P.M.*)

"Sit down, Pyne," said Vance, with peremptory kindness. "We have permission from Professor Dillard to question you; and we shall expect answers to all our questions."

"Certainly, sir," the man answered. "I'm sure there's nothing that Professor Dillard has any reason to hide."

"Excellent." Vance lay back lazily. "To begin with, then; what hour was breakfast served here this morning?"

"At half past eight, sir—the same as always."

"Were all the members of the family present?"

"Oh, yes, sir."

"Who calls the family in the morning? And at what time?"

"I do myself—at half past seven. I knock on the doors————"

"And wait for an answer?"

"Yes, sir—always."

"Now think, Pyne: did every one answer you this morning?"

The man inclined his head emphatically. "Yes, sir."

"And no one was late to breakfast?"

"Every one was on time promptly—as usual, sir."

Vance leaned over and deposited his cigarette ash in the grate.

"Did you happen to see any one leaving the house or returning to it this morning before breakfast?"

The question was put casually, but I noted a slight quiver of surprise in the butler's thin drooping eyelids.

"No, sir."

"Even though you saw no one," pursued Vance, "would it not have been possible for some member of the household to have gone out and returned without your knowing it?"

Pyne for the first time during the interview appeared reluctant to answer.

"Well, sir, the fact is," he said uneasily, "any one might have used the front door this morning without my knowing it, as I was in the dining-room setting table. And, for the matter of that, any one might have used the archery-room door, for my daughter generally keeps the kitchen door closed while preparing breakfast."

Vance smoked thoughtfully a moment. Then in an even, matter-of-fact tone he asked: "Does any one in the house own a revolver?"

The man's eyes opened wide.

"Not that I—know of, sir," he answered haltingly.

"Ever hear of the Bishop, Pyne?"

"Oh, no, sir!" His face blanched. "You mean the man who wrote those letters to the papers?"

"I merely meant the Bishop," said Vance carelessly. "But tell me: have you heard anything about a man being killed in Riverside Park this morning?"

408

"Yes, sir. The janitor next door was telling me about it."

"You knew young Mr. Sprigg, didn't you?"

"I'd seen him at the house here once or twice, sir."

"Was he here recently?"

"Last week, sir. Thursday I think it was."

"Who else was here at the time?"

Pyne frowned as if trying to remember.

"Mr. Drukker, sir," he said after a moment. "And, as I recall, Mr. Pardee came too. They were together in Mr. Arnesson's room talking until late."

"In Mr. Arnesson's room, eh? Is it custom'ry for Mr. Arnesson to receive callers in his room?"

"No, sir," Pyne explained; "but the professor was working in the library, and Miss Dillard was with Mrs. Drukker in the drawing-room here."

Vance was silent a while.

"That will be all, Pyne," he said at length. "But please send Beedle to us at once."

Beedle came and stood before us with sullen aggressiveness. Vance questioned her along the same lines as he had taken with Pyne. Her answers, for the most part monosyllabic, added nothing to what had already been learned. But at the end of the brief interview Vance asked her if she had happened to look out of the kitchen window that morning before breakfast.

"I looked out once or twice," she answered defiantly. "Why shouldn't I look out?"

"Did you see any one on the archery range or in the rear yard?"

"No one but the professor and Mrs. Drukker."

"No strangers?" Vance strove to give the impression that the fact of Professor Dillard's and Mrs. Drukker's presence in the rear yard that morning was of no importance; but, by the slow, deliberate way in which he reached into his pocket for his cigarette-case, I knew the information had interested him keenly.

"No," the woman replied curtly.

"What time did you notice the professor and Mrs. Drukker?"

"Eight o'clock maybe."

"Were they talking together?"

"Yes.—Anyway," she emended, "they were walking up and down near the arbor."

"Is it custom'ry for them to stroll in the yard before breakfast?"

"Mrs. Drukker often comes out early and walks about the flower beds. And I guess the professor has a right to walk in his own yard any time he wants to."

"I'm not questioning his rights in the matter, Beedle," said Vance mildly. "I was merely wondering if he was in the habit of exercising those rights at such an early hour."

"Well, he was exercising 'em this morning."

Vance dismissed the woman and, rising, went to the front window. He was patently puzzled, and he stood several minutes looking down the street toward the river.

"Well, well," he murmured. "It's a nice day for communin' with nature. At eight this morning the lark was on the wing no doubt, and—who knows?—

maybe there was a snail on the thorn. But—my word!—all wasn't right with the world."

Markham recognized the signs of Vance's perplexity.

"What do you make of it?" he asked. "I'm inclined to ignore Beedle's information."

"The trouble is, Markham, we can't afford to ignore anything in this case." Vance spoke softly, without turning. "I'll admit, though, that at present Beedle's revelation is meaningless. We've merely learned that two of the actors in our melodrama were up and about this morning shortly after Sprigg was snuffed out. The al-fresco rendezvous between the professor and Mrs. Drukker may, of course, be just one of your beloved coincidences. On the other hand, it may have some bearing on the old gentleman's sentimental attitude toward the lady. . . . I think we'll have to make a few discreet inquiries of him about his ante-prandial tryst, what? . . ."

He leaned suddenly toward the window.

"Ah! Here comes Arnesson. Looks a bit excited."

A few moments later there was the sound of a key in the front door, and Arnesson strode down the hall. When he saw us he came quickly into the drawing-room and, without a word of greeting, burst forth:

"What's this I hear about Sprigg being shot?" His eager eyes darted from one to the other of us. "I suppose you're here to ask me about him. Well, fire away." He threw a bulky brief-case on the centre-table and sat down abruptly on the edge of a straight chair. "There was a detective up at college this morning asking fool questions and acting like a burlesque sleuth in a comic opera. Very mysterious. . . . Murder—horrible murder! What did we know about a certain John E. Sprigg? And so on. . . . Scared a couple of juniors out of an entire semester's mental growth, and sent a harmless young English instructor into incipient nervous collapse. I didn't see the Dogberry myself—was in class at the time. But he had the cheek to ask what women Sprigg went around with. Sprigg and women! That boy didn't have a thought in his head but his work. Brightest man in senior math. Never missed a class. When he didn't answer roll-call this morning I knew something serious was the matter. At the lunch hour every one was buzzing about murder. . . . What's the answer?"

"We haven't the answer, Mr. Arnesson." Vance had been watching him closely. "However, we have another determinant for your formula. Johnny Sprig was shot this morning with a little gun through the middle of his wig."

Arnesson stared at Vance for some time without moving. Then he threw his head back and gave a sardonic laugh.

"Some more mumbo-jumbo, eh?—like the death of Cock Robin. . . . Read me the rune."

Vance gave him briefly the details of the crime.

"That's all we know at present," he concluded. "Could *you,* Mr. Arnesson, add any suggestive details?"

"Good Lord, no!" The man appeared genuinely amazed. "Not a thing. Sprigg . . . one of the keenest students I ever had. Something of a genius, by Gad! Too bad his parents named him John—plenty of other names. It sealed his doom apparently; got him shot through the head by a maniac. Obviously the same merry-andrew who did Robin in with an arrow." He rubbed his hands together,—the abstract philosopher in him had become uppermost. "A nice problem. You've told me everything? I'll need every known integer. Maybe I'll hit upon a new mathematical method in the process—like Kepler." He chuckled over the conceit. "Remember Kepler's 'Doliometrie'? It became the foundation of Infinitesimal Calculus. He arrived at it trying to construct a cask for his wine—a cask with a minimum amount of wood and a maximum cubical content. Maybe the formulas I work out to solve these crimes will open up new fields of scientific research. Ha! Robin and Sprigg will then become martyrs."

The man's humor, even taking into consideration his life's passion for abstractions, struck me as particularly distasteful. But Vance seemed not to mind his cold-blooded cynicism.

"There's one item," he said, "that I omitted to mention." Turning to Markham he asked for the piece of paper containing the formula, and handed it to Arnesson. "This was found beneath Sprigg's body."

The other scrutinized it superciliously.

"The Bishop, I see, is again involved. Same paper and typing as the notes. . . . But where did he get that Riemann-Christoffel tensor? Now, if it had been some other tensor—like the G-sigma-tau, for instance—any one interested in practical physics might have hit on it. But this one isn't common; and the statement of it here is arbitrary and unusual. Certain terms omitted. . . . *By George!* I was talking to Sprigg about this only the other night. He wrote it down, too."

"Pyne mentioned the fact that Sprigg had called here Thursday night," put in Vance.

"Oh, he did, did he? . . . Thursday—that's right. Pardee was here, too. And Drukker. We had a discussion on Gaussian co-ordinates. This tensor came up—Drukker mentioned it first, I think. And Pardee had some mad notion of applying the higher mathematics to chess. . . ."

"Do you play chess, by the by?" asked Vance.

"Used to. But no more. A beautiful game, though—if it wasn't for the players. Queer crabs, chess players."

"Did you ever make any study of the Pardee gambit?" (At the time I could not understand the seeming irrelevance of Vance's questions; and I noticed that Markham too was beginning to show signs of impatience.)

"Poor old Pardee!" Arnesson smiled unfeelingly. "Not a bad elementary mathematician. Should have been a high-school teacher. Too much money, though. Took to chess. I told him his gambit was unscientific. Even showed him how it could be beaten. But he couldn't see it. Then Capablanca, Vidmar and Tartakower came along and knocked it into a cocked hat. Just as I told him they would. Wrecked his life. He's been fussing around with another gambit for years, but can't make it cohere. Reads Weyl, Silberstein, Eddington and Mach in the hope of getting inspiration."

"That's most interestin'." Vance extended his match-case to Arnesson, who had been filling his pipe as he talked. "Was Pardee well acquainted with Sprigg?"

"Oh, no. Met him here twice—that's all. Pardee knows Drukker well, though. Always asking him about potentials and scalars and vectors. Hopes to hit on something that'll revolutionize chess."

"Was he interested in the Riemann-Christoffel tensor when you discussed it the other night?"

"Can't say that he was. A bit out of his realm. You can't hitch the curvature of space-time to a chess-board."

"What do you make of this formula being found on Sprigg?"

"Don't make anything of it. If it had been in Sprigg's handwriting I'd say it dropped out of his pocket. But who'd go to the trouble of trying to type a mathematical formula?"

"The Bishop apparently."

Arnesson took his pipe from his mouth and grinned.

"Bishop X. We'll have to find him. He's full of whimsies. Perverted sense of values."

"Obviously." Vance spoke languidly. "And, by the by, I almost forgot to ask you: does the Dillard house harbor any revolvers?"

"Oho!" Arnesson chuckled with unrestrained delight. "Sits the wind there? . . . Sorry to disappoint you. No revolvers. No sliding doors. No secret stairways. All open and above-board."

Vance sighed theatrically.

"Sad . . . sad! And I had such a comfortin' theory."

Belle Dillard had come silently down the hall, and now stood in the archway. She had evidently heard Vance's question and Arnesson's answer.

"But there *are* two revolvers in the house, Sigurd," she declared. "Don't you remember the old revolvers I used for target practice in the country?"

"Thought you'd thrown 'em away long ago." Arnesson rose and drew up a chair for her. "I told you when we returned from Hopatcong that summer that only burglars and bandits are allowed to own guns in this benevolent State. . . ."

"But I didn't believe you," the girl protested. "I never know when you're jesting and when you're serious."

"And you kept them, Miss Dillard?" came Vance's quiet voice.

"Why—yes." She shot an apprehensive glance at Heath. "Shouldn't I have done so?"

"I believe it was technically illegal. However"—Vance smiled reassuringly—"I don't think the Sergeant will invoke the Sullivan law against you.— Where are they now?"

"Down-stairs—in the archery-room. They're in one of the drawers of the tool-chest."

Vance rose.

"Would you be so good, Miss Dillard, as to show us where you put them? I have a gnawin' curiosity to see 'em, don't y' know."

The girl hesitated and looked to Arnesson for guidance. When he nodded she turned without a word and led the way to the archery-room.

"They're in that chest by the window," she said.

Going to it she drew out a small deep drawer in one end. At the rear, beneath a mass of odds and ends, was a .38 Colt automatic.

"Why!" she exclaimed. "There's only one here. The other is gone."

"It was a smaller pistol, wasn't it?" asked Vance.

"Yes. . . ."

"A .32?"

The girl nodded and turn bewildered eyes on Arnesson.

"Well, it's gone, Belle," he told her, with a shrug. "Can't be helped. Probably one of your young archers took it to blow out his brains with after he'd foozled at shooting arrows up the alley."

"Do be serious, Sigurd," she pleaded, a little frightened. "Where could it have gone?"

"Ha! Another dark mystery," scoffed Arnesson. "Strange disappearance of a discarded .32."

Seeing the girl's uneasiness Vance changed the subject.

"Perhaps, Miss Dillard, you'd be good enough to take us to Mrs. Drukker. There are one or two matters we want to speak to her about; and I assume, by your presence here, that the ride in the country has been postponed."

A shadow of distress passed over the girl's face.

"Oh, you mustn't bother her to-day." Her tone was tragically appealing. "Lady Mae is very ill. I can't understand it—she seemed so well when I was talking with her up-stairs. But after she'd seen you and Mr. Markham she changed: she became weak and . . . oh, something terrible seemed to be preying on her mind. After I'd put her to bed she kept repeating in an awful whisper: 'Johnny Sprig, Johnny Sprig.' . . . I phoned her doctor and he came right over. He said she had to be kept very quiet. . . .'"

"It's of no importance," Vance assured her. "Of course we shall wait.—Who is her doctor, Miss Dillard?"

"Whitney Barstead. He's attended her as long as I can remember."

"A good man," nodded Vance. "There's no better neurologist in the country. We'll do nothing without his permission."

Miss Dillard gave him a grateful look. Then she excused herself.

When we were again in the drawing-room Arnesson stationed himself before the fireplace and regarded Vance satirically.

" 'Johnny Sprig, Johnny Sprig.' Ha! Lady Mae got the idea at once. She may be cracked, but certain lobes of her brain are over-active. Unaccountable piece of machinery, the human brain. Some of the greatest mental computers of Europe are morons. And I know a couple of chess masters who need nurses to dress and feed 'em."

Vance appeared not to hear him. He had stopped by a small cabinet near the archway and was apparently absorbed in a set of jade carvings of ancient Chinese origin.

"That elephant doesn't belong there," he remarked casually, pointing to a tiny figure in the collection. "It's a *bunjinga*—decadent, don't y' know. Clever, but not authentic. Probably a copy of a Manchu piece." He stifled a yawn and turned toward Markham. "I say, old man, there's nothing more we can do. Suppose we toddle. We might have a brief word with the professor before we go, though. . . . Mind waiting for us here, Mr. Arnesson?"

Arnesson lifted his eyebrows in some surprise, but immediately crinkled his face into a disdainful smile.

"Oh, no. Go ahead." And he began refilling his pipe.

Professor Dillard was much annoyed at our second intrusion.

"We've just learned," said Markham, "that you were speaking to Mrs. Drukker before breakfast this morning. . . ."

The muscles of Professor Dillard's cheeks worked angrily.

"Is it any concern of the District Attorney's office if I speak to a neighbor in my garden?"

"Certainly not, sir. But I am in the midst of an investigation which seriously concerns your house, and I assumed that I had the privilege of seeking help from you."

The old man spluttered a moment.

"Very well," he acquiesced irritably. "I saw no one except Mrs. Drukker—if that's what you're after."

Vance projected himself into the conversation.

"That's not what we came to you for, Professor Dillard. We wanted merely to ask you if Mrs. Drukker gave you the impression this morning that she suspected what had taken place earlier in Riverside Park."

The professor was about to make a sharp retort, but checked himself. After a moment he said simply:

"No, she gave me no such impression."

"Did she appear in any way uneasy or, let us say, excited?"

"She did not!" Professor Dillard rose and faced Markham. "I understand perfectly what you are driving at; and I won't have it. I've told you, Markham, that I'll take no part in spying or tale-bearing where this unhappy woman is concerned. That's all I have to say to you." He turned back to his desk. "I regret I'm very busy to-day."

We descended to the main floor and made our adieus to Arnesson. He waved his hand to us cordially as we went out; but his smile held something of contemptuous patronage, as if he had witnessed, and was gloating over, the rebuff we had just received.

When we were on the sidewalk Vance paused to light a fresh cigarette.

"Now for a brief *causerie* with the sad and gentlemanly Mr. Pardee. I don't know what he can tell us, but I have a yearnin' to commune with him."

Pardee, however, was not at home. His Japanese servant informed us that his master was most likely at the Manhattan Chess Club.

"To-morrow will be time enough," Vance said to Markham, as we turned away from the house. "I'll get in touch with Doctor Barstead in the morning and try to arrange to see Mrs. Drukker. We'll include Pardee in the same pilgrimage."

"I sure hope" grumbled Heath, "that we learn more to-morrow than we did to-day."

"You overlook one or two consolin' windfalls, Sergeant," returned Vance. "We've found out that every one connected with the Dillard house was acquainted with Sprigg and could easily have known of his early morning walks along the Hudson. We've also learned that the professor and Mrs. Drukker were ramblin' in the garden at eight o'clock this morning. And we discovered that a .32 revolver has disappeared from the archery-room.—Not an embarrassment of riches, but something—oh, decidedly something."

As we drove down-town Markham roused himself from gloomy abstraction, and looked apprehensively at Vance.

"I'm almost afraid to go on with this case. It's becoming too sinister. And if the newspapers get hold of that Johnny-Sprig nursery rhyme and connect the two murders, I hate to think of the gaudy sensation that'll follow."

"I fear you're in for it, old man," sighed Vance. "I'm not a bit psychic—never had dreams that came true, and don't know what a telepathic seizure feels like—but something tells me that the Bishop is going to acquaint the press with that bit of Mother-Goose verse. The point of his new joke is even obscurer than his Cock-Robin comedy. He'll see to it that no one misses it. Even a grim humorist who uses corpses for his cap-and-bells must have his audience. Therein lies the one weakness of his abominable crimes. It's about our only hope, Markham."

"I'll give Quinan a ring," said Heath, "and find out if anything has been received."

But the Sergeant was saved the trouble. The *World* reporter was waiting for us at the District Attorney's office, and Swacker ushered him in at once.

"Howdy, Mr. Markham." There was a breezy impudence in Quinan's manner, but withal he showed signs of nervous excitement. "I've got something here for Sergeant Heath. They told me at Headquarters that he was handling the Sprigg case, and said he was parleying with you. So I blew over." He reached in his pocket and, taking out a sheet of paper, handed it to Heath. "I'm being mighty high, wide and handsome with you, Sergeant, and I expect a little inside stuff by way of reciprocity. . . . Cast your eye on that document. Just received by America's foremost family journal."

It was a plain piece of typewriting paper, and it contained the Mother-Goose melody of Johnny Sprig, typed in élite characters with a pale-blue ribbon. In the lower right-hand corner was the signature in capitals: THE BISHOP.

"And here's the envelope, Sergeant." Quinan again dug down into his pocket.

The official cancellation bore the hour of 9 A.M., and, like the first note, it had been mailed in the district of Post Office Station "N."

12

A MIDNIGHT CALL

(*Tuesday, April 12; 10 A.M.*)

THE FOLLOWING morning the front pages of the metropolitan press carried sensational stories which surpassed Markham's worst fears. In addition to the *World* two other leading morning journals had received notes similar to the one shown us by Quinan; and the excitement created by their publication was tremendous. The entire city was thrown into a state of apprehension and fear; and though half-hearted attempts were made here and there to dismiss the maniacal aspect of the crimes on the ground of coincidence, and to explain away the Bishop notes as the work of a practical joker, all the newspapers and the great majority of the public were thoroughly convinced that a new and terrible type of killer was preying upon the community.*

* A similar state of panic obtained in London in 1888 when Jack-the-Ripper was engaged in his grisly, abnormal debauch; and again in Hanover in 1923 when Haarmann, the werwolf, was busy with his anthropophagous slaugthers. But I can recall no other modern parallel for the atmosphere of gruesome horror that settled over New York during the Bishop murders.

Markham and Heath were beset by reporters, but a veil of secrecy was sedulously maintained. No intimation was given that there was any reason to believe that the solution lay close to the Dillard household; and no mention was made of the missing .32 revolver. Sperling's status was sympathetically dealt with by the press. The general attitude now was that the young man had been the unfortunate victim of circumstances; and all criticism of Markham's procrastination in prosecuting him was instantly dropped.

On the day that Sprigg was shot Markham called a conference at the Stuyvesant Club. Both Inspector Moran of the Detective Bureau and Chief Inspector O'Brien* attended. The two murders were gone over in detail, and Vance outlined his reasons for believing that the answer to the problem would eventually be found either in the Dillard house or in some quarter directly connected with it.

"We are now in touch," he ended, "with every person who could possibly have had sufficient knowledge of the conditions surrounding the two victims to perpetrate the crimes successfully; and our only course is to concentrate on these persons."

Inspector Moran was inclined to agree. "Except," he qualified, "that none of the *dramatis personæ* you have mentioned strikes me as a bloodthirsty maniac."

"The murderer is not a maniac in the conventional sense," returned Vance. "He's probably normal on all other points. His brain, in fact, may be brilliant except for this one lesion—too brilliant, I should say. He has lost all sense of proportion through sheer exalted speculation."

"But does even a perverted superman indulge in such hideous jests without a motive?" asked the Inspector.

"Ah, but there is a motive. Some tremendous impetus is back of the monstrous conception of these murders—an impetus which, in its operative results, takes the form of satanic humor."

O'Brien took no part in this discussion. Though impressed by its vague implications, he became nettled by its impractical character.

"That sort of talk," he rumbled ponderously, "is all right for newspaper editorials, but it ain't workable." He shook his fat black cigar at Markham. "What we gotta do is to run down every lead and get some kind of legal evidence."

It was finally decided that the Bishop notes were to be turned over to an expert analyst, and an effort made to trace both the typewriter and the stationery. A systematic search was to be instituted for witnesses who might have seen some one in Riverside Park between seven and eight that morning. Sprigg's habits and associations were to be the subject of a careful report; and a man was to be detailed to question the mail collector of the district in the hope that, when taking the letters from the various boxes, he had noticed the envelopes addressed to the papers and could say in which box they had actually been posted.

Various other purely routine activities were outlined; and Moran suggested that for a time three men be stationed day and night in the vicinity of the murders to watch for any possible developments or for suspicious actions on the

---

* Chief Inspector O'Brien was then in command of the entire Police Department.

part of those involved. The Police Department and the District Attorney's office were to work hand in hand. Markham, of course, in tacit agreement with Heath, assumed command.

"I have already interviewed the members of the Dillard and Drukker homes in connection with the Robin murder," Markham explained to Moran and O'Brien: "and I've talked the Sprigg case over with Professor Dillard and Arnesson. To-morrow I shall see Pardee and the Drukkers."

The next morning Markham, accompanied by Heath, called for Vance a little before ten o'clock.

"This thing can't go on," he declared, after the meagrest of greetings. "If any one knows anything, we've got to find it out. I'm going to put the screws on—and damn the consequences!"

"By all means, chivy 'em." Vance himself appeared despondent. "I doubt if it'll help though. No ordin'ry procedure is going to solve this riddle. However, I've phoned Barstead. He says we may talk with Mrs. Drukker this morning. But I've arranged to see him first. I have a hankerin' to know more of the Drukker pathology. Hunchbacks, d' ye see, are not usually produced by falls."

We drove at once to the doctor's home and were received without delay. Doctor Barstead was a large comfortable man, whose pleasantness of manner impressed me as being the result of schooled effort.

Vance went straight to the point.

"We have reason to believe, doctor, that Mrs. Drukker and perhaps her son are indirectly concerned in the recent death of Mr. Robin at the Dillard house; and before we question either of them further we should like to have you tell us—as far as professional etiquette will permit—something of the neurological situation we are facing."

"Please be more explicit, sir." Doctor Barstead spoke with defensive aloofness.

"I am told," Vance continued, "that Mrs. Drukker regards herself as responsible for her son's kyphosis; but it is my understanding that such malformations as his do not ordinarily result from mere physical injuries."

Doctor Barstead nodded his head slowly.

"That is quite true. Compression paraplegia of the spinal cord may follow a dislocation or injury, but the lesion thus produced is of the focal transverse type. Osteitis or caries of the vertebræ—what we commonly call Pott's disease—is usually of tubercular origin; and this tuberculosis of the spine occurs most frequently in children. Often it exists at birth. True, an injury may precede the onset by determining the site of infection or exciting a latent focus; and this fact no doubt gives rise to the belief that the injury itself produces the disease. But both Schmaus and Horsley have exposed the true pathological anatomy of spinal caries. Drukker's deformity is unquestionably of tubercular origin. Even his curvature is of the marked rounded type, denoting an extensive involvement of vertebræ; and there is no scholiosis whatever. Moreover, he has all the local symptoms of osteitis."

"You have, of course, explained the situation to Mrs. Drukker."

"On many occasions. But I have had no success. The fact is, a terrific instinct of perverted martyrdom bids her cling to the notion that she is responsible for her son's condition. This erroneous idea has become an *idée fixe* with her. It constitutes her entire mental outlook, and gives meaning to the life of service and sacrifice she had lived for forty years."

"To what extent," asked Vance, "would you say this psychoneurosis has affected her mind?"

"That would be difficult to say; and it is not a question I would care to discuss. I may say this, however: she is undoubtedly morbid; and her values have become distorted. At times there have been—I tell you this in strictest confidence—signs of marked hallucinosis centring upon her son. His welfare has become an obsession with her. There is practically nothing she would not do for him."

"We appreciate your confidence, doctor. . . . And would it not be logical to assume that her upset condition yesterday resulted from some fear or shock connected with his welfare?"

"Undoubtedly. She has no emotional or mental life outside of him. But whether her temporary collapse was due to a real or imaginary fear, one cannot say. She has lived too long on the borderland between reality and fantasy."

There was a short silence, and then Vance asked:

"As to Drukker himself: would you regard him as wholly responsible for his acts?"

"Since he is my patient," returned Doctor Barstead, with frigid reproach, "and since I have taken no steps to sequester him, I consider your question an impertinence."

Markham leaned over and spoke peremptorily.

"We haven't time to mince words, doctor. We're investigating a series of atrocious murders. Mr. Drukker is involved in those murders—to what extent we don't know. But it is our duty to find out."

The doctor's first impulse was to combat Markham; but he evidently thought better of it, for when he answered, it was in an indulgently matter-of-fact voice.

"I have no reason, sir, to withhold any information from you. But to question Mr. Drukker's responsibility is to impute negligence to me in the matter of public safety. Perhaps, however, I misunderstand this gentleman's question." He studied Vance for a brief moment. "There are, of course, degrees of responsibility," he went on, in a professional tone. "Mr. Drukker's mind is overdeveloped, as is often the case with kyphotic victims. All mental processes are turned inward, as it were; and the lack of normal physical reactions often tends to produce inhibitions and aberrancies. But I've noted no indications of this condition in Mr. Drukker. He is excitable and prone to hysteria; but, then, psychokinesia is a common accompaniment of his disease."

"What form do his recreations take?" Vance was politely casual.

Doctor Barstead thought a moment.

"Children's games, I should say. Such recreations are not unusual with cripples. In Mr. Drukker's case it is what we might term a waking wish-fulfillment. Having had no normal childhood, he grasps at whatever will give him a sense of youthful rehabilitation. His juvenile activities tend to balance the monotony of his purely mental life."

"What is Mrs. Drukker's attitude toward his instinct for play?"

"She very correctly encourages it. I've often seen her leaning over the wall above the playground in Riverside Park watching him. And she always presides at the children's parties and dinners which he holds in his home."

We took our leave a few minutes later. As we turned into 76th Street, Heath, as if arousing himself from a bad dream, drew a deep breath and sat upright in the car.

"Did you get that about the kid games?" he asked, in an awe-stricken voice. "Good God, Mr. Vance! What's this case going to turn into?"

A curious sadness was in Vance's eyes as he gazed ahead toward the misty Jersey cliffs across the river.

Our ring at the Drukker house was answered by a portly German woman, who planted herself stolidly before us and informed us suspiciously that Mr. Drukker was too busy to see any one.

"You'd better tell him, however," said Vance, "that the District Attorney wishes to speak to him immediately."

His words produced a strange effect on the woman. Her hands went to her face, and her massive bosom rose and fell convulsively. Then, as though panic-stricken, she turned and ascended the stairs. We heard her knock on a door; there was a sound of voices; and a few moments later she came back to inform us that Mr. Drukker would see us in his study.

As we passed the woman Vance suddenly turned and, fixing his eyes on her ominously, asked:

"What time did Mr. Drukker get up yesterday morning?"

"I—don't know," she stammered, thoroughly frightened. "*Ja, ja,* I know. At nine o'clock—like always."

Vance nodded and moved on.

Drukker received us standing by a large table covered with books and sheets of manuscript. He bowed sombrely, but did not ask us to have chairs.

Vance studied him a moment as if trying to read the secret that lay behind his restless, hollow eyes.

"Mr. Drukker," he began, "it is not our desire to cause you unnecess'ry trouble; but we have learned that you were acquainted with Mr. John Sprigg, who, as you probably know, was shot near here yesterday morning. Now, could you suggest any reason that any one might have had for killing him?"

Drukker drew himself up. Despite his effort at self-control there was a slight tremor in his voice as he answered.

"I knew Mr. Sprigg but slightly. I can suggest nothing whatever in regard to his death. . . ."

"There was found on his body a piece of paper bearing the Riemann-Christoffel tensor which you introduce in your book in the chapter on the finiteness of physical space." As Vance spoke he moved one of the typewritten sheets of papers on the table toward him, and glanced at it casually.

Drukker seemed not to notice the action. The information contained in Vance's words had rivetted his attention.

"I can't understand it," he said vaguely. "May I see the notation?"

Markham complied at once with his request. After studying the paper a moment Drukker handed it back; and his little eyes narrowed malevolently.

"Have you asked Arnesson about this? He was discussing this very subject with Sprigg last week."

"Oh, yes," Vance told him carelessly. "Mr. Arnesson recalled the incident, but couldn't throw any light on it. We thought perhaps you could succeed where he had failed."

"I regret I can't accommodate you." There was the suggestion of a sneer in Drukker's reply. "Any one might use the tensor. Weyl's and Einstein's works are full of it. It isn't copyrighted. . . ." He leaned over a revolving book case and drew out a thin octavo pamphlet. Here it is in Minkowski's 'Relativitätsprinzip,' only with different symbols—a T for the B, for instance; and Greek letters for the indices." He reached for another volume. "Poincaré also uses it in his 'Hypothèses Cosmogoniques,' with still other symbolic equivalents." He tossed the books on the table contemptuously. "Why come to me about it?"

"It wasn't the tensor formula alone that led our roving footsteps to your door," said Vance lightly. "For instance, we have reason to believe that Sprigg's death is connected with Robin's murder. . . ."

Drukker's long hands caught the edge of the table, and he leaned forward, his eyes glittering excitedly.

"Connected—Sprigg and Robin? You don't believe that newspaper talk, do you? . . . It's a damned lie!" His face had begun to twitch, and his voice rose shrilly. "It's insane nonsense. . . . There's no proof, I tell you—not a shred of proof!"

"Cock Robin and Johnny Sprig, don't y' know," came Vance's soft insistent voice.

"That rot! That crazy rot!—Oh, good God! Has the world gone mad! . . ." He swayed back and forth as he beat on the table with one hand, sending the papers flying in all directions.

Vance looked at him with mild surprise.

"Aren't you acquainted with the Bishop, Mr. Drukker?"

The man stopped swaying and, steadying himself, stared at Vance with terrible intensity. His mouth was drawn back at the corners, resembling the transverse laugh of progressive muscular dystrophy.

"You, too! You've gone mad!" He swept his eyes over us. "You damned, unutterable fools! There's no such person as the Bishop! There wasn't any such person as Cock Robin or Johnny Sprig. And here you are—men grown—trying to frighten me—*me,* a mathematician—with nursery tales! . . ." He began to laugh hysterically.

Vance went to him quickly, and taking his arm led him to his chair. Slowly his laughter died away, and he waved his hand wearily.

"Too bad Robin and Sprigg were killed." His tone was heavy and colorless. "But children are the only persons that matter. . . . You'll probably find the murderer. If you don't, maybe I'll help you. But don't let your imaginations run away with you. Keep to facts . . . facts. . . ."

The man was exhausted, and we left him.

"He's scared, Markham—deuced scared," observed Vance, when we were again in the hall. "I could bear to know what is hidden in that shrewd warped mind of his."

He led the way down the hall to Mrs. Drukker's door.

"This method of visiting a lady doesn't accord with the best social usage. Really, y' know, Markham, I wasn't born to be a policeman. I abhor snooping."

Our knock was answered by a feeble voice. Mrs. Drukker, paler than usual, was lying back on her chaise-longue by the window. Her white prehensile hands lay along the arms of the chair, slightly flexed; and more than ever she recalled to my mind the pictures I had seen of the ravening Harpies that tormented Phineus in the story of the Argonauts.

Before we could speak she said in a strained terrified voice: "I knew you would come—I knew you were not through torturing me. . . ."

"To torture you, Mrs. Drukker," returned Vance softly, "is the furthest thing from our thoughts. We merely want your help."

Vance's manner appeared to alleviate her terror somewhat, and she studied him calculatingly.

"If only I could help you!" she muttered. "But there's nothing to be done—nothing. . . ."

"You might tell us what you saw from your window on the day of Mr. Robin's death," Vance suggested kindly.

"No—no!" Her eyes stared horribly. "I saw nothing—I wasn't near the window that morning. You may kill me, but my dying words would be No—no—*no!*"

Vance did not press the point.

"Beedle tells us," he went on, "that you often rise early and walk in the garden."

"Oh, yes." The words came with a sigh of relief. "I don't sleep well in the mornings. I often wake up with dull boring pains in my spine, and the muscles of my back feel rigid and sore. So I get up and walk in the yard whenever the weather is mild enough."

"Beedle saw you in the garden yesterday morning."

The woman nodded absently.

"And she also saw Professor Dillard with you."

Again she nodded, but immediately afterward she shot Vance a combative inquisitive glance.

"He sometimes joins me," she hastened to explain. "He feels sorry for me, and he admires Adolph; he thinks he's a great genius. And he *is* a genius! He'd be a great man—as great as Professor Dillard—if it hadn't been for his illness. . . . And it was all my fault. I let him fall when he was a baby. . . ." A dry sob shook her emaciated body, and her fingers worked spasmodically.

After a moment Vance asked: "What did you and Professor Dillard talk about in the garden yesterday?"

A sudden wiliness crept into the woman's manner.

"About Adolph mostly," she said, with a too obvious attempt at unconcern.

"Did you see any one else in the yard or on the archery range?" Vance's indolent eyes were on the woman.

"No!" Again a sense of fear pervaded her. "But somebody else was there, wasn't there?—somebody who didn't wish to be seen." She nodded her head eagerly. "Yes! Some one else was there—and they thought I saw them. . . . But I didn't! Oh, merciful God, I didn't! . . ." She covered her face with her hands, and her body shook convulsively. "If only I had seen them! If only I knew! But it wasn't Adolph—it wasn't my little boy. He was asleep—thank God, he was asleep!"

Vance went close to the woman.

"Why do you thank God that it wasn't your son?" he asked gently.

She looked up with some amazement.

"Why, don't you remember? A little man shot Johnny Sprig with a little gun yesterday morning—the same little man that killed Cock Robin with a bow and arrow. It's all a horrible game—and I'm *afraid*. . . . But I mustn't tell—I *can't* tell. The little man might do something awful. Maybe"—her voice became dull with horror—"maybe he has some insane idea that I'm *the old woman who lived in a shoe! . . .*"

"Come, come, Mrs. Drukker." Vance forced a consoling smile. "Such talk is nonsense. You've let these matters prey on your mind. There's a perfectly rational explanation for everything. And I have a feeling that you yourself can help us find that explanation."

"No—no! I can't—I mustn't! I don't understand it myself." She took a deep, resolute inspiration, and compressed her lips.

"Why can't you tell us?" persisted Vance.

"Because I don't know," she cried. "I wish to God I did! I only know that something horrible is going on here—that some awful curse is hanging over this house. . . ."

"How do you know that?"

The woman began to tremble violently, and her eyes roamed distractedly about the room.

"Because"—her voice was barely audible—"because the little man came here last night!"

A chill passed up my spine at this statement, and I heard even the imperturbable Sergeant's sharp intake of breath. Then Vance's calm voice sounded.

"How do you know he was here, Mrs. Drukker? Did you see him?"

"No, I didn't see him; but he tried to get into this room—by that door." She pointed unsteadily toward the entrance to the hallway through which we had just come.

"You must tell us about it," said Vance; "or we will be driven to conclude that you manufactured the story."

"Oh, but I didn't manufacture it—may God be my witness!" There could be no doubt whatever of the woman's sincerity. Something had occurred which filled her with mortal fear. "I was lying in bed, awake. The little clock on the mantel had just struck midnight; and I heard a soft rustling sound in the hall outside. I turned my head toward the door—there was a dim night-light burning on the table here . . . and then I saw the door-knob turn slowly—silently—as if some one were trying to get in without waking me————"

"Just a moment, Mrs. Drukker," interrupted Vance. "Do you always lock your door at night?"

"I've never locked it until recently—after Mr. Robin's death. I've somehow felt insecure since then—I can't explain why. . . ."

"I quite understand.—Please go on with the story. You say you saw the door-knob move. And then?"

"Yes—yes. It moved softly—back and forth. I lay there in bed, frozen with terror. But after a while I managed to call out—I don't know how loud; but suddenly the door-knob ceased to turn, and I heard footsteps moving rapidly away—down the hall. . . . Then I managed to get up. I went to the door and listened. I was afraid—afraid for Adolph. And I could hear those soft footsteps descending the stairs————"

"Which stairs?"

"At the rear—leading to the kitchen. . . . Then the door of the screen porch shut, and everything was silent again. . . . I knelt with my ear to the keyhole a long time, listening, waiting. But nothing happened, and at last I rose. . . . Something seemed to tell me I must open the door. I was in deadly terror— and yet I knew I had to open the door. . . ." A shudder swept her body. "Softly I turned the key, and took hold of the knob. As I pulled the door slowly inward, a tiny object that had been poised on the outside knob fell to the floor with a clatter. There was a light burning in the hall—I always keep one burning at night,—and I tried not to look down. I tried—I *tried* . . . but I couldn't keep my eyes away from the floor. And there at my feet—oh, God in Heaven!—there lay *something! . . .*"

She was unable to go on. Horror seemed to paralyze her tongue. Vance's cool, unemotional voice, however, steadied her.

"What was it that lay on the floor, Mrs. Drukker?"

With difficulty the woman rose and, bracing herself for a moment at the foot of the bed, went to the dressing-table. Pulling out a small drawer she reached inside and fumbled among its contents. Then she extended her open hand to us. On the palm lay a small chessman—ebony black against the whiteness of her skin. It was the bishop!

13

IN THE BISHOP'S SHADOW

(Tuesday, April 12; 11 A.M.)

VANCE TOOK the bishop from Mrs. Drukker and slipped it into his coat pocket.

"It would be dangerous, madam," he said, with impressive solemnity, "if what happened here last night became known. Should the person who played this joke on you find out that you had informed the police, other attempts to frighten you might be made. Therefore, not one word of what you have told us must pass your lips."

"May I not even tell Adolph?" the woman asked distractedly.

"No one! You must maintain a complete silence, even in the presence of your son."

I could not understand Vance's emphasis on this point; but before many days had passed it was all too clear to me. The reason for his advice was revealed with tragic force; and I realized that even at the time of Mrs. Drukker's disclosure his penetrating mind had worked out an uncannily accurate ratiocination, and foreseen certain possibilities unsuspected by the rest of us.

We took our leave a few moments later, and descended the rear stairs. The staircase made a sharp turn to the right at a landing eight or ten steps below the second floor, and led into a small dark passageway with two doors—one on the left, opening into the kitchen, and another, diagonally opposite, giving on the screen porch.

We stepped out immediately to the porch, now flooded in sunshine, and stood without a word trying to shake off the atmosphere cast about us by Mrs. Drukker's terrifying experience.

Markham was the first to speak.

"Do you believe, Vance, that the person who brought that chessman here last night is the killer of Robin and Sprigg?"

"There can be no doubt of it. The purpose of his midnight visit is hideously clear. It fits perfectly with what has already come to light."

"It strikes me merely as a ruthless practical joke," Markham rejoined, "—the act of a drunken fiend."

Vance shook his head.

"It's the only thing in this whole nightmare that doesn't qualify as a piece of insane humor. It was a deadly serious excursion. The devil himself is never so solemn as when covering his tracks. Our particular devil's hand had been forced, and he made a bold play. 'Pon my soul, I almost prefer his jovial mood to the one that prompted him to break in here last night. However, we now have something definite to go on."

Heath, impatient of all theorizing, quickly picked up this last remark.

"And what might that be, sir?"

"*Imprimis*, we may assume that our chess-playing troubadour was thoroughly familiar with the plan of this house. The night-light in the upper hall may have cast its gleam down the rear stairs as far as the landing, but the rest of the way must have been in darkness. Moreover, the arrangement of the rear of the house is somewhat complicated. Therefore, unless he knew the lay-out he couldn't have found his way about noiselessly in the dark. Obviously, too, the visitor knew in which room Mrs. Drukker slept. Also, he must have known what time Drukker turned in last night, for he wouldn't have chanced making his call unless he had felt sure that the coast was clear."

"That don't help us much," grumbled Heath. "We've been going on the theory right along that the murderer was wise to everything connected with these two houses."

"True. But one may be fairly intimate with a family and still not know at what hour each of its members retires on a certain night, or just how to effect a surreptitious entry to the house. Furthermore, Sergeant, our midnight caller was some one who knew that Mrs. Drukker was in the habit of leaving her door unlocked at night; for he had every intention of entering her room. His object wasn't merely to leave his little memento outside and then depart. The silent stealthy way he tried the knob proves that."

"He may simply have wanted to waken Mrs. Drukker so she would find it at once," suggested Markham.

"Then why did he turn the knob so carefully—as if trying *not* to waken any one? A rattling of the knob, or a soft tapping, or even throwing the chessman against the door, would have answered that purpose much better. . . . No, Markham; he had a far more sinister object in mind; but when he found himself thwarted by the locked door and heard Mrs. Drukker's cry of fright, he placed the bishop where she would find it, and fled."

"Still and all, sir," argued Heath, "anyone mighta known she left her door unlocked at night; and any one coulda learned the lay of the house so's to find their way around in the dark."

"But who, Sergeant, had a key to the rear door? And who could have used it at midnight last night?"

"The door mighta been left unlocked," countered Heath; "and when we check up on the alibis of everybody we may get a lead."

Vance sighed.

"You'll probably find two or three people without any alibi at all. And if last night's visit here was planned, a convincing alibi may have been prepared. We're not dealing with a simpleton, Sergeant. We're playing a game to the death with a subtle and resourceful murderer, who can think as quickly as we can, and who has had long training in the subtleties of logic. . . ."

As if on a sudden impulse he turned and passed indoors, motioning us to follow. He went straight to the kitchen where the German woman who had admitted us earlier sat stolidly by a table preparing the midday meal. She rose as we entered and backed away from us. Vance, puzzled by her demeanor, studied her for several moments without speaking. Then his eyes drifted to the table where a large eggplant had been halved lengthwise and scooped out.

"Ah!" he exclaimed, glancing at the contents of the various dishes standing about. "*Aubergines à la Turque,* what? An excellent dish. But I'd mince the mutton a bit finer, if I were you. And not too much cheese: it detracts from the sauce *espagnole* which I see you're preparing." He looked up with a pleasant smile. "What's your name, by the by?"

His manner astonished the woman greatly, but it also had the effect of alleviating her fears.

"Menzel," she answered in a dull voice. "Grete Menzel."

"And how long have you been with the Drukkers?"

"Going on twenty-five years."

"A long time," Vance commented musingly. "Tell me: why were you frightened when we called here this morning?"

The woman became sullen, and her large hands closed tightly.

"I wasn't frightened. But Mr. Drukker was busy———"

"You thought perhaps we had come to arrest him," Vance broke in.

Her eyes dilated, but she made no answer.

"What time did Mr. Drukker rise yesterday morning?" Vance went on.

"I told you . . . nine o'clock—like always."

"What time did Mr. Drukker rise?" The insistent, detached quality of his voice was far more ominous than any dramatic intonation could have been.

"I told you—"

"*Die Wahrheit, Frau Menzel! Um wie veil Uhr ist er aufgestanden?*"

The psychological effect of this repetition of the question in German was instantaneous. The woman's hands went to her face, and a stifled cry, like a trapped animal's, escaped her.

"I don't—know," she groaned. "I called him at half past eight, but he didn't answer, and I tried the door. . . . It wasn't locked and—*Du lieber Gott!*—he was gone."

"When did you next see him?" asked Vance quietly.

"At nine. I went up-stairs again to tell him breakfast was ready. He was in the study—at his desk—working like mad, and all excited. He told me to go away."

"Did he come down to breakfast?"

"*Ja—ja.* He came down—half an hour later."

The woman leaned heavily against the drain-board of the sink, and Vance drew up a chair for her.

"Sit down, Mrs. Menzel," he said kindly. When she had obeyed, he asked: "Why did you tell me this morning that Mr. Drukker rose at nine?"

"I had to—I was told to." Her resistance was gone, and she breathed heavily like a person exhausted. "When Mrs. Drukker came back from Miss Dillard's yesterday afternoon she told me that if any one asked me that question about Mr. Drukker I was to say 'Nine o'clock.' She made me swear I'd say it. . . ." Her voice trailed off, and her eyes took on a glassy stare. "I was afraid to say anything else."

Vance still seemed puzzled. After several deep inhalations on his cigarette he remarked:

"There's nothing in what you've told us to affect you this way. It's not unnatural that a morbid woman like Mrs. Drukker should have taken such a fantastic measure to protect her son from possible suspicion, when a murder had been committed in the neighborhood. You've surely been with her long enough to realize how she might exaggerate every remote possibility where her son is concerned. In fact, I'm surprised you take it so seriously. . . . Have you any other reason to connect Mr. Drukker with this crime?"

"No—no!" The woman shook her head distractedly.

Vance strolled to the rear window, frowning. Suddenly he swung about. He had become stern and implacable.

"Where were you, Mrs. Menzel, the morning Mr. Robin was killed?"

An astounding change came over the woman. Her face paled; her lips trembled; and she clinched her hands with a spasmodic gesture. She tried to take her staring eyes from Vance, but some quality in his gaze held her.

"Where were you, Mrs. Menzel?" The question was repeated sharply.

"I was—here———" she began; then stopped abruptly and cast an agitated glance at Heath, who was watching her fixedly.

"You were in the kitchen?"

She nodded. The power of speech seemed to have deserted her.

"And you saw Mr. Drukker return from the Dillards'?"

Again she nodded.

"Exactly," said Vance. "And he came in the rear way, by the screen porch, and went up-stairs. . . . And he didn't know that you saw him through the kitchen door. . . . And later he inquired regarding your whereabouts at that hour. . . . And when you told him you had been in the kitchen he warned you to keep silent about it. . . . And then you learned of Mr. Robin's death a few minutes before you saw him enter here. . . . And yesterday, when Mrs. Drukker told you to say he had not risen until nine, and you heard that some one else had been killed near here, you became suspicious and frightened. . . . That's correct, is it not, Mrs. Menzel?"

The woman was sobbing audibly in her apron. There was no need for her to reply, for it was obvious that Vance had guessed the truth.

Heath took his cigar from his mouth and glared at her ferociously.

"So! You were holding out on me," he bellowed, thrusting forward his jaw. "You lied to me when I questioned you the other day. Obstructing justice, were you?"

She gave Vance a look of frightened appeal.

"Mrs. Menzel, Sergeant," he said, "had no intention of obstructing justice. And now that she has told us the truth, I think we may overlook her perfectly natural deception in the matter." Then before Heath had time to reply he turned to the woman and asked in a matter-of-fact tone: "Do you lock the door leading to the screen porch every night?"

"*Ja*—every night." She spoke listlessly: the reaction from her fright had left her apathetic.

"You are sure you locked it last night?"

"At half past nine—when I went to bed."

Vance stepped across the little passageway and inspected the lock.

"It's a snap-lock," he observed, on returning. "Who has a key to the door?"

"I have a key. And Mrs. Drukker—she has one, too."

"You're sure no one else has a key?"

"No one except Miss Dillard. . . ."

"Miss Dillard?" Vance's voice was suddenly resonant with interest. "Why should she have one?"

"She's had it for years. She's like a member of the family—over here two and three times a day. When I go out I lock the back door; and her having a key saves Mrs. Drukker the trouble of coming down and letting her in."

"Quite natural," Vance murmured. Then: "We sha'n't bother you any more, Mrs. Menzel." He strolled out on the little rear porch.

When the door had been closed behind us he pointed to the screen door that opened into the yard.

"You'll note that this wire mesh has been forced away from the frame, permitting one to reach inside and turn the latch. Either Mrs. Drukker's key or Miss Dillard's—probably the latter—was used to open the door of the house."

Heath nodded: this tangible aspect of the case appealed to him. But Markham was not paying attention. He stood in the background smoking with angry detachment. Presently he turned resolutely and was about to re-enter the house when Vance caught his arm.

"No—no, Markham! That would be abominable technique. Curb your ire. You're so dashed impulsive, don't y' know."

"But, damn it, Vance!" Markham shook off the other's hand. "Drukker lied to us about going out the Dillard gate before Robin's murder———"

"Of course he did. I've suspected all along that the account he gave us of his movements that morning was a bit fanciful. But it's useless to go upstairs now and hector him about it. He'll simply say that the cook is mistaken."

Markham was unconvinced.

"But what about yesterday morning? I want to know where he was when the cook called him at half past eight. Why should Mrs. Drukker be so anxious to have us believe he was asleep?"

"She, too, probably went to his room and saw that he was gone. Then when she heard of Sprigg's death her febrile imagination became overheated, and she proceeded to invest him with an alibi. But you're only inviting trouble when you plan to chivy him about the discrepancies in his tale."

"I'm not so sure." Markham spoke with significative gravity. "I may be inviting a solution to this hideous business."

Vance did not reply at once. He stood gazing down at the quivering shadows cast on the lawn by the willow trees. At length he said in a low voice:

"We can't afford to take that chance. If what you're thinking should prove to be true, and you should reveal the information you've just received, the little man who was here last night might prowl about the upper hall again. And this time he might not be content to leave his chessman *outside the door!*"

A look of horror came into Markham's eyes.

"You think I might be jeopardizing the cook's safety if I used her evidence against him at this time?"

"The terrible thing about this affair is that, until we know the truth, we face danger at every turn." Vance's voice was heavy with discouragement. "We can't risk exposing any one. . . ."

The door leading to the porch opened, and Drukker appeared on the threshold, his little eyes blinking in the sunlight. His gaze came to rest on Markham, and a crafty, repulsive smile contorted his mouth.

"I trust I am not disturbing you," he apologized, with a menacing squint; "but the cook has just informed me that she told you she saw me enter here by the rear door on the morning of Mr. Robin's unfortunate death."

"Oh, my aunt!" murmured Vance, turning away and busying himself with the selection of a fresh cigarette. "That tears it."

Drukker shot him an inquisitive look, and drew himself up with a kind of cynical fortitude.

"And what about it, Mr. Drukker?" demanded Markham.

"I merely desired to assure you," the man replied, "that the cook is in error. She has obviously confused the date,—you see, I come and go so often by this rear door. On the morning of Mr. Robin's death, as I explained to you, I left the range by the 75th-Street gate and, after a brief walk in the park, returned home by the front way. I have convinced Grete that she is mistaken."

Vance had been listening to him closely. Now he turned and met the other's smile with a look of bland ingenuousness.

"Did you convince her with a chessman, by any chance?"

Drukker jerked his head forward and sucked in a rasping breath. His twisted frame became taut; the muscles about his eyes and mouth began to twitch; and the ligaments of his neck stood out like whipcord. For a moment I thought he was going to lose his self-control; but with a great effort he steadied himself.

"I don't understand you, sir." There was the vibrancy of an intense anger in his words. "What has a chessman to do with it?"

"Chessmen have various names," suggested Vance softly.

"Are *you* telling *me* about chess?" A venomous contempt marked Drukker's manner, but he managed to grin. "Various names, certainly. There's the king and queen, the rook, the knight————" He broke off. *"The bishop! . . ."* He lay his head against the casement of the door and began to cackle mirthlessly. "So! That's what you mean? *The bishop! . . .* You're a lot of imbecile children playing a nonsense game."

"We have excellent reason to believe," said Vance, with impressive calmness, "that the game is being played by some one else—with the chess bishop as the principal symbol."

Drukker sobered.

"Don't take my mother's vagaries too seriously," he admonished. "Her imagination often plays tricks on her."

"Ah! And why do you mention your mother in this connection?"

"You've just been talking to her, haven't you? And your comments, I must say, sound very much like some of her harmless hallucinations."

"On the other hand," Vance rejoined mildly, "your mother may have perfectly good grounds for her beliefs."

Drukker's eyes narrowed, and he looked swiftly at Markham.

"Rot!"

"Ah, well," sighed Vance; "we sha'n't debate the point." Then in an altered tone he added: "It might help us though, Mr. Drukker, if we knew where you were between eight and nine yesterday morning."

The man opened his mouth slightly as if to speak, but quickly his lips closed again, and he stood staring calculatingly at Vance. At length he answered in a high-pitched insistent voice.

"I was working—in my study—from six o'clock until half past nine." He paused, but evidently felt that further explanation was desirable. "For several months I've been working on a modification of the ether-string theory to account for the interference of light, which the quantum theory is unable to explain. Dillard told me I couldn't do it";—a fanatical light came into his eyes—"but I awoke early yesterday morning with certain factors of the problem clarified; and I got up and went to my study. . . ."

"So that's where you were." Vance spoke carelessly. "It's of no great importance. Sorry we discommoded you to-day." He beckoned with his head to Markham, and moved toward the screen door. As we stepped upon the range he turned back and, smiling, said almost dulcetly: "Mrs. Menzil is under our protection. It would pain us deeply if anything should happen to her."

Drukker looked after us with a sort of hypnotized fascination.

The moment we were out of hearing Vance moved to Heath's side.

"Sergeant," he said in a troubled voice, "that forthright German *Hausfrau* may have put her head unwittingly in a noose. And—my word!—I'm afraid. You'd better have a good man watch the Drukker house to-night—from the rear, under those willow trees. And tell him to break in at the first scream or call. . . . I'll sleep better if I know there's a plain-clothes angel guarding Frau Menzel's slumbers."

"I get you, sir." Heath's face was grim. "There won't be no chess players worrying her to-night."

14

A GAME OF CHESS

(Tuesday, April 12; 11:30 A.M.)

As WE walked slowly toward the Dillard house it was decided that immediate inquiries should be made regarding the whereabouts the night before of every person connected in any way with this gruesome drama.

"We must be careful, however, to drop no hint of what befell Mrs. Drukker," warned Vance. "Our midnight bishop-bearer did not intend that we should learn of his call. He believed that the poor lady would be too frightened to tell us."

"I'm inclined to think," objected Markham, "that you're attaching too much importance to the episode."

"Oh, my dear fellow!" Vance stopped short and put both hands on the other's shoulders. "You're much too effete—that's your great shortcomin'. You don't feel—you are no child of nature. The poetry of your soul has run to prose. Now I, on the other hand, give my imagination full sway; and I tell you that the leaving of that bishop at Mrs. Drukker's door was no Hallowe'en prank, but the desperate act of a desperate man. It was meant as a warning."

"You think she knows something?"

"I think she saw Robin's body placed on the range. And I think she saw something else—something she would give her life not to have seen."

In silence we moved on. It was our intention to pass through the wall gate into 75th Street and present ourselves at the Dillards' front door; but as we passed the archery-room the basement door opened, and Belle Dillard confronted us anxiously.

"I saw you coming down the range," she said, with troubled eagerness, addressing her words to Markham. "For over an hour I've been waiting to get in touch with you—phoning your office. . . ." Her manner became agitated. "Something strange has happened. Oh, it may not mean anything . . . but when I came through the archery-room here this morning, intending to call on Lady Mae, some impulse made me go to the tool-chest again and look in the drawer,—it seemed so—so queer that the little revolver should have been stolen. . . . And there it lay—in plain sight—beside the other pistol!" She caught her breath. "Mr. Markham, some one returned it to the drawer last night!"

This information acted electrically on Heath.

"Did you touch it?" he asked excitedly.

"Why—no. . . ."

He brushed past her unceremoniously and, going to the tool-chest, yanked open the drawer. There, beside the larger automatic that we had seen the day before, lay a small pearl-handled .32. The Sergeant's eyes glistened as he ran his pencil through the trigger-guard and lifted it gingerly. He held it to the light and sniffed at the end of the barrel.

"One empty chamber," he announced, with satisfaction. "And it's been shot off recently. . . . This oughta get us somewheres." He wrapped the revolver tenderly in a handkerchief and placed it in his coat pocket. "I'll get Dubois busy on this for finger-prints; and I'll have Cap Hagedorn* check up on the bullets."

"Really now, Sergeant," said Vance banteringly; "do you imagine that the gentleman we're looking for would wipe a bow and arrow clean and then leave his digital monogram on a revolver?"

"I haven't got your imagination, Mr. Vance," returned Heath surlily. "So I'm going ahead doing the things that oughta be done."

"You're quite right." Vance smiled with good-natured admiration at the other's dogged thoroughness. "Forgive me for trying to damp your zeal."

He turned to Belle Dillard.

"We came here primarily to see the professor and Mr. Arnesson. But there's also a matter we'd like to speak about to you.—We understand you have a key to the rear door of the Drukker house."

She gave him a puzzled nod.

"Yes; I've had one for years. I run back and forth so much; and it saves Lady Mae a lot of bother. . . ."

"Our only interest in the key is that it might have been used by some one who had no right to it."

"But that's impossible. I've never lent it to any one. And I always keep it in my hand-bag."

"Is it generally known you have a key to the Drukkers'?"

"Why—I suppose so." She was obviously perplexed. "I've never made a secret of it. The family certainly know about it."

"And you may perhaps have mentioned or revealed the fact when there were outsiders present?"

"Yes—though I can't recall any specific instance."

"Are you sure you have the key now?"

She gave Vance a startled look, and without a word picked up a small lizard-skin hand-bag which lay on the wicker table. Opening it she felt swiftly in one of its inner compartments.

"Yes!" she announced, with relief. "It's where I always keep it. . . . Why do you ask me about it?"

"It's important that we know who had access to the Drukker house," Vance told her. Then, before she could question him further, he asked: "Could the key possibly have left your possession last night?—that is, could it have been extracted from your bag without your knowledge?"

A look of fright came into her face.

"Oh, what has happened———?" she began; but Vance interrupted her.

"Please, Miss Dillard! There's nothing for you to worry about. We're merely striving to eliminate certain remote possibilities in connection with our investigation.—Tell me: could any one have taken your key last night?"

"No one," she answered uneasily. "I went to the theatre at eight o'clock, and had my bag with me the entire time."

"When did you last make use of the key?"

---

* Captain Hagedorn was the fire-arms expert of the New York Police Department. It was he who, in the Benson murder case, gave Vance the data with which to establish the height of the murderer; and who made the examination of the three bullets fired from the old Smith & Wesson revolver in the Green murder case.

"After dinner last night. I ran over to see how Lady Mae was and to say good-night."

Vance frowned slightly. I could see that this information did not square with some theory he had formed.

"You made use of the key after dinner," he recapitulated, "and kept it with you in your hand-bag the rest of the evening, without letting it once go out of your sight.—Is that right, Miss Dillard?"

The girl nodded.

"I even held the bag in my lap during the play," she amplified.

Vance regarded the hand-bag thoughtfully.

"Well," he said lightly, "so ends the romance of the key.—And now we're going to bother your uncle again. Do you think you'd better act as our *avant-courier;* or shall we storm the citadel unannounced?"

"Uncle is out," she informed us. "He went for a walk along the Drive."

"And Mr. Arnesson, I suppose, has not yet returned from the university."

"No; but he'll be here for lunch. He has no classes Tuesday afternoons."

"In the meantime, then, we'll confer with Beedle and the admirable Pyne.—And I might suggest that it would do Mrs. Drukker no end of good if you'd pay her a visit."

With a troubled smile and a little nod the girl passed out through the basement door.

Heath at once went in search of Beedle and Pyne and brought them to the drawing-room, where Vance questioned them about the preceding night. No information, however, was obtained from them. They had both gone to bed at ten o'clock. Their rooms were on the fourth floor at the side of the house; and they had not even heard Miss Dillard when she returned from the theatre. Vance asked them about noises on the range, and intimated that the screen-porch door of the Drukkers might have slammed shut at about midnight. But apparently both of them had been asleep at that hour. Finally they were dismissed with a warning not to mention to any one the questions that had just been asked them.

Five minutes later Professor Dillard came in. Though surprised to see us, he greeted us amiably.

"For once, Markham, you've chosen an hour for your visit when I am not absorbed in work.—More questions, I suppose. Well, come along to the library for the inquisition. It'll be more comfortable there." He led the way upstairs, and when we were seated he insisted that we join him in a glass of port which he himself served from the sideboard.

"Drukker should be here," he remarked. "He has a fondness for my 'Ninety-six,' though he'll drink it only on rare occasions. I tell him he should take more port; but he imagines it's bad for him, and points to my gout. But there's no connection between gout and port—the notion is sheer superstition. Sound port is the most wholesome of wines. Gout is unknown in Oporto. A little physical stimulation of the right kind would be good for Drukker. . . . Poor fellow. His mind is like a furnace that's burning his body up. A brilliant man, Markham. If he had sufficient bodily energy to keep pace with his brain, he'd be one of the world's great physicists."

"He tells me," commented Vance, "that you twitted him on his inability to work out a modification of the quantum theory in regard to light-interference."

The old man smiled ruefully.

"Yes. I knew that such a criticism would spur him to a maximum effort. The fact is, Drukker is on the track of something revolutionary. He has already worked out some very interesting theorems. . . . But I'm sure this isn't what you gentlemen came here to discuss. What can I do for you, Markham? Or, perhaps you came to give me news."

"Unfortunately we have no news. We have come to solicit aid again. . . ." Markham hesitated as if uncertain how to proceed; and Vance assumed the rôle of questioner.

"The situation has changed somewhat since we were here yesterday. One or two new matters have arisen, and there is a possibility that our investigation would be facilitated if we knew the exact movements of the members of your household last night. These movements, in fact, may have influenced certain factors in the case."

The professor lifted his head in some surprise, but made no comment. He said merely: "That information is very easily given. To what members do you refer?"

"To no member specifically," Vance hastened to assure him.

"Well, let me see. . . ." He took out his old meerschaum pipe and began filling it. "Belle and Sigurd and I had dinner alone at six o'clock. At half past seven Drukker dropped in, and a few minutes later Pardee called. Then at eight Sigurd and Belle went to the theatre, and at half past ten Drukker and Pardee went away. I myself turned in shortly after eleven, after locking up the house—I'd let Pyne and Beedle go to bed early.—And that's about all I can tell you."

"Do I understand that Miss Dillard and Mr. Arnesson went to the theatre together?"

"Yes. Sigurd rarely patronizes the theatre, but whenever he does he takes Belle along. He attends Ibsen's plays, for the most part. He's a devout disciple of Ibsen's, by the way. His American upbringing hasn't in the least tempered his enthusiasm for things Norwegian. At heart he's quite loyal to his native country. He's as well grounded in Norwegian literature as any professor at the University of Oslo; and the only music he really cares for is Grieg's. When he goes to concerts or the theatre you're pretty sure to find that the programs are liberally Norwegian."

"It was an Ibsen play, then, he attended last night?"

" 'Rosmersholm,' I believe. There's a revival of Ibsen's dramas at present in New York."

Vance nodded. "Walter Hampden's doing them.—Did you see either Mr. Arnesson or Miss Dillard after they returned from the theatre?"

"No; they came in rather late, I imagine. Belle told me this morning they went to the Plaza for supper after the play. However, Sigurd will be here at any minute, and you can learn the details from him." Though the professor spoke with patience, it was plain that he was annoyed by the apparently irrelevant nature of the interrogation.

"Will you be good enough, sir," pursued Vance, "to tell us the circumstances connected with Mr. Drukker's and Mr. Pardee's visit here after dinner?"

"There was nothing unusual about their call. They often drop in during the evening. The object of Drukker's visit was to discuss with me the work he had done on his modification of the quantum theory; but when Pardee appeared the discussion was dropped. Pardee is a good mathematician, but advanced physics is beyond his depth."

"Did either Mr. Drukker or Mr. Pardee see Miss Dillard before she went to the theatre?"

Professor Dillard took his pipe slowly from his mouth, and his expression became resentful.

"I must say," he replied testily, "that I can see no valid object in my answering such questions.—However," he added, in a more indulgent tone, "if the domestic trivia of my household can be of any possible assistance to you, I will of course be glad to go into detail." He regarded Vance a moment. "Yes, both Drukker and Pardee saw Belle last night. All of us, including Sigurd, were together in this room for perhaps half an hour before theatre time. There was even a casual discussion about Ibsen's genius, in which Drukker annoyed Sigurd greatly by maintaining Hauptmann's superiority."

"Then at eight o'clock, I gather, Mr. Arnesson and Miss Dillard departed, leaving you and Mr. Pardee and Mr. Drukker alone here."

"That is correct."

"And at half past ten, I think you said, Mr. Drukker and Mr. Pardee went away. Did they go together?"

"They went down-stairs together," the professor answered, with more than a suggestion of tartness. "Drukker, I believe, went home; but Pardee had an appointment at the Manhattan Chess Club."

"It seems a bit early for Mr. Drukker to have gone home," mused Vance, "especially as he had come to discuss an important matter with you and had had no adequate opportunity to do so up to the time of his departure."

"Drukker is not well." The professor's voice was again studiously patient. "As I've told you, he tires easily. And last night he was unusually played out. In fact, he complained to me of his fatigue and said he was going immediately to bed."

"Yes . . . quite in keeping," murmured Vance. "He told us a little while ago that he was up working at six yesterday morning."

"I'm not surprised. Once a problem has posed itself in his mind he works on it incessantly. Unfortunately he has no normal reactions to counter-balance his consuming passion for mathematics. There have been times where I've feared for his mental stability."

Vance, for some reason, steered clear of this point.

"You spoke of Mr. Pardee's engagement at the Chess Club last night," he said, when he had carefully lighted a fresh cigarette. "Did he mention the nature of it to you?"

Professor Dillard smiled with patronizing lenity.

"He taked about it for fully an hour. It appears that a gentleman named Rubinstein—a genius of the chess world, I understand, who is now visiting this country—had taken him on for three exhibition games. The last one was yesterday. It began at two o'clock, and was postponed at six. It should have been played off at eight, but Rubinstein was the lion of some dinner downtown; so the hour set for the play-off was eleven. Pardee was on tenter-hooks, for he had lost the first game and drawn the second; and if he could have won last night's game he would have broken even with Rubinstein. He seemed to think he had an excellent chance according to the way the game stood at six o'clock; although Drukker disagreed with him. . . . He must have gone directly from here to the club, for it was fully half past ten when he and Drukker went out."

"Rubinstein's a strong player," observed Vance. A new note of interest, which he strove to conceal, had come into his voice. "He's one of the grand masters of the game. He defeated Capablanca at San Sebastian in 1911, and between 1907 and 1912 was considered the logical contender for the world's title held by Doctor Lasker.* . . . Yes, it would have been a great feather in Pardee's cap to have beaten him. Indeed, it was no small compliment to him that he should have been matched with Rubinstein. Pardee, despite the fame of his gambit, has never been ranked as a master.—Have you heard the result of last night's game, by the by?"

Again I noted a faint tolerant smile at the corners of the professor's mouth. He gave the impression of looking down benevolently on the foolish capers of children from some great intellectual height.

"No," he answered; "I didn't inquire. But my surmise is that Pardee lost; for when Drukker pointed out the weakness of his adjourned position, he was more positive than usual. Drukker by nature is cautious, and he rarely expresses a definite opinion on a problem without having excellent grounds for so doing."

Vance raised his eyebrows in some astonishment.

"Do you mean to tell me that Pardee analyzed his unfinished game with Drukker and discussed the possibilities of its ending? Not only is such a course unethical, but any player would be disqualified for doing such a thing."

"I'm unfamiliar with the punctilio of chess," Professor Dillard returned acidly; "but I am sure Pardee would not be guilty of a breach of ethics in that regard. And, as a matter of fact, I recall that when he was engaged with the chessmen at the table over there and Drukker stepped up to look on, Pardee requested him to offer no advice. The discussion of the position took place some time later, and was kept entirely to generalities. I don't believe there was a mention of any specific line of play."

Vance leaned slowly forward and crushed out his cigarette with that taut deliberation which I had long since come to recognize as a sign of repressed excitement. Then he rose carelessly and moved to the chess table in the corner. He stood there, one hand resting on the exquisite marquetry of the alternating squares.

"You say that Mr. Pardee was analyzing his position on this board when Mr. Drukker came over to him?"

"Yes, that is right." Professor Dillard spoke with forced politeness. "Drukker sat down facing him and studied the layout. He started to make some remark, and Pardee requested him to say nothing. A quarter of an hour or so later Pardee put the men away; and it was then that Drukker told him that his game was lost—that he had worked himself into a position which, though it looked favorable, was fundamentally weak."

Vance had been running his fingers aimlessly over the board; and he had

---

* Akiba Rubinstein was then, and is to-day, the chess champion of Poland and one of the great international masters of the game. He was born in Stavisk, near Lodz, in 1882, and made his début in international chess at the Ostend tournament in 1906. His recent visit to America resulted in a series of new triumphs.

taken two or three of the men from the box and tossed them back, as if toying with them.

"Do you remember just what Mr. Drukker said?" he asked without looking up.

"I didn't pay very close attention—the subject was not exactly one of burning moment to me." There was an unescapable note of irony in the answer. "But, as nearly as I can recall, Drukker said that Pardee could have won provided it had been a rapid-transit game, but that Rubinstein was a notoriously slow and careful player and would inevitably find the weak spot in Pardee's position."

"Did Pardee resent this criticism?" Vance now strolled back to his chair and selected another cigarette from his case; but he did not sit down again.

"He did—very much. Drukker has an unfortunately antagonistic manner. And Pardee is hypersensitive on the subject of his chess. The fact is, he went white with anger at Drukker's strictures. But I personally changed the subject; and when they went away the incident had apparently been forgotten."

We remained but a few minutes longer. Markham was profuse in his apologies to the professor and sought to make amends for the patent annoyance our visit had caused him. He was not pleased with Vance for his seemingly garrulous insistence on the details of Pardee's chess game, and when we had descended to the drawing-room he expressed his displeasure.

"I could understand your questions relating to the whereabouts of the various occupants of this house last night, but I could see no excuse for your harping on Pardee's and Drukker's disagreement over a game of chess. We have other things to do besides gossip."

"A hate of gossip parlance also crown'd Tennyson's Isabel thro' all her placid life," Vance returned puckishly. "But—my word, Markham!—our life is not like Isabel's. Speakin' seriously, there was method in my gossip. I prattled—and I learned."

"You learned what?" Markham demanded sharply.

With a cautious glance into the hall Vance leaned forward and lowered his voice.

"I learned, my dear Lycurgus, that a black bishop is missing from that set in the library, and that the chessman left at Mrs. Drukker's door matches the other pieces up-stairs!"

15

AN INTERVIEW WITH PARDEE

(*Tuesday, April 12; 12:30 P.M.*)

THIS PIECE of news had a profound effect on Markham. As was his habit when agitated, he rose and began pacing back and forth, his hands clasped behind him. Heath, too, though slower to grasp the significance of Vance's revelation, puffed vigorously on his cigar—an indication that his mind was busy with a difficult adjustment of facts.

Before either had formulated any comment the rear door of the hall opened and light footsteps approached the drawing-room. Belle Dillard, returning from Mrs. Drukker's, appeared in the archway. Her face was troubled, and letting her eyes rest on Markham, she asked:

"What did you say to Adolph this morning? He's in an awful state of funk. He's going about testing all the door-locks and window-catches as if he feared burglars; and he has frightened poor Grete by telling her to be sure to bolt herself in at night."

"Ah! He has warned Mrs. Menzel, has he?" mused Vance. "Very interestin'."

The girl's gaze turned swiftly to him.

"Yes; but he will give me no explanation. He's excited and mysterious. And the strangest thing about his attitude is that he refuses to go near his mother. . . . What does it mean, Mr. Vance? I feel as though something terrible were impending."

"I don't know just what it does mean." Vance spoke in a low, distressed voice. "And I'm afraid even to try to interpret it. If I should be wrong. . .'." He became silent for a moment. "We must wait and see. To-night perhaps we'll know.—But there's no cause for alarm on your part, Miss Dillard." He smiled comfortingly. "How did you find Mrs. Drukker?"

"She seemed much better. But there's still something worrying her; and I think it has to do with Adolph, for she talked about him the whole time I was there, and kept asking me if I'd noticed anything unusual in his manner lately."

"That's quite natural in the circumstances," Vance returned. "But you mustn't let her morbid attitude affect you.—And now, to change the subject: I understand that you were in the library for half an hour or so last night just before you went to the theatre. Tell me, Miss Dillard: where was your hand-bag during that time?"

The question startled her; but after a momentary hesitation she answered: "When I came into the library I placed it with my wrap on the little table by the door."

"It was the lizard-skin bag containing the key?"

"Yes. Sigurd hates evening dress, and when we go out together I always wear my day clothes."

"So you left the bag on the table during that half-hour, and then kept it with you the rest of the evening.—And what about this morning?"

"I went out for a walk before breakfast and carried it with me. Later I put it on the hat-rack in the hall for an hour or so; but when I started for Lady Mae's at about ten I took it with me. It was then I discovered that the little pistol had been returned, and I postponed my call. I left the bag down-stairs in the archery-room until you and Mr. Markham came; and I've had it with me ever since."

Vance thanked her whimsically.

"And now that the peregrinations of the bag have been thoroughly traced, please try to forget all about it." She was on the point of asking a question, but he anticipated her curiosity and said quickly: "You went to the Plaza for supper last night, your uncle told us. You must have been late in getting home."

"I never stay out very late when I go anywhere with Sigurd," she answered, with a maternal note of complaint. "He has a constitutional aversion to any kind of night life. I begged him to stay out longer, but he looked so miserable I hadn't the heart to remain. We actually got home at half past twelve."

Vance rose with a gracious smile.

"You've been awfully good to bear with our foolish questions so patiently.... Now we're going to drop in on Mr. Pardee and see if he has any illuminatin' suggestions to offer. He's generally in at this time, I believe."

"I'm sure he's in now." The girl walked with us to the hall. "He was here only a little while before you came, and he said he was returning home to attend to some correspondence."

We were about to go out when Vance paused.

"Oh, I say, Miss Dillard; there's one point I forgot to ask you about. When you came home last night with Mr. Arnesson, how did you know it was just half past twelve? I notice you don't wear a watch."

"Sigurd told me," she explained. "I was rather mean to him for bringing me home so early, and as we entered the hall here I asked him spitefully what time it was. He looked at his watch and said it was half past twelve...."

At that moment the front door opened and Arnesson came in. He stared at us in mock astonishment; then he caught sight of Belle Dillard.

"Hallo, sis," he called to her pleasantly. "In the hands of the *gendarmerie,* I see." He flashed us an amused look. "Why the conclave? This house is becoming a regular police station. Hunting for clews of Sprigg's murderer? Ha! Bright youth done away with by his jealous professor, and that sort of thing, eh?... Hope you chaps haven't been putting Diana the Huntress through a third degree."

"Nothing of the kind," the girl spoke up. "They've been most considerate. And I've been telling them what an old fogy you are—bringing me home at half past twelve."

"I think I was very indulgent," grinned Arnesson. "Much too late for a child like you to be out."

"It must be terrible to be senile and—and mathematically inclined," she retorted with some heat, and ran up-stairs.

Arnesson shrugged his shoulders and looked after her until she had disappeared. Then he fixed a cynical eye on Markham.

"Well, what glad tidings do you bring? Any news about the latest victim?" He led the way back to the drawing-room. "You know, I miss that lad. He'd have gone far. Rotten shame he had to be named Johnny Sprigg. Even 'Peter Piper' would have been safer. Nothing happened to Peter Piper aside from the pepper episode; and you couldn't very well work that up into a murder...."

"We have nothing to report, Arnesson," Markham broke in, nettled by the man's flippancy. "The situation remains unchanged."

"Just dropped in for a social call, I presume. Staying for lunch?"

"We reserve the right" said Markham coldly, "to investigate the case in whatever manner we deem advisable. Nor are we accountable to you for our actions."

"So! Something *has* happened that irks you." Arnesson spoke with sarcasm. "I thought I had been accepted as a coadjutor; but I see I am to be turned forth into the darkness." He sighed elaborately and took out his pipe. "Dropping the pilot!—Bismarck and me. Alas!"

Vance had been smoking dreamily near the archway, apparently oblivious of Arnesson's complaining. Now he stepped into the room.

"Really, y' know, Markham, Mr. Arnesson is quite right. We agreed to keep him posted; and if he's to be of any help to us he must know all the facts."

"It was you yourself," protested Markham, "who pointed out the possible danger of mentioning last night's occurrence. . . ."

"True. But I had forgotten at the time our promise to Mr. Arnesson. And I'm sure his discretion can be relied on." Then Vance related in detail Mrs. Drukker's experience of the night before.

Arnesson listened with rapt attention. I noticed that his sardonic expression gradually disappeared, and that in its place came a look of calculating sombreness. He sat for several minutes in contemplative silence, his pipe in his hand.

"That's certainly a vital factor in the problem," he commented at length. "It changes our constant. I can see that this thing has got to be calculated from a new angle. The Bishop, it appears, is in our midst. But why should he come to haunt Lady Mae?"

"She is reported to have screamed at almost the exact moment of Robin's death."

"Aha!" Arnesson sat up. "I grasp your implication. She saw the Bishop from her window on the morning of Cock Robin's dissolution, and later he returned and perched on her door-knob as a warning for her to keep mum."

"Something like that, perhaps. . . . Have you enough integers now to work out your formula?"

"I'd like to cast an eye on this black bishop. Where is it?"

Vance reached in his pocket, and held out the chessman. Arnesson took it eagerly. His eyes glittered for a moment. He turned the piece over in his hand, and then gave it back.

"You seem to recognize this particular bishop," said Vance dulcetly. "You're quite correct. It was borrowed from your chess set in the library."

Arnesson nodded a slow affirmative.

"I believe it was." Suddenly he turned to Markham, and an ironic leer came over his lean features. "Was that why I was to be kept in the dark? Under suspicion, am I? Shades of Pythagoras! What penalty attaches to the heinous crime of distributing chessmen among one's neighbors?"

Markham got up and walked toward the hall.

"You are not under suspicion, Arnesson," he answered, with no attempt to conceal his ill-humor. "The bishop was left at Mrs. Drukker's at exactly midnight."

"And I was half an hour too late to qualify. Sorry to have disappointed you."

"Let us hear if your formula works out," said Vance, as we passed out of the front door. "We've a little visit to pay to Mr. Pardee now."

"Pardee? Oho! Calling in a chess expert on the subject of bishops, eh? I see your reasoning—it at least has the virtue of being simple and direct. . . ."

He stood on the little porch and watched us, like a japish gargoyle, as we crossed the street.

Pardee received us with his customary quiet courtesy. The tragic, frustrated look which was a part of his habitual expression was even more pronounced than usual; and when he drew up chairs for us in his study his manner was that of a man whose interest in life had died, and who was merely going through the mechanical motions of living.

"We have come here, Mr. Pardee," Vance began, "to learn what we can of Sprigg's murder in Riverside Park yesterday morning. We have excellent reasons for every question we are about to ask you."

Pardee nodded resignedly.

"I shall not be offended at any line of interrogation you take. After reading the papers I realize just how unusual a problem you are facing."

"First, then, please inform us where you were yesterday morning between seven and eight."

A faint flush overspread Pardee's face, but he answered in a low, even voice.

"I was in bed. I did not rise until nearly nine."

"Is it not your habit to take a walk in the park before breakfast?" (I knew this was sheer guesswork on Vance's part, for the subject of Pardee's habits had not come up during the investigation.)

"That is quite true," the man replied, without a moment's hesitation. "But yesterday I did not go,—I had worked rather late the night before."

"When did you first hear of Sprigg's death?"

"At breakfast. My cook repeated the gossip of the neighborhood. I read the official account of the tragedy in the early edition of the evening *Sun.*"

"And you saw the reproduction of the Bishop note, of course, in this morning's paper.—What is your opinion of the affair, Mr. Pardee?"

"I hardly know." For the first time his lacklustre eyes showed signs of animation. "It's an incredible situation. The mathematical chances are utterly opposed to such a series of interrelated events being coincidental."

"Yes," Vance concurred. "And speaking of mathematics: are you at all familiar with the Riemann-Christoffel tensor?"

"I know of it," the man admitted. "Drukker uses it in his book on world lines. My mathematics, however, are not of the physicist's type. Had I not become enamored of chess"—he smiled sadly—"I would have been an astronomer. Next to manoeuvring the factors in a complicated chess combination, the greatest mental satisfaction one can get, I think, is plotting the heavens and discovering new planets. I even keep a five-inch equatorial telescope in a pent-house on my roof for amateur observations."

Vance listened to Pardee with close attention; and for several minutes discussed with him Professor Pickering's recent determination of the trans-Neptunean O,* much to Markham's bewilderment and to the Sergeant's annoyance. At length he brought the conversation back to the tensor formula.

"You were, I understand, at the Dillards' last Thursday when Mr. Arnesson was discussing this tensor with Drukker and Sprigg."

"Yes, I recall that the subject came up then."

"How well did you know Sprigg?"

"Only casually. I had met him with Arnesson once or twice."

"Sprigg, also, it seems, was in the habit of walking in Riverside Park before

* Since this discussion took place Professor Pickering has posited from the perturbations of Uranus, two other outer planets beyond Neptune: P and S.

breakfast," observed Vance negligently. "Ever run into him there, Mr. Pardee?"

The man's eyelids quivered slightly, and he hesitated before answering.

"Never," he said finally.

Vance appeared indifferent to the denial. He rose and, going to the front window, looked out.

"I thought one might be able to see into the archery range from here. But I note that the angle cuts off the view entirely."

"Yes, the range is quite private. There's even a vacant lot opposite the wall, so that no one can see over it. . . . Were you thinking of a possible witness to Robin's death?"

"That, and other things." Vance returned to his chair. "You don't go in for archery, I take it."

"It's a trifle too strenuous for me. Miss Dillard once tried to interest me in the sport, but I was not a very promising acolyte. I've been to several tournaments with her, however."

An unusually soft note had crept into Pardee's voice, and for some reason which I could not exactly explain I got the feeling that he was fond of Belle Dillard. Vance, too, must have received the same impression, for after a brief pause he said:

"You will realize, I trust, that it is not our intention to pry unnecessarily into any one's private affairs; but the question of motive in the two murders we are investigating still remains obscure, and as Robin's death was at first superficially attributed to a rivalry for Miss Dillard's affections, it might help us to know, in a general way, what the true situation is concerning the young lady's preference. . . . As a friend of the family you probably know; and we'd appreciate your confidence in the matter."

Pardee's gaze travelled out of the window, and the suggestion of a sigh escaped him.

"I've always had the feeling that she and Arnesson would some day be married. But that is only conjecture. She once told me quite positively that she was not going to consider matrimony until she was thirty." (One could easily guess in what connection Belle Dillard had made this pronouncement to Pardee. His emotional, as well as his intellectual life, had apparently met with failure.)

"You do not believe then," pursued Vance, "that her heart is seriously concerned with young Sperling?"

Pardee shook his head. "However," he qualified, "martyrdom such as he is undergoing at present has a tremendous sentimental appeal for women."

"Miss Dillard tells me you called on her this morning."

"I generally drop over during the day." He was obviously uncomfortable and, I thought, a little embarrassed.

"Do you know Mrs. Drukker well?"

Pardee gave Vance a quick, inquisitive look.

"Not particularly," he said. "I've naturally met her several times."

"You've called at her house?"

"On many occasions, but always to see Drukker. I've been interested for years in the relation of mathematics to chess. . . ."

Vance nodded.

"How did your game with Rubinstein come out last night, by the by? I didn't see the papers this morning."

"I resigned on the forty-fourth move." The man spoke hopelessly. "Rubinstein found a weakness in my attack which I had entirely overlooked when I sealed my move at the adjournment."

"Drukker, Professor Dillard tells us, foresaw the outcome when you and he were discussing the situation last night."

I could not understand why Vance referred so pointedly to this episode, knowing as he did how sore a point it was with Pardee. Markham, also, frowned at what appeared to be an unforgivably tactless remark on Vance's part.

Pardee colored, and shifted in his chair.

"Drukker talked too much last night." The statement was not without venom. "Though he's not a tournament player, he should know that such discussions are taboo during unfinished games. Frankly, though, I put little stock in his prophecy. I thought my sealed move had taken care of the situation, but Drukker saw farther ahead than I did. His analysis was uncannily profound." There was the jealousy of self-pity in his tone, and I felt that he hated Drukker as bitterly as his seemingly mild nature would permit.

"How long did the game last?" Vance asked casually.

"It was over a little after one o'clock. There were only fourteen moves in last night's session."

"Were there many spectators?"

"An unusually large number, considering the late hour."

Vance put out his cigarette and got up. When we were in the lower hall on our way to the front door he halted suddenly and, fixing Pardee with a gaze of sardonic amusement, said:

"Y' know, the black bishop was at large again last night around midnight."

His words produced an astonishing effect. Pardee drew himself up as if he had been struck in the face; and his cheeks went chalky white. For a full half-minute he stared at Vance, his eyes like live coals. His lips moved with a slight tremor, but no word came from them. Then, as if with superhuman effort, he turned stiffly away and went to the door. Jerking it open he held it for us to pass out.

As we walked up Riverside Drive to the District Attorney's car, which had been left in front of the Drukker house in 76th Street, Markham questioned Vance sharply in regard to the final remark he had made to Pardee.

"I was in hopes," explained Vance, "of surprising some look of recognition or understanding from him. But, 'pon my soul, Markham, I didn't expect any effect like the one I produced. Astonishin' how he reacted. I don't grasp it—I don't at all grasp it. . . ."

He became engrossed in his thoughts. But as the car swung into Broadway at 72nd Street he roused himself and directed the chauffeur to the Sherman Square Hotel.

"I have a gaspin' desire to know more of that chess game between Pardee and Rubinstein. No reason for it—sheer vagary on my part. But the idea has been workin' in me ever since the professor mentioned it. . . . From eleven until past one—that's a deuced long time to play off an unfinished game of only forty-four moves."

We had drawn up to the curb at the corner of Amsterdam Avenue and 71st Street, and Vance disappeared into the Manhattan Chess Club. It was fully five minutes before he returned. In his hand he carried a sheet of paper filled with notations. There was, however, no sign of jubilance in his expression.

"My far-fetched but charmin' theory," he said with a grimace, "has run aground on base prosaic facts. I just talked to the secret'ry of the club; and last night's session consumed two hours and nineteen minutes. It seems to have been a coruscatin' battle, full of esoteric quirks and strategical soul-searchin's. Along about half past eleven the onlooking genii had Pardee picked for the winner; but Rubinstein then staged a masterly piece of sustained analysis, and proceeded to tear Pardee's tactics to smithereens—just as Drukker had prognosticated. Astonishin' mind, Drukker's. . . ."

It was plain that even now he was not entirely satisfied with what he had learned; and his next words voiced his dissatisfaction.

"I thought while I was at it I'd take a page from the Sergeant's book, so to speak, and indulge in a bit of routine thoroughness. So I borrowed the score sheet of last night's game and copied down the moves. I may run over the game some day when time hangs heavy."

And, with what I thought unusual care, he folded the score and placed it in his wallet.

16

ACT THREE

(*Tuesday, April 12—Saturday, April 16.*)

AFTER LUNCH at the Élysée Markham and Heath continued down-town. A hard afternoon lay before them. Markham's routine work had accumulated; and the Sergeant, having taken on the Sprigg case in addition to the Robin investigation, had to keep two separate machines working, co-ordinate all his reports, answer innumerable questions from his superiors, and attempt to satisfy the voraciousness of an army of reporters. Vance and I went to an exhibition of modern French art at Knoedler's, had tea at the St. Regis, and met Markham at the Stuyvesant Club for dinner. Heath and Inspector Moran joined us at half past eight for an informal conference; but though it lasted until nearly midnight nothing of a tangible nature came out of it.

Nor did the following day bring anything but discouragement. The report from Captain Dubois stated that the revolver given him by Heath contained no sign of a finger-print. Captain Hagedorn identified the weapon as the one used in the shooting of Sprigg; but this merely substantiated our already positive belief. The man set to guard the rear of the Drukker residence spent an uneventful night. No one had entered or departed from the house; and by eleven o'clock every window had been dark. Nor had a sound of any kind come from the house until the next morning when the cook set about her chores for the day. Mrs. Drukker had appeared in the garden a little after eight; and at half past nine Drukker went out the front door and sat for two hours in the park reading.

Two days went by. A watch was kept on the Dillard house; Pardee was put under strict surveillance; and a man was stationed each night under the willow trees behind the Drukker house. But nothing unusual happened; and, despite the Sergeant's tireless activities, all promising lines of investigation seemed to be automatically closed. Both Heath and Markham were deeply worried. The newspapers were outdoing themselves in gaudy rhetoric; and the inability of the Police Department and the District Attorney's office to make the slightest headway against the mystery of the two spectacular murders was rapidly growing into a political scandal.

Vance called on Professor Dillard and discussed the case along general lines. He also spent over an hour on Thursday afternoon with Arnesson in the hope that the working out of the proposed formula had brought to light some detail that could be used as a starting-point for speculation. But he was dissatisfied with the interview, and complained to me that Arnesson had not been wholly frank with him. Twice he dropped in at the Manhattan Chess Club and attempted to lead Pardee into conversation; but each time he was met with the reticence of cold courtesy. I noticed that he made no effort to communicate with either Drukker or Mrs. Drukker; and when I asked him his reason for ignoring them, he answered:

"The truth cannot be learned from them now. Each is playing a game; and both are thoroughly frightened. Until we have some definite evidence, more harm than good will result from any attempt to cross-examine them."

This definite evidence was to come the very next day from a most unexpected quarter; and it marked the beginning of the last phase of our investigation—a phase fraught with such sinister, soul-stirring tragedy and unspeakable horror, with such wanton cruelty and monstrous humor, that even now, years later, as I set down this reportorial record of it, I find it difficult to believe that the events were not, after all, a mere grotesque dream of fabulous wickedness.

Friday afternoon Markham, in a mood of desperation, called another conference. Arnesson asked permission to attend; and at four o'clock we all met, including Inspector Moran, in the District Attorney's private room in the old Criminal Courts Building. Arnesson was unwontedly silent during the discussion, and not once did he indulge in his usual flippancy. He listened with close attention to all that was said, and seemed purposely to avoid expressing an opinion, even when directly appealed to by Vance.

We had been in conference perhaps half an hour when Swacker entered quietly and placed a memorandum on the District Attorney's desk. Markham glanced at it and frowned. After a moment he initialed two printed forms and handed them to Swacker.

"Fill these in right away and give them to Ben,"* he ordered. Then when the man had gone out through the outer-hall door, he explained the interruption. "Sperling has just sent a request to speak to me. He says he has information that may be of importance. I thought, in the circumstances, it might be well to see him now."

* Colonel Benjamin Hanlon, commanding officer of the Detective Division attached to the District Attorney's office.

Ten minutes later Sperling was brought in by a deputy sheriff from the Tombs. He greeted Markham with a friendly boyish smile, and nodded pleasantly to Vance. He bowed—a bit stiffly, I thought—to Arnesson, whose presence seemed both to surprise and disconcert him. Markham motioned him to a chair, and Vance offered him a cigarette.

"I wanted to speak to you, Mr. Markham," he began, a bit diffidently, "about a matter which may be of help to you. . . . You remember, when you were questioning me about my being in the archery-room with Robin, you wanted to know which way Mr. Drukker went when he left us. I told you I didn't notice, except that he went out by the basement door. . . . Well, sir, I've had a lot of time to think lately; and I've naturally gone over in my mind all that happened that morning. I don't know just how to explain it, but everything has become a lot clearer now. Certain—what you might call impressions—have come back to me. . . ."

He paused and looked down at the carpet. Then lifting his head, he went on:

"One of these impressions has to do with Mr. Drukker—and that's why I wanted to see you. Just this afternoon I was—well, sort of pretending I was in the archery-room again, talking to Robin; and all of a sudden the picture of the rear window flashed across my mind. And I remembered that when I had glanced out of the window that morning to see how the weather was for my trip, I had seen Mr. Drukker sitting in the arbor behind the house. . . ."

"At what time was this?" Markham demanded brusquely.

"Only a few seconds before I went to catch my train."

"Then you imply that Mr. Drukker, instead of leaving the premises, went to the arbor and remained there until you departed."

"It looks that way, sir." Sperling was reluctant to make the admission.

"You're quite sure you saw him?"

"Yes, sir. I remember distinctly now. I even recall the peculiar way he had his legs drawn up under him."

"You would swear to it," asked Markham gravely, "knowing that a man's life might rest on your testimony?"

"I'd swear to it, sir," Sperling returned simply.

When the sheriff had escorted his prisoner from the room, Markham looked at Vance.

"I think that gives us a foothold."

"Yes. The cook's testimony was of little value, since Drukker merely denied it; and she's the type of loyal stubborn German who'd back up his denial if any real danger threatened him. Now we're armed with an effective weapon."

"It seems to me," Markham said, after a few moments of speculative silence, "that we have a good circumstantial case against Drukker. He was in the Dillard yard only a few seconds before Robin was killed. He could easily have seen when Sperling went away; and, as he had recently come from Professor Dillard, he knew that the other members of the family were out. Mrs. Drukker denied she saw any one from her window that morning, although she screamed at the time of Robin's death and then went into a panic of fear when we came to question Drukker. She even warned him against us and called us 'the enemy.' My belief is she saw Drukker returning home immediately after Robin's body had been placed on the range.—Drukker was not in his room at the time Sprigg was killed, and both he and his mother have been at pains to cover up the fact. He has become excited whenever we broached the subject of the murders, and has ridiculed the idea that they were connected. In fact, many of his actions have been highly suspicious. Also, we know he is abnormal and unbalanced, and that he is given to playing children's games. It's quite possible—in view of what Doctor Barstead told us—that he has confused fantasy and reality, and perpetrated these crimes in a moment of temporary insanity. The tensor formula is not only familiar to him, but he may have associated it in some crazy way with Sprigg as a result of Arnesson's discussion with Sprigg about it.—As for the Bishop notes, they may have been part of the unreality of his insane games,—children all want an approving audience when they invent any new form of amusement. His choice of the word 'bishop' was probably the result of his interest in chess—a playful signature intended to confuse. And this supposition is further borne out by the actual appearance of a chess bishop on his mother's door. He may have feared that she saw him that morning, and thus sought to silence her without openly admitting to her that he was guilty. He could easily have slammed the screen-porch door from the inside, without having had a key, and thereby given the impression that the bearer of the bishop had entered and departed by the rear door. Furthermore, it would have been a simple matter for him to take the bishop from the library the night Pardee was analyzing his game. . . ."

Markham continued for some time building up his case against Drukker. He was thorough and detailed, and his summation accounted for practically all of the evidence that had been adduced. The logical and relentless way in which he pieced his various factors together was impressively convincing; and a long silence followed his résumé.

Vance at length stood up, as if to break the tension of his thoughts, and walked to the window.

"You may be right, Markham," he admitted. "But my chief objection to your conclusion is that the case against Drukker is too good. I've had him in mind as a possibility from the first; but the more suspiciously he acted and the more the indications pointed toward him, the more I felt inclined to dismiss him from consideration. The brain that schemed these abominable murders is too competent, too devilishly shrewd, to become entangled in any such net of circumstantial evidence as you've drawn about Drukker. Drukker has an amazing mentality—his intelligence and intellect are supernormal, in fact; and it's difficult to conceive of him, if guilty, leaving so many loopholes."

"The law," returned Markham with acerbity, "can hardly be expected to throw out cases because they're too convincing."

"On the other hand," pursued Vance, ignoring the comment, "it is quite obvious that Drukker, even if not guilty, knows something that has a direct and vital bearing on the case; and my humble suggestion is that we attempt to prise this information out of him. Sperling's testimony has given us the lever for the purpose. . . . I say, Mr. Arnesson, what's your opinion?"

"Haven't any," the man answered. "I'm a disinterested onlooker. I'd hate, however, to see poor Adolph in durance vile." Though he would not commit himself it was plain that he agreed with Vance.

Heath thought, characteristically, that immediate action was advisable, and expressed himself to that effect.

"If he's got anything to tell he'll tell it quick enough after he's locked up."

"It's a difficult situation," Inspector Moran demurred, in a soft judicial voice. "We can't afford to make an error. If Drukker's evidence should convict some one else, we'd be a laughing-stock if we had arrested the wrong man."

Vance looked toward Markham and nodded agreement.

"Why not have him on the tapis first, and see if he can't be persuaded to unburden his soul. You might dangle a warrant over his head, don't y' know, as a kind of moral inducement. Then, if he remains coy and reticent, bring out the gyves and have the doughty Sergeant escort him to the bastille."

Markham sat tapping indecisively on the desk, his head enveloped in smoke as he puffed nervously on his cigar. At last he set his chin firmly and turned to Heath.

"Bring Drukker here at nine o'clock to-morrow morning. You'd better take a wagon and a John-Doe warrant in case he offers any objection." His face was grim and determined. "Then I'll find out what he knows—and act accordingly."

The conference broke up immediately. It was after five o'clock, and Markham and Vance and I rode up-town together to the Stuyvesant Club. We dropped Arnesson at the subway, and he took leave of us with scarcely a word. His garrulous cynicism seemed entirely to have deserted him. After dinner Markham pleaded fatigue, and Vance and I went to the Metropolitan and heard Geraldine Farrar in "Louise."*

The next morning broke dark and misty. Currie called us at half past seven, for Vance intended to be present at the interview with Drukker; and at eight o'clock we had breakfast in the library before a light grate fire. We were held up in the traffic on our way down-town, and though it was quarter after nine when we reached the District Attorney's office, Drukker and Heath had not yet arrived.

Vance settled himself comfortably in a large leather-upholstered chair and lighted a cigarette.

"I feel rather bucked this morning," he remarked. "If Drukker tells his story, and if the tale is what I think it is, we'll know the combination to the lock."

His words had scarcely been uttered when Heath burst into the office and, facing Markham without a word of greeting, lifted both arms and let them fall in a gesture of hopeless resignation.

"Well, sir, we ain't going to question Drukker this morning—or no other time," he blurted. "He fell offa that high wall in Riverside Park right near his house last night, and broke his neck. Wasn't found till seven o'clock this morning. His body's down at the morgue now. . . . Fine breaks we get!" He sank disgustedly into a chair.

Markham stared at him unbelievingly.

"You're sure?" he asked, with startled futility.

"I was up there before they removed the body. One of the local men phoned me about it just as I was leaving the office. I stuck around and got all the dope I could."

* "Louise" was Vance's favorite modern opera, but he greatly preferred Mary Garden to Farrar in the title rôle.

"What did you learn?" Markham was fighting against an overwhelming sense of discouragement.

"There wasn't much to find out. Some kids in the park found the body about seven o'clock this morning—lots of kids around, it being Saturday; and the local men hopped over and called a police surgeon. The doc said Drukker musta fallen off the wall about ten o'clock last night—killed instantly. The wall at that spot—right opposite 76th Street—is all of thirty feet above the playground. The top of it runs along the bridle path; and it's a wonder more people haven't broke their necks there. Kids are all the time walking along the stone ledge."

"Has Mrs. Drukker been notified?"

"No. I told 'em I'd attend to it. But I thought I'd come here first and see what you wanted done about it."

Markham leaned back dejectedly.

"I don't see that there's much of anything we can do."

"It might be well," suggested Vance, "to inform Arnesson. He'll probably be the one who'll have to look after things.... My word, Markham! I'm beginning to think that this case is a nightmare, after all. Drukker was our principal hope, and at the very moment when there's a chance of our forcing him to speak, he tumbles off of a wall———" Abruptly he stopped. "Off of a wall!..." As he repeated these words he leapt to his feet. "*A hunchback falls off of a wall!... A hunchback!...*"

We stared at him as if he had gone out of his mind; and I admit that the look on his face sent a chill over me. His eyes were fixed, like those of a man gazing at a malignant ghost. Slowly he turned to Markham, and said in a voice that I hardly recognized:

"It's another mad melodrama—another Mother-Goose rhyme.... 'Humpty Dumpty' this time!"

The astonished silence that followed was broken by a strained harsh laugh from the Sergeant.

"That's stretching things, ain't it, Mr. Vance?"

"It's preposterous!" declared Markham, studying Vance with genuine concern. "My dear fellow, you've let this case prey on your mind too much. Nothing has happened except that a man with a hump has fallen from the coping of a wall in the park. It's unfortunate, I know; and it's doubly unfortunate at just this time." He went to Vance and put his hand on his shoulder. "Let the Sergeant and me run this show—we're used to these things. Take a trip and get a good rest. Why not go to Europe as you generally do in the spring———?"

"Oh, quite—quite." Vance sighed and smiled wearily. "The sea air would do me worlds of good, and all that. Bring me back to normal, what?—build up the wreck of this once noble brain.... I give up! The third act in this terrible tragedy is played almost before your eyes, and you serenely ignore it."

"Your imagination has got the better of you," Markham returned, with the patience of a deep affection. "Don't worry about it any more. Have dinner with me to-night. We'll talk it over then."

At this moment Swacker looked in, and spoke to the Sergeant.

"Quinan of the *World* is here. Wants to see you."

Markham swung about.

"*Oh, my God!* ... Bring him in here!"

Quinan entered, waved us a cheery salutation, and handed the Sergeant a letter.

"Another *billet-doux*—received this morning.—What privileges do I get for being so big-hearted?"

Heath opened the letter as the rest of us looked on. At once I recognized the paper and the faint blue characters of the élite type. The note read:

> Humpty Dumpty sat on a wall,
> Humpty Dumpty had a great fall;
> All the king's horses and all the king's men
> Cannot put Humpty Dumpty together again.

Then came that ominous signature, in capitals: THE BISHOP.

17

AN ALL–NIGHT LIGHT

(*Saturday, April 16; 9:30 A.M.*)

WHEN HEATH had got rid of Quinan with promises such as would have gladdened any reporter's heart,* there were several minutes of tense silence in the office. "The Bishop" had been at his grisly work again; and the case had now become a terrible triplicate affair, with the solution apparently further off than ever. It was not, however, the insolubility of these incredible crimes that primarily affected us; rather was it the inherent horror that emanated, like a miasma, from the acts themselves.

Vance, who was pacing sombrely up and down, gave voice to his troubled emotions.

"It's damnable, Markham—it's the essence of unutterable evil. . . . Those children in the park—up early on their holiday in search of dreams—busy with their play and make-believe . . . and then the silencing reality—the awful, overpowering disillusion. . . . Don't you see the wickedness of it? Those children found Humpty Dumpty—*their* Humpty Dumpty, with whom they had played—lying dead at the foot of the famous wall—a Humpty Dumpty they could touch and weep over, broken and twisted and never more to be put together. . . ."

He paused by the window and looked out. The mist had lifted, and a faint diffusion of spring sunlight lay over the gray stones of the city. The golden eagle on the New York Life Building glistened in the distance.

"I say; one simply mustn't get sentimental," he remarked with a forced

---

* It may be recalled that the *World's* accounts of the Bishop case were the envy of the other metropolitan newspapers. Sergeant Heath, though impartial in his statements of facts to the press, nevertheless managed to save several picturesque *bonnes-bouches* for Quinan, and permitted himself certain speculations which, while having no news value, gave the *World's* stories an added interest and color.

smile, turning back to the room. "It decomposes the intelligence and stultifies the dialectic processes. Now that we know Drukker was not the capricious victim of the law of gravity, but was given a helpin' hand in his departure from this world, the sooner we become energetic, the better, what?"

Though his change of mood was an obvious *tour de force,* it roused the rest of us from our gloomy apathy. Markham reached for the telephone and made arrangements with Inspector Moran for Heath to handle the Drukker case. Then he called the Medical Examiner's office and asked for an immediate *post-mortem* report. Heath got up vigorously, and after taking three cups of ice-water, stood with legs apart, his derby pulled far down on his forehead, waiting for the District Attorney to indicate a line of action.

Markham moved restlessly.

"Several men from your department, Sergeant, were supposed to be keeping an eye on the Drukker and Dillard houses. Did you talk to any of them this morning?"

"I didn't have time, sir; and, anyway, I figured it was only an accident. But I told the boys to hang around until I got back."

"What did the Medical Examiner have to say?"

"Only that it looked like an accident; and that Drukker had been dead about ten hours. . . ."

Vance interpolated a question.

"Did he mention a fractured skull in addition to the broken neck?"

"Well, sir, he didn't exactly say the skull was fractured, but he did state that Drukker had landed on the back of his head." Heath nodded understandingly. "I guess it'll prove to be a fracture all right—same like Robin and Sprigg."

"Undoubtedly. The technique of our murderer seems to be simple and efficacious. He strikes his victims on the vault, either stunning them or killing them outright, and then proceeds to cast them in the rôles he has chosen for them in his puppet-plays. Drukker was no doubt leaning over the wall, perfectly exposed for such an attack. It was misty, and the setting was somewhat obscured. Then came the blow on the head, a slight heave, and Drukker fell noiselessly over the parapet—the third sacrificial offering on the altar of old Mother Goose."

"What gets me," declared Heath with surly anger, "is why Guilfoyle,* the fellow I set to watch the rear of the Drukker house, didn't report the fact that Drukker was out all night. He returned to the Bureau at eight o'clock, and I missed him.—Don't you think, sir, it might be a good idea to find out what he knows before we go up-town?"

Markham agreed, and Heath bawled an order over the telephone. Guilfoyle made the distance between Police Headquarters and the Criminal Courts Building in less than ten minutes. The Sergeant almost pounced on him as he entered.

"What time did Drukker leave the house last night?" he bellowed.

"About eight o'clock—right after he'd had dinner." Guilfoyle was ill at ease, and his tone had the wheedling softness of one who had been caught in a dereliction of duty.

---

* Guilfoyle, it may be remembered, was one of the detectives who shadowed Tony Skeel in the Canary murder case.

"Which way did he go?"

"He came out the back door, walked down the range, and went into the Dillard house through the archery-room."

"Paying a social visit?"

"It looked that way, Sergeant. He spends a lot of time at the Dillards'."

"Huh! And what time did he come back home?"

Guilfoyle moved uneasily.

"It don't look like he came back home, Sergeant."

"Oh, it don't?" Heath's retort was ponderous with sarcasm. "I thought maybe after he'd broke his neck he mighta come back and passed the time of day with you."

"What I meant was, Sergeant———"

"You meant that Drukker—the bird you were supposed to keep an eye on—went to call on the Dillards at eight o'clock, and then you set down in the arbor, most likely, and took a little beauty nap.... What time did you wake up?"

"Say, listen!" Guilfoyle bristled. "I didn't take no nap. I was on the job all night. Just because I didn't happen to see this guy come back home don't mean I was laying down on the watch."

"Well, if you didn't see him come back, why didn't you phone in that he was spending his week-end out of town or something?"

"I thought he musta come in by the front door."

"Thinking again, were you? Ain't your brain worn out this morning?"

"Have a heart, Sergeant. My job wasn't to tail Drukker. You told me to watch the house and see who went in and out, and that if there was any sign of trouble to bust in.—Now, here's what happened. Drukker went to the Dillards' at eight o'clock, and I kept my eye on the windows of the Drukker house. Along about nine o'clock the cook goes up-stairs and turns on the light in her room. Half an hour later the light goes out, and says I: 'She's put to bed.' Then along about ten o'clock the lights are turned on in Drukker's room———"

"What's this?"

"Yeh—you heard me. The lights go on in Drukker's room about ten o'clock; and I can see a shadow of somebody moving about.—Now, I ask you, Sergeant: wouldn't you yourself have took it for granted that the hunchback had come in by the front door?"

Heath grunted.

"Maybe so," he admitted. "You're sure it was ten o'clock?"

"I didn't look at my watch; but I'm here to tell you it wasn't far off of ten."

"And what time did the lights go out in Drukker's room?"

"They didn't go out. They stayed on all night. He was a queer bird. He didn't keep regular hours, and twice before his lights were on till nearly morning."

"That's quite understandable," came Vance's lazy voice. "He has been at work on a difficult problem lately.—But tell us, Guilfoyle: what about the light in Mrs. Drukker's room?"

"Same as usual. The old dame always keeps a light burning in her room all night."

"Was there any one on guard in front of the Drukker house last night?" Markham asked Heath.

"Not after six o'clock, sir. We've had a man tailing Drukker during the day, but he goes off duty at six when Guilfoyle takes up his post in the rear."

There was a moment's silence. Then Vance turned to Guilfoyle.

"How far away were you last night from the door of the alleyway between the two apartment houses?"

The man paused to visualize the scene.

"Forty or fifty feet, say."

"And between you and the alleyway were the iron fence and some tree branches."

"Yes, sir. The view was more or less cut off, if that's what you mean."

"Would it have been possible for any one, coming from the direction of the Dillard house, to have gone out and returned by that door without your noticing him?"

"It mighta been done," the detective admitted; "provided, of course, the guy didn't want me to see him. It was foggy and dark last night, and there's always a lot of traffic noises from the Drive that woulda drowned out his movements if he was being extra cautious."

When the Sergeant had sent Guilfoyle back to the Bureau to await orders, Vance gave voice to his perplexity.

"It's a dashed complicated situation. Drukker called on the Dillards at eight o'clock, and at ten o'clock he was shoved over the wall in the park. As you observed, the note that Quinan just showed us was postmarked 11 P.M.— which means that it was probably typed *before the crime*. The Bishop therefore had planned his comedy in advance and prepared the note for the press. The audacity of it is amazin'. But there's one assumption we can tie to—namely, that the murderer was some one who knew of Drukker's exact whereabouts and proposed movements between eight and ten."

"I take it," said Markham, "your theory is that the murderer went and returned by the apartment-house alley."

"Oh, I say! I have no theory. I asked Guilfoyle about the alley merely in case we should learn that no one but Drukker was seen going to the park. In that event we could assume, as a tentative hypothesis, that the murderer had managed to avoid detection by taking the alleyway and crossing to the park in the middle of the block."

"With that possible route open to the murderer," Markham observed gloomily, "it wouldn't matter much who was seen going out with Drukker."

"That's just it. The person who staged this farce may have walked boldly into the park under the eyes of an alert myrmidon, or he may have hied stealthily through the alley."

Markham nodded an unhappy agreement.

"The thing that bothers me most, however," continued Vance, "is that light in Drukker's room all night. It was turned on at about the time the poor chap was tumbling into eternity. And Guilfoyle says that he could see some one moving about there after the light went on————"

He broke off, and stood for several seconds in an attitude of concentration.

"I say, Sergeant; I don't suppose you know whether or not Drukker's front-door key was in his pocket when he was found."

"No, sir; but I can find out in no time. The contents of his pockets are being held till after the autopsy."

Heath stepped to the telephone, and a moment later he was talking to the desk sergeant of the 68th-Street Precinct Station. Several minutes of waiting passed; then he grunted and banged down the receiver.

"Not a key of any kind on him."

"Ah!" Vance drew a deep puff on his cigarette and exhaled the smoke slowly. "I'm beginnin' to think that the Bishop purloined Drukker's key and paid a visit to his room after the murder. Sounds incredible, I know; but, for that matter, so does everything else that's happened in this fantastic business."

"But what, in God's name, would have been his object?" protested Markham incredulously.

"We don't know yet. But I have an idea that when we learn the motive of these astonishin' crimes, we'll understand why that visit was paid."

Markham, his face set austerely, took his hat from the closet.

"We'd better be getting out there."

But Vance made no move. He remained standing by the desk smoking abstractedly.

"Y' know, Markham," he said, "it occurs to me that we should see Mrs. Drukker first. There was tragedy in that house last night: something strange took place there that needs explaining; and now perhaps she'll tell us the secret that has been locked up in her brain. Moreover, she hasn't been notified of Drukker's death, and with all the rumor and gossip in the neighborhood, word of some kind is sure to leak through to her before long. I fear the result of the shock when she hears the news. In fact, I'd feel better if we got hold of Barstead right away and took him with us. What do you say to my phoning him?"

Markham assented, and Vance briefly explained the situation to the doctor.

We drove up-town immediately, called for Barstead, and proceeded at once to the Drukker house. Our ring was answered by Mrs. Menzel, whose face showed plainly that she knew of Drukker's death. Vance, after one glance at her, led her into the drawing-room away from the stairs, and asked in a low tone:

"Has Mrs. Drukker heard the news?"

"Not yet," she answered, in a frightened, quavering voice. "Miss Dillard came over an hour ago, but I told her the mistress had gone out. I was afraid to let her up-stairs. Something's wrong. . . ." She began to tremble violently.

"What's wrong, Mrs. Menzel?" Vance placed a quieting hand on her arm.

"I don't know. But she hasn't made a sound all morning. She didn't come down for breakfast . . . and I'm afraid to go and call her."

"When did you hear of the accident?"

"Early—right after eight o'clock. The paper boy told me; and I saw all the people down on the Drive."

"Don't be frightened," Vance consoled her. "We have the doctor here, and we'll attend to everything."

He turned back to the hall and led the way upstairs. When we came to Mrs. Drukker's room he knocked softly and, receiving no answer, opened the door. The room was empty. The night-light still burned on the table, and I noticed that the bed had not been slept in.

With a word Vance retraced his steps down the hall. There were only two other main doors, and one of them, we knew, led to Drukker's study. Unhesitatingly Vance stepped to the other and opened it without knocking. The window shades were drawn, but they were white and semi-transparent, and the gray daylight mingled with the ghastly yellow radiation from the old-fashioned chandelier. The lights which Guilfoyle had seen burning all night had not been extinguished.

Vance halted on the threshold, and I saw Markham, who was just in front of me, give a start.

"Mother o' God!" breathed the Sergeant, and crossed himself.

On the foot of the narrow bed lay Mrs. Drukker, fully clothed. Her face was ashen white; her eyes were set in a hideous stare; and her hands were clutching her breast.

Barstead sprang forward and leaned over. After touching her once or twice he straightened up and shook his head slowly.

"She's gone. Been dead probably most of the night." He bent over the body again and began making an examination. "You know, she's suffered for years from chronic nephritis, arteriosclerosis, and hypertrophy of the heart.... Some sudden shock brought on an acute dilatation.... Yes, I'd say she died about the same time as Drukker ... round ten o'clock."

"A natural death?" asked Vance.

"Oh, undoubtedly. A shot of adrenalin in the heart might have saved her if I'd been here at the time...."

"No signs of violence?"

"None. As I told you, she died from dilatation of the heart brought on by shock. A clear case—true to type in every respect."

18

THE WALL IN THE PARK

(*Saturday, April 16; 11 A.M.*)

WHEN THE doctor had straightened Mrs. Drukker's body on the bed and covered it with a sheet, we returned down-stairs. Barstead took his departure at once after promising to send the death certificate to the Sergeant within an hour.

"It's scientifically correct to talk of natural death from shock," said Vance, when we were alone; "but our immediate problem, d' ye see, is to ascertain the cause of that sudden shock. Obviously it's connected with Drukker's death. Now, I wonder...."

Turning impulsively, he entered the drawing-room. Mrs. Menzel was sitting where we had left her, in an attitude of horrified expectancy. Vance went to her and said kindly:

"Your mistress died of heart failure during the night. And it's much better that she should not have outlived her son."

"*Gott geb' ihr die ewige Ruh'!*" the woman murmured piously. "*Ja*, it is best. . . ."

"The end came at about ten last night.—Were you awake at that time, Mrs. Menzel?"

"All night I was awake." She spoke in a low, awed voice.

Vance contemplated her with eyes half shut.

"Tell us what you heard?"

"Somebody came here last night!"

"Yes, some one came at about ten o'clock—by the front door. Did you hear him enter?"

"No; but after I had gone to bed I heard voices in Mr. Drukker's room."

"Was it unusual to hear voices in his room at ten o'clock at night?"

"But it wasn't *him!* He had a high voice, and this one was low and gruff." The woman looked up in bewildered fright. "And the other voice was Mrs. Drukker's . . . and she never went in Mr. Drukker's room at night!"

"How could you hear so plainly with your door shut?"

"My room is right over Mr. Drukker's," she explained. "And I was worried—what with all these awful things going on; so I got up and listened at the top of the steps."

"I can't blame you," said Vance. "What did you hear?"

"At first it was like as though the mistress was moaning, but right away she began to laugh, and then the man spoke angry-like. But pretty soon I heard him laugh, too. After that it sounded like the poor lady was praying—I could hear her saying 'Oh, God—oh, God!' Then the man talked some more—very quiet and low. . . . And in a little while it seemed like the mistress was—reciting—a poem. . . ."

"Would you recognize the poem if you heard it again? . . . Was it

Humpty Dumpty sat on a wall;
Humpty Dumpty had a great fall. . . .?"

"*Bei Gott, das ist's!* It sounded just like that!" A new horror came into the woman's expression. "And Mr. Drukker fell from the wall last night. . . !"

"Did you hear anything else, Mrs. Menzel?" Vance's matter-of-fact voice interrupted her confused correlation of Drukker's death to the verse she had heard.

Slowly she shook her head.

"No. Everything was quiet after that."

"Did you hear any one leave Mr. Drukker's room?"

She gave Vance a panic-stricken nod.

"A few minutes later some one opened and shut the door, very soft; and I heard steps moving down the hall in the dark. Then the stairs creaked, and pretty soon the front door shut."

"What did you do after that?"

"I listened a little while, and then I went back to bed. But I couldn't sleep. . . ."

"It's all over now, Mrs. Menzel," Vance told her comfortingly. "There's nothing for you to fear.—You'd best go to your room and wait till we need you."

Reluctantly the woman went up-stairs.

"I think now," said Vance, "we can make a pretty close guess as to what happened here last night. The murderer took Drukker's key and let himself in by the front door. He knew Mrs. Drukker's quarters were at the rear, and he no doubt counted on accomplishing his business in Drukker's room and departing as he had come. But Mrs. Drukker heard him. It may be she associated him with 'the little man' who had left the black bishop at her door, and feared that her son was in danger. At any rate, she went at once to Drukker's room. The door may have been slightly open, and I think she saw the intruder and recognized him. Startled and apprehensive, she stepped inside and asked him why he was there. He may have answered that he had come to inform her of Drukker's death—which would account for her moans and her hysterical laughter. But that was only a prelimin'ry on his part—a play for time. He was devising some means of meeting the situation— he was planning now how he would kill her! Oh, there can be no doubt of that. He couldn't afford to let her leave that room alive. Maybe he told her so in as many words—he spoke 'angry-like,' you recall. And then he laughed. He was torturing her now—perhaps telling her the whole truth in a burst of insane egoism; and she could say only 'Oh God—oh God!' He explained how he had pushed Drukker over the wall. And did he mention Humpty Dumpty? I think he did; for what more appreciative audience could he have had for his monstrous jest than the victim's own mother? That last revelation proved too much for her hypersensitive brain. She repeated the nursery rhyme in a spell of horror; and then the accumulated shock dilated her heart. She fell across the bed, and the murderer was saved the necessity of sealing her lips with his own hands. He saw what had happened, and went quietly away."

Markham took a turn up and down the room.

"The least comprehensible part of last night's tragedy," he said, "is why this man should have come here after Drukker's death."

Vance was smoking thoughtfully.

"We'd better ask Arnesson to help us explain that point. Maybe he can throw some light on it."

"Yeh, maybe he can," chimed in Heath. Then after rolling his cigar between his lips for a moment, he added sulkily: "There's several people around here, I'm thinking, that could do some high-class explaining."

Markham halted before the Sergeant.

"The first thing we'd better do is to find out what your men know about the movements of the various persons hereabouts last night. Suppose you bring them here and let me question them.—How many were there, by the way?— and what were their posts?"

The Sergeant had risen, alert and energetic.

"There were three, sir, besides Guilfoyle. Emery was set to tail Pardee; Snitkin was stationed at the Drive and 75th Street to watch the Dillard house; and Hennessey was posted on 75th Street up near West End Avenue.— They're all waiting down at the place where Drukker was found. I'll get 'em up here *pronto.*"

He disappeared through the front door, and in less than five minutes returned with the three detectives. I recognized them all, for each had worked on one or more of the cases in which Vance had figured.* Markham questioned Snitkin first as the one most likely to have information bearing directly on the previous night's affair. The following points were brought out by his testimony:

> Pardee had emerged from his house at 6.30 and gone straight to the Dillards'.
>
> At 8.30 Belle Dillard, in an evening gown, had got into a taxi and been driven up West End Avenue. (Arnesson had come out of the house with her and helped her into the taxicab, but had immediately returned indoors.)
>
> At 9.15 Professor Dillard and Drukker had left the Dillard house and walked slowly toward Riverside Drive. They had crossed the Drive at 74th Street, and turned up the bridle path.
>
> At 9.30 Pardee had come out of the Dillard house, walked down to the Drive, and turned up-town.
>
> At a little after 10.00 Professor Dillard had returned to his house alone, recrossing the Drive at 74th Street.
>
> At 10.20 Pardee had returned home, coming from the same direction he had taken when going out.
>
> Belle Dillard had been brought home at 12.30 in a limousine filled with young people.

Hennessey was interrogated next; but his evidence merely substantiated Snitkin's. No one had approached the Dillard house from the direction of West End Avenue; and nothing of a suspicious nature had happened.

Markham then turned his attention to Emery, who reported that, according to Santos whom he had relieved at six, Pardee had spent the early part of the afternoon at the Manhattan Chess Club and had returned home at about four o'clock.

"Then, like Snitkin and Hennessey said," Emery continued, "he went to the Dillards' at half past six, and stayed till half past nine. When he came out I followed, keeping half a block or so behind him. He walked up the Drive to 79th Street, crossed to the upper park, and walked round the big grass bowl, past the rocks, and on up toward the Yacht Club. . . ."

"Did he take the path where Sprigg was shot?" Vance asked.

"He had to. There ain't any other path up that way unless you walk along the Drive."

"How far did he go?"

"The fact is, he stopped right about where Sprigg was bumped off. Then he came back the same way he'd gone and turned into the little park with the playground on the south side of 79th Street. He went slowly down the walk under the trees along the bridle path; and as he passed along the top of the wall under the drinking fountain, who should he run into but the old man and the hunchback, resting up against the ledge and talking. . . ."

---

* Hennessey had kept watch with Doctor Drumm over the Greene mansion from the Narcoss Flats, in the Greene murder case. Snitkin also had taken part in the Greene investigation, and had played a minor rôle in both the Benson and the Canary case. The dapper Emery was the detective who had unearthed the cigarette stubs from beneath the fire-logs in Alvin Benson's living-room.

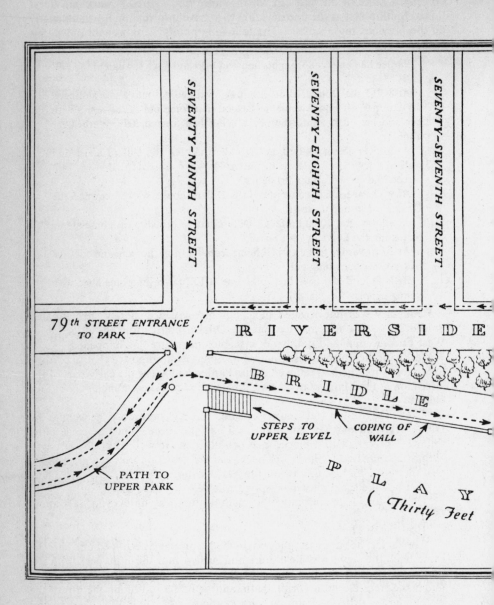

SEVENTY-NINTH STREET

SEVENTY-EIGHTH STREET

SEVENTY-SEVENTH STREET

79th STREET ENTRANCE
TO PARK

RIVERSIDE

BRIDLE

STEPS TO
UPPER LEVEL

COPING OF
WALL

PATH TO
UPPER PARK

P L A Y

(Thirty Feet

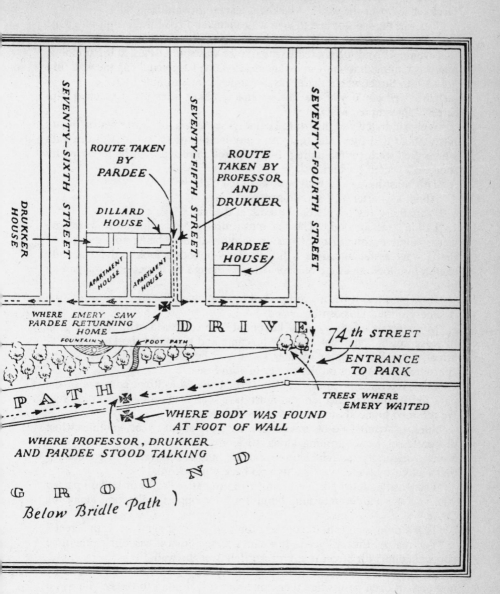

"You say he met Professor Dillard and Drukker at the very spot where Drukker fell over the wall?" Markham leaned forward hopefully.

"Yes, sir. Pardee stopped to visit with them; and I naturally kept on going. As I passed 'em I heard the hunchback say: 'Why ain't you practising chess this evening?' And it sounded to me like he was sore at Pardee for stopping, and was hinting that he wasn't wanted. Anyhow, I ambled along the wall till I got to 74th Street where there was a couple of trees to hide under. . . ."

"How well could you see Pardee and Drukker after you'd reached 74th Street?" interrupted Markham.

"Well, sir, to tell you the truth, I couldn't see 'em at all. It was getting pretty misty about that time, and there isn't any lamp-post at that part of the walk where they were confabulating. But I figured Pardee would be along pretty soon, so I waited for him."

"This must have been well on toward ten o'clock."

"About a quarter of, I should say, sir."

"Were there any people on the walk at that time?"

"I didn't see anybody. The fog musta driven 'em indoors—it wasn't no warm balmy evening. And it was on account of there being nobody around that I went as far ahead as I did. Pardee's nobody's fool, and I'd already caught him looking at me once or twice as though he suspected I was tailing him."

"How long was it before you picked him up again?"

Emery shifted his position.

"My figuring wasn't so good last night," he confessed, with a weak grin. "Pardee musta gone back the way he came and recrossed the Drive at 79th Street; for a half-hour or so later I saw him heading home in front of the apartment-house light on the corner of 75th Street."

"But," interposed Vance, "if you were at the 74th-Street entrance to the park until a quarter past ten you must have seen Professor Dillard pass you. He returned home about ten o'clock by that route."

"Sure, I saw him. I'd been waiting for Pardee about twenty minutes when the professor came strolling along all alone, crossed the Drive, and went home. I naturally thought Pardee and the hunchback were still gabbing,— that's why I took it easy and didn't go back to check up."

"Then, as I understand, about fifteen minutes after Professor Dillard passed you, you saw Pardee returning home from the opposite direction along the Drive."

"That's right, sir. And, of course, I took up my post again on 75th Street."

"You realize, Emery," said Markham gravely, "that it was during the time you waited at 74th Street that Drukker fell over the wall."

"Yes, sir. But you're not blaming me, are you? Watching a man on a foggy night on an open path when there ain't anybody around to screen you, is no easy job. You gotta take a few chances and do a little figuring if you don't want to get spotted."

"I realize your difficulty," Markham told him; "and I'm not criticizing you."

The Sergeant dismissed the three detectives gruffly. He was obviously dissatisfied with their reports.

"The farther we go," he complained, "the more gummed up this case gets."

"*Sursum corda,* Sergeant," Vance exhorted him. "Let not dark despair o'er-come you. When we have Pardee's and the Professor's testimony as to what took place while Emery was waiting beneath the trees at 74th Street, we may be able to fit some very interestin' bits together."

As he spoke Belle Dillard entered the front hall from the rear of the house. She saw us in the drawing-room and came in at once.

"Where's Lady Mae?" she asked in a troubled voice. "I was here an hour ago, and Grete told me she was out. And she's not in her room now."

Vance rose and gave her his chair.

"Mrs. Drukker died last night of heart failure. When you were here earlier Mrs. Menzel was afraid to let you go up-stairs."

The girl sat very quiet for some time. Presently the tears welled to her eyes.

"Perhaps she heard of Adolph's terrible accident."

"Possibly. But it's not quite clear what happened here last night. Doctor Barstead thinks Mrs. Drukker died at about ten o'clock."

"Almost the same time Adolph died," she murmured. "It seems too terri-ble.... Pyne told me of the accident when I came down to breakfast this morning,—every one in the quarter was talking about it,—and I came over at once to be with Lady Mae. But Grete said she had gone out, and I didn't know what to think. There's something very strange about Adolph's death...."

"What do you mean by that, Miss Dillard?" Vance stood by the window watching her covertly.

"I—don't know—what I mean," she answered brokenly. "But only yester-day afternoon Lady Mae spoke to me about Adolph and the—wall...."

"Oh, did she, now?" Vance's tone was more indolent than usual, but every nerve in his body was, I knew, vigilantly alert.

"On my way to the tennis courts," the girl went on, in a low, hushed voice, "I walked with Lady Mae along the bridle path above the playground—she often went there to watch Adolph playing with the children,—and we stood for a long time leaning over the stone balustrade of the wall. A group of chil-dren were gathered around Adolph: he had a toy aeroplane and was showing them how to fly it. And the children seemed to regard him as one of them-selves; they didn't look upon him as a grown-up. Lady Mae was very happy and proud about it. She watched him with shining eyes, and then she said to me: 'They're not afraid of him, Belle, because he's a hunchback. They call him Humpty Dumpty—he's their old friend of the story-book. My poor Humpty Dumpty! It was all my fault for letting him fall when he was little.' ..." The girl's voice faltered, and she put her handkerchief to her eyes.

"So she mentioned to you that the children called Drukker Humpty Dumpty." Vance reached slowly in his pocket for his cigarette-case.

She nodded, and a moment later lifted her head as if forcing herself to face something she dreaded.

"Yes! And that's what was so strange; for after a little while she shuddered and drew back from the wall. I asked her what was the matter, and she said in a terrified voice: 'Suppose, Belle—suppose that Adolph should ever fall off of this wall—the way the real Humpty Dumpty did!' I was almost afraid myself; but I forced a smile, and told her she was foolish. It didn't do any good, though. She shook her head and gave me a look that sent a chill through me. 'I'm not foolish,' she said. 'Wasn't Cock Robin killed with a bow and arrow, and wasn't Johnny Sprig shot with a little gun—*right here in New York?*" "The girl turned a frightened gaze upon us. "And it *did* happen, didn't it—just as she foresaw?"

"Yes, it happened," Vance nodded. "But we mustn't be mystical about it. Mrs. Drukker's imagination was abnormal. All manner of wild conjectures went through her tortured mind; and with these two other Mother-Goose deaths so vivid in her memory, it's not remarkable that she should have turned the children's sobriquet for her son into a tragic speculation of that kind. That he should actually have been killed in the manner she feared is nothing more than a coincidence. . . ."

He paused and drew deeply on his cigarette.

"I say, Miss Dillard," he asked negligently; "did you, by any chance, repeat your conversation with Mrs. Drukker to any one yesterday?"

She regarded him with some surprise before answering.

"I mentioned it at dinner last night. It worried me all the afternoon, and— somehow—I didn't want to keep it to myself."

"Were any comments made about it?"

"Uncle told me I shouldn't spend so much time with Lady Mae—that she was unhealthily morbid. He said the situation was very tragic, but that there was no need for me to share Lady Mae's suffering. Mr. Pardee agreed with uncle. He was very sympathetic, and asked if something could not be done to help Lady Mae's mental condition."

"And Mr. Arnesson?"

"Oh, Sigurd never takes anything seriously,—I hate his attitude sometimes. He laughed as though it was a joke; and all he said was: 'It would be a shame if Adolph took his tumble before he got his new quantum problem worked out.'"

"Is Mr. Arnesson at home now, by the by?" asked Vance. "We want to ask him about the necess'ry arrangements in regard to the Drukkers."

"He went to the university early this morning; but he'll be back before lunch. He'll attend to everything, I am sure. We were about the only friends Lady Mae and Adolph had. I'll take charge in the meantime and see that Grete gets the house in order."

A few minutes later we left her and went to interview Professor Dillard.

19

THE RED NOTE-BOOK

(Saturday, April 16; noon)

THE PROFESSOR was plainly perturbed when we entered the library that noon. He sat in an easy chair with his back to the window, a glass of his precious port on the table beside him.

"I've been expecting you, Markham," he said, before we had time to speak. "There's no need to dissemble. Drukker's death was no accident. I'll admit I felt inclined to discount the insane implications arising from the deaths of

Robin and Sprigg; but the moment Pyne related the circumstances of Drukker's fall I realized that there was a definite design behind these deaths: the probabilities of their being accidental would be incalculable. You know it, as well as I; otherwise you wouldn't be here."

"Very true." Markham had seated himself facing the professor. "We're confronted by a terrific problem. Moreover, Mrs. Drukker died of shock last night at almost the same time her son was killed."

"That, at least," returned the old man after a pause, "may be regarded as a blessing. It's better she didn't survive him—her mind unquestionably would have collapsed." He looked up. "In what way can I help?"

"You were probably the last person, with the exception of the actual murderer, to see Drukker alive; and we would like to know everything you can tell us of what took place last night."

Professor Dillard nodded.

"Drukker came here after dinner—about eight, I should say. Pardee had dined with us; and Drukker was annoyed at finding him here—in fact, he was openly hostile. Arnesson twitted him good-naturedly about his irascibility—which only made him more irritable; and, knowing that Drukker was anxious to thrash out a problem with me, I finally suggested that he and I stroll down to the park. . . ."

"You were not gone very long," suggested Markham.

"No. An unfortunate episode occurred. We walked up the bridle path to almost the exact spot where, I understand, the poor fellow was killed. We had been there for perhaps half an hour, leaning against the stone balustrade of the wall, when Pardee walked up. He stopped to speak to us, but Drukker was so antagonistic in his remarks that, after a few minutes, Pardee turned and walked away in the direction he had come. Drukker was very much upset, and I suggested we postpone the discussion. Furthermore, a damp mist had fallen, and I was beginning to get some twinges in my foot. Drukker straightway became morose, and said he didn't care to go indoors just yet. So I left him alone by the wall, and came home."

"Did you mention the episode to Arnesson?"

"I didn't see Sigurd after I got back. I imagine he'd gone to bed."

Later as we rose to take our leave, Vance asked casually: "Can you tell us where the key to the alley door is kept?"

"I know nothing about it, sir," the professor replied irritably, but added in a more equable tone: "However, as I remember, it used to hang on a nail by the archery-room door."

From Professor Dillard we went straight to Pardee, and were received at once in his study. His manner was rigid and detached, and even after we had seated ourselves he remained standing by the window, staring at us with unfriendly eyes.

"Do you know, Mr. Pardee," asked Markham, "that Mr. Drukker fell from the wall in the park at ten o'clock last night—shortly after you stopped and spoke to him?"

"I heard of the accident this morning." The man's pallor became more noticeable, and he toyed nervously with his watch chain. "It's very unfortunate." His eyes rested vacantly for a while on Markham. "Have you asked Professor Dillard about it? He was with Drukker——"

"Yes, yes; we've just come from him," interrupted Vance. "He said there was a ruffled atmosphere between you and Mr. Drukker last night."

Pardee slowly walked to the desk and sat down stiffly.

"Drukker was displeased for some reason to find me at the Dillards' when he came over after dinner. He hadn't the good taste to hide his displeasure, and created a somewhat embarrassing situation. But, knowing him as I did, I tried to pass the matter off. Soon, however, Professor Dillard took him out for a walk."

"You didn't remain long afterward," observed Vance indolently.

"No—about a quarter of an hour. Arnesson was tired and wanted to turn in, so I went for a walk myself. On my return I took the bridle path instead of the Drive, and came on Professor Dillard and Drukker standing by the wall talking. Not wishing to appear rude, I stopped for a moment. But Drukker was in a beastly mood and made several sneering remarks. I turned and walked back to 79th Street, crossed the Drive, and came home."

"I say; didn't you loiter a bit by the wayside?"

"I sat down near the 79th-Street entrance and smoked a cigarette."

For nearly half an hour Markham and Vance interrogated Pardee, but nothing more could be learned from him. As we came out into the street Arnesson hailed us from the front porch of the Dillard house and stalked forward to meet us.

"Just heard the sad news. Got home from the university a little while ago, and the professor told me you'd gone to rag Pardee. Learn anything?" Without waiting for an answer he ran on: "Frightful mess. I understand the entire Drukker family is wiped out. Well, well. And more story-book mumbo-jumbo to boot.... Any clews?"

"Ariadne has not yet favored us," responded Vance. "Are you an ambassador from Crete?"

"One never knows. Bring out your questionnaire."

Vance had led the way toward the wall gate, and we now stepped down on the range.

"We'll repair to the Drukker house first," he said. "There'll be a number of things to settle. I suppose you'll look after Drukker's affairs and the funeral arrangements."

Arnesson made a grimace.

"Elected! I refuse, however, to attend the funeral. Obscene spectacles, funerals. But Belle and I will see to everything. Lady Mae probably left a will. We'll have to find it. Now, where do women generally hide their wills? ..."

Vance halted by the Dillards' basement door and stepped into the archery-room. After glancing along the door's moulding he rejoined us on the range.

"The alley key isn't there.—By the by, what do you know about it, Mr. Arnesson?"

"You mean the key to yon wooden door in the fence? ... Haven't an idea on the subject. Never use the alley myself—much simpler going out the front door. No one uses it, as far as I know. Belle locked it up years ago: thought some one might sneak in off the Drive and get an arrow in the eye. I told her, let 'em get popped—serve 'em right for being interested in archery."

We entered the Drukker house by the rear door. Belle Dillard and Mrs. Menzel were busy in the kitchen.

"Hallo, sis," Arnesson greeted the girl. His cynical manner had been dropped. "Hard lines for a young 'un like you. You'd better run home now. I'll assume command." And taking her arm in a jocularly paternal fashion, he led her to the door.

She hesitated and looked back at Vance.

"Mr. Arnesson is right," he nodded. "We'll carry on for the present.—But just one question before you go. Did you always keep the key to the alley door hanging in the archery-room?"

"Yes—always. Why? Isn't it there now?"

It was Arnesson who answered, with burlesque irony.

"Gone! Disappeared!—Most tragic. Some eccentric key-collector has evidently been snooping around." When the girl had left us, he cocked an eye at Vance. "What, in the name of all that's unholy, has a rusty key to do with the case?"

"Perhaps nothing," said Vance carelessly. "Let's go to the drawin'-room. It's more comfortable there." He led the way down the hall. "We want you to tell us what you can about last night."

Arnesson took an easy chair by the front window, and drew out his pipe.

"Last night, eh? . . . Well, Pardee came to dinner—it's a sort of habit with him on Fridays. Then Drukker, in the throes of quantum speculation, dropped in to pump the professor; and Pardee's presence galled him. Showed his feelings too, by Gad! No control. The professor broke up the *contretemps* by taking Drukker for an airing. Pardee moped for fifteen minutes or so, while I tried to keep awake. Then he had the goodness to depart. I looked over a few test papers . . . and so to bed." He lighted his pipe. "How does that thrilling recital explain the end of poor Drukker?"

"It doesn't," said Vance. "But it's not without interest.—Did you hear Professor Dillard when he returned home?"

"Hear him?" Arnesson chuckled. "When he hobbles about with his gouty foot, thumping his stick down and shaking the banisters, there's no mistaking his arrival on the scene. Fact is, he was unusually noisy lasy night."

"Offhand, what do you make of these new developments?" asked Vance, after a short pause.

"I'm somewhat foggy as to the details. The professor was not exactly phosphorescent. Sketchy, in fact. Drukker fell from the wall, like Humpty Dumpty, round ten o'clock, and was found this morning—that's all plain. But under what conditions did Lady Mae succumb to shock? Who, or what, shocked her? And how?"

"The murderer took Drukker's key and came here immediately after the crime. Mrs. Drukker caught him in her son's room. There was a scene, according to the cook, who listened from the head of the stairs; and during it Mrs. Drukker died from dilatation of the heart."

"Thereby relieving the gentleman of the bother of killing her."

"That seems clear enough," agreed Vance. "But the reason for the murderer's visit here is not so lucid. Can you suggest an explanation?"

Arnesson puffed thoughtfully on his pipe.

"Incomprehensible," he muttered at length. "Drukker had no valuables, or no compromising documents. Straightforward sort of cuss—not the kind to mix in any dirty business. . . . No possible reason for any one prowling about his room."

Vance lay back and appeared to relax.

"What was this quantum theory Drukker was working on?"

"Ha! Big thing!" Arnesson became animated. "He was on the path of reconciling the Einstein-Bohr theory of radiation with the facts of interference, and of overcoming the inconsistencies inherent in Einstein's hypothesis. His research had already led him to an abandonment of causal space-time coordination of atomic phenomena, and to its replacement by a statistical description.* . . . Would have revolutionized physics—made him famous. Shame he was told off before he'd put his data in shape."

"Do you happen to know where Drukker kept the records of these computations?"

"In a loose-leaf note-book—all tabulated and indexed. Methodical and neat about everything. Even his chirography was like copperplate."

"You know, then, what the note-book looked like?"

"I ought to. He showed it to me often enough. Red limp-leather cover—thin yellow pages—two or three clips on every sheet holding notations—his name gold-stamped in large letters on the binding. . . . Poor devil! *Sic transit.* . . ."

"Where would this note-book be now?"

"One of two places—either in the drawer of his desk in the study or else in the escritoire in his bedroom. In the daytime, of course, he worked in the study; but he fussed day and night when wrapped up in a problem. Kept an escritoire in his bedroom, where he put his current records when he retired, in case he got an inspiration to monkey with 'em during the night. Then, in the morning, back they'd go to the study. Regular machine for system."

Vance had been gazing lazily out of the window as Arnesson rambled on. The impression he gave was that he had scarcely heard the description of Drukker's habits; but presently he turned and fixed Arnesson with a languid look.

"I say," he drawled; "would you mind toddling up-stairs and fetching Drukker's note-book? Look in both the study and the bedroom."

I thought I noticed an almost imperceptible hesitation on Arnesson's part; but straightway he rose.

"Good idea. Too valuable a document to be left lying round." And he strode from the room.

Markham began pacing the floor, and Heath revealed his uneasiness by puffing more energetically on his cigar. There was a tense atmosphere in the little drawing-room as we waited for Arnesson's return. Each of us was in a state of expectancy, though just what we hoped for or feared would have been difficult to define.

In less than ten minutes Arnesson reappeared at the door. He shrugged his shoulders and held out empty hands.

"Gone!" he announced. "Looked in every likely place—couldn't find it." He threw himself into a chair and relighted his pipe. "Can't understand it. . . . Perhaps he hid it."

"Perhaps," murmured Vance.

---

* An important step toward the solution of these complex problems was taken a few years later by the de Broglie-Schrödinger theory as laid down in de Broglie's "Ondes et Mouvements" and Schrödinger's "Abhandlungen zur Wellenmechanik."

20

THE NEMESIS

(*Saturday, April 16; 1 P.M.*)

IT WAS past one o'clock, and Markham, Vance and I rode to the Stuyvesant Club. Heath remained at the Drukker house to carry on the routine work, to draw up his report, and to deal with the reporters who would be swarming there shortly.

Markham was booked for a conference with the Police Commissioner at three o'clock; and after lunch Vance and I walked to Stieglitz's Intimate Gallery and spent an hour at an exhibition of Georgia O'Keefe's floral abstractions. Later we dropped in at Aeolian Hall and sat through Debussy's G-minor quartette. There were some Cézanne water-colors at the Montross Galleries; but by the time we had pushed our way through the late-afternoon traffic of Fifth Avenue the light had begun to fail, and Vance ordered the chauffeur to the Stuyvesant Club, where we joined Markham for tea.

"I feel so youthful, so simple, so innocent," Vance complained lugubriously. "So many things are happenin', and they're bein' manipulated so ingeniously that I can't grasp 'em. It's very disconcertin', very confusin'. I don't like it—I don't at all like it. Most wearin'." He sighed drearily and sipped his tea.

"Your sorrows leave me cold," retorted Markham. "You've probably spent the afternoon inspecting arquebuses and petronels at the Metropolitan Museum. If you'd had to go through what I've suffered————"

"Now, don't be cross," Vance rebuked him. "There's far too much emotion in the world. Passion is not going to solve this case. Cerebration is our only hope. Let us be calm and thoughtful." His mood became serious. "Markham, this comes very near being the perfect crime. Like one of Morphy's great chess combinations, it has been calculated a score of moves ahead. There are no clews; and even if there were, they'd probably point in the wrong direction. And yet . . . and yet there's something that's trying to break through. I feel it: sheer intuition—that is to say, nerves. There's an inarticulate voice that wants to speak, and can't. A dozen times I've sensed the presence of some struggling force, like an invisible ghost trying to make contact without revealing its identity."

Markham gave an exasperated sigh.

"Very helpful. Do you advise calling in a medium?"

"There's something we've overlooked," Vance went on, disregarding the sarcasm. "The case is a cipher, and the key-word is somewhere before us, but we don't recognize it. 'Pon my soul, it's dashed annoyin'. . . . Let's be orderly. Neatness—that's our desideratum. First, Robin is killed. Next, Sprigg is shot. Then Mrs. Drukker is frightened with a black bishop. After that, Drukker is shoved over a wall. Makin' four distinct episodes in the murderer's extravaganza. Three of 'em were carefully planned. One—the leaving of the bishop at Mrs. Drukker's door—was forced on the murderer, and was therefore decided on without preparation. . . ."

467

"Clarify your reasoning on that point."

"Oh, my dear fellow! The conveyor of the black bishop was obviously acting in self-defence. An unexpected danger developed along his line of campaign, and he took this means of averting it. Just before Robin's death Drukker departed from the archery-room and installed himself in the arbor of the yard, where he could look into the archery-room through the rear window. A little later he saw some one in the room talking to Robin. He returned to his house, and at that moment Robin's body was thrown on the range. Mrs. Drukker saw it, and at the same time she probably saw Drukker. She screamed—very natural, what? Drukker heard the scream, and told us of it later in an effort to establish an alibi for himself after we'd informed him that Robin had been killed. Thus the murderer learned that Mrs. Drukker had seen something—how much, he didn't know. But he wasn't taking any chances. He went to her room at midnight to silence her, and took the bishop to leave beside her body as a signature. But he found the door locked, and left the bishop outside, by way of warning her to say nothing on pain of death. He didn't know that the poor woman suspected her own son."

"But why didn't Drukker tell us whom he saw in the archery-room with Robin?"

"We can only assume that the person was some one whom he couldn't conceive of as being guilty. And I'm inclined to believe he mentioned the fact to this person and thus sealed his own doom."

"Assuming the correctness of your theory, where does it lead us?"

"To the one episode that wasn't elaborately prepared in advance. And when there has been no preparation for a covert act there is pretty sure to be a weakness in one or more of the details.—Now, please note that at the time of each of the three murders any one of the various persons in the drama could have been present. No one had an alibi. That, of course, was cleverly calculated: the murderer chose an hour when all of the actors were, so to speak, waiting in the wings. But that midnight visit! Ah! That was a different matter. There was no time to work out a perfect set of circumstances,—the menace was too immediate. And what was the result? Drukker and Professor Dillard were, apparently, the only persons on hand at midnight. Arnesson and Belle Dillard were supping at the Plaza and didn't return home until half past twelve. Pardee was hornlocked with Rubinstein over a chess-board from eleven to one. Drukker is now of course eliminated. . . . What's the answer?"

"I could remind you," returned Markham irritably, "that the alibis of the others have not been thoroughly checked."

"Well, well, so you could." Vance lay back indolently and sent a long regular series of smoke-rings toward the ceiling. Suddenly his body tensed, and with meticulous care he leaned over and put out his cigarette. Then he glanced at his watch and got to his feet. He fixed Markham with a quizzical look.

"*Allons, mon vieux.* It's not yet six. Here's where Arnesson makes himself useful."

"What now?" expostulated Markham.

"Your own suggestion," Vance replied, taking him by the arm and leading him toward the door. "We're going to check Pardee's alibi."

Half an hour later we were seated with the professor and Arnesson in the Dillard library.

"We've come on a somewhat unusual errand," explained Vance; "but it may have a vital bearing on our investigation." He took out his wallet, and unfolded a sheet of paper. "Here's a document, Mr. Arnesson, I wish you'd glance over. It's a copy of the official scoresheet of the chess game between Pardee and Rubinstein. Very interestin'. I've toyed with it a bit, but I'd like your expert analysis of it. The first part of the game is usual enough, but the play after the adjournment rather appeals to me."

Arnesson took the paper and studied it with cynical amusement.

"Aha! The inglorious record of Pardee's Waterloo, eh?"

"What's the meaning of this, Markham?" asked Professor Dillard contemptuously. "Do you hope to run a murderer to earth by dilly-dallying over a chess game?"

"Mr. Vance hoped something could be learned from it."

"Fiddlesticks!" The professor poured himself another glass of port and, opening a book, ignored us completely.

Arnesson was absorbed in the notations of the chess score.

"Something a bit queer here," he muttered. "The time's askew. Let's see. . . . The scoresheet shows that, up to the time of adjournment, White—that is, Pardee—had played one hour and forty-five minutes, and Black, or Rubinstein, one hour and fifty-eight minutes. So far, so good. Thirty moves. Quite in order. But the time at the end of the game, when Pardee resigned, totals two hours and thirty minutes for White, and three hours and thirty-two minutes for Black—which means that, during the second session of the game, White consumed only forty-five minutes whereas Black used up one hour and thirty-four minutes."

Vance nodded.

"Exactly. There were two hours and nineteen minutes of play beginning at 11 P.M., which carried the game to 1.19 A.M. And Rubinstein's moves during that time took forty-nine minutes longer than Pardee's.—Can you make out what happened?"

Arnesson pursed his lips and squinted at the notations.

"It's not clear. I'd need time."

"Suppose," Vance suggested, "we set up the game in the adjourned position and play it through. I'd like your opinion on the tactics."

Arnesson rose jerkily and went to the little chess table in the corner.

"Good idea." He emptied the men from the box. "Let's see now. . . . Oho! A black bishop is missing. When do I get it back, by the way?" He gave Vance a plaintive leer. "Never mind. We don't need it here. One black bishop was swapped." And he proceeded to arrange the men to accord with the position of the game at the time of adjournment. Then he sat down and studied the set-up.

"It doesn't strike me as a particularly unfavorable position for Pardee," ventured Vance.

"Me either. Can't see why he lost the game. Looks drawish to me." After a moment Arnesson referred to the scoresheet. "We'll run through the play and find out where the trouble lay." He made half a dozen moves; then, after several minutes' study, gave a grunt. "Ha! This is rather deep stuff of Rubinstein's. Amazing combination he began working up here. Subtle, by Gad! As I know Rubinstein, it took him a long time to figure it out. Slow, plodding chap."

"It's possible, isn't it," suggested Vance, "that the working out of that combination explains the discrepancy in time between Black and White?"

"Oh, undoubtedly. Rubinstein must have been in good form not to have made the discrepancy greater. Planning the combination took him all of forty-five minutes—or I'm a duffer."

"At what hour, would you say," asked Vance carelessly, "did Rubinstein use up that forty-five minutes?"

"Well, let's see. The play began at eleven: six moves before the combination started. . . . Oh, say, somewhere between half past eleven and half past twelve. . . . Yes, just about. Thirty moves before the adjournment: six moves beginning at eleven—that makes thirty-six: then on the forty-fourth move Rubinstein moved his pawn to Bishop-7-check, and Pardee resigned. . . . Yes—the working out of the combination was between eleven-thirty and twelve-thirty."

Vance regarded the men on the board, which were now in the position they had occupied at the time of Pardee's resignation.*

"Out of curiosity," he said quietly, "I played the game through to the checkmate the other night.—I say, Mr. Arnesson; would you mind doin' the same. I could bear to hear your comment on it."

Arnesson studied the position closely for a few minutes. Then he turned his head slowly and lifted his eyes to Vance. A sardonic grin overspread his face.

"I grasp the point. Gad! What a situation! Five moves for Black to win through. And an almost unheard-of finale in chess. Can't recall a similar instance. The last move would be Bishop to Knight-7, mating. In other words, Pardee was beaten by the black bishop! Incredible!"†

Professor Dillard put down his book.

"What's this?" he exclaimed, joining us at the chess table. "Pardee was defeated by the bishop?" He gave Vance a shrewd, admiring look. "You evidently had good reason, sir, for investigating that chess game. Pray overlook an old man's temper." He stood gazing down at the board with a sad, puzzled expression.

Markham was frowning with deep perplexity.

"You say it's unusual for a bishop alone to mate?" he asked Arnesson.

"Never happens—almost unique situation. And that it should happen to Pardee of all people! Incomprehensible!" He gave a short ironic laugh. "Inclines one to believe in a nemesis. You know, the bishop has been Pardee's *bête noir* for twenty years—it's ruined his life. Poor beggar! The black bishop is the symbol of his sorrow. Fate, by Gad! It's the one chessman that defeated the Pardee gambit. Bishop-to-Knight-5 always broke up his calculations—disqualified his pet theory—made a hissing and a mocking of his life's work. And now, with a chance to break even with the great Rubinstein, the bishop crops up again and drives him back into obscurity."

---

* For the benefit of the expert chess-player who may be academically interested I append the exact position of the game when Pardee resigned:—WHITE: King at QKtsq; Rook at QB8; Pawns at QR2 and Q2. BLACK: King at Q5; Knight at QKt5; Bishop at QR6; Pawns at QKt7 and QB7.

† The final five unplayed moves for Black to mate, as I later obtained them from Vance, were:—*45*. RxP; KtxR. *46*. KxKt; P—Kt8 (Queen). *47*. KxQ; K—Q6. *48*. K—Rsq; K—B7. *49*. P—Q3; B—Kt7 mate.

A few minutes later we took our departure and walked to West End Avenue, where we hailed a taxicab.

"It's no wonder, Vance," commented Markham, as we rode down-town, "that Pardee went white the other afternoon when you mentioned the black bishop's being at large at midnight. He probably thought you were deliberately insulting him—throwing his life's failure in his face."

"Perhaps. . . ." Vance gazed dreamily out into the gathering shadows. "Dashed queer about the bishop being his incubus all these years. Such recurring discouragements affect the strongest minds sometimes; create a desire for revenge on the world, with the cause of one's failure exalted to an Astræn symbol."

"It's difficult to picture Pardee in a vindictive rôle," objected Markham. Then, after a moment: "What was your point about the discrepancy in time between Pardee's and Rubinstein's playing? Suppose Rubinstein did take forty-five minutes or so to work out his combination. The game wasn't.over until after one. I don't see that your visit to Arnesson put us ahead in any way."

"That's because you're unacquainted with the habits of chess players. In a clock game of that kind no player sits at the table all the time his opponent is figuring out moves. He walks about, stretches his muscles, takes the air, ogles the ladies, imbibes ice-water, and even indulges in food. At the Manhattan Square Masters Tournament last year there were four tables, and it was a common sight to see as many as three empty chairs at one time. Pardee's a nervous type. He wouldn't sit through Rubinstein's protracted mental speculations."

Vance lighted a cigarette slowly.

"Markham, Arnesson's analysis of that game reveals the fact that Pardee had three-quarters of an hour to himself around midnight."

21

MATHEMATICS AND MURDER

(*Saturday, April 16; 8:30 P.M.*)

LITTLE WAS said about the case during dinner, but when we had settled ourselves in a secluded corner of the club lounge-room Markham again broached the subject.

"I can't see," he said, "that finding a loophole in Pardee's alibi helps us very much. It merely complicates an already intolerable situation."

"Yes," sighed Vance. "A sad and depressin' world. Each step appears to tangle us a little more. And the amazin' part of it is, the truth is staring us in the face; only, we can't see it."

"There's no evidence pointing to any one. There's not even a suspect against whose possible culpability reason doesn't revolt."

"I wouldn't say that, don't y' know. It's a mathematician's crime; and the landscape has been fairly cluttered with mathematicians."

Throughout the entire investigation no one had been indicated by name as the possible murderer. Yet each of us realized in his own heart that one of the persons with whom we had talked was guilty; and so hideous was this knowledge that we instinctively shrank from admitting it. From the first we had cloaked our true thoughts and fears with generalities.

"A mathematician's crime?" repeated Markham. "The case strikes me as a series of senseless acts committed by a maniac running amuck."

Vance shook his head.

"Our criminal is supersane, Markham. And his acts are not senseless: they're hideously logical and precise. True, they have been conceived with a grim and terrible humor, with a tremendously cynical attitude; but within themselves they are exact and rational."

Markham regarded Vance thoughtfully.

"How can you reconcile these Mother-Goose crimes with the mathematical mind?" he asked. "In what way can they be regarded as logical? To me they're nightmares, unrelated to sanity."

Vance settled himself deeper in his chair, and smoked for several minutes. Then he began an analysis of the case, which not only clarified the seeming madness of the crimes themselves, but brought all the events and the characters into a uniform focus. The accuracy of this analysis was brought home to us with tragic and overwhelming force before many days had passed.*

"In order to understand these crimes," he began, "we must consider the stock-in-trade of the mathematician, for all his speculations and computations tend to emphasize the relative insignificance of this planet and the unimportance of human life.—Regard, first, the mere scope of the mathematician's field. On the one hand he attempts to measure infinite space in terms of parsecs and light-years, and, on the other, to measure the electron which is so infinitely small that he has to invent the Rutherford unit—a millionth of a millimicron. His vision is one of transcendental perspectives, in which this earth and its people sink almost to the vanishing point. Some of the stars— such as Arcturus, Canopus and Betelgeuse—which he regards merely as minute and insignificant units, are many times more massive than our entire solar system. Shapleigh's estimate of the diameter of the Milky Way is 300,000 light-years; yet we must place 10,000 Milky Ways together to get the diameter of the universe—which gives us a cubical content a thousand milliard times greater than the scope of astronomical observation. Or, to put it relatively in terms of mass:—the sun's weight is 324,000 times greater than the weight of the earth; and the weight of the universe is postulated as that of a trillion†—a milliard times a milliard—suns. . . . Is it any wonder that workers in such stupendous magnitudes should sometimes lose all sense of earthly proportions?"

Vance made an insignificant gesture.

* I am obviously unable to set down Vance's exact words, despite the completeness of my notes; but I sent him a proof of the following passages with a request that he revise and edit them; so that, as they now stand, they represent an accurate paraphrase of his analysis of the psychological factors of the Bishop murders.

† Vance was here using the English connotation of "trillion," which is the third power of a million, as opposed to the American and French system of numeration which regards a trillion as a mere million millions.

"But these are element'ry figures—the every-day facts of journeyman cal-culators. The higher mathematician goes vastly further. He deals in abstruse and apparently contradict'ry speculations which the average mind can not even grasp. He lives in a realm where time, as we know it, is without meaning save as a fiction of the brain, and becomes a fourth co-ordinate of three-di-mensional space; where distance also is meaningless except for neighboring points, since there are an infinite number of shortest routes between any two given points; where the language of cause and effect becomes merely a conve-nient shorthand for explanat'ry purposes; where straight lines are non-existent and insusceptible of definition; where mass grows infinitely great when it reaches the velocity of light; where space itself is characterized by curvatures; where there are lower and higher orders of infinites; where the law of gravita-tion is abolished as an acting force and replaced by a characteristic of space— a conception that says, in effect, that the apple does not fall because it is at-tracted by the earth, but because it follows a geodesic, or world-line. . . .

"In this realm of the modern mathematician, curves exist without tangents. Neither Newton nor Leibnitz nor Bernoulli even dreamed of a continuous curve without a tangent—that is, a continuous function without a differential co-efficient. Indeed, no one is able to picture such a contradiction,—it lies be-yond the power of imagination. And yet it is a commonplace of modern math-ematics to work with curves that have no tangents.—Moreover, *pi*—that old friend of our school-days, which we regarded as immutable—is no longer a constant; and the ratio between diameter and circumference now varies ac-cording to whether one is measuring a circle at rest or a rotating circle. . . . Do I bore you?"

"Unquestionably," retorted Markham. "But pray continue, provided your observations have an earthly direction."

Vance sighed and shook his head hopelessly, but at once became serious again.

"The concepts of modern mathematics project the individual out of the world of reality into a pure fiction of thought, and lead to what Einstein calls the most degenerate form of imagination—pathological individualism. Sil-berstein, for instance, argues the possibility of five- and six-dimensional space, and speculates on one's ability to see an event before it happens. The conclu-sions contingent on the conception of Flammarion's Lumen—a fictive person who travels faster than the velocity of light and is therefore able to experience time extending in a reverse direction—are in themselves enough to distort any natural and sane point of view.* But there is another conceptual Homunculus

---

* Lumen was invented by the French astronomer to prove the possibility of the reversal of time. With a speed of 250,000 miles per second, he was conceived as soaring into space at the end of the battle of Waterloo, and catching up all the light-rays that had left the battlefield. He attained a gradually increasing lead, until at the end of two days he was witnessing, not the end, but the beginning of the battle; and in the meantime he had been viewing events in reverse order. He had seen projectiles leaving the objects they had pen-etrated and returning to the cannon; dead men coming to life and arranging themselves in battle formation. Another hypothetical adventure of Lumen was jumping to the moon, turning about instantaneously, and seeing himself leaping from the moon to the earth backwards.

even weirder than Lumen from the standpoint of rational thinking. This hypothetical creature can traverse all worlds at once with infinite velocity, so that he is able to behold all human history at a glance. From Alpha Centauri he can see the earth as it was four years ago; from the Milky Way he can see it as it was 4,000 years ago; and he can also choose a point in space where he can witness the ice-age and the present day simultaneously! . . ."

Vance settled himself more deeply in his chair.

"Toying with the simple idea of infinity is enough to unhinge the average man's mind. But what of the well-known proposition of modern physics that we cannot take a straight and ever-advancing path into space without returning to our point of departure? This proposition holds, in brief, that we may go straight to Sirius and a million times further without changing direction, but we can never leave the universe: we at last return to our starting-point *from the opposite direction!* Would you say, Markham, that this idea is conducive to what we quaintly call normal thinking? But however paradoxical and incomprehensible it may seem, it is almost rudiment'ry when compared with other theorems advanced by mathematical physics. Consider, for example, what is called the problem of the twins. One of two twins starts to Arcturus at birth— that is, with accelerated motion in a gravitational field—and, on returning, discovers that he is much younger than his brother. If, on the other hand, we assume that the motion of the twins is Galilean and that they are therefore travelling with uniform motion relative to each other, then each twin will find that his brother is younger than himself! . . .

"These are not paradoxes of logic, Markham: they're only paradoxes of feeling. Mathematics accounts for them logically and scientifically.* The point I'm trying to make is that things which seem inconsistent and even absurd to the lay mind, are commonplaces to the mathematical intelligence. A mathematico-physicist like Einstein announces that the diameter of space—of *space,* mind you—is 100,000,000 light-years, or 700 trillion miles; and considers the calculation abecedarian. When we ask what is beyond this diameter, the answer is: 'There is no beyond: these limitations include everything.' To wit, infinity is finite! Or, as the scientist would say, space is unbounded but finite.—Let your mind meditate on this idea for half an hour, Markham, and you'll have a sensation that you're going mad."

He paused to light a cigarette.

"Space and matter—that's the mathematician's speculative territ'ry. Eddington conceives matter as a characteristic of space—a bump in nothingness; whereas Weil conceives space as a characteristic of matter,—to him empty space is meaningless. Thus Kant's noumenon and phenomenon become interchangeable; and even philosophy loses all significance. But when we come to the mathematical conceptions of finite space all rational laws are abrogated. De Sitter's conception of the shape of space is globular, or spherical. Einstein's space is cylindrical; and matter approaches zero at the periphery, or 'border condition.' Weyl's space, based on Mach's mechanics, is saddle-shaped. . . . Now, what becomes of nature, of the world we live in, of human existence,

---

* Vance requested me to mention here A. d'Abro's recent scholarly work, "The Evolution of Scientific Thought," in which there is an excellent discussion of the paradoxes associated with space-time.

when we weigh them against such conceptions? Eddington suggests the conclusion that there are no natural laws—namely, that nature is not amenable to the law of sufficient reason. Alas, poor Schopenhauer!* And Bertrand Russell sums up the inevitable results of modern physics by suggesting that matter is to be interpreted merely as a group of occurrences, and that matter itself need not be existent! . . . Do you see what it all leads to? If the world is non-causative and non-existent, what is a mere human life?—or the life of a nation?—or, for that matter, existence itself? . . ."

Vance looked up, and Markham nodded dubiously.

"So far I follow you, or course," he said. "But your point seems vague—not to say esoteric."

"Is it surprising," asked Vance, "that a man dealing in such colossal, incommensurable concepts, wherein the individuals of human society are infinitesimal, might in time lose all sense of relative values on earth, and come to have an enormous contempt for human life? The comparatively insignificant affairs of this world would then become mere petty intrusions on the macrocosmos of his mental consciousness. Inevitably such a man's attitude would become cynical. In his heart he would scoff at all human values, and sneer at the littleness of the visual things about him. Perhaps there would be a sadistic element in his attitude; for cynicism is a form of sadism. . . ."

"But deliberate, planned murder!" objected Markham.

"Consider the psychological aspects of the case. With the normal person, who takes his recreations daily, a balance is maintained between the conscious and the unconscious activities: the emotions, being constantly dispersed, are not allowed to accumulate. But with the abnormal person, who spends his entire time in intense mental concentration and who rigorously suppresses all his emotions, the loosening of the subconscious is apt to result in a violent manifestation. This long inhibition and protracted mental application, without recreation or outlet of any kind, causes an explosion which often assumes the form of deeds of unspeakable horror. No human being, however intellectual, can escape the results. The mathematician who repudiates nature's laws is nevertheless amenable to those laws. Indeed, his rapt absorption in hyperphysical problems merely increases the pressure of his denied emotions. And outraged nature, in order to maintain her balance, produces the most grotesque fulminations—reactions which, in their terrible humor and perverted gaiety, are the exact reverse of the grim seriousness of abstruse mathematical theories. The fact that Sir William Crookes and Sir Oliver Lodge—both great mathematical physicists—became confirmed spiritists, constitutes a similar psychological phenomenon."

Vance took several deep inhalations on his cigarette.

"Markham, there's no escaping the fact: these fantastic and seemingly incredible murders were planned by a mathematician as forced outlets to a life of tense abstract speculation and emotional repression. They fulfil all the indicated requirements: they are neat and precise, beautifully worked out, with every minute factor fitting snugly in place. No loose ends, no remainders, apparently no motive. And aside from their highly imaginative precision, all

* Vance's M. A. thesis, I recall, dealt with Schopenhauer's "Ueber die vierfache Wurzel des Satzes vom zureichenden Grunde."

their indications point unmistakably to an abstrusely conceptive intelligence on the loose—a devotee of pure science having his fling."

"But why their grisly humor?" asked Markham. "How do you reconcile the Mother-Goose phase of them with your theory?"

"The existence of inhibited impulses," explained Vance, "always produces a state favorable to humor. Dugas designates humor as a *'détente'*—a release from tension; and Bain, following Spencer, calls humor a relief from restraint. The most fertile field for a manifestation of humor lies in accumulated potential energy—what Freud calls *Besetzungsenergie*—which in time demands a free discharge. In these Mother-Goose crimes we have the mathematician reacting to the most fantastic of frivolous acts in order to balance his superserious logical speculations. It's as if he were saying cynically: 'Behold! This is the world that you take so seriously because you know nothing of the infinitely larger abstract world. Life on earth is a child's game—hardly important enough to make a joke about.' ... And such an attitude would be wholly consistent with psychology; for after any great prolonged mental strain one's reactions will take the form of reversals—that is to say, the most serious and dignified will seek an outlet in the most childish games. Here, incidentally, you have the explanation for the practical joker with his sadistic instincts. . . .

"Moreover, all sadists have an infantile complex. And the child is totally amoral. A man, therefore, who experiences these infantile psychological reversals is beyond good and evil. Many modern mathematicians even hold that all convention, duty, morality, good, and the like, could not exist except for the fiction of free will. To them the science of ethics is a field haunted by conceptual ghosts; and they even arrive at the disintegrating doubt as to whether truth itself is not merely a figment of the imagination. . . . Add to these considerations the sense of earthly distortion and the contempt for human life which might easily result from the speculations of higher mathematics, and you have a perfect set of conditions for the type of crimes with which we are dealing."

When Vance had finished speaking Markham sat silent for a long time. Finally he moved restively.

"I can understand," he said, "how these crimes might fit almost any of the persons involved. But, on the basis of your argument, how do you account for the notes to the press?"

"Humor must be imparted," returned Vance. " 'A jest's prosperity lies in the ear of him who hears it.' Also, the impulse toward exhibitionism enters into the present case."

"But the 'Bishop' alias?"

"Ah! That's a most vital point. The *raison d'être* of this terrible orgy of humor lies in that cryptic signature."

Markham turned slowly.

"Does the chess player and the astronomer fulfil the conditions of your theory as well as the mathematical physicist?"

"Yes," Vance replied. "Since the days of Philidor, Staunton and Kieseritzki, when chess was something of a fine art, the game has degenerated almost into an exact science; and during Capablanca's régime it has become largely a matter of abstract mathematical speculation. Indeed, Maroczy, Doctor Lasker and Vidmar are all well-known mathematicians. . . . And the astronomer, who actually views the universe, may get an even more intense impression of the unimportance of this earth than the speculative physicist. Imagination runs riot through a telescope. The mere theory of existing life on distant planets tends to reduce earthly life to second'ry consideration. For hours after one has looked at Mars, for instance, and dallied with the notion that its inhabitants outnumber and surpass in intelligence our own population, one has difficulty in readjusting oneself to the petty affairs of life here on earth. Even a reading of Percival Lowell's romantic book* temporarily takes away from the imaginative person all consciousness of the significance of any single planet'ry existence."

There was a long silence. Then Markham asked:

"Why should Pardee have taken Arnesson's black bishop that night instead of one from the club where it would not have been missed?"

"We don't know enough of the motive to say. He may have taken it with some deliberate purpose in view.—But what evidence have you of his guilt? All the suspicions in the world would not permit you to take any step against him. Even if we knew indubitably who the murderer was, we'd be helpless. . . . I tell you, Markham, we're facing a shrewd brain—one that figures out every move, and calculates all the possibilities. Our only hope is to create our own evidence by finding a weakness in the murderer's combination."

"The first thing in the morning," declared Markham grimly, "I'm going to put Heath to work on Pardee's alibi that night. There'll be twenty men checking it up by noon, questioning every spectator at that chess game, and making a door-to-door canvass between the Manhattan Chess Club and the Drukker house. If we can find some one who actually saw Pardee in the vicinity of the Drukkers' around midnight, then we'll have a very suspicious piece of circumstantial evidence against him."

"Yes," agreed Vance; "that would give us a definite starting-point. Pardee would have considerable difficulty in explaining why he was six blocks away from the club during his set-to with Rubinstein at the exact hour that a black bishop was being left at Mrs. Drukker's door. . . . Yes, yes. By all means have Heath and his minions tackle the problem. It may lead us forward."

But the Sergeant was never called upon to check the alibi. Before nine o'clock on the following morning Markham called at Vance's house to inform him that Pardee had committed suicide.

* I do not know whether Vance was here referring to "Mars and Its Canals" or "Mars as the Abode of Life."

22

THE HOUSE OF CARDS

(*Sunday, April 17; 9 A.M.*)

THE ASTOUNDING news of Pardee's death had a curiously disturbing effect on Vance. He stared at Markham unbelievingly. Then he rang hastily for Currie and ordered his clothes and a cup of coffee. There was an eager impatience in his movements as he dressed.

"My word, Markham!" he exclaimed. "This is most extr'ordin'ry.... How did you hear of it?"

"Professor Dillard phoned me at my apartment less than half an hour ago. Pardee killed himself in the archery-room of the Dillard home some time last night. Pyne discovered the body this morning and informed the professor. I relayed the news to Sergeant Heath, and then came here. In the circumstances I thought we ought to be on hand." Markham paused to light his cigar. "It looks as if the Bishop case was over.... Not an entirely satisfactory ending, but perhaps the best for every one concerned."

Vance made no immediate comment. He sipped his coffee abstractedly, and at length got up and took his hat and stick.

"Suicide...," he murmured, as we went down the stairs. "Yes, that would be wholly consistent. But, as you say, unsatisfact'ry—dashed unsatis-fact'ry...."

We rode to the Dillard house, and were admitted by Pyne. Professor Dillard had no more than joined us in the drawing-room when the door-bell rang, and Heath, pugnacious and dynamic, bustled in.

"This'll clean things up, sir," he exulted to Markham, after the usual ritual-istic handshake. "Those quiet birds ... you never can tell. Yet, who'd've thought...?"

"Oh, I say, Sergeant," Vance drawled; "let's not think. Much too wearin'. An open mind—arid like a desert—is indicated."

Professor Dillard led the way to the archery-room. The shades at all the windows were drawn, and the electric lights were still burning. I noticed, too, that the windows were closed.

"I left everything exactly as it was," explained the professor.

Markham walked to the large wicker centre-table. Pardee's body was slumped in a chair facing the range door. His head and shoulders had fallen forward over the table; and his right arm hung at his side, the fingers still clutching an automatic pistol. There was an ugly wound in his right temple; and on the table beneath his head was a pool of coagulated blood.

Our eyes rested but a moment on the body, for a startling and incongruous thing diverted our attention. The magazines on the table had been pushed aside, leaving an open space in front of the body; and in this cleared area rose a tall and beautifully constructed house of playing cards. Four arrows marked the boundaries of the yard, and matches had been laid side by side to repre-sent the garden walks. It was a reproduction that would have delighted a

478

child's heart; and I recalled what Vance had said the night before about serious minds seeking recreation in children's games. There was something unutterably horrible in the juxtaposition of this juvenile card structure and violent death.

Vance stood looking down at the scene with sad, troubled eyes.

"*Hic jacet* John Pardee," he murmured, with a sort of reverence. "And this is the house that Jack built . . . a house of cards. . . ."

He stepped forward as if to inspect it more closely; but as his body struck the edge of the table there was a slight jar, and the flimsy edifice of cards toppled over.

Markham drew himself up and turned to Heath.

"Have you notified the Medical Examiner?"

"Sure." The Sergeant seemed to find it difficult to take his eyes from the table. "And Burke's coming along, in case we need him." He went to the windows and threw up the shades, letting in the bright daylight. Then he returned to Pardee's body and stood regarding it appraisingly. Suddenly he knelt down and leaned over.

"That looks to me like the .38 that was in the tool-chest," he remarked.

"Undoubtedly," nodded Vance, taking out his cigarette-case.

Heath rose and, going to the chest, inspected the contents of its drawer. "I guess that's it, all right. We'll get Miss Dillard to identify it after the doc has been here."

At this moment Arnesson, clothed in a brilliant red-and-yellow dressing-gown, burst excitedly into the room.

"By all the witches!" he exclaimed. "Pyne just told me the news." He came to the table and stared at Pardee's body. "Suicide, eh? . . . But why didn't he choose his own home for the performance? Damned inconsiderate of him to muss up some one else's house this way. Just like a chess player." He lifted his eyes to Markham. "Hope this won't involve us in more unpleasantness. We've had enough notoriety. Distracts the mind. When'll you be able to take the beggar's remains away? Don't want Belle to see him."

"The body will be removed as soon as the Medical Examiner has seen it," Markham told him in a tone of frosty rebuke. "And there will be no necessity to bring Miss Dillard here."

"Good." Arnesson still stood staring at the dead man. Slowly a look of cynical wistfulness came over his face. "Poor devil! Life was too much for him. Hypersensitive—no psychic stamina. Took things too seriously. Brooded over his fate ever since his gambit went up in smoke. Couldn't find any other diversion. The black bishop haunted him; probably tipped his mind from its axis. By Gad! Wouldn't be surprised if the idea drove him to self-destruction. Might have imagined he was a chess bishop—trying to get back at the world in the guise of his nemesis."

"Clever idea," returned Vance. "By the by, there was a house of cards on the table when we first saw the body."

"Ha! I wondered what the cards were doing there. Thought he might have sought solace in solitaire during his last moments. . . . A card house, eh? Sounds foolish. Do you know the answer?"

"Not all of it. 'The house that Jack built' might explain something."

"I see." Arnesson looked owlish. "Playing children's games to the end—

even on himself. Queer notion." He yawned cavernously. "Guess I'll get some clothes on." And he went up-stairs.

Professor Dillard had stood watching Arnesson with a look at once distressed and paternal. Now he turned to Markham with a gesture of annoyance.

"Sigurd's always protecting himself against his emotions. He's ashamed of his feelings. Don't take his careless attitude too seriously."

Before Markham could make a reply Pyne ushered Detective Burke into the room; and Vance took the opportunity of questioning the butler about his discovery of Pardee.

"How did it happen you entered the archery-room this morning?" he asked.

"It was a bit close in the pantry, sir," the man returned, "and I opened the door at the foot of the stairs to get a little more air. Then I noticed that the shades were down———"

"It's not custom'ry to draw the shades at night, then?"

"No, sir—not in this room."

"How about the windows?"

"I always leave them slightly open from the top at night."

"Were they left open last night?"

"Yes, sir."

"Very good.—And after you opened the door this morning?"

"I started to put out the lights, thinking Miss Dillard had forgotten to turn the switch last night; but just then I saw the poor gentleman there at the table, and went straight up and informed Professor Dillard."

"Does Beedle know about the tragedy?"

"I told her of it right after you gentlemen arrived."

"What time did you and Beedle retire last night?"

"At ten o'clock, sir."

When Pyne had left us Markham addressed Professor Dillard.

"It might be well for you to give us what details you can while we're waiting for Doctor Doremus.—Shall we go up-stairs?"

Burke remained in the archery-room, and the rest of us went to the library.

"I'm afraid there's little I can tell you," the professor began, settling himself and taking out his pipe. There was a noticeable reserve in his manner—a kind of detached reluctance. "Pardee came here last night after dinner, ostensibly to chat with Arnesson, but actually, I imagine, to see Belle. Belle, however, excused herself early and went to bed—the child had a bad headache—and Pardee remained until about half past eleven. Then he went out; and that was the last I saw of him until Pyne brought me the terrible news this morning. . . ."

"But if," put in Vance, "Mr. Pardee came to see your niece, how do you account for his staying so late after she had retired?"

"I don't account for it." The old man exhibited perplexity. "He gave the impression, though, that there was something on his mind and that he desired a sense of human contact. The fact is, I had to hint rather broadly about being tired before he finally got up to go."

"Where was Mr. Arnesson during the evening?"

"Sigurd remained here talking with us for an hour or so after Belle had retired, and then went to bed. He'd been busy with Drukker's affairs all afternoon, and was played out."

"What time would that have been?"

"About half past ten."

"And you say," continued Vance, "that Mr. Pardee impressed you as being under a mental strain?"

"Not a strain exactly." The professor drew on his pipe, frowning. "He appeared depressed, almost melancholy."

"Did it strike you that he was in fear of something?"

"No; not in the least. He was more like a man who had suffered a great sorrow and couldn't shake the effects of it."

"When he went out did you go with him into the hall—that is, did you note which direction he took?"

"No. We always treated Pardee very informally here. He said good-night and left the room. I took it for granted he went to the front door and let himself out."

"Did you go to your own room at once?"

"In about ten minutes. I stayed up only long enough to arrange some papers I'd been working on."

Vance lapsed into silence—he was obviously puzzled over some phase of the episode; and Markham took up the interrogation.

"I suppose," he said, "that it is useless to ask if you heard any sound last night that might have been a shot."

"Everything in the house was quiet," Professor Dillard replied. "And anyway no sound of a shot would carry from the archery-room to this floor. There are two flights of stairs, the entire length of the lower hall and a passageway, and three heavy doors between. Moreover, the walls of this old house are very thick and solid."

"And no one," supplemented Vance, "could have heard the shot from the street, for the archery-room windows were carefully closed."

The professor nodded and gave him a searching look.

"That is true. I see you, too, noticed that peculiar circumstance. I don't quite understand why Pardee should have shut the windows."

"The idiosyncrasies of suicides have never been satisfactorily explained," returned Vance casually. Then, after a short pause, he asked: "What were you and Mr. Pardee talking about during the hour preceding his departure?"

"We talked very little. I was more or less engaged with a new paper of Millikan's in the *Physics Review* on alkali doublets, and I tried to interest him in it; but his mind, as I've said, was noticeably preoccupied, and he amused himself at the chess-board for the best part of the hour."

"Ah! Did he, now? That's most interestin'."

Vance glanced at the board. A number of pieces were still standing on the squares; and he rose quickly and crossed the room to the little table. After a moment he came back and reseated himself.

"Most curious," he murmured, and very deliberately lighted a cigarette. "He was evidently pondering over the end of his game with Rubinstein just before he went down-stairs last night. The pieces are set up exactly as they were at the time he resigned the contest—with the inevitable black-bishop-mate only five moves off."

Professor Dillard's gaze moved to the chess table wonderingly.

"The black bishop," he repeated in a low tone. "Could that have been what was preying on his mind last night? It seems unbelievable that so trivial a thing could affect him so disastrously."

"Don't forget, sir," Vance reminded him, "that the black bishop was the symbol of his failure. It represented the wreckage of his hopes. Less potent factors have driven men to take their own lives."

A few minutes later Burke informed us that the Medical Examiner had arrived. Taking leave of the professor we descended again to the archery-room, where Doctor Doremus was busy with his examination of Pardee's body.

He looked up as we entered and waved one hand perfunctorily. His usual jovial manner was gone.

"When's this business going to stop?" he grumbled. "I don't like the atmosphere round here. Murders—death from shock—suicides. Enough to give any one the creeps. I'm going to get a nice uneventful job in a slaughter house."

"We believe," said Markham, "that this is the end."

Doremus blinked. "So! That's it, is it?—the Bishop suicides after running the town ragged. Sounds reasonable. Hope you're right." He again bent over the body, and, unflexing the fingers, tossed the revolver to the table.

"For your armory, Sergeant."

Heath dropped the weapon in his pocket.

"How long's he been dead, doc?"

"Oh, since midnight, or thereabouts. Maybe earlier, maybe later.—Any other fool questions?"

Heath grinned. "Is there any doubt about it being suicide?"

Doremus glared passionately at the Sergeant.

"What does it look like? A black-hand bombing?" Then he became professional. "The weapon was in his hand. Powder marks on the temple. Hole the right size for the gun, and in the right place. Position of the body natural. Can't see anything suspicious.—Why? Got any doubts?"

It was Markham who answered.

"To the contrary, doctor. Everything from our angle of the case points to suicide."

"It's suicide all right, then. I'll check up a little further, though.—Here, Sergeant, give me a hand."

When Heath had helped to lift Pardee's body to the divan for a more detailed examination, we went to the drawing-room where we were joined shortly by Arnesson.

"What's the verdict?" he asked, dropping into the nearest chair. "I suppose there's no question that the chap committed the act himself."

"Why should you raise the point, Mr. Arnesson?" Vance parried.

"No reason. An idle comment. Lots of queer things going on hereabouts."

"Oh, obviously." Vance blew a wreath of smoke upward. "No; the Medical Examiner seems to think there's no doubt in the matter. Did Pardee, by the by, impress you as bent on self-destruction last night?"

Arnesson considered. "Hard to say," he concluded. "He was never a gay soul. But suicide? ... I don't know. However, you say there's no question about it; so there you are."

"Quite, quite. And how does this new situation fit into your formula?"

"Dissipates the whole equation, of course. No more need for speculation." Despite his words, he appeared uncertain. "What I can't understand," he added, "is why he should choose the archery-room. Lot of space in his own house for a *felo-de-se.*"

"There was a convenient gun in the archery-room," suggested Vance. "And that reminds me: Sergeant Heath would like to have Miss Dillard identify the weapon, as a matter of form."

"That's easy. Where is it?"

Heath handed it to him, and he started from the room.

"Also"—Vance halted him—"you might ask Miss Dillard is she kept playing cards in the archery-room."

Arnesson returned in a few minutes and informed us that the gun was the one which had been in the tool-chest drawer, and that not only were playing cards kept in the table drawer of the archery-room but that Pardee knew of their presence there.

Doctor Doremus appeared soon afterwards and iterated his conclusion that Pardee had shot himself.

"That'll be my report," he said. "Can't see any way out of it. To be sure, lots of suicides are fakes—but that's *your* province. Nothing in the least suspicious here."

Markham nodded with undisguised satisfaction.

"We've no reason to question your findings, doctor. In fact, suicide fits perfectly with what we already know. It brings this whole Bishop orgy to a logical conclusion." He got up like a man from whose shoulders a great burden had been lifted. "Sergeant, I'll leave you to arrange for the removal of the body for the autopsy; but you'd better drop in at the Stuyvesant Club later. Thank Heaven today is Sunday! It gives us time to turn round."

That night at the club Vance and Markham and I sat alone in the lounge-room. Heath had come and gone, and a careful statement had been drawn up for the press announcing Pardee's suicide and intimating that the Bishop case was thereby closed. Vance had said little all day. He had refused to offer any suggestion as to the wording of the official statement, and had appeared reluctant even to discuss the new phase of the case. But now he gave voice to the doubts that had evidently been occupying his mind.

"It's too easy, Markham—much too easy. There's an aroma of speciousness about it. It's perfectly logical, d' ye see, but it's not satisfyin'. I can't exactly picture our Bishop terminating his debauch of humor in any such banal fashion. There's nothing witty in blowin' one's brain out—it's rather commonplace, don't y' know. Shows a woeful lack of originality. It's not worthy of the artificer of the Mother-Goose murders."

Markham was disgruntled.

"You yourself explained how the crimes accorded with the psychological possibilities of Pardee's mentality; and to me it appears highly reasonable that, having perpetrated his gruesome jokes and come to the end of his rope, he should have done away with himself."

"You're probably right," sighed Vance. "I haven't any coruscatin' arguments to combat you with. Only, I'm disappointed. I don't like anticlimaxes, especially when they don't jibe with my idea of the dramatist's talent. Pardee's death at this moment is too deuced neat—it clears things up too tidily. There's too much utility in it, and too little imagination."

Markham felt that he could afford to be tolerant.

"Perhaps his imagination was exhausted on the murders. His suicide might be regarded merely as a lowering of the curtain when the play was over. In any event, it was by no means an incredible act. Defeat and disappointment and discouragement—a thwarting of all one's ambitions—have constituted cause for suicide since time immemorial."

"Exactly. We have a reasonable motive, or explanation, for his suicide, but no motive for the murders."

"Pardee was in love with Belle Dillard," argued Markham; "and he probably knew that Robin was a suitor for her hand. Also, he was intensely jealous of Drukker."

"And Sprigg's murder?"

"We have no data on that point."

Vance shook his head.

"We can't separate the crimes as to motive. They all sprang from one underlying impulse: they were actuated by a single urgent passion."

Markham sighed impatiently.

"Even if Pardee's suicide is unrelated to the murders, we're at a dead end, figuratively and literally."

"Yes, yes. A dead end. Very distressin'. Consolin' for the police, though. It lets them out—for a while, anyway. But don't misinterpret my vagaries. Pardee's death is unquestionably related to the murders. Rather intimate relationship, too, I'd say."

Markham took his cigar slowly from his mouth and scrutinized Vance for several moments.

"Is there any doubt in your mind," he asked, "that Pardee committed suicide?"

Vance hesitated before answering.

"I could bear to know," he drawled, "why that house of cards collapsed so readily when I deliberately leaned against the table————"

"Yes?"

"—and why it didn't topple over when Pardee's head and shoulders fell forward on the table after he'd shot himself."

"Nothing to that," said Markham. "The first jar may have loosened the cards————" Suddenly his eyes narrowed. "Are you implying that the card-house was built *after* Pardee was dead?"

"Oh, my dear fellow! I'm not indulgin' in implications. I'm merely givin' tongue to my youthful curiosity, don't y' know."

23

A STARTLING DISCOVERY

(*Monday, April 25; 8:30 P.M.*)

EIGHT DAYS went by. The Drukker funeral was held in the little house on 76th Street, attended only by the Dillards and Arnesson and a few men from the university who came to pay a last tribute of respect to a scientist for whose work they had a very genuine admiration.

Vance and I were at the house on the morning of the funeral when a little girl brought a small cluster of spring flowers she had picked herself, and asked Arnesson to give them to Drukker. I almost expected a cynical response from him, and was surprised when he took the flowers gravely and said in a tone almost tender:

"I'll give them to him at once, Madeleine. And Humpty Dumpty thanks you for remembering him." When the child had been led away by her governess, he turned to us. "She was Drukker's favorite.... Funny fellow. Never went to the theatre. Detested travel. His only recreation was entertaining youngsters."

I mention this episode because, in spite of its seeming unimportance, it was to prove one of the most vital links in the chain of evidence that eventually cleared up, beyond all question of doubt, the problem of the Bishop murders.

The death of Pardee had created a situation almost unique in the annals of modern crime. The statement given out by the District Attorney's office had only intimated that there was a possibility of Pardee's being guilty of the murders. Whatever Markham may have personally believed, he was far too honorable and just to cast any direct doubt on another's character without overwhelming proofs. But the wave of terror arising from these strange murders had reached such proportions that he could not, in view of the duty he owed to the community, refrain from saying that he believed the case to be closed. Thus, while no open accusation of guilt was made against Pardee, the Bishop murders were no longer regarded as a source of menace to the city, and a sigh of relief went up from all quarters.

In the Manhattan Chess Club there was probably less discussion of the case than anywhere else in New York. The members felt perhaps that the club's honor was in some way involved. Or there may have been a sense of loyalty toward a man who had done as much for chess as Pardee. But whatever the cause of the club's avoidance of the subject, the fact remained that its members attended, almost to a man, Pardee's funeral. I could not help admiring this tribute to a fellow chess player; for, whatever his personal acts, he had been one of the great sustaining patrons of the royal and ancient game to which they were devoted.*

Markham's first official act on the day after Pardee's death was to secure

---

* Pardee left in his will a large sum for the furtherance of chess; and in the autumn of that same year, it will be remembered, the Pardee Memorial Tournament was held at Cambridge Springs.

485

Sperling's release. The same afternoon the Police Department moved all its records of the Bishop murders to the file marked "shelved cases," and withdrew the guards from the Dillard house. Vance protested mildly against this latter step; but, in view of the fact that the Medical Examiner's *post-mortem* report had substantiated in every particular the theory of suicide, there was little that Markham could do in the matter. Furthermore, he was thoroughly convinced that the death of Pardee had terminated the case; and he scoffed at Vance's wavering doubts.

During the week following the finding of Pardee's body Vance was restive and more distrait than usual. He attempted to interest himself in various matters, but without any marked success. He showed signs of irritability; and his almost miraculous equanimity seemed to have deserted him. I got the impression that he was waiting for something to happen. His manner was not exactly expectant, but there was a watchfulness in his attitude amounting at times almost to apprehension.

On the day following the Drukker funeral Vance called on Arnesson, and on Friday night accompanied him to a performance of Ibsen's "Ghosts"—a play which, I happened to know, he disliked. He learned that Belle Dillard had gone away for a month's visit to the home of a relative in Albany. As Arnesson explained, she had begun to show the effects of all she had been through, and needed a change of scene. The man was plainly unhappy over her absence, and confided to Vance that they had planned to be married in June. Vance also learned from him that Mrs. Drukker's will had left everything to Belle Dillard and the professor in the event of her son's death—a fact which appeared to interest Vance unduly.

Had I known, or even suspected, what astounding and terrible things were hanging over us that week, I doubt if I could have stood the strain. For the Bishop murder case was not ended. The climactic horror was still to come; but even that horror, terrific and staggering as it proved, was only a shadow of what it might have been had not Vance reasoned the case out to two separate conclusions, only one of which had been disposed of by Pardee's death. It was this other possibility, as I learned later, that had kept him in New York, vigilant and mentally alert.

Monday, April 25, was the beginning of the end. We were to dine with Markham at the Bankers Club and go afterwards to a performance of "Die Meistersinger"*; but we did not witness the triumphs of *Walther* that night. I noticed that when we met Markham in the rotunda of the Equitable Building he seemed troubled; and we were no more than seated in the club grill when he told us of a phone call he had received from Professor Dillard that afternoon.

"He asked me particularly to come to see him tonight," Markham explained; "and when I tried to get out of it he became urgent. He made a point of the fact that Arnesson would be away the entire evening, and said that a similar opportunity might not present itself until it was too late. I asked him

---

* Of the Wagnerian operas this was Vance's favorite. He always asserted that it was the only opera that had the structural form of a symphony; and more than once he expressed the regret that it had not been written as an orchestral piece instead of as a conveyance for an absurd drama.

what he meant by that; but he refused to explain, and insisted that I come to his house after dinner. I told him I'd let him know if I could make it."

Vance had listened with the intensest interest.

"We must go there, Markham. I've been rather expecting a call of this kind. It's possible we may at last find the key to the truth."

"The truth about what?"

"Pardee's guilt."

Markham said no more, and we ate our dinner in silence.

At half past eight we rang the bell of the Dillard house, and were taken by Pyne direct to the library.

The old professor greeted us with nervous reserve.

"It's good of you to come, Markham," he said, without rising. "Take a chair and light a cigar. I want to talk to you—and I want to take my time about it. It's very difficult. . . ." His voice trailed off as he began filling his pipe.

We settled ourselves and waited. A sense of expectancy invaded me for no apparent reason, except perhaps that I caught some of the radiations of the professor's obviously distraught mood.

"I don't know just how to broach the subject," he began; "for it has to do, not with physical facts, but with the invisible human consciousness. I've struggled all week with certain vague ideas that have been forcing themselves upon me; and I see no way to rid myself of them but by talking with you. . . ."

He looked up hesitantly.

"I preferred to discuss these ideas with you when Sigurd was not present, and as he has gone to-night to see Ibsen's 'Pretenders'—his favorite play, by the way—I took the opportunity to ask you here."

"What do these ideas concern?" asked Markham.

"Nothing specifically. As I have said, they're very vague; but they have nevertheless grown fairly insistent. . . . So insistent, in fact," he added, "that I thought it best to send Belle away for a while. It's true that she was in a tortured state of mind as a result of all these tragedies; but my real reason for shipping her north was that I was beset by intangible doubts."

"Doubts?" Markham leaned forward. "What sort of doubts?"

Professor Dillard did not reply at once.

"Let me answer that question by asking another," he countered presently. "Are you wholly satisfied in your mind that the situation in regard to Pardee is exactly as it appears?"

"You mean the authenticity of his suicide?"

"That and his presumptive culpability."

Markham settled back contemplatively.

"Are *you* not wholly satisfied?" he asked.

"I can't answer that question." Professor Dillard spoke almost curtly. "You have no right to ask me. I merely wanted to be sure that the authorities, having all the data in their hands, were convinced that this terrible affair was a closed book." A look of deep concern came over his face. "If I knew that to be a fact, it would help me to repulse the vague misgivings that have haunted me day and night for the past week."

"And if I were to say that I am not satisfied?"

The old professor's eyes took on a distant, distressed look. His head fell slightly forward, as if some burden of sorrow had suddenly weighed him down. After several moments he lifted his shoulders and drew a deep breath.

"The most difficult thing in this world," he said, "is to know where one's duty lies; for duty is a mechanism of the mind, and the heart is forever stepping in and playing havoc with one's resolutions. Perhaps I did wrong to ask you here; for, after all, I have only misty suspicions and nebulous ideas to go on. But there was the possibility that my mental uneasiness was based on some deep hidden foundation of whose existence I was unaware.... Do you see what I mean?" Evasive as were his words, there was no doubt as to the disturbing mien of the shadowy image that lurked at the back of his mind.

Markham nodded sympathetically.

"There is no reason whatever to question the findings of the Medical Examiner." He made the statement in a forced matter-of-fact voice. "I can understand how the proximity of these tragedies might have created an atmosphere conducive to doubts. But I think you need have no further misgivings."

"I sincerely hope you're right," the professor murmured; but it was clear he was not satisfied. "Suppose, Markham———" he began, and then stopped. "Yes, I hope you're right," he repeated.

Vance had sat through this unsatisfactory discussion smoking placidly; but he had been listening with unwonted concentration, and now he spoke.

"Tell me, Professor Dillard, if there has been anything—no matter how indefinite—that may have given birth to your uncertainty."

"No—nothing." The answer came quickly and with a show of spirit. "I have merely been wondering—testing every possibility. I dared not be too sanguine without some assurance. Pure logic is all very well for principles that do not touch us personally. But where one's own safety is concerned the imperfect human mind demands visual evidence."

"Ah, yes." Vance looked up, and I thought I detected a flash of understanding between these two disparate men.

Markham rose to make his adieu; but Professor Dillard urged him to remain a while.

"Sigurd will be here before long. He'd enjoy seeing you again. As I said, he's at 'The Pretenders,' but I'm sure he will come straight home.... By the way, Mr. Vance," he went on, turning from Markham; "Sigurd tells me you accompanied him to 'Ghosts' last week. Do you share his enthusiasm for Ibsen?"

A slight lift of Vance's eyebrows told me that he was somewhat puzzled by this question; but when he answered there was no hint of perplexity in his voice.

"I have read Ibsen a great deal; and there can be little doubt that he was a creative genius of a high order, although I've failed to find in him either the aesthetic form or the philosophic depth that characterizes Goethe's 'Faust,' for instance."

"I can see that you and Sigurd would have a permanent basis of disagreement."

Markham declined the invitation to stay longer, and a few minutes later we were walking down West End Avenue in the brisk April air.

"You will please take note, Markham old dear," observed Vance, with a touch of waggishness, as we turned into 72nd Street and headed for the park, "that there are others than your modest collaborator who are hag-ridden with doubts as to the volition of Pardee's taking-off. And I might add that the professor is not in the least satisfied with your assurances."

"His suspicious state of mind is quite understandable," submitted Markham. "These murders have touched his house pretty closely."

"That's not the explanation. The old gentleman has fears. And he knows something which he will not tell us."

"I can't say that I got that impression."

"Oh, Markham—my dear Markham! Weren't you listening closely to his halting, reluctant tale? It was as if he were trying to convey some suggestion to us without actually putting it into words. We were supposed to guess. Yes! That was why he insisted that you visit him when Arnesson was safely away at an Ibsen revival———"

Vance ceased speaking abruptly and stood stock-still. A startled look came in his eyes.

"Oh, my aunt! Oh, my precious aunt! So that was why he asked me about Ibsen! . . . My word! How unutterably dull I've been!" He stared at Markham, and the muscles of his jaw tightened. "The truth at last!" he said with impressive softness. "And it is neither you nor the police nor I who has solved this case: it is a Norwegian dramatist who has been dead for twenty years. In Ibsen is the key to the mystery."

Markham regarded him as though he had suddenly gone out of his mind; but before he could speak Vance hailed a taxicab.

"I'll show you what I mean when we reach home," he said, as we rode east through Central Park. "It's unbelievable, but it's true. And I should have guessed it long ago; but the connotation of the signature on those notes was too clouded with other possible meanings. . . ."

"If it were midsummer instead of spring," commented Markham wrathfully, "I'd suggest that the heat had affected you."

"I knew from the first there were three possible guilty persons," continued Vance. "Each was psychologically capable of the murders, provided the impact of his emotions had upset his mental equilibrium. So there was nothing to do but to wait for some indication that would focus suspicion. Drukker was one of my three suspects, but he was murdered; and that left two. Then Pardee to all appearances committed suicide, and I'll admit that his death made reasonable the assumption that he had been the guilty one. But there was an eroding doubt in my mind. His death was not conclusive; and that house of cards troubled me. We were stalemated. So again I waited, and watched my third possibility. Now I know that Pardee was innocent, and that he did not shoot himself. He was murdered—just as were Robin and Sprigg and Drukker. His death was another grim joke—he was a victim thrown to the police in the spirit of diabolical jest. And the murderer has been chuckling at our gullibility ever since."

"By what reasoning do you arrive at so fantastic a conclusion?"

"It's no longer a question of reasoning. At last I have the explanation for the crimes; and I know the meaning of the 'Bishop' signature to the notes. I'll show you a piece of amazing and incontrovertible evidence very soon."

A few minutes later we reached his apartment, and he led us straight to the library.

"The evidence has been here within arm's reach all the time."

He went to the shelves where he kept his dramas, and took down Volume II of the collected works of Henrik Ibsen.* The book contained "The Vikings at Helgeland" and "The Pretenders"; but with the first of these plays Vance was not concerned. Turning to "The Pretenders" he found the page where the *dramatis personæ* were given, and laid the book on the table before Markham.

"Read the cast of characters of Arnesson's favorite play," he directed.

Markham, silent and puzzled, drew the volume toward him; and I looked over his shoulder. This is what we saw:

HÅKON HÅKONSSON, *the King elected by the Birchlegs.*
INGA OF VARTEIG, *his mother.*
EARL SKULE.
LADY RAGNHILD, *his wife.*
SIGRID, *his sister.*
MARGRETE, *his daughter.*
GUTHORM INGESSON.
SIGURD RIBBUNG.
NICHOLAS ARNESSON, *Bishop of Oslo.*
DAGFINN THE PEASANT, *Hakon's marshal.*
IVAR BODDE, *his chaplain.*
VEGARD VÆADAL, *one of his guard.*
GREGORIUS JONSSON, *a nobleman.*
PAUL FLIDA, *a nobleman.*
INGEBORG, *Andres Skialdarband's wife.*
PETER, *her son, a young priest.*
SIRA VILIAM, *Bishop Nicholas's chaplain.*
MASTER SIGARD OF BRABANT, *a physician.*
JATGEIR SKALD, *an Icelander.*
BÅRD BRATTE, *a chieftain from the Trondhiem district.*

But I doubt if either of us read beyond the line:

NICHOLAS ARNESSON, *Bishop of Oslo.*

My eyes became riveted on that name with a set and horrified fascination. And then I remembered. . . . *Bishop Arnesson* was one of the most diabolical villains in all literature—a cynical, sneering monster who twisted all the sane values of life into hideous buffooneries.

---

* Vance's set was the William Archer copyright edition, published by Charles Scribner's Sons.

24

THE LAST ACT

(Tuesday, April 26; 9 A.M.)

WITH THIS astounding revelation the Bishop murder case entered its final and most terrible phase. Heath had been informed of Vance's discovery; and it was arranged that we should meet in the District Attorney's office early the following day for a counsel of war.

Markham, when he took leave of us that night, was more troubled and despondent than I had ever seen him.

"I don't know what can be done," he said hopelessly. "There's no legal evidence against the man. But we may be able to devise some course of action that will give us the upper hand. . . . I never believed in torture, but I almost wish we had access today to the thumbscrew and the rack."

Vance and I arrived at his office a few minutes after nine the next morning. Swacker intercepted us and asked us to wait in the reception room for a little while. Markham, he explained, was engaged for the moment. We had no more than seated ourselves when Heath appeared, grim, pugnacious and sullen.

"I gotta hand it to you, Mr. Vance," he proclaimed. "You sure got a line on the situation. But what good it's going to do us I don't see. We can't arrest a guy because his name's in a book."

"We may be able to force the issue some way," Vance rejoined. "In any event, we now know where we stand."

Ten minutes later Swacker beckoned to us and indicated that Markham was free.

"Sorry to have kept you waiting," Markham apologized. "I had an unexpected visitor." His voice had a despairing ring. "More trouble. And, curiously enough, it's connected with the very section of Riverside Park where Drukker was killed. However, there's nothing I can do about it. . . ." He drew some papers before him. "Now to business."

"What's the new trouble in Riverside Park?" asked Vance casually.

Markham frowned.

"Nothing that need bother us now. A kidnapping, in all likelihood. There's a brief account of it in the morning papers, in case you're interested. . . ."

"I detest reading the papers." Vance spoke blandly, but with an insistence that puzzled me. "What happened?"

Markham drew a deep breath of impatience.

"A child disappeared from the playground yesterday after talking with an unknown man. Her father came here to solicit my help. But it's a job for the Bureau of Missing Persons; and I told him so.—Now, if your curiosity is appeased———"

"Oh, but it isn't," persisted Vance. "I simply must hear the details. That section of the park fascinates me strangely."

Markham shot him a questioning glance through lowered lids.

"Very well," he asquiesced. "A five-year-old girl, named Madeleine Moffat, was playing with a group of children at about half past five last evening. She

491

crawled up on a high mound near the retaining wall, and a little later, when her governess went to get her, thinking she had descended the other side, the child was nowhere to be found. The only suggestive fact is that two of the other children say they saw a man talking to her shortly before she disappeared; but, of course, they can give no description of him. The police were notified, and are investigating. And that's all there is to the case so far."

" 'Madeleine.' " Vance repeated the name musingly. "I say, Markham; do you know if this child knew Drukker?"

"Yes!" Markham sat up a little straighter. "Her father mentioned that she often went to parties at his house. . . ."

"I've seen the child." Vance rose and stood, hands in pockets, gazing down at the floor. "An adorable little creature . . . golden curls. She brought a handful of flowers for Drukker the morning of his funeral. . . . And now she has disappeared after having been seen talking with a strange man. . . ."

"What's going on in your mind?" demanded Markham sharply.

Vance appeared not to have heard the question.

"Why should her father appeal to you?"

"I've known Moffat slightly for years—he was at one time connected with the city administration. He's frantic—grasping at every straw. The proximity of the affair to the Bishop murders has made him morbidly apprehensive. . . . But see here, Vance; we didn't come here to discuss the Moffat child's disappearance. . . ."

Vance lifted his head: there was a look of startled horror on his face.

"Don't speak—oh, don't speak. . . ." He began pacing up and down, while Markham and Heath watched him in mute amazement. "Yes—yes; that would be it," he murmured to himself. "The time is right . . . it all fits. . . ."

He swung about, and going to Markham seized his arm.

"Come—quickly! It's our only chance—we can't wait another minute." He fairly dragged Markham to his feet and led him toward the door. "I've been fearing something like this all week————"

Markham wrenched his arm free from the other's grip.

"I won't move from this office, Vance, until you explain."

"It's another act in the play—the last act! Oh, take my word for it." There was a look in Vance's eyes I had never seen before. "It's 'Little Miss Muffet' now. The name isn't identical, but that doesn't matter. It's near enough for the Bishop's jest; he'll explain it all to the press. He probably beckoned the child to the tuffet, and sat down beside her. And now she's gone—frightened away. . . ."

Markham moved forward in a sort of daze; and Heath, his eyes bulging, leapt to the door. I have often wondered what went on in their minds during those few seconds of Vance's importunate urgings. Did they believe in his interpretation of the episode? Or were they merely afraid not to investigate, in view of the remote possibility that another hideous joke had been perpetrated by the Bishop? Whatever their convictions or doubts, they accepted the situation as Vance saw it; and a moment later we were in the hall, hastening toward the elevator. At Vance's suggestion we picked up Detective Tracy from the branch office of the Detective Bureau in the Criminal Courts Building.

"This affair is serious," he explained. "Anything may happen."

We emerged through the Franklin-Street entrance, and in a few minutes were on our way up-town in the District Attorney's car, breaking speed regulations and ignoring traffic signals. Scarcely a word was spoken on that momentous ride; but as we swung through the tortuous roads of Central Park Vance said:

"I may be wrong, but we will have to risk it. If we wait to see whether the papers get a note, it'll be too late. We're not supposed to know yet; and that's our one chance. . . ."

"What do you expect to find?" Markham's tone was husky and a little uncertain.

Vance shook his head despondently.

"Oh, I don't know. But it'll be something devilish."

When the car drew up with a lurch in front of the Dillard house Vance leapt out and ran up the steps ahead of us. Pyne answered his insistent ring.

"Where's Mr. Arnesson?" he demanded.

"At the university, sir," the old butler replied; and I imagined there was fright in his eyes. "But he'll be home for an early lunch."

"Then take us at once to Professor Dillard."

"I'm sorry, sir," Pyne told him; "but the professor is also out. He went to the Public Library———"

"Are you alone here?"

"Yes, sir. Beedle's gone to market."

"So much the better." Vance took hold of the butler and turned him toward the rear stairs. "We're going to search the house, Pyne. You lead the way."

Markham came forward.

"But, Vance, we can't do that!"

Vance wheeled round.

"I'm not interested in what you can do or can't do. I'm going to search this house. . . . Sergeant, are you with me?" There was a strange look on his face.

"You bet your sweet life!" (I never liked Heath as much as at that moment.)

The search was begun in the basement. Every hallway, every closet, every cupboard and waste space was inspected. Pyne, completely cowed by Heath's vindictiveness, acted as guide. He brought keys and opened doors for us, and even suggested places we might otherwise have overlooked. The Sergeant had thrown himself into the hunt with energy, though I am sure he had only a vague idea as to its object. Markham followed us disapprovingly; but he, too, had been caught in the sweep of Vance's dynamic purposefulness; and he must have realized that Vance had some tremendous justification for his rash conduct.

Gradually we worked our way upward through the house. The library and Arnesson's room were gone over carefully. Belle Dillard's apartment was scrutinized, and close attention was given to the unused rooms on the third floor. Even the servants' quarters on the fourth floor were overhauled. But nothing suspicious was discovered. Though Vance suppressed his eagerness I could tell what a nervous strain he was under by the tireless haste with which he pushed the search.

Eventually we came to a locked door at the rear of the upper hall.

"Where does that lead?" Vance asked Pyne.

"To a little attic room, sir. But it's never used———"

"Unlock it."

The man fumbled for several moments with his bunch of keys.

"I don't seem to find the key, sir. It's supposed to be here. . . ."

"When did you have it last?"

"I couldn't say, sir. To my knowledge no one's been in the attic for years."

Vance stepped back and crouched.

"Stand aside, Pyne."

When the butler had moved out of the way Vance hurled himself against the door with terrific force. There was a creaking and straining of wood; but the lock held.

Markham rushed forward and caught him round the shoulders.

"Are you mad!" he exclaimed. "You're breaking the law."

"The law!" There was scathing irony in Vance's retort. "We're dealing with a monster who sneers at all law. You may coddle him if you care to, but I'm going to search that attic if it means spending the rest of my life in jail.—Sergeant, open that door!"

Again I experienced a thrill of liking for Heath. Without a moment's hesitation he poised himself on his toes and sent his shoulders crashing against the door's panel just above the knob. There was a splintering of wood as the lock's bolt tore through the moulding. The door swung inward.

Vance, freeing himself from Markham's hold, ran stumbling up the steps with the rest of us at his heels. There was no light in the attic, and we paused for a moment at the head of the stairs to accustom our eyes to the darkness. Then Vance struck a match and, groping forward, sent up the window shade with a clatter. The sunlight poured in, revealing a small room, scarcely ten feet square, cluttered with all manner of discarded odds and ends. The atmosphere was heavy and stifling, and a thick coating of dust lay over everything.

Vance looked quickly about him, and an expression of disappointment came over his face.

"This is the only place left," he remarked, with the calmness of desperation.

After a more careful scrutiny of the room, he stepped to the corner by the little window and peered down at a battered suit-case which lay on its side against the wall. I noticed that it was unlatched and that its straps hung free. Leaning over he threw the cover back.

"Ah! Here, at least, is something for you, Markham."

We crowded about him. In the suit-case was an old Corona typewriter. A sheet of paper was in the carriage; and on it had already been typed, in pale-blue élite characters, the two lines:

> Little Miss Muffet
> Sat on a tuffet

At this point the typist had evidently been interrupted, or for some other reason had not completed the Mother-Goose rhyme.

"The new Bishop note for the press," observed Vance. Then reaching into the suit-case he lifted out a pile of blank paper and envelopes. At the bottom, beside the machine, lay a red-leather note-book with thin yellow leaves. He handed it to Markham with the terse announcement:

"Drukker's calculations on the quantum theory."

But there was still a look of defeat in his eyes; and again he began inspecting the room. Presently he went to an old dressing-table which stood against the wall opposite to the window. As he bent over to peer behind it he suddenly drew back and, lifting his head, sniffed several times. At the same moment he caught sight of something on the floor at his feet, and kicked it toward the centre of the room. We looked down at it with astonishment. It was a gas-mask of the kind used by chemists.

"Stand back, you chaps!" he ordered; and holding one hand to his nose and mouth he swung the dressing-table away from the wall. Directly behind it was a small cupboard door about three feet high, set into the wall. He wrenched it open and looked inside, then slammed it shut immediately.

Brief as was my view of the interior of the cupboard, I was able to glimpse its contents clearly. It was fitted with two shelves. On the lower one were several books lying open. On the upper shelf stood an Erlenmeyer flask clamped to an iron support, a spirit-lamp, a condenser tube, a glass beaker, and two small bottles.

Vance turned and gave us a despairing look.

"We may as well go: there's nothing more here."

We returned to the drawing-room, leaving Tracy to guard the door to the attic.

"Perhaps, after all, you were justified in your search," acknowledged Markham, studying Vance gravely. "I don't like such methods, however. If we hadn't found the typewriter————"

"Oh, that!" Vance, preoccupied and restless, went to the window overlooking the archery range. "I wasn't hunting for the typewriter—or the note-book, either. What do they matter?" His chin fell forward on his breast, and his eyes closed in a kind of lethargy of defeat. "Everything's gone wrong—my logic has failed. We're too late."

"I don't pretend to know what you're grumbling about," said Markham. "But at least you've supplied me evidence of a sort. I'll now be able to arrest Arnesson when he returns from the university."

"Yes, yes; of course. But I wasn't thinking of Arnesson, or the arrest of the culprit, or the triumph of the District Attorney's office. I was hoping————"

He broke off and stiffened.

"We're *not* too late! I didn't think far enough. . . ." He went swiftly to the archway. "It's the Drukker house we must search. . . . Hurry!" He was already half-running down the hall, Heath behind him, and Markham and I bringing up the rear.

We followed him down the rear stairs, across the archery-room, and out on the range. We did not know, and I doubt if any of us even guessed, what was in his mind; but some of his inner excitement had been communicated to us, and we realized that only a vital urgency could have shaken him so completely out of his usual attitude of disinterest and calm.

When we came to the screen-porch of the Drukker house he reached through the broken wire-netting and released the catch. The kitchen door, to my astonishment, was unlocked; but Vance seemed to expect this, for he un-hesitatingly turned the knob and threw it open.

"Wait!" he directed, pausing in the little rear hallway. "There's no need to search the entire house. The most likely place. . . . Yes! Come along . . . up-stairs . . . somewhere in the centre of the house . . . a closet most likely . . .

where no one could hear. . . ." As he spoke he led the way up the rear stairs, past Mrs. Drukker's room and the study, and thence to the third floor. There were but two doors on this upper hall—one at the extreme end, and a smaller door set midway in the right wall.

Vance went straight to the latter. There was a key protruding from the lock, and, turning it, he drew open the door. Only a shadowy blackness met our eyes. Vance was on his knees in a second, groping inside.

"Quick, Sergeant. Your flash-light."

Almost before he had uttered the words a luminous circle fell on the floor of the closet. What I saw sent a chill of horror over me. A choked exclamation burst from Markham; and a soft whistle told me that Heath too was appalled by the sight. Before us on the floor, in a limp, silent heap, lay the little girl who had brought flowers to her broken Humpty Dumpty on the morning of his funeral. Her golden hair was dishevelled; her face was deathly pale, and there were streaks down her cheeks where the futile tears had welled forth and dried.

Vance bent over and put his ear to her heart. Then he gathered her tenderly in his arms.

"Poor little Miss Muffet," he whispered, and rising went toward the front stairs. Heath preceded him, flashing his light all the way so there would be no chance of his stumbling. In the main lower hall he paused.

"Unbolt the door, Sergeant."

Heath obeyed with alacrity, and Vance stepped out on the sidewalk.

"Go to the Dillards' and wait for me there," he flung back over his shoulder. And with the child clasped closely to his breast he started diagonally across 76th Street to a house on which I could make out a doctor's brass name-plate.

25

THE CURTAIN FALLS

(*Tuesday, April 26; 11 A.M.*)

TWENTY MINUTES later Vance rejoined us in the Dillard drawing-room.

"She's going to be all right," he announced, sinking into a chair and lighting a cigarette. "She was only unconscious, had fainted from shock and fright; and she was half-suffocated." His face darkened. "There were bruises on her little wrist. She probably struggled in that empty house when she failed to find Humpty Dumpty; and then the beast forced her into the closet and locked the door. No time to kill her, d' ye see. Furthermore, killing wasn't in the book. 'Little Miss Muffet' wasn't killed—merely frightened away. She'd have died, though, from lack of air. And *he* was safe: no one could hear her crying. . . ."

Markham's eyes rested on Vance affectionately.

"I'm sorry I tried to hold you back," he said simply. (For all his conventionally legal instincts, there was a fundamental bigness to his nature.) "You were right in forcing the issue, Vance.... And you, too, Sergeant. We owe a great deal to your determination and faith."

Heath was embarrassed.

"Oh, that's all right, sir. You see, Mr. Vance had me all worked up about the kid. And I like kids, sir."

Markham turned an inquisitive look on Vance.

"You expected to find the child alive?"

"Yes; but drugged or stunned perhaps. I didn't think of her as dead, for that would have contravened the Bishop's joke."

Heath had been pondering some troublous point.

"What I can't get through my head," he said, "is why this Bishop, who's been so damn careful about everything else, should leave the door of the Drukker house unlocked."

"We were expected to find the child," Vance told him. "Everything was made easy for us. Very considerate of the Bishop, what? But we weren't supposed to find her till to-morrow—after the papers had received the Little-Miss-Muffet notes. They were to have been our clew. But we anticipated the gentleman."

"But why weren't the notes sent yesterday?"

"It was no doubt the Bishop's original intention to post his poetry last night; but I imagine he decided it was best for his purpose to let the child's disappearance attract public attention first. Otherwise the relationship between Madeleine Moffat and little Miss Muffet might have been obscured."

"Yeh!" snarled Heath through his teeth. "And by to-morrow the kid woulda been dead. No chance then of her identifying him."

Markham looked at his watch and rose with determination.

"There's no point in waiting for Arnesson's return. The sooner we arrest him the better." He was about to give Heath an order when Vance intervened.

"Don't force the issue, Markham. You haven't any real evidence against the man. It's too delicate a situation for aggression. We must go carefully or we'll fail."

"I realize that the finding of the typewriter and the note-book is not conclusive," concurred Markham. "But the identification by the child——"

"Oh, my dear fellow! What weight would a jury attach to a frightened five-year-old girl's identification without powerful contribut'ry evidence? A clever lawyer could nullify it in five minutes. And even assuming you could make the identification hold, what would it boot you? It wouldn't connect Arnesson in any way with the Bishop murders. You could only prosecute him for attempted kidnapping,—the child's unharmed, remember. And if you should, through a legal miracle, get a doubtful conviction, Arnesson would receive at most a few years in the bastille. That wouldn't end this horror.... No, no. You mustn't be precipitate."

Reluctantly Markham resumed his seat. He saw the force of Vance's argument.

"But we can't let this thing go on," he declared ferociously. "We must stop this maniac some way."

"Some way—yes." Vance began pacing the room restlessly. "We may be able to wangle the truth out of him by subterfuge: he doesn't know yet that we've found the child.... It's possible Professor Dillard could assist us——"

He halted and stood looking down at the floor. "Yes! That's our one chance. We must confront Arnesson with what we know when the professor is present. The situation is sure to force an issue of some kind. The professor now will do all in his power to help convict Arnesson."

"You believe he knows more than he had told us?"

"Undoubtedly. I've told you so from the first. And when he hears of the Little-Miss-Muffet episode, it's not unlikely he'll supply us with the evidence we need."

"It's a long chance." Markham was pessimistic. "But it can do no harm to try. In any event, I shall arrest Arnesson before I leave here, and hope for the best."

A few moments later the front door opened and Professor Dillard appeared in the hall opposite the archway. He scarcely acknowledged Markham's greeting—he was scanning our faces as if trying to read the meaning of our unexpected visit. Finally he put a question.

"You have, perhaps, thought over what I said last night?"

"Not only have we thought it over," said Markham, "but Mr. Vance has found the thing that was disturbing you. After we left here he showed me a copy of 'The Pretenders.' "

"Ah!" The exclamation was like a sigh of relief. "For days that play has been in my mind, poisoning every thought. . . ." He looked up fearfully. "What does it mean?"

Vance answered the question.

"It means, sir, that you've led us to the truth. We're waiting now for Mr. Arnesson.—And I think it would be well if we had a talk with you in the meantime. You may be able to help us."

The old man hesitated.

"I had hoped not to be made an instrument in the boy's conviction." His voice held a tragic paternal note. But presently his features hardened; a vindictive light shone in his eyes; and his hand tightened over the knob of his stick. "However, I can't consider my own feelings now. Come; I will do what I can."

On reaching the library he paused by the sideboard and poured himself a glass of port. When he had drunk it he turned to Markham with a look of apology.

"Forgive me. I'm not quite myself." He drew forward the little chess table and placed glasses on it for all of us. "Please overlook my discourtesy." He filled the glasses and sat down.

We drew up chairs. There was none of us, I think, who did not feel the need of a glass of wine after the harrowing events we had just passed through.

When we had settled ourselves the professor lifted heavy eyes to Vance, who had taken a seat opposite to him.

"Tell me everything," he said. "Don't try to spare me."

Vance drew out his cigarette-case.

"First, let me ask you a question. Where was Mr. Arnesson between five and six yesterday afternoon?"

"I—don't know." There was a reluctance in the words. "He had tea here in the library; but he went out about half past four, and I didn't see him again until dinner time."

Vance regarded the other sympathetically for a moment, then he said:

"We've found the typewriter on which the Bishop notes were printed. It was in an old suit-case hidden in the attic of this house."

The professor showed no sign of being startled.

"You were able to identify it?"

"Beyond any doubt. Yesterday a little girl named Madeleine Moffat disappeared from the playground in the park. There was a sheet of paper in the machine, and on it had already been typed: 'Little Miss Muffet sat on a tuffet.' "

Professor Dillard's head sank forward.

"Another insane atrocity! If only I hadn't waited till last night to warn you———!"

"No great harm has been done," Vance hastened to inform him. "We found the child in time: she's out of danger now."

"Ah!"

"She had been locked in the hall-closet on the top floor of the Drukker house. We had thought she was here somewhere—which is how we came to search your attic."

There was a silence; then the professor asked:

"What more have you to tell me?"

"Drukker's note-book containing his recent quantum researches was stolen from his room the night of his death. We found this note-book in the attic with the typewriter."

"He stooped even to that?" It was not a question, but an exclamation of incredulity. "Are you sure of your conclusions? Perhaps if I had made no suggestion last night—had not sowed the seed of suspicion. . . ."

"There can be no doubt," declared Vance softly. "Mr. Markham intends to arrest Mr. Arnesson when he returns from the university. But to be frank with you, sir: we have practically no legal evidence, and it is a question in Mr. Markham's mind whether or not the law can even hold him. The most we can hope for is a conviction for attempted kidnapping through the child's identification."

"Ah, yes . . . the child would know." A bitterness crept into the old man's eyes. "Still, there should be some means of obtaining justice for the other crimes."

Vance sat smoking pensively, his eyes on the wall beyond. At last he spoke with quiet gravity.

"If Mr. Arnesson were convinced that our case against him was a strong one, he might choose suicide as a way out. That perhaps would be the most humane solution for every one."

Markham was about to make an indignant protest, but Vance anticipated him.

"Suicide is not an indefensible act *per se*. The Bible, for instance, contains many accounts of heroic suicide. What finer example of courage than Rhazis', when he threw himself from the tower to escape the yoke of Demetrius?*

---

* I admit that the name of Rhazis was unfamiliar to me; and when I looked it up later I found that the episode to which Vance referred does not appear in the Anglican Bible, but in the second book of Maccabees in the Apocrypha.

There was gallantry, too, in the death of Saul's sword-bearer, and in the self-hanging of Ahithophel. And surely the suicides of Samson and Judas Iscariot had virtue. History is filled with notable suicides—Brutus and Cato of Utica, Hannibal, Lucretia, Cleopatra, Seneca.... Nero killed himself lest he fall into the hands of Otho and the Pretorian guards. In Greece we have the famous self-destruction of Demosthenes; and Empedocles threw himself in the crater of Etna. Aristotle was the first great thinker to advance the dictum that suicide is an anti-social act, but, according to tradition, he himself took poison after the death of Alexander. And in modern times let us not forget the sublime gesture of Baron Nogi...."

"All that is no justification of the act," Markham retorted. "The law————"

"Ah, yes—the law. In Chinese law every criminal condemned to death has the option of suicide. The Codex adopted by the French National Assembly at the end of the eighteenth century abolished all punishments for suicide; and in the *Sachsenspiegel*—the principal foundation of Teuton law—it is plainly stated that suicide is not a punishable act. Moreover, among the Donatists, Circumcellions and Patricians suicide was considered pleasing to the gods. And even in More's Utopia there was a synod to pass on the right of the individual to take his own life.... Law, Markham, is for the protection of society. What of a suicide that makes possible that protection? Are we to invoke a legal technicality, when, by so doing, we actually lay society open to continued danger? Is there no law higher than those on the statute books?"

Markham was sorely troubled. He rose and walked the length of the room and back, his face dark with anxiety. When he sat down again he looked at Vance a long while, his fingers drumming with nervous indecision on the table.

"The innocent of course must be considered," he said in a voice of discouragement. "As morally wrong as suicide is, I can see your point that at times it may be theoretically justified." (Knowing Markham as I did, I realized what this concession had cost him; and I realized, too, for the first time, how utterly hopeless he felt in the face of the scourge of horror which it was his duty to wipe out.)

The old professor nodded understandingly.

"Yes, there are some secrets so hideous that it is well for the world not to know them. A higher justice may often be achieved without the law taking its toll."

As he spoke the door opened, and Arnesson stepped into the room.

"Well, well. Another conference, eh?" He gave us a quizzical leer, and threw himself into a chair beside the professor. "I thought the case had been adjudicated, so to speak. Didn't Pardee's suicide put *finis* to the affair?"

Vance looked straight into the man's eyes.

"We've found little Miss Muffet, Mr. Arnesson."

The other's eyebrows went up with sardonic amusement.

"Sounds like a charade. What am I supposed to answer: 'How's little Jack Horner's thumb?' Or, should I inquire into the health of Jack Sprat?"

Vance did not relax his steady gaze.

"We found her in the Drukker house, locked in a closet," he amplified, in a low, even tone.

Arnesson became serious, and an involuntary frown gathered on his forehead. But this slackening of pose was only transient. Slowly his mouth twisted into a smirk.

"You policemen are so efficient. Fancy finding little Miss Muffet so soon. Remarkable." He wagged his head in mock admiration. "However, sooner or later it was to be expected.—And what, may I ask, is to be the next move?"

"We also found the typewriter," pursued Vance, ignoring the question. "And Drukker's stolen note-book."

Arnesson was at once on his guard.

"Did you really?" He gave Vance a canny look. "Where were these tell-tale objects?"

"Up-stairs—in the attic."

"Aha! Housebreaking?"

"Something like that."

"Withal," Arnesson scoffed, "I can't see that you have a cast-iron case against any one. A typewriter is not like a suit of clothes that fits only one person. And who can say how Drukker's note-book found its way into our attic?—You must do better than that, Mr. Vance."

"There is, of course, the factor of opportunity. The Bishop is a person who could have been on hand at the time of each murder."

"That is the flimsiest of contributory evidence," the man countered. "It would not help much toward a conviction."

"We might be able to show why the murderer chose the sobriquet of Bishop."

"Ah! That unquestionably would help." A cloud settled on Arnesson's face, and his eyes became reminiscent. "I'd thought of that, too."

"Oh, had you, now?" Vance watched him closely. "And there's another piece of evidence I haven't mentioned. Little Miss Muffet will be able to identify the man who led her to the Drukker house and forced her into the closet."

"So! The patient has recovered?"

"Oh, quite. Doing nicely, in fact. We found her, d' ye see, twenty-four hours before the Bishop intended us to."

Arnesson was silent. He was staring down at his hands which, though folded, were working nervously. Finally he spoke.

"And if, in spite of everything, you were wrong. . . ."

"I assure you, Mr. Arnesson," said Vance quietly, "that I *know* who is guilty."

"You positively frighten me!" The man had got a grip on himself, and he retorted with biting irony. "If, by any chance, I myself were the Bishop, I'd be inclined to admit defeat. . . . Still, it's quite obvious that it was the Bishop who took the chessman to Mrs. Drukker at midnight; and I didn't return home with Belle until half past twelve that night."

"So you informed her. As I recall, you looked at your watch and told her what time it was.—Come, now: what time was it?"

"That's correct—half past twelve."

Vance sighed and tapped the ash from his cigarette.

"I say, Mr. Arnesson; how good a chemist are you?"

"One of the best," the man grinned. "Majored in it.—What then?"

"When I was searching the attic this morning I discovered a little wall-closet in which some one had been distilling hydrocyanic acid from potassium ferrocyanide. There was a chemist's gas-mask on hand, and all the paraphernalia. Bitter-almond odor still lurking in the vicinity."

"Quite a treasure-trove, our attic. A sort of haunt of Loki, it would seem."

"It was just that," returned Vance gravely, "—the den of an evil spirit."

"Or else the laboratory of a modern Doctor Faustus. . . . But why the cyanide, do you think?"

"Precaution, I'd say. In case of trouble the Bishop could step out of the picture painlessly. Everything in readiness, don't y' know."

Arnesson nodded.

"Quite a correct attitude on his part. Really decent of him, in fact. No use putting people to unnecessary bother if you're cornered. Yes, very correct."

Professor Dillard had sat during this sinister dialogue with one hand pressed to his eyes, as though in pain. Now he turned sorrowfully to the man he had fathered for so many years.

"Many great men, Sigurd, have justified suicide————" he began; but Arnesson cut him short with a cynical laugh.

"Faugh! Suicide needs no justification. Nietzsche laid the bugaboo of voluntary death. *'Auf eine stolze Art sterben, wenn es nicht mehr möglich ist, auf eine stolze Art zu leben. Der Tod unter den verächtlichsten Bedingungen, ein unfreier Tod, ein Tod zur unrechten Zeit ist ein Feiglings-Tod. Wir haben es nicht in der Hand, zu verhindern, geboren zu werden: aber wir können diesen Fehler—denn bisweilen ist es ein Fehler—wieder gut machen. Wenn man sich abschafft, tut man die achtungswürdigste Sache, die es giebt: man verdient beinahe damit, zu leben.'*—*Memorized that passage from 'Götzen-Dämmerung' in my youth. Never forgot it. A sound doctrine."

"Nietzsche had many famous predecessors who also upheld suicide," supplemented Vance. "Zeno the Stoic left us a passionate dithyramb defending voluntary death. And Tacitus, Epictetus, Marcus Aurelius, Cato, Kant, Fichte, Diderot, Voltaire and Rousseau, all wrote apologias for suicide. Schopenhauer protested bitterly against the fact that suicide was regarded as a crime in England. . . . And yet, I wonder if the subject can be formulated. Somehow I feel that it's too personal a matter for academic discussion."

The professor agreed sadly.

"No one can know what goes on in the human heart in that last dark hour."

During this discussion Markham had been growing impatient and uneasy; and Heath, though at first rigid and watchful, had begun to unbend. I could not see that Vance had made the slightest progress; and I was driven to the conclusion that he had failed signally in accomplishing his purpose of ensnaring Arnesson. However, he did not appear in the least perturbed. I even got the impression that he was satisfied with the way things were going. But I did notice that, despite his outer calm, he was intently alert. His feet were drawn

---

* "One should die proudly when it is no longer possible to live proudly. The death which takes place in the most contemptible circumstances, the death that is not free, the death which occurs at the wrong time, is the death of a coward. We have not the power to prevent ourselves from being born; but this error—for sometimes it is an error—can be rectified if we choose. The man who does away with himself, performs the most estimable of deeds; he almost deserves to live for having done so."

back and poised; and every muscle in his body was taut. I began to wonder what the outcome of this terrible conference would be.

The end came swiftly. A short silence followed the professor's remark. Then Arnesson spoke.

"You say you know who the Bishop is, Mr. Vance. That being the case, why all this palaver?"

"There was no great haste." Vance was almost casual. "And there was the hope of tying up a few loose ends,—hung juries are so unsatisfact'ry, don't y' know. . . . Then again, this port is excellent."

"The port? . . . Ah yes." Arnesson glanced at our glasses, and turned an injured look on the professor. "Since when have I been a teetotaler, sir?"

The other gave a start, hesitated, and rose.

"I'm sorry, Sigurd. It didn't occur to me . . . you never drink in the forenoon." He went to the sideboard and, filling another glass, placed it, with an unsteady hand, before Arnesson. Then he refilled the other glasses.

No sooner had he resumed his seat than Vance uttered an exclamation of surprise. He had half risen and was leaning forward, his hands resting on the edge of the table, his eyes fixed with astonishment on the mantel at the end of the room.

"My word! I never noticed that before. . . . Extr'ordin'ry!"

So unexpected and startling had been his action, and so tense was the atmosphere, that involuntarily we swung about and looked in the direction of his fascinated gaze.

"A Cellini plaque!" he exlaimed. "The Nymph of Fontainebleau! Bereson told me it was destroyed in the seventeenth century. I've seen its companion piece in the Louvre. . . ."

A red flush of angry indignation mounted to Markham's cheeks; and for myself I must say that, familiar as I was with Vance's idiosyncrasies and intellectual passion for rare antiques, I had never before known him to exhibit such indefensible bad taste. It seemed unbelievable that he would have let himself be distracted by an *objet-d'art* in such a tragic hour.

Professor Dillard frowned at him with consternation.

"You've chosen a strange time, sir, to indulge your enthusiasm for art," was his scathing comment.

Vance appeared abashed and chagrined. He sank back in his seat, avoiding our eyes, and began turning the stem of his glass between his fingers.

"You are quite right, sir," he murmured. "I owe you an apology."

"The plaque, incidentally," the professor added, by way of mitigating the severity of his rebuke, "is merely a copy of the Louvre piece."

Vance, as if to hide his confusion, raised his wine to his lips. It was a highly unpleasant moment: every one's nerves were on edge; and, in automatic imitation of his action, we lifted our glasses too.

Vance gave a swift glance across the table and, rising, went to the front window, where he stood, his back to the room. So unaccountable was his hasty departure that I turned and watched him wonderingly. Almost at the same moment the edge of the table was thrust violently against my side, and simultaneously there came a crash of glassware.

I leapt to my feet and gazed down with horror at the inert body sprawled forward in the chair opposite, one arm and shoulder flung across the table. A short silence of dismay and bewilderment followed. Each of us seemed momentarily paralyzed. Markham stood like a graven image, his eyes fastened on the table; and Heath, staring and speechless, clung rigidly to the back of his chair.

"*Good Gad!*"

It was Arnesson's astonished ejaculation that snapped the tension.

Markham went quickly round the table and bent over Professor Dillard's body.

"Call a doctor, Arnesson," he ordered.

Vance turned wearily from the window and sank into a chair.

"Nothing can be done for him," he said, with a deep sigh of fatigue. "He prepared for a swift and painless death when he distilled his cyanide.—The Bishop case is over."

Markham was glaring at him with dazed incomprehension.

"Oh, I've half-suspected the truth ever since Pardee's death," Vance went on, in answer to the other's unspoken question. "But I wasn't sure of it until last night when he went out of his way to hang the guilt on Mr. Arnesson."

"Eh? What's that?" Arnesson turned from the telephone.

"Oh, yes," nodded Vance. "You were to pay the penalty. You'd been chosen from the first as the victim. He even suggested the possibility of your guilt to us."

Arnesson did not seem as surprised as one would have expected.

"I knew the professor hated me," he said. "He was intensely jealous of my interest in Belle. And he was losing his intellectual grip—I've seen that for months. I've done all the work on his new book, and he's resented every academic honor paid me. I've had an idea he was back of all this deviltry; but I wasn't sure. I didn't think, though, he'd try to send me to the electric-chair."

Vance got up and, going to Arnesson, held out his hand.

"There was no danger of that.—And I want to apologize for the way I've treated you this past half hour. Merely a matter of tactics. Y' see, we hadn't any real evidence, and I was hopin' to force his hand."

Arnesson grinned sombrely.

"No apology necessary, old son. I knew you didn't have your eye on me. When you began riding me I saw it was only technique. Didn't know what you were after, but I followed your cues the best I could. Hope I didn't bungle the job."

"No, no. You turned the trick."

"Did I?" Arnesson frowned with deep perplexity. "But what I don't understand is why he should have taken the cyanide when he thought it was I you suspected."

"That particular point we'll never know," said Vance. "Maybe he feared the girl's identification. Or he may have seen through my deception. Perhaps he suddenly revolted at the idea of shouldering you with the onus. . . . As he himself said, no one knows what goes on in the human heart during the last dark hour."

Arnesson did not move. He was looking straight into Vance's eyes with penetrating shrewdness.

"Oh, well," he said at length; "we'll let it go at that. . . . Anyway, thanks!"

26

HEATH ASKS A QUESTION

(Tuesday, April 26; 4 P.M.)

WHEN MARKHAM and Vance and I departed from the Dillard house an hour later, I thought the Bishop affair was over. And it was over as far as the public was concerned. But there was another revelation to come; and it was, in a way, the most astounding of all the facts that had been brought to light that day.

Heath joined us at the District Attorney's office after lunch, for there were several delicate official matters to be discussed; and later that afternoon Vance reviewed the entire case, explaining many of its obscure points.

"Arnesson has already suggested the motive for these insane crimes," he began. "The professor knew that his position in the world of science was being usurped by the younger man. His mind had begun to lose its force and penetration; and he realized that his new book on atomic structure was being made possible only through Arnesson's help. A colossal hate grew up in him for his foster son; Arnesson became in his eyes a kind of monster whom he himself, like Frankenstein, had created, and who was now rising to destroy him. And this intellectual enmity was augmented by a primitive emotional jealousy. For ten years he had centred in Belle Dillard the accumulated affection of a life of solit'ry bachelorhood—she represented his one hold on every-day existence— and when he saw that Arnesson was likely to take her from him, his hatred and resentment were doubled in intensity."

"The motive is understandable," said Markham. "But it does not explain the crimes."

"The motive acted as a spark to the dry powder of his pent-up emotions. In looking about for a means to destroy Arnesson, he hit upon the diabolical jest of the Bishop murders. These murders gave relief to his repressions; they met his psychic need for violent expression; and at the same time they answered the dark question in his mind how he could dispose of Arnesson and keep Belle Dillard for himself."

"But why," Markham asked, "didn't he merely murder Arnesson and have done with it?"

"You overlook the psychological aspects of the situation. The professor's mind had disintegrated through long intense repression. Nature was demanding an outlet. And it was his passionate hatred of Arnesson that brought the pressure to an explosion point. The two impulses were thus combined. In committing the murders he was not only relieving his inhibitions, but he was also venting his wrath against Arnesson, for Arnesson, d' ye see, was to pay the penalty. Such a revenge was more potent, and hence more satisfying, than the mere killing of the man would have been,—it was the great grim joke behind the lesser jokes of the murders themselves. . . .

"However, this fiendish scheme had one great disadvantage, though the professor did not see it. It laid the affair open to psychological analysis; and at the outset I was able to postulate a mathematician as the criminal agent. The difficulty of naming the murderer lay in the fact that nearly every possible suspect was a mathematician. The only one I knew to be innocent was Arnesson, for he was the only one who consistently maintained a psychic balance—that is, who constantly discharged the emotions arising from his protracted abstruse speculations. A general sadistic and cynical attitude that is volubly expressed, and a violent homicidal outburst, are psychologically equivalent. Giving full rein to one's cynicism as one goes along produces a normal outlet and maintains an emotional equilibrium. Cynical, scoffing men are always safe, for they are farthest removed from sporadic physical outbreaks; whereas the man who represses his sadism and accumulates his cynicism beneath a grave and stoical exterior is always liable to dangerous fulminations. This is why I knew Arnesson was incapable of the Bishop murders and why I suggested your letting him help us with the investigation. As he admitted, he suspected the professor; and his request to assist us was, I believe, actuated by a desire to keep posted so that he could better protect Belle Dillard and himself in case his suspicions should prove correct."

"That sounds reasonable," acceded Markham. "But where did Dillard get his fantastic ideas for the murders?"

"The Mother-Goose motif was probably suggested to him when he heard Arnesson jestingly tell Robin to beware of an arrow from Sperling's bow. He saw in that remark a means of venting his hatred against the man who had made it; and he bided his time. The opportunity to stage the crime came shortly after. When he saw Sperling pass up the street that morning, he knew that Robin was alone in the archery-room. So he went below, engaged Robin in conversation, struck him over the head, drove a shaft into his heart, and shoved him out on the range. He then wiped up the blood, destroyed the cloth, posted his notes at the corner, put one in the house letter-box, returned to the library, and called up this office. One unforeseen factor cropped up, however:—Pyne was in Arnesson's room when the professor said he went out on the balcony. But no harm came of it, for though Pyne knew something was amiss when he caught the professor lying, he certainly didn't suspect the old gentleman of being a murderer. The crime was a decided success."

"Still and all," put in Heath, "you guessed that Robin hadn't been shot with a bow and arrow."

"Yes. I saw from the battered condition of the nock of the arrow that it had been hammered into Robin's body; and I concluded therefore that the chap had been killed indoors, after having first been stunned with a blow on the head. That was why I assumed that the bow had been thrown to the range from the window,—I didn't know then that the professor was guilty. The bow of course was never on the range.—But the evidence on which I based my deductions cannot be held as an error or oversight on the professor's part. As long as his Mother-Goose joke was accomplished, the rest didn't matter to him."

"What instrument do you think he used?" Markham put the question.

"His walking stick, most likely. You may have noticed it has an enormous gold knob perfectly constructed as a lethal weapon.* Incidentally, I'm inclined

---

* It was discovered later that the large weighted gold handle, which was nearly eight inches long, was loose and could be easily removed from the stick. The handle weighed nearly two pounds and, as Vance had observed, constituted a highly efficient "black jack." Whether or not it had been loosened for the purpose to which it was put, is of course wholly a matter of conjecture.'

to think he exaggerated his gout to attract sympathy and to shunt any possible suspicion from himself."

"And the suggestion for the Sprigg murder?"

"After Robin's death he may have deliberately looked about for Mother-Goose material for another crime. In any event, Sprigg visited the house the Thursday night preceding the shooting; and it was at that time, I imagine, that the idea was born. On the day chosen for the gruesome business he rose early and dressed, waited for Pyne's knock at half past seven, answered it, and then went to the park—probably through the archery-room and by way of the alley. Sprigg's habit of taking daily morning walks may have been casually mentioned by Arnesson, or even by the lad himself."

"But how do you explain the tensor formula?"

"The professor had heard Arnesson talking to Sprigg about it a few nights before; and I think he placed it under the body to call attention—through association—to Arnesson. Moreover, that particular formula subtly expressed the psychological impulse beneath the crimes. The Riemann-Christoffel tensor is a statement of the infinity of space—the negation of infinitesimal human life on this earth; and subconsciously it no doubt satisfied the professor's perverted sense of humor, giving added homogeneity to his monstrous conception. The moment I saw it I sensed its sinister significance; and it substantiated my theory that the Bishop murders were the acts of a mathematician whose values had become abstract and incommensurable."

Vance paused to light another cigarette, and after a moment's thoughtful silence continued.

"We come now to the midnight visit to the Drukker house. That was a grim *entr'acte* forced on the murderer by the report of Mrs. Drukker's scream. He feared the woman had seen Robin's body thrown to the range; and when, on the morning of Sprigg's murder, she had been in the yard and met him returning from the kill, he was more worried than ever that she would put two and two together. No wonder he tried to prevent our questioning her! And at the earliest opportunity he attempted to silence her for all time. He took the key from Belle Dillard's handbag before the theatre that night, and replaced it the next morning. He sent Pyne and Beedle to bed early; and at half past ten Drukker complained of fatigue and went home. At midnight he figured that the coast was clear for his grisly visit. His taking the black bishop as a symbolic signature to the contemplated murder was probably suggested by the chess discussion between Pardee and Drukker. Then again, it was Arnesson's chessman, and I even suspect him of telling us of the chess discussion to call attention to Arnesson's chess set in case the black bishop should fall into our hands."

"Do you think he had any idea of involving Pardee at that time?"

"Oh, no. He was genuinely surprised when Arnesson's analysis of the Pardee-Rubinstein game revealed the fact that the bishop had long been Pardee's nemesis. . . . And you were undoubtedly right about Pardee's reaction to my mention of the black bishop the next day. The poor chap thought I was deliberately ridiculing him as a result of his defeat at Rubinstein's hands. . . ."

Vance leaned over and tapped the ashes from his cigarette.

"Too bad," he murmured regretfully. "I owe him an apology, don't y' know." He shrugged his shoulders slightly, and, settling back in his chair, took up his narrative. "The professor got his idea for Drukker's murder from Mrs. Drukker herself. She expressed her imaginative fears to Belle Dillard, who repeated them at dinner that night; and the plan took shape. There were no complications to its execution. After dinner he went to the attic and typed the notes. Later he suggested a walk to Drukker, knowing Pardee wouldn't remain long with Arnesson; and when he saw Pardee on the bridle path he of course knew Arnesson was alone. As soon as Pardee had walked away, he struck Drukker and tipped him over the wall. Immediately he took the little path to the Drive, crossed to 76th Street, and went to Drukker's room, returning by the same route. The whole episode couldn't have occupied more than ten minutes. Then he calmly walked past Emery and went home with Drukker's note-book under his coat. . . ."

"But why," interposed Markham, "if you were sure that Arnesson was innocent, did you make such a point of locating the key to the alley door? Only Arnesson could have used the alley on the night of Drukker's death. Dillard and Pardee both went out by the front door."

"I wasn't interested in the key from the standpoint of Arnesson's guilt. But if the key was gone, d' ye see, it would have meant that some one had taken it in order to throw suspicion on Arnesson. How simple it would have been for Arnesson to slip down the alley after Pardee had gone, cross the Drive to the little path and attack Drukker after the professor had left him. . . . And, Markham, that is what we were supposed to think. It was, in fact, the obvious explanation of Drukker's murder."

"What I can't get through my head, though," complained Heath, "is why the old gent should have killed Pardee. That didn't throw any suspicion on Arnesson, and it made it look like Pardee was guilty and had got disgusted and croaked himself."

"That spurious suicide, Sergeant, was the professor's most fantastic joke. It was at once ironical and contemptuous; for all during that comic interlude plans were being made for Arnesson's destruction. And, of course, the fact that we possessed a plausible culprit had the great advantage of relaxing our watchfulness and causing the guards to be removed from the house. The murder, I imagine, was conceived rather spontaneously. The professor invented some excuse to accompany Pardee to the archery-room, where he had already closed the windows and drawn the shades. Then, perhaps pointing out an article in a magazine, he shot his unsuspecting guest through the temple, placed the gun in his hand, and, as a bit of sardonic humor, built the house of cards. On returning to the library he set up the chessmen to give the impression that Pardee had been brooding over the black bishop. . . .

"But, as I say, this piece of grim grotesquerie was only a side-issue. The Little-Miss-Muffet episode was to be the *dénouement;* and it was carefully planned so as to bring the heavens crashing down on Arnesson. The professor was at the Drukker house the morning of the funeral when Madeleine Moffat brought the flowers for Humpty Dumpty; and he undoubtedly knew the child by name—she was Drukker's favorite and had been to the house on numerous occasions. The Mother-Goose idea being now firmly implanted in his mind, like a homicidal obsession, he very naturally associated the name Moffat with Muffet. Indeed, it's not unlikely that Drukker or Mrs. Drukker had called the child 'Little Miss Moffat' in his presence. It was easy for him to attract her attention and summon her to the mound by the wall yesterday afternoon. He probably told her that Humpty Dumpty wanted to see her; and she came with him eagerly, following him under the trees by the bridle path, thence across the Drive, and through the alley between the apartment houses. No one would have noticed them, for the Drive is teeming with children at that hour. Then last night he planted in us the seed of suspicion against Arnesson, believing that when the Little-Miss-Muffet notes reached the press we would look for the child and find her, dead from lack of air, in the Drukker house.... A clever, devilish plan!"

"But did he expect us to search the attic of his own home?"

"Oh, yes; but not until to-morrow. By then he would have cleaned out the closet and put the typewriter in a more conspicuous place. And he would have removed the note-book, for there's little doubt that he intended to appropriate Drukker's quantum researches. But we came a day too soon, and upset his calculations."

Markham smoked moodily for a time.

"You say you were convinced of Dillard's guilt last night when you remembered the character of *Bishop Arnesson.* . . ."

"Yes—oh, yes. That gave me the motive. At that moment I realized that the professor's object was to shoulder Arnesson with the guilt, and that the signature to the notes had been chosen for that purpose."

"He waited a long time before he called our attention to 'The Pretenders,' " commented Markham.

"The fact is, he didn't expect to have to do it at all. He thought we'd discover the name for ourselves. But we were duller than he anticipated; and at last, in desperation, he sent for you and beat cleverly round the bush, accentuating 'The Pretenders.' "

Markham did not speak for several moments. He sat frowning reproachfully, his fingers tapping a tattoo on the blotter.

"Why," he asked at length, "did you not tell us last night that the professor and not Arnesson was the Bishop? You let us think————"

"My dear Markham! What else could I do? In the first place, you wouldn't have believed me, and would most likely have suggested another ocean trip, what? Furthermore, it was essential to let the professor think we suspected Arnesson. Otherwise, we'd have had no chance to force the issue as we did. Subterfuge was our only hope; and I knew that if you and the Sergeant suspected him you'd be sure to give the game away. As it was, you didn't have to dissemble; and lo! it all worked out beautifully."

The Sergeant, I noticed, had, for the past half hour, been regarding Vance from time to time with a look of perplexed uncertainty; but for some reason he had seemed reluctant to give voice to his troubled thoughts. Now, however, he shifted his position uneasily and, taking his cigar slowly from his mouth, asked a startling question.

"I ain't complaining about your not putting us wise last night, Mr. Vance, but what I would like to know is: why, when you hopped up and pointed at that plate on the mantel, did you switch Arnesson's and the old gent's glasses?"

Vance sighed deeply and gave a hopeless wag of the head.

"I might have known that nothing could escape your eagle eye, Sergeant."

Markham thrust himself forward over the desk, and glared at Vance with angry bewilderment.

"What's this!" he spluttered, his usual self-restraint deserting him. "You changed the glasses? You deliberately————"

"Oh, I say!" pleaded Vance. "Let not your wrathful passions rise." He turned to Heath with mock reproach. "Behold what you've got me in for, Sergeant."

"This is no time for evasion." Markham's voice was cold and inexorable. "I want an explanation."

Vance made a resigned gesture.

"Oh, well. Attend. My idea, as I've explained to you, was to fall in with the professor's plan and appear to suspect Arnesson. This morning I purposely let him see that we had no evidence, and that, even if we arrested Arnesson, it was doubtful if we could hold him. I knew that, in the circumstances, he would take some action—that he would try to meet the situation in some heroic way—for the sole object of the murders was to destroy Arnesson utterly. That he would commit some overt act and give his hand away, I was confident. What it would be I didn't know. But we'd be watching him closely.... Then the wine gave me an inspiration. Knowing he had cyanide in his possession, I brought up the subject of suicide, and thus planted the idea in his mind. He fell into the trap, and attempted to poison Arnesson and make it appear like suicide. I saw him surreptitiously empty a small phial of colorless fluid into Arnesson's glass at the sideboard when he poured the wine. My first intention was to halt the murder and have the wine analyzed. We could have searched him and found the phial, and I could have testified to the fact that I saw him poison the wine. This evidence, in addition to the identification by the child, might have answered our purpose. But at the last moment, after he had re-filled all our glasses, I decided on a simpler course————"

"And so you diverted our attention and switched the glasses!"

"Yes, yes. Of course. I figured that a man should be willing to drink the wine he pours for another."

"You took the law in your own hands!"

"I took it in my arms—it was helpless.... But don't be so righteous. Do you bring a rattlesnake to the bar of justice? Do you give a mad dog his day in court? I felt no more compunction in aiding a monster like Dillard into the Beyond than I would have in crushing out a poisonous reptile in the act of striking."

"But it was murder!" exclaimed Markham in horrified indignation.

"Oh, doubtless," said Vance cheerfully. "Yes—of course. Most reprehensible.... I say, am I by any chance under arrest?"

The "suicide" of Professor Dillard terminated the famous Bishop murder case, and automatically cleared Pardee's reputation of all suspicion. The following year Arnesson and Belle Dillard were married quietly and sailed for Norway, where they made their home. Arnesson had accepted the chair of applied mathematics at the University of Oslo; and it will be remembered that two years later he was awarded the Nobel prize for his work in physics. The old Dillard house in 75th Street was torn down, and on the site now stands a modern apartment house on whose façade are two huge terra-cotta medallions strongly suggestive of archery targets. I have often wondered if the architect was deliberate in his choice of decoration.

The Scarab Murder Case

La vérité n'a point cet air impétueux.

—*Boileau*

DEDICATED
WITH APPRECIATION
TO
AMBROSE LANSING
LUDLOW BULL
AND
HENRY A. CAREY
OF THE EGYPTIAN DEPARTMENT OF
THE METROPOLITAN MUSEUM
OF ART

CHARACTERS OF THE BOOK

PHILO VANCE

JOHN F.-X. MARKHAM
District Attorney of New York County.

ERNEST HEATH
Sergeant of the Homicide Bureau.

DR. MINDRUM W. C. BLISS
Egyptologist; head of the Bliss Museum of Egyptian Antiquities.

BENJAMIN H. KYLE
Philanthropist and art patron.

MERYT-AMEN
Wife of Dr. Bliss.

ROBERT SALVETER
Assistant Curator of the Bliss Museum; nephew of Benjamin H. Kyle.

DONALD SCARLETT
Technical Expert of the Bliss Expeditions in Egypt.

ANÛPU HANI
Family retainer of the Blisses.

BRUSH
The Bliss butler.

DINGLE
The Bliss cook.

HENNESSEY
Detective of the Homicide Bureau.

SNITKIN
Detective of the Homicide Bureau.

EMERY
Detective of the Homicide Bureau.

GUILFOYLE
Detective of the Homicide Bureau.

CAPTAIN DUBOIS
Finger-print expert.

DETECTIVE BELLAMY
Finger-print expert.

517

DR. EMANUEL DOREMUS
    Medical Examiner
CURRIE
    Vance's valet.

1

MURDER!

(Friday, July 13; 11 A. M.)

PHILO VANCE was drawn into the Scarab murder case by sheer coincidence, although there is little doubt that John F.-X. Markham—New York's District Attorney—would sooner or later have enlisted his services. But it is problematic if even Vance, with his fine analytic mind and his remarkable *flair* for the subtleties of human psychology, could have solved that bizarre and astounding murder if he had not been the first observer on the scene; for, in the end, he was able to put his finger on the guilty person only because of the topsy-turvy clews that had met his eye during his initial inspection.

Those clews—highly misleading from the materialistic point of view—eventually gave him the key to the murderer's mentality and thus enabled him to elucidate one of the most complicated and incredible criminal problems in modern police history.

The brutal and fantastic murder of that old philanthropist and art patron, Benjamin H. Kyle, became known as the Scarab murder case almost immediately, as a result of the fact that it had taken place in a famous Egyptologist's private museum and had centred about a rare blue scarabæus that had been found beside the mutilated body of the victim.

This ancient and valuable seal, inscribed with the names of one of the early Pharaohs (whose mummy had, by the way, not been found at the time), constituted the basis on which Vance reared his astonishing structure of evidence. The scarab, from the police point of view, was merely an incidental piece of evidence that pointed somewhat obviously toward its owner; but this easy and specious explanation did not appeal to Vance.

"Murderers," he remarked to Sergeant Ernest Heath, "do not ordinarily insert their visitin' cards in the shirt bosoms of their victims. And while the discovery of the lapis-lazuli beetle is most interestin' from both the psychological and evidential standpoints, we must not be too optimistic and jump to conclusions. The most important question in this pseudo-mystical murder is why—and how—the murderer left that archæological specimen beside the

519

defunct body. Once we find the reason for that amazin' action, we'll hit upon the secret of the crime itself."

The doughty Sergeant had sniffed at Vance's suggestion and had ridiculed his scepticism; but before another day had passed he generously admitted that Vance had been right, and that the murder had not been so simple as it had appeared in first view.

As I have said, a coincidence brought Vance into the case before the police were notified. An acquaintance of his had discovered the slain body of old Mr. Kyle, and had immediately come to him with the gruesome news.

It happened on the morning of Friday, July 13th. Vance had just finished a late breakfast in the roof-garden of his apartment in East Thirty-eighth Street, and had returned to the library to continue his translation of the Menander fragments found in the Egyptian papyri during the early years of the present century, when Currie—his valet and majordomo—shuffled into the room and announced with an air of discreet apology:

"Mr. Donald Scarlett has just arrived, sir, in a state of distressing excitement, and asks that you hasten to receive him."

Vance looked up from his work with an expression of boredom.

"Scarlett, eh? Very annoyin'.... And why should he call on me when excited? I infinitely prefer calm people.... Did you offer him a brandy-and-soda—or some triple bromides?"

"I took the liberty of placing a service of Courvoisier brandy before him," explained Currie. "I recall that Mr. Scarlett has a weakness for Napoleon's cognac."

"Ah, yes—so he has.... Quite right, Currie." Vance leisurely lit one of his *Régie* cigarettes and puffed a moment in silence. "Suppose you show him in when you deem his nerves sufficiently calm."

Currie bowed and departed.

"Interestin' johnny, Scarlett," Vance commented to me (I had been with Vance all morning arranging and filing his notes.) "You remember him, Van—eh, what?"

I had met Scarlett twice, but I must admit I had not thought of him for a month or more. The impression of him, however, came back to me now with considerable vividness. He had been, I knew, a college mate of Vance's at Oxford, and Vance had run across him during his sojourn in Egypt two years before.

Scarlett was a student of Egyptology and archæology, having specialized in these subjects at Oxford under Professor F. Ll. Griffith. Later he had taken up chemistry and photography in order that he might join some Egyptological expedition in a technical capacity. He was a well-to-do Englishman, an amateur and dilettante, and had made of Egyptology a sort of fad.

When Vance had gone to Alexandria Scarlett had been working in the Museum laboratory at Cairo. The two had met again and renewed their old acquaintance. Recently Scarlett had come to America as a member of the staff of Doctor Mindrum W. C. Bliss, the famous Egyptologist, who maintained a private museum of Egyptian antiquities in an old house in East Twentieth Street, facing Gramercy Park. He had called on Vance several times since his arrival in this country, and it was at Vance's apartment that I had met him. He had, however, never called without an invitation, and I was at a loss to understand his unexpected appearance this morning, for he possessed all of the well-bred Englishman's punctiliousness about social matters.

Vance, too, was somewhat puzzled, despite his attitude of lackadaisical indifference.

"Scarlett's a clever lad," he drawled musingly. "And most proper. Why should he call on me at this indecent hour? And why should he be excited? I hope nothing untoward has befallen his erudite employer. . . . Bliss is an astonishin' man, Van—one of the world's great Egyptologists."*

I recalled that during the winter which Vance had spent in Egypt he had become greatly interested in the work of Doctor Bliss, who was then endeavoring to locate the tomb of Pharaoh Intef V who ruled over Upper Egypt at Thebes during the Hyksos domination. In fact, Vance had accompanied Bliss on an exploration in the Valley of the Tombs of the Kings. At that time he had just become attracted by the Menander fragments, and he had been in the midst of a uniform translation of them when the Bishop murder case interrupted his labors.

Vance had also been interested in the variations of chronology of the Old and the Middle Kingdoms of Egypt—not from the historical standpoint but from the standpoint of the evolution of Egyptian art. His researches led him to side with the Bliss-Weigall, or short, chronology† (based on the Turin Papyrus), as opposed to the long chronology of Hall and Petrie, who set back the Twelfth Dynasty and all preceding history one full Sothic cycle, or 1,460 years. After inspecting the art works of the pre-Hyksos and the post-Hyksos eras, Vance was inclined to postulate an interval of not more than 300 years between the Twelfth and Eighteenth Dynasties, in accordance with the shorter chronology. In comparing certain statues made during the reign of Amen-em-hêt III with others made during the reign of Thut-mosè I—thus bridging the Hyksos invasion, with its barbaric Asiatic influence and its annihilation of indigenous Egyptian culture—he arrived at the conclusion that the maintenance of the principles of Twelfth-Dynasty æsthetic attainment could not have been possible with a wider lacuna than 300 years. In brief, he concluded that, had the interregnum been longer, the evidences of decadence in Eighteenth-Dynasty art would have been even more pronounced.

These researches of Vance's ran through my head that sultry July morning as we waited for Currie to usher in the visitor. The announcement of Scarlett's call had brought back memories of many wearying weeks of typing and tabulating Vance's notes on the subject. Perhaps I had a feeling—what we loosely call a premonition—that Scarlett's surprising visit was in some way connected

---

* Doctor Mindrum W. C. Bliss, M.A., A.O.S.S., F.S.A., F.R.S., Hon. Mem. R.A.S., was the author of "The Stele of Intefoe at Koptos"; a "History of Egypt during the Hyksos Invasion"; "The Seventeenth Dynasty"; and a monograph on the Amen-hotpe III Colossi.

† According to the Bliss-Weigall chronology the period between the death of Sebk-nefru-Rê and the overthrow of the Shepherd Kings at Memphis was from 1898 to 1577 B.C.—to wit: 321 years—as against the 1800 years claimed by the upholders to the longer chronology. This short chronology is even shorter according to Breasted and the German school. Breasted and Meyer dated the same period as from 1788 to 1580. These 208 years, by the way, Vance considered too short for the observable cultural changes.

with Vance's æsthetico-Egyptological researches. Perhaps I was even then arranging in my mind, unconsciously, the facts of that winter two years before, so that I might cope more understandingly with the object of Scarlett's present call.

But surely I could have had not the slightest idea or suspicion of what was actually about to befall us. It was far too appalling and too bizarre for the casual imagination. It lifted us out of the ordinary routine of daily experience and dashed us into a frowsty, miasmic atmosphere of things at once incredible and horrifying—things fraught with the seemingly supernatural black magic of a Witches' Sabbat. Only, in this instance it was the mystic and fantastic lore of ancient Egypt—with its confused mythology and its grotesque pantheon of beast-headed gods—that furnished the background.

Scarlett almost dashed through the portières of the library when Currie had pulled back the sliding door for him to enter. Either the Courvoisier had added to his excitement or else Currie had woefully underrated the man's nervous state.

"Kyle has been murdered!" the newcomer blurted, leaning against the library table and staring at Vance with gaping eyes.

"Really, now! That's very distressin'." Vance held out his cigarette-case. "Do have one of my *Régies*. . . . And you'll find that chair beside you most comfortable. A Charles chair: I picked it up in London. . . . Beastly mess, people getting murdered, what? But it really can't be helped, don't y' know. The human race is so deuced blood-thirsty."

His indifference had a salutary effect on Scarlett, who sank limply into the chair and began lighting his cigarette with trembling hands.

Vance waited a moment and then asked:

"By the by, how do you know Kyle has been murdered?"

Scarlett gave a start.

"I saw him lying there—his head bashed in. A frightful sight. No doubt about it." (I could not help feeling that the man had suddenly assumed a defensive attitude.)

Vance lay back in his chair languidly and pyramided his long tapering hands.

"Bashed in with what? And lying where? And how did you happen to discover the corpse? . . . Buck up, Scarlett, and make an effort at coherence."

Scarlett frowned and took several deep inhalations on his cigarette. He was a man of about forty, tall and slender, with a head more Alpine than Nordic—a Dinaric type. His forehead bulged slightly, and his chin was round and recessive. He had the look of a scholar, though not that of a sedentary bookworm, for there was strength and ruggedness in his body; and his face was deeply tanned like that of a man who has lived for years in the sun and wind. There was a trace of fanaticism in his intense eyes—an expression that was somehow enhanced by an almost completely bald head. Yet he gave the impression of honesty and straightforwardness—in this, at least, his British institutionalism was strongly manifest.

"Right you are, Vance," he said after a brief pause, with a more or less successful effort at calmness. "As you know, I came to New York with Doctor Bliss in May as a member of his staff; and I've been doing all the technical work for him. I have my diggings round the corner from the museum, in Irving Place. This morning I had a batch of photographs to classify, and reached the museum shortly before half past ten. . . ."

"Your usual hour?" Vance put the question negligently.

"Oh, no. I was a bit latish this morning. We'd been working last night on a financial report of the last expedition."

"And then?"

"Funny thing," continued Scarlett. "The front door was slightly ajar—I generally have to ring. But I saw no reason to disturb Brush——

"Brush?"

"The Bliss butler. . . . So I merely pushed the door open and entered the hallway. The steel entrance door to the museum, which is on the right of the hallway, is rarely locked, and I opened it. Just as I started to descend the stairs into the museum I saw some one lying in the opposite corner of the room. At first I thought it might be one of the mummy cases we'd unpacked yesterday—the light wasn't very good—and then, as my eyes got adjusted, I realized it was Kyle. He was crumpled up, with his arms extended over his head. . . . Even then I thought he had only fallen in a faint; and I started down the steps toward him."

He paused and passed his handkerchief—which he drew from his cuff—across his shining head.

"By Jove, Vance!—it was a hideous sight. He'd been hit over the head with one of the new statues we placed in the museum yesterday, and his skull had been crushed in like an egg-shell. The statue still lay across his head."

"Did you touch anything?"

"Good heavens, no!" Scarlett spoke with the emphasis of horror. "I was too ill—the thing was ghastly. And it didn't take half an eye to see that the poor beggar was dead."

Vance studied the man closely.

"I say, what was the first thing you did?"

"I called out for Doctor Bliss—he has his study at the top of the little spiral stairs at the rear of the museum. . . ."

"And got no answer?"

"No—no answer. . . . Then—I admit—I got frightened. Didn't like the idea of being found alone with a murdered man, and toddled back toward the front door. Had a notion I'd sneak out and not say I'd been there. . . ."

"Ah!" Vance leaned forward and carefully selected another cigarette. "And then, when you were again in the street, you fell to worryin'."

"That's it precisely! It didn't seem cricket to leave the poor devil there—and still I didn't want to become involved. . . . I was now walking up Fourth Avenue threshing the thing out with myself and bumping against people without seeing 'em. And I happened to think of you. I knew you were acquainted with Doctor Bliss and the outfit, and could give me good advice. And another thing, I felt a little strange in a new country—I wasn't just sure how to go about reporting the matter. . . . So I hurried along to your flat here." He stopped abruptly and watched Vance eagerly. "What's the procedure?"

Vance stretched his long legs before him and lazily contemplated the end of his cigarette.

"I'll take over the procedure," he replied at length. "It's not so dashed complicated, and it varies according to circumstances. One may call the police station, or stick one's head out the window and scream, or confide in a traffic officer, or simply ignore the corpse and wait for some one else to stumble on it. It amounts to the same thing in the end—the murderer is almost sure to get safely away. . . . However, in the present case I'll vary the system a bit by telephoning to the Criminal Courts Building."

He turned to the mother-of-pearl French telephone on the Venetian tabouret at his side, and asked for a number. A few moments later he was speaking to the District Attorney.

"Greetings, Markham old dear. Beastly weather, what?" His voice was too indolent to be entirely convincing. "By the by, Benjamin H. Kyle has passed to his Maker by foul means. He's at present lying on the floor of the Bliss Museum with a badly fractured skull. . . . Oh, yes—quite dead, I understand. Are you interested, by any chance? Thought I'd be unfriendly and notify you. . . . Sad—sad. . . . I'm about to make a few observations *in situ criminis*. . . . Tut, tut! This is no time for reproaches. Don't be so deuced serious. . . . Really, I think you'd better come along. . . . Right-o! I'll await you here."

He replaced the receiver on the bracket and again settled back in his chair.

"The District Attorney will be along anon," he announced, "and we'll probably have time for a few observations before the police arrive."

His eyes shifted dreamily to Scarlett.

"Yes . . . as you say . . . I'm acquainted with the Bliss outfit. Fascinatin' possibilities in the affair: it may prove most entertainin'. . . ." (I knew by his expression that his mind was contemplating—not without a certain degree of anticipatory interest—a new criminal problem.) "So, the front door was ajar, eh? And when you called out no one answered?"

Scarlett nodded but made no audible reply. He was obviously puzzled by Vance's casual reception of his appalling recital.

"Where were the servants? Couldn't they have heard you?"

"Not likely. They're in the other side of the house—down-stairs. The only person who could have heard me was Doctor Bliss—provided he'd been in his study."

"You could have rung the front door-bell, or summoned someone from the main hall," Vance suggested.

Scarlett shifted in his chair uneasily.

"Quite true," he admitted. "But—dash it all, old man!—I was in a funk. . . ."

"Yes, yes—of course. Most natural. *Prima-facie* evidence and all that. Very suspicious, eh what? Still, you had no reason for wanting the old codger out of the way, had you?"

"Oh, my God, no!" Scarlett went pale. "He footed the bills. Without his support the Bliss excavations and the museum itself would go by the board."

Vance nodded.

"Bliss told me of the situation when I was in Egypt. . . . Didn't Kyle own the property in which the museum is situated?"

"Yes—both houses. You see, there are two of 'em. Bliss and his family and young Salveter—Kyle's nephew—live in one, and the museum occupies the other. Two doors have been cut through, and the museum-house entrance has been bricked up. So it's practically one establishment."

"And where did Kyle live?"

"In the brownstone house next to the museum. He owned a block of six or seven adjoining houses along the street."

Vance rose and walked meditatively to the window.

"Do you know how Kyle became interested in Egyptology? It was rather out of his line. His weakness was for hospitals and those unspeakable English portraits of the Gainsborough school. He was one of the bidders for the *Blue Boy*. Luckily for him, he didn't get it."

"It was young Salveter who wangled his uncle into financing Bliss. The lad was a pupil of Bliss's when the latter was instructor of Egyptology at Harvard. When he was graduated he was at a loose end, and old Kyle financed the expedition to give the lad something to do. Very fond of his nephew, was old Kyle."

"And Salveter's been with Bliss ever since?"

"Very much so. To the extent of living in the same house with him. Hasn't left his side since their first visit to Egypt three years ago. Bliss made him Assistant Curator of the Museum. He deserved the post, too. A bright boy—lives and eats Egyptology."

Vance returned to the table and rang for Currie.

"The situation has possibilities," he remarked, in his habitual drawl. . . . "By the by, what other members of the Bliss ménage are there?"

"There's Mrs. Bliss—you met her in Cairo—a strange girl, half Egyptian, much younger than Bliss. And then there's Hani, an Egyptian, whom Bliss brought back with him—or, rather, whom *Mrs.* Bliss brought back with *her*. Hani was an old dependent of Meryt's father. . . ."

"Meryt?"

Scarlett blinked and looked ill at ease.

"I meant Mrs. Bliss," he explained. "Her given name is Meryt-Amen. In Egypt, you see, it's customary to think of a lady by her native name."

"Oh, quite." A slight smile flickered at the corner of Vance's mouth. "And what position does this Hani occupy in the household?"

Scarlett pursed his lips.

"A somewhat anomalous one, if you ask me. Fellahîn stock—a Coptic Christian of sorts. He accompanied old Abercrombie—Meryt's father—on his various tours of exploration. When Abercrombie died, he acted as a kind of foster-father to Meryt. He was attached to the Bliss expedition this spring in some minor capacity as a representative of the Egyptian Government. He's a sort of high-class handy-man about the museum. Knows a lot of Egyptology, too."

"Does he hold any official post with the Egyptian Government now?"

"That I don't know . . . though I wouldn't be surprised if he's doing a bit of patriotic spying. You never can tell about these chaps."

"And do these persons complete the household?"

"There are two American servants—Brush, the butler, and Dingle, the cook."

Currie entered the room at this moment.

"Oh, I say, Currie," Vance addressed him; "an eminent gentleman has just been murdered in the neighborhood, and I am going to view the body. Lay out a dark gray suit and my Bangkok. A sombre tie, of course. . . . And, Currie—the Amontillado first."

"Yes, sir."

Currie received the news as if murders were everyday events in his life, and went out.

"Do you know any reason, Scarlett," Vance asked, "why Kyle should have been put out of the way?"

The other hesitated almost imperceptibly.

"Can't imagine," he said, knitting his brows. "He was a kindly, generous old fellow—pompous and rather vain, but eminently likable. I'm not acquainted with his private life, though. He may have had enemies. . . ."

"Still," suggested Vance, "it's not exactly likely that an enemy would have followed him to the museum and wreaked vengeance on him in a strange place, when any one might have walked in."

Scarlett sat up abruptly.

"But you're not implying that any one in the house——"

"My dear fellow!"

Currie entered the room at this moment with the sherry, and Vance poured out three glasses. When we had drunk the wine he excused himself to dress. Scarlett paced up and down restlessly during the quarter of an hour Vance was absent. He had discarded his cigarette and lighted an old briar pipe which had a most atrocious smell.

Almost at the moment when Vance returned to the library an automobile horn sounded raucously outside. Markham was below waiting for us.

As we walked toward the door Vance asked Scarlett:

"Was it custom'ry for Kyle to be in the museum at this hour of the morning?"

"No, most unusual. But Doctor Bliss had made an appointment with him for this morning, to discuss the expenditures of the last expedition and the possibilities of continuing the excavations next season."

"You knew of this appointment?" Vance asked indifferently.

"Oh, yes. Doctor Bliss called him by phone last night during the conference, when we were assembling the report."

"Well, well." Vance passed out into the hall. "So there were others who also knew that Kyle would be at the museum this morning."

Scarlett halted and looked startled.

"Really, you're not intimating——" he began.

"Who heard the appointment made?" Vance was already descending the stairs.

Scarlett folowed him with puzzled, downcast eyes.

"Well, let me see. . . . There was Salvester, and Hani, and . . ."

"Pray, don't hesitate."

"And Mrs. Bliss."

"Every one in the household, then, but Brush and Dingle?"

"Yes. . . . But see here, Vance; the appointment was for eleven o'clock; and the poor old duffer was done in before half past ten."

"That's most inveiglin'," Vance murmured.

2

THE VENGEANCE OF SAKHMET

(Friday, July 13; 11:30 A. M.)

MARKHAM GREETED Vance with a look of sour reproach.

"What's the meaning of this?" he demanded tartly. "I was in the midst of an important committee meeting——"

"The meaning is still to be ascertained," Vance interrupted lightly, stepping into the car. "The cause of your ungracious presence, however, is a most fascinatin' murder."

Markham shot him a shrewd look, and gave orders to the chauffeur to drive with all possible haste to the Bliss Museum. He recognized the symptoms of Vance's perturbation: a frivolous outward attitude on Vance's part was always indicative of an inner seriousness.

Markham and he had been friends for fifteen years, and Vance had aided him in many of his investigations. In fact, he had come to depend on Vance's assistance in the more complicated criminal cases that came under his jurisdiction.*

It would be difficult to find two men so diametrically opposed to each other temperamentally. Markham was stern, aggressive, straightforward, grave, and a trifle ponderous. Vance was debonair, whimsical, and superficially cynical—an amateur of the arts, and with only an impersonal concern in serious social and moral problems. But this very disparateness in their natures seemed to bind them together.

On our way to the museum, a few blocks distant, Scarlett recounted briefly to the District Attorney the details of his macabre discovery.

Markham listened attentively. Then he turned to Vance.

"Of course, it may be just an act of thuggery—some one from the street. . . ."

"Oh, my aunt!" Vance sighed and shook his head lugubriously. "Really, y' know, thugs don't enter conspicuous private houses in broad daylight and rap persons over the head with statues. They at least bring their own weapons and chose *mises-en-scène* which offer some degree of safety."

"Well, anyway," Markham grumbled, "I've notified Sergeant Heath.† He'll be along presently."

---

* As legal adviser, monetary steward and constant companion of Philo Vance, I kept a complete record of the principal criminal cases in which he participated during Markham's incumbency. Four of these cases I have already recorded in book form—"The Benson Murder Case," "The 'Canary' Murder Case," "The Greene Murder Case," and "The Bishop Murder Case."

† Sergeant Ernest Heath, of the Homicide Bureau, had worked with Markham on most of his important cases. He was an honest, capable, but uninspired police officer, who, after the Benson and the "Canary" murder cases, had come to respect Vance highly. Vance admired the Sergeant; and the two—despite their fundamental differences in outlook and training—collaborated with admirable smoothness.

At the corner of Twentieth Street and Fourth Avenue he halted the car. A uniformed patrolman stood before a call-box, who, on recognizing the District Attorney, came to attention and saluted.

"Hop in the front seat, officer," Markham ordered. "We may need you."

When we reached the museum Markham stationed the officer at the foot of the steps leading to the double front door; and we at once ascended to the vestibule.

I made a casual mental note of the two houses, which Scarlett had already briefly described to us. Each had a twenty-five-foot frontage, and was con- structed of large flat blocks of brownstone. The house on the right had no en- trance—it had obviously been walled up. Nor were there any windows on the areaway level. The house on the left, however, had not been altered. It was three stories high; and a broad flight of stone stairs, with high stone banisters, led to the first floor. The "basement," as was usual in such structures, was a little below the street level. The two houses had at one time been exactly alike, and now, with the alterations and the one entrance, gave the impression of being a single establishment.

As we entered the shallow vestibule—a characteristic of all the old brown- stone mansions along the street—I noticed the heavy oak entrance door, which Scarlett had said was ajar earlier in the morning, was now closed. Vance, too, remarked the fact, for he at once turned to Scarlett and asked:

"Did you close the door when you left the house?"

Scarlett looked seriously at the massive panels, as if trying to recall his ac- tions.

"Really, old man, I can't remember," he answered. "I was devilishly upset. I may have shut the door. . . ."

Vance tried the knob, and the door opened.

"Well, well. The latch has been set anyway. Very careless on some one's part. . . . Is that unusual?"

Scarlett looked astonished.

"Never knew it to be unlatched."

Vance held up his hand, indicating that we were to remain in the vestibule, and stepped quietly inside to the steel door on the right leading to the mu- seum. We could see him open it gingerly but could not distinguish what was beyond. He disappeared for a moment.

"Oh, Kyle's quite dead," he announced sombrely on his return. "And ap- parently no one has discovered him yet." He cautiously reclosed the front door. "We sha'n't take advantage of the latch being set," he added. "We'll abide by the conventions and see who answers." Then he pressed the bell- button.

A few moments later the door was opened by a cadaverous, chlorotic man in butler's livery. He bowed perfunctorily to Scarlett, and coldly inspected the rest of us.

"Brush, I believe." It was Vance who spoke.

The man bowed slightly without taking his eyes off of us.

"Is Doctor Bliss in?" Vance asked.

Brush shifted his gaze interrogatively to Scarlett. Receiving an assuring nod, he opened the door a little wider.

"Yes, sir," he answered. "He's in his study. Who shall I say is calling?"

"You needn't disturb him, Brush." Vance stepped into the entrance hall, and we followed him. "Has the doctor been in his study all morning?"

The butler drew himself up and attempted to reprove Vance with a look of haughty indignation.

Vance smiled, not unkindly.

"Your manner is quite correct, Brush. But we're not wanting lessons in etiquette. This is Mr. Markham, the District Attorney of New York; and we're here for information. Do you care to give it voluntarily?"

The man had caught sight of the uniformed officer at the foot of the stone steps, and his face paled.

"You'll be doing the doctor a favor by answering," Scarlett put in.

"Doctor Bliss has been in his study since nine o'clock," the butler replied, in a tone of injured dignity.

"How can you be sure of that fact?" Vance asked.

"I brought him his breakfast there; and I've been on this floor ever since."

"Doctor Bliss's study," interjected Scarlett, "is at the rear of this hall." He pointed to a curtained door at the end of the wide corridor.

"He should be able to hear us now," remarked Markham.

"No, the door is padded," Scarlett explained. "The study is his *sanctum sanctorum;* and no sounds can reach him from the house."

The butler, his eyes like two glittering pin-points, had started to move away.

"Just a moment, Brush." Vance's voice halted him. "Who else is in the house at this time?"

The man turned, and when he answered it seemed to me that his voice quavered slightly.

"Mr. Hani is up-stairs. He has been indisposed——"

"Oh, has he, now?" Vance took out his cigarette-case. "And the other members of the household?"

"Mrs. Bliss went out about nine—to do some shopping, so I understood her to say—Mr. Salveter left the house shortly afterward."

"And Dingle?"

"She's in the kitchen below, sir."

Vance studied the butler appraisingly.

"You need a tonic, Brush. A combination of iron, arsenic and strychnine would build you up."

"Yes, sir. I've been thinking of consulting a doctor. . . . It's lack of fresh air, sir."

"Just so." Vance had selected one of his beloved *Régies*, and was lighting it with meticulous care. "By the by, Brush; what about Mr. Kyle? He called here this morning, I understand."

"He's in the museum now. . . . I'd forgotten, sir. Doctor Bliss may be with him."

"Indeed! And what time did Mr. Kyle arrive?"

"About ten o'clock."

"Did you admit him?"

"Yes, sir."

"And did you notify Doctor Bliss of his arrival?"

"No, sir. Mr. Kyle told me not to disturb the doctor. He explained that he was early for his appointment, and wished to look over some curios in the museum for an hour or so. He said he'd knock on the doctor's study door later."

"And he went direct into the museum?"

"Yes, sir—in fact, I opened the door for him."

Vance drew luxuriously on his cigarette for a moment.

"One more thing, Brush. I note that the latch on the front door has been set, so that any one from the outside could enter the house without ringing. . . ."

The man gave a slight start and, going quickly to the door, bent over and inspected the lock.

"So it is, sir. . . . Very strange."

Vance watched him closely.

"Why strange?"

"Well, sir, it wasn't unlatched when Mr. Kyle came at ten o'clock. I looked at it specially when I let him in. He said he wished to be left alone in the museum, and as members of the house sometimes leave the door on the latch when they go out for a short time, I made sure that no one had done so this morning. Otherwise they might have come in and disturbed Mr. Kyle without my warning them."

"But, Brush," interjected Scarlett excitedly; "when I got here at half past ten the door was open——"

Vance made an admonitory gesture.

"That's all right, Scarlett." Then he turned back to the butler. "Where did you go after admitting Mr. Kyle?"

"Into the drawing-room." The man pointed to a large sliding door half-way down the hall on the left, at the foot of the stairs.

"And remained there till when?"

"Till ten minutes ago."

"Did you hear Mr. Scarlett come in and go out the front door?"

"No, sir. . . . But then, I was using the vacuum cleaner. The noise of the motor——"

"Quite so. But if the vacuum cleaner's motor was hummin', how do you know that Doctor Bliss did not leave his study?"

"The drawing-room door was open, sir. I'd have seen him if he came out."

"But he might have gone into the museum and left the house by the front door without your hearing him. Y' know, you didn't hear Mr. Scarlett enter."

"That would have been out of the question, sir. Doctor Bliss wore only a light dressing-gown over his pyjamas. His clothes are all up-stairs."

"Very good, Brush. . . . And now, one more question. Has the front door-bell rung since Mr. Kyle's arrival?"

"No, sir."

"Maybe it rang and Dingle answered it. . . . That motor hum, don't y' know."

"She would have come up and told me, sir. She never answers the door in the morning. She's not in presentable habiliments till afternoon."

"Quite characteristically feminine," Vance murmured. . . . "That will be all for the present, Brush. You may go down-stairs and wait for our call. An accident has happened to Mr. Kyle, and we are going to look into it. You are to say nothing . . . understand?" His voice had suddenly become stern and ominous.

Brush drew himself up with a quick intake of breath: he appeared positively ill, and I almost expected him to faint. His face was like chalk.

"Certainly, sir—I understand." His words were articulated with great effort. Then he walked away unsteadily and disappeared down the rear stairs to the left of Doctor Bliss's study door.

Vance spoke in a low voice to Markham, who immediately beckoned to the officer in the street below.

"You are to stand in the vestibule here," he ordered. "When Sergeant Heath and his men come, bring them to us at once. We'll be in there." He indicated the large steel door leading into the museum. "If anyone else calls, hold them and notify us. Don't let any one ring the bell."

The officer saluted and took up his post; and the rest of us, with Vance leading the way, passed through the steel door into the museum.

A flight of carpeted stairs, four feet wide, led down along the wall to the floor of the enormous room beyond, which was on the street level. The first-story floor—the one which had been even with the hallway of the house we had just quitted—had been removed so that the room of the museum was two stories high. Two huge pillars, with steel beams and diagonal joists, had been erected as supports. Moreover, the walls marking the former rooms had been demolished. The result was that the room we had entered occupied the entire width and length of the house—about twenty-five by seventy feet—and had a ceiling almost twenty feet high.

At the front was a series of tall, leaded-glass windows running across the entire width of the building; and at the rear, above a series of oak cabinets, a similar row of windows had been cut. The curtains of the front windows were drawn, but those at the rear were open. The sun had not yet found its way into the room, and the light was dingy.

As we stood for a moment at the head of the steps I noted a small circular iron stairway at the rear leading to a small steel door on the same level as the door through which we had entered.

The arrangement of the museum in relation to the house which served as living quarters for the Blisses, was to prove of considerable importance in Vance's solution of Benjamin H. Kyle's murder, and for purposes of clarity I am including in this record a plan of the two houses. The floor of the museum, as I have said, was on the street level—it had formerly been the "basement" floor. And it must be borne in mind that the rooms indicated on the left-hand half of the plan were one story above the museum floor and half-way between the museum floor and the ceiling.

My eyes at once searched the opposite corner of the room for the murdered man; but that part of the museum was in shadow, and all I could see was a dark mass, like a recumbent human body, in front of the farthest rear cabinet.

Vance and Markham had descended the stairs while Scarlett and I waited on the upper landing. Vance went straightway to the front of the museum and pulled the draw-cords of the curtains. Light flooded the semi-darkness; and for the first time I took in the beautiful and amazing contents of that great room.

In the centre of the opposite wall rose a ten-foot obelisk from Heliopolis, commemorating an expedition of Queen Hat-shepsut of the Eighteenth Dynasty, and bearing her cartouche. To the right and left of the obelisk stood two plaster-cast portrait statues—one of Queen Teti-shiret of the Seventeenth Dynasty, and the other a black replica of the famous Turin statue of Ramses II—considered one of the finest pieces of sculptured portraiture in antiquity.

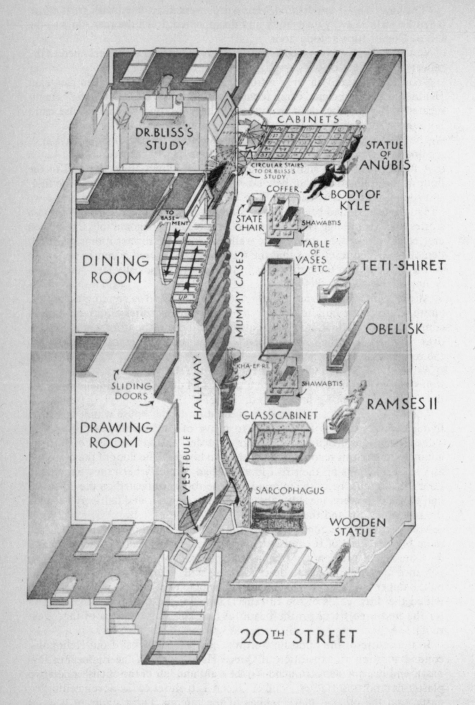

DR. BLISS'S STUDY

CABINETS

STATUE OF ANUBIS

CIRCULAR STAIRS TO DR. BLISS'S STUDY

COFFER

BODY OF KYLE

TO BASEMENT

STATE CHAIR

SHAWABTIS

DINING ROOM

TABLE OF VASES ETC.

TETI-SHIRET

MUMMY CASES

OBELISK

KHA-EF-RE

UP

SLIDING DOORS

SHAWABTIS

RAMSES II

DRAWING ROOM

GLASS CABINET

VESTIBULE HALLWAY

SARCOPHAGUS

WOODEN STATUE

20TH STREET

Above and beside them hung several papyri, framed and under glass, their faded burnt-orange backgrounds—punctuated with red, yellow, green and white patches—making splashes of attractive color against the dingy gray plaster of the wall. Four large limestone bas-reliefs, taken from a Nineteenth-Dynasty tomb at Memphis and containing passages from the Book of the Dead, were aligned above the papyri.

Beneath the front windows stood a black granite Twenty-second-Dynasty sarcophagus fully ten feet long, its front and sides covered with hieroglyphic inscriptions. It was surmounted by a mummy-shaped lid, showing the soul bird, or Ba—with its falcon's form and human head. This sarcophagus was one of the rarest in America, and had been brought to this country by Doctor Bliss from the ancient necropolis at Thebes. In the corner beyond was a cedar-wood statue of an Asiatic, found in Palestine—a relic of the conquests of Thut-mosè III.

Near the foot of the stairs on which I stood loomed the majestic Kha-ef-Rê statue from the Fourth Dynasty. It was made of gray plaster of Paris, varnished and polished in imitation of the original diorite. It stood nearly eight feet high; and its dignity and power and magistral calm seemed to dominate the entire museum.*

To the right of the statue, and extending all the way to the spiral stairs at the rear, was a row of anthropoid mummy cases, gaudily decorated in gold and brilliant colors. Above them hung two enormously enlarged tinted photographs—one showing the Colossi of Amen-hotpe III,† the other depicting the great Amûn Temple at Karnak.

Around the two supporting columns in the centre of the museum deep shelves had been built, and on them reposed a fascinating array of *shawabtis*—beautifully carved and gaily painted wooden figures.

Extending between the two pillars was a long, low, velvet-covered table, perhaps fourteen feet in length, bearing a beautiful collection of alabaster perfumery and canopic vases, blue lotiform jars, kohl pots of polished obsidian, and several cylindrical carved cosmetic jars of semi-translucent and opaque alabaster. At the rear of the room was a squat coffer with inlays of blue glazed faience, white and red ivory and black ebony; and beside it stood a carved chair of state, decorated in gesso and gilt, and bearing a design of lotus flowers and buds.

Across the front of the room ran a long glass show-case containing pectoral collars of cloisonné, amulets of majolica, shell pendants, girdles of gold cowries, rhombic beads of carnelian and feldspar, bracelets and anklets and finger-rings, gold and ebony fans, and a collection of scarabs of most of the Pharaohs down to Ptolemaic times.

Around the walls, just below the ceiling, ran a five-foot frieze—a sectional copy of the famous Rhapsody of Pen-ta-Weret, commemorating the victory of Ramses II over the Hittites at Kadesh in Syria.

As soon as Vance had opened the heavy curtains of the front windows he

---

* Kha-ef-Rê was the originator of the great Sphinx, and also of one of the three great Gizeh pyramids—*Wer Kha-ef-Rê* (Kha-ef-Rê is mighty), now known as the Second Pyramid.

† Popularly, and incorrectly, called the Memnon Colossi.

and Markham moved toward the rear of the room. Scarlett and I descended the stairs and followed them. Kyle was lying on his face, his legs slightly drawn up under him, and his arms reaching out and encircling the feet of a life-sized statue in the corner. I had seen reproductions of this statue many times, but I did not know its name.

It was Vance who enlightened me. He stood contemplating the huddled body of the dead man, and slowly his eyes shifted to the serene sculpture—a brown limestone carving of a man with a jackal's head, holding a sceptre.

"Anûbis," he murmured, his face set tensely. "The Egyptian god of the underworld. Y' know, Markham, Anûbis was the god who prowled about the tombs of the dead. He guided the dead through Amentet—the shadowy abode of Osiris. He plays an important part in the Book of the Dead—he symbolized the grave; and he weighed the souls of men, and assigned each to its abode. Without Anûbis's help the soul would never have found the Realm of Shades. He was the only friend of the dying and the dead. . . . And here is Kyle, in an attitude of final and pious entreaty before him."

Vance's eyes rested for a moment on the benignant features of Anûbis. Then his gaze moved dreamily to the prostrate man who, but for the hideous wound in his head, might have been paying humble obeisance to the underworld god. He pointed to the smaller statue which had caused Kyle's death.

This statue was about two feet long and was black and shiny. It still lay diagonally across the back of the murdered man's skull: it seemed to have been caught and held there in the concavity made by the blow. An irregular pool of dark blood had formed beside the head, and I noted—without giving the matter any particular thought—that one point of the periphery of the pool had been smeared outward over the polished maple-wood floor.

"I don't like this, Markham," Vance was saying in a low voice. "I don't like it at all. . . . That diorite statue, which killed Kyle, is Sakhmet, the Egyptian goddess of vengeance—the destroying element. She was the goddess who protected the good and annihilated the wicked—the goddess who slew. The Egyptians believed in her violent power; and there are many strange legend'ry tales of her dark and terrible acts of revenge. . . ."

3

SCARABÆUS SACER

(Friday, July 13; noon)

VANCE FROWNED slightly and studied the small black figure for a moment.

"It may mean nothing—surely nothing supernatural—but the fact that this particular statue was chosen for the murder makes me wonder if there may be something diabolical and sinister and superstitious in this affair."

"Come, come, Vance!" Markham spoke with forced matter-of-factness. "This is modern New York, not legendary Egypt."

"Yes . . . oh, yes. But superstition is still a ruling factor in so-called human nature. Moreover, there are many more convenient weapons in this room—weapons fully as lethal and more readily wielded. Why should a cumbersome, heavy statue of Sakhmet have been chosen for the deed? . . . In any event, it took a strong man to swing it with such force."

He looked toward Scarlett, whose eyes had been fastened on the dead man with a stare of fascination.

"Where was this statue kept?"

Scarlett blinked.

"Why—let me see. . . ." He was obviously trying to collect his wits. "Ah, yes. On the top of that cabinet." He pointed unsteadily to the row of wide shelves in front of Kyle's body. "It was one of the new pieces we unpacked yesterday. Hani placed it there. You see, we used that end cabinet temporarily for the new items, until we could arrange and catalogue 'em properly."

There were ten sections in the row of cabinets that extended across the rear of the museum, each one being about two and a half feet wide and a little over seven feet high. These cabinets—which in reality were but open shelves—were filled with all manner of curios: scores of examples of pottery and wooden vases, scent bottles, bows and arrows, adzes, swords, daggers, sistra, bronze and copper hand-mirrors, ivory game boards, perfume boxes, whip handles, palm-leaf sandals, wooden combs, palettes, head rests, reed baskets, carved spoons, plasterers' tools, sacrificial flint knives, funerary masks, statuettes, necklaces, and the like.

Each cabinet had a separate curtain of a material which looked like silk rep, suspended with brass rings on a small metal rod. The curtains to all the cabinets were drawn open, with the exception of the one on the end cabinet before which the dead body of Kyle lay. The curtain of this cabinet was only partly drawn.

Vance had turned around.

"And what about the Anûbis, Scarlett?" he asked. "Was it a recent acquisition?"

"That came yesterday, too. It was placed in that corner—to keep the shipment together."

Vance nodded, and walked to the partly curtained cabinet. He stood for several moments peering into the shelves.

"Very interestin'," he murmured, almost as if to himself. "I see you have a most unusual post-Hyksos bearded sphinx. . . . And that blue-glass vessel is very lovely . . . though not so lovely as yon blue-paste lion's-head. . . . Ah! I note many evidences of old Intef's bellicose nature—that battle-ax, for instance. . . . And—my word!—there are some scimitars and daggers which look positively Asiatic. And"—he peered closely into the top shelf—"a most fascinatin' collection of ceremonial maces."

"Things Doctor Bliss picked up on his recent expedition," explained Scarlett. "Those flint and porphyry maces came from the antechamber of Intef's tomb. . . ."

At this moment the great metal door of the museum creaked on its hinges, and Sergeant Ernest Heath and three detectives appeared at the head of the stairs. The Sergeant immediately descended into the room, leaving his men on the little landing.

He greeted Markham with the usual ritualistic handshake.

"Howdy, sir," he rumbled. "I got here as soon as I could. Brought three of the boys from the Bureau, and sent word to Captain Dubois and Doc Doremus* to follow us up."

"It looks as if we might be in for another unpleasant scandal, Sergeant." Markham's tone was pessimistic. "That's Benjamin H. Kyle."

Heath stared aggressively at the dead man and grunted.

"A nasty job," he commented through his teeth. "What in hell is that thing he was croaked with?"

Vance, who had been leaning over the shelves of the cabinet, his back to us, now turned round with a genial smile.

"That, Sergeant, is Sakhmet, an ancient goddess of the primitive Egyptians. But she isn't in hell, so to speak. This gentleman, however,"—he touched the tall statue of Anûbis—"is from the nether regions."

"I mighta known you'd be here, Mr. Vance." Heath grinned with genuine friendliness, and held out his hand. "I've got you down on my suspect list. Every time there's a fancy homicide, who do I find on the spot but Mr. Philo Vance! . . . Glad to see you, Mr. Vance. I reckon you'll get your psychological processes to working now and clean this mystery up *pronto.*"

"It'll take more than psychology to solve this case, I'm afraid." Vance had grasped the Sergeant's hand cordially. "A smatterin' of Egyptology might help, don't y' know."

"I'll leave that nifty stuff to you, Mr. Vance. What I want, first and foremost, is the finger-prints of that—that——" He bent over the small statue of Sakhmet. "That's the damnedest thing I ever saw. The guy who sculptured that was cuckoo. It's got a lion's head with a big platter on the dome."

"The lion's head of Sakhmet is undoubtedly totemistic, Sergeant," explained Vance, good-naturedly. "And that 'platter' is a representation of the solar disk. The snake peering from the forehead is a cobra—or uræus—and was the sign of royalty."

"Have it your own way, sir." The Sergeant had become impatient. "What I want is the finger-prints."

He swung about and walked toward the front of the museum.

"Hey, Snitkin!" he called belligerently to one of the men on the stair landing. "Relieve that officer outside—send him back to his beat. And bring Dubois in here as soon as he shows up." Then he returned to Markham. "Who'll give me the low-down on this, sir?"

Markham introduced him to Scarlett.

"This gentleman," he said, "found Mr. Kyle. He can tell you all we know of the case thus far."

Scarlett and Heath talked together for five minutes or so, the Sergeant maintaining throughout the conversation an attitude of undisguised suspicion. It was a basic principle with him that every one was guilty until his innocence had been completely and irrefutably established.

Vance in the meantime had been bending over Kyle's body with an intentness that puzzled me. Presently his eyes narrowed slightly and he went down on one knee, thrusting his head forward to within a foot of the floor. Then he

---

* Captain Dubois was then the finger-print expert of the New York Police Department; and Doctor Emanuel Doremus was the Medical Examiner.

SCARAB OF INTEF V

took out his monocle, polished it carefully, and adjusted it. Markham and I both watched him in silence. After a few moments he straighened up.

"I say, Scarlett; is there a magnifyin' glass handy?"

Scarlett, who had just finished talking to Sergeant Heath, went at once to the glass case containing the scarabs and opened one of the drawers.

"What sort of museum would this be without a magnifier?" he asked, with a feeble attempt at jocularity, holding out a Coddington lens.

Vance took it and turned to Heath.

"May I borrow your flash-light, Sergeant?"

"Sure thing!" Heath handed him a push-button flash.

Vance again knelt down, and with the flash-light in one hand and the lens in the other, inspected a tiny oblong object that lay about a foot from Kyle's body.

"*Nisut Biti . . . Intef . . . Se Rê . . . Nub-Kheper-Rê.*" His voice was low and resonant.

The Sergeant put his hands in his pockets and sniffed.

"And what language might that be, Mr. Vance?" he asked.

"It's the transliteration of a few ancient Egyptian hieroglyphs. I'm reading from this scarab. . . ."

The Sergeant had become interested. He stepped forward and leaned over the object that Vance was inspecting.

"A scarab, huh?"

"Yes, Sergeant. Sometimes called a scarabee, or scarabæid, or scarabæus—that is to say, beetle. . . . This little oval bit of lapis-lazuli was a sacred symbol of the old Egyptians. . . . This particular one, by the by, is most fascinatin'. It is the state seal of Intef V—a Pharaoh of the Seventeenth Dynasty. About 1650 B.C.—or over 3,500 year ago—he wore it. It bears the title and throne name of Intef-o, or Intef. His Horus name was Nefer-Kheperu, if I remember correctly. He was one of the native Egyptian rulers at Thebes during the reign of the Hyksos in the Delta.* The tomb of this gentleman is the one that Doctor Bliss has been excavating for several years. . . . And you of course note, Sergeant, that the scarab is set in a modern scarf-pin. . . ."

---

* The daughter of this particular Pharaoh—Nefra—incidentally is the titular heroine of H. Rider Haggard's romance, "Queen of the Dawn." Haggard, following the chronology of H. R. Hall, placed Intef in the Fourteenth Dynasty instead of the Seventeenth, making him a contemporary of the great Hyksos Pharaoh, Apopi, whose son Khyan—the hero of the book—marries Nefra. The researches of Bliss and Weigall seem to have demonstrated that this relationship is an anachronism.

Heath grunted with satisfaction. Here, at least, was a piece of tangible evidence.

"A beetle, is it? And a scarf-pin! . . . Well, Mr. Vance, I'd like to get my hands on the bird who wore that blue thingumajig in his cravat."

"I can enlighten you on that point, Sergeant." Vance rose to his feet and looked toward the little metal door at the head of the circular stairway. "That scarf-pin is the property of Doctor Bliss."

4

TRACKS IN THE BLOOD

(Friday, July 13; 12:15 P.M.)

SCARLETT HAD been watching Vance intently, a look of horrified amazement on his round bronzed face.

"I'm afraid you're right, Vance," he said, nodding with reluctance. "Doctor Bliss found that scarab on the site of the excavation of Intef's tomb two years ago. He didn't mention it to the Egyptian authorities; and when he returned to America he had it set in a scarf-pin. But surely its presence here can have no significance. . . ."

"Really, now!" Vance faced Scarlett with a steady gaze. "I remember quite well the episode at Dirâ Abu 'n-Nega. I was *particeps criminis,* as it were, to the theft. But since there were other scarabs of Intef, as well as a cylindrical seal, in the British Museum, I turned my eyes the other way. . . . This is the first time I've had a close look at the scarab. . . ."

Heath had started toward the front stairs.

"Say, you—Emery!" he bawled, addressing one of the two men on the landing. "Round up this guy Bliss, and bring 'im in here——"

"Oh, I say, Sergeant!" Vance hastened after him and put a restraining hand on his arm. "Why so precipitate? Let's be calm. . . . This isn't the correct moment to drag Bliss in. And when we want him all we have to do is to knock on that little door—he's undoubtedly in his study, and he can't run away. . . . And there's a bit of prelimin'ry surveying to be done first."

Heath hesitated and made a grimace. Then:

"Never mind, Emery. But go out in the back yard, and see that nobody tries to make a getaway. . . . And you, Hennessey,"—he addressed the other man—"stand in the front hall. If any one tries to leave the house, grab 'em and bring 'em in—see?"

The two detectives disappeared with a stealth that struck me as highly ludicrous.

"Got something up your sleeve, sir?" the Sergeant asked, eying Vance hopefully. "This homicide, though, don't look very complicated to me. Kyle gets bumped off by a blow over the head, and beside him is a scarf-pin belonging to Doctor Bliss. . . . That's simple enough, ain't it?"

"Too dashed simple, Sergeant," Vance returned quietly, contemplating the dead man. "That's the whole trouble. . . ."

Suddenly he moved toward the statue of Anûbis, and leaning over, picked up a folded piece of paper which had lain almost hidden beneath one of Kyle's outstretched hands. Carefully unfolding it, he held it toward the light. It was a legal-sized sheet of paper, and was covered with figures.

"This document," he remarked, "must have been in Kyle's possession when he passed from this world. . . . Know anything about it, Scarlett?"

Scarlett stepped forward eagerly and took the paper with an unsteady hand.

"Good Heavens!" he exclaimed. "It's the report of expenditures we drew up last night. Doctor Bliss was working on this tabulation——"

"Uh-huh!" Heath grinned with vicious satisfaction. "So! Our dead friend here musta seen Bliss this morning—else how could he have got that paper?"

Scarlett frowned.

"I must say it looks that way," he conceded. "This report hadn't been made out when the rest of us knocked off last night. Doctor Bliss said he was going to draw it up before Mr. Kyle got here this morning." He seemed utterly nonplussed as he handed the paper back to Vance. "But there's something wrong somewhere. . . . You know, Vance, it's not reasonable——"

"Don't be futile, Scarlett." Vance's admonition cut him short. "If Doctor Bliss had wielded the statue of Sakhmet, why should he have left this report here to incriminate himself? . . . As you say, something is wrong somewhere."

"Wrong, is it!" Heath scoffed. "There's that beetle—and now we find this report. What more do you want, Mr. Vance?"

"A great deal more." Vance spoke softly. "A man doesn't ordinarily commit murder and leave such obvious bits of direct evidence strewn all about the place. . . . It's childish."

Heath snorted.

"Panic—that's what it was. He got scared and beat it in a hurry. . . ."

Vance's eyes rested on the little metal door of Doctor Bliss's study.

"By the by, Scarlett," he asked; "when did you last see that scarab scarf-pin?"

"Last night." The man had begun to pace restlessly up and down. "It was beastly hot in the study, and Doctor Bliss took off his collar and four-in-hand and laid 'em on the table. The scarab pin was sticking in the cravat."

"Ah!" Vance's gaze did not shift from the little door. "The pin lay on the table during the conference, eh? . . . And, as you told me, Hani and Mrs. Bliss and Salveter and yourself were present."

"Right."

"Any one, then, might have seen it and taken it?"

"Well—yes, . . . I suppose so."

Vance thought a moment.

"Still, this report . . . most curious! . . . I could bear to know how it got in Kyle's hands. You say it hadn't been completed when the conference broke up?"

"Oh, no." Scarlett seemed hesitant about answering. "We all turned in our figures, and Doctor Bliss said he was going to add 'em up and present them to Kyle to-day. Then he telephoned Kyle—in our presence—and made an appointment with him for eleven this morning."

"Is that all he said to Kyle on the phone?"

"Practically . . . though I believe he mentioned that new shipment that came yesterday——"

"Indeed? Very interestin'. . . . And what did Doctor Bliss say about the shipment?"

"As I remember—I really didn't pay much attention—he told Kyle that the crates had been unpacked, and added that he wanted Kyle to inspect their contents. . . . You see, there was some doubt whether Kyle would finance another expedition. The Egyptian Government had been somewhat snooty, and had retained most of the choicest items for the Cairo Museum. Kyle didn't like this, and as he had already put oodles of money in the enterprise, he was inclined to back out. No *kudos* for him, you understand. . . . In fact, Kyle's attitude was the cause of the conference. Doctor Bliss wanted to show him the exact cost of the former excavations and try to induce him to finance a continuation of the work. . . ."

"And the old boy refused to do it," supplemented Heath; "and then the doctor got excited and cracked him over the head with that black statue."

"You *will* insist that life is so simple, Sergeant," sighed Vance.

"I'd sure hate to think it was as complex as you make it, Mr. Vance." Heath's retort came very near to an expression of dignified sarcasm.

The words were scarcely out of his mouth when the main door was opened quietly and a middle-aged, dark-complexioned man in native Egyptian costume appeared at the head of the front stairs. He surveyed us with inquisitive calm, and slowly and with great deliberation of movement, descended into the museum.

"Good-morning, Mr. Scarlett," he said, with a sardonic smile. He glanced at the murdered man. "I observe that tragedy has visited this household."

"Yes, Hani." Scarlett spoke with a certain condescension. "Mr. Kyle has been murdered. These gentlemen"—he made a slight gesture in our direction—"are investigating the crime."

Hani bowed gravely. He was of medium height, somewhat slender, and gave one the impression of contemptuous aloofness. There was a distinct glint of racial animosity in his close-set eyes. His face was relatively short—he was markedly dolichocephalic—and his straight nose had the typical rounded extremity of the true Copt. His eyes were brown—the color of his skin—and his eyebrows bushy. He wore a close-cut, semi-gray beard, and his lips were full and sensual. His head was covered by a soft dark tarbûsh bearing a pendant tassel of blue silk, and about his shoulders hung a long kaftan of red-and-white striped cotton, which fell to his ankles and barely revealed his yellow-leather babûshes.

He stood for a full minute looking down at Kyle's body, without any trace of repulsion or even regret. Then he lifted his head and contemplated the statue of Anûbis. A queer devotional expression came over his face; and presently his lips curled in a faint sardonic smile. After a moment he made a sweeping gesture with his left hand and, turning slowly, faced us. But his eyes were not on us—they were fixed on some distant point far beyond the front windows.

"There is no need for an investigation, gentlemen," he said, in a sepulchral tone. "It is the judgment of Sakhmet. For many generations the sacred tombs of our forefathers have been violated by the treasure-seeking Occidental. But the gods of Egypt were powerful gods and protected their children. They have been patient. But the despoilers have gone too far. It was time for the wrath of their vengeance to strike. And it has struck. The tomb of Intef-o has been saved from the vandal. Sakhmet has pronounced her judgment, just as she did when she slaughtered the rebels at Henen-ensu* to protect her father, Rê, against their treason."

He paused and drew a deep breath.

"But Anûbis will never guide a sacrilegious giaour to the Halls of Osiris— however reverently he may plead. . . ."

Both Hani's manner and his words were impressive; and as he spoke I remembered, with an unpleasant feeling, the recent tragedy of Lord Carnarvon and the strange tales of ancient sorcery that sprang up to account for his death on supernatural grounds.

"Quite unscientific, don't y' know." Vance's voice, cynical and drawling, brought me quickly back to the world of reality. "I seriously question the ability of that piece of black igneous rock to accomplish a murder unless wielded by ordin'ry human hands. . . . And if you *must* talk tosh, Hani, we'd be tremendously obliged if you'd do it in the privacy of your bedchamber. It's most borin'."

The Egyptian shot him a look of hatred.

"The West has much to learn from the East regarding matters of the soul," he pronounced oracularly.

"I dare say." Vance smiled blandly. "But the soul is not now under discussion. The West, which you despise, is prone to practicality; and you'd do well to forgo the metempsychosis for the nonce and answer a few questions which the District Attorney would like to put to you."

Hani bowed his aequiescence; and Markham, taking his cigar from his mouth, fixed a stern look upon him.

"Where were you all this forenoon?" he asked.

"In my room—up-stairs. I was not well."

"And you heard no sounds in the museum here?"

"It would have been impossible for me to hear any sound in this room."

"And you saw no one enter or leave the house?"

"No. My room is at the rear, and I did not leave it until a few moments ago."

Vance put the next question.

"Why did you leave it then?"

"I had work to do here in the museum," the man replied sullenly.

"But I understand you heard Doctor Bliss make an appointment with Mr. Kyle for eleven this morning." Vance was watching Hani sharply. "Did you intend to interrupt the conference?"

"I had forgotten about the appointment." The answer did not come spontaneously. "If I had found Doctor Bliss and Mr. Kyle in conference I would have returned to my room."

"To be sure." Vance's tone held a tinge of sarcasm. "I say, Hani, what's your full name?"

The Egyptian hesitated, but only for a second. Then he said:

"Anûpu Hani."†

---

* The ancient Egyptian name of Heracleopolis.

† This unusual name, I learned later, was the result of his father's interest in Egyptian mythology while in Maspero's service.

Vance's eyebrows went up, and there was irony in the slow smile that crept to the corners of his mouth.

" 'Anûpu'," he repeated. "Most allurin'. *Anûpu,* I believe, was the Egyptian form for Anûbis, what? You would seem to be identified with that unpleasant-lookin' gentleman in the corner, with the jackal's head."

Hani compressed his thick lips and made no response.

"It really doesn't matter, y' know," Vance remarked lightly. . . . "By the by, wasn't it you who placed the small statue of Sakhmet atop the cabinet yonder?"

"Yes. It was unpacked yesterday."

"And was it you who drew the curtain across the end cabinet?"

"Yes—at Doctor Bliss's request. The objects in it were in great disarray. We had not yet had time to arrange them."

Vance turned thoughtfully to Scarlett.

"Just what was said by Doctor Bliss to Mr. Kyle over the phone last night?"

"I think I've told you everything, old man." Scarlett appeared both puzzled and startled at Vance's persistent curiosity on this point. "He simply made the appointment for eleven o'clock, saying he'd have the financial report ready at that time."

"And what did he say about the new shipment?"

"Nothing, except that he was desirous of having Mr. Kyle see the items."

"And did he mention their whereabouts?"

"Yes; I recall that he said they had been placed in the end cabinet—the one with the closed curtains."

Vance nodded with a satisfaction I did not then understand.

"That accounts probably for Kyle's having come early to inspect the—what shall I say?—loot."

He faced Hani again with an engaging smile.

"And is it not true that you and the others at the conference last night heard this phone call?"

"Yes—we all heard it." The Egyptian had become morose; but I noticed that he was studying Vance surreptitiously from the corner of his eye.

"And—I take it—," mused Vance, "any one who knew Kyle might have surmised that he would come early to inspect the items in that end cabinet. . . . Eh, Scarlett?"

Scarlett shifted uneasily and looked at the great figure of the serene Kha-ef-Rê.

"Well—since you put it that way—yes. . . . Fact is, Vance, Doctor Bliss suggested that Mr. Kyle come early and have a peep at the treasures."

These ramifications had begun to irritate Sergeant Heath.

"Pardon me, Mr. Vance," he blurted, with ill-concealed annoyance; "but do you happen to be the defense attorney for this Doctor Bliss? If you aren't working hard to alibi him, I'm the Queen of Sheba."

"You're certainly not Solomon, Sergeant," returned Vance. "Don't you care to weigh all the possibilities?"

"Weigh hell!" Heath was losing his temper. "I want a heart-to-heart talk with this guy who wore that beetle-pin and drew up that report. I know clean-cut evidence when I see it."

"I don't doubt that for a moment," Vance spoke dulcetly. "But even clean-cut evidence may have various interpretations. . . ."

Snitkin threw open the door noisily at this point, and Doctor Doremus, the Medical Examiner, tripped jauntily down the stairs. He was a thin, nervous man, with a seamed, prematurely old face which carried a look at once crabbed and jocular.

"Good morning, gentlemen," he greeted us breezily. He shook hands perfunctorily with Markham and Heath, and squaring off, gave Vance an exaggeratedly disgruntled look.

"Well, well!" he exclaimed, tilting his straw hat at an even more rakish angle. "Wherever there's a murder I find you, sir." He glanced at his wristwatch. "Lunch time, by George!" His flashing gaze moved about the museum and came to rest on one of the anthropoid mummy cases. "This place don't look healthy. . . . Where's the body, Sergeant?"

Heath had been standing before the prostrate body of Kyle. He now moved aside and pointed to the dead man.

"That's him, doc."

Doremus came forward and peered indifferently at the corpse.

"Well, he's dead," he pronounced, cocking his eye at Heath.

"Honest to Gawd?" The Sergeant was good-naturedly sarcastic.

"That's the way it strikes me—though since Carrel's experiments you never can tell. . . . Anyway, I'll stand by my decision." He chuckled, and kneeling down, touched one of Kyle's hands. Then he moved one of the dead man's legs sidewise. "And he's been dead for about two hours—not longer, maybe less."

Heath took out a large handkerchief and, with great care, lifted the black statue of Sakhmet from Kyle's head.

"I'm saving this for finger-prints. . . . Any signs of a struggle, doc?"

Doremus turned the body over and made a careful inspection of the face, the hands, and the clothes.

"Don't see any," he returned laconically. "Was struck from the rear, I'd say. Fell forward, arms outstretched. Didn't move after he'd hit the floor."

"Any chance, doctor, of his having been dead when the statue hit him?" asked Vance.

"Nope." Doremus rose and teetered on his toes impatiently. "Too much blood for that."

"Simple case of assault, then?"

"Looks like it. . . . I'm no wizard, though." The doctor had become irritable. "The autopsy will settle that point."

"Can we have the *post-mortem* report immediately?" Markham made the request.

"As soon as the Sergeant gets the body to the mortuary."

"It'll be there by the time you've finished lunch, doc," said Heath. "I ordered the wagon before I left the Bureau."

"That being that, I'll run along." Again Doremus shook hands with Markham and Heath, and throwing a friendly salutation to Vance, walked briskly out of the room.

I had noticed that ever since Heath had placed the statue of Sakhmet to one side he had stood staring impatiently at the small pool of blood. As soon as

Doremus had departed he knelt down and became doggedly interested in something on the floor. He took out his flashlight, which Vance had returned to him, and focussed it on the edge of the blood-pool at the point where I had noted the outward smear. Then, after a moment, he moved a short distance away, and again shot his light on a faint smudge which stained the yellow wood floor. Once more he shifted his position—this time toward the little spiral stairs. A grunt of satisfaction escaped him now, and rising, he walked, in a wide circle, to the stairs themselves. There he again knelt down and ran the beam of his flash-light over the lower steps. On the third step the ray of light suddenly halted, and the Sergeant's face shot forward in an attitude of intense concentration.

A grin slowy overspread his broad features, and straightening up, he brought a gaze of triumph to bear on Vance.

"I've got the case tied up in a sack now, sir," he announced.

"I take it," replied Vance, "you've found the spoor of the murderer."

"I'll say!" Heath nodded with the deliberate emphasis of finality. "It's just like I told you. . . ."

"Don't be too positive, Sergeant." Vance's face had grown sombre. "The obvious explanation is often the wrong one."

"Yeah?" Heath turned to Scarlett. "Listen, Mr. Scarlett, I got a question to ask you—and I want a straight answer." Scarlett bristled, but the Sergeant paid no attention to his resentment. "What kind of shoes does this Doctor Bliss generally wear around the house?"

Scarlett hesitated, and looked appealingly at Vance.

"Tell the Sergeant whatever you know," Vance advised him. "This is no time for reticence. You can trust me. There's no question of disloyalty now. The truth, d' ye see, is all that matters."

Scarlett cleared his throat nervously.

"Rubber tennis shoes," he said, in a low voice. "Ever since his first expedition in Egypt he has had weak feet—they troubled him abominably. He got relief by wearing white canvas sneakers with rubber soles."

"Sure he did." Heath walked back toward the body of Kyle. "Step over here a minute, Mr. Vance. I got something to show you."

Vance moved forward, and I followed him.

"Take a look at that footprint," the Sergeant continued, pointing toward the smear at the edge of the pool of blood where Kyle's head had lain. "It don't show up much till you get close to it . . . but, once you spot it, you'll notice that it has marks of a rubber-soled shoe, with crossings like a checker-board on the sole and round spots on the heel."

Vance bent over and inspected the footprint in the blood.

"Quite right, Sergeant." He had become very grave and serious.

"And now look here," Heath went on, pointing to two other smudges on the floor half-way to the iron stairs.

Vance leaned over the spots, and nodded.

"Yes," he admitted. "Those marks were probably made by the murderer. . . ."

"And once more, sir." Heath went to the stairs and flashed his pocket-light on the third step.

Vance adjusted his monocle and looked closely. Then he rose and stood still for a moment, his chin resting in the palm of his hand.

"How about it, Mr. Vance?" the Sergeant demanded. "Is that evidence enough for you?"

Markham stepped to the foot of the circular stairway, and placed his hand on Vance's shoulder.

"Why this stubbornness, old friend?" he asked in a kindly voice. "It begins to look like a clear case."

Vance lifted his eyes.

"A clear case—yes! But a clear case of what? . . .It doesn't make sense. Does a man of Bliss's mentality brutally murder a man with whom he is known to have had an appointment, and then leave his scarab-pin and a financial report, which no one else could have produced, on the scene of the crime, to involve himself? And, lest that evidence wasn't enough, is he going to leave bloody footprints, of a distintive and personal design, leading from the body to his study? . . . Is it reasonable?"

"It may not be reasonable," Markham conceded; "but these things are nevertheless facts. And there's nothing to be done but confront Doctor Bliss with them."

"I suppose you're right." Vance's eyes again drifted toward the little metal door at the head of the spiral stairs. "Yes . . . the time has come to put Bliss on the carpet. . . . But I don't like it, Markham. There's something awry. . . . Maybe the doctor himself can enlighten us. Let me fetch him— I've known him for several years."

Vance turned and ascended the stairs, taking care not to step on the telltale footprint the Sergeant had discovered.

5

MERYT-AMEN

(Friday, July 13; 12:45 P.M.)

VANCE KNOCKED on the narrow door and reached into his pocket for his cigarette-case. We on the floor below watched the metal panel in silent expectancy. A feeling of dread, for some unknown reason, assailed me, and my muscles went tense. To this day I cannot explain the cause of my fear; but at that moment a chill came over my heart. All the evidence that had come to light pointed unmistakably toward the great Egyptologist in the little room beyond.

Vance alone seemed unconcerned. He casually lit his cigarette, and when he had replaced the lighter in his pocket, he knocked again at the door—this time more loudly. Still no answer.

"Very curious," I heard him murmur.

Then he raised his arm and pounded on the metal with a force that sent reverberating echoes through the great room of the museum.

At last, after several moments of ominous silence, there was a sound of a knob turning, and the heavy door swung slowly inward.

In the opening stood a tall, slender figure of a man in his middle forties. He wore a peacock-blue dressing-gown of self-figured silk, which reached to his ankles, and his sparse yellow hair was tousled as if he had just risen from bed. Indeed, his entire appearance was that of one who had suddenly been roused from a deep sleep. His eyes were hazy, and their lids drooped; and he clung to the inside knob of the door for support. He actually swayed a little as he peered dully at Vance.

Withal, he was a striking figure. His face was long and thin, rugged and deeply tanned. His forehead was high and narrow—a scholar's brow; but his nose, which was curved like an eagle's beak, was his most prominent characteristic. His mouth was straight, and surmounted a chin that was so square as to be cubic. His cheeks were sunken, and I got the distinct impression of a man who was physically ill but who overrode the ravages of disease by sheer nervous vitality.

For a moment he stared at Vance uncomprehendingly. Then—like a person coming out of an anæsthetic—he blinked several times and took a deep inspiration.

"Ah!" His voice was thick and a trifle rasping. "Mr. Vance! . . . A long time since I've seen you. . . ." His eyes drifted about the museum and came to rest on the little group at the foot of the stairs. "I don't quite understand. . . ." He passed his hand slowly over the top of his head, and ran his fingers through his rumpled hair. "My head feels so heavy . . . please forgive me . . . I—I must have been asleep. . . . Who are these gentlemen below? . . . I recognize Scarlett and Hani. . . . It's been devilishly hot in my study."

"A serious accident has happened, Doctor Bliss," Vance informed him, in a low voice. "Would you mind stepping down into the museum? . . . We need your help."

"An accident!" Bliss drew himself up, and for the first time since he appeared at the door his eyes opened wide. "A serious accident? . . . What has happened? Not burglars, I hope. I've always been worried——"

"No, there have been no burglars, doctor." Vance steadied him as he walked nervously down the circular stairs.

When he reached the floor of the museum every eye in the room, I felt sure, was focussed on his feet. Certainly my own initial instinct was to inspect them; and I noticed that Heath, who stood beside me, had concentrated his gaze on the doctor's foot-covering. But if any of us expected to find Bliss shod in rubber-soled tennis shoes, he was disappointed. The man wore a pair of soft vici-kid bedroom slippers, dyed blue to match his dressing gown and adorned with orange trimmings.

I did note, however, that his gray-silk pyjamas, which showed through the deep V-opening of his gown, had a broad, turned-over collar in which a mauve four-in-hand had been loosely knotted.

His eyes swept the little group before him and returned to Vance.

"You say there have been no burglars?" His voice was still vague and thick. "What, then, was the accident, Mr. Vance?"

"An accident far more serious than burglars, doctor," replied Vance, who had not released his hold on the other's arm. "Mr. Kyle is dead."

"Kyle dead!" Bliss's mouth sagged open, and a look of hopeless amazement came into his eyes. "But—but . . . I talked to him last night. He was to come here this morning . . . regarding the new expedition. . . . Dead? All my work—my life's work—ended!" He slumped into one of the small folding wooden chairs of which there were perhaps a score scattered about the museum. A look of tragic resignation settled on his face. "This is terrible news."

"I'm very sorry, doctor," Vance murmured consolingly. "I fully understand your great disappointment...."

Bliss rose to his feet. His lethargy had fallen from him, and his features became hard and resolute. He looked squarely at Vance.

"Dead?" His voice was menacing. "How did he die?"

"He was murdered." Vance pointed to the body of Kyle before which Markham and Heath and I were standing.

Bliss stepped toward Kyle's prostrate figure. For a full minute he stood staring down at the body; then his gaze shifted to the small statue of Sakhmet, and a moment later he lifted his eyes to the lupine features of Anûbis.

Suddenly he swung round and faced Hani. The Egyptian took a backward step, as though he feared violence from the doctor.

"What do you know about this?—you jackal!" Bliss threw the question at him venomously, a passionate hate in his voice. "You've spied on me for years. You've taken my money and pocketed bribes from your stupid and grasping government. You've poisoned my wife against me. You've stood in the way of all I've endeavored to accomplish. You tried to murder the old native who showed me the site of the two obelisks in front of Intef's pyramid.* You've hampered me at every turn. And because my wife believed in you and loved you, I've kept you. And now, when I've found the site of Intef's tomb and actually entered the antechamber and am about to give the fruits of my researches to the world, the one man who could make possible the success of my life's work is found murdered." Bliss's eyes were like burning coals. "What do you know about it, Anûpu Hani? Speak—you contemptible dog of a fellah!"

Hani had retreated several paces. Bliss's vitriolic tirade had pitifully cowed him. But he did not grovel: he had become grim and morose, and there was a snarl in his voice when he answered.

"I know nothing of the murder. It was the vengeance of Sakhmet! *She* killed the one who would have paid for the desecration of Intef's tomb...."

"Sakhmet!" Bliss's scorn was devastating. "A piece of stone belonging to a hybrid mythology! You're not among illiterate witch-doctors now—you're confronted with civilized human beings who want the truth.... Who killed Kyle?"

"If it wasn't Sakhmet, I don't know, Your Presence." Despite the Egyptian's subservient attitude there was an underlying contempt in his manner and in

---

* I learned from Vance that Doctor Bliss had read, in the British Museum, the Abbott Papyrus of the Twentieth Dynasty, which reported the inspection of this and other tombs. The report stated that, in early times, Intef V's tomb had been entered but not robbed: the raiders had evidently been unable to penetrate to the actual grave chamber. Bliss, therefore, had concluded that the mummy of Intef would still be found in the original tomb. An old native named Hasan had showed him where two obelisks had stood in front of the pyramid of Intef (Intef-o); and through this information he had succeeded in locating the pyramid, and had excavated at that point.

the intonation of his voice. "I have been in my room all morning. . . . You, *hadretak,*" he added, with a sneer, "were very close to your rich patron when he departed this world for the Land of Shades."

Two red patches of anger shone through the tan of Bliss's cheeks. His eyes blazed abnormally, and his hands plucked spasmodically at the folds of his dressing-gown. I feared that he would fly at the throat of the Egyptian.

Vance, too, had some such apprehension, for he moved to the doctor's side and touched him reassuringly on the arm.

"I understand perfectly how you feel, sir," he said in a soothing voice. "But temper won't help us get at the root of this matter."

Bliss sank back into his chair without a word, and Scarlett, who had been looking on at the scene with troubled amazement, stepped quickly up to Vance.

"There's something radically wrong here," he said. "The doctor isn't himself."

"So I observe." Vance spoke dryly, but there was a puzzled frown on his face. He scrutinized Bliss for a moment. "I say, doctor; what time did you fall asleep in your study this morning?"

Bliss looked up lethargically. His wrath seemed to have left him, and his eyes were again heavy.

"What time?" he repeated, like a man attempting to collect his thoughts. "Let me see. . . . Brush brought me my breakfast about nine, and a few minutes later I drank the coffee . . . some of it, at any rate——" His gaze wandered off into space. "That's all I remember until—until there was a pounding on the door. . . . What time is it, Mr. Vance?"

"It's well past noon," Vance informed him. "You evidently fell asleep as soon as you had your coffee. Quite natural, don't y' know. Scarlett tells me you worked late last night."

Bliss nodded heavily.

"Yes—till three this morning. I wanted to have the report in order for Kyle when he arrived. . . . And now"—he looked hopelessly toward the outstretched body of his benefactor—"I find him dead—murdered. . . . I can't understand."

"Neither can we—for the moment," Vance returned. "But Mr. Markham—the District Attorney—and Sergeant Heath of the Homicide Bureau are here for the purpose of ascertaining the facts; and you may rest assured, sir, that justice will be done. Just now you can help us materially by answering a few questions. Do you feel equal to it?"

"Of course I'm equal to it," Bliss replied, with a slight show of nervous vitality. "But," he added, running his tongue over his dry lips, "I'm horribly thirsty. A drink of water——"

"Ah! I thought you might be wanting a drink. . . . How about it, Sergeant?"

Heath was already on his way toward the front stairs. He disappeared through the door, and we could hear his voice giving staccato orders to some one outside. A minute or two later he returned to the museum with a glass of water.

Doctor Bliss drank it like a man parched with thirst, and when he set the glass down Vance asked him:

"When did you finish your financial report for Mr. Kyle?"

"This morning—just before Brush brought me my breakfast." Bliss's voice was stronger: there was even animation in his tone. "I had practically completed it before retiring last night—all but about an hour's work. So I came down to the study at eight this morning."

"And where is that report now?"

"On my desk in the study. I intended to check the figures after breakfast, before Kyle arrived. . . . I'll get it."

He started to rise, but Vance restrained him.

"That won't be necess'ry, sir. I have it here. . . . It was found in Mr. Kyle's hand."

Bliss looked at the paper, which Vance showed him, with dumbfounded eyes.

"In—Kyle's hand?" he stammered. "But . . . but. . . ."

"Don't disturb yourself about it." Vance's manner was casual. "Its presence there will be explained when we've come to know the situation better. The report was no doubt taken from your study while you were asleep. . . ."

"Maybe Kyle himself——"

"It's possible, but hardly probable." It was obvious that Vance scouted the idea of Kyle's having personally taken the report. "By the bý, is it custom'ry for you to leave the door leading from your study into the museum unlocked?"

"Yes. I never lock it. No necessity to. As a matter of fact I couldn't tell you offhand where the key is."

"That bein' the case," mused Vance, "any one in the museum might have entered the study and taken the report after nine o'clock or so, when you were asleep."

"But who, in Heaven's name, Mr. Vance——?"

"We don't know yet. We're still in the conjectural stage of our investigation.—And if you'll be so good, doctor, permit me to ask the questions. . . . Do you happen to know where Mr. Salveter is this morning?"

Bliss turned his head toward Vance with a resentful gesture.

"Certainly I know where he is," he responded, setting his jaws firmly. (I got the impression that he intended to protect Kyle's nephew from any suspicion.) "I sent him to the Metropolitan Museum——"

"You sent him? When?"

"I asked him last night to go the first thing this morning and inquire regarding the duplicate set of reproductions of the tomb furniture in the recently discovered grave of Hotpeheres, the mother of Kheuf of the Fourth Dynasty——"

"Hotpeheres? Kheuf? . . . Do you refer to Hetep-hir-es and Khufu?"

"Certainly!" The doctor's tone was tart. "I use the transliteration of Weigall. In his 'History of the Pharaohs'——"

"Yes, yes. Forgive me, doctor. I recall now that Weigall has altered many of the accepted transliterations from the Egyptian. . . . But, if my memory is correct, the expedition which unearthed the tomb of Hetep-hir-es—or Hotpeheres—was sponsored by Harvard University and the Boston Museum of Fine Arts."

"Quite true. But I knew that my old friend, Albert Lythgoe, the Curator of the Egyptian department of the Metropolitan Museum, could supply me with the information I desired."

"I see," Vance paused. "Did you speak to Mr. Salveter this morning?"

"No." Bliss became indignant. "I was in my study from eight o'clock on; and the lad wouldn't think of disturbing me. He probably left the house about nine-thirty,—the Metropolitan Museum opens at ten."

Vance nodded.

"Yes; Brush said he went out about that time. But shouldn't he be back by now?"

Bliss shrugged his shoulders.

"Perhaps," he said, as if the matter was of no importance. "He may have had to wait for the Curator, however. Anyway, he'll be back as soon as he has finished his mission. He's a good conscientious lad: both my wife and I are extremely fond of him. It was he who, by interceding with his uncle, made possible the excavations of Intef's tomb."

"So Scarlett told me." Vance spoke with the offhandedness of complete uninterest, and drawing up a collapsible wooden chair sat down lazily. As he did so he gave Markham an admonitory glance—a glance which said as plainly as words could have done: "Let me do the talking for the time being." Then he leaned back and folded his hands behind his head.

"I say, doctor," he went on, with a slight yawn; "speaking of old Intef, I was present, don't y' know, when you appropriated that fascinatin' lapis-lazuli scarab...."

Bliss's hand went to his four-in-hand, and he glanced guiltily toward Hani, who had moved before the statue of Teti-shiret and now stood with his back to us in a pose of detached and absorbed adoration. Vance pretended not to have seen the doctor's movements, and, gazing dreamily out of the rear windows, he continued:

"A most interestin' scarab—unusually marked. Scarlett tells me you had it made into a scarf-pin.... Have you it with you? I'd jolly well like to see it."

"Really, Mr. Vance,"—again Bliss's hand went to his cravat—"it must be up-stairs. If you'll call Brush——"

Scarlett had moved forward beside Bliss.

"It was in your study last night, doctor," he said, "—on the desk...."

"So it was!" Bliss was in perfect control of himself now. "You'll find it on my desk, stuck in the necktie I was wearing yesterday."

Vance rose and confronted Scarlett with an arctic look.

"Thanks awfully," he said coldly. "When I need your assistance I'll call on you." Then he turned to Bliss. "The truth is, doctor, I was endeavorin' to ascertain when you last remembered havin' your scarab pin.... It's not in your study, d' ye see. It was lyin' beside the body of Mr. Kyle when we arrived here."

"My Intef scarab here!" Bliss leapt to his feet and gazed, with a panic-stricken stare, at the murdered man. "That's impossible!"

Vance stepped to Kyle's body and picked up the scarab.

"Not impossible, sir," he said, displaying the pin; "but very mystifyin'.... It was probably taken from your study at the same time as the report."

"It's beyond me," Bliss remarked slowly, in a hoarse whisper.

"Maybe it fell outa your necktie," Heath suggested antagonistically, thrusting his jaw forward.

"What do you mean?" The doctor's tone was dull and frightened. "I didn't have it in this necktie. I left it in the study——"

"Sergeant!" Vance gave Heath a look of stern reproval. "Let's go at this thing calmly and with discretion."

"Mr. Vance,"—Heath's aggressiveness did not relax—"I'm here to find out who croaked Kyle. And the person who had every opportunity to do it is this Doctor Bliss. On top of that fact we find a financial report and a stick-pin that hooks Doctor Bliss up to the dead man. And there's those footprints——"

"All you say is true, Sergeant." Vance cut him short. "But ballyragging the doctor will not give us the explanation of this extr'ordin'ry situation."

Bliss had shrunk back in his chair.

"Oh, my God!" he moaned. "I see what you're getting at. You think *I* killed him!" He turned his eyes to Vance in desperate entreaty. "I tell you I've been asleep since nine o'clock. I didn't even know Kyle was here. It's terrible—terrible. . . . Surely, Mr. Vance, you can't believe——"

There was a sound of angry voices at the main door of the museum, and we all looked in that direction. At the head of the stairs stood Hennessey, his arms wide, protesting volubly. On the door-sill was a young woman.

"This is my house," she said in a shrill, angry voice. "How dare you tell me I can't enter here?. . ."

Scarlett at once hurried toward the stairs.

"Meryt!"

"It's my wife," Bliss informed us. "Why is she refused admittance, Mr. Vance?"

Before Vance could answer, Heath was shouting:

"That's all right, Hennessey. Let the lady come in."

Mrs. Bliss hastened down the stairs, and almost ran to her husband.

"Oh, what is it, Mindrum? What has happened?" She dropped to her knees and put her arms about the doctor's shoulders. At that instant she caught sight of Kyle's body and, with a gasp and a shudder, turned her eyes away.

She was a striking-looking woman, whose age, I surmised, was about twenty-six-or-seven. Her large eyes were dark and heavily lashed, and her skin was a deep olive. Her Egyptian blood was most marked in the sensual fullness of her lips and in her high prominent cheekbones, which gave her face a decidedly Oriental character. There was something about her that recalled to my mind the beautiful reconstructed painting made of Queen Nefret-îti by Winifred Brunton.* She wore a powder-blue toque hat not unlike the headdress of Nefret-îti herself; and her gown of cinnamon-brown georgette crêpe clung closely to her slender, well-rounded body, bringing out and emphasizing its sensuous curves. There were both strength and beauty in her supple figure, which followed the lines of the old Oriental ideal such as we find in Ingres' "Bain Turc."

Despite her youth she possessed a distinct air of maturity and poise: there were undeniable depths to her nature; and I could easily imagine, as I watched

---

* This colored portrait (with the Queen's name spelled Nefertiti) appears in "Kings and Queens of Ancient Egypt."

her kneeling beside Bliss, that she might be capable of powerful emotions and equally powerful deeds.*

Bliss patted her shoulder in an affectionately paternal manner. His eyes, though, were abstracted.

"Kyle is dead, my dear," he told her in a hollow voice. "He's been killed . . . and these gentlemen are accusing me of having done it."

"You!" Mrs. Bliss was instantly on her feet. For a moment her great eyes stared uncomprehendingly at her husband; then she turned on us in a flashing rage. But before she could speak Vance stepped toward her.

"The doctor is not quite accurate, Mrs. Bliss," he said in a low, even tone. "We have not accused him. We are merely making an investigation of this tragic affair; and it happens that the doctor's scarab-pin was found near Mr. Kyle's body. . . ."

"What of it?" She had become strangely calm. "Any one might have dropped it there."

"Exactly, madam," Vance returned, with friendly assurance. "Our main object in this investigation is to ascertain who that person was."

The woman's eyes were half-closed, and she stood rigid, as if transfixed by a sudden devastating thought.

"Yes . . . yes," she breathed. "Some one placed the scarab-pin there . . . some one. . . ." Her voice died out, and a cloud, as of pain, came over her face. But quickly she drew herself together and, taking a deep breath, looked resolutely into Vance's eyes.

"Whoever it was that did this terrible thing, I want you to find him." Her expression became set and hard. "And I will help you. Do you understand?—*I* will help you."

Vance studied her briefly before replying.

"I believe you will, Mrs. Bliss. And I shall call on you for that help." He bowed slightly. "But there is nothing you can do at this moment. A few prelimin'ry routine things must be done first. In the meantime, I would appreciate your waiting for us in the drawing-room—there will be several questions we shall want to ask you presently. . . . Hani may accompany you."

---

* I learned subsequently from Scarlett that Mrs. Bliss's mother had been a Coptic lady of noble descent who traced her lineage from the last Saïte Pharaohs, and who, despite her Christian faith, had retained her traditional veneration for the native gods of her country. Her only child, Meryt-Amen ("Beloved of Amûn"), had been named in honor of the great Ramses II, whose full title as Son of the Sun-God was Ra-mosê-su Mery-Amûn. (The more correct English spelling of Mrs. Bliss's name would have been Meryet-Amûn, but the form chosen was no doubt based on the transliterations of Flinders Petrie, Maspero, and Abercrombie.) Meryet-Amûn was not an uncommon name among the queens and princesses of ancient Egypt. Three queens of that name have already been found— one (of the family of Ah-mosè I) whose mummy is in the Cairo Museum; another (of the family of Ramses II) whose tomb and sarcophagus are in the Valley of the Queens; and a third, whose burial chamber and mummy were recently found by the Egyptian Expedition of the Metropolitan Museum of Art on the hillside near the temple of Deir el Bahri at Thebes. This last Queen Meryet-Amûn was the daughter of Thut-mosè III and Meryet-Rê, and the wife of Amen-hotpe II. The story of the finding of her tomb is told in Section II of the Bulletin of the Metropolitan Museum of Art for November 1929.

I had been watching the Egyptian with one eye during this little scene. When Mrs. Bliss had entered the museum he had barely turned in her direction, but when she had begun speaking to Vance he had moved silently toward them. He now stood, his arms folded, just behind the inlaid coffer, with his eyes fixed upon the woman, in an attitude of protective devotion.

"Come, Meryt-Amen," he said. "I will remain with you till these gentlemen wish to consult you. There is nothing to fear. Sakhmet has had her just revenge, and she is beyond the mundane power of Occidental law."

The woman hesitated a moment. Then, going to Bliss, she kissed him lightly on the forehead, and walked toward the front stairway, Hani servilely following her.

6

A FOUR-HOUR ERRAND

(Friday, July 13, 1:15 P.M.)

SCARLETT'S EYES followed her with a troubled, sympathetic look.

"Poor girl!" he commented, with a sigh. "You know, Vance, she was devoted to Kyle—her father and Kyle were great cronies. When old Abercrombie died Kyle cared for her as though she'd been his daughter.... This affair is a terrible blow to her."

"One can well understand that," Vance murmured perfunctorily. "But she has Hani to console her.... By the by, doctor, your Egyptian servant appears to be quite *en rapport* with Mrs. Bliss."

"What's that—what's that?" Bliss lifted his head and made an effort at concentration. "Ah, yes ... Hani. A faithful dog—where my wife's concerned. He practically brought her up, after her father's death. He's never forgiven me for marrying her." He smiled grimly and lapsed into a state of brooding despondency.

Heath's cigar had gone out, but he still chewed viciously on it.

He was standing beside Kyle's body, his legs apart, his hands in his pockets, glaring with frustrated animosity at the doctor.

"What's all this palaver about, anyhow?" he asked sullenly. He faced Markham. "Listen, Chief: haven't you got enough evidence for an indictment?"

Markham was sorely troubled. His instinct was to order Bliss's arrest, but his faith in Vance halted him. He knew that Vance was not satisfied with the situation, and he no doubt felt, as a result of Vance's attitude, that there were certain things connected with Kyle's murder which did not show on the surface. Moveover, there was perhaps an uncertainty in his own mind as to the authenticity of the evidence that pointed to the Egyptologist.

He was on the point of answering Heath when Hennessey put his head in the door and called out:

"Hey, Sergeant; the buggy from the Department of Public Welfare is here."

"Well, it's about time." Heath was in a vicious mood. He turned to Markham. "Any reason, sir, why we shouldn't get the body outa the way?"

Markham glanced toward Vance, who nodded.

"No, Sergeant," he answered. "The sooner it reaches the mortuary, the sooner we'll have the *post-mortem* report."

"Right!" Heath cupped his hands to his mouth and bawled to Hennessey: "Send 'em in."

A moment later two men—one the driver of the car, the other an unkempt "pick-up"—came down the stairs carrying a large wicker basket shaped like a coffin. Without a word they callously lifted Kyle's body into it, and started toward the front door with their gruesome burden, the "pick-up" at the rear end of the basket doing a playful dance step as he moved across the hardwood floor.

"Sweet sympathetic laddie," grinned Vance.

With the removal of Kyle's body a pall seemed to lift from the museum. But there was still that pool of blood and the recumbent statue of Sakhmet to tell the terrible story of the tragedy.

Heath stood eyeing the huddled, silent figure of Doctor Bliss.

"Where do we go from here?" His question contained both disgust and resignation.

Markham was growing restless and, beckoning Vance to one side, spoke to him in low tones. I could not hear what was said; but Vance talked earnestly to the District Attorney for several minutes. Markham listened attentively and then shrugged his shoulders.

"Very well," he answered, as they strolled back toward us. "But unless you reach some conclusion pretty soon we'll have to take action. . . ."

"Action—oh, my aunt!" Vance sighed deeply. "Always action—always pyrotechnics. The Rotarian ideal! Get busy—stir things up. Efficiency! . . . Why do the powers of justice have to emulate the whirling dervish? The human brain, after all, has certain functions."

He paced slowy back and forth in front of the cabinets, his eyes on the floor, while the rest of us watched him. Even Doctor Bliss roused himself and gazed at him with a curious and hopeful expression.

"None of these clews ring true, Markham," Vance said. "There's something here that doesn't meet the eye. It's like a cypher that says one thing and means another. I tell you the obvious explanation is the wrong one. . . . There's a key to this affair—somewhere. And it's staring us in the face . . . yet we can't see it."

He was deeply perplexed and dissatisfied, and he walked to and fro with that quiet, disguised alertness which I had long since come to recognize.

Suddenly he halted in front of the pool of blood before the end cabinet, and bent over. He studied it for a moment, and then his eyes moved to the cabinet. Slowly his gaze ascended the partly drawn curtain and came to rest on the beaded wooden ledge above the curtain rod. After a while his eyes drifted back to the pool of blood, and I got the impression that he was measuring distances and trying to determine the exact relationship between the blood, the cabinet, the curtain, and the moulding along the top of the shelves.

Presently he straightened up and stood very close to the curtains, his back to us.

"Really, now, that's most interestin'," he murmured. "I wonder. . . ."

He turned, and, drawing up one of the folding wooden chairs, placed it directly in front of the cabinet on the exact spot where Kyle's head had lain. Then he mounted the chair, and stood for a considerable time inspecting the top of the cabinet.

"My word! Extr'ordin'ry!" His voice was barely audible.

Taking out his monocle, he placed it in his eye. Then his hand reached out over the edge of the cabinet, and he picked up something very near to where Hani said he had placed the small statue of Sakhmet. Just what it was none of us could see; but presently he slipped the object into his coat pocket. A moment later he descended from the chair and faced Markham with a grim, satisfied look.

"This murder has amazin' possibilities," he observed.

Before he could explain his cryptic remark Hennessey again appeared at the head of the stairs and called out to Sergeant Heath:

"There's a guy named Salveter who says he wants to see Doc Bliss."

"Ah—*bon!*" Vance, for some reason, seemed highly pleased. "Supppose we have him in, Sergeant."

"Oh, sure!" Heath made an elaborate grimace of boredom. "O.K., Hennessey. Show in the gent. The more the merrier. . . . What is this, anyway?" he groused. "A convention?"

Young Salveter walked down the stairs and approached us with a startled, questioning air. He gave Scarlett a curt, cold nod; then he caught sight of Vance.

"How do you do?" he said, obviously surprised at Vance's presence. "It's been a long time since I saw you . . . in Egypt. . . . What's all the excitement about? Have we been invested by the military?" His pleasantry did not ring true.

Salveter was an earnest, aggressive-looking man of about thirty, with sandy hair, wide-set gray eyes, a small nose, and a thin, tight mouth. He was of medium height, stockily built, and might have been an athlete in his college days. He was dressed simply in a tweed suit that did not fit him, and the polka-dot tie in his soft-shirt collar was askew. I doubt if his cordovan blucher oxfords had ever been polished. My first instinct was to like him. The impression he gave was that of boyish frankness; but there was a quality in his make-up,—I could not analyze it at the time,—that signalled to one to be wary and not attempt to force an issue against his stubbornness.

As he spoke to Vance his eyes shifted with intense curiosity about the room, as if he were looking for something amiss.

Vance, who had been watching him appraisingly, answered after a slight pause in a tone that struck me an unnecessarily devoid of sympathy.

"No, it's not the milit'ry, Mr. Salveter. It's the police. The fact is, your uncle is dead—he has been murdered."

"Uncle Ben!" Salveter appeared stunned by the news; but presently an angry scowl settled on his forehead. "So—that's it!" He drew in his head and squinted pugnaciously at Doctor Bliss. "He had an appointment with you this morning, sir. . . . When—and how—did it happen?"

It was Vance, however, who made reply.

"Your uncle, Mr. Salveter, was struck over the head with that statue of

Sakhmet, about ten o'clock. Mr. Scarlett found the body here at the foot of Anûbis, and notified me. I, in turn, notified the District Attorney. . . . This, by the by, is Mr. Markham—and this is Sergeant Heath of the Homicide Bureau."

Salveter scarcely glanced in their direction.

"A damned outrage!" he muttered, setting his square, heavy jaw.

"An outrage—yes!" Bliss lifted his head, and his eyes, pitifully discouraged, met Salveter's. "It means the end of all our excavations, my boy——"

"Excavations!" Salveter continued to study the older man. "What do they matter! I want to lay my hands on the dog who did this thing." He swung about aggressively and faced Markham. "What can I do, sir, to help you?" His eyes were mere slits—he was like a dangerous wild beast waiting to pounce.

"Too much energy, Mr. Salveter," Vance drawled, sitting down indolently. "Far too much energy. I can apprehend exactly how you feel, don't y' know. But aggressiveness, while bein' a virtue in some circumstances, is really quite futile in the present situation. . . . I say; why not walk round the block vigorously a couple of times, and then return to us? We crave a bit of polite intercourse with you, but calmness and self-control are most necess'ry."

Salveter glared ferociously at Vance, who met his gaze with languid coldness; and for fully thirty seconds there was an unflinching ocular clash between them. But I have seen other men attempt to stare Vance out of countenance—without the least success. His quiet power and strength of character were colossal, and I would wish no one the task of outgazing him.

Finally Salveter shrugged his broad shoulders. A slight, compromising grin flickered along his set mouth.

"I'll pass up the promenade," he said, with admiring sheepishness. "Fire away."

Vance took a deep inhalation on his cigarette, and let his eyes wander lazily along the great frieze of Pen-ta-Weret's Rhapsody.

"What time did you leave the house this morning, Mr. Salveter?"

"About half past nine." Salveter was now standing relaxed, his hands in his coat pockets. All of his aggressiveness was gone, and, though he watched Vance closely, there was neither animosity nor tenseness in his manner.

"And you did not, by any chance, leave the front door unlatched—or open?"

"No! . . . Why should I?"

"Really, y' know, I couldn't say." Vance conferred on him a disarming smile. "A more or less vital question, however. Mr. Scarlett, d' ye see, found the door open when he arrived between ten and ten-thirty."

"Well, I didn't leave it that way. . . . What next?"

"You went to the Metropolitan Museum of Art, I understand."

"Yes. I went to inquire about some reproductions of the tomb furniture of Hotpeheres."

"And you got the information?"

"I did."

Vance looked at his watch.

"Twenty-five after one," he read. "That means you have been absent about four hours. Did you, by any hap, walk to Eighty-second Street and back?"

Salveter clamped his teeth tight for a moment, and stared antagonistically at Vance's nonchalant figure.

"I didn't walk either way, thank you." (I could not determine whether he was merely exerting great self-control or whether he was actually frightened.) "I took a 'bus up the Avenue, and came back in a taxi."

"Let us say one hour coming and going, then. That allowed you three hours to obtain your information, eh, what?"

"Mathematically correct." Again Salveter grinned savagely. "But it happened I dropped into the rooms on the right of the entrance to take a look at Per-nêb's Tomb. I'd heard recently that they'd added some objects to their collection of the contents of the burial-chamber.... Per-nêb, you see, was Fifth Dynasty——"

"Yes, yes.... And as Khufu, Hetep-hir-es' offspring, belonged to the preceding dynasty, you were æsthetically interested in the burial-chamber contents. Quite natural.... And how long did you prowl and commune among the Per-nêb fragments?"

"See here, Mr. Vance"—Salveter was growing apprehensive—"I don't know what you're trying to get at; but if it's going to help you in your investigation of Uncle Ben's death, I'll take your gaff.... I hung around the cabinets in the Egyptian rooms for nearly an hour. Got interested and didn't hurry—I knew Uncle Ben had an appointment with Doctor Bliss this morning, and I figured that if I got back at lunchtime it would be all right."

"But you didn't get back at lunch time," Vance remarked.

"What if I didn't? I had to cool my feet for nearly an hour in the Curator's outer office after I went upstairs—Mr. Lythgoe was talking with Lindsley Hall about some drawings. And then I had to hang around another half hour or so while he was phoning to Doctor Reisner at the Boston Museum of Fine Arts. I'm lucky to be back now."

"Quite.... I know how those things are. Very tryin'."

Vance apparently accepted his story without question. He rose lazily and drew a small note-book from his pocket, at the same time feeling in his waistcoat as if for something with which to write.

"Sorry and all that, Mr. Salveter; but could you lend me a pencil? Mine seems to have disappeared."

(I immediately became interested, for I knew Vance never carried a pencil but invariably used a small gold fountain-pen which he always wore on his watch-chain.)

"Delighted." Salveter reached in his pocket and held out a long hexagonal yellow pencil.

Vance took it and made several notations in his book. Then, as he was about to return the pencil, he paused and looked at the name printed on it.

"Ah, a Mongol No. 1, what?" he said. "Popular pencils these Fabers-482.... Do you always use them?"

"Never anything else...."

"Thanks awfully." Vance returned the pencil, and dropped the note-book into his pocket. "And now, Mr. Salveter, I'd appreciate it if you'd go to the drawing-room and wait for us. We'll want to question you again.... Mrs. Bliss, by the by, is there," he added casually.

Salveter's eyelids dropped perceptibly, and he gave Vance a swift sidelong glance.

"Oh, is she? Thanks. . . . I'll wait for you in the drawing-room." He went up to Bliss. "I'm frightfully sorry, sir," he said. "I know what this means to you. . . ." He was going to add something but halted himself. Then he walked doggedly toward the front door.

He was half-way up the stairs when Vance, who now stood regarding the statue of Sakhmet meditatively, suddenly turned and called to him.

"Oh, I say, Mr. Salveter. Tell Hani we'd like to see him here—there's a good fellow."

Salveter made a gesture of assent, and passed through the great steel door without looking back.

7

THE FINGER-PRINTS

(Friday, July 13, 1:30 p.m.)

HANI JOINED us a few moments later.

"I am at your service, gentlemen," he announced, looking from one to the other of us superciliously.

Vance had already drawn up a second chair beside the one on which he had stood during his inspection of the top of the cabinet; and he now made a beckoning gesture to the Egyptian.

"We appreciate your passionate spirit of co-operation, Hani," he replied lightly. "Would you be so amiable as to stand on this chair and point out to me exactly where you set the statue of Sakhmet yesterday?"

I was watching Hani closely, and I could have sworn that his eyebrows contracted slightly. But there was almost no hesitation in his compliance with Vance's request. Making a slow, deep bow, he approached the cabinet.

"Don't put your hands on the woodwork," Vance admonished. "And don't touch the curtain."

Awkwardly, because of his long flowing kaftan, Hani mounted one of the chairs; and Vance stepped upon the seat of the other.

The Egyptian squinted for a moment at the top of the cabinet, and then pointed a bony finger to a spot near the edge, exactly half-way across the two-and-a-half-foot opening.

"Just here, *effendi*," he said. "If you look closely you can see where the base of Sakhmet disturbed the dust. . . ."

"Oh, quite." Vance, though in an attitude of concentration, was nevertheless studying Hani's face. "But if one looks even more closely one can see other disturbances in the dust."

"The wind, perhaps, from yonder window. . . ."

Vance chuckled.

"*Blasen ist nicht flöten, ihr müsst die Finger bewegen*—to quote Goethe figuratively. . . . Your explanation, Hani, is a bit too poetic." He indicated a point near the moulding at the edge of the cabinet. "I doubt if even your simoon—

or, as you may prefer to call it, samûn*—could have made that scratch at the edge of the statue's base, what? . . . Or, it may be, you set down the statue with undue violence."

"It is possible, of course—though not likely."

"No, not likely—considerin' your superstitious reverence for the leonine lady." Vance descended from his perch. "However, Sakhmet seems to have been standing on the very edge of the cabinet, directly in the centre, when Mr. Kyle arrived this morning to inspect the new treasures."

We had all been watching him with curiosity. Heath and Markham were especially interested, and Scarlett—frowning·and immobile—had not taken his eyes from Vance. Even Bliss, who had seemed utterly broken by the tragedy and in a state of complete hopelessness, had followed the episode with intentness. That Vance had discovered something of importance was evident. I knew him too well to underestimate his persistence, and I waited, with a sense of inner excitement, for the time when he would share his new knowledge with us.

Markham, however, voiced his impatience.

"What have you in mind, Vance?" he asked irritably. "This is hardly the time to be secretive and dramatic."

"I'm merely delving into the subtler possibilities of this inveiglin' case," he replied, in an offhand manner. "I'm a complex soul, Markham old dear. I don't, alas! possess a simple, forthright nature. I'm a sworn enemy of the obvious and the trite. . . . You remember what the heart of the young man said to the Psalmist?—'Things are not what they seem.' "

Markham had long since come to understand this kind of evasive garrulousness on Vance's part, and no further question was asked. Moreover, there was an interruption at this moment, which was to place an even more complicated and more sinister aspect on the entire case.

The front door was opened by Hennessey, and Captain Dubois and Detective Bellamy, the finger-print experts, clattered down the stairs.

"Sorry to keep you waiting, Sergeant," Dubois said, shaking hands with Heath; "but I was tied up with a safe-breaking job on Fulton Street." He looked about him. "How d' ye do, Mr. Markham?" He extended his hand to the District Attorney. . . . "And Mr. Vance, is it?" Dubois spoke civilly but without enthusiasm: I believe his tiff with Vance during the "Canary" murder case still rankled in him.

"There ain't much of a job for you here, Captain," Heath interrupted impatiently. "The only thing I want you to check up on is that black statue laying there."

Dubois at once became seriously professional.

"That won't take long," he muttered, bending over the diorite figure of Sakhmet. "What might it be, Sergeant?—one of those Futuristic works of art that don't mean anything?"

"It don't mean anything to me," the Sergeant growled, "unless you can find some nice identifiable prints on it."

---

* I am not quite sure why Vance added this parenthetical phrase, unless it was because the word *simoon* comes from the Arabic *samma* (meaning *to be poisoned*), and he thought that Hani would better recognize the word in its correct etymological form.

Dubois grunted and snapped his fingers toward his assistant. Bellamy, who had stood imperturbably in the background during the exchange of greetings, came ponderously forward and opened a black hand-bag which he had brought with him. Dubois, using a large handkerchief and the palms of his hands, carefully lifted the statue and placed it upright on the seat of a chair. Then he reached in the hand-bag and took out an insufflator, or tiny hand-bellows, and puffed a fine pale-saffron powder over the entire figure. Following this operation, he gently blew away all the surplus powder, and fixing a jeweller's-glass in his eye, knelt down and made a close inspection of every part of the statue.

Hani had watched the performance with the keenest interest. He had slowly moved toward the finger-print men until now he stood within a few feet of them. His eyes were concentrated on their labors, and his hands, which hung at his sides, were tightly flexed.

"You'll find no finger-prints of mine on Sakhmet, gentlemen," he proclaimed in a low, tense voice. "I polished them off. . . . Nor will there be any finger-prints to guide you. The Goddess of Vengeance strikes of her own volition and power, and no human hands are needed to assist her in her acts of justice."

Heath threw the Egyptian a glance of scathing contempt; but Vance turned in his direction with a considerable show of interest.

"How do you know, Hani," he asked, "that your sign-manuals will not appear on the statue? It was you who placed it upon the cabinet yesterday."

"Yes, *effendi*," the man answered, without taking his eyes from Dubois. "I place it there—but with reverence. I rubbed and polished it from top to bottom when it was unpacked. And then I took it in my hands and stood it on the top of the cabinet, as Bliss *effendi* had directed. But when it was in place I could see where my hands had made marks upon its polished surface; and again I rubbed it with a chamois cloth so that it would be pure and untouched while the spirit of Sakhmet looked down sorrowfully over the stolen treasures of this room. . . . There was no mark or print on it when I left it."

"Well, my friend, there's finger-prints on it now," declared Dubois unemotionally. He had taken out a powerful magnifying glass and was centring his gaze on the thick ankles of the statue. "And they're damn clear prints, too. . . . Looks to me like they'd been made by some guy who'd lifted up this statue. . . . Both hands show around the ankles. . . . Pass me the camera, Bellamy."

Bliss had paid scant heed to the entrance of the finger-print men, but when Hani had begun to speak, he had roused himself from his despondent lethargy and concentrated his attention on the Egyptian. Then, when Dubois had announced the presence of finger-prints, he had stared, with terrible intentness, at the statue. A startling change had come over him. He was like a man in the grip of some consuming fear; and before Dubois had finished speaking he leapt to his feet and stood in a frozen attitude of stark horror.

"*God help me!*" he cried; and the sound of his voice sent a chill over me. "Those are *my* finger-prints on that statue!"

The effect of this admission was dumbfounding. Even Vance seemed momentarily shaken out of his habitual calm, and going to a small standard ashtray he abstractedly crushed out his cigarette, though he had smoked less than half of it.

Heath was the first to break the electric silence that followed Bliss's cry of anguish. He took his dead cigar from his lips, and thrust out his chin.

"Sure, they're your finger-prints!" he snapped unpleasantly. "Who else's would they be?"

"Just a moment, Sergeant!" Vance had wholly recovered himself, and his voice was casual. "Finger-prints can be very misleadin', don't y' know. And a few digital signatures on a lethal weapon don't mean that their author is necessarily a murderer. It's most important, d' ye see, to ascertain when and under what circumstances the signatures were made."

He approached Bliss, who had remained staring at the statue of Sakhmet like a stricken man.

"I say, doctor;"—he had assumed an easy, off-hand manner— "how do you know those finger-prints are yours?"

"How do I know?" Bliss repeated the question in a resigned, colorless tone. He appeared to have aged before our very eyes; and his white, sunken cheeks made him resemble a death's-head. "Because—oh, my God!—because I made them! . . . I made them last night—or, rather, early this morning, before I turned in. I took hold of the statue—around the ankles—exactly where that gentleman says there are the marks of two hands."

"And how did you happen to do that, doctor?" Vance asked quietly.

"I did it without thought—I'd even forgotten doing it till the finger-prints were mentioned." Bliss spoke with feverish earnestness: he seemed to feel that his very life depended on his being believed. "When I had finished arranging all the figures of the report early this morning, at about three o'clock, I came down here to the museum. I'd told Kyle about the new shipment, and I wanted to make sure that everything was in order for his inspection. . . . You see, Mr. Vance, a great deal depended on the impression the new treasures made on him. . . . I looked over the items in that end cabinet, and then re-drew the curtain. Just as I was about to depart I noticed that the statue of Sakhmet had not been placed evenly on the top of the cabinet—it was not in the exact centre, and was slightly sidewise. So I reached up and staightened it—taking hold of it by the ankles. . . ."

"Pardon me for intruding, Vance,"—Scarlett, a troubled look on his face, had stepped forward—"but I can ssure you that such an act was quite natural with Doctor Bliss. He's a stickler for orderliness—it's a good-natured joke among the rest of us. We never dare leave anything out of place: he's constantly criticising us and rearranging things after us."

Vance nodded.

"Then, as I understand you, Scarlett, if a statue was left a bit askew, it would be practically inevitable that Doctor Bliss, on seeing it, would set it right."

"Yes—I think that's a reasonable conclusion."

"Many thanks." Vance turned again to Bliss. "Your explanation is that you adjusted the statue of Sakhmet, by taking hold of its ankles, and forthwith went to bed?"

"That's the truth—so help me God!" The man searched Vance's eyes eagerly. "I turned out the lights and went up-stairs. And I've not set foot in the museum till you knocked on my study door."

Heath was obviously not satisfied with this story. It was plain that he had no intention of relinquishing his belief in Bliss's guilt.

"The trouble with that alibi," he retorted doggedly, "is that you haven't got any witnesses. And it's the sort of alibi any one would pull when they'd got caught with the goods."

Markham diplomatically intervened. He himself was patently not convinced one way or the other.

"I think, Sergeant," he said, "that it might be advisable to have Captain Dubois verify the identity of those finger-prints. We'll at least know definitely then if the prints are the ones Doctor Bliss made. . . . Can you do that now, Captain?"

"Sure thing."

Dubois reached in the hand-bag and drew forth a tiny inked roller, a narrow glass slab, and a small paper pad.

"I guess the thumbs'll be enough," he said. "There's only one set of hands showing on the statue."

He ran the inked roller over the glass slab, and going to Bliss, asked him to hold out his hands.

"Press your thumbs on the ink and then put 'em down on this paper," he ordered.

Bliss complied without a word; and when the impressions had been made Dubois again placed the jeweller's-glass in his eye and inspected the marks.

"Looks like 'em," he commented. "Ulnar loops—same like those on the statue. . . . Anyhow, I'll check 'em."

He knelt down beside the statue and held the pad close to its ankles. For a minute or so he studied the two sets of finger-prints.

"They match," he announced at length. "No doubt about it. . . . And there ain't another visible mark on the statue. This gentleman"—he gestured contemptuously toward Bliss—"is the only person who's laid hands on the statue, so far as I can see."

"That's bully with me," grinned Heath. "Let me have the enlargements as soon as you can—I got a feeling I'm going to need 'em." He took out a fresh cigar and bit the end off with gloating satisfaction. "I guess that'll be all Captain. Many thanks. . . . Now you can go and victual up."

"And let me tell you I need it." Dubois passed his camera and paraphernalia to Bellamy, who packed them with stodgy precision; and the two of them walked noisily out of the museum.

Heath finally got his cigar going, and for several moments stood puffing on it voluptuously, one eye cocked at Vance.

"That sorta sews things up—don't it, sir?" he asked. "Or maybe you've swallowed the doctor's abili." He addressed himself to Markham. "I put it up to you, sir. There's only one set of finger-prints on that statue; and if those prints were made last night, I'd like to have somebody drive up in a hearse and tell me what became of the finger-prints of the bird who cracked Kyle over the head. Kyle was hit with the top of the statue, and whoever did it musta had hold of it by the legs. . . . Now, Mr. Markham, I ask you: is any one going to rub off his own finger-prints and leave those of the doctor? He couldn't have done it if he'd wanted to."

Before Markham could reply, Vance spoke.

"How do you know, Sergeant, that the person who killed Mr. Kyle actually wielded the statue?"

Heath gave Vance a look of amazement.

"Say! You don't seriously think, do you, that this lion-headed dame did the job by herself—like this Yogi says?" He jerked his thumb at Hani without turning his eyes.

"No, Sergeant." Vance shook his head. "I haven't yet gone in for the supernatural. And I don't think the murderer erased his finger-prints and left those of Doctor Bliss. But I do think, d' ye see, that there's some explanation which will account for all the contradict'ry phases of this astonishin' case."

"Maybe there is." Heath felt that he could be tolerant and magnanimous. "But I'm pinning my opinion on finger-prints and tangible evidence."

"A very dangerous procedure, Sergeant," Vance told him, with unwonted seriousness. "I doubt if you could ever get a conviction against Doctor Bliss on the evidence you possess. It's far too obvious—too imbecile. You're bogged with an *embarras de richesse*—meanin' that no sane man would commit a crime and leave so many silly bits of damnin' evidence around. . . . And I believe Mr. Markham will agree with me."

"I'm not so sure," said Markham dubiously. "There's something in what you say, Vance; but on the other hand——"

"Excuse *me,* gentlemen!" Heath had suddenly become animated. "I gotta see Hennessey—I'll be back in a minute." And he stalked with vigorous determination to the front door and disappeared.

Bliss, to all appearances, had taken no interest in the discussion of his possible guilt. He had sunk back in his chair, where he sat staring resignedly at the floor—a tragic, broken figure. When the Sergeant had left us he moved his head slowly toward Vance.

"Your detective is fully justified in his opinion," he said. "I can see his point of view. Everything is against me—everything!" His tone, though flat and colorless, was bitter. "If only I hadn't fallen asleep this morning, I'd know the meaning of all this. . . . My scarab-pin, that financial report, those finger-prints. . . ." He shook his head like a man in a daze. "It's damnable—damnable!" His trembling hands went to his face, and he placed his elbows on his knees, bending forward in an attitude of utter despair.

"It's too damnable, doctor," Vance replied soothingly. "Therein lies our hope of a solution."

Again he walked to the cabinet and remained for some time in *distrait* contemplation. Hani had returned to his ascetic adoration of Teti-shiret; and Scarlett, frowning and unhappy, was pacing nervously up and down between the delicate state chair and the shelves holding the *shawabtis.* Markham stood in a brown study, his hands clasped behind him, gazing at the shaft of sunshine which had fallen diagonally through the high rear windows.

I noted that Hennessey had silently entered the main door and taken his post on the stair landing, one hand resting ominously in his right coat pocket.

Then the little metal door at the head of the iron spiral stairs swung open, and Heath appeared at the entrance to Doctor Bliss's study. One hand was behind him, out of sight, as he descended to the floor of the museum. He walked directly to Bliss and stood for a moment glowering grimly at the man whose guilt he believed in. Suddenly his hand shot forward—it was holding a white canvas tennis shoe.

"That yours, doctor?" he barked.

Bliss gazed at the shoe with perplexed astonishment.

"Why . . . yes. Certainly it's mine. . . ."

"You bet your sweet life it's yours!" The Sergeant strode to Markham and held up the sole of the shoe for inspection. I was standing at the District Attorney's side, and I saw that the rubber sole was criss-crossed with ridges and that there was a pattern of small hollow circles on the heel. But that which sent an icy breath of horror through me was the fact that the entire sole was red with dried blood.

"I found that shoe in the study, Mr. Markham," Heath was saying. "It was wrapped in a newspaper at the bottom of the waste-basket, covered up with all kinds of trash . . . hidden!"

It was several moments before Markham spoke. His eyes moved from the shoe to Bliss and back again; finally they rested on Vance.

"I think that clinches it." His voice was resolute. "I have no alternative in the matter now——"

Bliss sprang to his feet and hurried toward the Sergeant, his hypnotized gaze fastened on the shoe.

"What is it?" he cried. "What has that shoe to do with Kyle's death. . . ? He caught sight of the blood. "Oh, God in Heaven!" he moaned.

Vance placed a hand on the man's shoulder.

"Sergeant Heath found footprints here, doctor. They were made by one of your canvas shoes. . . ."

"How can that be?" Bliss's fascinated eyes were riveted on the bloody sole. "I left those shoes upstairs in my bedroom last night, and I came down this morning in my slippers. . . . *There's something diabolical going on in this house.*"

"Something diabolical, yes!—something unspeakable devilish. . . . And rest assured, Doctor Bliss, I am going to find out what it is. . . ."

"I'm sorry, Vance," Markham's stern voice rang forth ominously. "I know you don't believe Doctor Bliss is guilty. But I have a duty to perform. I'd be betraying the people who elected me if, in view of the evidence, I didn't take action.—And, after all, you may be wrong." (He said this with the kindliness of an old friend.) "In any event, my duty is clear."

He nodded to Heath.

"Sergeant, place Doctor Bliss under arrest, and charge him with the murder of Benjamin H. Kyle."

8

IN THE STUDY

(Friday, July 13; 2 P.M.)

I HAD often seen Vance in crucial moments of violent disagreement with Markham's judgment, but, whatever his feelings had been, he had always assumed a cynical and nonchalant attitude. Now, however, no lightness or playfulness marked his manner. He was grim and serious: a deep frown had settled on his forehead, and a look of baffled exasperation had come into his cold gray eyes. He compressed his lips tightly and crammed his hands deep into his coat pockets. I expected him to protest vigorously against Markham's action, but he remained silent, and I realized that he was confronted by one of the most difficult and unusual problems in his career.

His eyes drifted from Bliss to the immobile back of Hani and rested there. But they were unseeing eyes—eyes that were turned inward as if seeking for some means of counteracting the drastic step about to be taken against the great Egyptologist.

Heath, on the contrary, was elated. A grin of satisfaction had overspread his dour face at Markham's order, and without moving from in front of Bliss, he called stridently to the ominous figure of the detective on the stair landing.

"Hey, Hennessey! Tell Snitkin to phone Precinct Station 8 for a wagon. . . . Then go out back and get Emery, and bring him in here."

Hennessey disappeared, and Heath stood watching Bliss like a cat, as though he expected the doctor to make a dash for liberty. Had the situation not been so tragic the Sergeant's attitude would have appeared humorous.

"You needn't book and finger-print the doctor at the local station," Markham told him. "Send him direct to Headquarters. I'll assume all responsibility."

"That's fine with me, sir." The Sergeant seemed greatly pleased. "I'll want to talk confidentially with this baby myself later on."

Bliss, once the blow had fallen, had drawn himself together. He sat upright, his head thrown slightly back, his eyes gazing defiantly out of the rear windows. There was no cowering, no longer any fear, in his manner. Faced with the inevitable, he had apparently decided to accept it with stoical intrepidity. I could not help admiring the man's fortitude in extremity.

Scartlet stood like a man paralyzed, his mouth hanging partly open, his eyes fixed on his employer with a kind of unbelieving horror. Hani, of all the persons in the room, was the least perturbed: he had not even turned round from his rapt contemplation of Teti-shiret.

Vance, after several moments, dropped his chin on his chest, and his perplexed frown deepened. Then, as if on sudden impluse, he swung about and walked to the end cabinet. He stood absorbed, leaning against the statue of Anûbis; but soon his head moved slowly up and down and from side to side as he inspected various parts of the cabinet and its partly-drawn curtain.

Presently he came back to Heath.

"Sergeant, let me have another look at that tennis slipper." His voice was slow and strained.

Heath, without relaxing his vigilance, reached in his pocket and held out the shoe. Vance took it and, again adjusting his monocle, scrutinized the sole. Then he returned the shoe to the Sergeant.

"By the by," he said; "the doctor has more than one foot. . . . What about the other slipper?"

"I didn't look for it," snapped Heath. "This one was enough for me. It's the right shoe—the one that made the footprints."

"So it is." Vance's drawl informed me that his mind was more at ease. "Still, I could bear to know where the other shoe is."

"I'll find it—don't worry, sir." Heath spoke with contemptuous cocksureness. "I've got a little investigating to do as soon as I get the doctor safely booked at Headquarters."

"Typical police procedure," murmured Vance. "Book your man and then investigate. A sweet practice."

Markham was ruffled by this comment.

"It seems to me, Vance," he remarked with angry indignity, "that the investigation has already led to something fairly definite. Whatever else we find will be in the nature of supplementary evidence."

"Oh, will it now? Fancy that!" Vance smiled tauntingly. "I observe you've gone in for fortune-telling. Do you crystal-gaze in your moments of leisure, by any chance? . . . I myself am not what you'd call clairvoyant, but, Markham old dear, I can read the future better than you. And I assure you that when this investigation is continued there will be no supplement'ry evidence against Doctor Bliss. Indeed, you'll be amazed at what will turn up."

He came nearer to the District Attorney and dropped his scoffing tone.

"Can't you see, Markham, that you're playing into the murderer's hands? The person who killed Kyle planned the affair so you'd do exactly what you are doing. . . . And, as I've already told you, you'll never get a conviction with the preposterous evidence you have."

"I'll come mighty close to it," Markham retorted. "In any event, my duty is plain. I'll have to take a chance on the conviction. . . . But for once, Vance, I think you've permitted your theories to override a simple, obvious fact."

Before Vance could reply Hennessey and Emery came into the museum.

"Here, boys," the Sergeant ordered, "take this bird up-stairs and get some clothes on him, and bring him back here. Make it snappy."

Bliss went out between the two detectives.

Markham turned to Scarlett.

"You'd better wait in the drawing-room. I'll want to question every one, and I think you can give us some of the information we want. . . . And take Hani with you."

"I'll be glad to do what I can." Scarlett spoke in an awed voice. "But you're making a terrible mistake——"

"I'll settle that point for myself," Markham interrupted coldly. "Be good enough to wait in the drawing-room."

Scarlett and Heath walked slowly up the museum and passed out through the great steel door.

Vance had gone to the front of the spiral stairs and was pacing up and down with suppressed anxiety. A tense atmosphere had settled over the room. No one spoke. Heath was inspecting the small statue of Sakhmet with forced curiosity; and Markham had lapsed into a state of solemn abstraction.

A few minutes later Hennessey and Emery returned with Doctor Bliss in street cothes. They had hardly reached the rear of the museum when Snitkin put his head in the front door and called:

"The wagon's here, Sergeant."

Bliss turned immediately, and the two detectives swung about alertly. The three men had taken only a few steps when Vance's voice cracked out like a whip.

"Stop!" He looked squarely at Markham. "You can't do this! The thing is a farce. You're making an unutterable ass of yourself."

I had never seen Vance so fiery—he was quite unlike his usual frigid self—and Markham was noticeably taken aback.

"Give me ten minutes," Vance hurried on. "There's something I want to find out—there's an experiment I want to make. Then, if you're not satisfied, you can go ahead with this imbecile arrest."

Heath's face grew red with anger.

"Look here, Mr. Markham," he protested; "we've got the goods——"

"Just a minute, Sergeant." Markham held up his hand: he had obviously been impressed by Vance's unusual earnestness. "Ten minutes is not going to make any material difference. And if Mr. Vance has any evidence we don't know of, we might as well learn it now." He turned brusquely to Vance. "What's on your mind? I'm willing to give you ten minutes. . . . Has your request anything to do wth what you found on top of the cabinet and put in your pocket?"

"Oh, a great deal." Vance had again assumed his habitual easy-going manner. "And many thanks for the respite. . . . I'd suggest, however, that these two myrmidons take the doctor into the front hall and hold him there for further instructions."

Markham, after a brief hesitation, nodded to Heath, who gave Hennessey and Emery the necessary order.

When we were alone Vance turned toward the spiral stairs.

"Imprimis," he said almost gaily, "I passionately desire to make a curs'ry inspection of the doctor's study. I've a premonition that we will find something there of the most entrancin' interest."

He was now half-way up the stairs, with Markham, Heath and me following.

The study was a spacious room, about twenty feet square. It had two large windows at the rear and a smaller window on the east side giving on a narrow court. There were several massive embayed bookcases about the walls; and stacked in the corners were piles of paper pamphlets and cardboard folders. Along the wall which contained the door leading into the hall, stretched a long divan. Between the two rear windows stood a large flat-topped mahogany desk, before which was a cushioned swivel chair. Several other chairs were drawn up about the desk—evidences of the conference that had been held the previous night.

It was an orderly room, and there was a striking neatness about all of its appointments. Even the papers and books on the desk were carefully arranged, attesting to Bliss's meticulous nature. The only untidiness in the study was where Heath had upset the wicker waste-basket in his search for the tennis shoe. The curtains of the rear windows were up, and the afternoon sunlight flooded in.

Vance stood for a while just inside the door glancing slowly about him. His eyes tarried for a moment on the disposition of the chairs, but more especially, I thought, on the doctor's swivel seat, which stood several feet away from the desk. He looked at the heavily padded hall door, and let his gaze rest on the drawn curtain of the side window. After a pause he went to the window and raised the shade,—the window was shut.

"Rather strange," he commented. "A torrid day like this—and the window closed. Bear that in mind, Markham. . . . You observe, of course, that there's a window opposite in the next house."

"What possible significance could that have?" asked Markham irritably.

"I haven't the foggiest notion, don't y' know. . . . Unless," Vance added whimsically, "something went on in here that the occupant—or occupants— of the room didn't wish the neighbors to know about. The trees in the yard completely preclude any spying through the rear windows."

"Huh! That looks like a point in our favor," Heath rejoined. "The doc shuts the side window and pulls the shade down so's nobody'll hear him going in and out of the museum, or'll see him hiding the shoe."

Vance nodded.

"Your reasoning, Sergeant, is good as far as it goes. But you might carry the equation to one more decimal point. Why, for instance, didn't your guilty doctor open the window and throw up the shade after the dire deed was done? Why should he leave another obvious clew indicating his guilt?"

"Guys who commit murder, Mr. Vance," argued the Sergeant pugnaciously, "don't think of everything."

"The trouble with this crime," Vance returned quietly, "is that the murderer thought of too many things. He erred on the side of prodigality, so to speak."

He stepped to the desk. On one end lay a low starched turn-over collar with a dark-blue four-in-hand pulled through it.

"Behold," he said, "the doctor's collar and cravat which he removed last night during the conference. The scarab pin was in the cravat. Any one might have taken it—eh, what?"

"So you remarked before." Markham's tone held a note of bored sarcasm. "Did you bring us here to show us the necktie? Scarlett told us it was here. Forgive me, Vance, if I confess that I am not stunned by your discovery."

"No, I didn't lead you here to exhibit the doctor's neckwear." Vance spoke with calm assurance. "I merely mentioned the four-in-hand *en passant.*"

He brushed the spilled papers of the waste-basket back and forth with his foot.

"I am rather anxious to know where the doctor's other tennis shoe is. I have a feelin' its whereabouts might tell us something."

"Well, it ain't in the basket," declared Heath. "If it had been I'd have found it."

"Ah! But, Sergeant, why wasn't it in the basket? That's a point worth considerin', don't y' know."

"Maybe it didn't have any blood on it. And that being the case, there wasn't any use in hiding it."

"But, my word! It strikes me that the blameless left shoe is hidden even better than was the incriminatin' right shoe." (During the discussion Vance had made a fairly thorough search of the study for the missing tennis shoe.) "It's certainly not round here."

Markham, for the first time since we quitted the museum, showed signs of interest.

"I see your point, Vance," he conceded reluctantly. "The telltale shoe was hidden here in the study, and the other one has disappeared. . . . I admit that's rather odd. What's your explanation?"

"Oh, I say! Let's locate the shoe before we indulge in speculation. . . ." Vance then addressed himself to Heath. "Sergeant, if you should get Brush to conduct you to Doctor Bliss's bedchamber, I'm rather inclined to think you'll find the missing shoe there. You remember the doctor said he wore his tennis shoes up-stairs last night and came down this morning in his house slippers."

"Huh!" Heath scouted the suggestion. Then he gave Vance a sharp, calculating look. After a moment he changed his mind. Shrugging his shoulders in capitulation, he went swiftly out into the hall, and we could hear him calling down the rear stairs for the butler.

"If the Sergeant finds the shoe up-stairs," Vance observed to Markham, "it will be fairly conclusive evidence that the doctor didn't wear his tennis shoes this morning; for we know that he did not return to his bedroom after descending to his study before breakfast."

Markham looked perplexed.

"Then who brought the other shoe from his room this morning? And how did it get in the waste-basket? And how did it become blood-stained? . . . Surely, the murderer wore the shoe that Heath found here. . . ."

"Oh, yes—there can be no doubt of that." Vance nodded gravely. "And my theory is that the murderer wore only the one tennis shoe and left the other up-stairs."

Markham clicked his tongue with annoyance.

"Such a theory doesn't make sense."

"Forgive me, Markham, for disagreeing with you," Vance returned dulcetly. "But I think it makes more sense than the clews on which you're so trustfully counting to convict the doctor."

Heath burst into the room at this moment, holding the left tennis shoe in his hand. His expression was sheepish, but his eyes blinked with excitement.

"It was there, all right," he announced, "—at the foot of the bed. . . . Now, how did it get there?"

"Perhaps," softy suggested Vance, "the doctor wore it up-stairs last night, as he said."

"Then how the hell did the other shoe get down here?" The Sergeant was now holding the two shoes, one in each hand, staring at them in wrathful bewilderment.

"If you knew who brought that other shoe downstairs this morning," returned Vance, "you'd now who killed Kyle." Then he added: "Not that it would do us any particular good at the present moment."

Markham had been standing scowling at the floor and smoking furiously. The shoe episode had disconcerted him. But now he looked up and made an impatient gesture.

"You're making a mountain out of this affair, Vance," he asserted aggressively. "A number of simple explanations suggest themselves. The most plausible one seems to be that Doctor Bliss, when he came down-stairs this morning, picked up his tennis shoes to have them handy in his study, and in his nervousness—or merely accidentally—dropped one, or even failed to pick both of them up, and did not discover the fact until he was here——"

"And then," continued Vance, with a japish grin, "he took off one slipper and put on the tennis shoe, murdered Kyle, re-exchanged it for his temporarily discarded slipper, and tucked the tennis shoe in the waste-basket."

"It's possible."

Vance sighed audibly.

"Possible—yes. I suppose that almost anything is possible in this illogical world. But really, Markham, I can't subscribe enthusiastically to your touchin' theory of the doctor's having picked up one shoe instead of two and not having known the difference. He's much to orderly and methodical—too conscious of details."

"Let us assume then," Markham persisted, "that the doctor actually wore one tennis shoe and one bedroom slipper when he came to the study this morning. Scarlett told us his feet troubled him a great deal."

"If that hypothesis is correct," countered Vance, "how did the other bedroom slipper get down-stairs? He would hardly have put it in his pocket and carried it along."

"Brush perhaps. . . ."

Heath had been following the discussion closely, and now he went into action.

"We can check that one *pronto,* Mr. Vance," he said; and going briskly to the hall door, he called down the stairs to the butler.

But no help came from Brush. He declared that neither he nor any member of the household had been near the study after Bliss had gone there at eight o'clock, with the exception of the time when he carried the doctor's breakfast to him. When asked what shoes the doctor was wearing, Brush answered that he had taken no notice.

When the butler had gone Vance shrugged his shoulders.

"Let's not fume and whirret ourselves over the mysteriously separated pair of tennis shoes. My prim'ry reason for luring you to the study was to inspect the remains of the doctor's breakfast."

Markham gave a perceptible start, and his eyes narrowed.

"Good Heavens! You don't believe. . . ? I'll confess I thought of it, too. But then came all that other evidence. . . ."

"Thought of what, sir?" Heath was frankly exasperated, and his tone was irritable.

"Both Mr. Markham and I," explained Vance soothingly, "noted the dazed condition of Doctor Bliss when he appeared this morning in answer to my continued pounding on the door."

"He'd been asleep. Didn't he tell us so?"

"Quite. And that's why I'm so dashed interested in his matutional coffee."

Vance walked to the end of the desk upon which rested a small silver tray containing a rack of toast and a cup and saucer. The toast had not been touched, the the cup was practically empty. Only the congealed brown dregs of what had evidently been coffee remained in the bottom. Vance leant over and looked into the cup. Then he lifted it to his nose.

"There's a slightly acrid odor here," he remarked.

He touched the tip of his finger to the inside of the cup and placed it on his tongue.

"Yes! . . . Just what I thought," he nodded, setting the cup down. "Opium. And it's powered opium—the kind commonly used in Egypt. The other forms and derivatives of opium—such as laudanum, morphine, heroin, thebain, and codein—are not easily obtainable there."

Heath had come forward and stood peering belligerently into the cup.

"Well, suppose there was opium in the coffee," he rumbled. "What does that mean?"

"Ah, who knows?" Vance was lighting a cigarette, his eyes in space. "It might, of course, account for the doctor's long siesta this morning and for his confused condition when he answered my knock. Also, it might indicate that some one narcotized his coffee for a purpose. The fact is, Sergeant, the opium in the doctor's coffee might mean various things. At the present moment I'm expressing no opinion. I'm merely calling Mr. Markham's attention to the drug. . . . I'll say this, however: as soon as I saw the doctor this morning and observed the way he acted, I guessed that there would be evidences of an opiate in the study. And, being fairly familiar with conditions in Egypt, I surmised that the opiate would prove to be powdered opium—*opii pulvis.* Opium makes one very thirsty: that is why I wasn't in the least astonished when the doctor asked for a drink of water." He looked at Markham. "Does this discovery of the opium affect the doctor's legal status?"

"It's certainly a strong point in his favor," Markham returned after several moments.

That he was deeply perplexed was only too apparent. But he was loath to forgo his belief in Bliss's guilt; and when he spoke again it was obvious that he was arguing desperately against Vance's new discovery.

"I realize that the presence of the opium will have to be explained away before a conviction can be assured. But, on the other hand, we don't know how much opium he took. Nor do we know when he took it. He may have drunk the coffee *after* the murder—we have only his word that he drank it at nine o'clock. . . . No, it certainly doesn't affect the fundamental issue—though it does raise a very grave question. But the evidence against him is too strong to be counterbalanced by this one point in his favor. Surely, you must see, Vance, that the mere presence of opium in that cup is not conclusive evidence that Bliss was asleep from nine o'clock until you knocked on the study door."

"The perfect Public Prosecutor," sighed Vance. "But a shrewd defense lawyer could sow many fecund seeds of doubt in the jurors' so-called minds—eh, what?"

"True." The admission came after a moment's thought. "But we can't overlook the fact that Bliss was practically the only person who had the opportunity to kill Kyle. Every one else was out of the house, with the exception of Hani; and Hani impresses me as a harmless fanatic who believes in the supernatural power of his Egyptian dieties. So far as we know, Bliss was the only person who was actually on hand when Kyle was murdered."

Vance studied Markham for several seconds. Then he said:

"Suppose it had not been necess'ry for the murderer to have been anywhere near the museum when Kyle was killed with the statue of Sakhmet."

Markham took his cigar slowly from his mouth.

"What do you mean? How could that statue have been wielded by an absent person? It strikes me you're talking nonsense."

"Perhaps I am." Vance was troubled and serious. "And yet, Markham, I found something on top of that end cabinet which makes me think that maybe the murder was planned with diabolical cleverness. . . . As I told you, I want to make an experiment. Then, when I have made it, your course of action must rest entirely on your own convictions. . . . There's something both terrible and subtle about this crime. All its outward appearances are misleading—deliberately so."

"How long will this experiment take?" Markham was patently impressed by Vance's tone.

"Only a few minutes. . . ."

Heath had taken a sheet of newspaper from the basket and was carefully wrapping up the cup.

"This goes to our chemist," he explained sullenly. "I'm not doubting you, Mr. Vance, but I want an expert analysis."

"You're quite right, Sergeant."

Vance's eye at that moment caught sight of a small bronze tray on the desk, containing several yellow pencils and a fountain pen. Leaning over casually, he picked up the pencils, glanced at them, and put them back on the tray. Markham noted the action, as did I, but he refrained from asking any questions.

"The experiment will have to be made in the museum," Vance said; "and I'll need a couple of sofa pillows for it."

He walked to the divan and tucked two large pillows under his arm. Then he went to the steel door and held it open.

Markham and Heath and I passed down the spiral stairs; and Vance followed us.

9

VANCE MAKES AN EXPERIMENT

(Friday, July 13, 2:15 P.M.)

VANCE WENT direct to the end cabinet before which Kyle's body had been found, and dropped the two sofa pillows on the floor. Then he looked again speculatively at the upper edge of the cabinet.

"I wonder. . . ," he murmured. "Dash it all! I'm almost afraid to carry on. If I should be wrong, this entire case would come topplin' about my head. . . ."

"Come, come!" Markham was growing impatient. "Soliloquies have gone out of date, Vance. If you have anything to show me, let's get it over with."

"Right you are."

Vance stepped to the ash-tray and resolutely crushed out his cigarette. Returning to the cabinet he beckoned to Markham and Heath.

"By way of *præludium*," he began, "I want to call your attention to this curtain. You will observe that the brass ring at the end has been slipped off of the rod and is now hanging down."

For the first time I noticed that the small ring on the corner of the curtain was not strung on the rod, and that the left edge of the curtain sagged correspondingly.

"You will also observe," Vance continued, "that the curtain of this cabinet is only half drawn. It's as if some one had started to draw the curtain and, for some reason, had stopped. When I saw the partly-drawn curtain this morning it struck me as a bit peculiar, for obviously the curtain should have been entirely closed or else entirely open. We may assume that the curtain was closed when Kyle arrived here—we have Hani's word for it that he had pulled shut the curtain of this particular cabinet because of the disorder of its contents; and Doctor Bliss mentioned to Kyle on the telephone that the new treasures were in the end cabinet—*the cabinet with the drawn curtain.* . . . Now, in order to open the curtain, one has only to make a single motion of the arm—that is to say, one has only to take hold of the left-hand edge of it and pull it to the right: the brass rings would slide easily over the metal pole. . . . But what do we find? We find the curtain only half drawn! Kyle unquestionably would not have opened the curtain half-way to inspect the contents of the cabinet. Therefore, I concluded that something must have halted the curtain at the half-way point, and that Kyle died before he could draw the curtain entirely open. . . . I say, Markham; are you with me?"

"Go on." Markham had become interested. Heath, too, was watching Vance with close attention.

"Perpend, then. Kyle was found dead directly in front of this end cabinet; and he had died as the result of having been struck over the head by the heavy diorite statue of Sakhmet. This statue, as we know, had been placed by Hani on the top of the cabinet. When I observed that the curtain of the cabinet had been only partly opened and then discovered that the first brass ring of the curtain—the ring on the extreme left end—was not on the rod, I began to speculate—especially as I was familiar with Doctor Bliss's orderly habits. Had the ring been off of the rod last night when Doctor Bliss came into the museum, you may rest assured he would have seen it. . . ."

"Are you suggesting, Vance," asked Markham, "that the ring was deliberately taken off of the rod sometime this morning—and for a purpose?"

"Yes! At some time between Doctor Bliss's phone call to Kyle last night and Kyle's arrival this morning, I believe that some one removed the ring from the rod—and, as you say, for a purpose!"

"What purpose?" Heath put the question. His voice was aggressive and antagonistic.

"That remains to be seen, Sergeant." Vance spoke with scarcely any modulation of tone. "I'll admit I have a rather definite theory about it. In fact, I had a theory about it the moment I saw the position in which Kyle's body lay and learned that Hani had placed the statue atop the end cabinet. The partly drawn curtain and the unstrung brass ring substantiated that theory."

"I think I understand what's in your mind, Vance." Markham nodded slowly. "Was that why you inspected the top of the cabinet and got Hani to show you exactly where he had placed the statue?"

"Precisely. And not only did I find what I was looking for, but Hani confirmed my suspicions when he pointed to the spot where he had set the statue. That spot was several inches back from the edge of the cabinet; but there was also a deep scratch at the very edge and a second outline of the statue's base in the dust, showing that the statue had been moved forward after Hani had put it in place."

"But Doctor Bliss admitted he moved it last night before retiring," suggested Markham.

"He said only that he had straightened the statue," Vance answered. "And the two impressions made in the dust by the front of the statue's base are exactly parallel, so that the adjustment to which Doctor Bliss referred could not have been the moving of the statue six inches forward."

"I see what you mean. . . . Your theory is that some one moved the statue to the very edge of the cabinet after Doctor Bliss had straightened it. And it's not an unreasonable assumption."

Heath, who had been listening sullenly with half-shut eyes, suddenly mounted one of the chairs in front of the cabinet and peered over the moulding.

"I want to see this," he mumbled. Presently he descended and wagged his head heavily at Markham. "It's like Mr. Vance says, all right. . . . But what's all this hocus-pocus got to do with the case?"

"That's what I'm endeavorin' to ascertain, Sergeant," smiled Vance. "It may have nothing to do with it. On the other hand. . . ."

He leaned over and, with considerable effort, lifted the statue of Sakhmet. (As I have said, the statue was about two feet high. It was solidly sculptured and had a heavy thick base. I later lifted the statue to test it, and I should say it weighed at least thirty pounds.) Vance, stepping on a chair, placed the statue, with great precision, on top of the cabinet at the very edge of the moulding. Having carefully superimposed its base over the outlines in the dust, he drew the curtain shut. Then he took the free brass ring in his left hand, turned the corner of the curtain back until the ring reached the left-hand edge of the statue, tipped the statue to the right, and placed the ring just under the forward edge of the statue's base.

Having done this, he reached into his coat pocket and drew forth the object he had found on the top of the cabinet. He held it up to us.

"What I discovered, Markham," he explained, "was a three-inch section of a pencil, carefully cut and trimmed. I assumed that it was a home-made 'upright' such as is used in figure-4 traps. . . . Let us see if it works."

He tipped the statue forward and propped the piece of pencil under the rear edge of the statue's base. He took his hands away, and the statue stood leaning toward us, perilously balanced. For a moment it seemed as if it might topple over of its own accord, but the prepared pencil was apparently the exact length necessary to tilt the statue forward without quite upsetting its equilibrium.

"So far my theory checks." Vance stepped down from the chair. "Now, we will proceed with the experiment."

He moved the chair to one side, and arranged the two sofa pillows over the spot where Kyle's head had lain at the foot of Anûbis. Then he straightened up, and faced the District Attorney.

"Markham," he said sombrely, "I present you with a possibility. Regard the positon of that curtain; consider the positon of the loose brass ring—under the edge of the statue; observe the tilting attitude of Our Lady of Vengeance; and then picture the arrival of Kyle this morning. He had been informed that the new treasures were in the end cabinet, with the curtain drawn. He told Brush not to disturb Doctor Bliss because he was going into the museum to inspect the contents of the recent shipment."

He paused and deliberately lighted a cigarette. By his slow, lazy movements I knew that his nerves were tense.

"I am not suggesting," he continued, "that Kyle met his end as the result of a death trap. In fact, I do not even know if my reconstructed trap will work. But I am advancing the theory as a possibility; for if the defense attorneys can show that Kyle could have been murdered by some one other than Doctor Bliss—that is, *by an absent person*—then your case against him would receive a decided setback. . . ."

He stepped over to the statue of Anûbis. Lifting up the lower left-hand corner of the curtain, he stood close against the west wall of the museum.

"Let us say that Kyle, after taking his position before this end cabinet, reached out and drew the curtain aside. Now, what would have happened— provided the death trap had actually been set? . . ."

He gave the curtain a sharp jerk to the right. It moved over the rod until it was caught and held half-way across by the brass ring that had been inserted beneath Sakhmet's base. The jar dislodged the statue from its perilously balanced position. It toppled forward and fell with a terrific thud upon the sofa pillows, in the exact spot where Kyle's head had lain.

There were several moments of silence. Markham continued to smoke, his eyes focussed on the fallen statue. He was frowning and thoughtful. Heath, however, was frankly astounded. Apparently he had not considered the possibility of a death trap, and Vance's demonstration had everted, to a great extent, all his set theories. He glared at the statue of Sakhmet with perplexed amazement, his cigar held tightly between his teeth.

Vance was the first to speak.

"The experiment seems to have worked, don't y' know. Really, I think I've demonstrated the possibility of Kyle's having been killed while alone in the museum. . . . Kyle was rather short in stature, and there was sufficient distance between the top of the cabinet and Kyle's head for the statue to have gained a deadly momentum. The width of the cabinet is only a little over two feet, so that it would have been inevitable that the statue would hit him on the head, provided he had been standing in front of it. And he obviously would have stood directly in front of it when he pulled the curtain. The weight of the statue is sufficient to have caused the terrific fracture of his skull; and the position of the statue across the back of his head is wholly consistent with his having been killed by a carefully planned trap."

Vance made a slight gesture of emphasis.

"You must admit, Markham, that the demonstration I've just given you makes plausible the guilt of any absent person, and consequently removes one of your strongest counts against Doctor Bliss—namely, proximity and opportunity. . . . And this fact, taken in connection with the opium found in the coffee, gives him a convincing, though not an absolute, alibi."

"Yes. . . ." Markham spoke with deliberate and pensive slowness. "The negative clews you have found tend to counteract the direct clews of the scarab and the financial report and the bloody footprints. There's no doubt about it: the doctor could present a strong defense. . . ."

"A reasonable doubt, as it were—eh, what?" Vance grinned. "A beautiful phrase—meaningless, of course, but typically legal. As if the mind of man were ever capable of being reasonable! . . . And don't overlook the fact, Markham, that, if the doctor had merely intended to brain Kyle with the statue of Sakhmet, the evidences of the death trap would not have been present. If his object was only to kill Kyle, why should the whittled pencil—in the shape of an 'upright'—have been on top of the cabinet?"

"You're perfectly right," Markham admitted. "A shrewd defense attorney could make a shambles of the case I have against the doctor."

"And consider your direct evidence for a moment." Vance seated himself and crossed his legs. "The scarab pin, which was found beside the body, could have been palmed by any one at the conference last night, and deliberately placed beside the murdered body. Or, if the doctor had been put to sleep by the opium in his coffee, it would have been an easy matter for the murderer to have taken the pin from the desk this morning—the door into the study, y' know, was never locked. And what would have been simpler than to have taken the financial report at the same time, and slipped it into Kyle's dead hand? . . . As for the bloody footprints: any member of the household could have taken the tennis shoe from Doctor Bliss's bedroom and made the prints in the blood and then chucked the shoe in the waste-basket while the doctor slept under the influence of the opiate. . . . And that closed east window on the court: doesn't that closed window, with its drawn shade, indicate that someone in the study didn't want the neighbors next door to see what was going on?"

Vance took a slow draw on his cigarette and blew out a long spiral of smoke.

"I'm no Demosthenes, Markham, but I'd take Doctor Bliss's case in any court, and guarantee him an acquittal."

Markham had begun walking up and down, his hands behind his back.

"The presence of this death trap and of the opium in the coffee cup," he conceded at length, "casts an entirely new light on the case. It throws the affair wide open and makes possible and even plausible some one else's guilt." He stopped suddenly and looked sharply at Heath. "What's your opinion, Sergeant?"

Heath was obviously in a quandary.

"I'm going cuckoo," he confessed, after a pause. "I thought we had the damn affair sewed up in an air-tight bag, and now Mr. Vance pulls a lot of his subtle stuff and hands the doc a loophole." He gave Vance a belligerent glare. "Honest to Gawd, Mr. Vance, you shoulda been a lawyer." His contempt was devastating.

Markham could not help smiling, but Vance shook his head sadly and looked at the Sergeant with an exaggeratedly injured air.

"Oh, I say, Sergeant; must you be insultin'?" he protested whimsically. "I'm only tryin' to save you and Mr. Markham from making a silly blunder. And what thanks do I get? I'm told I should have been a lawyer! Alack and wella-day!"

"Let's forgo the cynicism." Markham was too upset to fall in with Vance's frivolous attitude. "You've made your point. And, in doing so, you've saddled me with a serious and weighty problem."

"Still and all," pursued Heath, "there's plenty of evidence against Bliss."

"Quite true, Sergeant." Vance had again become thoughtful. "But I'm afraid that evidence will not bear the closest scrutiny."

"You think, I take it," said Markham, "that the evidence was deliberately planted—that the actual murderer maliciously placed these clews so that they would point to Doctor Bliss."

"Is such a technic so unusual?" asked Vance. "Hasn't many a murderer sought to throw suspicion on some one else? Isn't criminal history filled with cases of innocent men being convicted on convincing circumstantial evidence? And is it not entirely possible that the misleading evidence in such cases was deliberately planted by the real culprits?"

"Still," Markham returned, "I can't afford, at this stage of the game, to ignore entirely the indicatory evidence pointing to Doctor Bliss. I must be able to prove a plot against him before I can completely exonerate him."

"And the arrest?"

Markham hesitated. He realized, I think, the hopelessness of his case now that Vance had unearthed so many contradictory bits of evidence.

"It's impossible, of course," he concluded, "to order the doctor's arrest at present, in view of the extenuating factors you've brought to light. . . . But," he added grimly, "I'm certainly not going to ignore altogether the evidence against him."

"And just what does one do in such legalistically complicated circumstances?"

Markham smoked for a while in troubled silence.

"I'm going to keep Bliss under close surveillance," he pronounced finally. Then he turned to Heath. "Sergeant, you may order your men to release the doctor. But make arrangements to have him followed day and night."

"That suits me, sir." Heath started toward the front stairs.

"And Sergeant," Markham called; "tell Doctor Bliss he is not to leave the house until I have seen him."

Heath disappeared on his errand.

10

THE YELLOW PENCIL

(Friday, July 13, 2:30 P.M.)

MARKHAM SLOWLY lighted a fresh cigar and sat down heavily on one of the folding chairs near the inlaid coffer, facing Vance.

"The situation is beginning to look serious—and complex," he said, with a weary sigh.

"More serious than you think," Vance returned. "And far more complex. . . . I assure you, Markham, that this murder is one of the most astounding and subtle criminal plots you have ever been faced with. Superficially it appears simple and direct—it was intended to appear that way, d'ye see—and your first reading of the clews was exactly what the murderer counted on."

Markham regarded Vance shrewdly.

"You have an idea of what that plot is?' His words were more a statement than a question.

"Yes . . . oh, yes." Vance at once became aloof. "An idea? . . . Quite. But not what you'd term a blindin' illumination. I immediately suspected a plot; and all the subsequent findings verified my theory. But I've only a nebulous idea regardin' it. And the precise object of the plot is totally obfuscated. However, since I know that the surface indications are deliberately misleading, there's a chance of getting at the truth."

Markham sat up aggressively.

"What's on your mind?"

"Oh, my dear chap! You flatter me abominably." Vance smiled blandly. "My mind is beclouded and adumbrated. It is shot with mist and mizzle, with vapor and haze and steam; it is cirrous and nubiferous, cumulous and vaporous; it is filled with woolpacks, mare's-tails, colt's-tails, cat's-tails, frost smoke, and spindrift. 'The lowring element scowls o'er the darkened landscip.' . . . My mind, in fact, is nephological——"

"Spare me your meteorological vocabulary. Remember, I'm only an ignorant District Attorney." Markham's sarcasm was measured by his exasperation. "Perhaps, however, you can suggest our next step. I frankly admit that, aside from cross-examining the members of the Bliss household, I can't see any means of approach to this problem; for, if Bliss isn't guilty, the crime was obviously committed by some one who was not only intimate with the domestic situation here but who had access to the house."

"I think, don't y' know," suggested Vance, "that we should first acquaint ourselves with the conditions and relationships existing in the ménage. It would give us a certain equipment, what? And it might indicate some fertile line of inquiry." He bent forward in his chair. "Markham, the solution of this problem depends almost entirely on our finding the motive. And there are sinister ramifications to that motive. Kyle's murder was no ordin'ry crime. It was planned with a finesse and a cunning amounting to genius. Only a tremendous incentive could have produced it. There's fanaticism behind this crime—a powerful, devastating *idée fixe* that is cruel and unspeakably ruthless. The actual murder was merely a prelimin'ry to something far more devilish—it was the means to an end. And that ultimate object was infinitely more terrible and despicable than Kyle's precipitous demise. . . . A nice, clean, swift murder can sometimes be justified, or at least extenuated. But the criminal in this instance did not stop with murder: he used it as a weapon to crush and ruin an innocent person. . . ."

"Granted what you say is true,"—Markham rose uneasily and leaned against the shelves containing the *shawabtis*—"how can we discover the interrelationships of this household without interviewing its members?"

"By questioning the one man who stands apart from the actual inmates."

"Scarlett?"

Vance nodded.

"He undoubtedly knows more than he has told us. He has been with the Bliss expedition for two years. He has lived in Egypt, and is acquainted with the family history. . . . Why not have him in here for a brief *causerie* before tackling the members of the establishment? There are several points I could endure to know ere the investigation proceeds."

Markham was watching Vance closely. Presently he moved his head up and down slowly.

"You've something in mind, Vance, and it's neither nimbus, cumulus, stratus, nor cirrus. . . . Very well. I'll get Scarlett here and let you question him."

Heath returned to the museum at this moment.

"Doc Bliss has gone to his bedroom, with orders to stay there," he reported. "The rest of 'em are in the drawing-room, and Hennessey and Emery are keeping their eye on things. Also, I sent the wagon away—and Snitkin's watching the front door." I had rarely seen Heath in so discouraged a mood.

"How did Doctor Bliss act when you ordered his release?" Vance asked.

"Didn't seem to care one way or another," the Sergeant told him, with an intonation of disgust. "Didn't even say anything. Just went up-stairs with his head down, stunned-like. . . . Queer bird, if you ask me."

"Most Egyptologists are queer birds, Sergeant," Vance remarked consolingly.

Markham was again growing impatient. He addressed himself curtly to Heath.

"Mr. Vance and I have decided to find out what Mr. Scarlett can tell us before going on with the investigation. Will you ask him to step here?"

The Sergeant extended his arms and let them fall in a broad gesture of resignation. Then he went from the museum. In a few moments he returned with Scarlett in tow.

Vance drew up several chairs. By his serious, deliberate manner I realized that he regarded the conference with Scarlett as highly important. At the time I was not aware of what was in his mind; nor did I understand why he had chosen Scarlett as his chief source of information. But before the day was over it was only too clear to me. With subtle accuracy and precision he had chosen the one man who could supply the data that were needed to solve the murder of Kyle. And the things Vance learned from Scarlett that afternoon proved to be the determining factors in his solution of the case.

Without preliminaries Vance informed Scarlett of the altered status of Doctor Bliss.

"Mr. Markham has decided to postpone the doctor's arrest. The evidence at present is most conflicting. We've discovered several things, which, from the legal point of view, throw serious doubt on his guilt. The fact is, Scarlett, we've come to the conclusion that further investigation is necess'ry before we can make any definite move."

Scarlett appeared greatly relieved.

"By Jove, Vance, I'm frightfully glad of that!" he exclaimed with complete conviction. "Doctor Bliss's guilt is unthinkable. What could possibly have been the man's motive? Kyle was his benefactor——"

"Have you any ideas on the subject?" Vance interrupted.

Scarlett shook his head emphatically.

"Not the ghost of an idea. The thing has stunned me. I can't imagine how it could have happened."

"Yes . . . most mysterious," Vance murmured. "We'll have to get at the matter by tryin' to discover the motive. . . . That's why we're appealin' to you. We want to know just what the inner workings are in the Bliss ménage. You, bein' more or less of an outsider, can possibly lead us to the truth. . . . For instance, you mentioned an intimate relationship between Kyle and Mrs. Bliss's father. Let us have the whole story."

"It's a bit romantic, but quite simple." Scarlett paused and took out his briar pipe. When he had got it going he continued: "You know the story of old

Abercrombie, Meryt's father. He went to Egypt in 1885, and became Grébaut's assistant the following year when Sir Gaston Maspero returned to France to resume his chair at the Collège de France. Maspero returned to Egypt in 1899 and retained his position as head of the Egyptian *Service des Antiquités* at Cairo until his resignation in 1914, at which time he was elected permanent Secretary of the Académie des Inscriptions et Belles-Lettres in Paris. Abercrombie then succeeded Maspero as Director of Antiquities at the Cairo Museum. In 1898, however, Abercrombie had fallen in love with a Copt lady, and had married her. Meryt was born two years later—in 1900."

Scarlett seemed to be having difficulty with his pipe, and used two matches to relight it.

"Kyle entered the picture four years before Meryt's birth," he went on. "He came to Egypt in 1896 as a representative of a group of New York bankers who had become financially interested in the proposed Nile irrigation system.* He met Abercrombie—then Grébaut's assistant—and their acquaintance developed into a close friendship. Kyle returned to Egypt nearly every year during the process of the dam's construction—that is, until 1902. He naturally met the Coptic lady whom Abercrombie subsequently married, and, I have every reason to believe, was much smitten with her. But being Abercrombie's friend and a gentleman, he refrained from any trespassing. However, when the lady died, at Meryt's birth, he quite openly transferred his affections from the mother to the daughter. He became Meryt's godfather and, in a big-hearted way, looked out for her as though she had been his own child. . . .Kyle wasn't a bad scout."

"And Bliss?"

"Bliss first went to Egypt in the winter of 1913. He met Abercrombie at that time, and they became friendly. He also met Meryt, who was then only thirteen years old. Seven years later—in 1920—young Salveter introduced Bliss to Kyle; and the first expedition to Egypt was made in the winter of 1921–22. Abercrombie died in Egypt in the summer of 1922, and Meryt was fathered, after a fashion, by Hani, who had been an old family retainer. The second Bliss expedition was in 1922–23; and Bliss again met Meryt. She was now twenty-three; and the following spring Bliss married her. . . . You met Meryt, Vance, on the third Bliss expedition in 1924. . . . Bliss brought Meryt back to America with him after the second expedition; and last year he added Hani to his personal staff. Hani had then been made an under inspector by the Egyptian Government. . . . That sums up the relationship between Bliss and Kyle and Abercrombie and Meryt. Is it what you wanted?"

"Exactly." Vance looked at the tip of his cigarette thoughtfully. "Briefly, then, Kyle was interested in Mrs. Bliss because of his love for her mother and his friendship for her father; and no doubt he had an added interest in financing Bliss's later expeditions because of the fact that Bliss married the daughter of his lost love."

"Yes, the assumption is perfectly reasonable."

"That bein' the case, Kyle probably has not forgotten Mrs. Bliss in his will. Do you happen to know, Scarlett, if he made any provision for her?"

---

* The irrigation to which Scarlett referred was the system that resulted in the Aswân Dam, the Asyût Weir, and the Esneh Barrage.

"As I understand it, " Scarlett explained, "he left a very considerable fortune to Meryt. I have only Hani's word for it; but he once mentioned to me that Kyle had willed her a large amount. Hani was elated over the fact, for there's no doubt he has a very deep, dog-like affection for her."

"And what of Salveter?"

"I presume that Kyle has taken care of him generously. Kyle was not married—whether his loyalty to Meryt's mother was responsible for his bachelorhood, I can't say—and Salveter was his only nephew. Moreover, he liked Salveter immensely. I'm inclined to think that, when the will is read, it'll be found he left Meryt and Salveter equal amounts."

Vance turned to Markham.

"Could you have one of your various diplomatic coadjutors find out confidentially about Kyle's will? I've a notion the data would help us materially."

"It might be done," Markham returned. "The moment this thing breaks in the papers Kyle's attorneys will come forward. I'll use a little pressure."

Vance again addressed Scarlett.

"I believe you told me that Kyle had recently begun to balk at the expenses of the Bliss expeditions.—Can you suggest any reason for his deflection other than lack of immediate results?"

"No-o." Scarlett pondered a moment. "You know, expeditions such as Doctor Bliss had planned are deucedly expensive luxuries, and the results, of course, are highly problematic. Furthermore, however successful they are, it takes a long time to produce any tangible evidence of their value. Kyle was getting impatient; he was not an Egyptologist and knew little of such matters; and he may have thought that Doctor Bliss was on an extravagant wild-goose chase at his expense. Fact is, he intimated last year that unless some definite results were obtained during the new excavations he'd not go on doling out money. That was why the doctor was so anxious last night to present a financial report and to have Kyle see the new treasures that arrived yesterday."

"There was nothing personal in Kyle's attitude?"

"To the contrary. All the realtionships were very friendly. Kyle liked Bliss personally and respected him immensely. And Bliss had only praise and gratitude for Kyle. . . . No, Vance, you'll find nothing by going at it from that angle."

"How did the doctor feel last night about the possible outcome of his interview with Kyle?—Was he worried or sanguine?"

Scarlett knit his brows and puffed at his pipe.

"Neither, I should say," he answered at length. "His state of mind was what might be described as philosophic. He's inclined to be easy-going—takes things as they come—and he has a rare amount of self-control. The serious scholar at all times—if you comprehend me."

"Quite. . . ." Vance put out his cigarette and folded his hands behind his head. "But what do you think would have been the effect on Doctor Bliss if Kyle had refused to finance the expedition further?"

"That's hard to say. . . . He'd probably have looked for capital elsewhere—remember, he had made great strides in his work despite the fact that he had not actually entered Intef's tomb."

"And what was young Salveter's attitude in the face of a possible cessation of the excavations?"

"He was more upset about it than the doctor. Salveter has unbounded enthusiasm, and he made several pleas to his uncle to continue financing the work. If Kyle had refused to go on, it would have come pretty near breaking the lad's heart. I understand he even offered to forgo his inheritance if Kyle would see the expedition through."

"There's no mistakin' Salveter's earnestness," Vance acceded. Then he was silent for a considerable time. Finally he reached for his cigarette-case; but he did not open it, and sat tapping it with his fingers. "There's another point I want to ask you about, Scarlett," he said presently. "How does Mrs. Bliss regard her husband's work?"

The question was vague—purposely so, I imagine; and Scarlett was a little puzzled. But after moment he replied:

"Oh, Meryt is quite the loyal wife. During the first year or so of her marriage she was most interested in all the doctor did—in fact, she accompanied him, as you know, on his 1924 expedition. Lived in a tent and all that sort of thing, and seemed perfectly happy. But—to tell you the truth, Vance—her interest has been waning of late. A racial reaction, I take it. The Egyptian blood in her is a powerful influence. Her mother was almost fanatical on the subject of Egyptian sanctity, and very proud; resented the so-called desecration of the tombs of her ancestors by western barbarians—as she designated all Occidental scientists. But Meryt has never voiced her own opinions,—I'm merely assuming that some of the mother's antagonism has recently cropped out in her. Nothing serious though, please understand. Meryt has been absolutely loyal to Bliss and his chosen work."

"Hani may have had something to do with her state of mind," commented Vance.

Scarlett shot him a questioning look.

"It's barely possible," he admitted reluctantly, and lapsed into silence.

Vance tenaciously pursued the subject.

"Most probably, I'd say. And I'd go even further. I've a suspicion that Doctor Bliss himself recognized Hani's influence on his wife, and became bitterly resentful. You recall the tirade he launched against Hani when he came into the museum this morning. He openly accused Hani of poisoning Mrs. Bliss's mind."

Scarlett moved uneasily in his chair and chewed the stem of his pipe.

"There's never been any love between the doctor and Hani," he remarked evasively. "Bliss brought him to America solely because Meryt insisted on it. I think he believes Hani is spying on him for the Egyptian Government."

"Is it entirely unlikely?" Vance put the question offhandedly.

"Really, Vance, I can't answer that." Scarlett suddenly leaned forward, and his features became tense. "But I'll tell you this: Meryt is incapable of any fundamental disloyalty to her husband. Even though she may think she made a mistake in marrying Doctor Bliss—who's much older than she is and completely absorbed in his work—she'd stand by her bargain . . . like a thoroughbred."

"Ah . . . just so." Vance nodded slightly and selected a *Régie* from his case. "And that brings me to a most delicate question. . . . Do you think that Mrs. Bliss has any—what shall I say?—interests outside of her husband? That is, aside from Doctor Bliss's life work, is it possible that her more intimate emotions are involved elsewhere?"

Scarlett got to his feet and began spluttering.

"Oh, really, Vance.... Dash it all!... You've no right to ask me such a question.... I'm no quidnunc.... One doesn't talk about such things; it's not done—really it isn't, old man.... You put me in a most embarrassing position...." (Scarlett's predicament roused my sympathy.)

"Neither is murder done in the best circles," returned Vance equably. "We're dealin' with a most unusual situation. And somebody translated Kyle from this world into the hereafter in a very distressin' fashion.... But since your sensitivities are so deuced lacerated I'll withdraw the question." He smiled disarmingly. "You're not entirely impervious to the lady's charms yourself—eh, what Scarlett?"

The man whirled about and glared at Vance ferociously. Before he could answer, Vance stood up and looked him steadily in the eyes.

"A man has been murdered," he said quietly; "and a devilish plot has been introduced into that murder. Another human life is at stake. And I'm here to find out who concocted this hideous scheme and to save an innocent person from the electric chair. Therefore I'm not going to let any squeamish conventional taboos stand in my way." His voice softened somewhat. "I appreciate your reticence. Under ordin'ry circumstances it would be most admirable. But just now it's rather silly."

Scarlett met Vance's gaze squarely, and after a few seconds he sat down again.

"You're quite right, old man," he acquiesced, in a low voice. "I'll tell you anything you want to know."

Vance nodded indifferently and smoked for a while.

"I think you've told me everything," he said finally. "But we may call on you later.... It's far past lunch time. Suppose you toddle along home."

Scarlett drew a deep sigh of relief and got to his feet.

"Thanks awfully." And without another word he went out.

Heath followed him, and we could hear him giving instructions to Snitkin to let Scarlett leave the house.

"Well," said Markham to Vance, when the Sergeant had returned; "how has Scarlett's information helped you? I can't see that it has thrown any very dazzling light on our problem."

"My word!" Vance shook his head with commiserating incredulity. "Scarlett has put us infinitely forrader. He was most revealin'. We now have a definite foundation on which to stand when we chivy the members of the household."

"I'm glad you feel so confident." Markham rose and regarded Vance sternly. "You can't really believe——?" He broke off, as if he did not quite dare to articulate his thought.

"Yes, I believe this crime was merely a means to an end," Vance returned. "Its real object, I'm convinced, was to involve an innocent person and thus wash the slate clean of several annoyin' elements."

Markham stood stock-still for several seconds.

"I think I see what you mean," he nodded. "It's possible of course."

He walked up the museum and back again, his head clouded in cigar smoke.

"See here;"—he stood looking grimly down at Vance—"I want to ask you a question. I recall your asking Salveter for a pencil.... What make of pencil was used for the 'upright' which you found on top of the end cabinet?—Was it a Mongol No. 1?"

Vance shook his head.

"No. It was not a Mongol. It was a Koh-i-noor—an HB, a much harder lead than the No. 1 Mongol, which is very soft.... Y' know, Mongols and Koh-i-noors look exactly alike: they're both hexagonal and yellow. The Koh-i-noor is made by Hardtmuth in Czecho-Slovakia—one of the oldest firms in Europe. Originally the Koh-i-noors were Austrian pencils, but after the World War the Austrian empire was divided——"

"Never mind the kindergarten lesson in history." Markham's face became suddenly overcast. "So it wasn't a Mongol that was used in the death trap...." He came closer to Vance. "Another question—and all your garrulousness about the Austrian Successor States can't divert me: What make of pencil were those you looked at on Doctor Bliss's desk in the study?"

Vance sighed.

"I feared you'd ask that question. And, y' know, I'm almost afraid to tell you—you're so impulsive...."

Markham glowered with exasperation and started toward Bliss's study.

"Oh, it won't be necess'ry for you to trudge up the spiral stairs," Vance called after him. "I'll tell you.... They were Koh-i-noors."

"Ah!"

"But I say; are you goin' to let that fact influence you?"

There was a slight pause before Markham answered.

"No.... After all, the pencil is not a particularly convincing piece of evidence, especially as every one had access to the study."

Vance grinned and looked puckish.

"Such broadmindedness in a district attorney is positively amazin'," he said.

11

THE COFFEE PERCOLATOR

(Friday, July 13; 2:45 P.M.)

MARKHAM RESUMED his seat. He was far too dismayed to resent Vance's good-natured irony. The murder of Kyle, which at first had appeared so straightforward and simple, was becoming more and more involved. Subtle and terrible undercurrents were beginning to make themselves felt; and it was now clear to everyone, I think, that the crime, instead of being a mere brutal braining, was a sinister factor in a deep, ramified plot. Even Heath had at last begun to sense the hidden significations of the obvious clews to which he had at first pinned his hope for a speedy solution.

"Yes," he admitted, his cigar bobbing up and down between his thin lips; "that pencil don't mean anything in particular.... This case—as you'd say, Mr. Vance—is getting a bit thick. Nobody with a brain is going to smear the whole works with clews pointing to himself, if he's guilty." He frowned at Markham. "What about that opium in the coffee, Chief?"

Markham pursed his lips.

"I was just thinking about that. And it might be advisable to try to find out at once who could have drugged Bliss. . . . What's your opinion, Vance?"

"A coruscatin' idea." Vance was smoking thoughtfully. "It's most essential to know who could have put the sleepin' powder in the doctor's coffee, for there's no doubt that the person who did it is the one who sent Kyle on his long pilgrimage. In fact, the key to the whole plot lies in the question of who had the opportunity to meddle with that cup of coffee."

Markham sat up decisively.

"Sergeant, get the butler. Bring him through the study so that the people in the drawing-room won't see him come in."

Heath rose with alacrity and swung up the spiral stairs three steps at a time. A minute or two later he reappeared at the study door, unceremoniously urging Brush before him.

The man was palpably in a state of fright; his face was very pale and he held his hands tightly clinched. He approached us unsteadily, but bowed with instinctive correctness and stood quite erect, like a well-trained servant waiting for orders.

"Sit down and relax, Brush." Vance busied himself with lighting a fresh cigarette. "I can't blame you for being wrought up, don't y' know. A most tryin' situation. If you'll try to be calm you can help us. . . . I say, stop fidgetin'! . . ."

"Yes, sir." The man sat down on the edge of a chair, and gripped his knees tensely with his hands. "Very good, sir. But I'm very much upset. I've been in the employ of gentlemen for fifteen years, and never before——"

"Oh, quite. I fully sympathize with your predicament." Vance smiled pleasantly. "Emergencies do arise, though. And this may be your great opportunity to enlarge your field of activities. The fact is, Brush, you may be able to lead us to the truth concerning this unfortunate affair."

"I hope so, sir." The butler had perceptibly calmed down under Vance's casual attitude.

"Tell us, then, about the breakfast arrangements in the house." Vance, with Markham's tacit consent, assumed the rôle of interrogator. "Where does the family indulge in its morning coffee?"

"In the breakfast-room down-stairs." Brush was now controlling himself admirably. "There's a small room at the front of the house in the basement, which Mrs. Bliss had decorated in Egyptian style. Only luncheon and dinner are served in the main dining-room up-stairs."

"Ah! And does the family break its fast together?"

"Generally, sir. I call every one at eight; and at eight-thirty breakfast is served."

"And just who appears at this unearthly hour?"

"Doctor and Mrs. Bliss, and Mr. Salveter—and Mr. Hani."

Vance's eyebrows went up slightly.

"Does Hani eat with the family?"

"Oh, no, sir." Brush seemed perplexed. "I don't exactly understand Mr. Hani's status—if you know what I mean, sir. He is treated by Doctor Bliss as a servant, and yet he calls the mistress by her first name. . . . He has his meals in an alcove off the kitchen—he will not eat with me and Dingle." There was a certain resentment in his tone.

Vance sought to console him.

"Hani, you must realize, is a very old retainer of Mrs. Bliss's family—and he is also an official of the Egyptian Government. . . ."

"Oh, the arrangement suits Dingle and me perfectly, sir," was the evasive answer.

Vance did not pursue the subject, but asked:

"Does Mr. Scarlett ever breakfast with the Blisses?"

"Quite often, sir—especially when there's work to be done in the museum."

"Did he come this morning?"

"No, sir."

"Then, if Hani was in his room all the morning and Doctor Bliss was in his study, Mrs. Bliss and Mrs. Salveter must have breakfasted alone together, what?"

"That's correct, sir. Mrs. Bliss came down-stairs a little before half past eight and Mr. Salveter a few minutes later. The doctor had told me at eight o'clock on his way to the study that he had work to do and the others should not wait for him."

"And who informed you of Hani's indisposition?"

"Mr. Salveter, sir. He told me that Mr. Hani had asked him to tell me he wouldn't be down for breakfast. . . . Their rooms, you see, face each other on the third floor, and I have noticed that Mr. Hani always leaves his door open at night."

Vance nodded approvingly.

"You're most limpid, Brush. . . . Therefore, as I understand it, at half past eight this morning the disposition of the members of the house was as follows:—Mrs. Bliss and Mr. Salveter were in the breakfast-room down-stairs; Hani was in his bedroom on the third floor; and Doctor Bliss was in his study. Mr. Scarlett was presumably at home. . . . And where were you and Dingle?"

"Dingle was in the kitchen, and I was between the kitchen and the break-fast-room, serving."

"And to your knowledge there was no one else in the house?"

The butler appeared mildly surprised.

"Oh, no, sir. There could not have been any one else in the house."

"But if you were down-stairs," Vance persisted, "how do you know no one came in the front door?"

"It was locked."

"You are quite sure?"

"Positive, sir. One of my duties is to see that the latch is thrown the last thing before retiring each night; and no one rang the bell or used the door this morning before nine o'clock."

"Very good." Vance smoked meditatively for several moments. Then he lay back lazily in his chair and closed his eyes. "By the by, Brush, how and where is the morning coffee prepared?"

"The coffee?" The man gave a start of astonishment, but quickly recovered himself. "The coffee is a fad of the doctor's—if you understand me, sir. He orders it from some Egyptian firm on Ninth Avenue. It's very black and damp, and somewhat burnt in the roasting. It tastes like French coffee—if you know how French coffee tastes."

"Unfortunately I do." Vance sighed and made a wry face. "An excruciatin' beverage. No wonder the French fill it full of hot milk. . . . And do you yourself drink this coffee, Brush?"

The butler looked a trifle disconcerted.

"No, sir. I can't say that I care for the taste of it. Mrs. Bliss has kindly given me and Dingle permission to make our own coffee in the old-fashioned way."

"Oh!" Vance half-closed his eyes. "So Doctor Bliss's coffee is not made in the old-fashioned way."

"Well, sir, I may have used the wrong word, but it's certainly not made in the customary way."

"Tell us about it." Vance again relaxed. "There's so much pother in this world about the correct way to make coffee. People get positively fanatical on the subject. I shouldn't be surprised if one day we had a civil war between the boilers and the non-boilers, or perhaps the drippers and the percolators. Silly notion . . . as if coffee were of any importance. Now, tea, on the other hand. . . . But go ahead and unfold the doctor's ideas on the subject."

Markham had begun beating an irritable tattoo with his foot, and Heath was wagging his head with elaborate impatience. But Vance, by his irrelevant loquacity, had produced exactly the effect he desired. He had succeeded in allaying Brush's nervousness and diverting his mind from the direct object of the interrogation.

"Well, sir," the man explained, "the coffee is made in a kind of percolator like a large samovar——"

"And where is this outlandish machine situated?"

"It always stands on the end of the breakfast table. . . . It has a spirit lamp under it to keep the coffee hot after it has—has——"

" 'Trickled' is probably the word."

"Trickled, sir. The percolator is in two sections—one fits into the other like a French coffee pot. You first lay a piece of filter paper over the holes and then put in the pulverized coffee—which Dingle grinds fresh every morning. Then there's a small plate which you set over the coffee—Doctor Bliss calls it the water-distributor. When that's in place you pour boiling water into the top of the samovar, and the coffee drips into the bottom. It is drawn off by a little spigot."

"Very interestin'. . . . And if one lifts off the top section of this apparatus one would have direct access to the liquid itself, what?"

Brush was frankly puzzled by this question.

"Yes, sir—but that isn't necessary because the spigot—"

"I can visualize the process perfectly, Brush. I was just wonderin' how one might go about doctorin' the coffee before it was drawn off."

"Doctoring the coffee?" The man appeared genuinely amazed.

"Just a passin' fancy." Vance spoke with utter negligence. "And now, Brush, to return to this morning's breakfast.—You say that Mrs. Bliss and Mr. Salveter were the only persons present. How much of the time were you actually in the breakfast-room during the repast?"

"Very little, sir. I merely brought in the breakfast and retired at once to the kitchen. Mrs. Bliss always serves the coffee herself."

"Did Hani go breakfastless this morning?"

"Not exactly, sir. Mrs. Bliss asked me to take him a cup of coffee."

"At what time was this?"

Brush thought a moment.

"At about quarter of nine, I should say, sir."

"And you of course took it to him."

"Certainly, sir. Mrs. Bliss had already prepared it when she called me."

"And what about the doctor's breakfast?"

"Mrs. Bliss suggested that I take his coffee and toast to the study. I would not have disturbed him myself unless he rang for me."

"And when was this suggestion made by Mrs. Bliss?"

"Just before she and Mr. Salveter left the breakfast-room."

"At about nine, I think you said."

"Yes, sir—perhaps a few minutes before."

"Did Mrs. Bliss and Mr. Salveter leave the breakfast-room together?"

"I couldn't say, sir. The fact is, Mrs. Bliss called me in just as she had finished breakfast, and told me to take some coffee and toast to the doctor. When I returned to the breakfast-room to get the coffee, she and Mr. Salveter had gone."

"And had Mrs. Bliss prepared the coffee for the doctor?"

"No, sir. I drew it myself."

"When?"

"The toast was not quite ready, sir; but I drew the coffee within five minutes after Mrs. Bliss and Mr. Salveter had gone up-stairs."

"And during those five minutes you were, I presume, in the kitchen?"

"Yes, sir. That is to say, except when I was in the rear hall telephoning—the usual daily orders to the tradespeople."

Vance roused himself from his apparent lethargy and crushed out his cigarette.

"The breakfast-room, then, was empty for about five minutes between the time when Mrs. Bliss and Mr. Salveter went up-stairs and the time when you went in to draw Doctor Bliss's coffee?"

"Just about five minutes, sir."

"Now, focus your brain on those five minutes, Brush.—Did you hear any sound in the breakfast-room during that time?"

The butler looked critically at Vance, and made an attempt at concentration.

"I wasn't paying much attention, sir," he replied at length. "And I was telephoning most of the time. But I can't recall hearing any sound. As a matter of fact, no one could have been in the breakfast-room during those five minutes."

"Mrs. Bliss or Mr. Salveter might have returned for some reason," Vance suggested.

"It's possible, sir," Bursh admitted dubiously.

"Moreover, could not Hani have come down-stairs in the interim?"

"But he was not well, sir. I took him his coffee——"

"So you told us. . . . I say, Brush, was Hani in bed when you presented him with this abominable coffee?"

"He was lying down—on the sofa."

"Dressed?"

"He had on that striped robe he usually wears round the house."

Vance was silent for several moments. Presently he turned to Markham.

"It's not what one would call a crystalline situation," he commented. "The samovar containing the coffee seems to have been in an almost indecent state of exposure this morning. Observe that Mrs. Bliss and Salveter were alone with it during breakfast, and that either one of 'em might have lingered behind for a few moments at the conclusion of the meal, or perhaps returned. Also, Hani could have descended to the breakfast-room as soon as Mrs. Bliss and Salveter came up-stairs. In fact, every one in the house had an opportunity to meddle with the coffee before Brush took the doctor's breakfast to him."

"It looks that way." Markham considered the matter morosely for a while. Then he addressed himself to the butler. "Did you notice anything unusual about the coffee you drew for Doctor Bliss?"

"Why no, sir." Brush sought unsuccessfully to hide his astonishment at the question. "It seemed perfectly all right, sir."

"The usual color and consistency?"

"I didn't see anything wrong with it, sir." The man's apprehension was growing, and again an unhealthy pallor overspread his sallow features. "It might have been a little strong," he added nervously. "But Doctor Bliss prefers his coffee very strong."

Vance got to his feet and yawned.

"I could bear to have a peep at this breakfast-room and its weird percolator. A bit of observation might help us, don't y' know."

Markham readily acceded.

"We'd better go through the doctor's study," said Vance, "so as not to rouse the curiosity of the occupants of the drawing-room...."

Brush led the way silently. He looked ghastly, and as he ascended the spiral stairs ahead of us I noticed that he held tightly to the iron railing. I could not figure him out. At times he appeared to be entirely dissociated from the tragic events of the forenoon; but at other times I got the distinct impression that some racking secret or suspicion was undermining his poise.

The breakfast-room extended, except for a small hallway, across the entire front of the house; but it was no more than eight feet deep. The front windows, which gave on the areaway of the street, were paned with opaque glass and heavily curtained. The room was fitted in exotic fashion and decorated with Egyptian designs. The breakfast-table was at least twelve feet long and very narrow, inlaid and painted in the decadent, rococo-esque style of the New Empire—not unlike the baroque furniture found in the tomb of Tut-ankh-Amûn.

On the end of the table stood the coffee samovar. It was of polished copper and about two feet high, elevated on three sprawling legs. Beneath it was an alcohol lamp.

Vance, after one glance, paid scant attention to it, much to my perplexity. He seemed far more interested in the arrangment of the lower rooms. He put his head in the butler's pantry between the breakfast-room and the kitchen, and stood for several moments in the main doorway looking up and down the narrow hallway which led from the rear stairs to the front of the house.

"A simple matter for any one to come to the breakfast-room without being seen," he observed. "I note that the kitchen door is behind the staircase."

"Yes, sir—quite so, sir." Brush's agreement was almost eager.

Vance appeared not to notice his manner.

"And you say you took the doctor's coffee to him about five minutes after Mrs. Bliss and Mr. Salveter had gone up-stairs. . . . What did you do after that, Brush?"

"I went to tidy up the drawing-room, sir."

"Ah, yes—so you told us." Vance was running his finger over the inlaid work of one of the chairs. "And I believe you said Mrs. Bliss left the house shortly after nine. Did you see her go?"

"Oh, yes, sir. She stopped at the drawing-room door on her way out and said she was going shopping, and that I should so inform Doctor Bliss in case he asked for her."

"You're sure she went out?"

Brush's eyes opened wide: the question seemed to startle him.

"Quite sure, sir," he replied with much emphasis. "I opened the front door for her. . . . She walked toward Fourth Avenue."

"And Mr. Salveter?"

"He came down-stairs fifteen or twenty minutes later, and went out."

"Did he say anything to you?"

"Only, 'I'll be back for lunch.' "

Vance sighed deeply and looked at his watch.

"Lunch! . . . My word! I'm positively famished." He gave Markham a doleful look. "It's nearly three o'clock . . . and I've had nothing today but tea and muffins at ten. . . . I say; must one starve to death simply because a silly crime has been committed?"

"I can serve you gentlemen——" Brush began, but Vance cut him short.

"An excellent idea. Tea and toast would sustain us. But let us speak to Dingle first."

Brush bowed and went to the kitchen. A few moments later he reappeared with a corpulent, placid woman of about fifty.

"This is Dingle, sir," he said. "I took the liberty of informing her of Mr. Kyle's death."

Dingle regarded us stolidly and waited, unperturbed, her hands on her generous hips.

"Good-afternoon, Dingle." Vance sat on the edge of the table. "As Brush has told you, a serious accident has happened in this house. . . ."

"An accident, is it?" The woman nodded her head sagely. "Maybe. Anyhow, you couldn't knock me over with a feather. What surprises me is that something didn't happen long ago—what with young Mr. Salveter living in the house, and Mr. Scarlett hanging around, and the doctor fussing with his mummies day and night. But I certainly didn't expect anything to happen to Mr. Kyle,—he was a very nice and liberal gentleman."

"To whom did you expect something to happen, Dingle?"

The woman set her face determinedly.

"I'm not saying—it's none of my business. But things here ain't according to nature. . . ." Again she wagged her head shrewdly. "Now, I've got a young good-looking niece who wants to marry a man of fifty, and I says to her——"

"I'm sure you gave her excellent advice, Dingle," Vance interrupted; "but we'd much prefer to hear your views on the Bliss family."

"You've heard 'em." The woman's jaws went together with a click, and it was obvious that neither threats nor wheedling could get any more out of her on the subject.

"Oh, that's quite all right." Vance treated her refusal as of no importance. "But there's one other matter we'd like to know about. It won't compromise you in the slightest to tell us.—Did you hear any one in this room after Mrs. Bliss and Mr. Salveter had gone up-stairs this morning—that is, during the time you were making the toast for the doctor's breakfast?"

"So that's it, is it?" Dingle squinted and remained silent for several moments. "Maybe I did and maybe I didn't," she said at length. "I wasn't paying any particular attention. . . . Who could've been in here?"

"I haven't the faintest notion." Vance smiled engagingly. "That's what we're tryin' to find out."

"Is it, now?" The woman's eyes drifted to the percolator. "Since you ask me," she returned, with a malevolence I could not understand at the time, "I'll tell you that I thought I heard some one drawing a cup of coffee."

"Who did you think it was?"

"I thought it was Brush. But at that moment he came out of the rear hall and asked me how the toast was getting along. So I knew it wasn't him."

"And what did you think then?"

"I didn't do any thinking."

Vance nodded abruptly and turned to Brush.

"Maybe we could have that toast and tea now."

"Certainly, sir." He started toward the kitchen, waving Dingle before him; but Markham halted them.

"Bring me a small container of some kind, Brush," he ordered. "I want to take away the rest of the coffee in this percolator."

"There ain't no coffee in it," Dingle informed him aggressively. "I cleaned that pesky contraption out and polished it at ten o'clock this morning."

"Thank Heaven for that," sighed Vance. "Y' know, Markham, if you had any of that coffee to analyze, you'd be farther away from the truth than ever."

With this cryptic remark he slowy lighted a cigarette and began inspecting one of the stencilled figures on the wall.

12

THE TIN OF OPIUM

(Friday, July 13; 3:15 P.M.)

A few minutes later Brush served us tea and toast.

"It is oolong tea, sir—Taiwan," he explained proudly to Vance. "And I did not butter the toast."

"You have rare intuition, Brush." Vance spoke appreciatively. "And what of Mrs. Bliss and Mr. Salveter? They have had no lunch."

"I took tea to them a little while ago. They did not wish anything else."

"And Doctor Bliss?"

"He has not rung for me, sir. But then, he often goes without lunch."

Ten minutes later Vance called Brush in from the kitchen.

"Suppose you fetch Hani."

The butler's eyelids fluttered.

"Yes, sir." He bowed stiffly and departed.

"There are one or two matters," Vance explained to Markham, "that we should clear up at once; and Hani may be able to enlighten us. . . . The actual murder of Kyle is the least devilish thing about this plot. I'm countin' extravagantly on what we'll learn from Salveter and Mrs. Bliss—which is why, d' ye see, I want to accumulate beforehand as much ammunition as possible."

"Still and all," put in Heath, "a guy was bumped off, and if I could put my hands on the bird who did it I wouldn't lay awake night worrying about plots."

"You're so dashed pristine, Sergeant." Vance sipped his tea dolefully. "Findin' the murderer is simple. But even if you had him gyved, it wouldn't do you a tittle of good. He'd have you apologizin' to him within forty-eight hours."

"The hell he would!" snapped Heath. "Slip me the baby that croaked Kyle, and I'll show you some inside stuff that don't get into the newspapers."

"If you were to arrest the murderer now," Vance returned mildly, "both of you would get into the newspapers—and the stories would all go against you. I'm savin' you from your own impetuosity."

Heath snorted, but Markham looked at Vance seriously.

"I'm begining to fall in with your views," he said. "The elements in this case are damnably confused."

At this moment soft, measured footsteps sounded in the hall, and Hani appeared at the door. He was calm and aloof as usual, and his immobile face registered not the least surprise at our being in possession of the breakfast-room.

"Come in and sit down, Hani." Vance's invitation was almost too pleasant.

The Egyptian moved slowly toward us, but he did not take a seat.

"I prefer to stand, *effendi.*"

"It's of course more comfortin' to stand in moments of stress," Vance commented.

Hani inclined his head slightly, but made no answer. His poise, typically oriental, was colossal.

"Mr. Scarlett tells us," Vance began, without looking up, "that Mrs. Bliss had been well provided for in Mr. Kyle's will. This information, Mr. Scarlett said, came from you."

"Is it not natural," asked Hani, in a quiet voice, "that Mr. Kyle should provide for his god-child?"

"He told you he had done so?"

"Yes. He always confided in me, for he knew I loved Meryt-Amen like a father."

"When did he give you his confidence?"

"Years ago—in Egypt."

"Who else, Hani, knew of this bequest?"

"I think every one knew of it. He told me in the presence of Doctor Bliss. And naturally I told Meryt-Amen."

"Did Mr. Salveter know about it?"

"I told him myself." There was a curious note in Hani's voice, which I could not understand at the time.

"And you also told Mr. Scarlett." Vance raised his eyes and studied the Egyptian impersonally. "You're not what I'd call the ideal reposit'ry for a secret."

"I did not consider the matter a secret," Hani returned.

"Obviously not." Vance rose and walked languidly to the samovar.

"Do you happen to know if Mr. Salveter was also to be an object of Mr. Kyle's benefactions?"

"I could not say with assurance." Hani's eyes rested dreamily on the opposite wall. "But from certain remarks dropped by Mr. Kyle, I gathered that Mr. Salveter was also well provided for in the will."

"You like Mr. Salveter—eh, what, Hani?" Vance lifted the top of the samovar and peered into its interior.

"He is, I have reason to think, an admirable young man."

"Oh, quite." Vance smiled faintly, and replaced the samovar's lid. "And he is much nearer Mrs. Bliss's age than Doctor Bliss."

Hani's eyes flickered, and it seemed to me that he gave a slight start. It was a momentary reaction, however. Slowly he folded his arms, and stood like a sphinx, silent and detached.

"Mrs. Bliss and Mr. Salveter will both be rich, now that Mr. Kyle is dead." Vance spoke casually without glancing toward the Egyptian. After a pause he asked: "But what of Doctor Bliss's excavations?"

"They are probably at an end, *effendi.*" Despite Hani's monotonous tone there was a discernible note of triumphal satisfaction in his words. "Why should the sacred resting-places of our noble Pharaohs be ravaged?"

"I'm sure I don't know," Vance said blandly. "The art unearthed is scarcely worth considerin'. The only true art of antiquity is Chinese; and all modern æsthetic beauty stems from the Greeks. . . . But this isn't an appropriate time to discuss the creative instinct. . . . Speakin' of the doctor's researches, isn't it possible that Mrs. Bliss will continue to finance her husband's work?"

A black cloud fell across Hani's face.

"It's possible. Meryt-Amen is a loyal wife. . . . And no one can tell what a woman will do."

"So I've been told—by those unversed in feminine psychology." Vance's manner was light and almost flippant. "Still, even should Mrs. Bliss decline to assist in the continuance of the work. Mr. Salveter—with his fanatical enthusiasm for Egyptology—might be persuaded to act as the doctor's financial angel."

"Not if it offended Meryt-Amen——" began Hani, and then stopped abruptly.

Vance appeared not to notice the sudden break in the other's response.

"You would, I suppose," he remarked, "attempt to influence Mrs. Bliss against helping her husband complete his excavations."

"Oh, no, *effendi.*" Hani shook his head. "I would not presume to advise her. She knows her own mind—and her loyalty to Doctor Bliss would dictate her decision, whatever I might say."

"Ah! . . . Tell me, Hani, who do you consider was the most benefited by the death of Mr. Kyle?"

"The *ka* of Intef."*

Vance raised his eyes and gave an exasperated smile.

"Ah, yes—of course. . . . Most helpful," he murmured.

"For that reason," Hani continued, a visionary look on his face, "the spirit of Sakhmet returned to the museum this morning and struck down the desecrator——"

"And," interjected Vance, "put the financial report in the desecrator's hand, placed the doctor's scarab pin beside the body, and made bloody footprints leading to the study. . . . Not very fairminded, your lady of vengeance—in fact, a rather bad sport, don't y' know, tryin' to get some one else punished for her little flutter in crime." He studied the Egyptian closely through narrowed eyes; then he leaned forward over the end of the table. When he spoke again his voice was severe and resonant. "You're trying to shield some one, Hani! . . . Who is it?"

The other took a deep breath, and the pupils of his eyes dilated.

"I have told you all I know, *effendi.*" His voice was scarcely audible. "I believe that Sakhmet——"

"Rubbish!" Vance cut him short. Then he shrugged his shoulders and grinned. *"Jawâb ul ahmaq sakût."*†

A shrewd gleam came into Hani's eyes, and I thought I detected a sneer on his mouth.

Vance was in no wise disconcerted, however. Somehow I felt that, despite the Egyptian's evasiveness, he had learned what he wanted. After a brief pause he tapped the samovar.

"Leaving mythology to one side," he said complaisantly, "I understand that Mrs. Bliss sent Brush to you this morning with a cup of coffee."

Hani merely nodded.

"What, by the by, was the nature of your illness?" Vance asked.

"Since coming to this country," the man returned, "I have suffered from indigestion. When I awoke this morning——"

"Most unfortunate," Vance murmured sympathetically. "And did you find that the one cup of coffee was sufficient for your needs?"

Hani obviously resented the question, but there was no indication of his feeling in his answer.

"Yes, *effendi.* I was not hungry. . . ."

Vance looked mildly surprised.

"Indeed! I was rather under the impression you came down-stairs and drew yourself a second cup from this percolator."

---

* Sir E. A. Wallis Budge defines *ka* (or, more correctly, *ku*) both as "the double of a man" and "a divine double." Breasted, explaining the *ka,* says it was the "vital force" which was supposed to animate the human body and also to accompany it into the next world. G. Elliot Smith calls the *ka* "one of the twin souls of the dead." (The other soul, *ba,* became deified in identification with Osiris.) *Ka* was the spirit of a mortal person, which remained in the tomb after death; and if the tomb were violated or destroyed, the *ka* had no resting-place. Our own word "soul" is not quite an accurate rendition of *ka,* but is perhaps as near as we can come to it in English. The German word *Doppelgänger,* however, is an almost exact translation.

† An old Arabic proverb meaning: "The only answer to a fool is silence."

Once more a cautious expression came over Hani's face, and he hesitated perceptibly before answering.

"A second cup?" he repeated. "Here in the breakfast-room? . . . I was not aware of the fact."

"It doesn't matter in the least," Vance returned. "Some one was alone with the percolator this morning. And whoever it was—that is to say, whoever might have been alone with it—was involved in the plot of Mr. Kyle's death."

"How could that be, *effendi?*" Hani, for the first time, appeared vitally worried.

Vance did not answer his query. He was leaning over the table, looking critically at the inlay.

"Dingle said she thought she heard some one in here after Mrs. Bliss and Mr. Salveter had gone up-stairs after breakfast, and it occurred to me it might have been you. . . ." He glanced up sharply. "It's possible, of course, that Mrs. Bliss returned for another cup of coffee . . . or even Mr. Salveter. . . ."

"It was I who was here!" Hani spoke with slow and impressive emphasis. "I came down-stairs almost immediately after Meryt-Amen had returned to her room. I drew myself another cup of coffee, and at once went back up-stairs. It was I whom Dingle heard. . . . I lied to you a moment ago because I had already told you, in the museum, that I had remained in my room all the morning—my trip to the breakfast-room had slipped my mind. I did not regard the matter as of any importance."

"Well, well! That explains everything." Vance smiled musingly. "And now that you have recalled your little pilgrimage for coffee, will you tell us who in the house possesses powdered opium?"

I was watching Hani, and I expected to see him show some sign of fear at Vance's question. But only an expression of profound puzzlement came over his stolid features. A full half minute passed before he spoke.

"At last I comprehend why you have questioned me concerning the coffee," he said. "But you are being cleverly deceived."

"Fancy that!" Vance stifled a yawn.

"Bliss *effendi* was not put to sleep this morning," the Egyptian continued; and, despite the oracular monotone of his voice, there was an undercurrent of hatred beneath his words.

"Really, now! . . . And who said he had been put to sleep, Hani?"

"Your interest in the coffee . . . your question regarding the opium. . . ." His voice trailed off.

"Well?"

"I have no more to say."

"Opium," Vance informed him, "was found in the bottom of the doctor's coffee cup."

Hani appeared genuinely startled by this news.

"You are sure, *effendi?* . . . I cannot understand."

"Why should you understand?" Vance stepped forward and stood before the man, searching him with a fixed look. "How much do you know about this crime, Hani?"

The veil of detachment again fell over the Egyptian.

"I know nothing," he returned sullenly.

Vance made a gesture of impatient resignation.

"You at least know who owned powdered opium hereabouts."

"Yes, I know that. Powered opium was part of the medical equipment on our tours of exploration in Egypt. Bliss *effendi* had charge of it."

Vance waited.

"There is a large cabinet in the hall up-stairs," Hani continued. "All the medical supplies are kept there."

"Is the door kept locked?"

"No, I do not believe so."

"Would you be so good as to toddle up-stairs and see if the opium is still there?"

Hani bowed and departed without a word.

"Look here, Vance";—Markham had risen and was pacing up and down—"what earthly good can it do us to know whether the rest of the opium is in the cabinet? . . . Moreover, I don't trust Hani."

"Hani has been most revealin'," Vance replied. "Let me dally with him in my own way for a time,—he has ideas, and they're most interestin'. . . . As for the opium, I have a distinct feelin' that the tin of brown powder in the medicine chest will have disappeared——"

"But why," interrupted Markham, "should the person who extracted some of the opium remove it all from the cabinet? He wouldn't leave the container on his dressing-table for the purpose of leading us directly to him."

"Not exactly." Vance's tone was grave. "But he may have sought to throw suspicion on some one else. . . . That's mere theory, however. Anyway, I'll be frightfully disappointed if Hani finds the tin in the cabinet."

Heath was glowering.

"It looks to me, sir," he complained, "that one of *us* ought look for that opium. You can't trust anything that Swami says."

"Ah, but you can trust his reactions, Sergeant," Vance answered. "Furthermore, I had a definite object in sending Hani up-stairs alone."

Again came the sound of Hani's footsteps in the hall outside. Vance walked to the window. Under his drooping lids he was watching the door eagerly.

The Egyptian entered the room with a resigned, martyr-like air. In one hand he held a small circular tin container bearing a white-paper label. He placed it solemnly on the table and lifted heavy eyes to Vance.

"I found the opium, *effendi.*"

"Where?" The word was spoken softly.

Hani hesitated and dropped his gaze.

"It was not in the cabinet," he said. "The place on the shelf were it was generally kept, was empty. . . . And then I remembered——"

"Most convenient!" There was a sneer in Vance's tone. "You remembered that you yourself had taken the opium some time ago—eh, what? . . . Couldn't sleep—or something of the kind."

"The *effendi* understands many things." Hani's voice was flat and expressionless. "Several weeks ago I was lying awake—I had not slept well for nights—and I went to the cabinet and took the opium to my room. I placed the container in the drawer of my own cabinet——"

"And forgot to return it," Vance concluded. "I do hope it cured your insomnia." He smiled ironically. "You are an outrageous liar, Hani. But I do not blame you altogether——"

"I have told you the truth."

"Se non è vero, è molto ben trovato." Vance sat down, frowning.

"I do not speak Italian. . . ."

"A quotation from Bruno." He inspected the Egyptian speculatively. "Clawed into the vulgate, it means that, although you have not spoken the truth, you have invented your lie very well."

"Thank you, *effendi.*"

Vance sighed and shook his head with simulated weariness. Then he said:

"You were not gone long enough to have made any extensive search for the opium. You probably found it in the first place you looked—you had a fairly definite idea where you'd find it. . . ."

"As I told you——"

"Dash it all! Don't be so persistent. You're becoming very borin'. . . ." Menacingly Vance rose and stepped toward the Egyptian. His eyes were cold and his body was tense. "Where did you find that tin of opium?"

Hani shrank away and his arms fell to his sides.

"Where did you find the opium?" Vance repeated the question.

"I have explained, *effendi.*" Despite the doggedness of Hani's manner, his tone was not convincing.

"Yes! You've explained—but you haven't told the truth. The opium was not in your room—although you have a reason for wanting us to think so. . . . A reason! What is it? . . . Perhaps I can guess that reason. You lied to me because you found the opium—"

"Effendi! . . . Don't continue. You are being deceived. . . ."

"I am not being deceived by you, Hani." (I had rarely seen Vance so earnest.) "You unutterable ass! Don't you understand that I knew where you'd find that opium? Do you think I'd have sent you to look for it if I hadn't been pretty certain where it was? And you've told me—in your circuitous Egyptian way you've informed me most lucidly." Vance relaxed and smiled. "But my real reason for sending you to search for the sleeping-powder was to ascertain to what extent you were involved in the plot."

"And you found out, *effendi?*" There were both awe and resignation in the Egyptian's question.

"Yes . . . oh, yes." Vance casually regarded the other. "You're not at all subtle, Hani. You're only involved—you have characteristics in common with the ostrich, which is erroneously said to bury its head in the sand when in danger. You have merely buried your head in a tin of opium."

"Vance *effendi* is too erudite for my inferior comprehension. . . ."

"You're extr'ordin'rily tiresome, Hani." Vance turned his back and walked to the other end of the room. "Go away, please—go quite away."

At this moment there was a disturbance in the hall outside. We could hear angry voices at the end of the corridor. They became louder, and presently Snitkin appeared at the door of the breakfast-room holding Doctor Bliss firmly by the arm. The doctor, fully clothed and with his hat on, was protesting volubly. His face was pale, and his eyes had a hunted, frightened look.

"What's the meaning of this?" He addressed no one in particular. "I wanted to go out to get a bit of fresh air, and this bully dragged me downstairs—"

Snitkin looked toward Markham.

"I was told by Sergeant Heath not to let any one leave the house, and this guy tries to make a getaway. Full of hauchoor, too. . . . Whaddya want done with him?"

"I see no reason why the doctor shouldn't take an airin', don't y' know." Vance spoke to Markham. "We sha'n't want to confer with him till later."

"It's bully with me," Heath agreed. "There's too many people in this house anyway."

Markham nodded to Snitkin.

"You may let the doctor go for a walk, officer." He shifted his gaze to Bliss. "Please be back, sir, in half an hour or so. We'll want to question you."

"I'll be back before that—I only want to go over in the park for a while." Bliss seemed nervous and distraught. "I feel unusually heavy and suffocated. My ears are ringing frightfully."

"And, I take it," put in Vance, "you've been inordinately thirsty."

The doctor regarded him with mild surprise.

"I've consumed at least a gallon of water since going to my room. I hope I'm not in for an attack of malaria. . . ."

"I hope not, sir. I believe you'll feel perfectly normal later on."

Bliss hesitated at the door-sill.

"Anything new?" he asked.

"Oh, much." Vance spoke without enthusiasm. "But we'll talk of that later."

Bliss frowned and was about to ask another question; but he changed his mind, and bowing, went away, Snitkin trailing after him sourly.

13

AN ATTEMPTED ESCAPE

(Friday, July 13; 3:45 P.M.)

It was Hani who broke the silence after Bliss's departure.

"You wish me to go away, *effendi?*" he asked Vance, with a respect that struck me as overdone.

"Yes, yes." Vance had become *distrait* and introspective. I knew something was preying on his mind. He stood near the table, his hands in his pockets, regarding the samovar intently. "Go up-stairs, Hani. Take some sodium bicarbonate—and meditate. Divinely bend yourself, so to speak; indulge in a bit of 'holy exercise,' as Shakespeare calls it in—is it *Richard III?*"

"Yes, *effendi*—in Act III. Catesby uses the phrase to the Duke of Buckingham."

"Astonishin'!" Vance studied the Egyptian critically. "I had no idea the fallahîn were so well versed in the classics."

"For hours at a time I read to Meryt-Amen when she was young——"

"Ah, yes." Vance dropped the matter. "We'll send for you when we need you. In the meantime wait in your room."

Hani bowed and moved toward the hall.

"Do not be deceived by appearances, *effendi,*" he said solemnly, turning at the door. "I do not fully understand the things that have happened in this house to-day; but do not forget——"

"Thanks awfully." Vance waved his hand in dismissal. "I at least shall not forget that your name is Anûpu."

With a black look the man went out.

Markham was growing more and more impatient.

"Everything in this case seems to peter out," he complained. "Any one in the household could have put the opium in the coffee—which leaves us just where we were before we came here to the breakfast-room. . . . By the way, where do you think Hani found the can of opium?"

"Oh, that? Why, in Salveter's room, of course. . . . Rather obvious, don't y' know."

"I'm damned if I see anything obvious about it. Why should Salveter have left it there?"

"But he didn't leave it there, old dear. . . . My word! Don't you see that some one in the house had ideas? There's a *deus ex machina* in our midst, and he's troublin' himself horriby about the situation. The plot has been far too clever; and there's a tutelary genius who's attempting to simplify matters for us."

Heath made a throaty noise of violent disgust.

"Well, I'm here to tell you he's making a hell of a job of it."

Vance smiled sympathetically.

"A hellish job, let us say, Sergeant."

Markham regarded him with a quizzical frown.

"Do you believe, Vance, that Hani was in this room after Mrs. Bliss and Salveter had gone up-stairs?"

"It's possible. In fact, it seems more likely that it was Hani than either Mrs. Bliss or Salveter."

"If the front door had been unlatched," Markham offered, "it might conceivably have been some one from the outside."

"Your hypothetical thug?" asked Vance dryly. "Dropped in here, perhaps, for a bit of caffein stimulant before tackling his victim in the museum." He did not give Markham time to reply, but went to the door. "Come. Let's chivy the occupants of the drawing-room. We need more data—oh, many more data."

He led the way up-stairs. As we walked along the heavily carpeted upper hall toward the drawing-room door, the sound of an angry high-pitched voice came to us. Mrs. Bliss was speaking; and I caught the final words of a sentence.

". . . should have waited."

Then Salveter answered in a hoarse, tense tone:

"Meryt! You're insane. . . ."

Vance cleared his throat, and there was silence.

Before we entered the room, however, Hennessey beckoned mysteriously to Heath from the front of the hall. The Sergeant stepped forward past the drawing-room door, and the rest of us, sensing some revelation, followed him.

"You know that bird Scarlett who you told me to let go," Hennessey reported in a stage whisper; "well, just as he was going out he turned suddenly and ran up-stairs. I was going to chase him, but since you O.K.'d him, I

thought it was all right. A coupla minutes later he came down and went away
without a word. Then I got to thinking that maybe I shoulda followed him
up-stairs. . . ."

"You acted correctly, Hennessey." Vance spoke before the Sergeant could
reply. "No reason why he shouldn't have gone up-stairs—probably went there
to speak to Doctor Bliss."

Hennessey appeared relieved and looked hopefully toward Heath, who
merely grunted disdainfully.

"And, by the by, Hennessey," Vance continued; "when the Egyptian came
up-stairs the first time, did he go directly to the floor above, or did he tarry in
the drawing-room *en route?*"

"He went in and spoke to the missus. . . ."

"Did you hear anything he said?"

"Naw. It sounded to me like they was parleying in one of those foreign languages."

Vance turned to Markham and said in a low voice: "That's why I sent Hani
up-stairs alone. I had an idea he'd grasp the opportunity to commune with
Mrs. Bliss." He spoke again to Hennessey. "How long was Hani in the drawing-room?"

"A minute or two maybe—not long." The detective was growing apprehensive. "Shouldn't I have let him go in?"

"Oh, certainly. . . . And then what happened?"

"The guy comes outa the room, looking worried, and goes up-stairs. Pretty
soon he comes down again carrying a tin can in his hand. 'What you got there,
Abdullah?' I asks. 'Something Mr. Vance sent me to get. Any objection?' he
says. 'Not if you're on the level; but I don't like your looks,' I answers. And
then he gives me the high hat and goes down-stairs."

"Perfect, Hennessey." Vance nodded encouragingly and, taking Markham
by the arm, walked back toward the drawing-room. "I think we'd better question Mrs. Bliss."

As we entered the woman rose to greet us. She had been sitting by the front
window, and Salveter was leaning against the folding doors leading to the
dining-room. They had obviously taken these positions when they heard us in
the hall, for as we came up-stairs they had been speaking at very close quarters.

"We are sorry to have to annoy you, Mrs. Bliss," Vance began, courteously.
"But it's necess'ry that we question you at this time."

She waited without the slightest movement or change of expression, and I
distinctly received the impression that she was resentful of our intrusion.

"And you, Mr. Salveter," Vance went on, shifting his gaze to the man, "will
you please go to your room. We'll confer with you later."

Salveter seemed disconcerted and worried.

"May I not be present——?" he began.

"You may not," Vance cut in with unwonted serverity; and I noticed that
even Markham was somewhat surprised at his manner. "Hennessey!" Vance
called toward the door, and the detective appeared almost simultaneously.
"Escort this gentleman to his room, and see that he communicates with no one
until we send for him."

Salveter, with an appealing look toward Mrs. Bliss, walked out of the room,
the detective at his side.

"Pray be seated, madam." Vance approached the woman and, after she had sat down, took a chair facing her. "We are going to ask you several intimate questions, and if you really want the murderer of Mr. Kyle brought to justice you will not resent those questions but will answer them frankly."

"The murderer of Mr. Kyle is a despicable and unworthy creature," she answered in a hard, strained voice; "and I will gladly do anything I can to help you." She did not look at Vance, but concentrated her gaze on an enormous honey-colored carnelian ring of intaglio design which she wore on the forefinger of her right hand.

Vance's eyebrows went up slightly.

"You think, then, we did right in releasing your husband?"

I could not understand the purport of Vance's question; and the woman's answer confused me still further. She raised her head slowly and regarded each one of us in turn. Finally she said:

"Doctor Bliss is a very patient man. Many people have wronged him. I am not even sure that Hani is altogether loyal to him. But my husband is not a fool—he is even too clever at times. I do not put murder beyond him—or beyond any one, for that matter. Murder may sometimes be the highest form of courage. However, if my husband had killed Mr. Kyle he would not have been stupid about it—certainly he would have not left evidence pointing to himself. . . ." She glanced again at her folded hands. "But if he had been contemplating murder, Mr. Kyle would not have been the object of his crime. There are others whom he had more reason for wanting out of the way."

"Hani, for instance?"

"Perhaps."

"Or Mr. Salveter?"

"Almost any one but Mr. Kyle," the woman answered, without a perceptible modulation of voice.

"Anger could have dictated the murder." Vance spoke like a man discussing a purely academic topic. "If Mr. Kyle had refused to continue financing the excavations——"

"You do not know my husband. He has the most equable temper I have ever seen. Passion is alien to his nature. He makes no move without long deliberation."

"The scholar's mind," Vance murmured. "Yes, I have always had that impression of him." He took out his cigarette-case. "Do you mind if I smoke?"

"Do you mind if *I* do?"

Vance leapt to his feet and extended his case.

"Ah—*Régies!*" She selected a cigarette. "You are very fortunate, Mr. Vance. There were none left in Turkey when I applied for a shipment."

"I am doubly fortunate that I am able to offer you one." Vance lighted her cigarette and resumed his seat. "Who, do you think, Mrs. Bliss, was most benefited by Mr. Kyle's death?" he put the question carelessly, but I could see he was watching her closely.

"I couldn't say." The woman was clearly on her guard.

"But surely," pursued Vance, "some one benefited by his death. Otherwise he would not have been murdered."

"That point is one the police should ascertain. I can give you no assistance along that line."

"It may be that the police have satisfied themselves, and that I merely asked you for corroboration." Vance, while courteous, spoke with somewhat pointed significance. "Lookin' at the matter coldly, the police might argue that the sudden demise of Mr. Kyle would remove a thorn from Hani's side and end the so-called desecration of his ancestors' tombs. Then again, the police might hold that Mr. Kyle's death would enrich both you and Mr. Salveter."

I expected the woman to resent this remark of Vance's, but she only glanced up with a frigid smile and said in a dispassionate tone:

"Yes, I do believe there was a will naming Mr. Salveter and myself as the principal beneficiaries."

"Mr. Scarlett informed us to that effect," Vance returned. "Quite understandable, don't y' know. . . . And by the by, would you be willing to use your inheritance to perpetuate Doctor Bliss's work in Egypt?"

"Certainly," she replied with unmistakable emphasis. "If he asked me to help him, the money would be his to do with as he desired. . . . Especially now," she added.

Vance's face had grown cold and stern, and after a quick upward glance he dropped his eyes and contemplated his cigarette.

Markham rose at this moment.

"Who, Mrs. Bliss," he asked, with what I regarded as unnecessary aggression, "would have had an object in attempting to saddle your husband with this crime?"

The woman's gaze faltered, but only momentarily.

"I'm sure I don't know," she returned. "Did some one really try to do that?"

"You suggested as much yourself, madam, when the scarab pin was called to your attention. You said quite positively that some one had placed it beside Mr. Kyle's body."

"What if I did?" She became suddenly defiant. "My initial instinct was naturally to defend my husband."

"Against whom?"

"Against you and the police."

"Do you regret that 'initial instinct'?" Markham put the question brusquely.

"Certainly not!" the woman stiffened in her chair and glanced surreptitiously toward the door.

Vance noted her action and drawled:

"It is only one of the detectives in the hall. Mr. Salveter is sojourning in his boudoir—quite out of hearing."

Quickly she covered her face with her hands, and a shudder ran over her body.

"You are torturing me," she moaned.

"And you are watching me through your fingers," said Vance with a mild grin.

She rose swiftly and glared ferociously at him.

"Please don't say 'How dare you?' " Vance spoke banteringly. "The phrase is so trite. And do sit down again. . . . Hani informed you, I believe—in your native language—that Doctor Bliss was supposed to have been given opium in his coffee this morning. What else did he tell you?"

"That was all he said." The woman resumed her seat: she appeared exhausted.

"Did you know that opium was kept in the cabinet up-stairs?"

"I wasn't aware of it," she replied listlessly; "though I'm not surprised."

"Did Mr. Salveter know of it?"

"Oh, undoubtedly—if it was actually there. He and Mr. Scarlett had charge of the medical supplies."

Vance shot her a quick look.

"Although Hani would not admit it," he said, "I am pretty sure that the tin of opium was found in Mr. Salveter's room."

"Yes?" (I could not help feeling that she rather expected this news. Certainly, it was no surprise to her.)

"On the other hand," pursued Vance, "it might have been found by Hani in *your* room."

"Impossible! It couldn't have been in my room!" She flared up, but on meeting Vance's steady gaze, subsided. "That is, I don't see how it could be possible," she ended weakly.

"I'm probably wrong," Vance murmured. "But tell me, Mrs. Bliss: did you return to the breakfast-room this morning for another cup of coffee, after you and Mr. Salveter had gone up-stairs?"

"I—I. . . ." She took a deep breath. "Yes! . . .Was there any crime in that?"

"Did you meet Hani there?"

After a brief hesitation she answered:

"No. He was in his room—ill. . . . I sent him his coffee."

Heath grunted disgustedly.

"A lot we're finding out," he growled.

"Quite right, Sergeant," Vance agreed pleasantly. "An amazin' amount. Mrs. Bliss is helpin' us no end." He turned to the woman again. "You know, of course, who killed Mr. Kyle?" he asked blandly.

"Yes . . . . I know!" The words were spoken with impulsive venom.

"And you also know why he was killed?"

"I know that, too." A sudden change had come over her. A strange combination of fear and animus possessed her; and the tragic bitterness of her attitude stunned me.

Heath let forth a queer, inarticulate ejaculation.

"You tell us who it was," he blurted vindictively, shaking his cigar in her face, "or I'll arrest you as an accessory, or as a material witness. . . ."

"Tut, tut, Sergeant!" Vance rose and placed his hand pacifyingly on the other's shoulder. "Why be so precipitate? It wouldn't do you the slightest good to incarcerate Mrs. Bliss at this time. . . . And, d' ye see, she may be wholly wrong in her diagnosis of the case."

Markham projected himself into the scene.

"Have you any definite reasons for your opinion, Mrs. Bliss?" he asked. "Have you any specific evidence against the murderer?"

"Not legal evidence," she answered quietly. "But—but. . . ." Her voice faltered, and her head fell forward.

"You left the house about nine o'clock this morning, I believe." Vance's calm voice seemed to steady her.

"Yes—shortly after breakfast."

"Shopping?"

"I took a taxi at Fourth Avenue to Altman's. I didn't see what I wanted there, and walked to the subway. I went to Wanamaker's, and later returned to Lord and Taylor's. Then I went to Saks's, and finally dropped in at a little shop on Madison Avenue. . . ."

"The usual routine," sighed Vance. "You of course bought nothing?"

"I ordered a hat on Madison Avenue. . . ."

"Remarkable!" Vance caught Markham's eye and nodded significantly. "I think that will be all for the present, Mrs. Bliss," he said. "You will kindly go to your room and wait there."

The woman pressed a small handkerchief to her eyes, and left us without a word.

Vance walked to the window and gazed out into the street. He was, I could see, deeply troubled as a result of the interview. He opened the window, and the droning summer noises of the street drifted in to us. He stood for several minutes in silence, and neither Markham nor Heath interrupted his meditations. At length he turned and, without looking at us, said in a quiet, introspective tone:

"There are too many cross-currents in this house—too many motives, too many objects to be gained, too many emotional complications. A plausible case could be made out of almost any one. . . ."

"But who could have benefited by Bliss's entanglement in the crime?" Markham asked.

"Oh, my word!" Vance leaned against the centre-table and gazed at a large oil portrait of the doctor which hung on the east wall. "Every one apparently. Hani doesn't like his employer and writhes in psychic agony at each basketful of sand that is excavated from Intef's tomb. Salveter is infatuated with Mrs. Bliss, and naturally her husband is an obstacle to his suit. As for the lady herself: I do not wish to wrong her, but I'm inclined to believe she returns the young gentleman's affection. If so, the elimination of Bliss would not drive her to suicidal grief."

Markham's face clouded.

"I got the impression, too, that Scarlett was not entirely impervious to her charms and that there was a chilliness between him and Salveter."

"Quite. *Ça crève les yeux.*" Vance nodded abstractedly. "Mrs. Bliss is undeniably fascinatin'. . . . I say; if only I could find the clew I'm looking for! Y' know, Markham, I've an idea that something new is going to happen anon. The plot thus far has gone awry. We've been led into a Moorish maze by the murderer, but the key hasn't yet been placed in our hands. When it is, I'll know which door it'll unlock—and it won't be the door the murderer intends us to use it on. Our difficulty now is that we have too many clews; and not one of 'em is the real clew. That's why we can't make an arrest. We must wait for the plot to unfold."

"It's unfolding, as you call it, too swift for me," Heath retorted impatiently. "And I don't mind admitting that I think we're getting sidetracked. After all's said and done, weren't Bliss's finger-prints found on the statue, and no one else's? Wasn't his stick-pin found beside the body? And didn't he have every opportunity to bump Kyle off? . . ."

"Sergeant,"—Vance spoke patiently—"would a man of intelligence and profound scientific training commit a murder and not only overlook his finger-prints on the weapon, but also be so careless as to drop his scarf-pin at the scene of the murder, and then calmly wait in the next room for the police to arrest him, after having made bloody footprints to guide them?"

"And there's the opium, too, Sergeant," added Markham. "It seems pretty clear to me that the doctor was drugged."

"Have it your own way, sir." Heath's tone bordered on impoliteness. "But I don't see that we're getting anywheres."

As he spoke Emery came to the door.

"Telephone call for you, Sergeant," he announced. "Down-stairs."

Heath hurried eagerly from the room and disappeared down the hall. Three or four minutes later he returned. His face was wreathed in smiles, and he swaggered as he walked toward Vance.

"Huh!" He inserted his thumbs in the armholes of his waistcoat. "Your good friend Bliss has just tried to make a getaway. My man, Guilfoyle,* who I'd phoned to tail the doctor, picked him up as he came out of this house for his walk in the park. But he didn't go to the park, Mr. Vance. He beat it over to Fourth Avenue and went to the Corn Exchange Bank at Twenty-ninth Street. It was after hours, but he knew the manager and didn't have no trouble getting his money. . . ."

"Money?"

"Sure!" He drew out everything he had in the bank—got it in twenties, fifties and hundreds—and then took a taxi. Guilfoyle hopped another taxi and followed him up-town. He got off at Grand Central Station and hurried to the ticket office. 'When's the next train for Montreal?' he asked. 'Four forty-five,' the guy told him. 'Gimme a through ticket,' he said. . . . It was then four o'clock; and the doc walked to the gate and stood there, waiting. Guilfoyle came up to him and said: 'Going for a jaunt to Canada?' The doc got haughty and refused to answer. 'Anyway,' said Guilfoyle, 'I don't think you'll leave the country to-day.' And taking the doc by the arm, he led him to a telephone booth. . . . Guilfoyle's on his way here with your innocent friend." The Sergeant rocked back and forth on his feet. "What do you think of that, sir?"

Vance regarded him lugubriously.

"And that is taken as another sign of the doctor's guilt?" He shook his head hopelessly. "Is it possible that you regard such a childish attempt of escape as incriminating? . . . I say, Sergeant; mightn't that come under the head of panic on the part of an impractical scientist?"

"Sure it might." Heath laughed unpleasantly. "All crooks and killers get scared and try to make a getaway. But it don't prove their lily-white innocence."

"Still, Sergeant,"—Vance's voice was discouraged—"a murderer who accidentally left clews on every hand pointing directly to himself and then indulged in this final stupid folly of trying to escape would not be exactly bright. And, I assure you, Doctor Bliss is neither an imbecile nor a lunatic."

"Them's mere words, Mr. Vance," declared the Sergeant doggedly. "This bird made a coupla mistakes and, seeing he was caught, tried to get outa the country. And, I'm here to tell you, that's running true to form."

"Oh, my aunt—my precious, dodderin' aunt!" Vance sank into a large chair and let his head fall back wearily against the lace antimacassar.

---

* Guilfoyle, I recalled, was the detective of the Homicide Bureau who was set to watch Tony Skeel in the "Canary" murder case, and who reported on the all-night light at the Drukker house in the Bishop murder case.

14

A HIEROGLYPHIC LETTER

(Friday, July 13; 4:15 P.M.)

MARKHAM GOT up irritably and walked the length of the room and back. As always in moments of perplexity his hands were clasped behind him, and his head was projected forward.

"Damn your various aunts!" he growled, as he came abreast of Vance. "You're always calling on an aunt. Haven't you any uncles?"

Vance opened his eyes and smiled blandly.

"I know how you feel." Despite the lightness of his tone there was unmistakable sympathy in his words. "No one is acting as he should in this case. It's as if every one were in a conspiracy to confuse and complicate matters for us."

"That's just it!" Markham fumed. "On the other hand, there's something in what the Sergeant says. Why should Bliss——?"

"Too much theory, Markham old dear," Vance interrupted. "Oh, much too much theory . . . too much speculation . . . to many futile questions. There's a key coming, and it'll explain everything. Our immediate task, it seems to me, is to find that key."

"Sure!" Heath spoke with heavy sarcasm. "Suppose I begin punching the furniture with hat-pins and ripping up the carpets. . . ."

Markham snapped his fingers impatiently, and Heath subsided.

"Let's get down to earth." He regarded Vance with vindictive shrewdness. "You've got some pretty definite idea; and all your maunderings couldn't convince me to the contrary.—What do you suggest we do next?—interview Salveter?"

"Precisely." Vance nodded with unwonted seriousness. "That bigoted lad fits conspicuously into the picture; and his presence on the tapis now is, as the medicos say, indicated."

Markham made a sign to Heath, who immediately rose and went to the drawing-room door and bellowed up the staircase.

"Hennessey! . . . Bring that guy down here. We got business with him."

A few moments later Salveter was piloted into the room. His eyes were flashing, and he planted himself aggressively before Vance, cramming his hands violently into his trousers' pockets.

"Well, here I am," he announced with belligerence. "Got the handcuffs ready?"

Vance yawned elaborately and inspected the newcomer with a bored expression.

"Don't be so virile, Mr. Salveter," he drawled. "We're all worn out with this depressin' case, and simply can't endure any more vim and vigor. Sit down and let the joints go free. . . . As for the manacles, Sergeant Heath has 'em beautifully polished. Would you like to try 'em on?"

"Maybe," Salveter returned, watching Vance calculatingly. "What did you say to Meryt—to Mrs. Bliss?"

606

"I gave her one of my *Régies*," Vance told him carelessly. "Most appreciative young woman.... Would you care for one yourself? I've two left."

"Thanks—I smoke Deities."

"Ever dip 'em in opium?" Vance asked dulcetly.

"Opium?"

"The concrete juice of the poppy, so to speak—obtained from slits in the cortex of the capsule of *Papaver somniferum*. Greek word: *opion*—to wit: omicron, pi, iota, omicron, nu."

"No!" Salveter sat down suddenly and shifted his gaze. "What's the idea?"

"There seems to be an abundance of opium in the house, don't y' know."

"Oh, is there?" The man looked up warily.

"Didn't you know?" Vance selected one of his two remaining cigarettes. "We thought you and Mr. Scarlett had charge of the medical supplies."

Salveter started and remained silent for several moments.

"Did Meryt-Amen tell you that?" he asked finally.

"Is it true?" There was a new note in Vance's voice.

"In a way," the other admitted. "Doctor Bliss——"

"What about the opium?" Vance leaned forward.

"Oh, there has always been opium in the cabinet up-stairs—nearly a canful."

"Have you had it in your room lately?"

"No ... yes ... I——"

"Thanks awfully. We take our choice of answers, what?"

"Who said there was opium in my room?" Salveter squared his shoulders.

Vance leaned back in his chair.

"It really doesn't matter. Anyway, there's no opium there now.... I say, Mr. Salveter; did you return to the breakfast-room this morning after you and Mrs. Bliss had gone up-stairs?"

"I did not!... That is," he amended, "I don't remember...."

Vance rose abruptly and stood menacingly before him.

"Don't try to guess what Mrs. Bliss told us. If you don't care to answer my questions, I'll turn you over to the Homicide Bureau—and God help you!... We're here to learn the truth, and we want straight answers.—Did you return to the breakfast-room?"

"No—I did not."

"That's much better—oh, much!" Vance sighed and resumed his seat. "And now, Mr. Salveter, we must ask you a very intimate question.—Are you in love with Mrs. Bliss?"

"I refuse to answer!"

"Good! But you would not be entirely brokenhearted if Doctor Bliss should be gathered to his fathers?"

Salveter clamped his jaws and said nothing.

Vance contemplated him ruminatingly.

"I understand," he said amicably, "that Mr. Kyle has left you a considerable fortune in his will.... If Doctor Bliss should ask you to finance the continuation of his excavations in Egypt, would you do it?"

"I'd insist upon it, even if he did not ask me." A fanatical light shone in Salveter's eyes. "That is," he added, as a reasoned afterthought, "if Meryt-Amen approved. I would not care to go against her wishes."

"Ah!" Vance had lit his cigarette and was smoking dreamily. "And do you think she would disapprove?"

Salveter shook his head.

"No, I think she would do whatever the doctor wanted."

"A dutiful wife—*quo?*"

Salveter bristled and sat up.

"She's the straightest, most loyal——"

"Yes, yes." Vance exhaled a spiral of cigarette smoke. "Spare me your adjectives. . . . I take it, however, she's not entirely ecstatic with her choice of a life mate."

"If she wasn't," Salveter returned angrily, "she wouldn't show it."

Vance nodded uninterestedly.

"What do you think of Hani?" he asked.

"He's a dumb beast—a good soul, though. Adores Mrs. Bliss. . . ." Salveter stiffened and his eyes opened wide. "Good God, Mr. Vance! You don't think——" He broke off in horror; then he shook himself. "I see what you're getting at. But . . . but. . . . Those degenerate modern Egyptians! They're all alike—oriental dogs, every one of 'em. No sense of right and wrong—superstitious devils—but loyal as they make 'em. I wonder. . . ."

"Quite. We're all wonderin'." Vance was apparently unimpressed by Salveter's outbreak. "But, as you say, he's pretty close to Mrs. Bliss. He'd do a great deal for her—eh, what? Might even risk his neck, don't y' know, if he thought her happiness was at stake. Of course, he might need a bit of coaching. . . ."

A hard light shone in Salveter's eyes.

"You're on the wrong tack. Nobody coached Hani. He's capable of acting for himself——"

"And throwing the suspicion on some one else?" Vance looked at the other. "I'd say the planting of that scarab pin was a bit too subtle for a mere fellah."

"You think so?" Salveter was almost contemptuous. "You don't know those people the way I do. The Egyptians were working out intricate plots when the Nordic race were arboreans."

"Bad anthropology," murmured Vance. "And you're doubtless thinkin' of Herodotus's silly story of the treausre house of King Rhampsinitus. Personally, I think the priests were spoofing the papa of history. . . . By the by, Mr. Salveter; do you know any one round here, besides Doctor Bliss, who uses Koh-i-noor pencils?"

"Didn't even know the doctor used 'em." The man flicked his cigarette ashes on the carpet and brushed his foot over them.

"You didn't by any chance see Doctor Bliss this morning?"

"No. When I came down to breakfast Brush told me he was working in the study."

"Did you go into the museum this morning before you went on your errand to the Metropolitan?"

Salveter's eyes blinked rapidly.

"Yes!" he blurted finally. "I generally go into the museum every morning after breakfast—a kind of habit. I like to see that everything is all right—that nothing has happened during the night. I'm the assistant curator; and, aside from my responsibility, I'm tremendously interested in the place. It's my duty to keep an eye on things."

Vance nodded understandingly.

"What time did you enter the museum this morning?"

Salveter hesitated. Then throwing his head back he looked challengingly at Vance.

"I left the house a little after nine. When I got to Fifth Avenue it suddenly occurred to me I hadn't made an inspection of the museum; and for some reason I was worried. I couldn't tell you why I felt that way—but I did. Maybe because of the new shipment that arrived yesterday. Anyway, I turned back, let myself in with my key, and went into the museum——"

"About half past nine?"

"That would be about right."

"And no one saw you re-enter the house?"

"I hardly think so. In any event, I didn't see any one."

Vance gazed at him languidly.

"Suppose you finish the recital. . . . If you don't care to, I'll finish it for you."

"You won't have to." Salveter tossed his cigarette into a cloisonné dish on the table and drew himself resolutely to the edge of his chair. "I'll tell you all there is to tell. Then if you're not satisfied, you can order my arrest—and the hell with you!"

Vance sighed and let his head fall back.

"Such energy!" he breathed. "But why be vulgar? . . . I take it you saw your uncle before you finally quitted the museum for the Great American Mausoleum on the Avenue."

"Yes—I saw him!" Salveter's eyes flashed and his chin shot forward. "Now, make something out of that."

"Really, I can't be bothered. Much too fatiguin'." Vance did not even look at the man: his eyes, half closed, were resting on an old-fashioned crystal chandelier which hung low over the centre-table. "Since you saw your uncle," he said, "you must have remained in the museum for at least half an hour."

"Just about," Salveter obviously could not understand Vance's indifferent attitude. "The fact is I got interested in a papyrus we picked up last winter, and tried to work out a few of the words that stumped me. There were the words *ankhet, wash,* and *tema* that I couldn't translate."

Vance frowned slightly; then his eyebrows lifted.

"*Ankhet . . . wash . . . tema. . . .*" He iterated the words slowly. "Was the *ankhet* written with or without a determinative?"

Salveter did not answer at once.

"With the animal-skin determinative," he said presently.

"And was the next word really *wash* and not *was?*"

Again he hesitated, and looked uneasily at Vance.

"It was *wash,* I think. . . . And *tema* was written with a double flail."

"Not the sledge ideogram, eh? . . . Now, that's most interestin'.—And during your linguistic throes your uncle walked in."

"Yes. I was sitting at the little desk-table by the obelisk when Uncle Ben opened the door. I heard him say something to Brush, and I got up to greet him. It was rather dark, and he didn't see me till he'd reached the floor of the museum."

"And then?"

"I knew he wanted to inspect the new treasures; so I ran along. Went to the Metropolitan——"

"Your uncle seemed in normal good spirits when he came into the museum?"

"About as usual—a bit grouchy perhaps. He was never over-pleasant in the forenoons. But that didn't mean anything."

"You left the museum immediately after greeting him?"

"At once. I hadn't realized I'd been so long fussing over the papyrus; and I hurried away. Another thing, I knew he'd come to see Doctor Bliss on a pretty important matter, and I didn't want to be in the way."

Vance nodded but gave no indication whether or not he unreservedly accepted the other's statements. He sat smoking lazily, his eyes impassive and mild.

"And during the next twenty minutes," he mused, "—that is between ten o'clock and ten-twenty, at which time Mr. Scarlett entered the museum—your uncle was killed."

Salveter winced.

"So it seems," he mumbled. "But"—he shot his jaw out—"I didn't have anything to do with it! That's straight,—take it or leave it."

"There, now; don't be indelicate," Vance admonished him quietly. "I don't have to take it and I don't have to leave it, d' ye see? I may choose merely to dally with it."

"Dally and be damned!"

Vance got to his feet leisurely, and there was a chilly smile on his face—a smile more deadly than any contortion of anger could have been.

"I don't like your language, Mr. Salveter," he said slowly.

"Oh, don't you!" The man sprang up, his fists clenched, and swung viciously. Vance, however, stepped back with the quickness of a cat, and caught the other by the wrist. Then he made a swift, pivotal movement to the right, and Salveter's pinioned arm was twisted upward behind his shoulder-blades. With an involuntary cry of pain, the man fell to his knees. (I recalled the way in which Vance had saved Markham from an attack in the District Attorney's office at the close of the Benson murder case.) Heath and Hennessey stepped forward, but Vance motioned them away with his free hand.

"I can manage this impetuous gentleman," he said. Then he lifted Salveter to his feet and shoved him back into his chair. "A little lesson in manners," he remarked pleasantly. "And now you will please be civil and answer my questions, or I'll be compelled to have you—and Mrs. Bliss—arrested for conspiring to murder Mr. Kyle."

Salveter was completely subdued. He looked at his antagonist in ludicrous amazement. Then suddenly Vance's words seemed to seep into his astonished brain.

"Mrs. Bliss? . . . She had nothing to do with it, I tell you!" His tone, though highly animated, was respectful. "If it'll save her from any suspicion, I'll confess to the crime. . . ."

"No need for any such heroism." Vance had resumed his seat and was again smoking calmly. "But you might tell us why, when you came into the museum this afternoon and learned of your uncle's death, you didn't mention the fact that you'd seen him at ten o'clock."

"I—I was too upset—too shocked," the man stammered. "And I was afraid. Self-protective instinct, maybe. I can't explain—really I can't. I should have told you, I suppose . . . but—but——"

Vance helped him out.

"But you didn't care to involve yourself in a crime of which you were innocent. Yes . . . yes. Quite natural. Thought you'd wait and find out if any one had seen you. . . . I say, Mr. Salveter; don't you know that if you had admitted being with your uncle at ten o'clock, it would have been a point in your favor?"

Salveter had become sullen, and before he could answer Vance went on.

"Leavin' these speculations to one side, could we prevail upon you to tell us exactly what you did in the museum between half past nine and ten o'clock?"

"I've already told you." Salveter was troubled and *distrait*. "I was comparing an Eighteenth-Dynasty papyrus recently found by Doctor Bliss at Thebes with Luckenbill's translation of the hexagonal prism of the Annals of Sennacherib* in order to determine certain values for——"

"You're romancing frightfully, Mr. Salveter," Vance broke in quietly. "And you're indulgin' in an anachronism. The Sennacherib prism is in Babylonian cuneiform, and dates almost a thousand years later." He lifted his eyes sternly. "What were you doing in the museum this morning?"

Salveter started forward in his chair, but at once sank back.

"I was writing a letter," he answered weakly.

"To whom?"

"I'd rather not say."

"Naturally." Vance smiled faintly. "In what language?"

An immediate change came over the man. His face went pale, and his hands, which were lying along his knees, convulsed.

"What language?" he repeated huskily. "Why do you ask that? . . . What language would I be likely to write a letter in—Bantu, Sanskrit, Walloon, Ido. . . ?"

"No-o." Vance's gaze came slowly to rest on Salveter. "Nor did I have in mind Aramaic, or Agao, or Swahili, or Sumerian. . . . The fact is, it smote my brain a moment ago that you were composin' an epistle in Egyptian hieroglyphics."

The man's eyes dilated.

"Why, in Heaven's name," he asked lamely, "should I do a thing like that?"

"Why? Ah, yes—why, indeed?" Vance sighed deeply. "But, really, y' know, you were composin' in Egyptian—weren't you?"

"Was I? What makes you think so?"

"Must I explain? . . . It's so deuced simple." Vance put out his cigarette and made a slight deprecatory gesture. "I could even guess for whom the epistle

---

* The prism referred to by Salveter was the terra-cotta one acquired by the Oriental Institute of the University of Chicago during its reconnoitering expedition of 1919-20. The document was a variant duplicate of the Taylor prism in the British Museum, written about two years earlier under another eponym.

was intended. Unless I'm hopelessly mistaken, Mrs. Bliss was to have been the recipient." Again Vance smiled musingly. "Y' see, you mentioned three words in the imagin'ry papyrus, which you have not yet satisfactorily translated—*ankhet, wash,* and *tema.* But since there are scores of Egyptian words that have thus far resisted accurate translation, I wondered why you should have mentioned these particular three. And I further wondered why you should have mentioned three words whose meaning you did not recall, which so closely approximate three very familiar words in Egyptian. . . . And then I bethought me as to the meaning of these three familiar words. *Ankh*—without a determinative—can mean the 'living one.' *Was*—which is close to *wash*—means 'happiness' or 'good fortune'; though I realize there is some doubt about it,— Erman translates it, with a question-mark, as *Glück.* The *tema* you mentioned with a double flail is unknown to me. But I of course am familiar with *tem* spelt with a sledge ideograph. It means 'to be ended' or 'finished.' . . . Do you follow me?"

Salveter stared like a man hypnotized.

"Good God!" he muttered.

"And so," Vance continued, "I concluded that you had been dealin' in the well-known forms of these three words, and had mentioned them because, in their other approximate forms, their transliterative meanings are unknown. . . . And the words fitted perfectly with the situation. Indeed, Mr. Salveter, it wouldn't take a great deal of imagination to reconstruct your letter, being given the three verbal salients—to wit, *the living one, happiness* or *good fortune,* and *to be ended* or *finished.*"

Vance paused briefly, as if to arrange his words.

"You probably composed a communication in which you said that the 'living one' (*ankh*) was standing in the way of your 'happiness' or 'good fortune' (*was*), and expressed a desire for the situation 'to be ended' or 'finished' (*tem*). . . . I'm right, am I not?"

Salveter continued staring at Vance in a kind of admiring astonishment.

"I'm going to be truthful with you," he said at length. "That's exactly what I wrote. You see, Meryt-Amen, who knows the Middle Egyptian heiroglyphic language better than I'll ever know it, suggested long ago that I write to her at least once a week in the language of her ancestors, as a kind of exercise. I've been doing it for years; and she always corrects me and advises me—she's almost as well versed as any of the scribes who decorated the ancient tombs. . . . This morning, when I returned to the museum, I realized that the Metropolitan did not open until ten o'clock, and on some sudden impulse I sat down and began working on this letter."

"Most unfortunate," Vance sighed; "for your phraseology in that letter made it appear that you were contemplating taking drastic measures."

"I know it!" Salveter caught his breath. "That's why I lied to you. But the fact is, Mr. Vance, the letter was innocent enough. . . . I know it was foolish, but I didn't take it very seriously. Honest, sir, it was really a lesson in Egyptian composition—not an actual communication."

Vance nodded non-committally.

"And where is this letter now?" he asked.

"In the drawer of the table in the museum. I hadn't finished it when Uncle Ben came in; and I put it away."

"And you had already made use of the three words, *ankh* and *was* and *tem?*"

Salveter braced himself and took a deep breath.

"Yes! Those three familiar words were in it. And then, when you first asked me about what I'd been doing in the museum I made up the tale about the papyrus——"

"And mentioned three words which were suggested to you by the three words you had actually used—eh, what?"

"Yes, sir! That's the truth."

"We're most grateful for your sudden burst of honesty." Vance's tone was frigid. "Will you be so good as to bring me the uncompleted epistle? I'd dearly love to see it; and perhaps I can decipher it."

Salveter leapt to his feet and fairly ran out of the room. A few minutes later he returned, to all appearances dazed and crestfallen.

"It isn't there!" he announced. "It's gone!"

"Oh, is it now? . . . Most unfortunate."

Vance lay back pensively for several moments. Then suddenly he sprang to his feet.

"It's not there! . . . It's gone!" he murmured. "I don't like this situation, Markham—I don't at all like it. . . . Why should the letter have disappeared? Why . . . why?"

He swung about to Salveter.

"What kind of paper did you write that indiscreet letter on?" he asked, with suppressed excitement.

"On a yellow scratch-pad—the kind that's generally kept on the table. . . ."

"And the ink—did you draw your characters with pen or pencil?"

"With a pen. Green ink. It's always in the museum. . . ."

Vance raised his hand in an impatient gesture.

"That's enough. . . . Go up-stairs—go to your room . . . and stay there."

"But, Mr. Vance, I—I'm worried about that letter. Where do you think it is?"

"Why should I know where it is?—provided, of course, you ever wrote it. I'm no divining-rod." Vance was deeply troubled, though he sought to hide the fact. "Didn't you know better than to leave such a missive lying loosely about?"

"It never occurred to me——"

"Oh, didn't it? . . . I wonder." Vance looked at Salveter sharply. "This is no time to speculate. . . . Please go to your room. I'll speak to you again. . . . Don't ask any questions—do as I tell you!"

Salveter, without a word, turned and disappeared through the door. We could hear his heavy footsteps ascending the stairs.

15

VANCE MAKES A DISCOVERY

(Friday, July 13; 4:45 P.M.)

VANCE STOOD for a long time in uneasy silence. At length he lifted his eyes to Hennessey.

"I wish you'd run up-stairs," he said, "and take a post where you can watch all the rooms. I don't want any communication between Mrs. Bliss and Salveter and Hani."

Hennessey glanced at Heath.

"Those are orders," the Sergeant informed him; and the detective went out with alacrity.

Vance turned to Markham.

"Maybe that priceless young ass actually wrote the silly letter," he commented; and a worried look came over his face. "I say; let's take a peep in the museum."

"See here, Vance,"—Markham rose—"why should the possibility of Salveter's having written a foolish letter upset you?"

"I don't know—I'm not sure." Vance went to the door; then pivoted suddenly. "But I'm afraid—I'm deuced afraid! Such a letter would give the murderer a loophole—that is, if what I think is true. If the letter *was* written, we've got to find it. If we don't find it, there are several plausible explanations for its disappearance—and one of 'em is fiendish. . . . But come. We'll have to search the museum—on the chance that it was written, as Salveter says, and left in the table-drawer."

He went swiftly across the hall and threw open the great steel door.

"If Doctor Bliss and Guilfoyle return while we're in the museum," he said to Snitkin, who stood leaning against the front door, "take them in the drawing-room and keep them there."

We passed down the steps into the museum, and Vance went at once to the little desk-table beside the obelisk. He looked at the yellow pad and tested the color of the ink. Then he pulled open the drawer and turned out its contents. After a few minutes' inspection of the odds and ends, he restored the drawer to order and closed it. There was a small mahogany waste-basket beneath the table, and Vance emptied it on the floor. Going down on his knees he looked at each piece of crumpled paper. At length he rose and shook his head.

"I don't like this, Markham," he said. "I'd feel infinitely better if I could find that letter."

He strolled about the museum looking for places where a letter might have been thrown. But when he reached the iron spiral stairs at the rear he leaned his back against them and regarded Markham hopelessly.

"I'm becoming more and more frightened," he remarked in a low voice. "If this devilish plot should work! . . ." He turned suddenly and ran up the stairs, beckoning to us as he did so. "There's a chance—just a chance," he called over his shoulder. "I should have thought of it before."

We followed him uncomprehendingly into Doctor Bliss's study.

614

"The letter should be in the study," he said, striving to control his eagerness. "That would be logical . . . and this case is unbelievably logical, Markham— so logical, so mathematical, that we may eventually be able to read it aright. It's too logical, in fact—that's its weakness. . . ."

He was already on all fours delving into the spilled contents of Doctor Bliss's waste-basket. After a moment's search he picked up two torn pieces of yellow paper. He glanced at them carefully, and we could see tiny markings on them in green ink. He placed them to one side, and continued his search. After several minutes he had amassed a small pile of yellow paper fragments.

"I think that's about all," he said, rising.

He sat down in the swivel chair and laid the torn bits of yellow paper on the blotter.

"This may take a little time, but since I know Egyptian heiroglyphs fairly well I ought to accomplish the task without too much difficulty, don't y' know."

He began arranging and fitting the scraps together, while Markham, Heath and I stood behind him looking on with fascination. At the end of ten min- utes he had reassembled the letter. Then he took a large sheet of white paper from one of the drawers of the desk and covered it with mucilage. Care- fully he transferred the reconstructed letter, piece by piece, to the gummed paper.

"There, Markham old dear," he sighed, "is the unfinished letter which Sal- veter told us he was working on this morning between nine-thirty and ten."

The document was unquestionably a sheet of the yellow scratch-pad we had seen in the museum; and on it were four lines of old Egyptian characters painstakingly limned in green ink.

Vance placed his finger on one of the groups of characters.

"That," he told us, "is the *ankh* heiroglyph." He shifted his finger. "And that is the *was* sign. . . . And here, toward the end, is the *tem* sign."

"And then what?" Heath was frankly nonplussed, and his tone was far from civil. "We can't arrest a guy because he drew a lot of cock-eyed pictures on a piece of yellow paper."

"My word, Sergeant! Must you always be thinkin' of clappin' persons into oubliettes? I fear you haven't a humane nature. Very sad. . . . Why not try to cerebrate occasionally?" He looked up and I was startled by his seriousness. "The young and impetuous Mr. Salveter confesses that he has foolishly penned a letter to his Dulcibella in the language of the Pharaohs. He tells us he has placed the unfinished *billet-doux* in the drawer of a table in the mu- seum. We discover that it is not in the table-drawer, but has been ruthlessly dismembered and thrown into the waste-basket in Doctor Bliss's study. . . . On what possible grounds could you regard the Paul of this epistle as a mur- derer?"

"I ain't regarding nobody as anything," retorted Heath violently. "But there's too much shenanigan going on around here to suit me. I want action."

Vance contemplated him gravely.

"For once I, too, want action, Sergeant. If we don't get some sort of action before long, we may expect something even worse than has already happened. But it must be intelligent action—not the action that the murderer wants us to take. We're caught in the meshes of a cunningly fabricated plot; and, unless we watch our step, the culprit will go free and we'll still be battling with the cobwebs."

Heath grunted and began poring over the reconstructed letter.

"That's a hell of a way for a guy to write to a dame," he commented, with surly disdain. "Give me a nice dirty shooting by a gangster. These flossy crimes make me sick."

Markham was scowling.

"See here, Vance," he said; "do you believe the murderer tore up that letter and threw it in Doctor Bliss's waste-basket?"

"Can there be any doubt of it?" Vance asked in return.

"But what, in Heaven's name, could have been his object?"

"I don't know—yet. That's why I'm frightened." Vance gazed out of the rear window. "But the destruction of that letter is part of the plot; and until we can get some definite and workable evidence, we're helpless."

"Still," persisted Markham, "if the letter was incriminating, it strikes me it would have been valuable to the murderer. Tearing it up doesn't help any one."

Heath looked first at Vance and then at Markham.

"Maybe," he offered, "Salveter tore it up himself."

"When?" Vance asked quietly.

"How do I know?" The Sergeant was nettled. "Maybe when he croaked the old man."

"If that were the case, he wouldn't have admitted having written it."

"Well," Heath persevered, "maybe he tore it up when you sent him to find it a few minutes ago."

"And then, after tearing it up he came here and put it in the basket where it might be found. . . . No, Sergeant. That's not entirely reasonable. If Salveter had been frightened and had decided to get rid of the letter, he'd have destroyed it completely—burned it, most likely, and left no traces of it about."

Markham, too, had become fascinated by the hieroglyphs Vance had pieced together. He stood regarding the conjoined bits of paper perplexedly.

"You think, then, we were intended to find it?" he asked.

"I don't know." Vance's far-away gaze did not shift. "It may be . . . and yet. . . . No! There was only one chance in a thousand that we would come across it. The person who put it in the wastebasket here couldn't have known, or even guessed, that Salveter would tell us of having written it and left it lying about."

"On the other hand,"—Markham was loath to relinquish his train of thought—"the letter might have been put here in the hope of involving Bliss still further—that is, it might have been regarded by the murderer as another planted clew, along with the scarab pin, the financial report, and the footprints."

Vance shook his head.

"No. That couldn't be. Bliss, d' ye see, couldn't have written the letter,—it's too obviously a communication from Salveter to Mrs. Bliss."

Vance picked up the assembled letter and studied it for a time.

"It's not particularly difficult to read for any one who knows something of Egyptian. It says exactly what Salveter said it did." He tossed the paper back on the desk. "There's something unspeakably devilish behind this. And the more I think of it the more I'm convinced we were not intended to find the letter. My feeling is, it was carelessly thrown away by some one—*after it had served its purpose."*

"But what possible purpose——?" Markham began.

"If we knew the purpose, Markham," said Vance with much gravity, "we might avert another tradegy."

Markham compressed his lips grimly. I knew what was going through his mind: he was thinking of Vance's terrifying predictions in the Greene and the Bishop cases—predictions which came true with all the horror of final and ineluctable catastrophe.

"You believe this affair isn't over yet?" he asked slowly.

"I know it isn't over. The plan isn't complete. We forestalled the murderer by releasing Doctor Bliss. And now he must carry on. We've seen only the dark preliminaries of his damnable scheme—and when the plot is finally revealed, it will be monstrous. . . ."

Vance went quietly to the door leading into the hall and, opening it a few inches, looked out.

"And, Markham," he said, reclosing the door, "we must be careful—that's what I've been insisting on right along. We must not fall into any of the murderer's traps. The arrest of Doctor Bliss was one of those traps. A single false step on our part, and the plot will succeed."

He turned to Heath.

"Sergeant, will you be so good as to bring me the yellow pad and the pen and ink from the table in the museum? . . . We, too, must cover up our tracks, for we are being stalked as closely as we are stalking the murderer."

Heath, without a word, went into the museum, and a few moments later returned with the requested articles. Vance took them and sat down at the doctor's desk. Then placing Salveter's letter before him he began copying roughly the phonograms and ideograms on a sheet of the yellow pad.

"It's best, I think," he explained as he worked, "that we hide the fact that we've found the letter. The person who tore it up and threw it in the basket may suspect that we've discovered it and look for the fragments. If they're not here, he will be on his guard. It's merely a remote precaution, but we can't afford to make a slip. We're confronted by a mind of diablolical cleverness. . . ."

When he had finished transcribing a dozen or so of the symbols, he tore the paper into pieces of the same size as those of the original letter, and mixed them with the contents of the waste-basket. Then he folded up Salveter's original letter and placed it in his pocket.

"Do you mind, Sergeant, returning the paper and ink to the museum?"

"You oughta been a crook, Mr. Vance," Heath remarked good-naturedly, picking up the pad and ink-stand and disappearing through the steel door.

"I don't see any light," Markham commented gloomily. "The farther we go, the more involved the case becomes."

Vance nodded sombrely.

"There's nothing we can do now but await developments. Thus far we've checked the murderer's king; but he still has several moves. It's like one of Alekhine's chess combinations—we can't tell just what was in his mind when he began the assault. And he may produce a combination that will clean the board and leave us defenseless. . . ."

Heath reappeared at this moment, looking uneasy.

"I don't like that damn room," he grumbled. "Too many corpses. Why do these scientific bugs have to go digging up mummies and things? It's what you might call morbid."

"A perfect criticism of Egyptologists, Sergeant," Vance replied with a sympathetic grin. "Egyptology isn't an archæological science—it's a pathological condition, a cerebral visitation—*dementia scholastica.* Once the *spirillum terrigenum* enters your system, you're lost—cursed with an incurable disease. If you dig up corpses that are thousands of years old, you're an Egyptologist; if you dig up recent corpses you're a Burke or a Hare, and the law swoops down on you. It all comes under the head of body-snatching. . . ."*

"Be that as it may,"—Heath was still troubled and was chewing his cigar viciously—"I don't like the things in that morgue. And I specially don't like that black coffin under the front windows. What's in it, Mr. Vance?"

"The granite sarcophagus? Really, I don't know, Sergeant. It's empty in all probability, unless Doctor Bliss uses it as a storage chest—which isn't likely, considerin' the weight of the lid."

There came a knock on the hall door, and Snitkin informed us that Guilfoyle had arrived with Doctor Bliss.

"There are one or two questions," Vance said, "that I want to ask him. Then, I think, Markham, we can toddle along: I'm fainting for muffins and marmalade. . . ."

"Quit now?" demanded Heath in astonished disgust. "What's the idea? We've just begun this investigation!"

"We've done more than that," Vance told him softly. "We've avoided every snare laid for us by the murderer. We've upset all his calculations and forced him to reconstruct his trenches. As the case stands now, it's a stalemate. The board will have to be set up again—and, fortunately for us, the murderer gets the white pieces. It's his first move. He simply *has* to win the game, d' ye see. We can afford to play for a draw."

"I'm beginning to understand what you mean, Vance." Markham nodded slowly. "We've refused to follow his false moves, and now he must rebait his trap."

"Spoken with a precision and clarity wholly unbecoming a lawyer," returned Vance, with a forced smile. Then he sobered again. "Yes, I think he will rebait the trap before he takes any final steps. And I'm hopin' that the new bait will give us a solution to the entire plot and permit the Sergeant to make his arrest."

"Well, all I've gotta say," Heath complained, "is that this is the queerest case I was ever mixed up in. We go and eat muffins, and wait for the guilty guy to spill the beans! If I was to outline that technic to O'Brien† he'd call an ambulance and send me to Bellevue."

"I'll see you don't go to a psychopathic ward, Sergeant," Markham said irritably, walking toward the door.

---

* Vance was here indulging in hyperbole, and believed it no more than John Dennis believed that "a man who could make so vile a pun would not scruple to pick a pocket." Vance knew several Egyptologists and respected them highly. Among them were Doctor Ludlow Bull and Doctor Henry A. Carey of the Metropolitan Museum of Art, who had once generously assisted him in his work on the Menander fragments.

† Chief Inspector O'Brien was at that time in charge of the entire Police Department of the City of New York.

16

A CALL AFTER MIDNIGHT

(Friday, July 13; 5:15 P.M.)

WE FOUND Doctor Bliss in the drawing-room, slumped in a deep sprawling chair, his tweed hat pulled down over his eyes. Beside him stood Guilfoyle smirking triumphantly.

Vance was annoyed, and took no pains to hide the fact.

"Tell your efficient bloodhound to wait outside, will you, Sergeant?"

"O.K." Heath looked commiseratingly at Guilfoyle. "Out on the cement, Guil," he ordered. "And don't ask any questions. This ain't a murder case—it's a Hallowe'en party in a bug-house."

The detective grinned and left us.

Bliss lifted his eyes. He was a dejected-looking figure. His face was flushed, and apprehension and humiliation were written on his sunken features.

"Now, I suppose," he said in a quavering voice, "you'll arrest me for this heinous murder. But—oh, my God, gentlemen!—I assure you——"

Vance had stepped toward him.

"Just a moment, doctor," he broke in. "Don't upset yourself. We're not going to arrest you; but we would like an explanation of your amazin' action. Why should you, if you are innocent, attempt to leave the country?"

"Why . . . why?" The man was nervous and excited. "I was afraid—that's why. Everything is against me. All the evidence points toward me. . . . There's some one here who hates me and wants me out of the way. It's only too obvious. The planting of my scarab pin beside poor Kyle's body, and that financial report found in the murdered man's hand, and those terrible footprints leading to my study—don't you think I know what it all means? It means that I must pay the price—I, *I*." He struck his chest weakly. "And other things will be found; the person who killed Kyle won't rest content until I'm behind the bars—or dead. I know it—I know it! . . . That's why I tried to get away. And now you've brought me back to a living death—to a fate more awful than the one that befell my old benefactor. . . ."

His head dropped forward and a shudder ran through his body.

"Still, it was foolish to attempt to escape, doctor," Markham said gently. "You might have trusted us. I assure you no injustice will be done you. We have learned many thngs in the course of our investigation; and we have reason to believe that you were drugged with powdered opium during the period of the crime——"

"Powdered opium!" Bliss almost leapt out of his chair. "That's what I tasted! There was something the matter with the coffee this morning—it had a curious flavor. At first I thought Brush hadn't made it the way I'd instructed him. Then I got drowsy, and forgot all about it. . . . Opium! I know the taste. I once had dysentery in Egypt, and took opium and capsicum—my Sun Chol-

619

era Mixture* had run out." His mouth sagged open, and he gave Markham a look of terrified appeal. "Poisoned in my own house!" Suddenly a grim vindictiveness shone in his eyes. "You're right, sir," he said, with metallic hardness. "I shouldn't have attempted to run away. My place is here, and my duty is to help you——"

"Yes, yes, doctor." Vance was palpably bored. "Regrets are very comfortin', but we're tryin' to deal with facts. And thus far you haven't been very helpful. . . . I say, who had charge of the medical supplies?" He put the question abruptly.

"Why . . . why . . . let me see. . . ." Bliss averted his eyes and began fidgeting with the crease in his trousers.

"We'll drop the matter." Vance made a resigned gesture. "Maybe you're willing to tell us how well Mrs. Bliss knows Egyptian hieroglyphs."

Bliss looked surprised, and it took him several moments to regain his equanimity.

"She knows them practically as well as I do," he answered at length. "Her father, Abercrombie, taught her the old Egyptian language when she was a child, and she has worked with me for years in the deciphering of inscriptions. . . ."

"And Hani?"

"Oh, he has a smattering of hieroglyphic writing—nothing unusual. He lacks the trained mind——"

"And how well does Mr. Salveter know Egyptian?"

"Fairly well. He's weak on grammatical points, but his knowledge of the signs and the vocabulary is rather extensive. He has studied Greek and Arabic; and I believe he had a year or two of Assyrian. Coptic, too. The usual linguistic foundation for an archæologist.—Scarlett, on the other hand, is something of a wizard, though he's a loyal adherent of Budge's system—like many amateurs.† And Budge, of course, is antiquated. Don't misunderstand me. Budge is a great man—his contributions to Egyptology are invaluable; and his publication of the Book of the Dead——"

"I know." Vance nodded with impatience. "His Index makes it possible to find almost any passage in the Papyrus of Ani. . . ."

"Just so." Bliss had begun to reveal a curious animation: his scientific enthusiasm was manifesting itself. "But Alan Gardiner is the true modern scholar. His 'Egyptian Grammar' is a profound and accurate work. The most important *opus* on Egyptology, however, is the Erman-Grapow 'Wörterbuch der aegyptischen Sprache.' . . ."

Vance had become suddenly interested.

"Does Mr. Salveter use the Erman-Grapow 'Wörterbuch'?" he asked.

---

* The Sun Cholera Mixture for dysentery (a recipe of Doctor G. W. Busteed) was so named because its formula had been published by the New York *Sun* during the cholera excitement in New York in June, 1849. It was admitted to the first edition of the National Formulary in 1883. Its constituents were tincture of capsicum, tincture of rhubarb, spirits of camphor, essence of peppermint, and opium.

† Sir E. A. Wallis Budge was for many years Keeper of the Egyptian and Assyrian Antiquities in the British Museum.

"Certainly. I insisted upon it. I ordered three sets from Leipzig—one for myself, and one each for Salveter and Scarlett."

"The signs differ considerably, I believe, from the Theinhardt type used by Budge."

"Oh, yes." Bliss removed his hat and threw it on the floor. "The consonant transliterated *u* by Budge—the quail chick—appears as *w* in the 'Wörterbuch' and every other modern work. And, of course, there's the cursive spiral sign which is also the hieroglyphic adaptation of the hieratic abbreviated form of the quail. . . ."

"Thank you, doctor." Vance took out his cigarette-case, saw he had only one *Régie* left, and returned it to his pocket. "I understand that Mr. Scarlett, before leaving the house this afternoon, went up-stairs. I rather thought, don't y' know, that he dropped in to see you."

"Yes." Bliss sank back in his chair. "A very sympathetic fellow, Scarlett."

"What did he say to you?"

"Nothing of any importance. He wished me good luck—said he'd stand by, in case I wanted him. That sort of thing."

"How long was he with you?"

"A minute or so. He went away immediately. Said he was going home."

"One more question, doctor," Vance said, after several moments' pause. "Who in this house would have any reason for wanting to saddle you with the crime of killing Mr. Kyle?"

A sudden change came over Bliss. His eyes glared straight ahead, and the lines of his face hardened into almost terrifying contours. He clutched the arms of his chair and drew in his feet. Both fear and hatred possessed him; he was a man about to leap at a mortal enemy. Then he stood up, every muscle in his body tense.

"I can't answer that question; I refuse to answer it! . . . I don't know—I don't know! But there is some one—isn't there?" He reached out and grasped Vance's arm. "You should have let me escape." A wild look came into his eyes, and he glanced hurriedly toward the door as if he feared some imminent danger lurking in the hall. "Have me arrested, Mr. Vance! Do anything but ask me to stay here. . . ." His voice had become pitifully appealing.

Vance drew away from him.

"Pull yourself together, doctor," he said in a matter-of-fact tone. "Nothing is going to happen to you. . . . Go to your room and remain there till to-morrow. We'll take care of the criminal end of the case."

"But you have no idea who did this frightful thing," Bliss protested.

"Oh, but we have, don't y' know." Vance's calm asurance seemed to have a quieting effect on him. "It's only necess'ry for us to wait a bit. At present we haven't enough evidence to make an arrest. But since the murderer's main object has failed, it's almost inevitable that he will make another move. And when he does, we may get the necess'ry evidence against him."

"But suppose he takes direct action—against me?" Bliss remonstrated. "The fact that he has failed to involve me may drive him to more desperate measures."

"I hardly think so," returned Vance. "But if anything happens, you can reach me at this telephone number." He wrote his private number on a card and handed it to Bliss.

The doctor took the card eagerly, glanced at it, and slipped it into his pocket.

"I'm going up-stairs now," he said, and walked distractedly out of the room.

"Are you sure, Vance," Markham asked in a troubled voice, "that we're not subjecting Doctor Bliss to unnecessary risk?"

"Pretty sure." Vance had become thoughtful. "Anyway, it's a delicate game, and there's no other way to play it." He went to the window. "I don't know...," he murmured. Then after several moments: "Sergeant, I'd like to speak to Salveter.—And there's no need for Hennessey to remain up-stairs. Let him go."

Heath, nonplussed and helpless, went into the hall and called to Hennessey.

When Salveter came into the drawing-room, Vance did not even glance in his direction.

"Mr. Salveter," he said, looking out at the dusty trees in Gramercy Park, "if I were you I'd lock my door to-night. . . . And don't write any more letters," he added. "Also, keep out of the museum."

Salveter appeared frightened by these admonitions. He studied Vance's back for some time, and then set his jaw.

"If any one starts anything round here——" he began with an almost ferocious aggressiveness.

"Oh, quite." Vance sighed. "But don't project your personality so intensively. I'm fatigued."

Salveter, after a moment's hesitation, swung about and strode from the room.

Vance came to the centre-table and rested heavily against it.

"And now, a word with Hani, and we can depart."

Heath shrugged his shoulders resignedly, and went to the door.

"Hey, Snitkin, round up that Ali Baba in the kimono."

Snitkin leapt to the staircase, and a few minutes later the Egyptian stood before us, serene and detached.

"Hani," said Vance, with an impressiveness wholly uncharacteristic, "you will do well to watch over this household to-night."

"Yes, *effendi*. I comprehend perfectly. The spirit of Sakhmet may return and complete the task she has begun——"

"Exactly." Vance gave a tired smile. "Your feline lady foozled things this morning, and she'll probably be back to tie up a few loose ends. . . . Watch for her—do you understand?"

Hani inclined his head.

"Yes, *effendi*. We understand each other."

"That's positively rippin'. And incidentally, Hani, what is the number of Mr. Scarlett's domicile in Irving Place?"

"Ninety-six." The Egyptian revealed considerable interest in Vance's question.

"That will be all. . . . And give my regards to your lion-headed goddess."

"It may be Anûbis who will return, *effendi*," said Hani sepulchrally, as he left us.

Vance looked whimsically at Markham.

"The stage is set, and the curtain will go up anon. . . . Let's move on. There's nothing more we can do here. And I'm totterin' with hunger."

As we passed out into Twentieth Street Vance led the way toward Irving Place.

"I rather think we owe it to Scarlett to let him know how things stand," he explained negligently. "He brought us the sad tidings and is probably all agog and aflutter. He lives just round the corner."

Markham glanced at Vance inquisitively, but made no comment. Heath, however, grunted impatiently.

"It looks to me like we're doing 'most everything but clean up this homicide," he groused.

"Scarlett's a shrewd lad; he may have conjured up an idea or two," Vance returned.

"I got ideas, too," the Sergeant declared maliciously. "But what good are they? If *I* was handling this case, I'd arrest the whole outfit, put 'em in separate cells, and let 'em sweat. By the time they got *habeas-corpus* proceedings started I'd know a damn sight more than I do now."

"I doubt it, Sergeant." Vance spoke mildly. "I think you'd know even less. . . . Ah, here's number ninety-six."

He turned into the Colonial entrance of an old brick house a few doors from Twentieth Street, and rang the bell.

Scarlett's quarters—two small rooms with a wide, arched doorway between—were on the second floor at the front. They were furnished severely but comfortably in Jacobean style, and typified the serious-minded bachelor. Scarlett had opened the door at our knock and invited us in with the stiff cordiality of the English host. He seemed relieved to see us.

"I've been in a frightful stew for hours," he said. "Been trying to analyze this affair. I was on the point of running round to the museum and finding out what progress you gentlemen had made."

"We've made a bit of progress," Vance told him; "but it's not of a tangible nature. We've decided to let matters float for a while in the anticipation that the guilty person will proceed with his plot and thus supply us with definite evidence."

"Ah!" Scarlett took his pipe slowly from his mouth and looked sharply at Vance. "That remark makes me think that maybe you and I have reached the same conclusion. There was no earthly reason for Kyle's having been killed unless his demise was to lead to something else——"

"To what, for example?"

"By Jove, I wish I knew!" Scarlett packed his pipe with his finger and held a match to it. "There are several possible explanations."

"My word! Are there? . . . Several? Well, well! Could you bear to outline one of them? We're dashed interested, don't y' know."

"Oh, I say, Vance! Really, now, I'd hate like the Old Harry to wrong any one," Scarlett spluttered. "Hani, however, didn't care a great deal for Doctor Bliss——"

"Thanks awfully. Astonishin' as it may seem, I noted that fact myself this morning. Have you any other little beam of sunshine you'd care to launch in our direction?"

"I think Salveter is hopelessly smitten with Meryt-Amen."

"Fancy that!"

Vance took out his cigarette-case and tapped his one remaining *Régie* on the lid. Deliberately he lighted it and, after a deep inhalation, looked up seriously.

"Yes, Scarlett," he drawled, "it's quite possible that you and I have arrived at the same conclusion. But naturally we can't make a move until we have something definite with which to back up our hypotheses. . . . By the by, Doctor Bliss attempted to leave the country this afternoon. If it hadn't been for one of Sergeant Heath's minions he presumably would be on his way to Montreal at this moment."

I expected to see Scarlett express astonishment at this news, but instead he merely nodded his head.

"I'm not surprised. He's certainly in a funk. Can't say that I blame him. Things appear rather black for him." Scarlett puffed on his pipe, and shot a surreptitious look at Vance. "The more I think about this affair, the more I'm impressed with the possibility that, after all——"

"Oh, quite." Vance cut him short. "But we're not pantin' for possibilities. What we crave is specific data."

"That's going to be difficult, I'm afraid." Scarlett grew thoughtful. "There's been too much cleverness—"

"Ah! That's the point—*too much cleverness.* Exactly! Therein lies the weakness of the crime. And I'm hopefully countin' on that *abundantia cautelæ.*" Vance smiled. "Really, y' know, Scarlett, I'm not as dense as I've appeared thus far. My object in stultifyin' my perceptions has been to wangle the murderer into new efforts. Sooner or later he'll overplay his hand."

Scarlett did not answer for some time. Finally he spoke.

"I appreciate your confidence, Vance. You're very sporting. But my opinion is, you'll never be able to convict the murderer."

"You may be right," Vance admitted. "Nevertheless, I'm appealing to you to keep an eye on the situation. . . . But I warn you to be careful. The murderer of Kyle is a ruthless johnnie."

"You don't have to tell me that." Scarlett got up and, walking to the fireplace, leaned against the marble mantel. "I could tell you volumes about him."

"I'm sure you could." To my astonishment Vance accepted the other's startling statement without the slightest manifestation of surprise. "But there's no need to go into that now." He, too, rose, and going to the door gave a casual wave of farewell to Scarlett. "We're toddlin' along. Just thought we'd let you know how things stood and admonish you to be careful."

"Very kind of you, Vance. Fact is, I'm frightfully upset—nervous as a Persian kitten. . . . Wish I could work; but all my materials are at the museum. I know I sha'n't sleep a wink to-night."

"Well, cheerio!" Vance turned the door-knob.

"I say, Vance!" Scarlett stepped forward urgently. "Are you, by any chance, going back to the Bliss house to-day?"

"No. We're through there for the time being." Vance's voice was quiet and droning, as with ennui. "Why do you ask?"

Scarlett fiddled at his pipe with a sort of sudden agitation.

"No reason." He looked at Vance with a constricted brow. "No reason at all. I'm anxious about the situation. There's no telling what may happen."

"Whatever happens, Scarlett," Vance said, with a certain abruptness,

"Mrs. Bliss will be perfectly safe. I think we can trust Hani to see to that."

"Yes—of course," the man murmured. "Faithful dog, Hani. . . . And who'd want to harm Meryt?"

"Who, indeed?" Vance was now standing in the hallway, holding the door open for Markham and Heath and me to pass through.

Scarlett, animated by some instinct of hospitality, came forward.

"Sorry you're going," he said perfunctorily. "If I can be of any help. . . . So you've ended your investigation at the house?"

"For the moment, at least." Vance paused. The rest of us had passed him and were waiting at the head of the stairs. "We're not contemplatin' returning to the Bliss establishment until something new comes to light."

"Right-o." Scarlett nodded with a curious significance. "If I learn anything I'll telephone to you."

We went out into Irving Place, and Vance hailed a taxicab.

"Food—sustenance," he moaned. "Let us see. . . . The Brevoort isn't far away. . . ."

We had an elaborate tea at the old Brevoort on lower Fifth Avenue, and shortly afterward Heath departed for the Homicide Bureau to make out his report and to pacify the newspaper reporters who would be swarming in on him the moment the case went on record.

"You had better stand by," Vance suggested to the Sergeant, as he left us; "for I'm full of anticipation, and we couldn't push forward without you."

"I'll be at the office till ten to-night," Heath told him sulkily. "And after that Mr. Markham knows where to reach me at home. But, I'm here to tell you, I'm disgusted."

"So are we all," said Vance cheerfully.

Markham telephoned to Swacker* to close the office and go home. Then the three of us drove to Longue Vue for dinner. Vance refused to discuss the case and insisted upon talking about Arturo Toscanini, the new conductor of the Philharmonic-Symphony Orchestra.

"A vastly overrated *Kapellmeister*," he complained, as he tasted his *canard Molière*. "It strikes me he is temperamentally incapable of sensing the classic ideals in the great symphonic works of Brahms and Beethoven. . . . I say, the tomato purée in this sauce is excellent, but the Madeira wine is too vineg'ry. Prohibiton, Markham, worked devastatin' havoc on the food of this country: it practically eliminated gastronomic æsthetics. . . . But to return to Toscanini. I'm positively amazed at the panegyrics with which the critics have showered him. His secret ideals, I'm inclined to think, are Puccini and Giordano and Respighi. And no man with such ideals should attempt to interpret the classics. I've heard him do Brahms and Beethoven and Mozart, and they all exuded a strong Italian aroma under his baton. But the Americans worship him. They have no sense of pure intellectual beauty, of sweeping classic lines and magistral form. They crave strongly contrasted *pianissimos* and *fortissimos*, sudden changes in tempi, leaping *accelerandos* and crawling *ritardandos*. And Toscanini gives it all to 'em. . . . Furtwängler, Walter, Klemperer, Mengelberg, Van Hoogstraaten—any one of these conductors is, in my opinion, superior to Toscanini when it comes to the great German classics. . . ."

---

* Swacker, a bright, energetic youth, was Markham's secretary.

"Would you mind, Vance," Markham asked irritably, "dropping these irrelevancies and outlining to me your theory of the Kyle case?"

"I'd mind terribly," was Vance's amiable reply. "After the *Bar-le-duc* and *Gervaise,* however. . . ."

As a matter of fact it was nearly midnight before the subject of the tragedy was again broached. We had returned to Vance's apartment after a long drive through Van Cortlandt Park; and Markham and he and I had gone up to the little roof garden to seek whatever air was stirring along East Thirty-eighth Street. Currie had made a delicious champagne cup—what the Viennese call a *Bowle*—with fresh fruit in it; and we sat under the summer stars smoking and waiting. I say, "waiting," for there is no doubt that each of us expected something untoward to happen.

Vance, for all his detachment, was inwardly tense—I could tell this by his slow, restrained movements. And Markham was loath to go home: he was far from satisfied with the way the investigation had progressed, and was hoping—as a result of Vance's prognostication—that something would develop to take the case out of the hazy realm of conjecture and place it upon a sound basis where definite action could be taken.

Shortly before twelve o'clock Markham held a long conversation with Heath on the telephone. When he hung up the receiver he heaved a hopeless sigh.

"I don't like to think of what the opposition papers are going to say to-morrow," he remarked gloomily, as he cut the tip off of a fresh cigar. "We've got absolutely nowhere in this investigation. . . ."

"Oh, yes, we have." Vance was staring up into the sultry night. "We've made amazin' progress. The case, d' ye see, is closed as far as the solution is concerned. We're merely waitin' for the murderer to get panic-stricken. The moment he does, we'll be able to take action."

"Why must you be so confounded mysterious?" Markham was in a vile humor. "You're always indulging in cabalistic rituals. The Delphic Pythia herself was no vaguer or more obscure than you. If you think you know who killed Kyle, why not come out with it?"

"I can't do it." Vance, too, was distressed. "Really, y' know, Markham, I'm not trying to be illusory. I'm strivin' to find some tangible evidence to corroborate my theory. And if we bide our time we'll secure that evidence." He looked at Markham seriously. "There's danger, of course. Something unforeseen may happen. But there's no human way to stop it. Whatever step we might take now would lead to tragedy. We have given the murderer an abundance of rope; let us hope he will hang himself. . . ."

It was exactly twenty minutes past twelve that night when the thing that Vance had been waiting for happened. We had been sitting in silence for perhaps ten minutes when Currie stepped out into the garden carrying a portable telephone.

"I beg your pardon, sir——" he began; but before he could continue Vance had risen and walked toward him.

"Plug it in, Currie," he ordered. "I'll answer the call."

Vance took the instrument and leaned against the French door.

"Yes . . . yes. What has happened?" His voice was low and resonant. He listened for perhaps thirty seconds, his eyes half closed. Then he said merely: "We'll be there at once," and handed the telephone to Currie.

He was unquestionably puzzled, and stood for several moments, his head down, deep in thought.

"It's not what I expected," he said, as if to himself. "It doesn't fit."

Presently he lifted his head, like one struck sharply.

"But it *does* fit! Of course it fits! It's what I should have expected." Despite the careless pose of his body his eyes were animated. "Logic! How damnable logical! . . . Come, Markham. Phone Heath—have him meet us at the museum as soon as he can get there. . . ."

Markham had risen and was glaring at Vance in ferocious alarm.

"Who was that on the phone?" he demanded. "And what has happened?"

"Please be tranquil, Markham." Vance spoke quietly. "It was Doctor Bliss who spoke to me. And, accordin' to his hysterical tale, there has been an attempted murder in his house. I promised him we'd look in. . . ."

Markham had already snatched the telephone from Currie's hands and was frantically asking for Heath's number.

17

THE GOLDEN DAGGER

(Saturday, July 14; 12:45 A.M.)

WE HAD to walk to Fifth Avenue to find a taxicab at that hour, and even then there was five minutes' wait until an unoccupied one came by. The result was that it was fully twenty minutes before we turned into Gramercy Park and drew up in front of the Bliss residence.

As we alighted another taxicab swung round the corner of Irving Place and nearly skidded into us as its brakes were suddenly thrown on. The door was flung open before the cab had come to a standstill, and the bulky figure of Sergeant Heath projected itself to the sidewalk. Heath lived in East Eleventh Street and had managed to dress and reach the museum almost simultaneously with our arrival.

"My word, Sergeant!" Vance hailed him. "We synchronize, don't y' know. We arrive at the same destination at the same time, but from opposite directions. Jolly idea."

Heath acknowledged the somewhat enigmatical pleasantry with a grunt.

"What's all the excitement anyway?" he asked Markham. "You didn't give me much of an earful over the phone."

"An attempt has been made on Doctor Bliss's life," Markham told him.

Heath whistled softly.

"I certainly didn't expect that, sir."

"Neither did Mr. Vance." The rejoinder was intended as a taunt.

We went up the stone steps to the vestibule, but before we could ring the bell Brush opened the door. He placed his forefinger to his lips and, leaning forward mysteriously, said in a stage whisper:

"Doctor Bliss requests that you gentlemen be very quiet so as not to disturb the other members of the household. . . . He's in his bedchamber waiting for you."

Brush was clad in a flannel robe and carpet slippers, but despite the hot sultriness of the night he was visibly shivering. His face, always pale, now appeared positively ghastly in the dim light.

We stepped into the hall, and Brush closed the door cautiously with trembling hands. Suddenly, Vance wheeled about and caught him by the arm, spinning him round.

"What do you know about the occurrence here to-night?" he demanded in a low tone.

The butler's eyes bulged and his jaw sagged.

"Nothing—nothing," he managed to stammer.

"Really, now! Then why are you so frightened?" Vance did not relax his hold.

"I'm afraid of this place," came the plaintive answer. "I want to leave here. Strange things are going on——"

"So they are. But don't fret; you'll be able to look for another berth before long."

"I'm glad of that, sir." The man seemed greatly relieved. "But what *has* happened to-night, sir?"

"If you're ignorant of what has taken place," returned Vance, "how do you happen to be here at this hour awaiting our arrival and acting like a villain in a melodrama?"

"I was told to wait for you, sir. Doctor Bliss came down-stairs to my room——"

"Where is your room, Brush?"

"In the basement, at the rear, just off the kitchen."

"Very good. Go on."

"Well, sir, Doctor Bliss came to my room about half an hour ago. He seemed very much upset, and frightened—if you know what I mean. He told me to wait at the front door for you gentlemen—that you'd arrive any minute. And he instructed me to make no noise and also to warn you——"

"Then he went up-stairs?"

"At once, sir."

"Where is Doctor Bliss's room?"

"It's the rear door on the second floor, just at the head of the stairs. The forward door is the mistress's bedchamber."

Vance released the man's arm.

"Did you hear any disturbance to-night?"

"None, sir. Everything has been quiet. Every one retired early, and I myself went to bed before eleven."

"You may go back to bed now," Vance told him.

"Yes, sir." And Brush went quickly away and disappeared through the door at the rear of the hall.

Vance made a gesture for us to follow him and led the way up-stairs. A small electric bulb was burning in the upper hall, but we did not need it to find Doctor Bliss's room, for his door was a few inches ajar and a shaft of light fell diagonally across the floor outside.

Vance, without knocking, pushed the door inward and stepped into the room. Bliss was sitting rigidly in a straight chair in the far corner, leaning slightly forward, his eyes riveted on the door. In his hand was a brutal-looking army revolver. At our entrance he leapt to his feet, and brought the gun up simultaneously.

"Tut, tut, doctor!" Vance smiled whimsically. "Put the firearms away and chant us the distressin' rune."

Bliss drew an audible sigh of relief, and placed the weapon on a small table at his side.

"Thank you for coming, Mr. Vance," he said in a strained tone. "And you, Mr. Markham." He acknowledged Heath's and my presence with a slight, jerky bow. "The thing you predicted has happened. . . . There's a murderer in this house!"

"Well, well! That would hardly come under the head of news." (I could not understand Vance's attitude.) "We've known that fact since eleven this morning."

Bliss, too, was perplexed and, I imagine, somewhat piqued by Vance's negligent manner, for he stepped stiffly to the bed and, pointing at the headboard, remarked irritably:

"And there's the proof!"

The bed was an old Colonial piece, of polished mahogany, with a great curving headboard rising at least four feet above the mattress. It stood against the left-hand wall at a right angle to the door.

The object at which Bliss pointed with a quivering finger was an antique Egyptian dagger, about eleven inches long, whose blade was driven into the headboard just above the pillow. The direction of penetration was on a line with the door.

We all moved forward and stood for several seconds staring at the sinister sight. The dagger had undoubtedly been thrown with great force to have entered the hard mahogany wood so firmly; and it was obvious that if any one had been lying on the pillow at the time it was hurled, he would have received the full brunt of it somewhere in the throat.

Vance studied the position of the dagger, gauging its alignment and angulation with the door, and then he reached out his hand to grasp it. But Heath intercepted the movement.

"Use your handkerchief, Mr. Vance," he admonished. "There'll be fingerprints——"

"Oh, no, there won't, Sergeant." Vance spoke with an impressive air of knowledge. "Whoever threw that dagger was careful to avoid any such incriminatin' tokens. . . ." Whereupon he drew the blade, with considerable difficulty, from the headboard, and took it to the table-lamp.

It was a beautiful and interesting piece of workmanship. Its handle was ornamented with decorations of granulated gold and with strips of cloisonné and semi-precious stones—amethysts, turquoises, garnets, carnelians, and tiny cuttings of obsidian, chalcedony and felspar. The haft was surmounted with a lotiform knob of rock crystal, and at the hilt was a chair-scroll design in gold wire. The blade was of hardened gold adorned with shallow central grooves ending with an engraved palmette decoration.*

---

* A similar dagger was found on the royal mummy in the tomb of Tut-ankh-Amûn by the late Earl of Carnarvon and Howard Carter, and is now in the Cairo Museum.

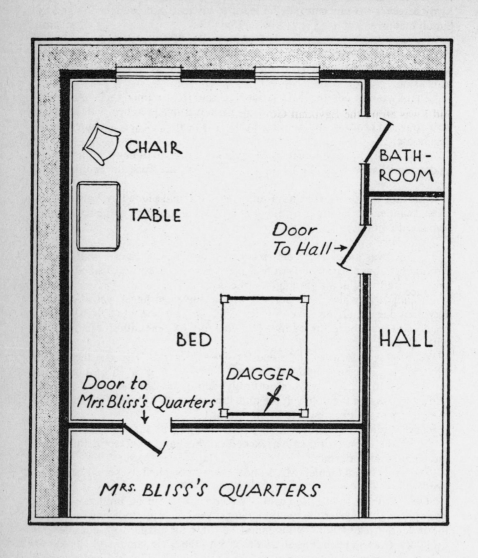

CHAIR

TABLE

BATH-ROOM

Door To Hall →

BED

DAGGER

HALL

Door to Mrs. Bliss's Quarters

M^{RS.} BLISS'S QUARTERS

DOCTOR BLISS'S BEDROOM

"Late Eighteenth Dynasty," murmured Vance, fingering the dagger and studying its designs. "Pretty, but decadent. The rugged simplicty of early Egyptian art went frightfully to pot during the opulent renaissance following the Hyksos invasion. . . . I say, Doctor Bliss; how did you come by this flamboyant gewgaw?"

Bliss was ill at ease, and when he answered his tone was apologetic and embarrassed.

"The fact is, Mr. Vance, I smuggled that dagger out of Egypt. It was an unusual and unexpected find, and purely accidental. It's a most valuable relic, and I was afraid the Egyptian Government would claim it."

"I can well imagine they'd want to keep it in their own country." Vance tossed the dagger to the table. "And where did you ordinarily keep it?"

"Under some papers in one of my desk drawers in the study," he replied presently. "It was a rather personal item, and I thought it best not to list it in the museum."

"Most discreet. . . . Who besides yourself knew of its existence?"

"My wife, of course, and——" He broke off suddenly, and a peculiar light came in his eyes.

"Come, come, doctor." Vance spoke with annoyance. "This won't do. Finish your sentence."

"It is finished. My wife was the only person I confided in."

Vance accepted the statement without further argument.

"Still," he said, "any one might have discovered it, what?"

Bliss nodded slowly.

"Provided he had been snooping through my desk."

"Exactly. When did you last see the dagger in your desk drawer?"

"This morning. I was searching for some foolscap paper on which to check my report for poor Kyle. . . ."

"And who, to your knowledge, has been in your study since we left the house this afternoon?"

Bliss pondered, and shortly a startled expression came over his face.

"I'd rather not say."

"We can't do anything to help you, doctor, if you take that attitude," Vance said severely. "Was it Mr. Salveter who was in the study?"

Bliss paused for several seconds. Then he set his jaw.

"Yes!" The word fairly burst from his lips. "I sent him to the study after dinner to-night to get me a memorandum book. . . ."

"And where did you keep the book?"

"In the desk." This information was given reluctantly. "But any attempt to connect Salveter——"

"We're not attemptin' just now to connect any one with this episode." Vance interrupted. "We're merely tryin' to accumulate all the information possible. . . . However, you must admit, doctor," Vance added, "that young Mr. Salveter is—how shall I put it?—rather interested in Mrs. Bliss——"

"What's that?" Bliss stiffened and glared at Vance ferociously. "How dare you intimate such a thing? My wife, sir——"

"No one has criticised Mrs. Bliss," Vance said mildly. "And one A.M. is hardly the time for indignant pyrotechnics."

Bliss sank into his chair and covered his face with his hands.

"It may be true," he conceded in a despairing voice. "I'm too old for her—too much absorbed in my work. . . . But that doesn't mean that the boy would attempt to kill me."

"Perhaps not." Vance spoke indifferently. "But who, then, do you suspect of endeavorin' to sever your carotid?"

"I don't know—I don't know." The man's voice rose pitifully.

At this moment the door leading into the front apartment opened, and Mrs. Bliss stood on the threshold, a long flowing robe of oriental pattern draped about her. She was perfectly calm, and her eyes were steady, if a bit brilliant, as they took in the scene before her.

"Why have you gentlemen returned at this hour?" she inquired imperiously.

"An attempt has been made on your husband's life, madam," Markham answered sombrely; "and he telephoned to us——"

"An attempt on his life? Impossible!" She spoke with over-emphasis, and her face turned perceptibly pale. Then she went to Bliss and put her arms about him in an attitude of affectionate protection. Her eyes were blazing as she lifted them to Vance. "What absurdity is this? Who would want to take my husband's life?"

"Who, indeed?" Vance met her gaze calmly. "If we knew, we could at least arrest the person for assault with a deadly weapon—I believe that's the phrase."

"A deadly weapon?" She frowned with obvious distress. "Oh, tell me what happened!"

Vance indicated the dagger on the table.

"All we know thus far is that yon golden dagger was projectin' from the head of the bed when we arrived. We were on the point of asking your husband for a full account of the affair when you appeared—a charming Nefret-îti—at the door. . . . Perhaps," he went on, turning to Bliss, "the doctor will recount the entire episode for us now."

"There's really little to tell." Bliss sat up and began nervously to make creases in the folds of his dressing-gown. "I came here to my room shortly after dinner, and went to bed. But I couldn't sleep, and got up. Just then Salveter passed my door on his way up-stairs and I asked him to fetch the memorandum book from the study,—I thought I might take my mind off the dreadful events of the day——"

"One moment, doctor," Vance interposed. "Was your door open?"

"Yes. I had opened it when I arose, in order to get a little more air in the room,—the atmosphere was stifling. . . . Then I went over a few old notes and entries relating to last winter's excavations. But I couldn't keep my mind on them, and finally I closed the door, switched off the lights, and lay down again on the bed."

"That would have been about what time?"

"Between half past ten and eleven, I should say. . . . I dozed intermittently till midnight—I could see the time by that clock with the luminous dial—and then became unaccountably restless. I got to thinking about poor Kyle, and all inclination to sleep left me. However, I was dog-tired physically, and lay quite still. . . . About a quarter past twelve—the house was very quiet, you understand—I thought I could hear footsteps on the stairs——"

"Which stairs, doctor?"

"I couldn't determine. The footsteps might have been coming down from the third floor, or they might have been ascending from the first floor. They were very quiet, and if I had not been wide awake and keyed up I wouldn't have noticed them. As it was, I couldn't be sure, though at one time I imagined I heard a slight creak as if a board were a little loose under the carpet."

"And then?"

"I lay speculating on who it might be, for I knew the other members of the house had retired early. I did not exactly worry about the sounds until I heard them approach my own door and suddenly halt. Then your warning, Mr. Vance, swept over me with full force, and I felt that some terrible unknown danger was lurking on the threshold. I was, I admit, temporarily paralyzed with fright: I could feel the roots of my hair tingle, and my body broke out in cold perspiration."

He took a deep breath, as if to rid himself of a haunting memory.

"Just then the door began to open slowly and softly. The light in the hall had been turned out and the room here was in almost pitch darkness, so I was unable to see anything. But I could hear the gentle swish of the door as it swung open, and I could feel the mild current of air that came in from the hall. . . ."

A tremor ran over his body, and his eyes glowed unnaturally.

"I would have called out, but my throat seemed constricted, and I did not want to imperil Mrs. Bliss, who might have answered my call and run unwittingly into something dangerous and deadly. . . . And then the blinding ray of a flash-light was thrown directly into my eyes, and I instinctively lurched to the far side of the bed. At that moment I heard a swift, brushing sound followed by a dull wooden detonation near my head. And immediately I became conscious of footsteps retreating——"

"In which direction?" Vance again interrupted.

"I'm not sure—they were very faint. I was aware only of their stealthy retreat. . . ."

"What did you do after that, doctor?"

"I waited several minutes. Then I cautiously closed the door and switched on the lights. It was at that moment I realized what had made the noise at the head of the bed, for the first thing I saw was the dagger. And I knew that I had been the object of a murderous attack."

Vance nodded and, picking up the dagger, weighed it on the palm of his hand.

"Yes," he mused; "it's blade-heavy and could easily have been thrown accurately even by an amateur. . . . A peculiar form of assassination, though," he went on, almost to himself. "Much simpler and surer for the wielder to have sneaked to the bed and thrust it into his intended victim's ribs. . . . Most peculiar! Unless, of course——" He stopped and glanced thoughtfully at the bed. Presently he shrugged his shoulders, and looked at Bliss. "After discovering the dagger, I opine, you telephoned to me."

"Within five minutes. I listened at the door a while and then went down to the study and called your number. After that I roused Brush and told him to watch for you at the front door. I came back up-stairs,—I'd armed myself with my revolver while in the study,—and awaited your arrival."

Mrs. Bliss had been watching her husband with a look of deep anxiety during his recital.

"I heard the sound of the dagger striking the headboard," she said in a low, fearful voice. "My bed is against the other side of the wall. It startled me and woke me up, but I didn't give it a second thought, and went to sleep again." She threw her head back and glared at Vance. "This is shameful and outrageous! You insist upon my husband staying in this house that harbors a murderer—a murderer who is plotting against him—and you do nothing to protect him."

"But nothing has happened to him, Mrs. Bliss," Vance replied with gentle sternness. "He has lost an hour's sleep, but really, y' know, that's not a serious catastrophe. And I can assure you that no further danger will beset him." He looked straight into the woman's eyes, and I was conscious that some understanding passed between them in that moment of mutual scrutiny.

"I do hope you find the guilty person," she said with slow, tragic emphasis. "I can bear the truth—now."

"You are very courageous, madam," Vance murmured. "And in the meantime you can best help us by retiring to your room and waiting there until you hear from us. You can trust me."

"Oh, I know I can!" There was a catch in her voice. Then she bent impulsively, touched her lips to Bliss's forehead, and returned to her room.

Vance's eyes followed her with a curious expression: I could not determine if it was one of regret or sorrow or admiration. When the door had closed after her he strolled to the table and replaced the dagger on it.

"I was just wonderin', doctor," he said. "Don't you lock or bolt your door at night?"

"Always," was the immediate reply. "It makes me nervous to sleep with an unlocked door."

"But what about to-night?"

"That is what puzzles me." Bliss's forehead was knit in perplexity. "I'm sure I locked it when I first came to my room. But, as I told you, I got up later and opened the door to get some air. The only explanation I can think of is that when I went back to bed I forgot to relock the door. It's possible of course, for I was very much upset. . . ."

"It couldn't have been unlocked from the outside?"

"No, I'm sure it couldn't. The key was in the lock, just as you see it now."

"What about finger-prints on the outside knob?" Heath queried. "That cut glass would take 'em easy."

"My word, Sergeant!" Vance shook his head despairingly. "The concocter of this plot knows better than to leave his visitin' card wherever he goes. . . ."

Bliss sprang to his feet.

"An idea has just struck me," he exclaimed. "There was a gold-and-cloisonné sheath to that dagger; and if the sheath should not be in my desk drawer now, perhaps—perhaps——"

"Yes, yes. Quite." Vance nodded. "I see your point. The sheath might still be in the frustrated assassin's possession. An excellent clew. . . . Sergeant, would you mind going with Doctor Bliss to the study to ascertan if the sheath was taken with the dagger? No use worryin' ourselves about it if it's still in the drawer."

Heath went promptly to the hall, followed by Bliss. We could hear them descending to the first floor.

"What do you make of this, Vance?" Markham asked, when we were alone. "It looks pretty serious to me."

"I make a great deal of it," Vance returned sombrely. "And it *is* pretty serious. But, thank Heaven, the *coup* was not very brilliant. The whole thing was frightfully botched."

"Yes, I can see that," Markham agreed. "Imagine any one hurling a knife six feet or more when he could have dealt a single thrust in a vital spot."

"Oh, that?" Vance lifted his eyebrows. "I wasn't thinking of the technic of the knife-thrower. There were other points about the affair still less intelligent. I can't understand it altogether. Perhaps too much panic. Anyway we may get a definite key to the plot through the doctor's suggestion about the sheath."

Bliss and Heath were heard returning up the stairs.

"Well, it's gone," the Sergeant informed us, as the two stepped into the room.

"No doubt taken with the dagger," Bliss supplemented.

"Suppose I send for a couple of the boys and give the house the once-over," Heath suggested.

"That's not necess'ry, Sergeant," Vance told him. "I've a feelin' it won't be hard to find."

Markham was becoming annoyed at Vance's vagueness.

"I suppose," he said, with a tinge of sarcasm, "you can tell us exactly where we can find the sheath."

"Yes, I rather think so." Vance spoke with thoughtful seriousness. "However, I'll verify my theory later. . . . In the meantime"—he addressed himself to Bliss—"I'd be greatly obliged if you'd remain in your room until we finish our investigation."

Bliss bowed in acquiescence.

"We're going to the drawing-room for a while," Vance continued. "There's a little work to be done there."

He moved toward the hall, then stopped as if on sudden impulse and, going to the table, slipped the dagger into his pocket. Bliss closed the door after us, and we could hear the key turn in the lock. Markham and Heath and I started down the stairs, Vance bringing up the rear.

We had descended but a few steps when a calm, flat voice from the upper hall arrested us.

"Can I be of any assistance, *effendi?*"

The unexpected sound in that dim quiet house startled us, and we instinctively turned. At the head of the stairs leading to the third floor stood the shadowy figure of Hani, his flowing kaftan a dark mass against the palely lighted wall beyond.

"Oh, rather!" Vance answered cheerfully. "We were just repairin' to the drawing-room to hold a little conversational *séance*. Do join us, Hani."

18

A LIGHT IN THE MUSEUM

(Saturday, July 14; 1:15 A.M.)

HANI JOINED us in the drawing room. He was very calm and dignified, and his inscrutable eyes rested impassively on Vance like those of an ancient Egyptian priest meditating before the shrine of Osiris.

"How do you happen to be up and about at this hour?" Vance asked casually. "Another attack of gastritis?"

"No, *effendi.*" Hani spoke in slow, measured tones. "I rose when I heard you talking to Brush. I sleep with my door open always."

"Perhaps, then, you heard Sakhmet when she returned to the house tonight."

"Did Sakhmet return?" The Egyptian lifted his head slightly in mild interest.

"In a manner of speaking. . . . But she's a most inefficient deity. She bungled everything again."

"Are you sure she did not intentionally bungle things?" Despite the droning quality of Hani's voice, there was a significant note in it.

Vance regarded him for a moment. Then:

"Did you hear footsteps on the stairs or along the second-floor corridor shortly after midnight?"

The man shook his head slowly.

"I heard nothing. But I was asleep for at least an hour before you arrived; and the soft tread of footsteps on the deep carpet would scarcely have been sufficient to rouse me."

"Doctor Bliss himself," Vance explained, "came down-stairs and telephoned to me. You did not hear him either?"

"The first sound I perceived was when you gentlemen came into the front hall and talked to Brush. Your voices, or perhaps the door opening, awakened me. Later I could hear your muffled tones in Doctor Bliss's bedroom, which is just below mine; but I could not distinguish anything that was said."

"And of course you were not aware that any one turned off the light in the second-story hall round midnight."

"Had I not been asleep I would certainly have noticed it, as the light shines dimly up the stairs into my room. But when I awoke the light was on as usual." Hani frowned slightly. "Who would have turned the hall light off at that hour?"

"I wonder. . . ." Vance did not take his eyes from the Egyptian. "Doctor Bliss has just told us that it was some one who had designs on his life."

"Ah!" The exclamation was like a sigh of relief. "But the attempt, I gather, was not successful."

"No. It was quite a fiasco. The technic, I might say, was both stupid and hazardous."

"It was not Sakhmet." Hani's pronouncement was almost sepulchral.

"Really, now!" Vance smiled slightly. "She is still reclinin', then, by the side

636

of the great west wind of heaven.* . . . I'm jolly glad to be able to rule her out. And since no occult force was at work, perhaps you can suggest who would have had a motive to cut the doctor's throat."

"There are many who would not weep if he were to quit this life; but I know of none who would take it upon himself to precipitate that departure."

Vance lighted a *Régie* and sat down.

"Why, Hani, did you imagine you might be of service to us?"

"Like you, *effendi,*" came the soft reply, "I expected that something distressing, and perhaps violent, would happen in this house to-night. And when I heard you enter and go to Doctor Bliss's room, it occurred to me that the looked-for event had come to pass. So I waited on the upper landing until you came out."

"Most considerate and thoughtful of you," Vance murmured, and took several puffs on his cigarette. After a moment he asked: "If Mr. Salveter had emerged from his room to-night after you had gone to bed, would you have known of the fact?"

The Egyptian hesitated, and his eyes contracted.

"I think I would. His room is directly opposite mine——"

"I'm familiar with the arrangement."

"It does not seem probable that Mr. Salveter could have unlocked his door and come out without my being cognizant of it."

"It's possible though, is it not?" Vance was insistent. "If you were asleep, and Mr. Salveter had good reason for not disturbing you, he might have emerged so cautiously that you would have slept on in complete ignorance of his act."

"It is barely possible," Hani admitted unwillingly. "But I am quite sure that he did not leave his room after retiring."

"Your wish, I fear, is father to your assurance," Vance sighed. "However, we sha'n't belabor the point."

Hani was watching Vance with lowering concern.

"Did Doctor Bliss suggest that Mr. Salveter left his room tonight?"

"Oh, to the contr'ry," Vance assured him. "The doctor said quite emphatically that any attempt to connect Mr. Salveter with the stealthy steps outside of his door at midnight would be a grave error."

"Doctor Bliss is wholly correct," the Egyptian declared.

"And yet, Hani, the doctor insisted that a would-be assassin was prowlin' about the house. Who else could it have been?"

"I cannot imagine." Hani appeared almost indifferent.

"You do not think that it could have been Mrs. Bliss?"

"Never!" The man's tone had become quickly animated. "Meryt-Amen would have had no reason to go into the hall. She has access to her husband's room through a communicating door——"

* Vance was referring jocularly to the declaration of Sakhmet in the Chapter of Opening the Mouth of Osiris Ani in the Egyptian *Book of the Dead:*

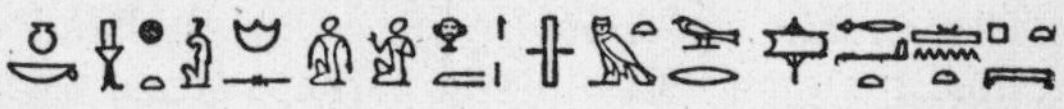

"I am the Goddess Sakhmet, and I take my seat upon the side of the great west (wind?) of the skies."

"So I observed a while ago,—she joined our *pour-parler* in the doctor's room. And I must say, Hani, that she was most anxious for us to find the person who had made the attempt on ther husband's life."

"Anxious—and sad, *effendi.*" A new note crept into Hani's voice. "She does not yet understand the things that have happened to-day. But when she does——"

"We won't speculate along those lines now," Vance cut in brusquely. He reached in his pocket and drew out the golden dagger. "Did you ever see that?" he asked, holding the weapon toward the Egyptian.

The man's eyes opened wide as he stared at the glittering, jewelled object. At first he appeared fascinated, but the next moment his face clouded, and the muscles of his jowls worked spasmodically. A smouldering anger had invaded him.

"Where did that Pharaonic dagger come from?" he asked, striving to control his emotion.

"It was brought from Egypt by Doctor Bliss," Vance told him.

Hani took the dagger and held it reverently under the table-lamp.

"It could only have come from the tomb of Ai. Here on the crystal knob is faintly engraved the king's cartouche. Behold: Kheper-kheperu-Rê Iry-Maët——"

"Yes, yes. The last Pharaoh of the Eighteenth Dynasty. The doctor found the dagger during his excavations in the Valley of the Tombs of the Kings." Vance was watching the other intently. "You are quite positive you have never seen it before?"

Hani drew himself up proudly.

"Had I seen it, I would have reported it to my Government. It would no longer be in the possession of an alien desecrator, but in the country where it belongs, cared for by loving hands at Cairo. . . . Doctor Bliss did well to keep it hidden."

There was a bitter hatred in his words, but suddenly his manner changed.

"May I be permitted to ask when you first saw this royal dagger?"

"A few minutes ago," Vance answered. "It was projectin' from the head-board of the doctor's bed—just behind the place where his head had lain a second earlier."

Hani's gaze travelled past Vance to some distant point, and his eyes became shrewdly thoughtful.

"Was there no sheath to this dagger?" he asked.

"Oh, yes." There was a flicker in the corners of Vance's eyes. "Gold and cloisonné—though I haven't seen it. The fact is, Hani, we're deuced interested in the sheath. It's disappeared—lying *perdu* somewhere hereabouts. We're going to make a bit of a search for it ere long."

Hani nodded his head understandingly.

"And if you find it, are you sure you'll know more than you do now?"

"It may at least verify my suspicions."

"The sheath would be an easy object to hide securely," Hani reminded him.

"I really don't anticipate any difficulty in putting my hands on it." Vance rose and confronted the man. "Could you perhaps suggest where we might best start our search?"

"No, *effendi,*" Hani returned, after a perceptible hesitation. "Not at this moment. I would need time to think about it."

"Very well. Suppose you go to your room and indulge in some lamaic concentration. You're anything but helpful."

Hani handed the dagger back, and turned toward the hall.

"And be so good," Vance requested, "as to knock on Mr. Salveter's door and tell him we would like to see him here at once."

Hani bowed, and disappeared.

"I don't like that bird," Heath grumbled, when the Egyptian was out of hearing. "He's too slippery. And he knows something he's not telling. I'd like to turn my boys loose on him with a piece of rubber hose—they'd make him come across. . . . I wouldn't be surprised, Mr. Vance, if he threw the dagger himself. Did you notice the way he held it, laying out flat in the palm of his hand with the point toward the fingers?—just like those knife-throwers in vaudeville."

"Oh, he might have been thinkin' caressingly of Doctor Bliss's trachea," Vance conceded. "However, the dagger episode doesn't worry me half as much as something that *didn't* happen to-night."

"Well, it looks to me like plenty happened," retorted Heath.

Markham regarded Vance inquisitively.

"What's in your mind?" he asked.

"The picture presented to us to-night, d' ye see, wasn't finished. I could still detect some of the underpainting. And there was no *vernissage*. The canvas needed another form—the generating line wasn't complete. . . ."

Just then we could hear footsteps on the stairs. Salveter, with a wrinkled Shantung dressing-gown wrapped about his pyjamas, blinked as he faced the lights in the drawing-room. He appeared only half awake, but when his pupils had become adjusted to the glare, he ran his eyes sharply over the four of us and then shot a glance at the bronze clock on the mantel.

"What now?" he asked. "What has happened?" He seemed both bewildered and anxious.

"Doctor Bliss phoned me that some one had tried to kill him," Vance explained. "So we hobbled over. . . . Know anything about it?"

"Good God, no!" Salveter sat down heavily in a chair by the door. "Some one tried to kill the doctor? When? . . . How?" He fumbled in his dressing-gown pockets, and Vance, reading his movements correctly, held out his cigarette-case. Salveter lighted a *Régie* nervously, and drew several deep inhalations on it.

"Shortly after midnight," Vance answered. "But the attempt failed dismally." He tossed the dagger in Salveter's lap. "Familiar with that knick-knack?"

The other studied the weapon a few seconds without touching it. A growing astonishment crept into his expression, and he carefully picked up the dagger and inspected it.

"I never saw it in my life," he said in an awed tone. "It's a very valuable archæological specimen—a rare museum piece. Where, in Heaven's name, did you unearth it? It certainly doesn't belong to the Bliss collection."

"Ah, but it does," Vance assured him. "A private item, so to speak. Always kept secluded from pryin' vulgar eyes."

"I'm amazed. I'll bet the Egyptian Government doesn't know about it." Salveter looked up abruptly. "Has this dagger anything to do with the attempt on the doctor's life?"

"Everything apparently," Vance replied negligently. "We found it lodged in the headboard of the doctor's bed, evidently thrown with great force at the spot where his throat should have been."

Salveter contracted his brow and set his lips.

"See here, Mr. Vance," he declared at length; "we haven't any Malayan jugglers in this house. . . . Unless," he added, as a startled afterthought, "Hani knows the art. Those orientals are full of unexpected lore and practices."

"The performance to-night was not, according to all accounts, what one would unqualifiedly call artistic. It was, in fact, somewhat amateurish. I'm sure a Malay could have done much better with his kris. In the first place, the intruder's footsteps and the opening of the door were plainly heard by Doctor Bliss; and, in the second place, there was sufficient delay between the projection of the flash-light and the actual hurling of the dagger to give the doctor time to remove his head from the line of propulsion. . . ."

At this moment Hani appeared at the door holding a small object in his hand. Walking forward he laid it on the centre-table.

"Here, *effendi*," he said in a low voice, "is the sheath of the royal dagger. I found it lying against the baseboard of the second-story hall, near the head of the stairs."

Vance scarcely glanced at it.

"Thanks awfully," he drawled. "I rather thought you'd find it. But of course it wasn't in the hall."

"I assure you——"

"Oh, quite." Vance looked straight into Hani's eyes, and presently a faint, gentle smile crept into his gaze. "Isn't it true, Hani," he asked pointedly, "that you found the sheath exactly where you and I believed it to be hidden?"

The Egyptian did not answer at once. Presently he said:

"I have told my story, *effendi*. You may draw your own conclusion."

Vance appeared satisfied and waved his hand toward the door.

"And now, Hani, go to bed. We sha'n't need you any more to-night. *Leiltak sa'îda.*"

"*Leiltak sa'îda wemubâraka.*" The man bowed and departed.

Vance picked up the sheath and, taking the dagger from Salveter, fitted the blade into its holder, looking at the gold embossing critically.

"Ægean influence," he murmured. "Pretty, but too fussy. These ornate floral devices of the Eighteenth Dynasty bear the same relation to early Egyptian art that the Byzantine ginger-bread does to the simple Greek orders." He held the sheath closer to his monocle. "And, by the by, here's a decoration that may interest you, Mr. Salveter. The formal scrolls terminate in a jackal's head."

"Anûpu, eh? Hani's given name. That's curious." Salveter rose and looked at the design. "And another point might be considered, Mr. Vance," he went on, after a pause. "These lower-class Copts are, for all their superficial Christian veneer, highly superstitious. Their minds run along one traditional groove: they like to fit everything to a preconceived symbolism. There have been nine more or less coincidental deaths of late among those connected with the excavations in Egypt,* and the natives ridiculously imagine that the afrîts

---

* Salveter was here referring to the Earl of Carnarvon, Colonel the Honorable Aubrey Herbert, General Sir Lee Stack, George J. Gould, Woolf Joel, Sir Archibald Douglas

of their ancestors lay in ambush in the various tombs to mow down the western intruders, as a kind of punitive measure. They actually believe in such malefic forces. . . . And here is Hani, at bottom a superstitious Egyptian, who resents the work of Doctor Bliss:—is it not possible he might consider the death of the doctor by a dagger once worn by a Pharaoh as a sort of mystical retribution in line with all these other irrational ghost stories? And Hani might even regard the jackal's head on that sheath as a sign that he—named after the jackal-headed god, Anûbis—had been divinely appointed the agent in this act of vengeance."

"A charmin' theory," was Vance's somewhat uninterested comment. "But a bit too specious, I fear. I'm comin' to the opinion that Hani is not nearly so stupid and superstitious as he would have us think. He's a kind of modern Theogonius, who has found it the part of wisdom to simulate mental inferiority."*

Salveter slowly nodded agreement.

"I've felt that same quality in him at times. . . . But who else——?"

"Ah! Who else?" Vance sighed. "I say, Mr. Salveter; what time did you go to bed to-night?"

"At ten-thirty," the man returned aggressively. "And I didn't wake up until Hani called me just now."

"You retired, then, immediately after you had fetched the memorandum-book from the study for Doctor Bliss."

"Oh, he told you about that, did he? . . . Yes, I handed him the book and went on up to my room."

"The book, I understand, was in his desk."

"That's right.—But why this cross-examination about a memorandum-book?"

"That dagger," Vance explained, "was also kept in one of the drawers of the doctor's desk."

Salveter leapt to his feet.

"I see!" His face was livid.

"Oh, but you don't," Vance mildly assured him. "And I'd appreciate it immensely if you'd try to be calm. Your vitality positively exhausts me.—Tell me, did you lock your bedroom door to-night?"

"I always lock it at night."

"And during the day?"

"I leave it open—to air the room."

"And you heard nothing to-night after retiring?"

"Nothing at all. I went to sleep quickly—the reaction, I suppose."

Vance rose.

"One other thing: where did the family have dinner to-night?"

Reid, Professor Lafleur, H. G. Evelyn-White, and Professor Georges-Aaron Bénédite. Since that time two more names have been added to the fatal list—those of the Honorable Richard Bethell, secretary to Howard Carter, and Lord Westbury.

* Theogonius was a friend of Simon Magus, who, because of his fear of the Emperor Caligula, pretended imbecility in order to hide his wisdom. Suetonius refers to him as Theogonius, but Scaliger, Casaubon and other historians give "Telegenius" as the correct spelling.

"In the breakfast-room. It could hardly be called dinner, though. No one was hungry. It was more like a light supper. So we ate down-stairs. Less bother."

"And what did the various members of the household do after dinner?"

"Hani went up-stairs at once, I believe. The doctor and Mrs. Bliss and I sat here in the drawing-room for an hour or so, when the doctor excused himself and went to his room. A little later Meryt-Amen went up-stairs, and I sat here until about half past ten trying to read."

"Thank you, Mr. Salveter. That will be all." Vance moved toward the hall. "Only, I wish you'd tell Mrs. Bliss and the doctor that we sha'n't disturb them any more to-night. We'll probably communicate with them to-morrow. . . . Let's go, Markham. There's really nothing more we can do here."

"I could do a whole lot more," Heath objected with surly antagonism. "But this case is being handled like a pink tea. Somebody in this house threw that dagger, and if I had my way I'd steam the truth out of him."

Markham endeavored diplomatically to soothe the Sergeant's ruffled feelings, but without any marked success.

We were now standing just inside the front door preparatory to departing, and Vance paused to light a cigarette. He was facing the great steel door leading into the museum, and I saw his frame suddenly go taut.

"Oh, just a moment, Mr. Salveter," he called; and the man, who was now nearly at the head of the first flight of stairs, turned and retraced his steps. "What are the lights doing on in the museum?"

I glanced toward the bottom of the steel door where Vance's gaze was resting, and for the first time saw a tiny illuminated line. Salveter, too, glanced at the floor, and frowned.

"I'm sure I don't know," he said in a puzzled voice. "The last person in the museum is supposed to turn off the switch. But no one to my knowledge has been in there to-night. . . . I'll see." He stepped toward the door, but Vance moved in front of him.

"Don't trouble yourself," he said peremptorily. "I'll attend to it. . . . Good-night."

Salveter took the dismissal uneasily but without another word he went up-stairs.

When he had disappeared round the banisters on the second floor, Vance gently turned the knob, and pushed the museum door open. Below us, on the opposite side of the room, seated at the desk-table near the obelisk, and surrounded by filing-boxes, photographs, and cardboard folders, was Scarlett. His coat and waistcoat were hanging over the back of his chair; a green celluloid shade covered his eyes; and a pen was in his hand, poised above a large note-book.

He looked up as the door opened.

"Oh, hallo!" he called cheerily. "Thought you were through with the Bliss ménage for to-day."

"It's to-morrow now," returned Vance, going down the stairs and crossing the museum.

"What!" Scarlett reached behind him and took out his watch. "Great Scott! So it is. Had no idea of the hour. Been working here since eight o'clock——"

"Amazin'." Vance glanced over a few of the upturned photographs. "Very interestin'. . . . Who let you in, by the by?"

"Brush, of course." Scarlett seemed rather astonished at the question. "Said the family were having dinner in the breakfast-room. I told him not to disturb 'em—that I had a bit of work to finish. . . ."

"He didn't mention your arrival to us." Vance was apparently engrossed in a photograph of four amuletic bracelets.

"But why should he, Vance?" Scarlett had risen and was getting into his coat. "It's a commonplace thing for me to come here and work in the evenings. I'm drifting in and out of the house constantly. When I work at night I always shut off the light on going and see that the front door is fastened. Nothing unusual about my coming here after dinner."

"That probably accounts for Brush's not telling us, don't y' know." Vance tossed the photographs back on the table. "But something out of the ordin'ry did happen here to-night." He laid the sheathed dagger before Scarlett. "What do you know about that bizarre parazonium?"

"Oh, much." The other grinned, and shot Vance an interrogatory look. "How did you happen on it? It's one of the doctor's dark secrets."

"Really?" Vance lifted his eyebrows in simulated surprise. "Then you're familiar with it?"

"Rather. I saw the old scalawag slip in into his khaki shirt when he found it. I kept mum—none of my business. Later, when we were here in New York, he told me he'd smuggled it out of Egypt, and confided to me that he was keeping it sequestered in his study. He was in constant fear that Hani would unearth it, and swore me to secrecy. I agreed. What's one dagger, more or less? The Cairo Museum has the cream of all the excavated items anyway."

"He kept it ensconced under some papers in one of his desk drawers."

"Yes, I know. Safe hiding-place. Hani rarely goes in the study. . . . But I'm curious——"

"We're all curious. Distressin' state, what?" Vance gave him no time to speculate. "Who else knew of the dagger's existence?"

"No one, as far as I know. The doctor certainly didn't disclose the fact to Hani; and I doubt seriously if he informed Mrs. Bliss. She has peculiar loyalties in regard to her native country, and the doctor respects them. No telling how she'd react to the theft of such a valuable treasure."

"What about Salveter?"

"I'd say no." Scarlett made an unpleasant grimace. "He'd be sure to confide in Meryt-Amen. Impulsive young cub."

"Well, some one knew of its whereabouts," Vance remarked. "Doctor Bliss phoned me shortly after midnight that he had escaped assassination by the proverbial hair's-breadth; so we sped hither and found the point of that poniard infixed in the head of his bed."

"By Jove! You don't say!" Scarlett seemed shocked and perplexed. "Some one must have discovered the dagger . . . and yet——" He stopped suddenly and shot Vance a quick look. "How do you account for it?"

"I'm not accountin' for it. Most mysterious. . . . Hani, by the by, found the sheath in the hall near the doctor's door."

"That's odd. . . ." Scarlett paused as if considering. Then he began arranging his papers and photographs in neat piles and stacking his filing-boxes under the table. "Couldn't you get any suggestions out of the rest of the house-hold?" he asked.

"Any number of suggestions. All of 'em conflictin', and most of 'em silly. So we're toddlin' along home. Happened to see the light under the door and was overcome with curiosity. . . . Quitting now?"

"Yes." Scarlett took up his hat. "I'd have knocked off long ago but didn't realize how late it was."

We all left the house together. A heavy silence had fallen over us, and it was not until Scarlett paused in front of his quarters that any one of us spoke. Then Vance said:

"Good-night. Don't let the dagger disturb your slumbers."

Scarlett waved an abstracted adieu.

"Thanks, old man," he rejoined. "I'll try to follow your advice."

Vance had taken several steps when he turned suddenly.

"And I say, Scarlett; if I were you I'd keep away from the Bliss house for the time being."

19

A BROKEN APPOINTMENT

(Saturday, July 14; 2 A.M.—10 P.M)

HEATH LEFT us at Nineteenth Street and Fourth Avenue; and Vance, Markham and I took a taxicab back to Vance's apartment. It was nearly two o'clock, but Markham showed no indication of going home. He followed Vance up-stairs to the library, and throwing open the French windows gazed out into the heavy, mist-laden night. The events of the day had not gone to his liking; and yet I realized that his quandary was so deep that he felt disinclined to make any decisive move until the conflicting factors of the situation became more clarified.

The case at the outset had appeared simple, and the number of possible suspects was certainly limited. But, despite these two facts, there was a subtle and mysterious intangibility about the affair that rendered a drastic step impossible. The elements were too fluid, the cross-currents of motives too contradictory. Vance had been the first to sense the elusory complications, the first to indicate the invisible paradoxes; and so surely had he put his finger upon the vital points of the plot—so accurately had he foretold certain phases of the plot's development—that Markham had, both figuratively and literally, stepped into the background and permitted him to deal with the case in his own way.

Withal, Markham was dissatisfied and impatient. Nothing definitely leading to the actual culprit had, so far as could be seen, been brought to light by Vance's unprofessional and almost casual process of investigation.

"We're not making headway, Vance," Markham complained with gloomy concern, turning from the window. "I've stood aside all day and permitted you to deal with these people as you saw fit, because I felt your knowledge of them and your familiarity with things Egyptological gave you an advantage over impersonal official cross-questioning. And I also felt that you had a plausible theory about the whole matter, which you were striving to verify. But Kyle's murder is as far from a solution as it was when we first entered the museum.

"You're an incorrigible pessimist, Markham," Vance returned, getting into a printed foulard dressing-gown. "It has been just fifteen hours since we found Sakhmet athwart Kyle's skull; and you must admit, painful as it may be to a District Attorney, that the average murder investigation has scarcely begun in so brief a time. . . ."

"In the average murder case, however," Markham retorted acidly, "we'd at least have found a lead or two and outlined a workable routine. If Heath had been handling the matter he'd have made an arrest by now—the field of possibilities is not an extensive one."

"I dare say he would. He'd no doubt have had every one in jail, including Brush and Dingle and the Curators of the Metropolitan Museum. Typical tactics: butcher innocent persons to make a journalistic holiday. I'm not entranced with that technic, though. I'm far too humane—I've retained too many of my early illusions. Sentimentality, alas! will probably be my downfall."

Markham snorted, and seated himself at the end of the table. For several moments he beat the devil's tattoo on a large, vellum-bound copy of "Malleus Maleficarum."

"You told me quite emphatically," he said, "that when this second episode happened—the attempt on Bliss's life—you'd understand all the phases of the plot and perhaps be able to adduce some tangible evidence against Kyle's murderer. It appears to me, however, that to-night's affair has simply plunged us more deeply into uncertainty."

Vance shook his head seriously in disagreement.

"The throwing of that dagger and the hiding and finding of the sheath have illuminated the one moot point in the plot."

Markham looked up sharply.

"You think you know now what the plot is?"

Vance carefully fitted a *Régie* into a long jet holder and gazed at a small Picasso still-life beside the mantel.

"Yes, Markham," he returned slowly; "I think I know what the plot is. And if the thing that I expect to happen to-night occurs, I can, I believe, convince you that I am right in my diagnosis. Unfortunately the throwing of the dagger was only part of the pre-arranged episode. As I said to you a while ago, the tableau was not completed. Something intervened. And the final touch—the rounding-out of the episode—is yet to come."

He spoke with impressive solemnity, and Markham, I could see, was strongly influenced by his manner.

"Have you any definite notion," he inquired, "what that final touch will prove to be?"

"Oh, quite. But just what shape it will take I can't say. The plotter himself probably doesn't know, for he must wait for a propitious opportunity. But it will centre about one specific object, or, rather, clew—a planted clew, Markham. That clew has been carefully prepared, and the placing of it is the only indefinite factor left. . . . Yes, I am waiting for a specific item to appear; and when it does, I can convince you of the whole devilish truth."

"When do you figure this final clew will turn up?" Markham asked uneasily.

"At almost any moment." Vance spoke in low, level and quiet tones. "Something prevented its taking shape to-night, for it is an intimate corollary of the dagger-throwing. And by refusing to take that episode too seriously, and by letting Hani find the sheath, I made the immediate planting of the final clew necess'ry. Once again we refused to fall into the murderer's trap—though, as I say, the trap was not fully baited."

"I'm glad to have some kind of explanation for your casual attitude to-night." Despite the note of sarcasm in Markham's voice, it was obvious that at bottom he was not indulging in strictures upon Vance's conduct. He was at sea and inclined, therefore, to be irritable. "You apparently had no interest in determining who hurled the dagger at Bliss's pillow."

"But, Markham old dear, I knew who hurled the bejewelled bodkin." Vance made a slight gesture of impatience. "My only concern was with what the reporters call the events leading up to the crime."

Markham realized it was of no use to ask, at this time, who had thrown the dagger; so he pursued his comments on Vance's recent activities at the Bliss house.

"You might have got some helpful suggestions from Scarlett—he evidently was in the museum during the entire time. . . ."

"Even so, Markham," Vance countered, "don't forget there is a thick double wall between the museum and the Bliss domicile, and that those steel doors are practially sound-proof. Bombs might have been exploded in the doctor's room without any one in the museum hearing them."

"Perhaps you're right." Markham rose and stood contemplating Vance appraisingly. "I'm putting a lot of trust in you—you confounded æsthete. And I'm going against all my principles and stultifying the whole official procedure of my office because I believe in you. But God help you if you fail me. . . . What's the programme for to-morrow?"

Vance shot him a grateful, affectionate look. Then, at once, a cynical smile overspread his face.

"I'm the unofficial straw, so to speak, at which the drowning District Attorney clutches—eh, what? Not an overwhelmin' compliment."

It was always the case with these two old friends that when one uttered a generous remark the other immediately scotched it, lest there be some outward show of sentiment.

"The programme for to-morrow?" Vance took up Markham's question. "Really, y' know, I hadn't given it any Cartesian consideration. . . . There's an exhibition of Gauguins at Wildenstein's. I might stagger in and bask in the color harmonics of the great Pont-Avenois. Then there's a performance of the Beethoven *Septet* at Carnegie Hall; and a preview of Egyptian wall paintings from the tombs of Nakhte and Menena and Rekh-mi-Rê——"

"And there's an orchid show at the Grand Central Palace," Markham suggested with vicious irony. "But see here, Vance: if we let this thing run on another day without taking some kind of action, there may be danger ahead for someone else, just as there was danger for Bliss to-night. If the murderer of Kyle is as ruthless as you say and his job hasn't been completed——"

"No, I don't think so." Vance's face clouded again. "The plot doesn't include another act of violence. I believe it has now entered upon a quiescent and subtle—and more deadly—stage." He smoked a moment speculatively. "And yet . . . there may be a remote chance. Things haven't gone according to the murderer's calculations. We've blocked his two most ambitious moves. But he has one more combination left, and I'm countin' on his trying it. . . ."

His voice faltered, and rising he walked slowly to the French window and back.

"Anyway, I'll take care of the situation in the morning," he said. "I'll guard against any dangerous possibility. And at the same time I'll hasten the planting of that last clew."

"How long is this rigmarole going to take?" Markham was troubled and nervous. "I can't go on indefinitely waiting for apocalyptic events to happen."

"Give me twenty-four hours. Then, if we haven't received further guidance from the gentleman who is pullin' the strings you may turn Heath loose on the family."

It was less than twenty-four hours when the culminating event occurred. The fourteenth of July will always remain in my memory as one of the most terrible and exciting days of my life; and as I set down this record of the case, years later, I can hardly refrain from a shudder. I do not dare think of what might have happened—of what soul-stirring injustice might have been perpetrated in good faith—had not Vance seen the inner machinations of the diabolical plot underlying Kyle's murder, and persisted in his refusal to permit Markham and Heath taking the obvious course of arresting Bliss.

Vance told me months later that never in his career had he been confronted by so delicate a task as that of placating Markham and convincing him that an impassive delay was the only possible means of reaching the truth. Almost from the moment Vance entered the museum in answer to Scarlett's summons, he realized the tremendous difficulties ahead; for everything had been planned in order to force Markham and the police into making the very move against which he had so consistently fought.

Though Markham did not take his departure from Vance's apartment on the night of the dagger episode until half past two, Vance rose the next morning before eight o'clock. Another sweltering day was promised, and he had his coffee in the roof-garden. He sent Currie to fetch all the morning newspapers, and spent a half hour or so reading the accounts of Kyle's murder.

Heath had been highly discreet about giving out the facts, and only the barest skeleton of the story was available to the press. But the prominence of Kyle and the distinguished reputation of Doctor Bliss resulted in the murder creating a tremendous furore. It was emblazoned across the front page of every metropolitan journal, and there were long reviews of Bliss's Egyptological work and the financial interest taken in it by the dead philanthropist. The general theory seemed to be—and I recognized the Sergeant's shrewd hand in it—that some one from the street had entered the museum, and, as an act of vengeance or enmity, had killed Kyle with the first available weapon.

Heath had told the reporters of the finding of the scarab beside the body, but had given no further information about it. Because of this small object, which was the one evidential detail that had been vouchsafed, the papers, always on the lookout for identifying titles, named the tragedy the Scarab murder case; and that appellation has clung to it to the present day. Even those persons who have forgotten the name of Benjamin H. Kyle still remember the sensation caused by his murder, as a result of that ancient piece of lapis-lazuli carved with the name of an Egyptian Pharaoh of the year 1650 B.C.

Vance read the accounts with a cynical smile.

"Poor Markham!" he murmured. "Unless something definite happens very soon, the anti-administration critics will descend on him like a host of trolls. I see that Heath has announced to the world that the District Attorney's office has taken full charge of the case. . . ."

He smoked meditatively for a time. Then he telephoned to Salveter and asked him to come at once to his apartment.

"I'm hopin' to remove every possibility of disaster," he explained to me as he hung up the receiver; "though I'm quite certain another attempt to hoodwink us will be made before any desperate measures are taken."

For the next fifteen minutes he stretched out lazily and closed his eyes. I thought he had fallen asleep, but when Currie softly opened the door to announce Salveter, Vance bade him show the visitor up before the old man could speak.

Salveter entered a minute later looking anxious and puzzled.

"Sit down, Mr. Salveter." Vance waved him indolently to a chair. "I've been thinkin' about Queen Hetep-hir-es and the Boston Museum. Have you any business that might reasonably take you to Boston to-night?"

Salveter appeared even more puzzled.

"I always have work that I can do there," he replied, frowning. "Especially in view of the excavations of the Harvard-Boston Expedition at the Gîzeh pyramids. It was in connection with these excavations that I had to go to the Metropolitan yesterday morning for Doctor Bliss. . . . Does that answer your question satisfactorily?"

"Quite. . . . And these reproductions of the tomb furniture of Hetep-hir-es: couldn't you arrange for them more easily if you saw Doctor Reisner personally?"

"Certainly. The fact is, I'll have to go north anyway in order to close up the business. I was merely on the trail of preliminary information yesterday."

"Would the fact that to-morrow is Sunday handicap you in any way?"

"To the contrary. I could probably see Doctor Reisner away from his office, and go into the matter at leisure with him."

"That being the case, suppose you hop a train to-night after dinner. Come back, let us say, to-morrow night. Any objection?"

Salveter's puzzlement gave way to astonishment.

"Why—no," he stammered. "No particular objection. But——"

"Would Doctor Bliss think it strange if you jumped out on such sudden notice?"

"I couldn't say. Probably not. The museum isn't a particularly pleasant place just now. . . ."

"Well, I want you to go, Mr. Salveter." Vance abandoned his lounging demeanor and sat up. "And I want you to go without question or argument. . . . There's no possibility of Doctor Bliss's forbidding you to go, is there?"

"Oh, nothing like that," Salveter assured him. "He may think it's queer, my running off at just this time; but he never meddles in the way I choose to do my work."

Vance rose.

"That's all. There's a train to Boston from the Grand Central at half past nine to-night. See that you take it. . . . And," he added, "you might phone me from the station, by way of verification. I'll be here between nine and nine-thirty. . . . You may return to New York any time you desire after to-morrow noon."

Salveter gave Vance an abashed grin.

"I suppose those are orders."

"Serious and important orders, Mr. Salveter," Vance returned with quiet impressiveness. "And you needn't worry about Mrs. Bliss. Hani, I'm sure, will take good care of her."

Salveter started to make a reply, changed his mind, and, turning abruptly, strode rapidly away.

Vance yawned and rose languorously.

"And now I think I'll take two more hours' sleep."

After lunch at Marguéry's, Vance went to the Gauguin exhibition, and later walked to Carnegie Hall to hear the Beethoven *Septet*. It was too late when the concert was over to see the Egyptian wall paintings at the Metropolitan Museum of Art. Instead, he called for Markham in his car, and the three of us drove to the Claremont for dinner.

Vance explained briefly what steps he had taken in regard to Salveter. Markham made scant comment. He looked tired and discouraged, but there was a distracted tensity about his manner that made me realize how greatly he was counting on Vance's prediction that something tangible would soon happen in connection with the Kyle case.

After dinner we returned to Vance's roof-garden. The enervating mid-summer heat still held, and there was scarcely a breath of air stirring.

"I told Heath I'd phone him——" Markham began, sinking into a large peacock wicker chair.

"I was about to suggest getting in touch with the Sergeant," Vance chimed in. "I'd rather like to have him on hand, don't y' know. He's so comfortin'."

He rang for Currie and ordered the telephone. Then he called Heath and asked him to join us.

"I have a psychic feelin'," he said to Markham, with an air of forced levity, "that we are going to be summoned anon to witness the irrefutable proof of some one's guilt. And if that proof is what I think it is. . . ."

Markham suddenly leaned forward in his chair.

"It has just come to me what you've been hinting about so mysteriously!" he exclaimed. "It has to do with that hieroglyphic letter you found in the study."

Vance hesitated but momentarily.

"Yes, Markham," he nodded. "That torn letter hasn't been explained yet. And I have a theory about it that I can't shake off—it fits too perfectly with the whole fiendish scheme."

"But you have the letter," Markham argued, in an effort to draw Vance out.

"Oh, yes. And I'm prizin' it."

"You believe it's the letter Salveter said he wrote?"

"Undoubtedly."

"And you believe he is ignorant of its having been torn up and put in the doctor's waste-basket?"

"Oh, quite. He's still wonderin' what became of it—and worryin', too."

Markham studied Vance with baffled curiosity.

"You spoke of some purpose to which the letter might have been put before it was thrown away."

"That's what I'm waiting to verify. The fact is, Markham, I expected that the letter would enter into the mystery of the dagger throwing last night. And I'll admit I was frightfully downcast when we'd got the whole family snugly back to bed without having run upon a single hieroglyph." He reached for a cigarette. "There was a reason for it, and I think I know the explanation. That's why I'm pinnin' my childlike faith on what may happen at any moment now. . . ."

The telephone rang, and Vance himself answered it at once. It was Salveter calling from the Grand Central Station; and after a brief verbal interchange, Vance replaced the instrument on the table with an air of satisfaction.

"The doctor," he said, "was evidently quite willin' to endure to-night and to-morrow without his assistant curator. So that bit of strategy was achieved without difficulty. . . ."

Half an hour later Heath was ushered into the roof-garden. He was glum and depressed, and his greeting was little more than a guttural rumble.

"Lift up your heart, Sergeant," Vance exhorted him cheerfully. "This is Bastille Day.* It may have a symbolic meaning. It's not beyond the realm of possibility that you will be able to incarcerate the murderer of Kyle before midnight."

"Yeah?" Heath was utterly sceptical. "Is he coming here to give himself up, bringing all the necessary proof with him? A nice, accommodating fella."

"Not exactly, Sergeant. But I'm expecting him to send for us; and I think he may be so generous as to point out the principal clew himself."

"Cuckoo, is he? Well, Mr. Vance, if he does that, no jury'll convict him. He'll get a bill of insanity with free lodging and medical care for the rest of his life." He looked at his watch. "It's ten o'clock. What time does the tip-off come?"

"Ten?" Vance verified the hour. "My word! It's later than I thought. . . ." A look of anxiety passed over his set features. "I wonder if I could have miscalculated this whole affair."

He put out his cigarette and began pacing back and forth. Presently he stopped before Markham, who was watching him uneasily.

"When I sent Salveter away," he began slowly, "I was confident that the expected event would happen forthwith. But I'm afraid something has gone wrong. Therefore I think I had better outline the case to you now."

He paused and frowned.

"However," he added, "it would be advisable to have Scarlett present. I'm sure he could fill in a few of the gaps."

Markham looked surprised.

"What does Scarlett know about it?"

* Vance of course was referring to the French *Fête Nationale* which falls on July 14th.

"Oh, much," was Vance's brief reply. Then he turned to the telephone and hesitated. "He hasn't a private phone, and I don't know the number of the house exchange. . . ."

"That's easy." Heath picked up the receiver and asked for a certain night official of the company. After a few words of explanation, he clicked the hook and called a number. There was considerable delay, but at length some one answered at the other end. From the Sergeant's questions it was evident Scarlett was not at home.

"That was his landlady," Heath explained disgustedly, when he had replaced the receiver. "Scarlett went out at eight o'clock—said he was going to the museum for a while and would be back at nine. Had an appointment at nine with a guy at his apartment, and the guy's still waiting for him. . . ."

"We can reach him at the museum, then." Vance rang up the Bliss number and asked Brush to call Scarlett to the phone. After several minutes he pushed the instrument from him.

"Scarlett isn't at the museum either," he said. "He came, so Brush says, at about eight, and must have departed unobserved. He's probably on his way back to his quarters. We'll wait a while and phone him there again."

"Is it necessary to have Scarlett here?" Markham asked impatiently.

"Not precisely necess'ry," Vance returned evasively; "but most desirable. You remember he admitted quite frankly he could tell me a great deal about the murderer——"

He broke off abruptly, and with tense deliberaton selected and lighted another cigarette. His lids drooped, and he stared fixedly at the floor.

"Sergeant," he said in a repressed tone, "I believe you said Mr. Scarlett had an appointment with some one at nine and had informed his landlady he would return at that hour."

"That's what the dame told me over the phone."

"Please see if he has reached home yet."

Without a word Heath again lifted the receiver and called Scarlett's number. A minute later he turned to Vance.

"He hasn't shown up."

"Deuced queer," Vance muttered. "I don't at all like this, Markham. . . ."

His mind drifted off in speculation, and it seemed to me that his face paled slightly.

"I'm becoming frightened," he went on in a hushed voice. "We should have heard about that letter by now. . . . I'm afraid there's trouble ahead."

He gave Markham a look of grave and urgent concern.

"We can't afford to delay any longer. It may even be too late as it is. We've got to act at once." He moved toward the door. "Come on, Markham. And you, Sergeant. We're overdue at the museum. If we hurry we may be in time."

Both Markham and Heath had risen as Vance spoke. There was a strange insistence in his tone, and a foreboding of terrible things in his eyes. He disappeared swiftly into the house; and the rest of us, urged by the suppressed excitement of his manner, followed in silence. His car was outside, and a few moments later we were swinging dangerously round the corner of Thirty-eighth Street and Park Avenue, headed for the Bliss Museum.

20

THE GRANITE SARCOPHAGUS

(Saturday, July 14; 10:10 P.M.)

WE ARRIVED at the museum in less than ten minutes. Vance ran up the stone steps, Markham and Heath and I at his heels. Not only was there a light burning in the vestibule, but through the frosted glass panels of the front door we could see a bright light in the hall. Vance pressed the bell vigorously, but it was some time before Brush answered our summons.

"Napping?" Vance asked. He was in a tense, sensitive mood.

"No, sir." Brush shrank from him. "I was in the kitchen——"

"Tell Doctor Bliss we're here, and want to see him at once."

"Yes, sir." The butler went down the hall and knocked on the study door. There was no answer, and he knocked again. After a moment he turned the knob and looked in the room. Then he came back to us.

"The doctor is not in his study. Perhaps he has gone to his bedroom. . . . I'll see."

He moved toward the stairs and was about to ascend when a calm, even voice halted him.

"Bliss *effendi* is not up-stairs." Hani came slowly down to the front hall. "It is possible he is in the museum."

"Well, well!" Vance regarded the man reflectively. "Amazin' how you always turn up. . . . So you think he may be potterin' among his treasures—eh, what?" He pushed open the great steel door of the museum. "If the doctor is in here, he's whiling away his time in the dark." Stepping to the stair-landing inside the museum door, he switched on the lights and looked about the great room. "You're apparently in error, Hani, regarding the doctor's whereabouts. To all appearances the museum is empty."

The Egyptian was unruffled.

"Perhaps Doctor Bliss has gone out for a breath of air."

There was a troubled frown on Vance's face.

"That's possible," he murmured. "However, I wish you'd make sure he is not up-stairs."

"I would have seen him had he come up-stairs after dinner," the Egyptian replied softly. "But I will follow your instructions nevertheless." And he went to search for Bliss.

Vance stepped up to Brush and asked in a low voice:

"At what time did Mr. Scarlett leave here to-night?"

"I don't know, sir." The man was mystified by Vance's manner. "I really don't know. He came at about eight—I let him in. He may have gone out with Doctor Bliss. They often take a walk together at night."

"Did Mr. Scarlett go into the museum when he arrived at eight?"

"No, sir. He asked for Doctor Bliss. . . ."

"Ah! And did he see the doctor?"

"Yes, sir. . . . That is,"—Brush corrected himself—"I suppose he did. I told him Doctor Bliss was in the study, and he at once went down the hall. I returned to the kitchen."

"Did you notice anything unusual in Mr. Scarlett's manner?"

The butler thought a moment.

"Well, sir, since you mention it, I might say that Mr. Scarlett was rather stiff and distant, like there was something on his mind—if you know what I mean."

"And the last you saw of him was when he was approaching the study door?"

"Yes, sir."

Vance nodded a dismissal.

"Remain in the drawing-room for the time being," he said.

As Brush disappeared through the folding door Hani came slowly down the stairs.

"It is as I said," he responded indifferently. "Doctor Bliss is not up-stairs."

Vance scrutinized him sternly.

"Do you know that Mr. Scarlett called here tonight?"

"Yes, I know." A curious light came into the man's eyes. "I was in the drawing-room when Brush admitted him."

"He came to see Doctor Bliss," said Vance.

"Yes. I heard him ask Brush——"

"Did Mr. Scarlett see the doctor?"

The Egyptian did not answer at once. He met Vance's gaze steadily as if trying to read the other's thoughts. At length, reaching a decision, he said:

"They were together—to my knowledge—for at least half an hour. When Mr. Scarlett entered the study he left the door open by the merest crack, and I was able to hear them talking together. But I could not distinguish anything that was said. Their voices were subdued."

"How long did you listen?"

"For half an hour. Then I went up-stairs."

"You have not seen either Doctor Bliss or Mr. Scarlett since?"

"No, *effendi.*"

"Where was Mr. Salveter during the conference in the study?" Vance was striving hard to control his anxiety.

"Was he here in the house?" Hani asked evasively. "He told me at dinner that he was going to Boston."

"Yes, yes—on the nine-thirty train. He needn't have left the house until nine.—Where was he between eight and nine?"

Hani shrugged his shoulders.

"I did not see him. He went out before Mr. Scarlett arrived. He was certainly not here after eight——"

"You're lying." Vance's tone was icy.

"*Wahyât en-nabi*——"

"Don't try to impress me—I'm not in the humor." Vance's eyes were like steel. "What do you think happened here to-night?"

"I think perhaps Sakhmet returned."

A pallor seemed to overspread Vance's face: it may, however, have been only the reflection of the hall light.

"Go to your room and wait there," he said curtly.

Hani bowed.

"You do not need my help now, *effendi.* You understand many things." And the Egyptian walked away with much dignity.

Vance stood tensely until he had disappeared. Then, with a motion to us, he hurried down the hall to the study. Throwing open the door he switched on the lights.

There was anxiety and haste in all his movements, and the electric atmosphere of his demeanor was transmitted to the rest of us. We realized that something tragic and terrible was leading him on.

He went to the two windows and leaned out. By the pale reflected light he could see the asphalt tiles on the ground below. He looked under the desk, and measured with his eyes the four-inch clearance beneath the divan. Then he went to the door leading into the museum.

"I hardly thought we'd find anything in the study; but there was a chance. . . ."

He was now swinging down the spiral stairs.

"It will be here in the museum," he called to us. "Come along, Sergeant. There's work to do. A fiend has been loose to-night. . . ."

He walked past the state chair and the shelves of *shawabtis,* and stood beside the long glass table case, his hands deep in his coat pockets, his eyes moving rapidly about the room. Markham and Heath and I waited at the foot of the stairs.

"What's this all about?" Markham asked huskily "What has taken place? And what, incidentally, are you looking for?"

"I don't know what has taken place." Something in Vance's tone sent a chill through me. "And I'm looking for something damnable. If it isn't here. . . ."

He did not finish the sentence. Going swiftly to the great replica of Kha-ef-Rê he walked round it. Then he went to the statue of Ramses II and inspected its base. After that he moved to Teti-shiret and tapped the pedestal with his knuckles.

"They're all solid," he muttered. "We must try the mummy cases." He recrossed the museum. "Start at that end, Sergeant. The covers should come off easily. If you have any difficulty, tear them off." He himself went to the anthropoid case beside Kha-ef-Rê and, inserting his hand beneath the upstanding lid, lifted it off and laid it on the floor.

Heath, apparently animated by an urgent desire for physical action, had already begun his search at the other end of the line. He was by no means gentle about it. He tore the lids off viciously, throwing them to the floor with unnecessary clatter.

Vance, absorbed in his own task, paid scant attention except to glance up as each lid was separated from the case. Markham, however, had begun to grow uneasy. He watched the Sergeant disapprovingly for several minutes, his face clouding over. Then he stepped forward.

"I can't let this go on, Vance," he remarked. "These are valuable treasures, and we have no right——"

Vance stood up and looked straight at Markham.

"And if there is a dead man in one of them?" he asked with a cold precision that caused Markham to stiffen.

"A dead man?"

"Placed here tonight—between eight and nine."

Vance's words had an ominous and impressive quality, and Markham said no more. He stood by, his features strained and set, watching the feverish inspection of the remaining mummy cases.

But no grisly discovery was made. Heath removed the lid of the last case in obvious disappointment.

"I guess something's gone wrong with your ideas, Mr. Vance," he commented without animus: indeed, there was a kindly note in his voice.

Vance, distraught and with a far-away look in his eyes, now stood by the glass case. His distress was so apparent that Markham went to him and touched him on the arm.

"Perhaps if we could re-calculate this affair along other lines——" he began; but Vance interrupted.

"No; it can't be re-calculated. It's too logical. There's been a tragedy here to-night—and we were too late to intercept it."

"We should have taken precautions." Markham's tone was bitter.

"Precautions! Every possible precaution was taken. A new element was introduced into the situation to-night—an element that couldn't possibly have been foreseen. To-night's tragedy was not part of the plot. . . ." Vance turned and walked away. "I must think this thing out. I must trace the murderer's reasoning. . . ." He made an entire circuit of the museum without taking his eyes from the floor.

Heath was puffing moodily on his cigar. He had not moved from in front of the mummy cases, and was pretending to be interested in the crudely colored hieroglyphs. Ever since the "Canary" murder case, when Tony Skeel had failed to keep his appointment in the District Attorney's office, he had, for all his protests, believed in Vance's prognostications; and now he was deeply troubled at the other's failure. I was watching him, a bit dazed myself, when I saw a frown of puzzled curiosity wrinkle his forehead. Taking his cigar from his mouth he bent over one of the fallen mummy cases and lifted out a slender metal object.

"That's a hell of a place to keep an automobile jack," he observed. (His interest in the jack was obviously the result of an unconscious attempt to distract his thoughts from the tense situation.)

He threw the jack back into the case and sat down on the base of Kha-ef-Rê's statue. Neither Vance nor Markham had apparently paid the slightest attention to his irrelevant discovery.

Vance continued pacing round the museum. For the first time since our arrival at the house he took out a cigarette and lighted it.

"Every line of reasoning leads here, Markham." He spoke in a low, hopeless tone. "There was no necessity for the evidence to have been taken away. In the first place, it would have been too hazardous; and, in the second place, we were not supposed to have suspected anything for a day or two. . . ."

His voice faltered and his body went suddenly taut. He wheeled toward Heath.

"An automobile jack!" A dynamic change had come over him. "Oh, my aunt! I wonder . . . I wonder. . . ."

He hurried toward the black sarcophagus beneath the front windows, and scrutinized it anxiously.

"Too high," he murmured. "Three feet from the floor! It couldn't have been done. . . . But it had to be done—somehow. . . ." He looked about him. "That taboret!" He pointed to a small solid oak stand, about twenty inches high, against the wall near the Asiatic wooden statue. "It was not there last night; it was beside the desk-table by the obelisk—Scarlett was using it." As he spoke he went to the taboret and picked it up. "And the top is scratched—there's an indentation. . . ." He placed the stand against the head of the sarcophagus. "Quick, Sergeant! Bring me that jack."

Heath obeyed with swiftness; and Vance placed the jack on the taboret, fitting its base over the scars in the wood. The lifting-head came within an inch of the under-side of the sarcophagus's lid where it extended a few inches over the end elevation between the two projecting lion-legged supports at the corners.

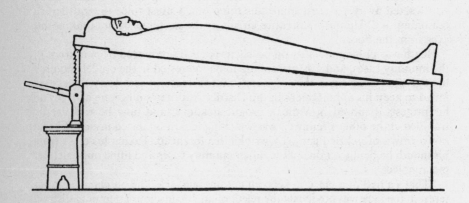

We had gathered about Vance in tense silence, not knowing what to expect but feeling that we were on the threshold of some appalling revelation.

Vance inserted the elevating lever, which Heath handed him, into the socket, and moved it carefully up and down. The jack worked perfectly. At each downward thrust of the lever there was a metallic click as the detent slipped into the groove of the rack. Inch by inch the end of the ponderous granite lid—which must have weighed over half a ton*—rose.

Heath suddenly stepped back in alarm.

* This was my guess during Vance's operation. Later I calculated the weight of the lid. It was ten feet long, four feet wide, and was surmounted by a large carved figure. A conservative estimate would give us ten cubic feet for the lid; and as the density of granite is approximately 2.70 grams per cubic centimeter, or 170 pounds per cubic foot, the lid would have weighed at least 1,700 pounds.

"Ain't you afraid, Mr. Vance, that the lid'll slide off the other end of the coffin?"

"No, Sergeant," Vance assured him. "The friction alone of so heavy a mass would hold it at a much greater angle than this jack could tilt it."

The head of the cover was now eight inches in the clear, and Vance was using both hands on the lever. He had to work with great care lest the jack slip from the smooth under-surface of the granite. Nine inches ... ten inches ... eleven ... twelve. ... The rack had almost reached its limit of elevation. With one final thrust downward, Vance released the lever and tested the solidity of the extended jack.

"It's safe, I think. . . ."

Heath had already taken out his pocket-light and flashed it into the dark recesses of the sarcophagus.

"Mother o' God!" he gasped.

I was standing just behind him, leaning over his broad shoulders; and simultaneously with the flare of his light I saw the horrifying thing that had made him call out. In the end of the sarcophagus was a dark, huddled human body, the back hunched upward and the legs hideously cramped, as if some one had hastily shoved it through the aperture, head first.

Markham stood bending forward like a person paralyzed in the midst of an action.

Vance's quiet but insistent voice broke the tension of our horror.

"Hold your light steady, Sergeant. And you, Markham, lend me a hand. But be careful. Don't touch the jack. . . ."

With great caution they reached into the sarcophagus and turned the body until the head was toward the widest point of the opening. A chill ran up my spine as I watched them for I knew that the slightest jar, or the merest touch on the jack, would bring the massive granite lid down upon them. Heath, too, realized this—I could see the glistening beads of sweat on his forehead as he watched the dangerous operation with fearful eyes.

Slowly the body emerged through the small opening, and when the feet had passed over the edge of the sarcophagus and clattered to the floor, the flashlight went out, and Heath sprawled back on his haunches with a convulsive gasp.

"Hell! I musta stumbled, Mr. Vance," he muttered. (I liked the Sergeant even more after that episode.)

Markham stood looking down at the inert body in stupefaction.

"Scarlett!" he exclaimed in a voice of complete incredulity.

Vance merely nodded, and bent over the prostrate figure. Scarlett's face was cyanosed, due to insufficient oxygenation of the blood; his eyes were set in a fixed bulging stare; and there was a crust formation of blood at his nostrils. Vance put his ear on the man's chest and took his wrist in one hand to feel the pulse. Then he drew out his gold cigarette-case and held it before Scarlett's lips. After a glance at the case he turned excitedly to Heath.

"The ambulance, Sergeant! Hurry! Scarlett's still alive. . . ."

Heath dashed up the stairs and disappeared into the front hall.

Markham regarded Vance intently.

"I don't understand this," he said huskily.

"Nor do I—entirely." Vance's eyes were on Scarlett. "I advised him to keep away from here. He, too, knew the danger, and yet. . . . You remember Rider Haggard's dedication of 'Allan Quartermain' to his son, wherein he spoke of the highest rank to which one can attain—the state and dignity of an English gentleman?*. . . Scarlett was an English gentleman. Knowing the peril, he came here to-night. He thought he might end the tragedy."

Markham was stunned and puzzled.

"We've got to take some sort of action—now."

"Yes. . . ." Vance was deeply concerned. "But the difficulties! There's no evidence. We're helpless. . . . Unless——" He stopped short. "That hieroglyphic letter! Maybe it's here somewhere. To-night was the time; but Scarlett came unexpectedly. I wonder if he knew about that, too. . . ." Vance's eyes drifted thoughtfully into space, and for several moments he stood rigid. Then he suddenly went to the sarcophagus and, striking a match, looked inside.

"Nothing." There was dire disappointment in his tone. "And yet, it should be here. . . ." He straightened up. "Perhaps . . . yes! That, too, would be logical."

He knelt down beside the unconscious man and began going through his pockets. Scarlett's coat was buttoned, and it was not until Vance had reached into the inner breast pocket that his search was rewarded. He drew out a crumpled sheet of yellow scratch paper of the kind on which Salveter's Egyptian exercise had been written, and after one glance at it thrust it into his own pocket.

Heath appeared at the door.

"O.K.," he called down, "I told 'em to rush it."

"How long will it take?" Vance asked.

"Not more'n ten minutes. I called Headquarters; and they'll relay it to the local station. They generally pick up the cop on the beat—but that don't delay things. I'll wait here at the door for 'em."

"Just a moment." Vance wrote something on the back of an envelope and handed it up to Heath. "Call Western Union and get this telegram off."

Heath took the message, read it, whistled softly, and went out into the hall.

"I'm wiring Salveter at New Haven to leave the train at New London and return to New York," Vance explained to Markham. "He'll be able to catch the Night Express at New London, and will get here early to-morrow morning."

Markham looked at him shrewdly.

"You think he'll come?"

"Oh, yes."

When the ambulance arrived, Heath escorted the interne, the blue-uniformed driver and the police officer into the museum. The interne, a pink-faced youth with a serious brow, bowed to Markham and knelt beside Scarlett. After a superficial examination, he beckoned to the driver.

"Go easy with his head."

---

* The actual dedication reads: "I inscribe this book of adventure to my son, Arthur John Rider Haggard, in the hope that in days to come he, and many other boys whom I shall never know, may in the acts and thoughts of Allan Quartermain and his companions, as herein recorded, find something to help him and them to reach to what, with Sir Henry Curtis, I hold to be the highest rank whereto we can obtain—the state of dignity of English gentlemen."

The man, assisted by the officer, lifted Scarlett to the stretcher.

"How bad is he, doctor?" Markham asked anxiously.

"Pretty bad, sir." The interne shook his head pompously. "A messy fracture at the base of the skull. Cheyne-Stokes breathing. If he lives, he's luckier than I'll ever be." And with a shrug he followed the stretcher out of the house.

"I'll phone the hospital later," Markham said to Vance. "If Scarlett recovers, he can supply us with evidence."

"Don't count on it," Vance discouraged him. "To-night's episode was isolated." He went to the sarcophagus and reversed the jack. Slowly the lid descended to its original position. "A bit dangerous, don't y' know, to leave it up."

Markham stood by frowning.

"Vance, what paper was that you found in Scarlett's pocket?"

"I imagine it was an incriminatin' document written in Egyptian hieroglyphs. We'll see."

He spread the paper out smoothly on the top of the sarcophagus. It was almost exactly like the letter Vance had pieced together in Bliss's study. The color of the paper was the same, and it contained four rows of hieroglyphs in green ink.

Vance studied it while Markham and Heath, who had returned to the museum, and I looked on.

"Let me see how well I remember my Egyptian," he murmured. "It's been years since I did any transliterating. . . ."

He placed his monocle in his eye and bent forward.

"*Meryt-Amûn, aha-y o er yu son maut-y en merya-y men seshem pen dya-y em yeb-y era-y en marwet mar-en yu rekha-t khet nibet hir-sa hetpa-t na-y kheft shewa-n em debat nefra-n entot hena-y. . . .* This is done very accurately, Markham. The nouns and adjectives agree as to gender, and the verb endings——"

"Never mind those matters," Markham interrupted impatiently. "What does that paper say?"

"I beg of you, Markham old dear!" Vance protested. "Middle-Kingdom Egyptian is a most difficult language. Coptic and Assyrian and Greek and Sanskrit are abecedarian beside it. However, I can give you a literal translation." He began reading slowly: " 'Beloved of Amûn, I stop here until comes the brother of my mother. Not do I wish that should-endure this situation. I have-placed in my heart that I should-act for the sake of our well-being. Thou shalt-know every-thing later. Thou shalt-be-satisfied toward me when we are-free from what-blocks-the-way, happy-are we, thou together-with me. . . .' Not what you'd call Harvardian. But such were the verbal idiosyncrasies of the ancient Egyptians."

"Well, it don't make sense to me," Heath commented sourly.

"But properly paraphrased it makes fiendish sense, Sergeant. Put into everyday English, it says: 'Meryt-Amen: I am waiting here for my uncle. I cannot endure this situation any longer; and I have decided to take drastic action for the sake of our happiness. You will understand everything later, and you will forgive me when we are free from all obstacles and can be happy together.' . . . I say, Sergeant; does that make sense?"

"I'll tell the world!" Heath looked at Vance with an air of contemptuous criticism. "And you sent that bird Salveter to Boston!"

THE HIEROGLYPHIC LETTER

"He'll be back to-morrow," Vance assured him.

"But see here";—Markham's eyes were fixed on the incriminating paper—"what about that other letter you pieced together? And how did this letter get in Scarlett's pocket?"

Vance folded the paper carefully and placed it in his wallet.

"The time has come," he said slowly, "to tell you everything. It may be, when you have the facts in hand, you can figure out some course of procedure. I can see legal difficulties ahead; but I now have all the evidence we can ever hope for." He was uneasy and troubled. "Scarlett's intrusion in to-night's happenings changed the murderer's plans. Anyway, I can now convince you of the incredible and abominable truth."

Markham studied him for several moments, and a startled light came in his eyes.

"*God Almighty!*" he breathed. "I see what you mean." He clicked his teeth together. "But first I must phone the hospital. There's a chance that Scarlett can help us—if he lives."

He went to the rear of the museum and mounted the spiral stairs to the study. A few minutes later he reappeared, his face dark and hopeless.

"I spoke to the doctor," he said. "There's not one chance in a thousand for Scarlett. Concussion of the brain—and suffocation. They've got the pulmotor on him now. Even if he does pull through he'll be unconscious for a week or two."

"I was afraid of that." I had rarely seen Vance so distressed. "We were too late. But—dash it all!—I couldn't have foreseen his quixotism. And I warned him. . . ."

"Come, old man." Markham spoke with paternal kindliness. "It's not your fault. There was nothing you could have done. And you were right in keeping the truth to yourself——"

"Excuse *me!*" Heath was exasperated. "I myself ain't exactly an enemy of truth. Why can't I get in on this?"

"You can, Sergeant." Vance placed his hand on the other's shoulder. "Let's go to the drawing-room. 'And every mountain and hill shall be made low; and the crooked shall be made straight, and the rough places plain.'"

He moved toward the stairs; and we followed him.

21

THE MURDERER

(Saturday, July 14; 10:40 P.M.)

As WE entered the drawing-room Brush rose. He was pale and palpably frightened.

"Why are you worried?" Vance asked.

"Suppose, sir, I should be blamed!" the man blurted. "It was I who left the front door open yesterday morning—I wanted to get some fresh air. And then you came and said something had happened to Mr. Kyle. I know I shouldn't have unlatched the door." (I realized then why he had acted in so terrified a manner.)

"You may cheer up," Vance told him. "We know who killed Mr. Kyle, and I can assure you, Brush, that the murderer didn't come in the front door."

"Thank you, sir." The words were like a sigh of relief.

"And now tell Hani to come here. Then you may go to your room."

Brush had scarcely left us when there was the sound of a key being inserted in the front door. A moment later Doctor Bliss appeared at the entrance to the drawing-room.

"Good-evening, doctor," Vance greeted him. "I hope we're not intrudin'. But there are several questions we wish to ask Hani during Mr. Salveter's absence."

"I understand," Bliss returned, with a sad nod. "You know, then, of Salveter's excursion to Boston."

"He phoned me and asked if he might go."

Bliss looked at Vance with heavy, inquisitive eyes.

"His wanting to go north at this time was most unusual," he said; "but I did not raise any objection. The atmosphere here is very depressing, and I sympathized with his desire to escape from it."

"What time did he leave the house?" Vance put the question carelessly.

"About nine. I offered to drive him to the station. . . ."

"At nine, what? And where was he between eight and nine?"

Bliss looked unhappy.

"He was with me in the study. We were going over details regarding the reproductions of Hotepheres' tomb furniture."

"Was he with you when Mr. Scarlett arrived?"

"Yes." Bliss frowned. "Very peculiar, Scarlett's visit. He evidently wanted to talk to Salveter alone. He acted most mysteriously—treated Salveter with a sort of resentful coldness. But I continued to discuss the object of Salveter's trip north——"

"Mr. Scarlett waited?"

"Yes. He watched Salveter like a hawk. Then, when Salveter went out, Scarlett went with him."

"Ah! And you, doctor?" Vance was apparently absorbed in selecting a cigarette from his case.

"I stayed in the study."

"And that's the last you saw of either Scarlett or Salveter?"

"Yes. . . . I went for a walk about half past nine. I looked in the museum on my way out, thinking possibly Scarlett had remained and would join me; but the room was dark. So I strolled down the avenue to Washington Square. . . ."

"Thank you, doctor." Vance had lighted his cigarette and was smoking moodily. "We sha'n't trouble you any more to-night."

Hani entered the room.

"You wish to see me?" His manner was detached and, I thought, a trifle bored.

"Yes." Vance indicated a chair facing the table. Then he turned quickly to Bliss who was on the point of going out.

"On second thought, doctor, it may be advisable for us to question you again regarding Mr. Salveter.—Would you mind waiting in the study?"

"Not at all." Bliss shot him a comprehending glance, and went down the hall. A few moments later we heard the study door close.

Vance gave Hani a curious look, which I did not understand.

"I have something I wish to tell Mr. Markham," he said. "Will you be good enough to stand in the hall and see that no one disturbs us?"

Hani rose.

"With pleasure, *effendi.*" And he took his post outside.

Vance closed the folding doors, and coming back to the centre-table, settled himself comfortably.

"You, Markham—and you, Sergeant—were both right yesterday morning when you concluded that Doctor Bliss was guilty of murdering Kyle——"

"Say, listen!" Heath leapt to his feet. "What the hell——!"

"Oh, quite, Sergeant. Please sit down and control yourself."

"I said he killed him! And you said——"

"My word! Can't you be tranquil? You're so upsettin', Sergeant." Vance made an exasperated gesture. "I'm aware you remarked inelegantly that Bliss had 'croaked' Mr. Kyle. And I trust you have not forgotten that I said to you last night that we often arrive at the same destination at the same time—but from opposite directions."

"That was what you meant, was it?" Heath resumed his seat surlily. "Then why didn't you let me arrest him?"

"Because that's what he wanted you to do."

"I'm floundering," Heath wailed. "The world has gone nuts."

"Just a moment, Sergeant." Markham spoke peremptorily. "I'm beginning to understand this affair. It's not insane in the least.—Let Mr. Vance continue."

Heath started to expostulate, but instead made a grimace of resignation, and began chewing on his cigar.

Vance regarded him sympathetically.

"I knew, Sergeant—or at least I strongly suspected—within five minutes after entering the museum yesterday morning, that Bliss was guilty. Scarlett's story about the appointment gave me the first clew. Bliss's telephone call in the presence of every one and his remarks about the new shipment struck me as fitting in perfectly with a preconceived plan. Then, when I saw the various clews, I felt positive they had been planted by Bliss himself. With him it was not only a matter of pointing suspicion to himself, but—on second view—of throwing suspicion on another. Fortunately he overstepped the grounds of plausibility; for had some one else committed the crime, the planted clews would have been less numerous and less obvious. Consequently, I leapt to the conclusion that Bliss had murdered Kyle and had, at the same time, striven to lead us to think that he was the victim of a plot——"

"But, Mr. Vance," interrupted Heath, "you said——"

"*I did not say one word to give you the definite impression that I exonerated Bliss. Not once did I say he was innocent.* . . . Think back. You'll remember I said only that the clews did not ring true—that things were not what they seemed. I knew the clews were traps, set by Bliss to deceive us. And I also knew—as Mr. Markham knew—that if we arrested Bliss on the outward evidence, it would be impossible to convict him."

Markham nodded thoughtfully.

"Yes, Sergeant. Mr. Vance is quite correct. I can't recall a single remark of his inconsistent with his belief in Bliss's guilt."

"Although I knew Bliss was guilty," Vance continued, "I didn't know what his ultimate object was or whom he was trying to involve. I suspected it was Salveter—though it might have been either Scarlett or Hani or Mrs. Bliss. I at once saw the necessity of determining the real victim of his plot. So I pretended to fall in with the obvious situation. I couldn't let Bliss think that I suspected him,—my only hope lay in pretending that I believed some one else was guilty. But I did avoid the traps set for us. I wanted Bliss to plant other clews against his victim and perhaps give us some workable evidence. That was why I begged you to play a waiting game with me."

"But what was Bliss's idea in having himself arrested?" Markham asked. "There was danger in that."

"Very little. He probably believed that even before an indictment he or his lawyer could persuade you of his innocence and of Salveter's guilt. Or, if he had been held for trial, he was almost sure of an acquittal, and would then be entirely safe on the caressin' principle of double jeopardy, or *autrefois acquit*. . . . No, he was running no great risk. And remember, too, he was playing a big game. Once he had been arrested, he would have felt justified in pointing openly to Salveter as the murderer and plotter. Hence I fought against your arresting him, for *it was the very thing he wanted*. As long as he thought he was free from suspicion, there was no point in his defending himself at Salveter's expense. And, in order to involve Salveter, he was forced to plant more evidence, to concoct other schemes. And it was on these schemes that I counted for evidence."

"I'm sunk!" The ashes of Heath's cigar toppled off and fell over his waist-coat, but he didn't notice them.

"But, Sergeant, I gave you many warnings. And there was the motive. I'm convinced that Bliss knew there was no more financial help coming from Kyle; and there's nothing he wouldn't have done to insure a continuation of his researches. Furthermore, he was intensely jealous of Salveter: he knew Mrs. Bliss loved the young cub."

"But why," put in Markham, "did he not merely kill Salveter?"

"Oh, I say! The money was a cardinal factor,—he wanted Meryt-Amen to inherit Kyle's wealth. His second'ry object was to eliminate Salveter from Meryt-Amen's heart: he had no reason for killing him. Therefore he planned subtly to disqualify him by making it appear that Salveter not only had murdered his uncle but had tried to send another to the chair for it."

Vance slowly lighted a fresh cigarette.

"Bliss was killing three birds with one stone. He was making himself a martyr in Meryt-Amen's eyes; he was eliminating Salveter; he was insuring his wife a fortune with which he could continue his excavations. Few murders have had so powerful a triple motive. . . . And one of the tragic things is that Mrs. Bliss more than half believed in Salveter's guilt. She suffered abominably. You recall how she took the attitude that she wanted the murderer brought to justice. And she feared all the time that it was Salveter. . . ."

"Still and all," said Heath, "Bliss didn't seem very anxious to get Salveter mixed up in the affair."

"Ah, but he was, Sergeant. He was constantly involving Salveter while pretending not to. A feigned reluctance, as it were. He couldn't be too obvious about it—that would have given his game away. . . . You remember my question of who had charge of the medical supplies. Bliss stuttered, as if trying to shield some one. Very clever, don't y' know."

"But if you knew this——" Heath began.

"I didn't know *all* of it, Sergeant. I knew only that Bliss was guilty. I was not sure that Salveter was the object of his plot. Therefore I had to investigate and learn the truth."

"Anyhow, I was right in the first place when I said Bliss was guilty," Heath declared doggedly.

"Of course you were, Sergeant." Vance spoke almost affectionately. "And I felt deuced bad to have to appear to contradict you." He rose and, going to Heath, held out his hand. "Will you forgive me?"

"Well . . . maybe." Heath's eyes belied his gruff tone as he grasped Vance's hand. "Anyhow, I was right!"

Vance grinned and sat down.

"The plot itself was simple," he continued after a moment. "Bliss phoned Kyle in the presence of every one and made the appointment for eleven. He specifically mentioned the new shipment, and suggested that Kyle should come early. You see, he had decided on the murder—and on the whole plot in fact—when he made the fatal rendezvous. And he deliberately left the scarab pin on the study desk. After killing Kyle he placed the pin and the financial report near the body. And note, Markham, that Salveter had access to both objects. Moreover, Bliss knew that Salveter was in the habit of going to the museum after breakfast; and he timed Kyle's appointment so that Salveter and his uncle would probably meet. He sent Salveter to the Metropolitan to get him out of the house while he himself killed Kyle. And he also fixed the statue of Sakhmet so that it would look like a trap. The murderer could easily have come back at any time before we arrived and planted the pin and the report and made the foot-prints—provided of course Bliss had been asleep with the opium. . . ."

Heath sat upright and squinted at Vance.

"That trap was only a stall?" he asked indignantly.

"Nothing else, Sergeant. It was set up after the murder, so that even if Salveter had had an alibi, he still could have been guilty. Furthermore, the possibility of Kyle's having been killed by an absent person was another point in favor of Bliss. Why should Bliss have made a death-trap when he had every opportunity to kill Kyle by direct contact? The trap was merely another counter-clew."

"But the pencil used in the trap," interposed Markham. "It was not the kind Salveter used."

"My dear Markham! Bliss used one of his own pencils for the 'upright' in order to create another clew against himself. A man actually planning a death-trap is not going to use his own pencil,—he would use the pencil of the man he was trying to involve. The doctor therefore used his own pencil—*in order to throw suspicion elsewhere.* But the trap did not fool me. It was too fortuitous. A murderer would not have taken such a chance. The falling statue might not have fallen exactly on Kyle's head. And another thing: a man struck in that fashion is not likely to fall in the positon we found Kyle, with his head just beneath the place where the statue struck him, and with his arms stretched out. When I made my experiment, and the statue fell exactly where Kyle's head had been, I realized how unlikely it was that he had actually been killed by the statue falling." Vance's eyes twinkled. "I did not raise the point at the time, for I wanted you to believe in the death-trap."

"Right again!" Heath slapped his forehead dramatically with his palm. "And I never thought of it! . . . Sure, I'll forgive you, Mr. Vance!"

"The truth is, Sergeant, I did everything I could to make you overlook the inconsistency of it. And Mr. Markham didn't see it either.* As a matter of fact, Kyle was killed while he was looking into the cabinet, by a blow from someone behind him. I have an idea, too, that one of those heavy flint or porphyry maces was used. His body was arranged in the position we found it, and the statue of Sakhmet was then dropped on his skull, obliterating the evidence of the first blow."

"But suppose," objected Markham, "you hadn't seen the loose ring on the curtain?"

"The trap was arranged so that we would discover it. If we had overlooked it, Bliss would have called our attention to it."

"But the finger-prints——" began Heath, in a kind of daze.

"They were purposely left on the statue. More evidence, d' ye see, against Bliss. But he had an alibi in reserve. His first explanation was so simple and so specious:—he had moved Sakhmet because it wasn't quite straight. But the second explanation why there were no other finger-prints on Sakhmet was to come later, after his arrest—to wit, no one had actually wielded the statue: it was a death-trap set by Salveter!"

Vance made an open-handed gesture.

"Bliss covered every clew against himself with a stronger clew pointing to Salveter. . . . Regard, for instance, the evidence of the footprints. Superficially these pointed to Bliss. But there was the omnipresent counter-clew—namely: he was wearing bedroom slippers yesterday morning, and only one tennis shoe was to be found in the study. The other tennis shoe was in his room, *exactly where he said he had left it the night before.* Bliss simply brought one shoe downstairs, made the footprints in the blood, and placed the shoe in the waste-basket. He wanted us to find the prints and to discover the shoe. And we did—that is, the Sergeant did. His answer to the footprints, after his arrest, would merely have been that some one who had access to his room had taken one tennis shoe down-stairs and made the tracks to involve him."

Markham nodded.

"Yes," he said; "I'd have been inclined to exonerate him, especially after the discovery of opium in his coffee cup."

"Ah, that opium! The perfect alibi! What jury would have convicted him after the evidence of the opium in his coffee? They would have regarded him as the victim of a plot. And the District Attorney's office would have come in for much severe criticism. . . . And how simple the opium episode was! Bliss took the can from the cabinet, extracted what he needed for the ruse, and placed the powder in the bottom of his coffee cup."

---

* Nor did I. But while this record of mine was running serially in the *American Magazine* several readers wrote to me pointing out the inconsistency.

"You didn't think he had been narcotized?"

"No. I knew he hadn't. A narcotic contracts the pupils; and Bliss's were distended with excitement. I knew he was pretending, and that made me suspect I'd find a drug in his coffee."

"But what about the can?" Heath put the question. "I never did get that can business straight. You sent Hani——"

"Now, Sergeant!" Vance spoke good-naturedly. "I knew where the can was, and I merely wanted to ascertain how much Hani knew."

"But I see the Sergeant's point," Markham put in. "We don't know that the opium can was in Salveter's room."

"Oh, don't we, now?" Vance turned toward the hall. "Hani!"

The Egyptian opened the sliding door.

"I say;"—Vance looked straight into the man's eyes—"I'm dashed admirin' of your deceptive attitude, but we could bear some facts for a change.— Where did you find the opium tin?"

"*Effendi,* there is no longer any need for dissimulation. You are a man of profound wisdom, and I trust you. The tin was hidden in Mr. Salveter's room."

"Thanks awfully." Vance was almost brusque. "And now return to the hall."

Hani went out and softly closed the door.

"And by not going down to breakfast yesterday morning," Vance continued, "Bliss knew that his wife and Salveter would be in the breakfast-room alone, and that Salveter might easily have put the opium in the coffee...."

"But," asked Markham, "if you knew Bliss put the opium in his own coffee, why all the interest in the samovar?"

"I had to be sure who it was Bliss's plot was aimed at. He was trying to make it appear that *he* was the victim of the plot; and since his object was to involve some one else, I knew the real victim would have had to have access to the coffee yesterday morning."

Heath nodded ponderously.

"That's easy enough. The old boy was pretending some one had fed him knock-out drops, but if the bird he was aiming at couldn't have fed him the drops, his plot would have gone blooey.... But look here, Mr. Vance;"—he suddenly remembered something—"what was the idea of the doc's trying to escape?"

"It was a perfectly logical result of what had gone before," Vance explained. "After we had refused to arrest him, he began to worry. Y' see, he yearned to be arrested; and we disappointed him frightfully. Sittin' in his room, he got to planning. How could he make us re-order his arrest and thus give him the chance to point out all the evidences of Salveter's heinous plot against him? He decided to attempt an escape. That gesture, he figured, would surely revive suspicion against him. So he simply went out, drew his money openly from the bank, taxied to the Grand Central Station, asked loudly about trains to Montreal, and then stood conspicuously by the gate waiting for the train.... He knew that Guilfoyle was following him; for, had he really intended making his escape, you may rest assured Guilfoyle would never have traced him. You, Sergeant, accepted Bliss's action at its face value; and I was afraid that his silly disappearance would produce the very result he in-

tended—namely, his re-arrest. That was why I argued against it so passionately."

Vance leaned back but did not relax. There was a rigid alertness in his attitude.

"And because you did not manacle him, Sergeant," he continued, "he
was forced to take a further step. He had to build up a case against Salveter.
So he staged the drama with the dagger. He deliberately sent Salveter to
the study to get a memorandum-book in the desk—where the dagger was
kept. . . ."

"And the sheath!" exclaimed Markham.

"Oh, quite. That was the real clew against Salveter. Having put the sheath
in Salveter's room, Bliss suggested to us that we might find the would-be
assassin by locating the sheath. I knew where it was the moment he so help-
fully mentioned it; so I gave Hani a chance to lie about it. . . ."

"You mean Hani didn't find the sheath in the hall?"

"Of course not."

Vance again called Hani from the hall.

"Where did you find the sheath of the royal dagger?" he asked.

Hani answered without a moment's hestitation.

"In Mr. Salveter's room, *effendi*—as you well know."

Vance nodded.

"And by the by, Hani, has any one approached this door to-night?"

"No, *effendi*. The doctor is still in his study."

Vance dismissed him with a gesture, and went on:

"Y' see, Markham, Bliss put the sheath in Salveter's room, and then threw
the dagger into the headboard of his bed. He phoned me and, when we arrived, told an elaborate but plausible tale of having been assaulted by an *inconnu.*"

"He was a damn good actor," Heath commented.

"Yes—in the main. But there was one psychological point he overlooked. If
he had actually been the victim of a murderous attack he would not have gone
down-stairs alone in the dark to phone me. He would have first roused the
house."*

"That's reasonable." Markham had become impatient. "But you said something about the picture not being complete——"

"The letter!" Vance sat up and threw away his cigarette. "That was the
missing factor. I couldn't understand why the forged hieroglyphic letter didn't
show up last night,—it was the perfect opportunity. But it was nowhere in
evidence; and that's what troubled me. . . . However, when I found Scarlett
working in the museum, I understood. The doctor, I'm convinced, intended to
plant the forged letter—which he had placed temporarily in the desk-table
drawer—in Meryt-Amen's room or some place where we'd find it. But when
he looked into the museum through the study door he saw Scarlett at work at
the desk-table. So he let the letter go, reserving it for future use—in case we
didn't arrest Salveter after the dagger episode. And when I deliberately

---

* It will be recalled in the Greene murder case the murderer, pretending to be frightened at the sinister danger lurking in the dim corridors of the old Greene mansion, made
a similar error in psychological judgment by descending to the pantry in the middle of the
night for no other reason than to gratify a mild appetite for food.

avoided the clews he had prepared against Salveter, I kenw the letter would appear very soon. I was afraid Scarlett might in some way block Bliss's scheme, so I warned him to keep away from the house. I don't know what more I could have done."

"Nor I." Markham's tone was consoling. "Scarlett should have followed your advice."

"But he didn't." Vance sighed regretfully.

"You think, then, that Scarlett suspected the truth?"

"Undoubtedly. And he suspected it early in the game. But he wasn't sure enough to speak out. He was afraid he might be doing the doctor an injustice; and, being an English gentleman, he kept silent. My belief is, he got to worrying about the situation and finally went to Bliss——"

"But something must have convinced him."

"The dagger, Markham. Bliss made a grave error in that regard. Scarlett and Bliss were the only two persons who knew about that smuggled weapon. And when I showed it to Scarlett and informed him it had been used in an attempt on Bliss's life, he knew pretty conclusively that Bliss had concocted the whole tale."

"And he came here to-night to confront Bliss. . . ?"

"Exactly. He realized that Bliss was trying to involve Salveter; and he wanted to let Bliss know that his monstrous scheme was seen through. He came here to protect an innocent man—despite the fact that Salveter was his rival, as it were, for the affections of Meryt-Amen. That would be like Scarlett. . . ." Vance looked sad. "When I sent Salveter to Boston I believed I had eliminated every possibility of danger. But Scarlett felt he had to take matters in his own hands. His action was fine, but ill-advised. The whole trouble was, it gave Bliss the opportunity he'd been waiting for. When he couldn't get the forged letter from the museum last night, and when we declined his invitation to find the sheath in Salveter's room, it was necessary for him to play his ace—the forged letter."

"Yes, yes. I see that. But just where did Scarlett fit?"

"When Scarlett came here to-night Bliss no doubt listened to his accusation diplomatically, and then on some pretext or other got him into the museum. When Scarlett was off guard Bliss struck him on the head—probably with one of those maces in the end cabinet—and put him in the sarcophagus. It was a simple matter for him to get the jack from his car, which he keeps parked in the street outside,—you recall that he offered to drive Salveter to the station. . . ."

"But the letter?"

"Can't you see how everything fitted? The attack on Scarlett took place between eight and eight-thirty. Salveter was probably up-stairs bidding adieu to Mrs. Bliss. At any rate, he was in the house, and therefore could have been Scarlett's murderer. In order to make it appear that Salveter *was actually the murderer of Scarlett* Bliss crumpled up the forged telltale letter and stuck in it Scarlett's pocket. He wanted to make it appear that Scarlett had come to the house to-night to confront Salveter, had mentioned the letter he'd found in the desk-table drawer, and had been killed by Salveter."

"But why wouldn't Salveter have taken the letter?"

"The assumption would have been that Salveter didn't know that Scarlett had the letter in his pocket."

"What I want to know," put in Heath, "is how Bliss found out about Salveter's original letter."

"That point is easily explained, Sergeant." Vance drew out his cigarette-case. "Salveter undoubtedly returned to the museum yesterday morning, as he told us, and was working on his letter when Kyle entered. He then put the letter in the table-drawer, and went to the Metropolitan Museum on his errand. Bliss, who was probably watching him through a crack in the study door, saw him put the paper away, and later took it out to see what it was. Being an indiscreet letter to Meryt-Amen, it gave Bliss an idea. He took it to his study and rewrote it, making it directly incriminating; and then tore up the original. When I learned that the letter had disappeared I was worried, for I suspected that Bliss had taken it. And when I saw it had been destroyed and thrown away, I was convinced we would find another letter. But since I had the original, I believed that the forged letter would, when it appeared, give us evidence against Bliss."

"So that's why you were so interested in those three words?"

"Yes, Sergeant. I hardly thought Bliss would use *tem* and *was* and *ankh* in rewriting the letter, for he couldn't have known that Salveter had told us about the letter and specifically mentioned these three words. And not one of the three words was in the forgery."

"But a handwriting expert——"

"Oh, I say, Sergeant! Don't be so *naïf*. A handwriting expert is a romantic scientist even when the writing is English script and familiar to him. And all his rules are based on chirographic idiosyncrasies. No art expert can tell with surety who drew a picture—and Egyptian writing is mostly pictures. Forged Michelangelo drawings, for instance, are being sold by clever dealers constantly. The only approach in such matters is an æsthetic one—and there is no æsthetics in Egyptian hieroglyphs."

Heath made a wry face.

"Well, if the forged letter couldn't be admitted as evidence, what was the doctor's idea?"

"Don't you see, Sergeant, that even if the letter couldn't be absolutely identified with Salveter, it would have made every one believe that Salveter was guilty and had escaped a conviction on a legal technicality. Certainly Meryt-Amen would have believed that Salveter wrote the letter; and that was what Bliss wanted."

Vance turned to Markham.

"It's a legal point which really doesn't matter. Salveter might not have been convicted; but Bliss's plot would none the less have succeeded. With Kyle dead, Bliss would have had access to one-half of Kyle's fortune—in his wife's name, to be sure—and Meryt-Amen would have repudiated Salveter. Thus Bliss would have won every trick. And even legally Salveter might have been convicted had it not been for Hani's removal of two direct clews from Salveter's room—the opium can and the sheath. Furthermore, there was the letter in Scarlett's pocket."

"But, Vance, how would the letter have been found?" Markham asked. "If you had not suspected the plot and looked for Scarlett's body, it might have remained in the sarcophagus almost indefinitely."

"No." Vance shook his head. "Scarlett was to have remained in the sarcophagus only for a couple of days. When it was discovered to-morrow that he was missing Bliss would probably have found the body for us, along with the letter."

He looked questioningly at Markham.

"How are we going to connect Bliss with the crime, since Salveter was in the house at the time of the attack?"

"If Scarlett should get well——"

"If!... Just so. But suppose he shouldn't— and the chances are against him. Then what? Scarlett at most could only testify that Bliss had made an abortive and unsuccessful attack on him. True, you might convict him for felonious assault, but it would leave Kyle's murder still unsolved. And if Bliss said that Scarlett attacked him and that he struck Scarlett in self-defense, you'd have a difficult time convicting him even for assault."

Markham rose and walked up and down the room. Then Heath asked a question.

"How does this Ali Baba fit into the picture, Mr. Vance?"

"Hani knew from the first what had happened; and he was shrewd enough to see the plot that Bliss had built up about Salveter. He loved Salveter and Meryt-Amen, and he wanted them to be happy. What could he do except lend his every energy to protecting them? And he has certainly done this, Sergeant. Egyptians are not like Occidentals. It was against his nature to come out frankly and tell us what he suspected. Hani played a clever game—the only game he could have played. He never believed in the vengeance of Sakhmet. He used his superstitious logomachy to cover up the truth. He fought with words for Salveter's safety."

Markham halted in front of Vance.

"The thing is incredible! I have never known a murderer like Bliss."

"Oh, don't give him too much credit." Vance lighted the cigarette he had been holding for the past five minutes. "He frightfully overdid the clews: he made them too glaring. Therein lay his weakness."

"Still," said Markham, "if you hadn't come into the case I'd have brought a murder charge against him."

"And you would have played into his hands. Because I didn't want you to, I appeared to argue against his guilt."

"A palimpsest!" Markham commented after a pause.

Vance took a deep draw on his cigarette.

"Exactly. *Palimpsestos*—'again rub smooth.' First came the true story of the crime, carefully indicated. Then it was erased, and the story of the murder, with Salveter as the villain, was written over it. This too, was erased, and the original story—in grotesque outline and filled with inconsistencies and loopholes—was again written. We were supposed to read the third version, become sceptical about it, and find the evidences of Salveter's guilt between the lines. My task was to push through to the first and original version—the twice written-over truth."

"And you did it, Mr. Vance!" Heath had risen and gone toward the door. "The doc is in the study, Chief. I'll take him to Headquarters myself."

22

THE JUDGMENT OF ANUBIS

(Saturday, July 14; 11 P.M.)

"I SAY, Sergeant! Don't be rash." Despite the drawling quality of Vance's tone Heath halted abruptly. "If I were you I'd take a bit of legal advice from Mr. Markham before arresting the doctor."

"Legal advice be damned!"

"Oh, quite. In principle I agree with you. But there's no need to be temerarious about these little matters. Caution is always good."

Markham, who was standing beside Vance, lifted his head.

"Sit down, Sergeant," he ordered. "We can't arrest a man on theory." He walked to the fireplace and back. "This thing has to be thought out. There's no evidence against Bliss. We couldn't hold him an hour if a clever lawyer got busy on the case."

"And Bliss knows it," said Vance.

"But he killed Kyle!" Heath expostulated.

"Granted." Markham sat down beside the table and rested his chin in his hands. "But I've nothing tangible to present to a grand jury. And, as Mr. Vance says, even if Scarlett should recover I'd have only an assault charge against Bliss."

"What wallops me, sir," moaned Heath, "is how a guy can commit murder almost before our very eyes, and get away with it. It ain't reasonable."

"Ah, but there's little that's reasonable in this fantastic and ironical world, Sergeant," remarked Vance.

"Well, anyhow," returned Heath, "I'd arrest that bird in a minute and take my chances at making the charge stick."

"I feel the same way," Markham said. "But no matter how convinced we are of the truth, we must be able to produce conclusive evidence. And this fiend has covered all the evidence so cleverly that any jury in the country would acquit him, even if we could hold him for trial—which is highly dubious."

Vance sighed and looked up.

"The law!" He spoke with unusual fervor. "And the rooms in which this law is put on public exhibition are called courts of justice. *Justice!*—oh, my precious aunt! *Summum jus, summa injuria.* How can there be justice, or even intelligence, in echolalia? . . . Here we three are—a District Attorney; a Sergeant of the Homicide Bureau; and a lover of Brahms' B-flat piano concerto—with a known murderer within fifty feet of us; and we're helpless! Why? Because this elaborate invention of imbeciles, called the law, has failed to provide for the extermination of a dangerous and despicable criminal, who not only murdered his benefactor in cold blood, but attempted to kill another decent man, and then endeavored to saddle an innocent third man with both crimes so that he could continue digging up ancient and venerated corpses! . . . No wonder Hani detests him. At heart Bliss is a ghoul; and Hani is an honorable and intelligent man."

"I admit the law is imperfect," Markham interrupted tartly. "But your dissertation is hardly helpful. We're confronted with a terrible problem, and a way must be found to handle it."

Vance still stood before the table, his eyes fixed on the door.

"But your law will never solve it," he said. "You can't convict Bliss; you don't even dare arrest him. He could make you the laughing-stock of the country if you tried it. And furthermore, he'd become a sort of persecuted hero who had been hounded by an incompetent and befuddled police, who had unjustly pounced on him in a moment of groggy desperation in order to save their more or less classic features."

Vance took a deep draw on his cigarette.

"Markham old dear, I'm inclined to think the gods of ancient Egypt were more intelligent than Solon, Justinian, and all the other law-givers combined. Hani was spoofing about the vengeance of Sakhmet; but, after all, that solar-disked lady would be just as effective as your silly statutes. Mythological ideas are largely nonsense; but are they more nonsensical than the absurdities óf present-day law? . . ."

"For God's sake, be still." Markham was irritable.

Vance looked at him in troubled concern.

"Your hands are tied by the technicalities of a legalistic system; and, as a result, a creature like Bliss is to be turned loose on the world. Moreover, a harmless chap like Salveter is to be put under suspicion and ruined. Also, Meryt-Amen—a courageous lady——"

"I realize all that." Markham raised himself, an agonized look on his face. "And yet, Vance, there's not one piece of convincing evidence against Bliss."

"Most distressin'. Your only hope seems to be that the eminent doctor will meet with a sudden and fatal accident. Such things do happen, don't y' know."

Vance smoked for a moment.

"If only Hani's gods had the supernatural power attributed to them!" he sighed. "How deuced simple! And really, Anûbis hasn't shown up at all well in this affair. He's been excruciatingly lazy. As the god of the underworld——"

"That's enough!" Markham rose. "Have a little sense of propriety. Being an æsthete without responsibilities is no doubt delightful, but the world's work must go on. . . ."

"Oh, by all means." Vance seemed wholly indifferent to the other's outburst. "I say, you might draw up a new law altering the existing rules of evidence, and present it to the legislature. The only difficulty would be that, by the time those intellectual Sandows got through debating and appointing committees, you and I and the Sergeant and Bliss would have passed forever down the dim corridors of time."

Markham slowly turned toward Vance. His eyes were mere slits.

"What's behind this childish garrulity?" he demanded. "You've got something on your mind."

Vance seated himself on the edge of the table and, putting out his cigarette, thrust his hands deep into his pockets.

"Markham," he said, with serious deliberation, "you know, as well as I, that Bliss is outside the law, and that there's no human way to convict him. The only means by which he can be brought to book is trickery."

"Trickery?" Markham was momentarily indignant.

"Oh, nothing reprehensible," Vance answered lightly, taking out another cigarette. "Consider, Markham. . . ." And he launched out into a detailed recapitulation of the case. I could not understand the object of his wordy repetitions, for they seemed to have little bearing on the crucial point at issue. And Markham, also, was puzzled. Several times he attempted to interrupt, but Vance held up his hand imperatively and continued with his résumé.

After ten minutes Markham refused to be silenced.

"Come to the point, Vance," he said somewhat angrily. "You've gone over all this before. Have you—or haven't you—any suggestion?"

"Yes, I have a suggestion." Vance spoke earnestly. "It's a psychological experiment; and there is a chance that it'll prove effective. I believe that if Bliss were confronted suddenly with what we know, and if a little forceful chicanery were used on him, he might be surprised into an admission that would give you a hold on him. He doesn't know we found Scarlett in the sarcophagus, and we might pretend that we have got an incriminatin' statement from the poor chap. We might go so far as to tell him that Mrs. Bliss is thoroughly convinced of the truth; for if he believes that his plot has failed and that there is no hope of his continuing his excavations, he may even confess everything. Bliss is a colossal egoist, and, if cornered, might blurt out the truth and boast of his cleverness. And you must admit that your one chance of shipping the old codger to the executioner lies in a confession."

"Chief, couldn't we arrest the guy on the evidence he planted against himself?" Heath asked irritably. "There was that scarab pin, and the bloody footmarks and the finger-prints——"

"No, no, Sergeant." Markham was impatient. "He has covered himself at every point. And the moment we arrested him he'd turn on Salveter. All we'd achieve would be the ruination of an innocent man and the unhappiness of Mrs. Bliss."

Heath capitulated.

"Yeah, I can see that," he said sourly, after a moment. "But this situation slays me. I've known some clever crooks in my day; but this bird Bliss has 'em all beat . . . . Why not take Mr. Vance's suggestion?"

Markham halted in his nervous pacing, and set his jaw.

"I guess we'll have to." He fixed his gaze on Vance. "But don't handle him with silk gloves."

"Really, now, I never wear 'em. Chamois, yes—on certain occasions. And in winter I'm partial to pigskin and reindeer. But silk! Oh, my word! . . ."

He went to the folding door and threw it open. Hani stood just outside in the hall, with folded arms, a silent, watchful sentinel.

"Has the doctor left the study?" Vance asked.

"No, *effendi.*" Hani's eyes looked straight ahead.

"Good!" Vance started down the hall. "Come, Markham. Let's see what a bit of extra-legal persuasion will do."

Markham and Heath and I followed him. He did not knock on the study door, but threw it open unceremoniously.

"Oh, I say! Something's amiss." Vance's comment came simultaneously with our realization that the study was empty. "Dashed queer." He went to the steel door leading to the spiral stairs, and opened it. "No doubt the doctor is communin' with his treasures." He passed through the door and descended the steps, the rest of us trailing along.

Vance drew up at the foot of the stairs and put his hand to his forehead. "We'll never interview Bliss again in this world," he said in a low voice.

There was no need for him to explain. In the corner opposite, in almost the exact place where we had found Kyle's body the preceding day, Bliss lay sprawled face downward in a pool of blood. Across the back of his crushed skull stretched the life-sized statue of Anûbis. The heavy figure of the underworld god had apparently fallen on him as he leaned over his precious items in the cabinet before which he had murdered Kyle. The coincidence was so staggering that none of us was able to speak for several moments. We stood, in a kind of paralyzed awe, looking down on the body of the great Egyptologist.

Markham was the first to break the silence.

"It's incredible!" His voice was strained and unnatural. "There's a divine retribution in this."

"Oh, doubtless." Vance moved to the feet of the statue and bent over. "However, I don't go in for mysticism myself. I'm an empiricist—same like Weininger said the English are."* He adjusted his monocle. "Ah! . . . Sorry to disappoint you, and all that. But there's nothing supernatural about the demise of the doctor. Behold, Markham, the broken ankles of Anûbis. . . . The situation is quite obvious. While the doctor was leaning over his treasure, he jarred the statue in some way, and it toppled over on him."

We all bent forward. The heavy base of the statue of Anûbis stood where it had been when we first saw it; but the figure, from the ankles up, had broken off.

"You see," Vance was saying, pointing to the base, "the ankles are very slender, and the statue is made of limestone—a rather fragile substance. The ankels no doubt were cracked in shipping, and the tremendous weight of the body weakened the flaw."

Heath inspected the statue closely.

"That's what happened, all right," he remarked, straightening up. . . . "I ain't had many breaks in my life, Chief," he added to Markham with feigned jauntiness; "but I never want a better one than this. Mr. Vance mighta lured the doc into a confession—and he mighta failed. Now we got nothing to worry about."

"Quite true." Markham nodded vaguely. He was still under the influence of the astounding change in the situation. "I'm leaving you in charge, Sergeant. You'd better call the local ambulance and get the Medical Examiner. Phone me at home as soon as the routine work is finished. I'll take care of the reporters in the morning. . . . The case is on the shelf, thank God!"

He stood for some time, his eyes fixed on the body. He looked almost hag-

---

* Vance was here referring to the famous passage in the Chapter—"Das Judentum"— in Otto Weininger's "Geschlecht und Charakter": *"Der Engländer hat dem Deutschen als tüchtiger, Empiriker, als Realpolitiker im Praktischen wie im Theoretischen, imponiert, aber damit ist seine Wichtigkeit für die Philosophie auch erschöpft. Es hat noch nie einen tieferen Denker gegeben, der beim Empirismus stehen geblieben is; und noch nie einen Engländer, der über ihn selbstständig hinausgekommen wäre."*

gard, but I knew a great weight had been taken off of his mind by Bliss's un-expected death.

"I'll attend to everything, sir," Heath assured him. "But what about break-ing the news to Mrs. Bliss?"

"Hani will do that," said Vance. He put his hand on Markham's arm. "Come along, old friend. You need sleep. . . . Let's stagger round to my hum-ble abode, and I'll give you a brandy-and-soda. I still have some *Napoléon-*'48 left."

"Thanks." Markham drew a deep sigh.

As we emerged into the front hall Vance beckoned to Hani.

"Very touchin', but your beloved employer has gone to Amentet to join the shades of the Pharaohs."

"He is dead?" the Egyptian lifted his eyebrows slightly.

"Oh, quite, Hani. Anûbis fell on him as he leaned over the end cabinet. A most effective death. But there was a certain justice in it. Doctor Bliss was guilty of Mr. Kyle's murder."

"You and I knew that all along, *effendi.*" The man smiled wistfuly at Vance. "But I fear that the doctor's death may have been my fault. When I unpacked the statue of Anûbis and set it in the corner, I noticed that the ankles were cracked. I did not tell the doctor, for I was afraid he might accuse me of hav-ing been careless, or of having deliberately injured his treasure."

"No one is going to blame you for Doctor Bliss's death," Vance said ca-sually. "We're leaving you to inform Mrs. Bliss of the tragedy. And Mr. Sal-veter will be returning early to-morrow morning. . . . *Es-salâmu alei-kum.*"

"*Ma es salâm, effendi.*"

Vance and Markham and I passed out into the heavy night air.

"Let's walk," Vance said. "It's only a little over a mile to my apartment, and I feel the need of exercise."

Markham fell in with the suggestion, and we strolled toward Fifth Avenue in silence. When we had crossed Madison Square and passed the Stuyvesant Club, Markham spoke.

"It's almost unbelievable, Vance. It's the sort of thing that makes one su-perstitious. Here we were, confronted by an insoluble problem. We knew Bliss was guilty, and yet there was no way to reach him. And while we were debat-ing the case he stepped into the museum and was accidentally killed by a fall-ing statue on practically the same spot where he murdered Kyle. . . . Damn it! Such things don't happen in the orderly course of the world's events. And what makes it even more fantastic is that you suggested that he might meet with an accident."

"Yes, yes. Interestin' coincidence." Vance seemed disinclined to discuss the matter.

"And that Egyptian," Markham rumbled on. "He wasn't in the least aston-ished when you informed him of Bliss's death. He acted almost as if he ex-pected some such news——"

He suddenly drew up short. Vance and I stopped, too, and looked at him. His eyes were blazing.

"*Hani killed Bliss!*"

Vance sighed and shrugged.

"Of course he did, Markham. My word! I thought you understood the situa-tion."

"Understood?" Markham was spluttering. "What do you mean?"

"It was all so obvious, don't y' know," Vance said mildly. "I realized, just as you did, that there was no chance of convicting Bliss; so I suggested to Hani how he could terminate the whole silly affair——"

"You suggested to Hani?"

"During our conversation in the drawing-room. Really, Markham old dear, I'm not in the habit of indulgin' in weird conversations about mythology unless I have a reason. I simply let Hani know there was no legal way of bringing Bliss to justice, and intimated how he could overcome the difficulty and incidentally save you from a most embarrassin' predicament. . . ."

"But Hani was in the hall, with the door closed." Markham's indignation was rising.

"Quite so. I told him to stand outside the door. I knew very well he'd listen to us. . . ."

"You deliberately——"

"Oh, most deliberately." Vance spread his hands in a gesture of surrender. "While I babbled to you and appeared foolish no doubt, I was really talking to Hani. Of couse, I didn't know if he would grasp the opportunity or not. But he did. He equipped himself with a mace from the museum—I do hope it was the same mace that Bliss used on Kyle—and struck Bliss over the head. Then he dragged the body down the spiral stairs and laid it at the feet of Anûbis. With the mace he broke the statue's sandstone ankles, and dropped the figure over Bliss's skull. Very simple."

"And all that rambling chatter of yours in the drawing-room——"

"Was merely to keep you and Heath away in case Hani decided to act."

Markham's eyes narrowed.

"You can't get away with that sort of thing, Vance. I'll send Hani up for murder. There'll be finger-prints——"

"Oh, no there won't, Markham. Didn't you notice the gloves on the hat-rack? Hani is no fool. He put on the gloves before he went to the study. You'd have a harder time convicting him than you'd have had convicting Bliss. Personally, I rather admire Hani. Stout fella!"

For a time Markham was too angry to speak. Finally, however, he gave voice to an ejaculation.

"It's outrageous!"

"Of course it is," Vance agreed amiably. "So was the murder of Kyle." He lighted a cigarette and puffed on it cheefully. "The trouble with you lawyers is, you're jealous and blood-thirsty. You wanted to send Bliss to the electric chair yourself, and couldn't; and Hani simplified everything for you. As I see it, you're merely disappointed because some one else took Bliss's life before you could get round to it. . . . Really, y' know, Markham, you're frightfully selfish."

I feel that a short postscript will not be amiss. Markham had no difficulty, as you will no doubt remember, in convincing the press that Bliss had been guilty of the murder of Benjamin H. Kyle, and that his tragic "accidental" death had in it much of what is commonly called divine justice.

Scarlett, contrary to the doctor's prediction, recovered; but it was many weeks before he could talk rationally. Vance and I visited him in the hospital late in August, and he corroborated Vance's theory about what had happened on that fatal night in the museum. Scarlett went to England early in September,—his father had died, leaving him an involved estate in Bedfordshire.

Mrs. Bliss and Salveter were married in Nice late the following spring; and the excavations of Intef's tomb, I see from the bulletins of the Archæological Institute, are continuing. Salveter is in charge of the work, and I am rather happy to note that Scarlett is the technical expert of the expedition.

Hani, according to a recent letter from Salveter to Vance, has become reconciled to the "desecration of the tombs of his ancestors." He is still with Meryt-Amen and Salveter, and I'm inclined to think that his personal love for these two young people is stronger than his national prejudices.